Joan Jonker was born and bred in Liverpool. Her childhood was a time of love and laughter with her two sisters, a brother, a caring but gambling father and an indomitable mother who was always getting them out of scrapes. Then came the Second World War – a period that Joan remembers so well – when she met and fell in love with her late husband, Tony.

For twenty-three years, Joan campaigned tirelessly on behalf of victims of violence, and her first book, *Victims of Violence*, is an account of those years. She has recently retired from charity work in order to concentrate on her writing. Joan has two sons and two grandsons and she lives in Southport. Her previous bestselling Liverpool sagas have won her legions of fans throughout the world:

'So happy and funny – the best books I've ever read!' Lesley Day, Australia

'I am proud to say I own all the books you have written. Thank you, Joan, for so many hours of pleasure' Ena Gardner, Newbold Verdon, Leicestershire

'Please keep your books coming, Joan. They are the best. You are my favourite author' Deborah Hulme, Hindley, Wigan

'Wonderful . . . The characters are so real I feel I am there in Liverpool with them' Athena Tooze, Brooklyn, New York

'Wonderful characters and humour' Mrs Ivy Decks, Essex

'When I'm low and feeling sorry for myself . . . all I need is to pick up one of your books . . . and I'm soon feeling better' Marion Carver, London

'Absolutely wonderful' Jean Bowers, Canada

The Pride
Of Polly Perkins
and
Home Is Where
the Heart Is

Joan Jonker

headline

THE PRIDE OF POLLY PERKINS first published in 1996
by HEADLINE BOOK PUBLISHING

HOME IS WHERE THE HEART IS first published in 1993
by HEADLINE BOOK PUBLISHING

First published in this omnibus edition in 2005
by HEADLINE BOOK PUBLISHING

A HEADLINE paperback

10 9 8 7 6 5 4 3 2 1

ISBN 0 7553 2659 8

Typeset in Plantin by Avon DataSet Ltd,
Bidford-on-Avon, Warwickshire

Printed and bound in Great Britain by
Clays Ltd, St Ives plc

Headline's policy is to use papers that are natural, renewable and
recyclable products and made from wood grown in sustainable
forests. The logging and manufacturing processes are expected to
conform to the environmental regulations of the country of origin.

HEADLINE BOOK PUBLISHING
A division of Hodder Headline
338 Euston Road
London NW1 3BH

www.headline.co.uk
www.hodderheadline.com

The Pride
Of Polly Perkins

To my dear friends Pat Scott and John Rowley

And to Josie, who, when she was growing up in a
poor area of Liverpool, used to sing this song:

> Mary Ellen at the pawn-shop door,
> A bundle in her hand,
> And a bundle on the floor.
> She asked for seven and six,
> But they only gave her four,
> Poor Mary Ellen at the pawn-shop door.

Chapter One

It was dark in the narrow street of two-up two-down houses, and the howling wind blowing in from the Mersey was bitterly cold. It wasn't a night to venture out if you didn't have to, and most people were sat huddled around their grates to keep warm. There wasn't a soul in sight except for two young girls playing swings on the gas lamp, which shed an eerie glow on the two slight figures. Polly Perkins and her friend Doreen Ashcroft had thrown a length of thick rope over one of the two arms of the gas lamp and were taking it in turns to swing around the iron post.

'Ay, Polly Perkins, I can count, yer know! That's ten swings yer've had an' we said six each. So come on, let's be havin' yer, it's my turn now.' Doreen bent down to pull up the thick black socks lying in folds like a concertina around her ankles. 'Me mam will be callin' me in for bed soon.'

'Yeah, okay.' Polly bent her legs back and scraped her shoes along the ground to slow down her speed. 'You be quick havin' your turn, then I'll climb up an' get the rope down before me dad comes in from work. If I've scuffed me shoes I'll get me ears boxed, 'cos they're the only pair I've got an' me mam said she can't afford to buy me new ones.'

This remark gave Doreen food for thought. Her father had put new soles on her shoes last week and had warned her about playing rough games or sliding down the railway embankment. If he knew she was using them as a brake she'd get more than a clip around the ears. She wiped the sleeve of her coat across her running nose before rubbing her arms briskly to warm herself up. The thin coat she was wearing was no barrier against the strong wind and she was frozen to the marrow.

1

'I'm not 'alf cold, Polly, so I think I'll skip my turn an' have an extra one temorrer.'

'Please yerself.' With the agility of a monkey, Polly climbed up the post to release the knot in the rope. She was eleven years old, slight of build and a real tomboy who was far happier playing cowboys and Indians or football with the lads in the street than cissie games like skipping or hopscotch. 'Come down the entry with us, Doreen, while I throw this rope into next door's yard. If me mam sees me with it I'll get a thick lip.'

Just then a door on the opposite side of the street opened and a voice yelled, 'Doreen, get yerself in here, quick, before I belt yer one.' The tone of her mother's voice warned Doreen that it was woe betide her if she didn't obey.

'Comin', Mam!' She took to her heels, calling over her shoulder, 'I'll knock for yer in the mornin' for school.'

Polly eyed the rope in her hands. She didn't fancy going into the dark entry on her own, but if she took the rope home her mam would take it off her and she'd never see it again. Neither would the boy next door, Steve Mitchell, and he'd only lent it to her. She wasn't going to let Steve down 'cos he was a good mate to her. When the lads were having a game of football, or marbles, they always told her to scram because they didn't want to play with a girl. But Steve always stuck up for her, and as he was a big, strong lad for a twelve-year-old, the others all gave in and let her play.

Polly ran as though her life depended on it. With wings on her heels she was down the entry in a flash, had flung the rope over the high yard wall and within seconds was back outside her own front door banging hard on the brass knocker her mam polished every day.

Ada Perkins shook her head when she saw her daughter standing on the step. 'It's a wonder yer don't catch yer death of cold playin' out in this weather. Yer want yer bumps feelin', yer know that, don't yer? I bet there's no one else out, they've all got more sense.'

'I've been playing with Doreen.' Polly smiled at her four-year-old brother, Joey. He was sitting at the table playing with coloured bricks, his nose running as usual. 'What yer buildin', Joey?'

'An 'ouse,' Joey said with pride. 'One with a chimney pot.'

'I'll help yer.' Polly pulled one of the wooden chairs close. She idolised her brother and acted as his guardian when he was playing in the street. Every kid in the neighbourhood knew that to upset Joey was asking for trouble. 'What colour shall we make the roof, Joey? Red or brown?'

Joey laid his arms flat on the table and rested his head on them. 'You build it, our Polly.' His blue eyes twinkled. 'An' when yer've finished it, I can knock it down.'

'Yer a little tinker, our Joey.' Polly laughed. 'I've a good mind not to play with yer.'

Ada was sitting by the fire darning a hole in the heel of one of her husband's working socks. It was a darn on top of a darn and she knew it was a waste of time because there was none of the original heel left to weave on to. But new socks cost money, which they didn't have, so there was no use complaining. She looked up from her task and studied her two children. They were as different in looks as chalk and cheese. Polly had her colouring – jet black curly hair and deep brown eyes, while Joey favoured his dad, with fair hair and blue eyes. And their natures were different, too. Polly was adventurous, outgoing, and as stubborn as a mule, while Joey was quiet, shy and would do anything for an easy life. Ada sighed as she lowered her head. She knew she'd never have to worry about Polly; her daughter would find her own way in life. With her pretty face, smiling eyes and deep dimples, she could charm the birds off a tree. And she wasn't backward in coming forward, either! If she thought she was in the right she'd argue till she was blue in the face, and as for being a chatterbox, she could talk the hind legs off a donkey. But Joey was different and Ada feared for him. He'd always been a sickly child, never without a cold, even in the summer, and he was always listless as though he had no energy. But he was five in the summer and Ada was hoping that when he started school it would bring him out more. He'd have to learn to stick up for himself then because Polly wouldn't be around to fight his battles for him.

'Mam, look at this!' Polly had tight hold of Joey's hands so he couldn't undo her handiwork. 'How would yer like to live in a house with a red roof, a blue chimney and green windows?'

Ada smiled. She was thirty-three years of age and a fine-looking woman with a warm, passionate nature. There were no strands of grey in her dark, luxuriant hair, her complexion was clear and she had a slim figure with curves in the right places. 'Make it a hundred times bigger, stick it in a field away from all the smokin' chimneys an' rotten middens, an' I'll buy it off yer.' She heard a key turn in the lock and quickly put her darning on the floor at the side of her chair. 'Here's yer dad, clear the table.'

Joey didn't need telling twice. He swept his arm through the bricks and sent them flying in all directions. He and Polly were laughing heartily when Tommy Perkins opened the door, bringing with him a draught of cold air. 'Oh, aye! What's all this, then?'

'Our Joey's just knocked me mam's new 'ouse down.' Polly ran to fling her arms around her father's waist and raised her face for a kiss. 'It took me ages to build an' now it's all over the floor.'

Tommy by-passed the puckered lips and kissed her on the cheek. Then he ruffled his son's hair before slipping his coat off. 'Hang this up for us, Polly.' Shivering from head to toe, he moved to the fireplace and held out his hands to feel the warmth. 'I don't think I've ever been so cold in all me life.'

Ada was carrying his dinner through from the kitchen when he began to cough. She stood by the door and sent a silent plea to God, asking why a good man like her husband

4

should have to go to work when anyone with half an eye could see he wasn't fit. She'd pleaded with him this morning to stay off, have a few days in bed, but he wouldn't hear of it. If he didn't go to work, he argued, he wouldn't get any wages. And how would they live without money to pay the rent, buy the coal and food? Look how they'd had to struggle the few times he had taken a day off when he wasn't well. By the time they'd paid the rent, bought a bag of coal and saved a few pennies for the gas, there was nothing left for food. Bread and dripping they'd lived on – and that was no good for growing children.

Ada banged the plate down on the table as anger built up within her. It just wasn't fair! The war was the cause of his ill-health, but nobody in the whole wide world cared. Men like her Tommy were used when they were needed to fight the enemy, but when it was over those in authority conveniently forgot they existed. She'd started courting Tommy in 1920, two years after the war was over. He was very nervous in those days and had admitted to having nightmares about the horrors he'd seen. But they had fallen in love and Ada thought with lots of care and kindness he would soon be better. And he had improved – the nightmares happened less frequently until they disappeared altogether. He'd had a cough then, but it hadn't been bad enough to cause concern and neither of them had worried unduly about it. But over the last few years it had gradually got worse and now Ada fretted constantly about him.

When the racking coughs eased off, she said softly, 'Come an' eat yer dinner, love, before it gets cold.'

'Aye, I'll do that.' Tommy took a deep breath and undid the stud in the neck of his shirt. He felt terrible, worse than he'd ever felt. He'd almost collapsed in work today, and if it hadn't been for his mates carrying his work load he'd never have completed his shift. 'I think I'll go to bed then, have a good night's rest. I'll take the oven shelf up with me to warm the bed up.'

Ada moved to the cupboard set in the recess at the side of the big black iron grate, and took out a piece of cloth that had once been a sheet. 'If I take it up now it'll warm the bed through before you go up.' She opened the oven door at the side of the fire and with her hands covered with the sheeting, pulled the heavy shelf out. 'But you're not goin' to work tomorrow, Tommy Perkins, yer goin' to see the doctor.' When she saw her husband open his mouth to protest, she held up her hand. 'The longer yer leave it, the worse it'll be, so don't argue.'

'I can't keep takin' time off work, love, otherwise I'll be gettin' me cards and then where will we be? Besides, it costs a shillin' to go to the doctor's an' we can't afford it.'

'Yer can have my penny pocket money on Saturday, Dad,' Polly said, a frown creasing her brow. If her father was having to go to the doctor's then he must be really sick. 'I don't mind, honest.'

'Yer can 'ave mine too,' Joey piped up. He didn't understand what was going on, but he could see his mother was worried and if his penny helped then he didn't mind going without his black jacks or bull's eyes. 'Yeah, Dad, yer can 'ave my penny as well.'

There was a sadness in Tommy's smile. He loved his children dearly and of late he had worried about what would happen to them and Ada if he was as ill as he thought he was. 'We'll see, we'll see. But thanks for the offer, it's very kind of yer.'

'Well, we want yer to get better, Dad.' Polly nodded her head solemnly. 'If me mam says yer should see the doctor, then that's what yer should do, 'cos me mam knows best.'

Ada hurried from the room with tears in her eyes. With the warm shelf held close to her chest she prayed softly as she climbed the steep narrow stairs. 'I don't ask You for much, God, but You know my Tommy's a good man. He wouldn't hurt a fly an' would give anyone his last ha'penny.' She slipped the oven shelf between the sheets on her husband's side of the bed, then made the sign of the cross. 'You're the only one I can turn to for help, God, and I'm at me wits' end. Please hear my prayer and make my Tommy better. You see, me an' the kids love him so much an' we need him. Don't let anythin' bad happen to him.'

Polly tutted as she dashed down the hall pulling her coat on. Her dad hadn't got up for work this morning so he must be really ill, and there was Doreen banging the door down and making enough noise to wake the dead.

'There's no need for that racket, I'm not deaf.' Polly stood on the top step and glared at her friend as she wound the woollen scarf around her neck and buttoned her coat up. 'It's only twenty to nine, we've got plenty of time.'

'It said a quarter to on our clock an' it's always dead right.' Doreen was hopping from one foot to the other. Being late for school meant three strokes of the cane and she didn't fancy that. 'Come on, slow coach.'

Polly closed the door slowly so as not to make a noise. She was worried about her dad, he hadn't half coughed a lot during the night. And her mam had been up a few times because she'd heard the stairs creaking. Sighing, she reached for Doreen's hand and pulled. 'Come on, let's make a run for it.'

But they'd only taken a few steps when a figure loomed in front of them. 'Blimey, Steve, yer gave me the fright of me life! I nearly jumped out of me skin!'

'I've been standing in the entry waitin' for yer.' Steve was a tall lad, well-built with a shock of sandy hair and eyes that were hazel one minute and green the next. 'Where's the rope? I told yer to throw it over the wall when yer'd finished with it.'

'I threw it over the wall,' Polly said, looking puzzled. 'Honest, I did!'

'Well, it's not in the yard an' me dad will belt me when he finds it's missing.' Steve's eyes were troubled. 'He didn't get taken on at the docks this mornin' so he said he'd go out with the handcart to try an' earn a few bob. He needs the rope to help him pull the cart.'

'Well, I definitely threw it over the wall,' Polly insisted before glaring at Doreen and pushing her hand away. 'Stop pullin', will yer? If yer that worried, you run on an' I'll catch yer up.'

'Yer'll be late an' yer'll get the cane.' Doreen hesitated. She didn't like leaving her friend but the thought of holding her hand out and seeing the cane descend to inflict a pain that would last for hours, filled her with dread. 'I'll go on 'cos yer can run quicker than me.' Neither Polly nor Steve noticed her running down the street as though the devil was on her heels.

'Are yer sure it was our wall yer threw it over?' Steve asked. ' 'Cos I've searched the yard an' there's no sign of it.'

'I'm not daft, Steve Mitchell! I should know which is your wall by now, seein' as it's right next to ours.' Polly was flummoxed. She didn't know what to make of it, but she did know she couldn't leave Steve to face the music on his own, not when she was the one who had coaxed him to lend them the rope in the first place. 'Let's go down the entry an' I'll show yer how I threw it.'

'We're both goin' to be late for school,' Steve grumbled as they walked side by side down the entry. 'If me dad doesn't get me first an' knock me into the middle of next week, then it'll be six of the best off Mr Grundy. I don't know which would be the least painful.'

'If they both get yer, yer'll end up in 'ospital with both yer legs in plaster.' When they stopped outside the Mitchells' yard door, Polly raised her eyes to the top of the wall. A sudden grin lit up her face as she pointed a finger to where she could see a short piece of the rope hanging from the roof of the lavatory. 'There yer are, Steve! That's one place yer didn't think of looking.'

Steve let out a sigh of relief. 'Put yer hands together an' give us a leg up, Polly.'

Bending her body forward, Polly laced her fingers. 'Make it snappy, Steve, before someone catches us.' She gritted her teeth while she took his full weight on the cradle she'd made of her hands, but she was determined not to cry out like a cissie.

'Thank the Lord for that!' Steve smiled as he wound the rope into a coil like he'd seen his dad do hundreds of times. 'You get goin', Polly. I'll just tie this up and heave it over. I hope me mam and dad don't happen to look out of the window when it sails over the wall.'

'It's all my fault an' I'm sorry,' Polly said before taking to her heels and running as fast as she could. By the time she turned into the street where her school was, her chest was burning and she was gasping for breath. It crossed her mind that Doreen must have made it because there was no sign of her, but she groaned inwardly when she saw Mr Grundy's head appear over the iron gates. His eyes narrowed as he watched her running towards him. She was within a few yards of the gates when he slammed them shut, bringing tears of anger to Polly's eyes.

'That's not fair, Mr Grundy, it's only nine o'clock.'

'Don't be impudent, girl!' The headmaster's nostrils flared. 'You will stay here until after prayers, then you're to go straight to Miss Wilton's office to receive your punishment.'

Polly heard running footsteps and turned her head to see Steve come up behind her. Shaking her head in disbelief, and for a moment forgetting Mr Grundy's reputation for cruelty, she blurted out, 'He shut the gate in me face! He's dead mean, that's what he is!'

Steve's eyes darted from Polly to Mr Grundy, and the look of anger on the headmaster's face caused him to say softly, 'All right, Polly, just leave it.'

'Keep a still tongue in your head, boy!' The man ran a

finger round the inside of his stiff collar. His wife had been heavy on the starch and it was digging into his neck, restricting the movement of his Adam's apple. His discomfort had put him in a foul temper and he vowed he would have strong words for his wife when he got home. Until then, providence had seen fit to send him two late-comers to vent his anger on. His view of children was that they should be seen and not heard, and they should, without question, be obedient to their elders at all times. Well, it was up to the headmistress, Miss Wilton, to chastise the girl, but he'd get a good deal of satisfaction out of punishing the boy. After six strokes of the cane he wouldn't be so cocky.

'You will both stay there until the caretaker comes to let you in.' He pointed to Steve. 'You, boy, will go straight to my office, and you, girl, will go to Miss Wilton's. I'll tell her to expect you and I will report your insolence to her.'

Polly had the sense to wait until his back was turned and he was walking away from them before she stuck out her tongue. 'He's the most horrible man in the whole world an' I hate him.' But for all her show of spirit she was worried. Her mam would go mad if she knew she'd got the cane for being naughty and Polly didn't want to pile any more trouble on to Ada when she had her plate full with her dad being sick. 'I'm not goin' to tell me mam if we get the cane, so don't let on, Steve, will yer?'

'Nah! I never tell the old girl when I get the cane 'cos she'd only say I must've done somethin' to deserve it an' she'd give me a clip around the ears.'

Polly sniffed up her tears and managed a half-smile. 'It'll be our secret, then – eh, Steve? That's what real mates are for, isn't it? To tell their secrets to each other?'

'Yeah, Polly, that's what real mates are for.' Steve looked down at the pavement. If the expression on old Grundy's face was anything to go by, he was really in for it. Still, the caning would be over in five minutes, even if the pain lasted all day. He'd just have to grin and bear it . . . but he'd make sure he was on time tomorrow. There was no point in asking for trouble.

'If you could just give me some medicine for me cough, Doctor, I'll be fine.' Tommy's breathing was laboured, his face grey. 'It'll pass off in a day or two, it always does.'

'Mr Perkins, you are a sick man and you should never have come here today. You should have sent for me.' Dr Rigby's kind blue eyes clouded over. The man sitting across the desk from him was a consumptive if ever he'd seen one. And he sensed that Tommy Perkins knew how ill he was, but he wouldn't give into it because he couldn't afford the luxury of being ill. Like most people in the area, the family were living from hand to mouth on the meagre wages Tommy brought in. If those wages stopped, it would be the poor-house for them. But even as these thoughts crossed his mind, he knew he couldn't just give the man a bottle of cough medicine and allow him to go back to work until he died on his feet. During all those years of training to become a doctor his one aim had been to help people live healthy lives, not to help them die. 'I'd like you to go to the hospital for a check-up.'

There was a flicker of fear in Tommy's eyes as he shook his head. 'I can't do that, Dr Rigby. I can't afford to take any time off work. I've got a wife an' two kids to provide for, and even with me workin' we have a struggle to keep our heads above water.'

The anger rising within the medical man wasn't against Tommy; it was against the unfairness of a society where the rich prospered and the poor became poorer. Most of the people who came to his surgery wouldn't need his help if they had a decent standard of living. How could they be healthy when they weren't able to feed their families as they should be fed? Kids were running around barefoot, no food in their bellies, no fire in their grate and no warm clothes to their backs. And their parents were old before their time, bowed down with worry and despair.

John Rigby let out a deep sigh. 'If you don't get yourself seen to soon, you'll be too ill to go to work – and where would that leave your wife and children?' He dropped his eyes to avoid seeing the haunted look of hopelessness on the face of the man sitting opposite him. 'Look, I understand your position, Mr Perkins, but as your doctor I have to be straight with you. A bottle of cough mixture isn't the answer to your problem, and you know it as well as I do. You need to see a specialist as soon as possible.'

Tommy dropped his head to stare at the flat cap he was holding in his hands. He knew in his heart that the doctor was right, and in an ideal world he wouldn't hesitate to go to the hospital and get himself seen to. But it wasn't an ideal world.

He raised his eyes and in a low voice said, 'I hear and understand what yer sayin', Doctor, an' I appreciate yer bein' straight with me. But there's no way I can take any time off work to go to the hospital, not just now, anyway. But if you'll just give me a bottle of cough mixture to ease me throat, I'll make yer a promise to come back, say in a couple of weeks, an' yer can make arrangements for me to see a specialist.'

'If you have no money now, what makes you think your circumstances will change in a few weeks?' John Rigby's voice was sharper than he intended and he mentally chastised himself. The poor man had no more control over his life than the man in the moon. 'Look, why don't you talk it over with your wife? It affects her, so it's only right she should know what the situation is. It would be very wrong to keep her in the dark.'

'I'll have a word with her, Doctor.' Tommy felt as though the room was closing in on him and he desperately needed to get some fresh air in his lungs. 'Can I have the cough mixture, please?'

The doctor sighed as he pushed his chair back. 'Yes, but it's against my better judgement, Mr Perkins. I can't force you to do anything, but I will stress that you need treatment as soon as possible.'

Tommy nodded his head. At that moment he would have promised anything just to get the bottle of mixture so the story he intended telling Ada would sound genuine.

Ada was peering through the net curtains when she saw Tommy walking up on the opposite side of the street and she had the door open before he had time to raise his hand to the knocker. 'I'd almost given yer up, yer've been ages!'

'There were a few people there ahead of me so I had to wait me turn. If yer didn't have a cold before yer went there, yer'd certainly have one when yer came out, what with all the coughing an' spluttering.'

'How did yer get on?' Ada held out her hand to take his coat. 'What did Dr Rigby have to say?'

Tommy held out the bottle of dark red syrupy medicine. 'He said I've got a bad case of bronchitis, but this should help.'

Ada tore her eyes away from his and turned to take his coat into the hall. He's keeping something from me, she told herself as tears threatened. I've lived with him too long not to know when he's lying, and right now he's lying through his teeth. She screwed her eyes up tight and shivered as the blood in her veins ran cold. He was lying to protect her from worry and she loved him for it. But she wasn't stupid, she knew that her husband was suffering from something worse than bronchitis. And she also knew the bottle of medicine he'd brought home was only a blind.

Taking a deep breath and squaring her shoulders, Ada returned to the living room. It was no good discussing it now, not with young Joey listening to every word. Better wait until the kids were in bed, then she could try and worm the truth out of him. If he still stuck to the same story, then rather than upset him, she'd go and see Dr Rigby on the sly.

Because, whatever the future held for her Tommy she intended to stand by his side and they'd face it together.

Chapter Two

Ada kicked angrily at a small stone and watched it bounce ahead of her, hitting the concrete path a few times before coming to rest on the grass verge. She paused outside the gates and looked back at the large double-fronted house which was both the doctor's private residence and his surgery. When she'd walked up the path half an hour earlier there'd been a glimmer of hope in her heart that she was worrying unduly, making a mountain out of a molehill. Now that hope had been extinguished and her worry had turned to fear. Not that Dr Rigby had told her much; he wouldn't commit himself on what he thought was wrong with Tommy, but then doctors never did commit themselves, did they? It was more than they dare do, in case they were wrong. But the little she'd been able to get out of him was enough to set the alarm bells off. Her husband was a sick man who needed treatment *now*. The two of them should sit down and discuss how they could manage for him to take time off work, and they should do it soon because the longer they left it, the worse it would be. The doctor hadn't been abrupt; in fact, he'd been kind and understanding. But no matter how kind he'd been it didn't alter the fact that Tommy was a very sick man and they were in trouble.

Taking a deep breath, Ada pushed her clenched fists deep into her pockets and started to walk in the direction of home. A lone tear ran down her cheek and she quickly brushed it away. How could she explain red-rimmed eyes to Dolly Mitchell, who was minding Joey for her? She'd told her neighbour she was nipping to T. J. Hughes' to see if they had any cheap working socks for Tommy, and while Dolly would believe her if she came back empty-handed, saying they were too dear, she wouldn't see it as something to cry about.

Ada bent her head and quickened her pace as her mind ticked over. They had to think of some way that Tommy could get the treatment he needed. But as with everything else, it all boiled down to money, the root of all evil. She would willingly go out to work to earn a few bob, but who would look after Joey? And even if she got a job, women were very poorly paid and she wouldn't earn enough to keep them. Tommy's wages barely covered the necessities, she was living from hand to mouth every week, so God help them if they had to rely on her bringing enough in. If only Polly was two years older she'd be leaving school in a couple of months and finding herself a job. With her earning, and Ada with a little job, they could just about manage.

Ada sighed. Wishing her daughter's life away wasn't going to help. But they had to find a solution or God knows what would happen to Tommy. She loved him too much to just stand by and watch him work himself to death for the sake of his family.

Two tears escaped to run down her cheeks and she was so busy wiping them away as she turned the corner of the street, that she missed seeing the woman coming in the opposite direction until she bumped into her.

'Glory be to God, Ada Perkins, is it meself yer after killing?'

Ada managed a smile for the woman who was struggling to steady the huge basket she carried on her head. 'I'm sorry, Mary, I was miles away.'

'Miles away, was it?' Mary, head slightly back and eyes rolled upwards, slowly took one hand from the heavy wicker basket, twisted her head slightly until she felt her burden was safely anchored, then she lowered both her arms. 'Sure wasn't it another world altogether yer were in, Ada, me darlin'?'

'Well, you were the last person I'd expect to bump into,' Ada said. 'What are yer doin' home this time of day?'

'I'm happy to be tellin' yer that I sold out in two hours, so I did. It was a day when the whole of Liverpool an' his friend wanted to buy flowers.' Mary was dressed in the uniform of a typical Liverpool Mary Ellen, with her long black skirt swirling around her ankles, a dark blouse fastened at the neck with a cameo-type brooch and a black knitted shawl around her shoulders. Her black hair was brushed straight back and plaited into a bun to rest in the nape of her neck. Leaning towards Ada she said in her soft Irish brogue, 'Sure, if business was like this every day wouldn't I be a rich woman in no time at all?'

'So yer've finished for the day?'

'Not while I've a breath in me body would I be restin' on me laurels this time of the day, Ada Perkins! I'm off to the market to replenish me stock, then back to Bold Street with a prayer in me heart to the good Lord that the people are still as generous this afternoon as they were this mornin'.' Once again she lowered her voice. 'I only nipped home to use the lavvy 'cos I was right desperate, so I was.'

An idea was forming in Ada's mind and she knew if she didn't voice it now she'd lose her nerve. 'Would I be any good as a flower-seller, Mary?'

Thinking it was said in humour, Mary laughed. 'Sure, with your looks, me darlin', wouldn't the men be buying flowers off yer even if they didn't want them? I'd not be lettin' yer set up next to me, an' that's the truth of it.' When there was no answering smile from Ada, the Irishwoman narrowed her eyes and studied her neighbour's face closely. 'Is everythin' all right with yer, girl? Sure, when yer bumped into me yer were wipin' yer eyes, an' didn't I think yer'd been crying?'

Ada shook her head. She was fond of Mary and knew she wasn't one for gossip, but not even with her would she share the burden she was carrying. 'No, somethin' blew in me eye, that's all. But I was serious when I asked about me sellin' flowers, or anythin' for that matter. We're havin' a hard time makin' ends meet an' I thought if I got a little job it would make life a bit easier.'

'Oh girl, yer wouldn't last five minutes! Sure, the women would run yer off the street in no time if they thought yer were queering their pitch. Most of the street-traders have been in business all their lives, so they have, and their mothers an' grandmothers before them. It's a trade handed down through the generations from mother to daughter, and they're fiercely proud. They're hard workers and they stick together, so any stranger threatening their livelihood would get short shrift from them.'

Ada pulled a face as she sighed. 'Ah well, it was only a thought.'

'Sure, it wasn't the best thought yer've ever had in yer life, me darlin', an' that's the truth of it. It's better for me to be straight with yer than fill yer head full of blarney.' Mary wrapped the shawl across her chest, folded her arms and stuck her hands under her armpits for warmth. 'If it's a few bob yer after, why don't yer look for a cleaning job? The pay's no good, I'll grant yer that, but it's better than a kick in the teeth when yer belly's rumbling.'

Once again Ada pulled a face. 'I wouldn't know where to start.'

Mary tutted impatiently. 'If yer were that desperate, Ada, sure yer'd soon find the place to start, and that's a fact.' She made to walk away, aware that if she didn't put a move on, the flower market would be closed. But her conscience brought her to a halt. The Perkinses were a good family and always the first to offer help if it was needed. 'D'yer know that overall factory, the one just around the corner from Northumberland Street? Well, as it so happens, me darlin', I know someone who works there as a cleaner. I see her most nights when I go to the pub for me glass of stout, an' she's a pleasant enough woman, so she is. Would it please yer if I asked her whether there's any jobs going?'

'Oh yes, please, Mary. I'd be that grateful.' Another

unwanted tear fell and she quickly flicked it away. 'I've either got a bit of dirt in me eye or I'm in for a cold.'

Mary wisely kept her thoughts to herself. She'd known Ada for about twelve years and wasn't fooled by the lame excuse for the tears. But she wasn't going to pry. 'I'll be on me way, me darlin', but if I see me friend tonight when I go for me nightcap, I'll let yer know tomorrow what she has to say.'

'Thanks, Mary.' As Ada watched the Irishwoman walk away she wondered why, after being neighbours for so many years, she still knew so little about her. Mary was alone when she first rented the house on the opposite side of the street, and she'd been alone since. No man in her life, no family and very few visitors. And although she was always polite and friendly with everyone in the street, she gave very little away about her personal life. They knew as much about her now as they had twelve years ago. Even her age was a mystery, although Ada would put it at a guess at about forty, or even younger. There were no strands of grey in her dark hair, her eyes were a clear blue, her cheeks a rosy red, and when she smiled she showed a set of strong white teeth. She had a slim figure and walked with an ease and grace that most women would envy. A striking woman like her, it was hard to believe that some man hadn't come along before now to claim her affections.

Ada shook her head to clear her mind. She'd better get moving or Dolly Mitchell would think she'd left home. Giving her eyes a last wipe, she crossed the cobbled street and knocked on her neighbour's door.

'Well, the wanderer returns!' Dolly held the door wide. 'I was beginnin' to think yer'd run off with the coalman.'

'It was a wasted journey, too!' Ada lowered her eyes as she told the lie. 'The socks are cheaper at the market.'

'Well, come in an' I'll make yer a cuppa.' Dolly closed the door and followed Ada down the hall. 'It'll be weak, 'cos I'm low on tea, but at least it'll be wet an' warm.' She pulled a chair from under the table and motioned for Ada to sit herself down.

'Where's Joey?' Ada asked, her eyes turned to the kitchen. 'He's not out playin', is he? It's bitterly cold.'

'He's just run down to the lavvy for a tinkle, he won't be long.' Dolly bent to stare into Ada's face. 'Yer eyes an' cheeks are all streaked as though yer've been cryin'.' Without waiting for an answer, Dolly put her two palms flat on her tummy and let out a roar of laughter. 'Ah, aye, girl! A pair of ruddy socks are not worth cryin' over! Tell yer what, I'll knit yer a pair while yer havin' yer cup of tea, eh? Mind you, they'll have no heels in 'cos I never learned how to turn a heel.' Her hearty laughter filled the room. 'An' as I've only got bits of old wool in, they'll have to be sky blue pink with a finny-haddy border! Still, if Tommy wears them for work for a few weeks no one will know the difference 'cos they'll be as black as the Ace of Spades.'

Even though laughter was the last thing on her mind, Ada couldn't help grinning. She was a caution was Dolly Mitchell, always good for a laugh. And she had a heart of gold. As poor as a church mouse, like the rest of them, she'd share her last loaf with you, and there'd be a smile on her face and a joke on her lips while she did it.

Just then the kitchen door opened and Joey dashed in, his pale face pinched with the cold. 'Yer back, Mam!'

'Yes, son, I'm back.' Ada held her arms wide. 'Come here while I warm yer up.' She held him close and kissed the top of his head. 'Have yer been a good boy for Auntie Dolly?'

'She said I'm a very good boy an' a credit to yer.'

'Blimey!' Dolly was pouring water from the soot-covered iron kettle on the fire hob into the brown earthen teapot. 'It's a good job I wasn't pullin' yer to pieces, isn't it? He'd have told yer that as well.'

Stroking her son's fine blond hair, Ada smiled at her neighbour. 'Why, Dolly, you don't gossip about people behind their backs, do yer?'

'Of course I don't!' Dolly plonked the teapot on the table before giving a mischievous smile. 'Unless I don't like yer, then to me yer fair game. Like that cow in number four, I can't stand her at any cost. I've only got to see her an' me hair stands on end. Now I could gossip about her until the cows come home . . . or until Donnelly docks, an' he hasn't even got a ruddy ship yet!'

'Who's Donnelly, Auntie Dolly?' Joey's eyes were full of interest. 'Did he have a ship an' lose it?'

'D'yer know, Joey, that's one of the big mysteries of life.' Dolly gave Ada a broad wink before folding her arms and hitching up her mountainous bosom. 'No one knows what happened to Donnelly's ship.'

The young boy's brow furrowed. 'Doesn't he know 'imself? Have yer ever asked 'im?'

'Just hang on a tick while I get a cup for yer mam before she starts spittin' feathers.' Dolly disappeared for a few seconds and came back carrying two cups and a chipped enamel mug. 'The cups 'ave got no handle on, Ada, so yer'll have to excuse me.'

Ada smiled. 'I'm not surprised, Dolly, 'cos yer very heavy-handed. It's a wonder yer've got a cup in the house.'

'Ay, I'm not takin' any lip off me guests, Ada Perkins! Cheeky sod, that's what yer are!' Dolly poured the tea out so quickly it splashed on to the oilcloth covering the table. 'Get it down yer an' think yerself lucky. Yer don't drink out of the ruddy handle, anyway!'

'Have yer got a drop of milk?' Ada asked. 'I can't drink black tea.'

'Huh! There's no flies on you, is there, girl?' Dolly huffed as she opened one of the sideboard cupboards. 'I've only got conny-onny, so yer can like it or lump it.' She put the tin on the table, but when she tried to let go of it she found her fingers stuck in the rivulets of the condensed milk which had trickled down the sides and set into a gel. 'Damn and blast the bloody stuff!'

21

'Patience!' Ada said, placing her fingers around the bottom of the tin which was clear of the sticky substance. 'Yer can take yer hand away now, I've got hold of it.'

Dolly licked each of her fingers in turn. 'I hate the flamin' stuff, but yer can't waste, can yer?'

Joey was getting impatient. 'Me mam's got 'er cup now, Auntie Dolly, so tell me about the man what lost 'is ship.'

'Well, I'll 'ave to put me thinkin' cap on for that, son.' Dolly ran her hands down the front of her wrap-around pinny, then pulled a chair out and sat down. How was she going to talk her way out of this? There was no such person as Donnelly, it was just an old Liverpool saying which meant it was a waste of time waiting for something because it was never going to happen. But how did you explain that to a four-year-old boy whose eyes were wide with interest? 'It's like this, yer see, Joey. Nobody knows the truth because Donnelly won't tell anyone about his ship. He sits down at the Pier Head every day, looking out to sea, and when anyone asks what he's doin', he says he's waitin' for his ship to come in.'

'Well, he must know where it is!'

'That's the mystery, son, yer see. No one 'as ever seen Donnelly's ship except him!'

Joey was disappointed. He'd been expecting to hear an exciting story and felt let down. 'That Donnelly, he's daft.'

The two women exchanged smiles. 'He's not only daft,' Dolly said, 'he's ruddy careless! I mean, anyone who can lose a flamin' big ship doesn't deserve to 'ave one, does he?'

'Well, if I 'ad a ship, I wouldn't lose it,' Joey said, nodding his head knowingly. 'I'd keep it tied up with a big piece of rope so no one could pinch it.'

'That's 'cos you're a clever boy,' Ada said, draining her cup. 'Now, you an' me are goin' to have to scarper so I can get some housework done.'

Dolly lifted her hand. 'Not so fast, Ada Perkins. Yer were talkin' about me gossipin' before, weren't yer? Well, yer a fine one to talk, I must say. Who was it I saw when I happened to glance out of the window a little while ago? Only yerself an' Irish Mary standin' on the corner havin' a right good gossip.'

'We were just talkin', Dolly, we were not gossiping!'

'Pull the other one, it's got bells on,' Dolly huffed. 'When two women get together for a jangle, they're not goin' to talk about the ruddy weather, are they? Not bloody likely they're not! Some poor bugger's gettin' pulled to pieces!'

'Mary doesn't gossip, yer should know that by now,' Ada said. 'In all the years we've known her, have yer ever heard her sayin' a wrong word about anyone? No yer haven't, 'cos she never has.'

Dolly laid her arms flat on the table. 'Tell me what yer were talkin' about then. Go on, don't be a meany. Yer know I'd rather 'ave a bit of juicy gossip than a hot dinner.'

Shaking her head, and knowing she wouldn't be able to leave until she'd told her neighbour enough to whet her appetite, Ada said, 'She was telling me she'd had a busy mornin', sold all her flowers in a couple of hours. When I saw her she was off to the market for more stock.'

'An' that's all?' Dolly looked disappointed. 'It took 'er ten minutes to tell yer that?'

Ada smiled. 'Watchin' the clock, were yer, Dolly? Timing me?'

There was no insulting Dolly when she had a bee in her bonnet. Resting her chin on a curled fist, she said, 'I might be cabbage-lookin', girl, but I ain't flaming well green! If she was supposed to have done all the talkin', how come your lips were movin' so much? An' don't tell me she's a ventriloquist an' had her hand up yer back, 'cos I'm not fallin' for that!'

For the first time in days, Ada chuckled. 'Yer a case, you are, Dolly Mitchell! I bet there's not a thing happens in this street that yer don't know about. In fact, I'd go as far as to say in the whole neighbourhood! Yer should get a job as the town crier, then we wouldn't have to buy the *Echo* to find out what's going on.'

Dolly slapped an open palm on her forehead. 'D'yer know, girl, yer've just reminded me. I knew there was somethin' I had to do, but it slipped me mind. I'm supposed to be cuttin' last night's *Echo* into squares to hang on the nail in the lavvy, as there's nothin' out there to wipe our backsides on. My feller had a right cob on this mornin', didn't half give me the length of 'is tongue.'

'I can do that, Auntie Dolly,' Joey piped in. 'I do it for me mam, don't I, Mam?'

Dolly shot up from the chair and lifted a cushion on the couch. Taking out a newspaper, she handed it to Joey. 'Are yer sure yer can do it, son?'

'Yeah, I just fold it over an' over until I get the right size, then I slit down the folds with a knife.'

Once the boy was seated on the floor with the bluntest knife she could find, Dolly sat down and faced Ada. 'Now, what were we talkin' about? Oh, I remember, yer were goin' to finish tellin' me what yer had to say to Irish Mary.'

Ada lowered her eyes and drummed her fingers on the table. 'Well, if yer must know, I was askin' her if she knew of any cleaning jobs. I could do with earnin' a few bob to help out. Tommy had a day off this week because he wasn't well, an' it'll be docked from his wages. That means missing me club woman again an' cutting right down to the bone on coal and food. I'm fed up bein' skint all the time, robbing Peter to pay Paul.'

'It's a bad cough your Tommy's got,' Dolly said. 'With these walls bein' so thin, we can hear him coughin' his heart out every night. He should get himself seen to – yer know that, don't yer, girl?'

'Easier said than done, Dolly.' Ada put a finger to her lips and nodded to where Joey was busy cutting the paper into squares. 'We'll talk about it again, eh? But now yer know why I'm desperate to get a job of some description.'

Lowering her voice to a whisper, she said, 'I'm out of me mind with worry.'

'I understand, girl.' Dolly stretched across to pat her hand. 'I wish I could help yer out, but it takes my feller all his time to bring in enough to keep us goin'. Twice this week he's been knocked back at the docks an' he's had to take the cart out. He doesn't make much on the rags and scrap he collects, but it helps keep the wolf from the door.'

'He's a grafter, your Les,' Ada said, 'an' I admire him for it. It's hard goin', pulling a cart around, particularly in this cold weather.'

'He covers some miles, too,' Dolly said proudly. 'As he says, it's no good goin' around streets where the people have no money; it's the big houses where he gets the best stuff.' Once again she slapped her forehead with an open palm. 'Honest to God, girl, I'd forget my head if it wasn't screwed on! I was supposed to tell yer he'd picked up a good quality coat yesterday. He got it from a house in Allerton an' he says the material's pure wool an' it's in good nick, except it's very faded. But with you bein' handy with a needle and thread, he said yer could unpick it an' turn the material so the faded part was on the inside. He reckons yer'd get a coat for Polly out of it, and trousers for the little feller.'

'I couldn't afford to buy it off him, Dolly. I'm stony broke.'

'He only gave coppers for it!' Dolly didn't know how much Les had paid the woman, but a little white lie wouldn't go amiss. 'The woman gave him a few things an' he only gave her a tanner for the lot. He said she was one of those posh people who look down their nose at yer, keep their distance in case yer've got fleas and speak as though they've got a mouthful of plums. He had me in stitches when he told me how she'd wrinkled her nose when she took the money off him. He said he'd bet a pound to a pinch of snuff that the money would be under the tap being scrubbed before he was at the end of the road.'

'What it is to be rich, eh?' Ada said. 'I'm not usually

envious, but right now I wish we had enough money to get Tommy the treatment he needs. It's not a lot to ask for, is it, Dolly?'

'Don't let yerself get downhearted, girl, otherwise yer'll upset Tommy an' that's the last thing yer want. Keep yer chin up, say a prayer an' hope for the best. Somethin' will turn up, I know it will. In the meantime, when Les goes to the coalyard where he keeps his cart, I'll tell him to bring the coat an' yer can pay him a penny a week. Yer could manage that, couldn't yer?'

'I think yer'd better ask him first,' Ada said. 'He might not like you bein' so generous with his money.'

Her neighbour laughed. 'Me an' my feller have an agreement that suits us fine. Seein' as I'm bigger than him, I get to win every argument.'

Ada glanced at the clock on the mantelpiece. 'Look at the time – an' I haven't even made the beds. I'll have to go, Dolly, but thanks for the tea an' the sympathy. I'm lucky to 'ave you for a neighbour.'

'Come on, Polly, how many times do I have to tell yer? It's nine o'clock an' yer should have been in bed ages ago.'

'Ah ray, Mam, can't I just finish this comic?' Polly pleaded. 'I've got to give it back to Doreen tomorrow 'cos she only borrowed it from a girl in our class.'

'Then get up a bit earlier in the mornin' and read it.' Ada plumped a cushion on the couch. If her daughter didn't go to bed soon, Tommy would beat her to it; he'd been going up early every night to get as much rest as possible. But she wanted to have a good talk to him tonight – tell him about her trip to the doctor's. He wouldn't be very happy with what she'd done, but the sooner it was out in the open the better. And she couldn't talk to him while Polly was there. 'Come on, no arguing an' no messing about.'

Pulling a face, Polly folded the comic. 'Will yer wake me a bit earlier in the mornin', then, Mam? An' if I don't make a move, pull me out of bed by me ankles?'

'Oh yeah, I'll do that all right! Listen to me, young lady, if yer so desperate to read the flaming comic, then it's up to you to get out of bed when I call yer.'

Polly pushed the chair back under the table then laid the comic carefully on the sideboard. 'I'll leave it there, where I can see it as soon as I come down.' She blew a kiss to Tommy. 'Good night and God bless, Dad – sleep well. I'll see yer in the mornin', Mam – good night an' God bless.'

Tommy waited until the door was closed before saying, 'Yer could have let her stay up another fifteen minutes so she could finish reading the comic.'

'I would 'ave done any other night, but I want to have a good talk to yer an' I couldn't do it in front of her.' Ada seated herself on top of the lidded coal scuttle next to Tommy's chair. Then she took one of his hands in hers and held it tight. 'Yer know I love yer, don't yer, Tommy?'

'I should hope so, after bein' married to me for fourteen years.' A look of puzzlement crossed his face. 'What's brought this on all of a sudden, love?'

'So yer'll understand why I did what I did.' Quickly, before she lost her nerve, Ada told him of her visit to the doctor and what had been said.

Tommy snatched his hand away. 'What did yer do that for? Yer had no right!'

'I had every right, Tommy, because I love yer an' don't want to lose yer.' Ada reached for his hand again and kept it in a tight grip. 'Not talking about it won't make it go away, sweetheart. You are ill an' yer need to take time off work to get yerself better. There's nothin' to be ashamed of in that! And because what happens to you affects me an' the kids, it's only right that we should all get stuck in and do something to help.'

Tommy's laugh was hollow. 'Got a rich uncle, have yer, Ada? Yer'd need one if I'm off work for any length of time.'

'Tommy, calm down an' be reasonable. What is the

alternative? That yer go on working until yer drop? Then what would happen to me and the kids, have yer thought of that?'

'I think of nothing else.' Tommy hung his head. 'But I feel so helpless an' don't know where to turn. If we had a few bob in the bank it would be different, but I've never earned enough to put money by for a rainy day. In fact, I've never brought enough in to give yer a decent life . . . It's a poor man that can't provide for his family.'

'Yer can cut that sort of talk out! Yer the best husband in the world bar none, an' the best father, so don't be putting yerself down.' The utter dejection on her husband's face filled Ada's heart with sadness. 'We're a family, you, me, Polly and Joey, and we'll see this through as a family.'

She raised herself from her seat to plant a kiss on his cheek. 'Are yer calmed down enough to listen to what I've got to say?' When he nodded, Ada went on to tell him about her chat with Irish Mary. 'Nothin' might come of the cleanin' job, but it's a start. And now I've made up me mind to get off me backside and do something, instead of sittin' worrying, I'm going out tomorrow and will ask around to see if there's any part-time jobs on offer. If necessary, I'll tramp the ruddy streets until I find something.'

'Ada, sweetheart, yer'd never manage on what you could earn as a cleaner, it's just not possible.'

'I haven't lost the run of me senses, Tommy. I know I'll never earn enough for our needs, but as I said it's a start. There's no way I'm goin' to stand idly by, twiddling me thumbs, while the man I love fades away before me eyes.'

Tommy's expression was tender as he held out his arms. 'Come here, sweetheart, an' let me hold yer.'

Ada moved to kneel between his legs, her head on his chest. 'I do love yer, Tommy, yer me whole life. Yer've got to get better for my sake, and the kids'. We wouldn't know what to do without yer.'

Tommy hugged her close, kissing the top of her head. His

voice cracking with emotion, he said, 'I'm glad yer went to see the doctor 'cos I was too frightened to tell yer what he said. Not that I needed him to tell me how sick I am, I knew that already. But d'yer know, love, now we've been able to talk about it, I feel as though a ton weight has been lifted off me shoulders.'

Ada's dark brown eyes sought his. 'From now on, Tommy Perkins, we keep nothing from each other, d'yer hear? We share everything.'

Chapter Three

Ada was in the kitchen the next morning at half-past seven when there was a ran-tan on the knocker. Tommy had not long left for work and her first thought was he'd taken bad. Her heart in her mouth, she flew to open the door – and when she saw the smiling face of Irish Mary she went weak in the knees with relief. 'Ooh, I got the fright of me life, Mary. I thought Tommy 'ad 'ad an accident.'

'I did think twice about knockin' this time of the morning, but sure wasn't I afraid that if I left it until tonight it might be too late. Yer'll not be wantin' to let the grass grow under yer feet, will yer, Ada?' The handle of her empty basket cradled in the crook of her arm, Mary smiled. 'I had a word with me friend last night and it could be you're in luck. There's only three cleaners workin' in the factory and one of them is leaving next week. According to me friend the woman is having a baby, but she didn't tell anyone because she needed the money and wanted to work until the last minute. But Maggie, that's me friend, said the poor woman couldn't hope to fool the boss because she's as big as a house and looks as though she's goin' to give birth any time. So the man gave her a week's notice, sayin' he couldn't keep her on any longer 'cos he couldn't be responsible for her safety.'

Ada's heart was beating fast. Had God answered her prayers? Was good fortune going to smile on them for a change? 'I feel a bit mean about being glad the poor woman's been given the sack; it's almost like stepping into a dead man's shoes. But it would be wonderful if I got the job, Mary, it really would.'

'Well, me darlin', no one knows the job's going yet, so it's a head start yer have.' Mary moved the basket to her other arm. 'Have yer had any experience doin' cleaning work?'

Ada shook her head, her spirits dropping. 'Only fourteen years doin' me own housework. I served behind the counter at Irwin's from the time I left school to getting married.'

Mary saw the doubt on her neighbour's face and said, 'Sure, yer keep yer house like a little palace, so yer do, an' isn't housework the hardest job of the lot? So if he asks yer if yer've had any experience, tell him yer have. He probably won't ask yer for references, not for that job, so just leave it at that. Sure God doesn't mind a little white lie if it's in a good cause.'

'When shall I go down – an' who do I ask for?'

'If it's serious yer are about a job, Ada, then get yerself down there this morning. Ask for Mr Donaldson, an' if he wants to know how yer knew there'd be a vacancy, me friend Maggie Tilsley said yer could use her name.'

'Mary, I don't know how to thank you. You're an angel!'

'I've been many things in my life, Ada Perkins, so I have, but an angel isn't one of them. And before yer start throwing yer arms around me, hadn't I better be puttin' yer straight on what the job is? It isn't all sweetness and light, believe me! It's six mornings a week, Monday to Saturday, from half-past five until eight o'clock, when the factory workers start. Maggie said it's hard graft, yer don't get time for a cup of tea or a breather. There's the factory to clean, plus the offices and lavatories. And for all that, me darlin', yer get paid the princely sum of twelve and six a week. So think hard before yer take a step. I don't want yer blaming me if yer get the job an' find yer don't like it.'

'I'm not frightened of hard work, Mary, an' I don't think twelve and six a week is bad. It'll go a long way in our house, I can tell yer! And yer know what they say – "beggars can't be choosers".'

'That's the spirit, me darlin'! Keep that up when yer go to see this Mr Donaldson. Even if yer knees are knockin' an' yer tummy's doing somersaults, don't let him see yer scared. After all, the man can't eat yer.'

Ada felt someone touch her skirt and turned to find Polly standing behind her, dressed only in her undervest and navy blue fleecy-lined knickers. 'Put somethin' on, yer daft ha'porth, before yer catch yer death of cold.'

But Polly was too interested to feel the cold. She hadn't heard all the conversation, just enough to make her curious. 'Hello, Miss Hanrahan.'

'Top of the mornin' to yer, Polly.' Mary was fond of the girl, who was always bright and cheerful. Looking at her now she could see the slight mounds under her thin vest, heralding the start of a budding bosom. She was going to be a real beauty, was Polly, with her mass of dark curls, velvety brown eyes and lovely dimpled smile. A few years from now she'd be a real heartbreaker. 'Sure is it meself that needs glasses, or have yer grown a few inches since the last time I saw yer?'

Polly preened. She couldn't wait to be old enough to leave school. 'I'm twelve in three weeks.'

'Is that right, now? Well, as a birthday present, I'll bake yer a cake an' put twelve candles on it . . . would yer like that? An' to give yer mam a break, you an' Joey can come to tea.'

Polly's face lit up. She'd never had a birthday cake before, not a proper one with candles on. Wait until she told Doreen, she'd be green with envy.

'Oh yes, please, Miss Hanrahan! It's very kind of yer an' I thank yer a million times over.'

'Now, in yer go,' Ada said, giving her daughter a push towards the living room. 'Get a swill in the sink before yer get dressed, there's some warm water in the kettle. And yer clean clothes are on the fireguard.' She turned back to Mary. 'Yer very good to her.'

'Sure, I'm fond of the girl, so I am.' There was pleasure on Mary's face when she said, 'That's one good turn I've done today for definite. Now when I call tonight I hope to see yer with a smile on yer face which will tell me that I've got a double up. And wouldn't I go to bed a happy woman if that happens?'

'I'll do me best, Mary, I promise. I'll keep me fingers crossed, and for good measure I'll even cross me legs an' me eyes.'

Mary began to move away, laughing. 'Sure I'd like to see the man's face if you walk in with cross eyes, twisted legs and deformed hands. He'd give yer the job out of pity, so he would.' She walked a few steps then turned. 'The best of luck, Ada me darlin'. May the good Lord smile down on yer.'

Polly had given herself a cat's lick and a promise at the kitchen sink, rubbing the wet towel under her chin so there was no tell-tale tide mark. She'd come down early to finish reading the comic, but that was forgotten in the light of what she'd heard. When her mother came into the room she was slipping her gymslip over her head. 'Ay, Mam, are yer really goin' after a job?'

Ada put a finger to her lips. 'You are not to repeat a word yer've heard, d'yer hear me? Not even to yer best mate, Doreen, 'cos she'd tell her mam an' it would be all over the street in no time.'

'I won't let on, Mam, I promise!'

'I know yer won't, because I'm not goin' to give yer the chance! Yer dad doesn't know about it yet, so I'm certainly not goin' to tell you before he knows. Anyway, nothin' might come of it, so just forget about it until tonight.'

'Mam, I'm nearly twelve, I'm not a baby any more!' Polly almost stamped her foot, so indignant was she. But she knew she'd get a fourpenny one if she showed any temper so common sense prevailed. 'Go on, Mam, tell us. Are yer goin' after a job?'

'I might be, Polly, and that's all I'm goin' to say for now. I know yer a sensible girl for yer age an' yer wouldn't go shoutin' yer mouth off if I asked yer not to. But I'm not goin' after a job just to earn a few bob, as Mary thinks; there's more to it than that. And I think yer old enough and sensible enough to be told the whole story. So just leave things as they are for now and tonight yer can sit down with me and yer dad and we'll tell yer the truth.'

Polly's eyes were wide. 'Me dad hasn't lost his job, has he?'

'No, sunshine, nothing like that.' Oh, if only that was all it was, Ada thought. We could cope with that. 'Now, you read yer comic while I see to yer breakfast, there's a good girl. And please, not another word on the subject until tonight.'

Ada was humming softly as she undressed Joey in front of the fire. She couldn't wait to get him into bed so she could tell Tommy her news, and she was thankful her son always went to bed without a fuss. He certainly didn't take after Polly, who at his age would kick up a stink every night and had to be carried upstairs crying in protest at what she thought was an injustice.

'There we are, sunshine! I've put the iron in the bed so it'll be nice an' warm for yer.' Ada gave him a big hug. 'Seein' as how yer big sister is honouring us with her presence tonight, instead of being out gallivantin', how would yer like her to tuck you up?'

'Ooh, yeah!' Joey ran to the couch where Polly was sitting and held out his hands. 'Come on, our Polly, yer can tell me a story.'

'It'll have to be a short one 'cos it's freezin' up there.' Polly had been on pins all day, wondering why her mother had been so mysterious. It must be something very important for her to behave like that, and at the back of Polly's mind was a nagging feeling that all was not well. 'How about Goldilocks and the Three Bears?'

Joey grinned as he pulled her forward. 'That's me very best favourite.'

'Aren't you forgetting somethin'?' Tommy asked. 'What about me goodnight kiss?'

Joey flung his arms around his dad's neck. 'Night an' God bless, Dad.'

'Night and God bless, son.' Tommy ruffled his hair. 'Sleep tight an' mind the fleas don't bite.'

Ada listened to their footsteps clattering on the lino-covered stairs, and when all was silent she sat on the arm of her husband's chair. 'I've got a lot to tell yer, but first I want yer to know why our Polly never went out to play tonight. I asked her to stay in so we could tell her what's going on. She's a big girl now, very sensible for her age, an' I think she should be told everything.'

Tommy shook his head. 'She's only a kid! It wouldn't be fair to fill her head with worry.'

'She's goin' to find out soon enough, anyway, and it won't be such a shock if she knows from the beginning. She's got a good little head on her shoulders, has our Polly, an' if we share our ups and downs with her, I think she'll appreciate it an' will put herself out to give us all the support an' help she can. The day might come, Tommy, when we'll be glad of her help.'

'Well, it's up to you, love, if you think it's best.'

'Shush, here she comes.' Ada busied herself folding Joey's clothes neatly in a pile ready for the next day. 'Has he gone off all right?'

'Yeah, he's dead to the world. I didn't even get halfway through the story.' Polly was feeling nervous. Part of her wanted to know what was going on, part of her didn't. 'Shall I put the kettle on an' make us a cup of tea?'

'No, love, we'll leave it until nearer bedtime.' Ada sighed as she sat down. It was a problem knowing where to start. 'I went after that job this mornin', Tommy – remember I told yer about it? Well, Irish Mary called just after yer'd left for work to say her friend had told her there was a vacancy comin' up an' I should go after it right away before someone

36

beat me to it. I was a bundle of nerves when I got to the factory, an' by the time I got in to see the boss, a Mr Donaldson, me teeth were chattering so much I could hardly speak. I felt a right fool an' thought he'd probably kick me out on me ear.' A broad smile lit up her face. 'But I got the job! I start a week on Monday.'

'Go 'way!' Tommy sat forward on the couch, his eyes showing interest and pleasure. 'When yer mentioned it last night, I didn't think anythin' would come of it.'

'Oh Mam, isn't that great!' Polly's heart lifted. If this was what her mam had been so secretive about, then she'd been worrying for nothing. 'Tell us about it, go on.'

Ada felt sadness in her heart that the beaming smile on her daughter's face would disappear when she knew the reason why she was going out to work. She idolised her dad and would be devastated when she knew he was ill. The only thing Ada could do was break the news gently, try and make light of it. 'I start at five-thirty and work until eight o'clock. It means yer gettin' yer own breakfast, I'm afraid, Tommy, but I'll make the porridge the night before an' yer'll only have to warm it up.'

'But what about the children? I don't fancy the idea of them bein' left on their own in the house.'

'I've thought it all through, love, an' yer know I wouldn't go to work if the children were being neglected. That's why I'm going to ask our Polly if she'll help me out. You don't leave the house until nearly half seven, I'll be home about ten past eight 'cos it's only a ten-minute walk at the most. If Polly will get up when you go out, and keep an eye on Joey until I arrive, we'll manage fine.'

'I'll do that, Mam,' Polly said eagerly. 'I don't mind, honest.' Then with childish curiosity, she asked, 'How much a week will yer get?'

Ada tapped her nose. 'Curiosity killed the cat, remember? But seein' as the three of us are in this together, I'll tell yer. The wages are twelve an' six a week.'

'Ooh er, won't we be well-off!'

'Polly, I'm not goin' out to work to make us rich. There's another reason for it.' Ada looked to her husband for guidance, but he had his head down gazing at his clasped hands. 'Yer know yer dad's had this cough for a long time, don't yer? Well, he went to see the doctor an' he has to go to the hospital to get himself seen to. That means he'll be off work for a while and there'll be no wages comin' in. Now I know twelve and six isn't goin' to keep us, but it's a start. Over the next few weeks we might come up with other ways of makin' money . . . I might get an extra job, perhaps cleaning in a shop or a pub.'

Tommy clicked his tongue on the roof of his mouth and shook his head. 'Yer'll kill yerself takin' too many jobs on an' having the house and kids to see to as well. Best leave things as they are.'

'No!' Polly cried. 'If yer sick, Dad, then yer've got to get yerself seen to an' get better. I'll help me mam with the housework, honest! An' I'll look after Joey an' run the messages.'

Tommy was crying inwardly as he gazed at his daughter. He knew then how much she meant to him and how much he meant to her. More than anything in the world he wanted to see her grow up, her and Joey. They needed him, needed a father, and Ada needed a husband. It was in those few seconds, as his gaze moved from his daughter to his wife, that Tommy resolved to seek help for what ailed him. Come hell or high water, he'd survive; he had to for their sake.

'If you can carry on workin' for another few weeks, love,' Ada said, 'it'll give me a chance to sort meself out. I'll put me wages away each week, plus anythin' I can save from the housekeeping, then yer can go and see the doctor with an easy mind, knowing we're all right for money for a month or so.'

'I'm truly blessed havin' two good women in my life, aren't I?' There was a catch in Tommy's voice. He knew in his heart he was more sick than Ada realised, and he just hoped he hadn't left it too late. 'How can I help but get better with you two behind me?'

'I'll tell yer what, Dolly, they don't half get their money's worth out of yer,' Ada said as she sat facing her neighbour across the table. 'Talk about slave labour! From the time yer clock in it's all go, non-stop.' She slipped her shoes off and wiggled her toes. 'Me flamin' feet are talkin' to me.'

Dolly pulled a face and held her nose between her finger and thumb. 'God strewth, Ada, is that your sweaty feet, or has me milk turned sour?'

Ada grinned. 'One thing I *don't* have is sweaty feet, Dolly. Me body, yeah, I get in a right lather at work, but not me feet.'

'I don't sweat much, either.' Dolly pulled the neck of her dress forward and looked down. 'Sometimes I do a bit, in the valley between me breasts, but it's only the sweet smell of me fine soft skin. My feller wallows in that smell every night, says it does him more good than a pint of bitter.' She leaned her arms on the table and her face became serious as she pinched at the flesh on her elbow. 'Pay day today, eh?'

'Yeah, I got me second pay packet. I didn't get paid the first week 'cos yer have to work a week in hand.' Ada had told Dolly everything in the strictest confidence, and true to her word her neighbour hadn't repeated it to a soul, not even her husband. 'If I can put as much away this week out of the housekeepin' as I did last, I'll have thirty bob saved up.'

'Yer've done wonders, girl, an' I take me hat off to yer. At least I would if I 'ad a hat, which I 'aven't.' A smile played around the corners of Dolly's mouth. 'An' it's a pity, that, 'cos I really look lovely in a hat. I can wear any style, they all look good on me. Mind you, with my looks I could wear a tea cosy on me head an' still look glamorous.'

'Can't you ever be serious for long, Dolly? I don't

know how yer can be so lively all the time.'

'Oh, I can be serious, girl, when I want to. I mean, if I was to dwell on how little I've got in me purse right now, I'd sit down an' cry me eyes out. But doin' that wouldn't put any money in me purse, would it, so what's the flamin' use?'

'I can lend yer a few bob if yer like, Dolly,' Ada said. 'I'd have to have it back in a few weeks 'cos Tommy's goin' to see the doctor next Saturday an' I think he'll send him to the hospital right away.'

'No, I wouldn't dream of borrowin' yer hard-earned money, girl, but I appreciate yer offer.'

'Don't be daft!' Ada huffed. 'How many times have you helped me out when I've been skint? Loads of times.'

'I'll be all right, girl, so don't be worryin' yer head about me. My feller's gone to get some rags weighed in, he'll be bringin' a few bob home soon, so we won't starve.'

'It's our Polly's birthday today, she's twelve. Her an' Joey have been invited over to Irish Mary's for tea.'

'I know it's your Polly's birthday. How could I forget it, with our Steve pesterin' the life out of me for a penny for a birthday card for her! He even talked me into lettin' him get one for *me* to give to her . . . me who's never sent a ruddy card in me life! I must be gettin' soft in me old age.'

'Dolly, yer neither old nor soft. Just a warm-hearted, generous woman who I'm glad to call me best mate.'

'God bless yer little cotton socks, girl, it's not often anyone pays me compliments.' A wicked glint in her eye, Dolly lowered her head and whispered out of the side of her mouth, loud enough for Ada to hear, 'Poor sod! If I'm the best she can come up with, things must be in a bad state.'

'Ha, ha, very funny! Yer so sharp, Dolly Mitchell, yer'll be cuttin' yerself one of these days.' Ada pushed her chair back and reached for the two shopping bags on the floor. 'I'd better get back and start on the dinner. I've cut everythin' down to the bone to save a few coppers, so it'll be a case of hide-and-seek tryin' to find any meat in the stew. Still, with plenty of vegetables and barley in, the goodness will be there.'

'Have yer done yer washin'?'

'No, but it won't take long once I've got the dinner on the go. I left it in to steep all night and our Polly's been busy with the dolly peg, so I've only got to rinse it and put it through the mangle. If I can get it pegged out before we have our meal it should be dry in a couple of hours 'cos there's a good breeze blowing.'

'Yer too bloody organised for me,' Dolly grumbled. 'Yer move that quick yer make me look as though I'm standin' still.'

Ada laughed. 'Most of the time you are, sunshine, admit it! But then yer older than me, so I'll let yer off.'

'Hey, yer just watch it, girl! Yer know I'm a very even-tempered woman as a rule, but even I have me limits. Older than you, indeed! There's six ruddy months between us, that's all!'

Ada waited until she reached the door before saying, 'Aye, but some women age quicker than others.' She saw a cushion come hurtling towards her and ducked her head just in time. 'Temper, temper!' She went on her way chuckling. Thank God for Dolly Mitchell, the only woman she knew who was guaranteed to make you forget your troubles for a while and brighten up the darkest of days.

Mary struck a match and lit each of the twelve candles spaced at intervals on the cake which had coloured paper around it, making it look very attractive. The top was iced in white, and written across it in blue icing were the words *Happy Birthday Polly*.

Blowing the match out before it could burn her fingers, Mary said, 'Now if yer make a wish and blow all the candles out with one puff, sure the fairies will get busy makin' sure yer wish comes true.'

Polly was beside herself with excitement. The table was

set with a pure white lace cloth, the likes of which she'd never seen before. She only wished her friend Doreen could see it, 'cos she'd never believe Polly when she told her how big the cake was, or that there were sandwiches, fairy cakes, chocolate biscuits and red and yellow jelly creams decorated with hundreds and thousands.

'Go on, our Polly, hurry up.' Joey had his eye on the red jelly creams and his mouth was watering. 'Take a big breath an' blow.'

Polly closed her eyes, concentrated hard on her wish, then took a deep breath and blew with all her might, extinguishing the flame on every candle. Her face flushed with excitement, she asked, 'Will I get me wish now, Miss Hanrahan?'

'I'm sure yer will, me darlin'. Now sit yerself down and tuck in. I want to see every last crumb eaten.'

Joey's eyes were popping out of his head. 'D'yer mean all of this is just for us?'

'Shut up, our Joey,' Polly said. 'Yer eyes are bigger than yer belly.'

'Just eat what yer can,' Mary told him. 'What yer can't eat yer can take home an' give yer mam and dad a treat.'

'My dad's sick.' Joey jumped when Polly gave him a sharp dig in the ribs. 'What did yer do that for? Me dad *is* sick – yer told me he was when he woke us up last night with 'is coughing.'

Polly's face was flushed. 'Yer tellin' fibs, our Joey. I never said nothing of the sort.'

Joey, usually so quiet, got in a huff. Why should he take the blame when he was only telling the truth. 'I'm not tellin' fibs, you are, an' I'm goin' to tell me mam on yer.'

When Mary looked at Polly's face she could see she'd been upset by what her brother had said, and it set the Irishwoman thinking. Then she brushed her thoughts aside; the first priority was to restore peace. 'Is it a fight yer after, an' on yer sister's birthday, too? Sure a birthday is supposed to be a grand day altogether, so it is.' She handed the boy a plate of brawn sandwiches. 'Here now, eat up an' let's not spoil the day for her.'

'Can I 'ave a jelly cream instead?'

When Polly's laugh joined Mary's the tension was broken, and the three chatted happily as they tucked into the goodies. Mary told of the colourful characters she encountered as she plied her wares in Liverpool city centre, and Polly had them in stitches as she related some of the antics her classmates got up to behind their teacher's back. Although her audience didn't know it, her impersonation of the headmistress, Miss Wilton, was very good. Standing up, she pointed a finger at Joey and said in a posh voice, 'You, Joseph Perkins, go and stand in the corner with your back to the class. Perhaps that will teach you not to be impudent in future.'

When Joey, looking all innocent, asked, 'Can I 'ave me jelly cream first, please, Miss?' Mary laughed until the tears rolled down her cheeks.

'It's a long time since I enjoyed meself so much,' she said. 'Sure, I think it's my birthday as well as Polly's.'

'An' mine!' Joey wasn't going to be left out. 'I've never been to a party before.'

'Well, I'll not be forgettin' when your birthday comes along, Joey. We'll have another party in your honour.' Mary began to gather up the plates. 'I'll wash these an' get them out of the way, then I've got some sweeties for yer.'

Polly jumped to her feet. 'I'll help yer with the dishes, Miss Hanrahan.'

'Yer a good girl, Polly, so you are.' Mary smiled at her. 'Why don't yer call me Auntie Mary? Sure, doesn't it sound altogether more friendly.'

'Why do they all call yer Irish Mary?' Joey asked, swinging his legs back and forth. 'It's a daft name, that.'

'With four women in the street all called Mary, they gave us nicknames so people would know who they were talkin' about. So we have fat Mary, skinny lizzie Mary, Mary with the bandy legs and meself, Irish Mary.'

Joey giggled. 'I think Mary with the bandy legs is the best. It's dead funny.'

'Yer wouldn't think it was funny if it was yerself had the bandy legs, Joey, an' that's a fact. Sure the poor soul can't help the way the good Lord made her.' Mary picked up the stacked plates before bending her head to look into his face. 'I'd not like to see a nice little feller like yerself poking fun at anyone. Sure, it would sadden me heart an' that's the truth of it.'

'Oh, I won't, Auntie Mary! Cross me heart an' hope to die.'

'It's pleased I am to hear it, me darlin'. Now, if you be a good boy while me an' Polly wash these dishes, then meself has a nice little surprise for yer.'

'Shall I wash, Auntie Mary?' Polly looked around the tiny kitchen, thinking how neat and tidy it was. Their kitchen at home was always in a mess with the dolly tub in the middle of the floor and the huge iron mangle taking up most of the space. Then Polly felt ashamed of herself. Her mam had four to wash and clean for, while Mary only had herself to worry about.

'I'll wash, Polly, you can dry.' Mary handed her a spotlessly clean tea towel. 'Sure, there's nothing really dirty, we'll have them done before yer can say Jack Robinson.'

'Thank you for me party, Auntie Mary, it was lovely.' Polly picked up one of the washed plates from the wooden draining board and began to dry it. 'It's the first time I've ever 'ad a proper party.'

'There's no need for thanks, me darlin'. Sure, the pleasure was all mine.' Mary looked up from the sink and into Polly's eyes. 'Yer'll not be gettin' the little feller into trouble by tellin' yer mam he said yer dad was sick, will yer? He's too young to understand, an' if he spoke out of turn, sure he wouldn't 'ave done it on purpose.'

'He had no right to say it,' Polly said, carefully putting a plate on the shelf which ran along the length of one wall. 'But I won't tell me mam on him. I wouldn't clat on me own brother.'

Mary swirled her hand around in the water for any spoons she'd missed, then slowly tipped the water out of the washing-up bowl. As she reached for the towel hanging on a nail behind the back door, she glanced at Polly. 'It's a funny thing for him to say, though, unless he heard it somewhere. I mean, it's not somethin' a child his age would make up, is it?'

Polly averted her eyes. 'I don't know, Miss . . . er . . . Auntie Mary.'

Mary dried her hands and hung the towel back on the nail. Little incidents came back to her, like the morning she'd met Ada and thought she'd been crying. And her neighbour so keen to get a job when she had her hands full with the two children. 'Polly, is it true that yer dad's sick?'

Polly screwed her eyes up. How could she lie to a woman who had been so good to her? But she'd made a promise to her mam and it was wrong to break a promise.

'Polly,' Mary said softly, 'I'm asking as a friend.'

'Yes, me dad is sick, but he's goin' to get better!' Polly was near to tears. 'He's goin' to see the doctor, then he's goin' to stay off work for a bit until he's properly well again.'

'I see.' Mary took the girl by the shoulders and pulled her towards her. Patting her back as she would a baby, she said, 'Don't feel bad about tellin' me, me darlin'. It'll not go any further than these walls. And it's sure I am that yer dad's goin' to be fine, so don't be worryin' yer pretty little head. But if yer ever think yer mam needs help, someone to talk to, then yer know where yer can find yer Auntie Mary.'

Chapter Four

Ada slipped the key out of the lock, stepped into the tiny hall and almost collided with her daughter who was waiting for her at the bottom of the stairs. Polly's face was white, her eyes wide with fear.

'Oh Mam, I'm not half glad yer've come, I didn't know what to do!'

'It's yer dad, isn't it?' Ada bent her leg backwards and kicked the door shut as a tight band circled her heart. 'It is, isn't it?'

Polly nodded, clasping her hands together tightly. 'I was lyin' in bed waitin' for him to come in an' say he was leaving for work, but he never came. He was coughin' real bad, so I went in to him an' got the fright of me life.' Polly's words came tumbling out with nerves. 'He looks terrible, Mam, an' he can hardly breathe.'

'I knew it!' Ada's eyes were on the stairs, her heart telling her to go up quickly to help the man she adored, but her mind keeping her rooted to the spot, fearful of what she might find when she got up there. 'He was bad in the night an' I wanted to get the doctor, but he got in such a state he was makin' himself worse. Said he only had today an' temorrer to do an' he could struggle on for the two days.'

'I've been so frightened, Mam! I didn't know whether to knock next door for Auntie Dolly, or run across for Auntie Mary.'

'It's the doctor we want, love, so slip something on an' run around to his house as fast as yer can. If his housekeeper opens the door an' tries to fob yer off, tell her I said it's urgent yer see Dr Rigby, an' stand there until she fetches him.' Ada put her hand on the bannister and steeled herself.

But before mounting the bottom stair she turned her head and said softly, 'On yer way back, Polly, give a knock next door an' ask Auntie Dolly to slip in, there's a good girl. She's very good in an emergency, is Dolly, an' I need someone with me.'

'I'll be with yer, Mam! I'll run as quick as I can, all the way there an' back.' Polly tossed her head defiantly. 'I'm not goin' to school today. I'm staying with you.'

Ada nodded and climbed the stairs with a heavy heart. She paused for a second on the landing and braced herself before opening the bedroom door. She was used to seeing her husband fighting for breath, but she had never seen him in the state he was in now. His nostrils were flared, their whiteness standing out in the grey pallor of a face wet with perspiration. His two hands were clutching at the bedding as he strove to force air into his lungs.

'Oh, love!' Ada ran to the bed and put out her arms to comfort him, but he raised a hand to ward her off.

'Don't . . . come . . . too close. Might . . . be . . . catching.' Tommy turned his head on the pillow as though the effort had sapped what little energy he had.

Ada stood looking down on him, feeling more useless than she'd ever felt in her life. The man she loved was suffering and she could do nothing to ease the pain. If it had been one of the neighbours lying there, she'd have been bustling about doing this, that and the other to help. But when it came to one of her own she was too numb with fear to even think straight. Tears built up in the corners of her eyes and as she felt the warmth of them running down her cheeks she mentally gave her head a good shake. With a finger and thumb, she nipped the flesh on her arm until the pain cleared her mind and brought her to her senses. 'Get moving,' she growled under her breath. 'Instead of standin' like one of the dummies in Blackler's window, get downstairs and bring a bowl of water an' a flannel up to wash him down. His vest is wringin' wet and so are the sheets, so get them changed.'

The thought was easier than the deed. There was no way she could lift Tommy up to change his vest or the sheets, so she had to be content with gently wiping his face, neck and hands with a damp flannel. She was doing this when Joey came to stand in the doorway. He'd heard Polly and his mam talking in the hall, sensed something bad was happening and had buried his head under the bedclothes until nature warned him that if he didn't get up he'd wet the bed.

'Mam – what's wrong with me dad?'

Ada turned her head. 'He's not well, son, and we've sent for the doctor. You be a good boy and go down an' get yerself dressed. When Polly comes back she'll get yer somethin' to eat.'

Dolly Mitchell appeared behind Joey and put her hands on his shoulders. 'Do as yer mam said, sweetheart, and show yer Auntie Dolly how big yer are by puttin' yer own clothes on. Yer can do that easy, can't yer?' Joey nodded, then after one last glance at the bed he made his way downstairs.

'He's a little love, that one,' Dolly said. 'I'll swap him for one of mine any day.' If she got a shock when she saw Tommy, she didn't let it show. 'Need any help, girl?'

'I wanted to change his vest, long johns an' the sheets before the doctor gets here, but I can't move him on me own.'

'I'll give yer a hand, we'll manage between us.' Dolly rolled her sleeves up to her elbows. 'I hope yer don't think I'm meddling, but I asked Polly to rake the grate out an' tidy the room up a bit, save you worryin'.'

'That's fine.' Having her neighbour there took some of the strain off Ada. Dolly never got ruffled, was always calm in a crisis. 'Shall we change his underclothes first, or the sheets?'

'It's easy to see yer were never a nurse, Ada Perkins.'

Ada's mouth gaped. 'Yer've never been a flamin' nurse!'

Looking all innocent, Dolly said, 'I never said I'd been a nurse, I just said it was easy to see *you* hadn't!' It was an

49

effort to sound cheerful because she was heartbroken, shocked to the core by the sight of Tommy. He had the look of a dying man if ever she'd seen one. And he was a good bloke, he didn't deserve this. All he lived for was to go out to work and look after his family. But she mustn't let her feelings show, mustn't deprive Ada of what hope she had in her heart. 'We'll change the bottom sheet first by rolling him on his side an' doin' it that way. Then his undies before the top sheet.' She saw Tommy's eyelids flicker and leaned down to whisper, 'I promise to keep me eyes closed when we change yer long johns, Tommy, so don't be worryin'. Anyway, yer've got nothin' that my feller hasn't got.'

They just had Tommy settled when Dr Rigby arrived. He took one look at the sick man and said, 'I can't do anything, he'll have to go into hospital. I'll telephone for an ambulance from the surgery.' He couldn't control his anger. 'It should never have been allowed to go on until he got into this state.'

'I know that, Doctor,' Ada said quietly, her voice choked with tears. 'But we weren't in a position to do anythin' about it.'

Dolly stood by, her face growing red with temper. As though Ada didn't have enough heartache without him laying the blame at her door! 'I'll show yer out, Doctor. I'm sure yer'll want to get back to telephone for an ambulance.'

Dr Rigby was stepping into the street when Dolly caught his arm. 'Just a word, Doctor, if yer don't mind.' She went on in no uncertain terms to tell him that what he'd said upstairs was uncalled for. 'She's been workin' for the last month as a cleaner, floggin' 'erself to death to save up enough for Tommy to take some time off. Have yer ever had meatless stew, Doctor? Have yer ever sat all night in the dark to save puttin' precious pennies in the gas meter? Have yer ever had to go to bed early because yer've no coal? Well, they've had to do all those things, and more. And d'yer know what the sad part is? He was comin' to see yer on Saturday to ask yer to arrange for him to see a specialist! They did everythin' they could, apart from robbin' a bank, but as yer can see, it wasn't enough. They're a good family, a loving family, an' I don't think yer should be layin' any blame at their door.'

John Rigby gave a half-smile. 'Well, that's putting me in my place, right enough! But there was no need for the lecture because as soon as the words were out of my mouth I'd have given anything to retract them. I will apologise to Mrs Perkins when I come back. My excuse is that I wasn't getting at her, I was getting at the system that keeps people like them down, on the bread line, living from hand to mouth. I see patients like Tommy every day, and every day I get angry. But unfortunately there is not a damn thing I can do about it.'

Dolly was speechless. Fancy a doctor saying things like that! He was right, everything he said was true, but it wasn't often a man in his position showed such concern for those not as well-off as himself. He'd even used a swearword! My, but he was a man after her own heart. Please God it would never happen, but if she ever got sick she'd be around to Dr Rigby in no time. She'd feel safe in his hands. The old doctor they had now was no good, he should have retired years ago. Whether you went to him with a sore throat, broken leg, measles, constipation or diarrhoea, you still came out of the surgery with the same bottle of red medicine. You'd be better off taking your chances with a ruddy witch doctor!

'Dolly, I've no pyjamas for him!' Ada was pacing the length of the room, stopping now and again to peep through the curtains to see if there was any sign of the ambulance. 'I can't let him go into hospital with no pyjamas, I'd be ashamed for him.'

'I can't help yer out there, girl, 'cos my feller hasn't got a pair to his name. He sleeps in 'is vest and long drawers, like your Tommy.' Dolly winked at Polly and Joey who were sitting close to each other on the couch looking like two scared rabbits. Poor buggers, she thought, they don't know what to do or say. Let's see if I can bring a smile to their faces. 'D'yer know what I've said to my feller time an' time again, Ada? I've said we'd look a right shower if the house ever went on fire while we were in bed. Can yer imagine us havin' to run into the street with him in his long johns, both knees with ruddy darns in an' a hole in the backside, an' me in me pink fleecy-lined drawers? Not a pretty sight, eh? We'd be the talk of the wash-house.'

Joey's chuckle was followed by a chortle from Polly. Ada turned to them and smiled. She was neglecting the children, she knew, but she couldn't help it when her mind was in a turmoil over Tommy. That's why she was glad when Dolly said she'd stay until the ambulance came and then take the children to her house. 'Your Auntie Dolly is tuppence short of a shilling, but she's harmless enough.'

A rap on the door sent Ada flying to the window. 'The doctor's car's outside but I can't see an ambulance.' With a hand to her mouth and her legs feeling as though they were going to give out any minute, she went to open the door. 'I wasn't expectin' you, Doctor.'

'The ambulance will be here any minute, but I wanted to have a word with you before it came. Where are the children?'

Ada frowned. 'In the living room, why?'

'I would prefer them not to be present because they might get upset. Is there anywhere they can go for half an hour?'

Dolly, who had been hovering near the door, made her presence known. 'I was takin' them home with me after the ambulance had been, but I can just as easy take them now.'

John Rigby took stock of the woman who had given him the length of her tongue just a short while ago. She looked strong and dependable, just the sort of person Mrs Perkins was going to need by her side when she heard what he had to say. 'I'd prefer you to stay, Mrs . . . er . . . ?'

'Mitchell's the name, Dolly Mitchell.' She popped her

head out of the door and jerked her thumb. 'I live next door.'

'Would the children be safe in your house on their own for a short time? I really do need to speak to Mrs Perkins and I would prefer them not to be here.'

Dolly stuck her hand in the pocket of the floral wrap-around pinny and brought out a penny. She always kept a penny there in case the gas went out, so she didn't have to fumble around in the dark looking for her purse. 'They can go to the shops for some sweets an' eat them in our 'ouse.'

'Come in, Doctor.' Ada was surprised to find her voice so steady because her mouth was dry with nerves and her heart thumping like mad. She asked herself why the children were being sent out and why Dolly had been asked to stay. It could only mean she was going to hear something she didn't even want to think about.

'Here's a penny, get yer coats on an' go and buy yerself some sweets.' Dolly offered the coin to Polly. 'It'll be better if yer sit in our 'ouse to eat them, 'cos if yer here when the ambulance comes yer dad might get upset.'

'No!' Polly shook her head vigorously. 'I want to see me dad before he goes!'

Ada dropped on her haunches in front of the two frightened children. She had to be brave for their sakes. 'Listen to me, both of you. Yer know how much yer dad loves yer, don't yer? Well, can't yer imagine how upset he'll be at havin' to leave yer? An' if he sees yer standin' there, it'll make it ten times harder for him. So be good children and do as Auntie Dolly tells yer . . . do it for yer dad.'

Joey put his coat on without a murmur. Too young to understand that the home life he was used to was in jeopardy, his mind was on the selection of sweets in the jars on the shelves of the corner shop. But Polly thought it was wrong that she couldn't see her dad before he went away. It wasn't fair on either of them. So without uttering a word, she made her feelings clear by the set of her face and her head held high. Taking Joey by the hand she marched out of the room, and if it wasn't for her dad lying sick upstairs, she'd have banged the front door behind them as a further show of her disapproval.

'Sit down, Mrs Perkins. We haven't long because the ambulance will be here any minute.' John Rigby stood in front of the grate, facing Ada and Dolly who were sitting side by side on the couch. 'There's no easy way of saying this but I think you should be warned in advance of what is facing you. The ambulance will be taking your husband to Fazakerley Hospital, and while you may go with him in the ambulance, you will not be allowed to go further than the entrance to the section he'll be admitted to.'

Ada gasped. 'Fazakerley! But that's miles away from here! I'd have to get two trams to get there an' it'd take ages! Why can't he go to the Northern, or even Walton?'

Dolly, in her wisdom, thought she knew the reason and she reached for Ada's hand. 'Steady on, girl, let the doctor finish.'

John Rigby ran a finger round the inside of his shirt collar. It was at a time like this he wished he'd taken up another profession. 'I may be wrong, Mrs Perkins, but I don't think so. I believe your husband has consumption, and in Fazakerley they have isolation wards that deal specifically with patients suffering from this disease.'

'Oh, no!' Ada beat her clenched fist on the arm of the couch. 'He hasn't got consumption, he hasn't, he hasn't!'

Dolly slipped an arm across her shoulders and held her tight. 'Lots of people catch it, girl, an' they get better. Don't be lookin' on the black side.'

'Your neighbour's right, you've got to think positive.' Why did it have to be me who put that look of despair on her face, John asked himself. He didn't have to do it, he could have let someone at the hospital break the sad news. But he couldn't have lived with himself if he'd done that. It would sound cold and impersonal coming from someone who spent their lives caring for the sick and dying but who couldn't allow themselves to get too involved with the patients or they'd never be able to do their job properly. 'I know it's hard, but try to put a brave face on for your husband's sake. I'll wait here for the ambulance while you go upstairs and talk to him. Try to make light of it, because the last thing he needs is to see you looking worried to death.'

'Will yer come up with me, Dolly? I'll be better if you're there.'

'Of course I will, girl.' Dolly shuffled to the edge of the couch and pushed herself up. 'Come on, let's go an' see how Tommy is.'

'Oh,' John called as they reached the door, 'in case I don't have time to speak to you again today, could you come to the surgery tomorrow to see me? I know you go to work very early, but I'll be there until a little after ten o'clock.'

Ada nodded. 'I'll be there about nine o'clock, after I've seen to the children's breakfast. Polly can keep an eye on Joey for me.'

The sigh that left Ada's lips as she sat down facing the doctor contained all the sadness and weariness she felt. She hadn't closed her eyes all night, seeing in her mind's eyes that picture of Tommy as they wheeled him through a door and away from her. It was a sight that would haunt her for the rest of her days. It had taken all her willpower to drag herself out of bed to go to work, but they needed every penny they could lay their hands on. She couldn't afford the luxury of staying in bed even though her mind was craving the oblivion of sleep and her body was crying out for rest.

John Rigby shuffled some papers on his desk, straightened his blotting pad and placed his fountain pen in the ink-stand next to a bottle of Quink. All the while he was watching Ada out of the corner of his eye and noting the black circles under her eyes and the dejected slump of her shoulders. She seemed to have aged years since yesterday and he was filled with compassion for her. 'I rang the hospital this morning to ask how your husband was.'

For a few seconds Ada held her breath. Please God, don't let it be bad news, I couldn't take any more. Then she managed to speak through the lump that had formed in her throat. 'What did they say?'

'It's too early for them to say anything, really, except that he's had a comfortable night. But that should ease your mind a little.'

'Thank you, Doctor. It was kind of you to do that an' I do appreciate it.' Ada fixed her gaze on the ink stain on the blotting paper. 'I'll be goin' to the hospital later, but first I've got to go into town to buy some pyjamas for him. I felt ashamed sending him into hospital the way he was, but yer see, pyjamas are a luxury people like us can't afford.'

'Well now, what a coincidence!' John leaned his elbows on the desk, his raised eyebrows feigning surprise. 'My wife was sorting my clothes out yesterday and I know she put two pairs of pyjamas aside to either give away or use as dusters. They're in quite good condition, and I think your husband is about my build, so if you wouldn't be offended I'll fetch them and you can see for yourself whether they're good enough.'

'Pride is another luxury I can't afford, Doctor,' Ada said. 'I'd be glad of them.'

'Good!' John pushed his chair back, deciding this was a job for his housekeeper rather than his wife, who would wonder why he was giving away two perfectly good pairs of pyjamas. She wouldn't object of course, she was a very kind and generous woman, but he didn't have the time to go into details with her right now. He had ten house calls to make when he'd finished his interview with Mrs Perkins, two of them urgent cases.

He left the room but was back within minutes. 'They'll be wrapped ready for you when you leave.' He sat down, laced the fingers of his two hands and rested his chin on them.

'Now to the purpose of your visit. Because of the nature of your husband's illness, you and the two children will have to have a thorough examination.'

'Why?' Ada cried. 'There's nothin' wrong with us!'

'Just a precaution, Mrs Perkins, nothing to worry about. Consumption is a disease which can be passed on to anyone who has been close to the person suffering from it. Coughing can produce germs in the air, saliva from a kiss . . . oh, there are many ways it can be passed on.'

Ada sat perfectly still, her brow furrowed. Then she said, 'He knew he had it! He's known for a long time but never said a word.' When she shook her head it was in sadness. 'He hasn't kissed the kids properly for ages, always a peck on the cheek. And he hasn't kissed me, either. We've never made . . . er, never been lovin' for months, but I thought it was because he was too tired.' She bit on her lip when she felt tears stinging her eyes. 'That man has gone to work every day knowin' he was killing himself, an' I was too stupid to see! Oh, I knew he was sick all right, but I never dreamed he was that bad or I'd have done somethin' about it before now.'

'You're not being fair to yourself, Mrs Perkins. You weren't in a position to do anything about it.'

'I've done it now, haven't I? I've got meself a job . . . I could have done that before now! Oh, what I earn won't keep us, but if necessary I'll scrub steps or even beg in the streets! If I'd have had any sense I'd have done it a year ago, not leave it until it's too late.'

'We don't know it's too late,' John Rigby said. 'Your husband's a very sick man and I'm not going to tell you otherwise, but people do get cured of consumption, so until we're told different, let's believe your Tommy's going to be one of the lucky ones. Don't give up hope, Mrs Perkins, you must never do that.'

Ada straightened her shoulders and sniffed up. 'You're right. No matter how bad I feel, or how worried I am, there's the children to think about. So I'll put a brave face on if it kills me, and I'll tell them their dad's goin' to get better.'

'That's the spirit!' John rose from his desk. 'Bring the children on Monday morning and I'll give the three of you a good examination.' He moved to open the door for her. 'If you knock on that door marked "Private", my housekeeper will have a parcel for you.'

'Thank you.' Ada passed him, then paused. 'I'll say a special prayer for you tonight.'

'How did yer get on?' Dolly was waiting by her front door for her neighbour. 'What did he want yer for?'

Ada glanced up and down the street. 'I'll come in for five minutes. The less people know, the better.'

'Oh aye, girl, if it wasn't so serious I'd be laughin' me bloody socks off! Mrs Gleeson in number sixteen said Tommy had a broken leg, Fat Mary said he'd had a heart attack, old Ma Pritchard said he had pneumonia an' my mate, that long string of misery in number four, she said she had it on good authority that he had a burst appendix.'

'Go 'way!' Ada's jaw dropped. 'Yer mean everyone in the street knows Tommy's in hospital?'

'Well, yer can't blame them for that, girl! They'd have to be ruddy blind to miss seein' a flamin' big ambulance.'

'Yer haven't told anyone what's wrong with him, have yer, Dolly? I don't want them to know, not yet anyway. I mean, we're not sure ourselves yet, are we? Although I know in me heart of hearts that Dr Rigby's not wrong, there's still a chance he could be.'

'I know yer think I'm a gossipin' old hag, girl, but I promise yer I've been the soul of discretion.' Dolly grinned into Ada's face. 'Doesn't that sound posh . . . the soul of discretion?'

Ada rolled her eyes to the ceiling. 'I bet yer couldn't write it down an' get the spellin' right.'

'Now what would I want to do that for, girl? It's not the sort of thing yer'd put in a letter, even if yer had someone to write to, which I haven't.' Dolly leaned against the sideboard and rubbed her hands together. 'Anyway, what did he want yer for?'

Ada quickly told her all that had been said and ended by holding out the paper bag she was carrying. 'He's a good man, there's no two ways about it. Just by chance I happened to mention I was goin' into town to get some pyjamas for Tommy, an' he said it was a coincidence because he had two old pair his wife was goin' to throw out. He asked if they'd be any use to me an', as yer can imagine, I jumped at them.'

It was Dolly's turn to gape. 'Blimey! I've never heard of a doctor givin' anythin' away before. Let's have a quick dekko, see how the other half live.'

Ada handed the bag over. 'See for yerself, nosy poke.'

The pyjamas were in a soft winceyette material, one pair maroon and cream stripes, the other dark blue and cream. 'Well, if these are old I'll eat me ruddy hat!' Dolly fingered the material. 'Look, there's not a break in them.'

'I can see that,' Ada said. 'I hopped in lucky there all right. Perhaps me luck's goin' to take a change for the better.'

'Do us a favour, girl?' Dolly asked, folding the pyjamas carefully before putting them back in the bag. 'When yer take a clean pair in to Tommy, let me wash the dirty ones. I can just see the face on her next door if she saw them hanging on me wash line. Blimey, she'd be callin' all the neighbours in to have a look-see.'

'Dolly Mitchell, I do believe yer a snob!'

'I would be if I 'ad anything to be a snob about.' Dolly handed the bag over and the smile dropped from her face. 'I'm goin' to give yer a bit of advice, girl, but yer don't have to take it if yer don't want to. If I were in your shoes, I wouldn't tell a soul about you an' the kids having to be checked over. Yer know what folk are like. If they hear the word "contagious", they'll avoid yer like the plague. Those yer think of as friends won't be so friendly, they'll cross the street when they see yer coming. An' don't tell Polly and

Joey what ails their dad, 'cos what they don't know they can't repeat.'

'I'd already thought of that, Dolly.' Ada gave a big sigh. 'I wouldn't care what they thought if it was only meself I had to worry about, but I wouldn't like the kids to be upset.' Again she sighed. 'You wouldn't cross the street to avoid me, would yer, Dolly?'

'Would I heckerslike! You're me mate, an' I stick by me mates. I'm not the only one, either. There's some good people in this street who think a lot of you an' yer family. Yer'll make it, girl, I promise.'

'Please God,' Ada said softly.

'Aye, an' Him as well. He's yer best friend.'

Chapter Five

'Can Polly come out for a game of ollies, Mrs Perkins?' Steve Mitchell asked, his face flushed with embarrassment and his eyes on a crack in the flagstone he was standing on. He dug his hand in his pocket and produced a large marble patterned in blue and white. 'I won this bobby dazzler off one of me mates an' I thought Polly would like to have a go with it.'

Ada ran the back of her hand across her forehead and smiled at the boy from next door. Gosh, he was a big lad for his age; must be as tall as his dad and he wasn't thirteen until next week. He would pass for sixteen if it weren't for the short grey trousers he was wearing, which were far too small for him. 'I won't stop her goin' out, Steve, but I don't think she will. The kids in the street haven't exactly been jumpin' over themselves to play with her. Even her mate, Doreen, has been givin' her a wide berth.'

'They're daft, all of them.' Steve shuffled his feet. 'Will yer ask her for us?'

'Come in an' ask her for yerself.' Ada held the door wide. 'She's only playin' Ludo with Joey.'

'Hello, Steve.' Polly looked up with surprise. 'Have yer come on a message for yer mam?'

'No, I came to show yer somethin'.' His chest puffed with pride, Steve opened his hand to reveal the prized marble. 'I won this off Mick Skelly an' I thought yer'd like a game with me.'

Polly pursed her lips and whistled. 'Ay, that's a whopper! Look, Joey, isn't that the biggest ollie yer've ever seen?'

Joey was really impressed. 'Can I hold it, Steve?'

'If yer mam will let yer, yer can come out and have a game

with me an' Polly. I'll teach yer how to play.'

His pale face aglow, Joey scrambled from the chair. 'I can go, can't I, Mam?' He saw the doubt on his mother's face and pleaded. 'Go on, Mam, say I can go.'

Ada wavered. 'Are you goin', Polly?'

Polly was torn. She didn't want to disappoint her brother, but her pride was against giving the kids in the street the satisfaction of ignoring her. Their attitude had puzzled and saddened her at first, until she'd mentioned it to her Auntie Mary. The Irishwoman had told her to pay them no heed, and that it was their parents who were to blame for their ignorance. After that she just got angry and stayed clear of them. It was her friend Doreen who had hurt her most. She didn't call for her for school any more, but once there she played with her as normal. Polly asked her the reason for this and was told Mrs Ashcroft had warned her daughter about playing with her in case she caught the disease. Polly was so mad she told her friend to take a running jump and stay away from her.

Joey tugged on her arm. 'Come on, our Polly!'

She looked into the bright blue eyes and her heart melted. 'As long as we play outside our front door.'

Ada watched from behind the curtains. Dolly had been right about finding out who her real friends were. But enough of the neighbours had rallied around to give her heart, and the rest she didn't care about. They didn't put the bread on the table or the pennies in the gas meter. But she worried about the children being upset. Particularly when it was unnecessary after Dr Rigby had given the three of them a clean bill of health.

Ada moved the net curtain aside to see more clearly. Steve and Polly were on their knees in the gutter, their thumbs flicking the marbles to try and knock their opponent out, while Joey stood looking on, waiting for his turn. Steve looked far too big to be kneeling in such an undignified position, but Ada reminded herself that although he might look grown-up he was still a boy at heart. She was about to turn away when she saw Sammy Whiteside, a lad from the top end of the street, saunter across the cobbles and approach Steve.

Ada's eyes narrowed. If Sammy had come to cause trouble she'd be out like a shot to give him a piece of her mind. Not that she didn't think Steve could handle himself 'cos she knew better, but she'd had enough and wasn't about to stand by and see her children humiliated any more. However, to her relief the boy knelt down and she could see his lips move as a smile crossed his face. She couldn't hear what was being said, but she heard his whoop of joy when Steve revealed his bobby dazzler. And whatever remark he made, it brought a smile to Polly's face. As she climbed the stairs, Ada told herself that the neighbours would all come round in the end, it was just a matter of time. And if she was honest, she couldn't really blame them. In their position she'd probably be acting the same way herself.

Ada hesitated at the top of the stairs and took a deep breath before entering the big bedroom. Every time she looked at the double bed she'd shared with Tommy for four-teen years, she felt like bursting into tears. She missed him so much, missed the comforting warmth of his body next to hers and his whispered 'I love you' before he went to sleep every night. He'd been gone three weeks now and it seemed like a lifetime. She hadn't told the children yet, but the doctor at the hospital said even if he responded to treatment it would be a year, perhaps two, before he was cured and able to come home. It would break Polly's heart if she knew it was going to be so long before she saw her dad again. They didn't allow children in the isolation wards but his bed was near a window, and when he was a bit better, Ada was hoping to take the children down and at least they could see each other, even if it was through a pane of glass. Seeing them would do Tommy the world of good, he fretted about them so much.

Ada tucked the blanket under the mattress and straightened the counterpane. The children weren't her husband's only worry. He kept asking how she was managing for money. She'd had to tell him she'd got another part-time job cleaning in a shop, otherwise he'd know she couldn't possibly be managing on what she was earning. If only she could tell herself a lie and get away with it. The trouble was, she was the one with the nearly empty purse. When he went into hospital she'd picked up three pounds ten shillings from Tommy's works, that was with his week in hand, and she had the two pounds she'd saved. But for the past three weeks she'd had to take twenty-seven shillings a week from the savings to add to her wages just to pay for the very bare necessities. She dreaded to think what would happen after next week when she only had her twelve and six a week to live on. The rent had to be paid come what may, or they'd be out on the street without a roof over their heads. She'd tried everywhere to get another job but without any luck.

Ada gripped the round brass knob on the bedhead and spoke to the empty room. 'I don't know what, but I've got to do something. It'll be over my dead body that my children end up in the workhouse.' She turned and left the room, and as she closed the door behind her she felt as though she was closing the door on her life.

'Mam, it's Steve's birthday next Monday. Can I 'ave a penny to buy a card for him?' Polly came into the room after putting Joey to bed. 'He gave me one on my birthday, remember?'

'I can't spare a penny, love, I'm sorry.'

'Ah, ay, Mam! I'd feel mean if I didn't give him one!'

'Polly, will yer shut up! I've told yer I haven't got a penny to spare so don't keep on about it.' Ada closed her eyes and groaned inwardly. What was she shouting at the kid for? It wasn't her fault they were in dire straits. She patted the arm of her chair and said, 'Come an' sit down, sunshine, I've got somethin' to tell yer.'

Polly didn't move. 'Is it somethin' bad about me dad?'

'No, it's nothing to do with yer dad.' Ada patted the arm of the chair again. 'Come on, love, yer've got to know. I can't keep it to meself any longer or I'll go out of me mind.'

Polly was at her side in a flash. 'What is it, Mam? You're not sick, are yer?'

Ada took hold of one of her daughter's hands and gazed into her face. Fancy having to burden someone so young, it just didn't seem right. But what was the alternative? 'Polly, if I had a penny to spare I'd give it to yer willingly because yer a good girl an' I love yer very much. But you see, I've got to make every farthing count 'cos there's not enough money comin' into the house. I've paid the rent for this week, but I'll not be able to pay it next week unless a miracle happens. An' miracles don't happen very often, not around here, anyway.'

Polly gazed at her mother with eyes like saucers. 'Yer mean yer won't be able to pay the rent an' we'll get put out on the street, like the Gregory family did last year? With the furniture on the back of a cart an' all the neighbours out gawping?'

'I hope it won't come to that.' Oh dear God, Ada thought, I'm trying to put an old head on young shoulders. But she couldn't alter what was a fact. Polly would know soon enough anyway, when there was no food on the table. 'I've tried everywhere for a job, but there's just none to be had. I don't need as much as when your dad was home 'cos I used to give him his tram fare, an' there was his carry-out. Another pound a week would see us eating from hand to mouth, but at least I could struggle through on that. The problem is, where do I get the pound from? I can't pluck it out of the air. But I'll keep on tryin', sunshine. I promise I won't just sit on me backside and do nothin'.'

'Have you asked Auntie Mary if she can help? She gets around to more places than you, she might know of some cleaning jobs going.'

'I can't go cryin' to the neighbours, Polly. They've all got enough troubles of their own.' Ada patted her daughter's hand. 'I'm glad yer know now the way things stand. It means I've got someone to talk to an' I don't have to bottle things up inside.'

Polly was silent for a while, wondering whether to say what was on her mind. She might get told off, but if it helped then it would be worth a ticking off. 'Mam, yer remember when Auntie Mary gave me a birthday party? Well, I didn't think anythin' of it at the time, but now I'm wondering if she knew me dad was sick 'cos when I was helping her wash the dishes, she said I was to tell her if I ever thought you needed any help.'

'I wonder why she said that?' Ada looked puzzled. 'Yer weren't gabbing yer mouth off to her, were yer?'

'No I wasn't, Mam, honest!' Polly wasn't going to tell tales on her brother; he was only a baby, he didn't know he was letting the cat out of the bag. 'She just came out with it for no reason at all. But she wasn't being nosy, Mam, she was just being kind.'

'I know she wasn't being nosy, love, she's too genuine a person for that. But I can't burden her with my troubles, it wouldn't be fair.'

'I'll help yer all I can, Mam, I promise.' What Polly said wasn't what she was thinking. If her mam wouldn't approach Auntie Mary, then there was no harm in doing it herself. They were in trouble, her mam looked worried to death, so who better to ask for help than a friend?

Polly was playing hopscotch outside her front door, her eyes peeled for a familiar figure who was due to turn the corner any minute. As soon as she saw her, she ran across the street. 'Can I carry yer basket for yer, Auntie Mary?'

'Sure it isn't heavy, me darlin', it's as empty as me head, so it is.' Mary smiled as she reached up and brought the basket down from its perch. 'But I'll not refuse a kind offer.'

'Can I try an' balance it on me head, like you do?'

'As long as yer keep yer hand on it.' Mary set the basket on the top of the black curly hair. 'Don't let go 'cos there's bits of wood stickin' out an' yer'll do yerself an injury.'

It looked so easy when Mary did it, but Polly found that even with one hand keeping it steady, the basket had a mind of its own and slithered about in all directions. She wasn't sorry when they reached the Irishwoman's house. 'Yer'll have to get it down for me, Auntie Mary. It's harder than it looks.'

'It is that, me darlin'! Didn't meself think I'd never get the hang of it at all, but like everythin' else, it takes time.' There was a wide, deep pocket in the thick black apron Mary wore around her waist to keep her money safe, and now she felt between the coins for the door key. 'Are yer comin' in, me darlin'? I wanted to have a word with yer an' intended to call at yer house later, but sure it'll save me the journey.' She laughed as she opened the door. 'Anyone would think yer lived miles away, instead of just across the street. If the truth was known, it's meself that's gettin' lazy in me old age.'

There was doubt on Polly's face as she gazed across the street at the front door she'd left ajar. 'Shall I go an' tell me mam where I am, in case she comes out lookin' for me?'

'It'll not take but a few minutes, Polly, an' then yer can tell yer mam what we've talked about an' see what she thinks.'

Polly marvelled once again at the spick and span living room. Not a cushion or ornament out of place, not a newspaper or shoes littering the floor, and the black grate polished until you could see your face in it. Considering she was out every day from early in the morning, her Auntie Mary kept the place like a little palace.

'Would yer mam be able to spare yer on a Saturday and Sunday if I could get yer a little job?' Mary kept her eyes averted as she pulled the shawl from her shoulders and folded it neatly before setting it down on the gleaming sideboard. 'It wouldn't pay much, but it would be pocket money for yer right enough.'

Polly's mouth dropped open. How did the Irishwoman know she'd been waiting for her just to ask that very question? Then Polly closed her mouth and mentally shook her head. She couldn't possibly have known, it was just a coincidence. Swallowing hard, and her voice no more than a whisper, Polly said, 'I'm sure me mam can spare me, but she doesn't get in from work on a Saturday until a quarter past eight an' I have to look out for Joey until then.' With hope surging in her heart, her voice grew stronger. 'I could come after that, though.'

'Sure, that'll be time enough, so it will.' Mary now looked the girl full in the face. 'Yer might not want the job when I tell yer what it is, but it's yerself that has the privilege of saying yea or nay.'

'Oh, I'll take it!' Polly tried in vain not to sound too eager but it came over in her voice. 'What is it, Auntie Mary?'

'Flower-selling.' Mary studied the pretty face to see if it clouded over with disappointment, but no, the eyes remained alive with excitement. 'There's ten of us work together at the bottom of Bold Street and one of them is an old lady called Sarah Jane. She's a lovely old lady, so she is, an' we all try an' help her as much as we can. She's really gone past working, but the poor old soul hasn't any family an' she's been working the same patch for donkey's years so she'd miss all the hustle an' bustle. Sure, if she had to give it up she'd fret so much she'd be dead in no time, an' that's the truth of it.'

'But what would I have to do?' Polly asked, her hopes fading. 'I mean, if she's not leavin', what would I be wanted for?'

'Well, Sarah Jane, God bless her, has trouble getting off her chair and bending down to pick the flowers out of the buckets.' Mary waved her arms. 'Sure, it's yerself would have to see it to understand. The old lady has about ten buckets in front of her, all filled with different flowers an' ferns. If a customer asks for a bunch of flowers from one of the buckets at the front, it's altogether too much for the old soul to get up from her chair, shuffle to where the flowers are and bend down and pick out a bunch. Then it's back she has to go to wrap them up. Because she's so slow, her trade has dropped to rock bottom. Although we do our best to help her, the top and bottom of it is we can't afford to lose custom ourselves. It's every man for himself an' the divil take the hindmost.'

Polly's doubts were growing by the minute. 'I don't think I could do that, Auntie Mary. I wouldn't know where to start.'

'Sure, wouldn't that be the least of yer worries, me darlin'. Sarah Jane knows the business inside out, she'd put yer wise. And wouldn't meself be around to show yer the ropes?'

The important question was whirling around in Polly's head and she had to put it into words. 'How much would I get, Auntie Mary?'

'I'll not be tellin' yer lies, me darlin', so I have to say I really don't know. It would all depend on how much business yer did for Sarah Jane. It could be sixpence a day, it could be a shilling a day. The more yer sell, the more yer earn.'

Once again Polly's hopes were raised. 'Yer mean I could earn a whole shilling a day? That would mean two shillings for the Saturday an' Sunday?'

'If yer keep a smile on yer pretty face an' a joke on those ruby lips, Sarah Jane could end up outselling the lot of us! But don't be too forward or pushy, 'cos yer'll upset the other traders. Just take yer lead from Sarah Jane an' meself, an' yer won't go far wrong. Yer've got yer head screwed on the right way, me darlin', you'll soon learn.'

Polly was hopping from one foot to the other, excitement bubbling inside of her. She couldn't wait to tell her mother the news. Two shillings a week would be a good help, and she'd make sure she earned that two bob. 'Can I go an' see what me mam says? She'll want to know all the ins and outs, so will it be all right if she comes over an' yer can explain it all to her?'

'Sure, it's only natural she'd want to know what her daughter was up to. She'd be a poor mother if she didn't, so she would.' Mary's look was sympathetic. 'Wouldn't it be grand now to have your own pocket money?'

Polly lowered her head. 'I'd give it all to me mam, I wouldn't keep a penny for meself.'

'I thought as much.' Mary held her arms out. 'It's a good daughter yer are, me darlin'.'

Polly flung her arms around the Irishwoman's neck. 'Oh Auntie Mary, me mam's in terrible trouble. She'll go mad if she knows I've told yer, so don't let on, will yer?'

'Hush now, sweetheart, don't be gettin' yerself in a state. I'll not tell yer mam that yer've said anythin', but the truth of it is, I didn't need telling. It doesn't take a brain box to figure out that if there's not enough money comin' in to cover what has to be paid, that's when the wolf comes knocking at yer door.'

Polly pulled away and brushed a hand across her eyes. 'I'll go an' tell me mam, see if it bucks her up. After all, two bob in the gas meter will give us light for the week.'

Mary sighed. Dear God, why are good people like the Perkins given such a heavy burden to carry? 'Tell yer mam to slip over, but give me half an hour to have a bite to eat. I'm so hungry I could eat a horse without takin' its saddle off.'

'I've just made a fresh pot of tea, but I'll let it brew for a few minutes. If there's one thing I can't abide it's weak tea.' Mary slipped a knitted tea cosy over the brown earthen pot. 'Sit yerself down, Ada me darlin', an' take the weight off yer feet.'

Ada chose the armchair at the side of the hearth. 'I've left our Polly pacing up an' down like a cat on hot bricks. She's been gabbling on about this job, but she was talkin' that fast I couldn't make head nor tail of her. All I could make out was that there's an old lady called Sarah Jane who can't sell flowers because she can't bend down. If Polly could help her on a Saturday an' Sunday, she'd be paid a shilling a day. And as if I can't do simple sums in me head, me daughter informs me that a shilling a day for two days equals two shillings.'

'I'll pour the tea an' we can sit down nice an' quiet while I tell yer what it's all about.' Mary didn't say another word until they were seated facing each other with a cup of tea in their hands. Then she went through the whole story again, slowly and in more detail. 'So there yer have it, me darlin', that's all there is to it.'

Ada sipped on the hot tea as her mind ticked over. It seemed too much of a coincidence to ring true. 'Mary, our Polly hasn't been pestering yer for a job, has she?'

'Glory be to God!' Mary put her drink down quickly on the arm of the chair, causing the tea to spill over the rim of the china cup and trickle into the saucer. 'I can't see into yer head, Ada Perkins, so I don't know what wild thoughts yer have runnin' around in there. But I'll not be beating around the bush, indeed I'll not! Your daughter has never pestered me for a job or anythin' else for that matter. Sure, wasn't she wide-eyed with surprise when I told her about it? And when I said she'd be able to earn some pocket money for herself, didn't the dear child say she didn't want any money for herself, she'd give anythin' she earned to her mam? It's a lucky woman yer are to have such a sensible, thoughtful daughter, an' it's grateful yer should be.' Mary leaned forward to rest her elbows on her knees. 'Ada, me darlin', pride is a good thing when yer can afford it, but it'll never put food on yer table, nor will the rent man take it as an excuse for not payin' yer rent. So pocket yer pride and take any help that's offered to yer. Especially when it comes from a friend who cares about yer.'

For a few seconds Ada watched a tea leaf floating on top of her tea. Around and around it went, mesmerizing and calming. 'Mary, we're on our uppers.' She looked across at her neighbour. 'I don't know what to do or where to turn.'

'What yer don't do, me darlin', is lose heart. Yer've been dealt a bitter blow, I'll not be sayin' otherwise. And it would be stupid of me to tell yer not to worry because yer have to worry about where next week's rent is coming from. But think of the good things in yer life an' it'll make the worry easier to bear. Yer have two of the grandest children in the world, so yer have, an' they're depending on you now that their dad is away for a while. It's father and mother yer have to be to them until Tommy comes home.'

Ada took a deep breath and blew it out slowly. 'Mary, apart from Dolly, I haven't told a soul, but it might be two years before Tommy comes home. I just don't see how I can keep the home together for all that time.'

Mary willed herself not to become emotional. The last thing Ada wanted or needed was sympathy. 'And have yer thought what will happen if yer *don't* keep yer home together? If yer get thrown out of this house, yer'll end up in a hovel with no runnin' water and the whole street sharing a lavvy. Is that what yer want Tommy to come out to?' She gave a deep sigh. 'I'm being cruel to be kind, Ada me darlin', so don't think badly of me. It's a heavy cross yer have to bear, an' that's the truth of it – but why don't yer let yer friends help yer carry it? I know it's money yer short of, an' they'll not be able to give yer that! Every family in the street is livin' from hand to mouth, wondering where the next day's meal is coming from. But help appears in different guises, Ada, an' yer shouldn't turn yer nose up at it, whether it's a kind word, a sympathetic ear or half a loaf of bread.'

There was a spark of admiration in Ada's eyes as she said, 'That job for Polly didn't just happen to come up, did it? You went out of yer way to get it for her.'

Mary smiled. 'Well, meself will have to be admittin' that old Sarah Jane hadn't thought about getting a young girl to help until I mentioned it. But once she'd had time to think about it, sure, wasn't she as pleased as Punch?'

'She really does need someone, does she? I mean, yer

didn't do it just to get a few bob for us?'

Mary shook her head. 'Sarah Jane's body might be showing its age, but sure, there's nowt wrong with her brains. Isn't it a fact now that the good Lord Himself couldn't talk her into doing somethin' she didn't want to do. It's a clever head she has on her shoulders, all right, an' no mistake.'

Ada leaned forward to put her cup on the table. 'I'm glad we've had this talk, Mary. I feel better already, more heartened, like. And I'm very grateful to yer. As they say, "A pal in need is a pal indeed". You've certainly made our Polly a very happy girl. She's over the moon because she'll be able to help me with what she earns.' She gave a low laugh. 'Seein' as it's confession time, yer may as well know exactly what this job means to her. I know it's wrong to burden a young girl with worries, but I had no one else to talk to. So, in desperation, last night I sat her down an' explained the situation to her. I said I needed a pound a week comin' in on top of my wages to keep the house going. Well, when she came back from talking to you, she had it all worked out. With the two shillings she'll earn, we've only got to find another eighteen shillings an' we'll be on Easy Street. She was so proud when she was tellin' me, it took me all me time to stop meself from crying.'

'God bless the child's innocence,' Mary said. 'On that money yer'd barely manage, there'd definitely be no cakes with yer Sunday night tea. But it's you that should be proud, Ada, me darlin' – proud to have a daughter who's as beautiful on the inside as she is to look at. They don't come like Polly very often.'

'I *am* proud of her. I'm proud of my Tommy and Joey as well. And right now I feel as though I could take the world on! I'm filled with determination to go out an' find a job that pays that extra eighteen shillings a week. I don't care how I do it, but by God, do it I will!'

Chapter Six

When she got to the bottom of Renshaw Street, Polly stopped to catch her breath. She'd run all the way from home, not wanting to be late on her first day. Leaning against one of the windows in Lewis's she looked around as she waited for her racing heartbeats to slow down. Her eyes lingered on the large Adelphi Hotel on the opposite side of the street, and she wondered what it was like inside. It was only for posh people with plenty of money so she'd probably never find out. Still, surprises could happen in life; it could be that one day she'd be all dolled up and walking up those wide steps and into a new world. When she left school and got a job, her dad would be back home and working, so with two wages coming in it wasn't beyond the realms of possibility that she'd be able to save up enough to just once walk into the imposing hotel and see how the other half live.

As Polly turned the corner of the large store and began to walk down Ranelegh Street she cast an eye over her coat. Her mam had pressed it last night and done her best to make it look presentable, but nothing could hide the frayed cuffs or the torn pockets. Still, it was the only one she had so it was Hobson's choice. There weren't many people around at that time on a Saturday morning, and long before she reached them she could hear the flower-sellers shouting to each other. 'How's your old man, Nellie?' Back came the reply: 'Moanin' as usual, Maggie! Says his corns are givin' 'im gyp. Bleedin' baby, that's what he is.'

Blind panic set in, and for a fleeting second Polly had the desire to turn on her heels and run back home to her mam. But it was the thought of her mother and the money she so badly needed that kept Polly's legs moving.

As she approached, Mary came to meet her. 'I've been keepin' me eye out for yer, me darlin'.' She took the girl's elbow and propelled her forward. 'There's someone waitin' to meet yer.' They skirted the buckets and the women who were busy filling them with colourful flowers and ferns. 'Sarah Jane, this is Polly, the girl I told yer about.'

Polly was dumbstruck. The old lady sitting on what appeared to be a stool, was older than anyone she'd ever seen. There wasn't an inch of space between the wrinkles and lines on her weatherbeaten face, and long hairs were growing from a wart on her chin. With a black shawl over her shoulders and her white hair brushed back from her face and plaited into a bun at the nape of her neck, she reminded the frightened girl of an old Indian squaw she'd once seen in a cowboy film. With her faded blue eyes narrowed and a severe expression on her face, she looked Polly up and down.

'Polly, say hello.' Mary pushed her forward. 'Don't be afraid of her. She looks tough, I'll grant yer that, but sure she's as soft as a pussy cat.'

'What do I call her?' Polly asked, wishing herself miles away. This wasn't going to work out 'cos she could see the old lady didn't like the looks of her.

'Yer can call me Sarah Jane, like everybody else does.' The voice was as rough as sandpaper. 'Unless yer want to be posh an' call me Miss Sarah Jane. If yer do that I'll think I've gone up in the world.' The old lady's face broke into a wide smile, showing a set of toothless gums. 'I 'ad yer there, girl, didn't I? Thought I was a wicked old witch, eh?'

Polly was amazed. With her toothless smile, the old lady looked so comical and yet so cuddly. 'I'll call yer Miss Sarah Jane.'

'Jesus Mary an' Joseph, don't do that, girl! Yer'll chase all the ruddy customers away!'

Polly's laugh rang out. 'I'm a good runner, I'll catch them an' bring them back.'

'If yer don't get the flowers out and arranged, yer won't *have* any customers,' Mary butted in. 'Yer can't waste time nattering.'

Sarah Jane grinned. 'If yer don't mind, missus, I'm interviewin' my young lady assistant.'

While this exchange had been going on, the other flower-sellers had kept themselves busy, but all the time they'd been maintaining a watchful eye on the oldest flower-seller in Liverpool. Sarah Jane was well-respected and loved, an adopted mother to all of them. They'd weighed Polly up and down and given each other the eye to say the kid didn't look bad and they were prepared to give her a chance.

'If you an' yer young lady assistant don't put a move on an' get those flowers out, yer'll be goin' home without any money in yer pocket,' the one called Nellie shouted. 'An' no money means no bottles of stout.'

Another voice piped up, 'What's yer name, girl?'

'Polly Perkins.'

'Well, Polly, get crackin' before town starts gettin' busy.'

Polly turned to Mary. 'Will yer tell me what to do, Auntie Mary?'

'All the flowers an' ferns bunched together in those buckets belong to Sarah Jane. Watch how me an' the others sort them out an' follow suit. Sure, it's slow yer'll be at first, it's only to be expected, but take yer time an' do it properly. Make them look as attractive as yer can to catch the eye of people goin' past. If yer get stuck, all yer've got to do is ask Sarah Jane.'

The next hour flew over as Polly watched, copied and learned. Ferns and gypsy grass in one bucket, carnations in another and so on. It was a pleasure to work with the wide variety of colourful flowers, and although she knew she had a long way to go to keep up with women who had been doing it all their lives, she would enjoy learning.

'How does that look, Sarah Jane?' Polly stood beside the old lady's stool. 'D'yer want me to change anythin', or move the buckets around? Just tell me an' I'll do it.'

'Yer've done fine, girl, they look a treat.' Sarah Jane smiled up at the pretty young girl. 'I think you an' me will make a good team.'

'I like it,' Polly said, her face breaking into a smile at the compliment. 'An' once I'm used to it I'll be a lot quicker.'

Florrie Cummins, sitting next to them on an upturned orange box, smiled across. 'Yer've done wonders, girl. They look a credit to yer.'

'Ay, don't be praisin' her too much,' said Sarah Jane, 'or she'll be askin' for a rise on 'er first day.'

The city centre started to throb with life about ten o'clock when people arrived to do their weekend shopping. Several stopped to gaze at the colourful displays and Polly was to have her first lesson in the art of selling. 'Come on, missus, yer can't miss a bargain like this,' yelled Florrie. 'Lovely daffs at three ha'pence a bunch, I'm practically givin' them away.'

'How much are the marguerites?' asked the woman.

'Tuppence a bunch to you, missus, an' cheap at half the price. They'd look a treat on yer sideboard with a nice piece of green fern to show them off.' As she was wrapping the flowers, Florrie winked at Polly and mouthed, 'Go on, have a go.'

But Polly was too shy; she left the shouting to Sarah Jane. And what a voice the old lady had! She could be heard above all the other women and their voices were certainly loud enough to wake the dead. Sarah Jane gave Polly a dig as a woman stopped to admire the blooms. 'Now's yer chance, girl.'

Polly moved to the side of the buckets and smiled broadly at the woman. 'Aren't they lovely? My mam would be over the moon if I took some of them home to her.'

'How much are they?'

Polly looked towards Sarah Jane. 'Those are tuppence each, an' a real bargain,' the old lady said. 'Yer only need two of them in a vase an' they'd set any room off.'

The woman hesitated. 'That's sixpence for three?'

Polly took one of the blooms out of the water and held it towards the customer. It was in a burnt orange colour and had a massive head. 'Isn't it beautiful? Or perhaps yer'd like a white or a yellow?' Quickly she pulled two more of the blooms out and bunched them together. 'I think they're the most beautiful flowers I've ever seen. If I had a tanner I'd buy the three of them for me mam.'

The remark was made with such sincerity that it decided the woman. 'I'll take the three of them,' she said impulsively.

'Oh, thank you, madam.' Polly's smile made the woman think the child was more beautiful than the flowers. 'I'll wrap them nice for yer.'

Sarah Jane slipped the sixpence into her wide pocket, a smile of satisfaction on her lined face. 'I knew the minute I clapped eyes on yer that you an' me would make a good team. That was yer first sale, girl – the next won't be so hard.' As Polly made to move away, frightened of missing any likely sales, the old lady pulled on her coat. 'Keep that smile on yer face, girl, 'cos it would melt a heart of stone.'

Mary left her place to come and give Polly a hug. 'Sure, that was good salesmanship, me darlin', so it was. I'm proud of yer.'

The other women all smiled encouragement and Polly felt as though she'd been accepted. Her next customer wanted a bunch of marguerites, and Polly decided to try her powers of persuasion once again. She took the bunch of white flowers out of the bucket, then picked out a piece of fern. 'See how nice the green looks with the white? It doesn't half set them off.'

The customer pursed her lips. These Mary Ellens would sell yer the flaming Town Hall if you were daft enough to buy it. Still, she had to admit the girl had a point. The green did set the white flowers off a treat. 'How much is the fern?'

'Only a penny, madam, an' definitely worth it.' Polly remembered Mary telling her not to be too forward so she added, 'But it's up to you. If yer don't want it then yer don't have to buy it.'

The woman opened her handbag and took out a purse. 'Go on, I'll take them both.'

Sarah Jane was beside herself with happiness as the day wore on and her pocket became heavier. Polly had picked things up so quick the old lady hadn't stirred from her stool all day. The girl definitely had a way with her, no doubt about that. She was doing as much business as any of the other vendors and it was all down to the smile that was forever present on the pretty face.

'Have yer got change of half a crown, Sarah Jane?' Polly handed the coin over. 'Two bunches of carnations and one gypsy grass.'

The old lady's eyes narrowed as she counted the change out. 'Here yer are, girl, an' tell them not to spend it all in one shop.'

All the women had brought sandwiches which they ate when there was a lull in trade, and Irish Mary had brought enough to share with Polly. The young girl was glad of them because her tummy was rumbling with hunger. 'I'm doin' all right, aren't I, Auntie Mary?'

'It's wonders yer workin', me darlin', an' that's the truth of it. Sure, just look at the smile on Sarah Jane's face. Doesn't that tell yer what yer want to know?'

'I think she's lovely.' Polly caught the old lady's eye and winked. 'I can't wait to tell me mam about her.'

'There's someone at me stall, I'd better go.' Mary beat a hasty retreat, calling over her shoulder, 'We start packing up about half-past five.'

The remark set Polly wondering how Sarah Jane managed when the day was over. What happened to her stool, the buckets and any flowers that were left? There wouldn't be much stock over today by the looks of things, but every day wasn't as busy as a Saturday. She went to stand next to the old lady while at the same time keeping an eye out for a potential customer. 'Are yer all right, Sarah Jane?'

'Right as rain, girl! It's the best day I've had for ages, thanks to you. I was just thinkin' it's a pity yer still at school, 'cos yer could work here every day – except Monday, that is. There's no use comin' on a Monday 'cos it wouldn't be worth the effort. Everyone's skint.'

'I wish I could come every day, I haven't half enjoyed meself.' But although it was true that she'd enjoyed herself, it was the money that was uppermost in Polly's mind. Just think, if she worked six days it would be six shillings a week! What a help to her mam that would be. 'Sarah Jane, me mam is very strict with me an' me brother, Joey, an' she's always saying we must be polite and respect our elders. She'd have me life if she heard me callin' yer by yer first name.'

'Well, that's me name, girl, an' everyone knows me as that.'

'I know it's only a pet name, but I've heard a few of the women callin' yer Ma.' Polly was blushing to the roots of her hair, afraid that what she was about to say might cause offence. 'I was wonderin' if I could call yer Grandma? Yer see, I haven't got a grandma or a grandad. Both me mam's an' me dad's parents died when I was only little. I've always wished I had a grandma.'

Sarah Jane was a tough old soul and she couldn't remember the last time she'd cried. But right now she could feel a lump in her throat and tears stinging the backs of her eyes. Coughing to clear her throat, she said in a choked voice, 'I'll be yer grandma, girl! I might not be a good one 'cos I've never had any experience, but I'll have a bleedin' good try at it.' She put a hand across her mouth. 'A grandma shouldn't swear, should she? Not a good one, anyhow. So I'll watch me mouth from now on, except on a Saturday night when I've had a few stouts down me, then I've no control over me tongue.'

Polly roared with laughter. 'Yer'll make a lovely grandma, an' as I won't be seein' yer on a Saturday night yer can swear as much as yer like.' She spotted a man giving their flowers the once-over. 'Watch this, Grandma. I'll bet yer I get a sale.'

She was soon back to hand over a shilling. 'That's all yer carnations gone, Grandma, an' he told me to keep the change.'

'Bloody hell, girl!' Sarah Jane looked down at the silver coin. 'I'll be able to get rotten drunk tonight!'

Polly wagged a finger. 'My Grandma doesn't get rotten drunk. An' anyway, I want me wages before yer spend it in the pub.'

'How much did Irish Mary say yer'd get?'

Polly didn't like asking for money but it was a case of having to. That's what she was there for. 'A shilling a day, but it would depend upon how much we sold.'

Sarah Jane had not moved from her stool all day. She looked like a sweet old lady who was only there to pass the time. But she had a clever head on her shoulders and she knew to the penny how much she had in her now very heavy pocket. She had worked out how much she'd spent on supplies and how much profit she'd made so far. But the day wasn't over yet and she wasn't going to build the girl's hopes up. 'So far so good, girl, yer well on target.'

Content that her shilling was safe, Polly went about selling the remaining stock with a will. And by five o'clock they were left with just a few bunches which Sarah Jane told her to sell off for half-price. Polly did this in no time, shouting out with the rest of them. 'Come on, ladies, half-price flowers! Don't yer know a bargain when yer see one?'

Finally, Polly emptied the water down the grid and stacked the empty buckets on top of each other. 'What do I do with these?' she asked Sarah Jane. 'D'yer take them home with yer?'

The old lady showed her toothless gums. 'Gerroutofit, girl! D'yer think we all walk home with ten buckets on our heads? Nah, there's a feller comes with a cart an' he takes them away an' brings them back on Tuesday mornin'. We give 'im a couple of coppers for his trouble.'

'Tuesday morning?' Polly's heart sank. 'But what about tomorrow? Auntie Mary said it was for two days, Saturday an' Sunday.'

Sarah Jane shook her head. 'The shops all close on a Sunday, girl, it would be a waste of time. No, the only places to sell flowers on a holy day is outside a hospital, church or cemetery.'

'Will I be comin' with you?'

Again the old lady shook her head. 'I don't work on a Sunday, girl, it's too much for me. It's not like 'ere where I can sit down, it's on yer feet all day an' me poor old plates of meat aren't up to it. The women go in pairs an' I'd just be a drag on whoever I was with.'

'So I won't be wanted tomorrow?' Polly was heartbroken. The elation she'd felt after a successful first day evaporated. 'I was lookin' forward to tomorrow.'

'If Irish Mary said yer'd be workin' tomorrow then she must 'ave somethin' in mind for yer.' There was a glint in the tired eyes as the old lady held out her two hands, both tightly clenched. 'Double or nothin', eh?'

'No!' Polly cried. 'I need the shillin' for me mam!'

'It was my idea of a joke, but it's not bleedin' funny, is it?' Sarah Jane shook her head and tutted. 'I'll have to remember to keep this tongue of mine under control when I'm with me granddaughter.' She opened her right hand to reveal a two-shilling piece nestling in the palm. 'Yer wages, girl.'

Polly stared. 'But that's too much! I only want a shilling.'

'Yer had quite a few coppers in tips, so that's about right. Anyway, yer worked hard an' yer deserve it.'

'Oh, thank you!' Polly bent to kiss the wrinkled cheek. 'I'll see yer next Saturday, then, shall I?'

'Before, if yer feel like bunkin' off school.' Sarah Jane gripped her hand. 'No, forget I said that, girl. God forbid that I should try an' lead yer astray.'

Polly turned when she heard her name being called. The flower-sellers had now cleared all their paraphernalia away and were standing in a group with Mary in the centre beckoning to her. 'I'll have to go, I'll see yer next week,' she said to Sarah Jane.

'Come here, we want yer,' Mary said, when Polly hovered on the edge of the group. She waited until the girl was standing beside her, then went on, 'We all think yer've done wonders for the old lady. Yer've brightened her life up no end, and that's the truth of it. An' everyone that's good to her, is good to us. So we've had a little whipround – not much, mind you, but just to show our appreciation here's a shilling that's been collected between us.'

It was all too much for Polly and the tears began to flow. Two shillings off Sarah Jane, and now this! She couldn't wait to see her mam's face. 'Thank you,' she stammered. 'I don't know what to say, yer've all been so good to me.'

'Just take the shillin' and stop blabberin',' Nellie said, in her thick Liverpool accent. She was a big woman was Nellie, with a mouth on her like a fog horn. But when you got to know her, you soon found out her heart was as big as her body. 'Yer a smashin' little worker an' yer did the old girl proud. She can go out tonight and sup as many bottles of stout as she can get down her.'

'An' yer've done us a favour as well,' Florrie chipped in. 'We usually give her a hand, which means we lose a bit of trade ourselves. But today, with you helpin' her, we haven't had to worry about 'er an' we've all had a good day.'

'Come on, let's go,' Maggie Murphy said. 'Me flamin' feet are killin' me. I'll be lucky if I make it to the pub tonight.'

'Oh, my God, will yer listen to her!' Nellie bawled. 'It's never been known for yer to miss a night at the ale-house, Maggie Murphy! If ever yer didn't turn up, I'd start collectin' for a wreath 'cos I know the only thing that would keep yer away was if yer were dead!'

Laughing, Mary put her arm across Polly's shoulders. 'Let's get yer home, Polly, before one of these ladies says somethin' not meant for young ears. Sure, 'tis the divil himself that gets into them sometimes.'

'Three shillings?' Ada shook her head. 'Pull the other one, sunshine, it's got bells on.'

Polly was bursting with pride as she held out her hand. 'See for yerself – a two-bob piece *an'* a shilling.'

'Oh love, where did you get all that?'

Polly quickly told the tale, words pouring from her mouth as though she had no control over them. 'I didn't half do good, Mam. Sarah Jane was over the moon an' the others said I'd done well for her.' She placed the coins on the table in front of her mother. 'That's a good help, isn't it, Mam?'

'It's more than good, love, it's marvellous. I feel that proud of yer I could cry.'

Joey had been listening wide-eyed. 'What d'yer want to cry for if it's good, Mam? Yer only cry when somethin' bad happens, like when yer've got the belly ache or a toothache.'

'No, yer don't, our Joey!' Polly said. 'Yer cry when nice things happen as well. I felt like bawlin' me eyes out when I got that much money and they were all so kind to me.'

Ada pushed the shilling towards her daughter. 'Take that to the corner shop an' get a birthday card for Steve. An' get a pennyworth of sweets between you and Joey.'

Polly shook her head. 'No, Mam, yer'd better keep hold of it 'cos I won't be gettin' much temorrer. They don't sell flowers in town on a Sunday, on account of the shops bein' closed, an' I'm goin' with Auntie Mary to Anfield cemetery. But I can't see her sellin' many flowers there, so I might only get coppers.'

'Go to the corner shop an' do as yer told.' Ada picked up the shilling and pressed it into her daughter's hand. 'It's only a penny for a card an' a penny for sweets, so I'll still have two and tenpence left, way over what I was expectin' yer to give me.'

'Can I come with yer, our Polly, an' choose me own ha'porth of sweets?' Joey stood beside her, pulling at her coat. 'Come on, it'll soon be me bedtime.'

'At last he's in the land of Nod. I thought he'd never go off.' Ada fell into the chair and stretched her legs. 'It's been a long day.' She was about to say she'd missed her daughter running the messages for her and looking after Joey, but bit her tongue before the words came out. 'Me legs are tired.'

'Why don't yer sit on the couch an' put yer feet up? Go on, Mam, take it easy for a change.'

'D'yer know, I think I will. I'll leave the flamin' washing until tomorrow when I'm off.' Ada stretched out on the couch with a cushion at her back. 'That's better. Now I can sit in comfort while yer tell me what yer did today and what Sarah Jane's like.'

'Oh Mam, she's lovely! I don't mean to look at 'cos she's very old an' her face is all wrinkled.' Polly didn't need to exaggerate when it came to describing the old lady. 'She frightened the life out of me when I first saw her, but once yer get used to her yer feel like cuddling her, she's that nice. I'm a bit sorry for her 'cos she's no family at all. Auntie Mary told me she has a room with a family and they look after her.'

'Yer seem to have enjoyed yerself.'

'Oh, I did! If I could go down there every day we'd nearly have enough money to keep us goin', wouldn't we, Mam?'

Ada looked startled. 'Don't you even think of saggin' school, young lady! It's me the School Board would be after, an' I'm in enough trouble as it is.'

'Just now an' again, Mam, just to see us through until me dad comes home and goes back to work.'

'I said "no", Polly, so leave it at that! I'd have the School Board on me like a ton of bricks.'

'Are yer goin' to see me dad temorrer?'

Ada's nod was accompanied by a sigh. 'I haven't been all week an' I feel terrible about it. But it's fourpence fare an' I can't afford that very often. Still, yer dad understands how we're placed. He won't think badly of me.'

'When will he be comin' home, Mam? Will he be home for the summer?'

'I don't think so, sunshine, he's still very sick.' Ada noticed her daughter's downcast face and added, 'But he's in the right place an' he's goin' to get better. If he comes home too soon, he'll end up sick again – an' we don't want that, do we?'

'When yer go in temorrer, will yer tell him about me job? An' tell him about Sarah Jane an' all the other women. It'll cheer him up an' make him laugh. An' don't forget to tell him me an' our Joey love him very much an' can't wait for him to come home.'

'I'll tell him, love,' Ada lied. Tommy was still very poorly indeed, and to inform him about his daughter having to go out and sell flowers would break his heart and just about finish him off. She'd not tell him anything that would upset him. As far as he knew, she had two cleaning jobs and they were managing to scrape along. She had no intention of telling him otherwise.

Chapter Seven

Ada let her body relax to sway in rhythm with the motions of the tram as it trundled along Walton Road. From side to side, backwards and forward she let herself go, the lightness of her body calming the turmoil in her mind. The visits to Tommy took their toll. The man lying in the bed was a mere shadow of her husband and she was heartbroken every time she saw him. The hospital conditions made it worse; with him in isolation she wasn't allowed to get near enough to comfort him. She thought he looked worse than the last time she'd visited, but when she collared the Sister, she was told that, although there was no sign of improvement, he certainly wasn't any worse. It was that small crumb of comfort that kept repeating itself in her mind. She had to believe he was going to get better otherwise she wouldn't be able to carry on, she'd go out of her mind. The part that hurt the most was Tommy's attempt to pretend he wasn't as ill as he looked. She could tell he was using up all his energy to ask after the kids. How was Joey, was he looking forward to going to school? What was Polly doing to help her in the house, and how was she managing with having two jobs? He'd said, 'Yer'll have to watch out, love, or yer'll wear yerself out.' The same old Tommy, thinking of everyone else but himself.

The conductor's voice brought Ada out of her reverie and, glancing through the window, she saw the tram was nearing her stop. She stood up and holding on to the rail at the back of the seats for support, she made her way down the aisle to the platform. She'd lied her head off to Tommy, painting a very rosy picture which was so far from the truth it would have been laughable if it weren't so serious. But at least he'd looked peaceful when she'd left him, believing every lie that had come out of her mouth.

Dolly Mitchell opened the door to Ada with a big smile on her face. 'Your Joey saw yer passin' the window an' ran like hell for his coat. He's so eager to get away anyone would think I'd been beatin' the livin' daylights out of him.'

'I'll come in for a minute, see if yer can cheer me up,' Ada said, pinching her neighbour's cheek as she passed. 'I always feel down in the dumps after I've been to the hospital.'

Dolly's husband Les had the *News of the World* spread out on the table and was poring over the football pages. When Ada entered he quickly closed the pages and folded the paper. 'Hello, Ada. Come in, girl.'

Joey had his coat on and, eager to get home, he grabbed his mother's hand and pulled. 'Come on, Mam, our Polly will be home soon.'

'Not so fast, young feller me lad!' Dolly chucked him under the chin. 'Yer mam's goin' to sit down an' have a nice cup of tea.'

'No thanks, Dolly, I'm stoppin' Les from readin' the paper. Thanks all the same, but I won't bother yer.'

'Oh, I'm not askin' yer, girl, I'm tellin' yer!' Dolly looked determined. 'An' yer'll find out why as soon as I've brewed up.'

Ada shrugged her shoulders as Dolly made for the kitchen. 'I'm sorry, Les, but I'm not about to argue with your wife 'cos she's bigger than me.'

'I don't blame yer, she throws a hefty punch. I should know 'cos she's landed one on me many a time.' Les pointed to a chair. 'Sit yerself down, girl, an' tell us how Tommy is.'

'He's just about the same, Les,' Ada said, choosing her words with care because she could feel her son's eyes on her. 'No better an' no worse. It's goin' to be a long haul, I'm 'fraid.'

'As long as he gets better, girl, that's the main thing. He's only a young man an' when he does come home he'll be as right as rain.'

Dolly kicked the kitchen door wide with her foot. 'Get that paper off the table, Les Mitchell, an' clear a space.' She came through carrying a tray which she set in front of Ada before standing back with a look of triumph on her chubby face. 'There yer are, Ada Perkins, aren't I posh!'

Ada smiled. On the tray were three delicate china cups and saucers with a milk jug and sugar basin to match. In white, decorated with pretty pink flowers, the set was very attractive. 'Oh, they're lovely, Dolly! Yer shouldn't be using them for me, keep them for best!'

'What the 'ell do I want with best cups? All me mates are like me, as common as muck. They wouldn't know china from mug.'

'Well, thanks very much, Dolly Mitchell.' Ada feigned anger. 'Sunday afternoon an' I have to come here to be insulted!' She looked to Les for support. 'I'm not as common as muck, am I, Les?'

'Ay, don't you be gettin' round my feller, fight yer own battles.' Dolly folded her arms and hitched up her bosom. 'I'm gettin' me own back on yer for sayin' I was heavy-handed with me crockery. Well, I'm not, yer see! I got those at five o'clock last night, that's twenty-four hours ago, an' I haven't broke one yet. So there!'

Mild-tempered Les muttered, 'The day's not over yet.'

'Ay, I heard that! Don't be gettin' cocky with me, throwin' yer weight around just 'cos we've got visitors, Les Mitchell! Ada here won't stop me from givin' yer a thick ear if I've a mind to.'

'Will yer stop shoutin' and pour me tea out?' Ada grinned, thinking how lonely she'd be without the humour of her neighbour to lift her spirits. 'I can't remember the last time I drank out of a china cup.'

Dolly's body shook with laughter. 'Well, enjoy it while yer

91

can, girl, 'cos they'll probably all be smashed to smithereens by tomorrow.'

'They're beautiful.' Ada watched the cup filling with weak tea. 'Where did yer get them?'

'Les got them on his round. Some posh, la-di-dah woman said she'd broken some and they were no use to her now as they weren't a full set.' Dolly handled the cup and saucer carefully. If she was going to break one it wouldn't be in front of Ada or she'd never hear the end of it. 'Pity about some folk, isn't it? Poor cow, I feel sorry for her.'

Ada reached for the sugar basin only to find it empty. Thinking it wouldn't hurt her to do without sugar, 'cos more often than not she never had any in her own house, she put the basin down and picked up the milk jug. That was empty too!

Realising she was having her leg pulled, Ada turned to Dolly. Her neighbour was holding her tummy and rocking with silent laughter. 'Ever been had, girl?' Dolly's bosom bounced up and down as her guffaws filled the room. 'What d'yer expect? A china cup and saucer, *an'* sugar an' milk! Blimey, there's no pleasin' some people.' Still laughing she bent to open the sideboard cupboard and brought forth a tin of condensed milk. She plonked the tin of conny-onny on the table, nudged Ada's shoulder and said, 'Get it down yer an' like it; beggars can't be choosers.' Again the room rang with her laughter. 'That poor bloody cup's come down in the world, hasn't it? Probably never had conny-onny in it before, so watch it doesn't crack with the shock.'

Grinning broadly, Ada looked on the tray for a spoon. 'What am I supposed to use for the conny-onny?'

'Yer could use yer finger, but I suppose I'd better get yer a spoon or yer'll be tellin' the neighbours I've got lovely new cups but bloody awful manners.'

'Every dog knows its own tricks best, Dolly.' Ada watched her open a drawer in the sideboard and chuckled when things started getting flung out in her search for a spoon.

Scarf, gloves, braces, a pair of socks and an odd lisle stocking were plonked on top of the sideboard, along with a few choice swearwords.

'Ah, here we are, I knew I 'ad one in there.' After wiping the spoon on the corner of her pinny, Dolly handed it to Ada with a flourish. 'I'm sorry it's not silver, but I pawned me best canteen last week.'

'Ha, ha, very funny.' Ada stirred her tea. 'Where's Steve and Clare?'

'Your guess is as good as mine, girl. Steve said he was goin' to the park with 'is mates, but where Clare is, God only knows.' Like Ada, the Mitchells only had the two children, but there wasn't such a big age gap between Dolly's as there was between Polly and Joey. Clare was eleven, only two years younger than Steve. 'They'll be in when their bellies are rumbling.'

'Steve's big day tomorrow, eh? One more year an' he'll be leaving school.'

'I can't wait, either. I won't know I'm born with a few more bob comin' in every week.' Dolly looked across at her husband. 'But we don't starve, do we, love? You make sure of that.'

'Just about, Dolly, just about. Times is hard but there's folk a damn sight worse off than us.'

'Not much doin' at the docks, then, Les?' Ada asked.

'I got three days in this week, which is better than it has been. But yer get fed up standin' there every morning hopin' yer'll be one of the lucky ones.' It wasn't often Les raised his voice, but he did now. 'It's a ruddy big fiddle! The gaffers have their favourites an' the same men get taken on every day. No one can tell me there's no back-handers given over 'cos it's as plain as the nose on yer face.'

'Don't be gettin' yerself all het up, love, or yer indigestion will start playin' yer up,' Dolly said, trying to calm him down. 'It's the same the world over an' always will be. No matter where yer go it's not what yer know, but *who* yer know.'

'It's a good job yer've got yer other little business, Les,' Ada said. 'At least yer've got that to fall back on.'

Les gave a wry smile. 'It's a case of havin' to, Ada – that, or go hungry. I can't say I enjoy it, but it brings in a few bob . . . an' some china cups for me dearly beloved.'

Dolly's bosom was hitched up once again as she preened herself. 'Did yer hear that, Ada? My feller called me his dearly beloved! Oh, he can be dead romantic when he feels like it, can my Les. The trouble is, he only feels like it every Preston Guild.'

Joey had had enough of grown-up talk by this time. He wanted to go home to see if Polly was there. They could have a game of snakes and ladders before he went to bed. 'Come on, Mam, let's go.' He pulled on her skirt. 'If Polly's back, she'll be hungry.'

That reminded Dolly, and she nodded her head knowingly. 'Oh, I saw Polly with Irish Mary this mornin' on me way to Mass. From what Mary said, your daughter did very well yesterday, worked as good as the older women.' She dropped her banter. 'She's a good kid is your Polly, always has been. An' her few bob will be a big help to yer.'

Ada nodded. What was the use of saying they'd need more than a few bob to survive? If all she ever did was moan she'd soon have doors closing in her face. People had enough troubles of their own without listening to her whining all the time. 'I'll get home an' see what we've got in the house to eat. With bein' in the fresh air all day, our Polly will be starving hungry.'

'The rain kept off for her anyway, that's a blessin'.' Dolly screwed up her face. 'Miserable bloody job standin' outside a cemetery at the best of times, but imagine if it was tippin' down.'

'Did yer ever do anythin' with that coat yer bought off me?' Les asked, picking up the Sunday paper. 'Good bit of stuff in that coat. It would be a shame to waste it.'

'Oh, it'll not get wasted, no fear of that! I'm goin' to start unpicking it tonight.' Ada laughed and pretended to stumble as Joey pulled her along the hall as though it was a matter of life and death. 'If I make a good job of it I might start takin' in sewing. Ta-ra for now.' Standing on the front step, she called in a loud voice, 'Thanks for the tea in those lovely china cups, Dolly. It was a treat.'

Dolly, who had followed her to the door, grinned. 'I hope that cow in number four heard yer, give her somethin' to talk about. While she's havin' a go at me she's leavin' some other poor bugger alone.'

Polly got in not long after them and she was carrying a bunch of daffodils which she proudly handed to her mother. 'These are for you, Mam, off Auntie Mary.'

'That was good of her. We haven't had flowers in the house for God knows how long.' Ada admired the bright yellow trumpets which seemed to bring sunshine into the room. 'How did yer get on?'

'It wasn't as good as yesterday, but then Auntie Mary had told me it wouldn't be. She only had her basket with her, an' a smaller one for me. I stood on one side of the cemetery gates an' she stood on the other so we wouldn't miss anyone. At first I thought it was goin' to be a waste of time, but we got really busy between two and three and sold out in no time.'

'Yer Auntie Mary knows the tricks of the trade, sunshine. She wouldn't bother goin' if she thought it wasn't worth it.'

Joey pulled on his sister's arm. 'Did yer get any money, our Polly? Can I have a ha'penny for sweets?'

Polly swept him up into her arms and held him tight. 'I'm sorry, Joey, but I only got a shillin' an' our mam needs it to buy bread.' When he looked crestfallen, she smiled into his face. 'Next Saturday I'll give yer a whole penny for yerself.'

The promise did the trick and he smiled back. 'All for meself?'

'Scout's honour.' She set him down and patted his head before facing her mother. 'I'm famished, Mam, is there anythin' to eat?'

'I've got some dripping in, will yer have fried bread? It's not much, but it's all there is.'

If Polly was disappointed she didn't let it show. 'Yeah, that sounds fine! I'll make it, Mam, you sit down. Oh, I nearly forgot,' she delved into her pocket and handed a shilling piece over, 'me wages.'

'I feel terrible mean takin' it off yer after yer've been on yer feet all day. Don't yer want to keep a couple of coppers for yerself?'

Polly shook her head. 'I don't need it, Mam, honest. I've got the card for Steve, so there's nothin' else I want. When I've had somethin' to eat I'll knock next door an' give it to him in case I miss him in the morning. It wouldn't be right to give it to him after school when the day's nearly over.'

'Is your Steve in, Auntie Dolly?'

'Yeah, he's just finished his tea, love.' Dolly was about to invite Polly in when she saw the card in her hand and had second thoughts. Steve was at an awkward age; he'd die of embarrassment if he was handed the card in front of the family. 'I'll tell him he's wanted.'

As she walked down the hall Dolly's mind was going back over the years. It was funny how her son and Polly had been friends since they were nippers. She'd never known them fall out or have a cross word, and that was very unusual for kids. Especially their Steve – he was often in trouble for fighting with other boys in the street. But with Polly he was different. Mind you, it would be hard to fall out with the girl because she was always very pleasant and easy to get along with.

'Yer body's wanted, Steve.' Dolly jerked her thumb. 'There's someone at the door for yer.'

Steve looked up from one of the comic books his dad had picked up on his round. 'Who is it?'

'Never mind who it is! Get that big backside off the chair an' go and see for yerself.'

'I'm not goin' out to play whoever it is.' Steve stood up and put the comic on his chair. 'They can go an' get lost.'

Dolly smiled but didn't enlighten him. 'Go an' tell them yerself. Do yer own dirty work.'

Steve was muttering as he went down the hall. He'd soon get rid of whoever it was and get back to the exciting fight that was going on between the goody and the baddy in the comic. But when he saw Polly his face lit up. 'Me mam didn't say it was you.'

'I've brought yer birthday card.' Polly handed the card over. 'I hope yer have a happy birthday.'

'Thanks, Polly!' Steve tore at the envelope, took out the card and opened it. When he saw the three kisses Polly had put under her signature he blushed to the roots of his hair. He hadn't put kisses on his card when it was her birthday, he'd just put his name. And this card was nice and clean; he remembered his had dirty fingermarks all over it. Still, boys weren't expected to be soppy, not like girls. He pushed the card back in the envelope, wondering what to do with it. If his mam saw the kisses she'd pull his leg soft and he'd never hear the end of it. But he wasn't going to tear it up, not a card from Polly, so he'd just have to find a hiding place. 'Me mam said yer've been out sellin' flowers with Irish Mary. How did yer get on?'

'Oh, yer'd never believe yesterday, Steve, it was brilliant! D'yer feel like comin' for a walk for ten minutes an' I'll tell yer all about it?'

'Yeah, okay!' Steve still had the card in his hand and nowhere to put it. 'Hang on till I tell me mam.' He took the stairs two at a time, pushed the card under his pillow, opened a drawer in the tallboy and took something out, then ran down to the living room. 'I'm goin' out for a few minutes with Polly. Don't touch my comic, Clare, or I'll belt yer one.'

'Who wants to look at yer silly comic?' Clare's blue eyes flashed. 'I've got me own book to read, so there!'

'I'll see yer. Ta-ra.' Steve ran down the hall with his mother's voice ringing in his ears. 'Half an hour, now, d'yer hear?'

'Let's walk down to Parliament Street, that's not too far.' Her hands in her pockets, Polly fell into step beside him. 'Yer won't believe me when I tell yer about yesterday.' She was so good at describing everything down to the smallest detail, Steve could see Sarah Jane in his mind's eye. And when she said the old lady didn't have a tooth in her head and looked like an Indian squaw, he bent double with laughter. The nice lady who bought the three blooms, the man who purchased all the carnations and gave her a tip, and the woman who didn't think she wanted a fern until Polly talked her into it . . . all were described in detail, making the whole scene come alive for Steve.

'I wish I'd been there,' he said. 'I wouldn't half have enjoyed it.' Polly gave a little skip to keep up with him. His legs were so long he covered the ground in half the time.

'You'd love Sarah Jane, she's dead funny. Perhaps yer can come down one Saturday, just to see, like?'

'Yeah, I'll do that.' Steve grinned. 'I could just stand there an' watch yer flog yer guts out.' His face sobered. 'I wish I could get a little weekend job meself. I haven't been to the Saturday matinée for ages 'cos me mam says she can't afford it.'

'If yer were workin' weekends, yer daft thing, then yer still couldn't go to the matinée.'

'I could go to the first house one night, get a grown-up to take me in. Yer can do that with a U-certificate picture.'

Polly stopped when they came to the junction of Parliament Street. 'We'd better make our way back.' They turned and began to walk back the way they'd come. Polly was silent for a while, then she said, 'I give all me money to me mam. She's havin' a hard time with me dad bein' in hospital so I'm tryin' to help her out.'

Her words caused Steve to feel guilty. 'Oh, I didn't mean

I'd keep all the money for meself! No, I'd give at least half to me mam.'

Polly glanced sideways, chewing on the inside of her lip. She could trust Steve; he wouldn't repeat anything she told him. 'If me mam doesn't get a job soon, we might end up on the streets.'

Steve halted in his tracks. 'Nah, don't be daft! Your mam's got a job, she'll be able to pay the rent.'

With a wisdom far beyond her years, Polly listed all the things her mother had to pay out for every week. 'Just the same as your mam, Steve. An' it's not just the big things, like rent, food, coal, gas, and the club woman. What about when the gas mantle goes, or we need shoes or clothes? That's without countin' bars of soap, Parr's Aunt Sally or a new mop when the old one falls to pieces . . . oh, there's dozens of things! Even with my few bob a week, it's nowhere near enough.'

Steve scratched his head as he carried on walking. He'd never given a thought to his mam having to fork out for all those things week in week out. She was always laughing and joking, no one would know she had all those worries on her shoulders. Polly had put him to shame.

More to himself than to her, he muttered, 'Here's me moanin' this mornin' 'cos I had to have dry bread with me boiled egg. No wonder me mam gave me a clip around the ear an' said I should count meself lucky I had an egg.'

Polly managed a smile. 'What's an egg, Steve? Is it one of them things shaped like Humpty Dumpty?'

'I'm thick, aren't I?' Steve kicked a loose stone out of his path. 'Too busy thinkin' of havin' a game of footie in the park, or a game of rounders.'

'You're not thick, Steve. It's just that men don't see things like women do because they don't have the worry of runnin' a home.'

Steve cheered up a bit at that. Polly had classed him in with the men and he began to walk tall. He'd be more thoughtful in future, take more notice of what was going on in the house. He wasn't a kid any more; this time next year he'd be looking for a job. And he should have known all these things without Polly having to tell him. Mind you, she had a head on her shoulders, did Polly Perkins. She always did well in school; she could read and write much better than him. And she couldn't half spell, even the hard words. But him, he was always nearer the bottom of the class than the top. It was his own fault; he'd never really tried. He was always getting the cane for talking, or staring out of the window when he should have been listening. Well, he only had one year left to make up for it, so he'd better pull his socks up. And he'd be nicer to his mam. If she gave him dry bread again, he'd eat it and keep his trap shut.

They were nearing their street when Steve pulled on Polly's arm. 'Hang on a tick, I've got somethin' for yer.'

Polly's face broke into a smile. 'It's not an egg, is it?'

'I'd look well walkin' around with an egg in me pocket, wouldn't I, yer daft nit.' Steve opened his clenched hand and held it towards her. 'I want yer to have this.'

Polly stared in disbelief at the bobby dazzler lying in his palm. He'd given it a good wash and the different shades of blue running through the white marble were lovely. It must have been filthy last time she saw it because it hadn't looked as colourful as it did now.

'I can't take that off yer, it's yer best ollie!'

'I want yer to have it.' Steve's eyes were looking some-where over her shoulder. 'Me mam said I'm too big an' ugly to be playin' ollies at my age. In fact she said, an' don't you dare tell me mates, that my backside reminded her of the rising sun.'

Polly's laugh rang out. 'Oh, she's a scream is your mam! Honest, she can turn anythin' into a joke.'

'Here yer are.' Steve pushed his hand nearer. 'I won't be playin' any more so I want you to have it.'

Polly felt a sinking sensation in the pit of her tummy. She'd miss playing marbles, 'cos if Steve wasn't there the other boys wouldn't let her play – even though she could knock spots off every one of them any day. 'Yer'll still be playin' out, won't yer, Steve? I mean, yer not too big to play footie, are yer?'

'Of course I'll be playin' out.' Steve's voice was in the process of breaking and ranged from high soprano to deep bass. 'I'll just be keepin' me backside out of sight, that's all.'

Polly took the marble from his hand and held it nearer for a closer inspection. 'It's beautiful. I'll never play with it, I'll keep it safe an' it'll always remind me of you.'

Blushing the colour of beetroot, Steve growled, 'An' I'll keep the birthday card yer gave me.' As they carried on walking, he asked himself how he was going to manage to keep the card hidden. And hidden it must stay if he was to have any peace. His mam wasn't the only joker in the family; their Clare was just as bad if not worse. She wouldn't only pull his leg, she'd have a go at Polly. And Steve wasn't going to give anyone the chance of showing Polly up. After all, she was his best mate.

Steve sighed. He'd have to take the card with him everywhere he went, that was the only solution. Unless, of course, he made his own bed every morning. But if he did that his mam would think he was sick and send for the doctor.

Chapter Eight

A hand flew to Ada's mouth as she let the curtain fall back into place and moved away from the window. She'd been keeping her eye out for the rent man and he was on the opposite side of the street now, knocking on Freda Ashcroft's door. But to Ada's horror it wasn't their usual collector, Mr James, it was the man who owned nearly all the houses in the street – Mr Roscoe. And if rumour was to be believed, he owned property all over Liverpool. It wasn't often he deigned to show himself in this neck of the woods; in fact, Ada could only remember seeing him about half a dozen times in all the years she'd lived there.

Biting on a nail already bitten down to the quick, Ada crossed to the sideboard and picked up the dark blue rent book. She flicked through the back pages, thinking she hadn't been a bad tenant. Now and again she'd been a few bob short but she'd always made it up the following week. The trouble was, she was four shillings short this time, and while it would have been bad enough telling Mr James, it would be a hundred times worse telling the owner of the house – the man who had the power to put her and the children out on the streets. It wasn't likely he'd do it this week because she was straight up to today, but what about next week when she knew she wouldn't be able to pay the full rent again, never mind making up the difference?

Ada went back to the window. Mr Roscoe was now at the Greens' house, the last before he crossed the street. In a few minutes he'd be knocking at her door . . . She began to panic. She'd taken Joey next door and asked Dolly to mind him so she could invite the collector in and explain the situation, but now all those plans had been sent haywire. She could hardly invite a man of Roscoe's standing into her living room. You only had to look at him to realise he was a man of substance and not used to slumming it.

Then an argument raged in Ada's head. *He's no better than I am!* After all, it was the rent of poor people like herself which made him into a rich man. A voice in her head came back to say, *That's all very well, but he's still the one who can put you and the children in the workhouse . . .*

Ada jumped when the knock came on the door. She put the rent book down on the sideboard, straightened her back, and telling herself she wasn't going to grovel to any man, she made for the door.

'Mrs Perkins? Good morning to you! Mr James is off ill so I'm filling in for him.'

Taken aback by the friendliness of the greeting and the smile on the quite handsome face, Ada was momentarily at a loss for words. She didn't return the smile, merely inclined her head. 'Would yer come in for a minute, Mr Roscoe, I would like to talk to yer.'

A look of surprise crossed the man's face, but it was brief. Closing the book he had open in his hands, he said, 'Of course.'

As he passed her, Ada took in the fine material of his beige and black small check suit, the heavy gold chain of his fob watch and the brown bowler hat he was now removing. She sighed. She didn't envy anyone their wealth, but it didn't seem right that a few should have so much while so many were reduced to living in poverty.

'Sit down, please.' Ada pointed to the one chair that still had its springs intact. 'I didn't want to discuss my business on the front step. I hope you understand?'

'Yes, I understand your desire for privacy.' John Roscoe placed his hat and his collecting book on the floor. 'How can I help you?'

Ada tried to swallow the lump in her throat but it refused to move. She needed a drink. 'I hope you won't think I'm trying to get round you, but would you like a cup of tea while we're talking?'

'What a good idea!' John Roscoe was intrigued. The woman appeared to be daring him to refuse. And what a striking-looking woman she was! The clothes she was wearing were almost threadbare, but they took nothing away from the trim figure. Her dark hair was luxuriant, her nose slightly turned up, and her eyes a deep velvety brown. Dressed in the right clothes, he thought, this woman would be a beauty.

When Ada went into the kitchen, John's eyes scanned the room. The furniture was old and scuffed, the pattern had been worn off the lino, and there was no fire in the grate even though it was cool outside. But the room was spotlessly clean and had an air of being lived in. Poor it might be, but it wasn't just a house, it was a home.

'I'm sorry I have no sugar.' Ada handed him one of the two china cups and saucers she'd borrowed off Dolly, before taking a seat on the couch. 'I was goin' to tell Mr James a sob story, Mr Roscoe, but I've made up me mind that it wouldn't get me anywhere. I've told more lies in the last couple of weeks than I've told in a lifetime, and I'm sick to death of it.' Cradling the saucer in her lap, she softly told the man everything. 'I intended paying yer four bob short and saying I'd make it up next week, but yer see that would be just one more lie. It was to buy me the time to look for another job so we wouldn't be thrown out on the street.'

John was going to put his cup and saucer down at the side of his chair when Ada jumped up. 'I'll take them off yer. You see, they don't belong to me. I borrowed them off Mrs Mitchell next door.'

Surprising himself, John began to chuckle. 'By Jove, that's honesty for you!'

'Lies haven't got me anywhere, so let's see how honesty works.' Ada carried the precious china out to the kitchen, saying over her shoulder, 'If I break these, I'll get me neck broken.'

Once again John chuckled. When he'd started out this morning he hadn't expected to get any satisfaction out of the day, but he found a certain contentment in sitting in the small, poorly furnished room. He remembered he'd been in a foul temper when he was told at short notice that Philip James had slipped and broken his ankle. It had been too late to delegate the job to one of his other collectors so he was lumbered – and he hated collecting the rents; it always made him miserable. He had to admit to a certain amount of shame when he saw people living from hand to mouth, doing without food to pay him their weekly rent, but he was a businessman and couldn't afford to let sympathy take over.

He was telling himself this when Ada came back into the room and fastened those soft brown eyes on him. 'We'll have the neighbours talkin' if yer here much longer, Mr Roscoe. It doesn't take much to start the tongues waggin'.'

'Well, shall we get down to business? Not that I'm worried about wagging tongues, but we have your good name to think of. So, what did you want of me, Mrs Perkins?'

Ada found she was no longer nervous of him. He was quite nice to talk to, really. 'A stay of execution, please. I'm four shillings short of me rent this week, an' I'll do me damnedest to make it up. But I can't promise it'll be next week or even the week after.' She lowered her head and her voice. 'I've told yer about me sick husband an' me two children. Our home isn't a palace, but I'm desperate to keep it together. I'll work me fingers to the bone to make it possible. If there's a job to be had, no matter what it is, I'll take it. But I need a little time an' I'm beggin' yer to give me that time.'

'Mrs Perkins, dear, you don't have to crawl to me.'

'Mr Roscoe, I crawl to no man for meself. But for me husband and me two children I'll crawl to the Devil himself.'

'I may not be as white as the driven snow, Mrs Perkins, but the Devil I am not! Now, I think you should pay me what you can afford for the next few weeks and we'll take it from there. I'll be around to deal with it myself because Mr James has broken his ankle and is likely to be absent for some time. So take that worried look off your face, fetch me your rent book, and we'll see how things go.'

When he was leaving, Ada couldn't thank him enough. She felt as though a ton weight had been lifted from her shoulders.

'No need for thanks, Mrs Perkins. Just do me a favour and keep our deal a secret. I'm known as a hard businessman, and I can't have people thinking I've gone soft.'

He'd only been gone five minutes when Dolly came up the yard and knocked on the window before pushing the kitchen door open. 'Eh, that's a turn-up for the books, isn't it? Fancy Mr Roscoe havin' a drink out of my china cups.'

Ada's mouth gaped. 'He told yer?'

'Yeah!' Dolly held her head high and looking down her nose she adopted a haughty pose. 'He complimented me on them, said I 'ad good taste.'

'What else did he tell yer?' Ada thought if he mentioned the china he might have mentioned other things. And although Dolly was her best mate she didn't want her to know she'd practically begged on her hands and knees.

'I thought he was very nice, considerin' he's such a toff. Let me see, what were his exact words?' Dolly opened the palm of one hand and crooked the fingers of her other as though holding a pen. 'He marked me book,' her fingers holding the imaginary pen moved across her palm. 'Then when he'd taken me money, he closed his book, then put his pen in a pocket of his waistcoat.' These words were accompanied by exaggerated actions. 'Then he looked up at me an' said, "Mrs Perkins is having a rough time of it. Pity, really, because she's such a nice lady".'

Ada laughed aloud. 'You lying hound!'

'May God strike me dead! If I never move from this spot, girl, that's what the man said.'

'I'll believe yer where thousands wouldn't.' Ada felt a

sense of relief. 'Yer right about him bein' a nice man, he really is. He was so easy to talk to I found meself tellin' him all me troubles an' asking him for a few weeks' grace.'

'And?' Dolly raised an eyebrow. 'Did yer get it – the grace, I mean?'

'He said to see how it goes for a couple of weeks. I've told him I'm tryin' everywhere for another job, an' I think he believed me. Anyway, he'll be comin' to collect the rents himself for a few weeks 'cos Mr James has broken his ankle.'

'Ooh, er!' Dolly pulled on her earlobe. 'I'd better put those cups an' saucers in a safe place if you're goin' to keep on havin' posh visitors. An' I'll try an' get me canteen of cutlery out of the pop shop in case he stops for dinner. An' seein' as half of my kitchen's goin' to be in your 'ouse, I want an invite as well.'

Ada gave her a friendly push. 'Go 'way with yer, yer daft ha'porth.'

'What's daft about that! If you're goin' up in the world, girl, yer ain't leavin' me behind.'

John Roscoe thought about Ada a lot on his rounds that day. And when he conjured up her handsome face and figure, her warmth and loyalty to her family, he found himself comparing her with Maureen, his wife – a woman who had never known what it was to want, who had never washed a cup or lifted a finger since the day they married. Living in a big double-fronted house on Queens Drive, she had a maid to do all the things she thought beneath her. The big gardens back and front were tended to by a gardener because Maureen refused to get her hands dirty. He would have enjoyed doing the gardening himself, but she complained so much about him trailing soil through the house, or having dirt under his nails that he soon gave it up.

And she was cold, his wife. She'd borne him a son a year after they were married, but the child was sickly and only lived for two days. Since then she'd refused to have him in her bed, saying the sex act was disgusting. He'd been hurt at first, wondering why she'd married him if she didn't love him, but it didn't take him long to realise she might not love him but she loved what his money could give her. Now they were like two strangers living in the same house. It was only when they had visitors or attended one of the functions Maureen was so fond of, that they put on a show of being happily married.

When he'd finished collecting, John walked to where he'd parked his car. He slipped into the driver's seat and sat for a while, deep in thought. Then he switched the engine on and turned the car in the opposite direction to the one which would take him home. He drove past the Perkins' house, slowing down so he could get a good look at it. She kept her house as neat on the outside as she did on the inside, and it wasn't done with money but with good old-fashioned elbow grease. Something his wife knew nothing about.

His mind elsewhere, he drove automatically down Smithdown Road on to Allerton Road, then forked left into Queens Drive. He turned into the driveway of his home and wondered what his wife had done with her day. Afternoon tea at the Adelphi, perhaps? Or had she been to Cripps in Bold Street for yet another evening gown? One thing she certainly wouldn't have been doing was humiliating herself in an effort to keep a roof over the heads of her family. What a pity she couldn't be forced to live for a while with no hot water, no central heating or bathroom, and a toilet at the bottom of the yard. She looked down her nose at people who lived in those conditions as though somehow it was their own fault. Because she'd never shown any interest in his background, only in the luxury he could provide for her, she didn't know that both his father and mother had been working-class people who spoke with a thick Liverpool accent and were proud of it. Through sheer hard work, and going without, they'd built up the business that had come to him when they died. And the irony of it was, Maureen was enjoying the fruits of their labour now, but if they'd been alive she wouldn't have even sat at the same table as them.

John was so deep in thought he didn't see the front door opening, nor did he hear his name being called. It was the loud banging on the car window that caused him to look up into a face that was twisted with anger. 'Are you going to sit there all day? You know we're having guests for dinner and you have to get changed.'

John wound the window down. 'I won't be in for dinner. I'm going down to the office to get some paperwork done.'

Maureen narrowed her hazel eyes. She was a stocky woman whose liking for rich food had played havoc with her face and figure. There was nothing feminine about her; even her hair, which she had marcel waved twice a week, didn't look real. 'You'll do no such thing! I've invited guests and you'll be here to greet them.'

'You invited them, you greet and entertain them. I'll have something to eat at the club then go to the office. If I don't get my work done by ten o'clock I'll sleep at the office.'

Maureen looked as though she'd been slapped across the face. 'You can't do this to me! What shall I tell our friends?'

'*Your* friends, Maureen, not mine. And I really don't care what you tell them. You're usually very good with words, I'm sure you'll come up with something.'

When she saw he was in earnest, his wife's expression changed. 'Come along, darling,' she wheedled. 'I know how you hate collecting and I understand. You'll feel better after a hot bath.'

John turned the key in the ignition and set the engine in motion. It had taken Ada Perkins, out of her head with worry over a few bob, to make him see his wife as she really was. He was just a meal ticket to her; there wasn't even a spark of love in her heart for him – never had been. He could never remember her hugging or kissing him, and any overtures he'd made had quickly been rebuffed.

'I'll be working again tomorrow, so have my dinner ready

for six o'clock,' he said brusquely. Looking over his shoulder to make sure the road was clear, he reversed out of the drive. Once on the wide road, he looked back to see his wife standing as though shell-shocked. She'd make some excuse for his absence, she was good at that. In fact she'd be the perfect hostess, as always. He was just glad he wouldn't be there to see how false her behaviour was. She was his wife and he wouldn't leave her, but he was tired of putting on a show of happily married bliss in front of her friends. She'd be as sweet as honey with him while they were there but as soon as they were gone she'd bid him a cool good night and retire to her own bedroom, closing the door on him.

'Did yer have any luck today, Mam?' Polly asked on the following Monday when she came in from school.

Ada shook her head. 'I've tried every shop an' pub in the vicinity but there's nothin' doing. They've all got cleaners. I've walked the length an' breadth of Lodge Lane, Park Road and Mill Street, me feet are killin' me, an' to add insult to injury I've got a hole in the sole of me shoe. Proper happy little soul, aren't I?'

'It's not your fault, Mam!' Polly threw her coat over the back of a chair. 'But what will happen when the rent man comes on Friday? Will he give yer more time, like he said, even though yer can't give him any extra off the arrears?'

'Polly, I've been honest with yer so far 'cos I think yer have a right to know, an' I'll be honest with yer now. The truth is, it doesn't look as though I'm goin' to have any rent for him this week at all. I've been dipping into the rent money already.' Ada saw the shocked look on her daughter's face and hastened to explain. 'I had to give the club woman a few bob today 'cos she hasn't been paid for weeks, an' she said her manager would be out to see me if she didn't get anythin' this week. An' I've had to buy food – we can't live on fresh air.'

'Oh Mam, what are we goin' to do?' There was a worried

frown on Polly's pretty face. 'Won't yer let me sag school for a few days, just for this week? Yer could give Doreen a note to take in to say I was sick.'

'I couldn't do that, yer dad would go mad if he knew.'

'But me dad won't know, will he? If I did Tuesday, Wednesday and Thursday it would be three bob. That could go to the rent man.'

Ada stroked her chin. It would be wrong to keep her daughter off school, and she shouldn't even consider it. But it was also wrong to have a twelve-year-old girl with worry lines on her forehead. The offer was tempting, no doubt about that. Three shillings would almost keep them in food until she got her wages on Saturday, so all the money she had left in the drawer could go towards their rent. 'What about yer mate, Doreen? She'll know yer not sick.'

'How will she? If you tell her I'm in bed with a cold, she won't know the difference. I'd be well away when she was goin' to school, and I could sneak in an' out the back way.'

'D'yer know, Polly, I never thought the day would come when I'd sink so low as to encourage me own daughter to tell lies.'

'Mam, did yer ever think the day would come when me dad would be in hospital an' we'd be sittin' here with no money, frightened of bein' thrown out?'

'No, love, I didn't.'

'Then write the note an' give it to Doreen in the morning when she knocks for me. I'll slip over to Auntie Mary's when I've had me tea and tell her I'll meet her in town at half eight.'

'May God forgive the pair of us for tellin' such lies, Polly. I just hope we don't get paid back for it.'

'God will understand, Mam. He knows we're not really bad.'

Ada looked around the room to make sure it was tidy, just in case Mr Roscoe came in. She didn't think he would; he probably wouldn't be as friendly as he had been last week. He might even have changed his mind about giving her a bit of leeway. But at least she had a full week's rent for him today, even though it was made up of the four shillings Polly had earned over the three days, and two bob she'd borrowed off Irish Mary until she got her wages. There was nothing to go off the arrears, and God knows how she'd manage next week, but she'd worry about that when the time came. All she could do was hope and pray. One thing was certain – no matter how bad things were, she wasn't going to allow Polly to sag school again. It just wasn't fair on the girl.

The rat-tat at the door sent her hand hovering over the rent book. Should she take it with her or not? Better had; he might get the wrong idea if she invited him in again – think she was a flighty piece.

'Good morning, Mrs Perkins.'

'Good morning, Mr Roscoe.' Ada held the book and the ten-shilling note out. 'I know I'm short, but I have done me best.'

John looked slightly taken aback. 'Oh, I wonder if I could come in for a moment? I won't keep you long.'

'Is it about the arrears?' Ada's heart started to thump. Surely he wasn't going to give her a lecture on the four shillings she owed?

'No, not at all. Something entirely different.'

Ada stood aside. 'Come in, please.'

Today he was wearing a navy-blue pin-striped suit with a white shirt and navy tie, and his bowler hat was in navy. Ada thought the dark colours made him look older, more sober. He was probably only a few years older than herself, perhaps around the forty mark, she guessed.

He stood inside the living room, hat in hand, and smiled. 'I don't suppose you've still got Mrs Mitchell's china cups, have you? I haven't had a drink since breakfast and I'm terribly thirsty.'

Ada clamped her lips together. She mustn't laugh, he'd

think she was making fun of him. But she couldn't hold it in and her head went back as she roared with laughter. 'She's put them in a safe place in case I wanted to borrow them again, an' she said if I ever invite yer to dinner she'll redeem her canteen of cutlery from the pawnshop.' Her laughter reduced to a chuckle, she went on, 'There's only one snag . . . she comes with the china and cutlery.'

John settled back in the chair and crossed his legs. Funny, but he felt perfectly at home here. It didn't enter his head that in his expensive clothes he looked completely out of place in the poorly furnished room. 'Your neighbour sounds a bundle of fun.'

'Oh, she is! I don't know what I'd have done without her since Tommy went in hospital. I've been out of me mind with worry, really down in the dumps, but she always manages to make me laugh.'

'I'll tell you what.' John leaned forward and laced his fingers together. 'Why don't we attend to our business, then invite Mrs Mitchell, and her cups and saucers, to join us for a cup of tea.'

'You don't know my neighbour, Mr Roscoe, an' don't think I'm making fun of yer 'cos I'm not. But if I said to Dolly Mitchell that she was being invited to join us for a cup of tea, she'd never stop laughin' for a week! If I said "brew's up", that's more her style.' Ada handed him rent book and money. 'When yer've done that, I'll go an' fetch her. She's mindin' me youngest, Joey, so he can come back with her.'

He ignored her outstretched hand and said, 'Will you sit down for a minute, I've got a proposition to put to you.'

For some unknown reason Ada felt as though she hadn't a care in the world. It was probably talking about Dolly that made her so lighthearted. Taking a seat, she chuckled, 'A proposition? Ooh, I hope it's not painful.'

John had thought of her as a fine-looking woman, but when she smiled her face was transformed and he changed the word from fine to beautiful. 'I may have the answer to your problems. I'm looking for a cleaner and wondered if you'd like the job.'

'You, lookin' for a cleaner? D'yer mean for your house?'

John shook his head. 'I have a property in Faulkner Square. It's a large three-storey house, the ground and first floor being used as offices. It's where the collectors pay their money in and where all the records are kept. The top floor is my inner sanctum, used solely by myself. I have an office there, a private sitting room and bedroom. Sometimes, when I'm working on the books and accounts, it can be quite late when I've finished and I'm too tired to drive home so I stay the night. It's also a place to escape to when I need a bit of peace and quiet.'

Ada looked doubtful. 'Haven't you got a cleaner? I'd have thought yer needed one for such a big place.'

'I do have one, but the work is getting too much for her. She won't admit it, though, keeps saying that because she's seventy it doesn't mean she can't do a good day's work. But to my knowledge she's been seventy for the last five years! She worked for my father until he died, and she's been with me since I took over, so I haven't the heart to sack her. But she definitely needs someone to give her a hand and I thought of you.'

Ada was telling herself not to build her hopes up in case there was a catch in it. It seemed too good to be true. 'Can yer tell me what the hours would be, please?'

'Agnes, the woman I've just been telling you about, starts at seven in the morning and has the offices cleaned by the time the staff arrive. But I know you have an early-morning job, so you could come after five-thirty when the offices close. That would suit old Agnes. She doesn't like having to get up early in the morning.'

'I'm pinchin' meself to make sure I'm not dreaming. It seems too good to be true.' Ada held his eyes. 'You are in earnest, aren't you, Mr Roscoe? I mean, yer wouldn't build me hopes up an' then let me down?'

'There's a job waiting for you if you want it,' he assured her. 'I'm afraid the place has been neglected because of Agnes's age, but that's not her fault. I should have got someone in to help her ages ago. She gets twelve shillings a week, and if you agree to take the job you'll get the same.'

Ada was silent for so long John thought she was going to turn his offer down. 'Have you lost your tongue?'

'I'm speechless! I'm that excited I feel like a kid that's been given a new toy.' Ada stood up and thrust the book and money at him. 'Mark that so I can go an' tell Dolly.' Suddenly remembering who he was, she added, 'If you please.' She twirled around, laughing. 'I'm so happy, if I don't tell someone soon, I'll burst.'

John looked down at the book and the ten-shilling note. 'Would it be impertinent of me to ask how you came by this money?'

Ada stood with her hands on her hips, a wide smile on her face. 'I'll tell yer the truth.'

When she'd finished, John shook his head. 'You mean you would have paid me this and starved the rest of the week?'

She nodded. 'But I'm going to be all right now, thanks to you. Oh, yer've no idea what yer've done for me. I'll be indebted to you for the rest of me life.'

'Would you allow me to do one thing more for you?'

Ada's face clouded. 'What's that?'

'Give you five shillings back so you can pay . . . what did you say her name was? Oh yes, Irish Mary. Pay her what you owe her, and put the rest to buying decent food for yourself and the children.' He saw she was about to protest and held up his hand. 'It's not charity, Mrs Perkins. You can pay me back at a shilling a week. If it makes you feel better, I will deduct it from your wages.'

While John was rummaging in his pocket for change of the ten-shilling note, Ada studied him. And when he handed her two half-crowns, she asked, 'Why are you bein' so good to me?'

He dropped the coins into her open hand and smiled. 'Perhaps one day I'll tell you, when you know me better. Until then, let me assure you I only wish you well and do not have an ulterior motive for my actions.'

'I believe yer, Mr Roscoe.' A glint of mischief appeared in her eyes. 'I know it's a terrible thing to say, but wasn't it lucky for me that Mr James broke his ankle?'

'I hope you feel the same way when you're scrubbing the front steps in Faulkner Square. They're the bane of Agnes's life. Because she's been there so long, she'll probably boss you around and give you all the jobs she finds hard going. But I would take it as a favour if you indulged her. You see, I'm very fond of the old girl.' John rubbed his hands together. 'Now, how about bringing in your neighbour? Not forgetting her cups, of course.'

Ada got halfway to the yard door, then turned. 'No, I'll not go out the back! I'll go out the front way an' give the neighbours somethin' to gossip about. If they see Dolly comin' in here, they'll think yer've got two fancy women.' She disappeared, calling, 'Won't be a tick!'

Chapter Nine

Polly stood beside the table and opened up the Snakes and Ladders board in front of Joey. He was sitting on one of the wooden chairs, elbows on the table, his hands cupping his chin and legs swinging back and forth. He had a mischievous glint in his eye, and as soon as Polly tipped the coloured counters out of the box he swiped them off the table with the back of his hand, chuckling with glee.

'If yer don't behave yerself, our Joey,' Polly said, playfully smacking his hand, 'I won't let yer cheat.'

At that moment Ada came into the room with her coat over her arm, and Joey gave her a sly wink. 'I don't cheat, do I, Mam?'

'No, of course yer don't cheat, sunshine.' Ada smiled as she slipped an arm into the sleeve of her coat. 'Yer just make a mistake in yer countin', that's all.'

'What time d'yer have to be there?' Polly bent down and picked up the counters, keeping them safe in her hand. 'Did yer say half-five?'

'That's when the office staff finish, so Mr Roscoe said if I got there just after, Agnes would be there to let me in.' Ada was getting a bit jittery, which was understandable. The first day at a new job was always a bit nerve-racking because you never knew what to expect. 'I hope this Agnes is easy to get on with.'

'Don't worry, Mam, you can get on with anyone.' Polly tilted her head to one side. 'Look at Mr Roscoe – he must like yer to be so good to yer.'

Ada grinned. 'He's on me prayer list, after you two an' yer dad.' She buttoned her coat then reached for the bag containing her wrap-around pinny. 'Will yer put me laddo there to bed at seven? I don't know what time I'll be home – probably between half-eight and nine.'

'Yer goin' to be tired, Mam. It's a long day from five o'clock this mornin' till nine tonight.'

'I put me feet up this afternoon for an hour after I'd finished me work. Me an' Joey got on the couch and had a little sleep, didn't we, sunshine?'

'Yeah, it was good, our Polly! Me mam brought a blanket down an' we snuggled up nice an' warm.' His pale face split into a smile. 'Me mam doesn't half snore, though.'

Ada gasped. 'I do not snore!'

'I was only kiddin', Mam. Yer were breathin' down me ear an' it sounded like a snore.'

'I'll let you off.' Ada heaved a sigh. 'I'd better get goin', it wouldn't do to be late on me first day.' She gave each of them a hug and a kiss before setting off for the unknown.

Ada gazed in awe at the houses she passed in Faulkner Square. They were very big and very beautiful. She hesitated outside one where the curtains were open and she could see a lovely chandelier hanging from the high ceiling. It was very ornate, with long fingers of glass shining and giving off different colours in the glow from the six candle-shaped light bulbs. 'I'd hate to have to clean that,' Ada spoke softly to herself as she walked on, looking at the numbers on the brass plates beside the huge front doors. 'Mind you, if yer had enough money to live here yer'd have enough to employ a couple of maids.'

She came to a stop outside her destination and stood for a while, her hand curled around one of the bars of the black railings. Then she crossed her fingers and took a deep breath before climbing the steps and ringing the bell.

The door was opened almost immediately by a woman who couldn't be anyone else but the cleaner. She had a piece of sacking over her wrap-around pinny and it was kept in place by a length of string tied around her waist. She had a mop and bucket in her hand and a mobcap on her head that was all skew-whiff and threatening to cover her eyes any second. She looked down on Ada and growled, 'Are you Mrs Thingy?'

Ada smiled. 'Me name's Ada Perkins, but I'm not fussy. If yer want to call me Mrs Thingy, I'll answer to it. In fact, I'll answer to anythin', even Rover!'

The lined face broke into a smile, showing yellow teeth dotted at intervals in her gums. 'Come in, girl, an' let's get this door shut. Those bleedin' steps give me nightmares just lookin' at 'em. I scrub them nice an' clean every day, then the collectors come and leave their dirty ruddy footmarks all over them.'

She closed the door and set the bucket on the black and white tiled floor. Then she ran a hand down the sacking before holding it out. 'Me name's Agnes Connelly, but me friends call me Aggie.'

Ada took her hand, noting the thick blue veins standing out against the thin, tissue-like skin. 'Pleased to meet yer, Aggie. I think you an' me are goin' to get on fine.'

''Course we are! If Mr John says yer all right, that's good enough for me.' Aggie picked up the bucket and made to walk down the huge, high-ceilinged hall. 'I'll show yer what's what, eh?'

'Would yer like me to do the front steps before it starts gettin' dark?' Ada slipped her coat off and hung it over the end of the bannister. 'I don't mind, and it'll be off yer mind then.'

The bucket was set down so heavily that water spilled over the sides, forming little pools on the diamond-shaped tiles. But Aggie didn't see them, she was too busy patting Ada on the shoulder, a huge grin on her wrinkled face. 'I knew the minute I clapped eyes on yer, girl, that yer were a woman after me own heart. You do those steps for me an' yer'll be me bleedin' friend for life.'

Ada laughed and reached over to straighten the mobcap.

'Yer look as though yer've had one over the eight.'

'I should be so lucky! No, girl, I like me drink an' I'll not deny it, but it's two bottles of stout a night, an' that's me limit.' She dropped her head and chuckled. 'Except on a Saturday – that's when I roll home singin' at the top of me voice. Not that I can sing, mind yer, 'cos I'm tone ruddy deaf! But as all me mates are as drunk as me they think I've got a voice like a bleedin' nightingale.'

Ada tutted. 'I'm ashamed of yer, Aggie! Now will yer get me the necessary cleaning stuff for the steps, otherwise we'll get no work done.'

Ada was on her hands and knees cleaning under a desk in an office on the second floor when Aggie called. 'Come on down for a cuppa.'

Surprised, Ada scrambled to her feet. She wasn't expecting to have a break. Rubbing her hands over her pinny, she ran down the wide staircase. 'Are yer allowed to make tea?'

'I dunno, girl, I've never asked!' Aggie handed her a nice white cup and saucer. 'Never ask a question if yer think the answer isn't goin' to be to yer satisfaction. I learned that early on in life, girl.'

'But who does the tea an' milk belong to, Aggie? And whose cups and saucers are they? Did yer bring them with yer?'

The older woman winked. 'If I'd of 'ad cups and saucers like them, girl, they'd have been well pawned by now.' She shook her head. 'Everythin' I've used belongs to the office. Mr John supplies them.'

'But what would Mr Roscoe say if he knew we were stoppin' our work to have a cuppa? Don't forget, this is me first day an' I don't want to get in his bad books.'

'Listen to me, Ada Perkins, I've known Mr John since he was a schoolboy an' he wouldn't begrudge me havin' a little break. An' seein' as you're me assistant, the same goes for you.'

Ada sat in one of the office chairs and ran a finger along the wooden desk. 'It's a beautiful house, isn't it? Comin' down that wide staircase I felt like Cinderella goin' to the ball. It's as near as I'll get to it, but it doesn't do any harm to dream, does it?'

Aggie cocked her head and her voice was sympathetic when she said, 'Mr John told me yer've got yer share of trouble.'

'You don't know the half of it, Aggie! If it hadn't been for Mr Roscoe givin' me this job, me an' the kids would be walking the streets in the not too distant future. I'll be grateful to him for the rest of me life.'

'He's a good man, one of the best yer'll ever meet.' Aggie tucked her white hair into her mobcap. 'Have yer ever met his wife?'

Ada shook her head. 'No! How would I ever meet her?'

'Well, a little word of warning, girl. If she ever comes when you're here, make yerself scarce. She's the most stuck-up, toffee-nosed bitch yer ever likely to meet. Looks down her nose at yer as though yer a piece of dirt. What Mr John ever saw in her, only God knows an' He won't snitch.'

'Go 'way! Fancy that, an' him being such a nice man!' Ada put her palms flat on the desk and pushed herself up. If they didn't get a move on they'd be here until ten o'clock. 'He must have loved her to have married her. Is she pretty?'

Aggie leaned across the table until their faces were nearly touching. 'Beauty is in the eye of the beholder, girl, an' as I can't stand the sight of her I think she's as ugly as sin.'

'Oh, dear.' Ada sucked in the air through her teeth. 'Anyway, I've got enough troubles without botherin' about anyone else. But I'll heed yer warning, Aggie. If she does come, I'll run an' stand behind you.'

'I'm not frightened of her, Ada, never 'ave been. An' that doesn't half get up her nose. She thinks she's only got to snap her fingers an' we'll all come runnin'. But she's got another think comin' with Agnes Theresa Connelly, 'cos I don't bow to no little upstart like her. Oh, I know she'd have had me out of 'ere long ago if she'd had her way. Mr John doesn't know, but I overheard them talkin' one day an' I heard her say I lowered the tone of the Square.'

'She didn't!' Ada felt angry for the woman she'd only met two hours ago but knew was going to be a friend. 'The cheeky madam! If I'd have heard her say that about *me* I'd have slapped her face – even if it did mean losin' me job!'

'I didn't need to. Mr John told her where to go in no uncertain terms. It was the first time I've ever heard him shout at her.'

'Good for him!' Ada waved a hand at the cups. 'Shall I wash these or get back an' finish the second floor? I'll have to make it snappy 'cos there's still the top floor to do.'

'Uh, uh! Mr John said to leave his quarters for today. Just do the stairs and his landing. He'll have locked all his doors because he keeps his important papers up there.'

It was half-past eight when Agnes pulled the door behind her and followed Ada down the steps. 'Yer a blessing in disguise, girl, an' that's the God's honest truth. I don't feel half as tired as I usually do.' She tucked her arm into Ada's. 'An' it's much better for me to work at night. I'm gettin' too old to be rising from me bed at half-past five every mornin'.'

Ada turned to smile at the woman who felt as familiar as an old friend. Aggie might be getting on in years but she was thin and wiry and could certainly pull her weight. They'd got through all the work and it hadn't been hard because it was a pleasure just to be in the lovely house. And there'd been plenty of laughter 'cos Aggie had such funny sayings; she had Ada in stitches every time their paths crossed. She was a real character, all right – no wonder Mr John thought so much of her. As they walked arm in arm down the Square, little did they know they were being watched from a window on the top floor. John had stayed behind to finish some paperwork and had heard Mrs Perkins ring the bell. He'd gone on to the landing and was about to make his presence known when he heard the two women chatting together and decided he'd leave them to get acquainted first. He was poised to return to his office when he heard Mrs Perkins offer to clean the front steps and this took him to the window of his sitting room which overlooked the Square. He watched as she got on her knees and began to scrub the wide steps with a stiff scrubbing brush before wiping them clean and then using a whitestone on them. He could feel himself growing angry as she toiled, but couldn't think of a reason for his emotion. After all, women up and down the country were scrubbing steps every day. Why did he think Mrs Perkins was any different to them? And she had needed the job; it was either that or starve.

John sighed as the chatting couple passed under a lamp and he saw Ada throw her head back and laugh at something Agnes had said. It was then he understood why he'd been drawn to her. With all the troubles she had to bear, she had the spirit and the guts to carry on, and he admired her for that. She was a woman with a warm compassionate nature and she didn't deserve the cards Fate had dealt her.

John placed the papers in the safe and turned the key. At least he'd helped her, but even with that help her life was going to be one of penny-pinching and drudgery. She was worthy of better than that.

'The kettle's on the boil, Mam, an' I'll make yer some toast.' Polly's eyes were questioning as she took her mother's coat. 'How did yer get on?'

'Marvellous! It's a doddle compared to me mornin' job.' Ada dropped on to the couch. 'Yer should see the house, Polly, it's so big! This place would fit into two of the rooms.'

'Don't tell me any more until I've made the tea an' toast.' Polly hastened to the tiny hall where she hung her mother's coat on a hook on the wall, then she passed through the living room and into the kitchen in a flash saying, 'I can't wait to hear all about it.'

When she came back into the room she was carrying a plate with a thick slice of toast on it and a mug of tea. 'There yer are, Mam, get that down yer.'

Ada watched as her daughter pulled one of the chairs from the table and turned it to face her. 'Aren't you havin' any toast, love?'

'There's not much bread left, Mam, only enough for in the mornin'. But I'm all right, I'm not hungry.'

Ada split the slice of toast into two pieces and passed half over to her daughter. 'We'll share.'

Polly didn't argue because she was so hungry, she could hear her tummy rumbling. 'Go on, Mam, I want to know all about the house an' how yer got on with Agnes.'

'Oh, Agnes is a real character, somethin' like yer Auntie Dolly. She's got an answer to everythin' an' it's always funny. She can swear, mind yer, but somehow it doesn't sound bad coming from her.' Ada licked her lips and leaned forward to put the plate on the table. 'I enjoyed that bit of toast, sunshine, it'll keep me goin' until the morning.' She then went on to describe Agnes in detail and recounted the tale about her Saturday-night drinking and singing sessions. 'You'd like her, Polly, she's real kind and friendly.'

'What about the house, Mam?' Polly had seen the houses in Faulkner Square and had often wondered what they were like inside. Now she was eager for details. 'Only posh people live in them, don't they?'

'Yes.' Ada nodded her head. 'I don't know why Mr Roscoe has his offices there, 'cos from what I could see all the other houses have families livin' in them. When we were comin' home, one of the doors was opened by a maid and she had a white lace-trimmed apron on over a black dress, an' she had a white thing on her head an' that was trimmed with lace, too! Polly, love, we don't know how the other half live.'

'Tell me what the house was like inside.' Polly leaned forward, eager for every little detail. 'Don't leave anythin' out.'

'Put that on the table for us, there's a good girl.' Ada passed the empty mug to her daughter. 'Now, where shall I start? Well, there's black wrought-iron railings in front of the house and very wide steps up to the massive front door.' Ada took her time and her description was so vivid, Polly could feel herself walking through each room. And she laughed with pleasure when her mother told her about feeling like Cinderella when she walked down the wide staircase. 'Honest, Polly, the wood the bannister was made of felt like silk under me hands. The only word I can find to describe it is magnificent.'

'I'm glad it turned out good for yer,' Polly said. 'An' I can tell you enjoyed it by yer face. Yer look so young an' happy.'

'Oh, thanks, sunshine! Are yer sayin' I usually look like a miserable old hag?'

'Yer know I didn't mean that!' Polly said hotly. 'Yer the best-looking woman in this street.'

Ada remembered Agnes saying beauty was in the eye of the beholder, and she smiled at her daughter. 'Yer'll find that Steve, and Doreen, an' every other kid in the street for that matter, thinks their mam's the best-looking.'

'They wouldn't be right, though,' Polly laughed, "cos you are.' The smile slipped and her face became serious. 'Mam, are we goin' to be all right for money now? I mean, will yer be able to pay yer rent an' everything now yer've got this job?'

'We won't have to worry about bein' put out on the street, sunshine, but we're still going to be hard-up. My wages, and what you earn, only comes to about twenty-five bob and that's not enough to pay all me ways an' put decent clothes on our backs or good food on the table. But don't look so downhearted – we're a damn sight better off than we were this time last week. At least we're sure of a roof over our heads, a couple of bob for the club woman, pennies for the gas an' a bag of coal for when the weather's cold. And even if we can't buy food that we fancy, we won't starve. There's thousands worse off than us, so let's thank God for what we've got.'

'Yeah, and it's only till me dad comes home. We'll be well-off then.' Polly lowered her head. 'I wish he was home, Mam, I don't half miss him.'

'So do I, love, so do I.' Ada blinked to clear the blur of tears from her eyes. Oh God, how she missed Tommy. He was in her thoughts all the time, even when she was working. But night-time was the time she dreaded most. The bed seemed so big and empty without him. She longed to feel his arms around her holding her tight, yearned for the nights when their need brought their bodies together with a passion that was a sign of the deep love they had for each other. It had been a long time since they'd made love, and being a passionate woman there were nights when Ada's body cried out with need.

She was so wrapped up in her thoughts she didn't hear Polly talking to her until her daughter leaned forward and touched her arm. 'Mam, I asked yer if yer saw Mr Roscoe?'

'No, he wasn't there, love. He was probably at home sitting down to his dinner . . . lucky feller.'

John slipped the key from the lock and closed the door behind him. It was nine o'clock and Maureen would probably go into one of her sulking moods because he was late. His arm was stretched to hang his coat on the wooden coatstand when he heard his wife's high-pitched laugh. Oh, dear lord, Maureen had visitors again. He felt like putting his coat back on and returning to Faulkner Square, but his eyes were tired with staring at figures all day and he didn't relish driving in the dark. So, pulling down the front of his waistcoat and making sure his tie was straight, he opened the lounge door with a smile on his face and a greeting on his lips.

'Oh, it's you!' Then Maureen remembered she had guests and her manner changed completely. Rising from her chair she came towards him and pecked his cheek. 'Your dinner's in the oven, darling, keeping warm. Be careful when you get it out because the plate will be hot.'

The uncomfortable silence of the visitors was enough to inflame John. He wouldn't start an argument with her in front of them, he'd bide his time until they'd gone. In the meanwhile though, he had no intention of allowing himself to be made a fool of. 'I'm sure your guests won't mind you leaving them for a minute to see to your husband's dinner. After all, I've been working all day and can't be expected to come home and wait on myself.'

Maureen was facing him and he could see hatred and anger in her eyes. And when she spoke it was through clenched teeth. 'It's impolite to leave guests, darling, and I was brought up never to be impolite.'

'Maureen, I'm very tired and have no intention of debating the issue. I'm going up to the bathroom for a swill, and when I come down I'll expect my dinner to be on the dining-room table. Is that understood . . . darling?'

John came down to find his dinner and the evening paper laid out on the table in the front dining room, plus a full pot of coffee and his box of cigars. He gave a tight smile. This was his wife's way of saying he wouldn't be welcome in the lounge. He'd been naughty and had to be punished. But she needn't have worried because he was in no mood to sit making polite conversation. He wasn't really hungry so he only ate part of the meal, but he had two cups of coffee whilst reading the paper and enjoying one of his favourite cigars. He could hear the hum of voices and occasional laughter, and in his mind he could see his wife posing with a smile on her face, the perfect hostess.

It was eleven o'clock when he heard the front door open and farewells being called, but he didn't stir. He knew his wife would come barging in and accuse him of humiliating her in front of her guests. So he was ready when the door burst open.

'How dare you!' She was beside herself with rage. Her face was contorted as she screamed at him, 'If you ever humiliate me in front of my friends again you'll be sorry.'

'Why? What will you do to me, Maureen? Stop my pocket money like you would a child? But you can't do that, can you, because I'm the one who gives you pocket money. So I'll be interested to know what you can do to make me squirm.'

Her nostrils flared, Maureen was too filled with anger to see she was flirting with danger. John was usually so placid, too eager to give in rather than face her wrath. It never entered her head he could change, that she had at last gone too far. 'Oh, there's plenty of ways of making you sorry you made a fool out of me. For instance, how would you like to have to cook your own meals, make your own bed or iron your own shirts? And that's only the beginning, the list is endless.'

'But you don't do any of those things for me, anyway, so what difference does it make?' John spoke quietly and calmly. 'Mildred does all the housework.'

There was a look of triumph on his wife's face. 'Precisely! And Mildred does as *I* tell her. She works for me.'

'Oh, I'm sorry, I've been under a misapprehension all these years.' John picked up a cigar and slowly bit off the end. 'I was under the impression that *I* paid Mildred's wages.'

It was at that moment that his wife began to have second thoughts. She was no longer sure of her hold over him. 'Well, of course you pay her wages, but she works for me.'

'She works for you simply because I've been prepared to pay her wages! You have no money, so if I didn't pay her she wouldn't be working here, would she? And you would have to do the cooking, make the beds and see to the ironing . . . isn't that the reality of it, Maureen?'

'But I pay her out of the housekeeping allowance you give me.' Maureen could feel the ground slipping beneath her feet. Why hadn't she kept her stupid mouth shut?

'And a very generous allowance you've been enjoying since we got married.' John motioned to a chair. 'Sit down, Maureen.'

'But I'm tired, I wish to go to bed.'

'Sit down, Maureen!'

'Look, I'm sorry about asking you to get your stupid dinner out of the oven. I really didn't think it would upset you like this. But is it so important that we discuss it now? Surely it will keep until tomorrow when I'm not so tired?'

John didn't even bother to answer. Instead he asked, 'How many hours does Mildred work and how much does she get?'

Maureen was now looking decidedly flustered. 'Five hours a day, unless I'm having guests for dinner, then it could be eight hours.'

'All those hours for a cleaner just for this place?' John tried to keep control of his temper. 'Do you ever do any work yourself, Maureen – or is that a stupid question?' He saw his wife was trying desperately to think of something convincing. 'Don't bother, Maureen, I've been married to you for ten years and have never yet seen you do a tap. Anyway, how much a week does Mildred get?'

She coughed nervously. 'Two pounds a week. But she does put a lot of hours in, and she's a good cleaner.'

John wondered how long he could keep a rein on his anger. He had nothing against Mildred, she was a nice woman and a good worker. But she wasn't a poor woman; her husband had a decent job. She didn't need two pounds a week! No wonder she dressed well – a fact in her favour so far as his wife was concerned. She wouldn't have anyone coming to the house who, in her eyes, looked scruffy.

Without conscious thought, Ada Perkins came to John's mind. If she got two pound a week she'd consider herself rich. But John didn't use her to press home his point. 'I have collectors working for me who have big families to provide for and they don't take home much more than your cleaner's getting. From now on, Mildred will work three hours a day and no more. And her wages will be one pound a week.'

'I'm not standing for that! Have you gone out of your mind? What am I supposed to do if I have a dinner party?'

'That's entirely up to you. If you require Mildred's services at night, then you do without her during the day. Or have you forgotten how to make a bed?'

'Something's happened today to put you in a bad temper,' Maureen said, keen to get away. 'We'll talk about it in the morning when you're more rational.'

'I haven't finished yet, so you'd better sit down.' His tone brooked no argument and Maureen quickly seated herself. 'I'm also cutting your clothing allowance. You will no longer have a credit account at Cripps or any of the other stores.' He heard her sharp intake of breath but carried on. 'In future you will ask me for any money you want for clothes or household items. I won't be miserly with you, far from it, but your free-spending days are over and you've only yourself to blame. For ten years you've treated me like a stranger in my own home. The only use you had for me was my money, which you have spent without a thought of where it came from. You have never once asked how my business was doing because as long as the money was there you didn't care.'

John stood and looked down on his wife, who was dumbstruck. 'One thing more. Tonight was the last time *you* humiliate *me* in front of your so-called friends. And by the way, just out of curiosity, have you never wondered why these friends of yours never invite you to their homes?'

He reached the door and turned. 'In future when you're having guests I'll stay the night at my flat.'

Chapter Ten

'Hello, Grandma!' Polly kissed the old woman's nose, and with a cheeky grin whispered in her ear, 'Close yer legs, everyone can see yer bloomers.'

'Right,' said Sarah Jane, making no effort to cover her indignity, 'put a penny on all the flowers. If they're gettin' a peepshow thrown in, it'll cost a bit more.'

'I don't know what I'm goin' to do with you,' Polly said, her curls swinging as she shook her head. 'Our neighbour, me Auntie Dolly, would call yer a shameless hussy.' She put a hand on each of Sarah Jane's knees and pushed them together. 'There, that's better.'

'I can't sit like this all day, all prim an' proper like a ruddy school-teacher! Anyway, I'm not comfortable, an' I can't sit not bein' comfortable for hours on end.'

'Then pull the legs of yer bloomers up, they're round yer ankles.'

'The ruddy elastic has gone, they won't stay up.' The old lady bent down and fumbled under her skirt. 'There, if I don't move they'll stay like that an' no one will see them.'

'We should be busy today without your little peepshow,' Polly said. 'The sun's goin' to shine an' everyone will be comin' into town.'

Sarah Jane gave her toothless smile as she gazed up at the girl whom she'd grown very fond of over the last six months. 'We don't need the sun when we've got that sunny smile of yours. It's that that sells me flowers, girl, make no mistake.'

'Go on, yer old flatterer.' Polly took off her coat and folded it before laying it on the ground beside the stool. 'I'll get the flowers sorted out, then yer can tell me the prices.' She was a dab hand at arranging the flowers now and could have the stall set out in no time. And she loved the job. Particularly now with the wide variety of summer flowers. 'Ooh, I love these red roses, they look like velvet.'

'The ones yer holdin' are threepence a bunch. The others, the ones just in bud, yer sell them single at tuppence each 'cos they'll last a long time.' Sarah Jane grimaced as she rubbed her knees. 'Me ruddy legs are givin' me gyp today; it took me all me time to get out of bed this mornin'.'

Polly was at once concerned. 'If yer feel like goin' home, Grandma, I can manage on me own. I could give Auntie Mary the money an' she could take it to your house.'

'No, I'll be all right. It's just that I like to moan now an' again just to let people know I'm still alive. Anyway, if I went home I'd only be starin' at the four bare walls until it was time to go to the pub.' Sarah Jane's laugh was so loud and hearty most of the flower-sellers stopped what they were doing to listen. 'When I was a young girl an' didn't feel like goin' to work, I used to try an' pull a fast one on me mother. I'd lie in bed moanin', sayin' I had a belly-ache or a sore throat. But I don't know why I bothered because I never got away with it. She'd drag me out of bed by me ear an' say if I was fit to go dancin', then I was fit to go to work.'

'My God, you've got a bloody good memory, Sarah Jane!' Florrie shouted, laughing as she waved a bunch of iris. 'That must be all of a hundred years ago!'

'I'll take your word for it, Florrie.' Sarah Jane took after her mother in at least one respect. No one ever got the better of her. 'You should know 'cos yer were there, weren't yer, girl?'

'Yer cheeky sod!' Florrie laughed good-naturedly and went back to her flower-arranging while she tried to think of a witty reply.

Polly's first customer bought two bunches of roses and after that business became brisk. As she'd predicted, the warm sunny weather had brought the people out in large numbers and the city was bustling. Many just wanted to get out of the house and had only come to window shop, but their presence added to the happy atmosphere.

'Those rose buds are not goin', Grandma. I haven't sold one yet.' Polly handed over the twopence she'd taken for a bunch of sweet william. 'I think they're too dear. As soon as I tell anyone the price they pull a face an' shake their head.'

Sarah Jane rubbed her chin thoughtfully. 'I'm not sellin' them off cheap, Polly. I've got to get back what I've paid for them an' make a bit of profit. What yer could do, if a woman has a husband with her, is work yer charm on him. Tell him he'd look very handsome with one in his buttonhole.'

Polly looked doubtful. To have a buttonhole you had to have a suit, and none of the men in her street possessed a suit. Most of them had jackets which they wore with odd trousers. And like her dad's, they usually came from a second-hand stall at the market. She couldn't imagine any of them walking down the street with a flower in their lapel, even if they were given one free. But it would be such a shame if they didn't sell because they really were beautiful.

Polly picked a stem out of the bucket and was admiring it when she saw a smartly dressed man approaching. He seemed to be in a hurry but there was no harm in trying. She stepped from behind the array of buckets and when he was almost on top of her, she moved into his path. 'Buy a lovely flower, mister, for yer buttonhole?'

He brushed past her, seemingly oblivious to her presence, but after half a dozen paces he slowed down and turned his head. 'I'm sorry, were you speaking to me?'

Scenting a customer, Polly ran towards him, the rose in her outstretched hand. 'Would yer like to buy a flower, please, mister? Only tuppence, an' it would look lovely in yer buttonhole.'

The man turned and came towards her, his eyes quickly taking in the scruffy shoes and the shabby clothing. It was only when he was facing her and saw the mass of curly hair framing a smiling visage that the beauty of the rose was put in the shade. 'You're very young to be selling flowers, aren't you? Are you with someone?'

Polly's first thought was that he was a School Board official. Then she remembered it was Saturday, so she was safe. 'I'm helpin' me grandma 'cos she's not well.'

'I see.' The man looked down at the flower. 'How much did you say it was?'

'Tuppence, mister. But it's worth it 'cos it isn't opened up yet an' will last a long time.'

The man's lips curved at the corners but he kept the smile at bay. 'If you'll make the stem shorter, I'll take one.'

'Oh, thank you, mister! I won't be a tick.' Polly nearly knocked a bucket flying in her haste to get to Sarah Jane. 'How short shall I make it?'

'Three inches, just enough so it won't stick out of the side of his lapel.' The old lady winked. 'Nice goin', girl.'

'There yer are, mister.' Polly pushed the end of the stem through his buttonhole and stepped back. 'Yer look dead posh an' dead handsome.'

At this, the man's smile broke through. 'If it makes me look handsome then it is indeed worth the money because it must be magic.' His hand was in his pocket jingling the coins there, when he asked, 'Do you have any decent wrapping paper? If you have I'll take half a dozen as a present for my wife.'

Polly's face fell. 'We haven't, mister. Not nice enough for what you want it for. I'd run to Woollies an' get a piece for yer, but I can't leave the stall.' She looked dejected at losing the sale. 'It's a shame 'cos . . .' she almost said because they hadn't been selling well, but caught the words back just in time and replaced them with, 'I'm sure yer wife would like them.'

'I'll be passing again in about an hour. Perhaps you'll have been able to purchase the wrapping paper by then?'

Irish Mary had been keeping a watchful eye. The man looked very respectable but you never could tell. She walked

136

over and stood next to Polly. 'We'll have them ready for you, sir. In an hour, did you say?'

The man nodded. 'I'm meeting a colleague in the Athenaeum Club around the corner. I'll be at least an hour.'

Irish Mary nodded. 'They'll be ready for you, sir.'

The man took a handful of change from his pocket. Looking directly at Polly, he asked, 'Let's see now, how much will seven at twopence each be?'

'One an' tuppence, of course.' Fancy that, thought Polly. Dressed up like a toff and he can't add up!

'Here's one and six.' He handed the coins over. 'That should cover the cost of the paper as well. Any change, buy yourself some sweets.'

'Oh, thank you, mister!'

Sarah Jane was beside herself with delight. Watching Polly, and the way she had with people, was better than going to the pictures. 'The paper will only be a ha'penny, girl, so yer've made yerself a threepence ha'penny tip! How about that, eh?'

'Yes, me darlin', yer did very well.' Irish Mary gave her a quick, noisy kiss. 'It's daft I must have been to let Sarah Jane have yer. I should have kept yer for meself.'

'Could I have two of the roses instead of the money, Grandma?' Polly asked. 'Me mam can take them to the hospital with her tomorrow an' give them to me dad.'

Sarah Jane turned her head. This young girl didn't have a selfish bone in her body. The sole was hanging off her shoe, she wasn't wearing any socks today, which meant she didn't have any, she handed all her money over to her mother, and now when she had a bit extra which she could have spent on herself, she wanted to use in on flowers for her dad. 'I'll buy one for him as well.' The old woman blinked away a tear. 'After all, if it weren't for you I wouldn't be lookin' forward to me Saturday night out 'cos I'd be stony broke. And three roses will look better than two.'

'Make that four,' Irish Mary said. 'Sure, I'll not be lettin'

137

Sarah Jane get the better of me, that I'll not.'

Polly's smile couldn't have been wider. She knew this morning when she got out of bed that it was going to be a good day, and how right she'd been.

Charles Denholme walked away bemused. What on earth had come over him? The last thing his wife needed was more flowers . . . the house was full of them! It was the girl who'd caught his eye. It was obvious by her clothes that the family were as poor as church mice, but even when she was asking him to buy a twopenny flower there was nothing subservient in her manner. When she spoke she looked you in the eye as an equal. And she was so unaffected, she didn't realise she was prettier than the flowers she was selling. By Jove, it would do his two children good to swap places with her for a week. Perhaps then they'd appreciate what they had and not take it for granted.

He walked through the doors of the Athenaeum Club and as he looked around for his colleague, he was thinking that if she was dressed in decent clothes and had some elocution lessons, that little lady would hold her own in any company.

Ada turned into Faulkner Square on the run. The offices closed at twelve-thirty on a Saturday and usually she met Aggie at half-five, like the other nights. But last night Aggie had asked if she'd come early so they'd be finished about half-three and she could have a lie down until it was time to go to the pub. But it had been one mad rush for Ada after she finished her morning job. Running home on the double so Polly could go out, then tidying up and getting the washing on the line before seeing to Joey. Then she had to get some shopping in or they'd have had nothing in the house to eat. It's a good job it wasn't Saturday every day, she'd never be able to keep up the pace.

Aggie opened the door, heard Ada's hard breathing and

pulled her inside. 'Yer shouldn't have rushed, girl. Yer'll be doin' yerself an injury if yer keep that up.'

Ada leaned against the wall. 'It's yer fault! You an' yer ruddy pub, yer'll be the death of me!'

'Hold yer horses now, girl, 'cos yer'll be singin' a different tune in a minute.' Aggie tapped the side of her nose. 'Who is it that thinks so much of her mate she'd come in an hour early an' get started on the work? Go on, just tell me.'

Ada chuckled. 'Agnes Theresa Connelly, who else?'

'Right first time! I wasn't very popular with the staff, mind you. They didn't like me chasing them while I did under their desks. Still, I redeemed meself by makin' them a nice cup of tea an' worming me way back into their good books.' Aggie took hold of Ada's arm and pulled her along the hall. 'I've got the kettle on the boil so we can have a quick cuppa.'

'Aggie, yer an angel.'

'I know that, girl. Them's not me shoulder blades stickin' out of me back, I'll have yer know – it's me ruddy wings! Anyway, all the ground floor's done. So when we've had a drink an' yer get yer second wind back, I'll start on the next floor an' you can do Mr John's place. We can be finished in an hour.'

After working there for five months Ada was used to the routine and knew the house like the back of her hand. She started on the stairs up to the top floor, then the landing followed by Mr John's sitting room and his bedroom. He often left clothes lying around and she was no longer shy about putting them away in drawers or hanging them in the wardrobe. As she handled the fine materials, she found herself wondering why he kept such a selection there. But she reminded herself that he was a busy man, and if he needed to change during the day it made sense to have the clothes on hand rather than have to travel home.

Ada had left Mr John's office until the last and she was on her hands and knees in front of the fireplace when he came in unexpectedly. 'Oh yer gave me a fright!' she gasped. 'I wasn't expectin' yer.'

He was immediately apologetic. 'I'm so sorry, Mrs Perkins. Agnes told me you were here and I did whistle on my way up the stairs. Obviously I didn't whistle loud enough.'

'It's me own fault, I was miles away.' Ada sat back on her heels. 'I'm goin' in to see me husband temorrer an' I'm always a bit on edge the day before.'

John walked around his desk and was about to sit down when he noticed the hole in the sole of Ada's shoe. He dropped his eyes quickly, not wanting to embarrass her. 'I should think your husband is out of danger now, surely?'

Ada shrugged her shoulders. 'He's a hell of a lot better than when he went in; he could hardly hold his head up then, or even speak. But he's still in what they call isolation because of the disease being catching. I mean, they won't let the kids go in to see him. But they take him out in the hospital grounds so he gets plenty of fresh air.'

John nodded, trying to keep his eyes off the sole of her shoe. 'He will pull through, Mrs Perkins, it will just take time.'

'Yeah, about another eighteen months!' Ada threw the floor cloth into the bucket of water. 'Eighteen months . . . sounds like a lifetime.'

'They won't let him home until they're absolutely sure he's clear of it, and that's not only for his sake, but also for you and the children.'

'Yeah, I know, Mr John.' Ada went back to polishing the fireguard. 'I keep tellin' meself I should count meself lucky, 'cos he was awful sick an' I really thought he was goin' to die. But it gets lonely without him. The kids are good, but it's not like having a man to cuddle up to.'

John knew only too well what loneliness was. He'd grown accustomed to it over the years and had accepted that this was how it was going to be for the rest of his life. It was Ada

Perkins who had opened his eyes to what he was missing. A wife who was considerate, warm-hearted and loving.

'Well, that's me lot.' Ada struggled to her feet and picked up the bucket and the wooden box which contained the furniture polish, Brasso, blacklead and dusters. 'There's nothin' else yer want doin', is there, Mr John?'

'No, that's fine, thank you.' He was willing himself to say something that would keep her there, but no words would come until she was walking through the door. 'Ada!'

She stopped but didn't turn around right away. That was the first time he'd used her first name and she was taken by surprise. 'Yes, did yer want something?' she asked, her back still to him.

'Would you come back for a minute, please?'

After laying down the working utensils, she wiped her hands down the front of her pinny before walking back to stand in front of the highly polished desk. 'Yes?'

John coughed nervously as his mind sought the right words. 'I just wondered how you were managing for money. I know it's none of my business and you are within your rights to tell me so. But I want you to know I'm asking as a friend.'

'We're doin' all right, Mr John. We're not livin' in the lap of luxury an' I'd be tellin' lies if I said it wasn't a struggle. But we scrape along.'

'Ada, I'm going to ask you something. But before I do, will you promise not to take umbrage and put your coat on and walk away from this house for ever?'

Ada, though mystified, smiled. 'If umbrage means will I take the huff, then no, of course not. Yer've been too good to me for me to do that.'

'If you do get mad, throw the bucket of water over me. But don't stand on your pride and walk out.' John took a deep breath. 'You're not really managing for money, are you?'

'I've just said it's a struggle, but we get along. Don't you worry about us, Mr John, we're fine.'

John looked away from the forced brightness of her eyes. 'Then why are you wearing a pair of shoes with the soles worn through?'

It was anger and not pride that made Ada say, 'Because I haven't had time to go to Paddy's market to get a pair of second-hand ones, that's why!' Then she banged a clenched fist on his desk. 'No, that's a lie! I *did* go to the market one day for a pair of shoes, but they were for me son, Joey. His had gone too small for him an' the poor kid could hardly walk. So he was me first priority. This afternoon I'm goin' to the market again for a pair of shoes, this time for Polly, me daughter. The sole's hangin' off hers. Next week will be my turn, then we'll all have decent shoes on our feet. All second-hand, mind, but we can't afford to be proud. At least we won't be barefoot.'

This was a long speech for Ada, and John watched with admiration the changing emotions mirrored on her face. Anger had put colour in her cheeks and a sparkle in her deep brown eyes.

'I'm sorry if I've upset you, Ada, but I did it out of concern for you. Now, do you want to get that bucket of water and throw it over me, or are we still on speaking terms?'

Ada glared at him for several seconds, before shaking her head. 'I'm not in that much of a temper that I'd spoil that expensive suit. An' I'm not falling out with yer, Mr John, 'cos I know yer mean well. But I'm livin' on a shoe-string an' have to do the best I can. What I haven't got, or can't afford, we have to do without.'

'You don't have to go without, I'll help you.' John saw her eyes widen and quickly went on, 'There'd be no strings attached, I can assure you my intentions are strictly honourable. I have more money than I need, and helping you would be one way of getting satisfaction out of the money I have.'

'I can't take money off yer, Mr John, not without earnin' it. What would that make me!'

John knew he would have to tread carefully if he wasn't to offend her pride. 'There is a way you can earn it, unless you've too much work on already. As you know, I keep a lot of clothes here but have to take my shirts and other items home to be washed and ironed. It would be of enormous help to me if you could work an extra hour to keep my wardrobe in order.'

Ada looked at him through narrowed eyes. 'What about Aggie? She's been here a long time, she'd think I was pushin' her nose out an' I wouldn't want that. She's been good to me, has Aggie.'

'I'll ask Agnes if it would make you feel better, but I know beforehand what she'll say.' To Ada's amazement he adopted Aggie's voice. 'Here, Mr John, what d'yer think I am, a ruddy horse! Yer can iron yer own bleedin' shirts, or get that wife of yours to do 'em.'

Ada laughed aloud. 'I can almost hear her! She does have a certain way with words, does Aggie.'

'Usually words that are not in the English Dictionary.' It was John's turn to laugh aloud and Ada was surprised at the difference it made to him.

'D'yer know, yer look ten years younger when yer laugh.'

'In that case I'll go around with a permanent grin on my face.' Why does she have the power to make me feel a different man when she's around? John asked himself. The answer came back promptly. Because she's warm and natural, with no falseness about her. No made-up face, no fancy expensive clothes, no cloying smell of perfume and no putting on airs. And above all, she treats me like a man. 'I'll put it to Agnes so there's no ill-feeling, but as I know what she'll say, can I ask if you'd be prepared to work an extra hour or so?'

'Yeah, it suits me as long as it doesn't upset me mate downstairs. I can't work over on a Saturday, though, 'cos it's too much of a rush. But I'll stay an extra hour at night, as long as I have notice. I don't want me children to worry if

I'm late home. They might think I've run off with the coalman.'

Ada walked into the ward to find Tommy sitting in a chair at the side of his bed. His pale face lit up when he saw her, and at the sight of the bunch of roses his eyebrows almost touched his hairline. 'Have yer come into money, love?'

'These are off Polly, aren't they lovely? They come with all her love, an' Joey's.'

Tommy had been told about his daughter's weekend work, but without the real reason for it. He thought she was doing it as a favour to an old lady, although he knew she got a few bob for it. 'She shouldn't be spendin' her money on me,' he said, but inwardly he was delighted that he was still in the thoughts of his children. 'Give her my thanks an' a whoppin' big kiss. An' Joey, of course. Don't leave him out.'

'Joey won't be left out! He's come on a lot in the last few months, even starting to answer me back, the little tinker.'

Tommy laughed. 'He'll need to stick up for himself when he starts school, otherwise he'll get picked on.'

Ada saw a nurse further down the ward. 'I'll give these to the nurse an' she can put them in water. I won't be a tick.'

When she came back she sat on the side of the bed. 'How are yer, love? Yer look a lot brighter.'

'I've been for a walk in the grounds an' the fresh air an' sunshine have cheered me up a bit. But I do get fed up, Ada, the days seem to drag. All I've got to look forward to is seein' you on a Sunday. I miss yer so much, an' I miss the children.'

'Ay, never mind sayin' yer've got nothing to look forward to – of course yer have! When yer better yer'll be coming home, isn't that somethin' to look forward to? An' as for missing me an' the kids, the same goes for us as well. The kids never stop asking when yer'll be home, they miss yer somethin' terrible. As for me – well, that bed is awful lonely without yer.'

'I haven't been capable of being a real husband to yer for a long time, have I, love?'

'There's more to marriage than what goes on in bed, Tommy, an' to me yer always have been, an' always will be, the best husband in the world. I wouldn't swap yer for a big clock.'

'An' I wouldn't swap you for all the tea in China.' Tommy reached for her hand and stroked it with his thumb. 'How are the jobs goin', love? Not overdoin' it, are yer?'

'No, I'm fine. The mornin' one is hard going, but the one with Mr Roscoe is a doddle. In fact, it's a pleasure to work there. Me an' Aggie get on like a house on fire – she's an absolute scream. When yer come home I'll invite her down to meet yer. Her language is a bit choice, but yer get used to it after a while.' Ada smiled into his eyes. 'I know yer won't be able to work for a while after they let you out of here, but when yer are well enough I'm still goin' to keep one of the jobs on so we're never down to rock bottom again. Unless Polly gets a decent job when she leaves school, o' course. In that case, I'll retire an' live the life of Riley.'

'I don't care how we live as long as I get home.' There was a catch in Tommy's voice. 'I love me family an' I just want to be back with them, back where I belong.'

Chapter Eleven

Ada was pegging Polly's gymslip on the line when she heard her neighbour emptying her ashcan into the bin set in the wall, and singing at the top of her voice. Ada chuckled. 'Is that you, Dolly?'

'No, it's Jeanette MacDonald,' came the reply. 'Practisin' for me next film.'

Ada laughed. 'Yer know, it's times like this when I'm glad I never 'ave the time or money to go to the pictures. I always thought Jeanette MacDonald was a good singer.'

'Well, people thought so until I came on the scene. She's not a patch on me for singin', or for looks come to that.' Dolly banged the bin lid down. 'Have yer got time for a cuppa? I've got somethin' I think yer'll be interested in.'

'Yeah, all right. Put the kettle on an' I'll have the rest of me washing out by the time it's boiled.'

When Ada opened the front door the noise out in the street was deafening. Children seemed to be everywhere . . . girls jumping with their skipping ropes or playing hopscotch, several groups of boys were playing footie and two were even swinging from the lamp-posts. Thank goodness it was the last week of the school summer holidays. There'd been no peace in the street for the past seven weeks, what with the kids fighting between themselves, balls being kicked through windows and arguments between neighbours over whose child was responsible and who was going to fork out for a new pane of glass.

The trouble was, Ada thought as she pulled the door behind her, the holidays were far too long and the children got bored. There was no money around for them to go to a matinée every afternoon, so the only place they could play was in the street.

Joey was sat on the kerb with his feet in the gutter, watching what the other children got up to. He turned his head when he heard the door bang. 'Where yer goin', Mam?'

'Only next door, sunshine, I won't be long. Yer can come with me if yer like.'

'Nah, I'll stay here. It's better than sittin' in the house.'

'Don't yer move away from yer own front door, d'yer hear?' Ada gave a brisk rap on Dolly's knocker. 'Tap on the window if yer want me, but do it gently. Don't put the ruddy glass in.'

'Come in, girl, the tea's made.' Dolly pressed back against the wall to let her neighbour pass. 'And I've got fresh milk so yer in luck.'

When she was seated with a cup of steaming tea in front of her, Ada asked, 'What have yer got that might interest me?'

'Some things Les picked up on his round.' Dolly pointed to a neat pile of clothing on the couch. 'There's a couple of dresses there that look brand new. They won't fit me, I can't get them over me bust. But with you not havin' no bust, they'd fit you.'

Ada placed her cup back in the saucer. They weren't the china ones – those were long gone. Dolly had kept them especially for when Mr Roscoe collected the rent, but as soon as their old collector was back on the round they'd been put out for everyday use and had been smashed in no time. 'What d'yer mean, missus, I've got no bust? What d'yer think these two things are?'

'Plums. They're not big enough for oranges, that's a dead cert.' Dolly let out a hoot of laughter. 'You should see yer face, girl – it's a picture no artist could paint.'

'I should flaming well think so! It's not that I've got a small bust, it's you whose got two ruddy mountains!'

'Don't exaggerate now, girl. Hills perhaps, but never mountains.'

'Well, I think we've just about exhausted the topic of who's got the biggest bust, so can I have a look at these dresses?'

Dolly closed one eye. 'As long as we agree that I've got hills an' not mountains.'

'Aye, okay.' Ada smothered a laugh. 'But I've seen hills smaller than your bust.'

'You're jealous, that's your trouble. My Les thinks I've got a smashin' pair of . . . er . . . er . . .'

'Mountains?'

Oh, she's not getting away with that, Dolly vowed. This is my house and I'll have the last laugh if it kills me. 'D'yer know, yer may be right! I've never thought of it before, but d'yer think that's why me feller tries to climb them every night?'

Ada had just taken a mouthful of tea and now it spluttered all over her dress. 'Dolly Mitchell, you really are past the post!'

'*First* past the post, girl. With my bust I couldn't be anythin' but first. Me backside might come in last, but me bust would definitely come in first.'

'I give up.' Ada wiped the front of her dress with the corner of her pinny. 'Now, can I see the dresses, please?'

Dolly pushed herself up and walked to the couch. 'This is my favourite. If it fitted me yer wouldn't get a look in.' She held up a long-sleeved soft wool dress in deep maroon. 'Whoever bought this paid a pretty penny for it. Feel the quality, girl.'

'I can see, it's beautiful.' Ada fingered the soft material. 'Who'd give a dress like this away? It's just like new.'

'Them what have more money than sense, girl, that's who.'

'Well, whoever, they had good taste.' Ada admired the plain round neck, the nipped-in waist that flared out into a full skirt, and the straight sleeves. 'It's plain but well-cut, and definitely expensive.'

149

'Try it on, girl, see if it fits.'

Ada shook her head. She'd be ashamed getting undressed in front of anyone because her underclothes, although clean, were well worn. 'I'm a sight underneath.'

'Oh, sod off, Ada Perkins! Who the hell d'yer think's goin' to see yer? Yer've only got the same as me, even if I do have a bit more of it. Go in the ruddy kitchen if it makes you feel better.'

When Ada came out of the kitchen wearing the dress, Dolly whistled. 'My God, girl, yer look a million dollars! It fits yer a treat an' the colour doesn't half suit yer.'

Ada ran her hands over her waist and hips. 'It feels as though it's been made for me. Fits like a glove.'

'If yer say yer can't afford that, yer want yer ruddy bumps feelin'.' Dolly nodded to emphasise her strong feelings. 'Yer'll never get another chance like it.'

'How much does Les want for it?' Ada knew she was going to have the dress come what may. She'd do without food rather than let a bargain like this go. Anyway, she wasn't too badly off these days. The extra ten bob a week she got for doing Mr Roscoe's laundry had made all the difference. It meant she could pay all her ways and they didn't have to have blind stew to fill their tummies. And for the past six weeks Polly had been flower-selling every day and she'd been handing over six shillings every Saturday. She would have given more, but Ada told her to save up while she had the chance and buy herself a new pair of shoes or a pretty dress.

'There's another one here just as nice,' Dolly was saying when Ada had collected her thoughts. 'Les wants a shillin' for the two of them. An' yer couldn't fall out with the price, girl, he's not makin' hardly any profit on them. It's only because it's you he's lettin' them go so cheap.'

'Where's the other one?'

'Here.' Dolly held up a dress in midnight blue. It was in the same soft wool and the same simple pattern, except this had a square neck and three-quarter sleeves. 'It's the same size so it'll fit yer.'

'I'll give Les one and six for them – would that do?'

'He'd be over the moon, girl! But are yer sure yer can afford it?'

Ada nodded. 'I've been doing well for the past few weeks, what with me extra few bob from Mr Roscoe and Polly's money, so the dresses turned up at the right time.'

'I keep forgettin' to ask yer, but did yer ever do anythin' with that green coat?' Dolly asked. 'Yer never mention it an' I just wondered.'

'I unpicked it, but never seem to have any spare time to get down to tacking it together. That's good material, too, an' if I turn it inside out where it isn't faded, it'll look all right. I was thinkin' of makin' Polly a coat out of it, but I might just keep it for meself and try an' get her one from the market.'

'Ay, girl, I can just see your Tommy's face if yer walk in the hospital with one of those dresses on an' a posh coat. He'll think yer've got a rich fancy man tucked away somewhere.'

'He'll more likely think I've robbed a bank. He knows I've no time for a rich fancy man. I work twice a day, every day but Sunday, an' then I go in to see him. Me life's all planned out for me, Dolly, all ruddy work an' no play.'

'It won't be like that for ever. Time passes quickly an' yer'll soon have Tommy home again.' Dolly grinned. 'Life's not all pain an' misery, girl. Yer've got one good thing to look forward to.' She saw Ada's puzzled look. 'Your Joey starts school next week, or had yer forgotten?'

'I'd have a job to forget, he talks about nothing else. I've got to kit him out at the weekend . . . new shirt, kecks, socks an' shoes. I can't keep up with him with shoes, he grows out of them so quick.'

'If you think you've got problems, what about me with our Steve? I can't get short trousers to fit him! He's gone

151

out today in the first pair of long kecks he's ever worn. They're a pair his dad got on his round an' they fit him a treat.'

'He can't wear long trousers for school, though. They won't allow it, will they?'

'Nah.' Dolly clicked her tongue on the roof of her mouth. 'But the pair he's got on today are the pair he'll be wearin' to school on Monday, whether he likes it or the school likes it. It's not worth buying him any more short trousers, he'll be startin' work after Christmas.'

'Ah, don't let the lad get into trouble with his headmaster.'

'He'll not get into trouble, don't worry. I'm goin' to chop the legs off the trousers at the knees, put a hem on, an' no one will know any difference.'

'Yer a crafty beggar, Dolly Mitchell.'

'Thanks, girl.'

'Hello, Mr Denholme.' Polly gave a wide smile to the man she considered one of her regular, twice a week, customers. 'Is it a rose today, or will yer have a carnation?'

'I'll let you choose, Polly.'

'A carnation,' Polly said without hesitation. She tilted her head and closed one eye as she inspected him. 'Seein' as yer wearing a grey suit, I think a pink one will be best.' She glanced to where Sarah Jane was looking on with interest. 'What do you think, Grandma?'

'You're a better judge than me, girl,' Sarah Jane cackled. 'My taste is in me . . . er . . . in me . . . er . . .' The old woman was stuck. If she said 'backside' in front of the toff, Polly would have her guts for garters. But she couldn't think of a word to replace it with so she said, 'I've got no taste, yer know that.'

Polly was dying to laugh but she kept her face straight. She'd laugh about it tonight when she was telling her mam that it was the first time she'd seen Sarah Jane stuck for words. 'Right, pink it is then.' She pushed the shortened stem through his buttonhole and pulled it down behind his lapel. 'There yer are, an' very nice yer look too.'

Going through the change in his hand, Charles Denholme asked, 'Is the lady really your grandmother, Polly?'

'No.' Polly took his threepenny bit. 'But I wish she was 'cos I love the bones of her.'

'And that boy, the one standing at the back – I've seen him here a few times lately, but he's always been in short trousers before. Is he your brother?'

'No, me brother's only five!' Polly's infectious laugh rang out. 'That's Steve Mitchell, he lives next door to me. During the school holidays he's been comin' down to give a hand clearin' away.'

'Ah, a secret boyfriend, eh?'

Again her laugh rang out. 'I'm too young to have a boyfriend, but Steve's me very best mate.' She could see several people who seemed interested in the flowers and Polly didn't want to lose a customer. 'I'll 'ave to go, Mr Denholme, but I'll see yer again, I hope?'

'Yes, of course, Polly.' Doffing his bowler hat first to Polly, and then to Sarah Jane, Charles went on his way.

'If he wasn't old enough to be yer dad, I'd think he fancied yer,' Sarah Jane called.

'Don't be daft, Grandma, he's just a nice man. A real gent, that's what he is.'

Steve had also been watching with interest. He marvelled at Polly's ability to get on with people. Rich or poor she treated everyone alike. The old lady who'd asked her to split a bunch of flowers because she could only afford a penny got the same friendly treatment as that toff in the bowler hat who spoke as though he had a plum in his mouth. Polly was good with folk, there was no doubt about that. And she was a good mate, better than any of the boys in the street. Look how she'd got him this little job for during the summer holidays. It wasn't really a job, he just helped the women empty their buckets and brushed the pavement when they'd cleared everything away. He only got threepence a day for it but it was better than hanging about in the street or kicking a ball around in the park. Just standing here watching was an eye-opener. The different expressions on the faces of people passing by, or listening to the flower-sellers laughing and cracking jokes with customers who tried to bargain them down, it was all new and exciting. He wouldn't half miss it when school started. The only good thing about next Monday was that it was the start of the last four months of his schooldays.

Steve pushed his hands into the pockets of his long trousers. They didn't half feel good on him and they fitted him perfect. He could see by his reflection in the window of a shop opposite that they made him look grown-up. He reckoned he looked at least sixteen.

When the day was over, the flower-sellers were in high spirits because it had been a good day. There was a lot of banter as they began to clear away, and with Steve's willing hands to help them they were finished and on their way home in no time. Only Sarah Jane and Irish Mary were left with the two youngsters.

'Are yer goin' to be able to get home on yer own, Grandma?' Polly looked anxious when she saw the pain on the old woman's face as she tried to walk.

'Me legs are playin' me up, girl, with sittin' in the same position all day. But once I can get them movin' I'll be all right.' Sarah Jane took a faltering step. 'That's the worst of growin' old. All yer bits an' pieces start to give up on yer.'

'I'll see her home, she doesn't live far,' Irish Mary said. 'You two toddle off home.'

'Are yer sure?' Polly still looked anxious. 'Me an' Steve could take her.'

'It's only a stone's throw, Polly, me darlin', an' she'll be sittin' in her rocking chair in no time at all, so she will.' Mary held out her large wicker basket. 'Would yer be after takin' this for me? If I have me two hands free Sarah Jane can lean her weight on me.'

'I could give her a piggy-back,' Steve said, smiling. 'I often give our Clare a piggy-back.'

Sarah Jane gave him a gentle push. 'Ah, but your Clare doesn't wear fleecy-lined bloomers, does she?'

Steve blushed. 'I don't know what she wears.'

'Come on now,' Mary said briskly. 'Let's get goin' before yer have the poor lad not knowin' where to put his face.'

So to Steve's delight, he had Polly to himself on the walk home. 'I'll carry the basket, Polly.'

'Thank yer kindly, sir.' Every Saturday Polly bought a bunch of flowers for her mam to take into the hospital. Today she'd chosen carnations and she placed them carefully in the basket before handing it over. 'Me dad will like those, they've got a lovely smell.'

Steve glanced sideways at her. She had a smile on her face and it struck him that he'd never seen her in a bad temper. Not like his sister, who was always throwing tantrums and moaning if she couldn't get her own way. But Polly wasn't like that. She wasn't a cissie like most girls; she was one of the lads, mucked in with everything.

Steve swung his arm and puffed out his chest. He felt so proud in his long trousers, and Polly was a pretty girl to have walking by his side. In fact, he told himself, he'd never seen a prettier girl.

'Have yer still got that marble, Polly?'

'Of course I have!' Polly looked surprised. 'I told yer I'd always keep it to remind me of yer.'

Steve's chest expanded a few inches. 'I've still got the birthday card yer gave me. I'll never throw that away.' He wasn't going to tell her the trouble he had keeping it a secret. Every Monday morning he had to take it out of his pillowcase and find a new hiding place for it. Monday was wash-day in their house, the day his mam changed the bedding. Still, like he told Polly, he'd never throw it away. 'School again on Monday, Polly.'

'Oh, don't remind me. I dread it! But it's all right for you – only four months before yer leave.'

'Yeah, an' it can't come quick enough. I'll be a workin' man just after Christmas.'

'Have yer made up yer mind what yer want to be?'

'Me dad doesn't want me to go near the docks, said it's not a steady job. He reckons I'd be better to try an' get an apprenticeship in one of the trades. The wages would be lousy until I was twenty-one, but he said if yer've got a trade at yer fingertips then yer've likely got a job for life.'

'He's right.' Polly nodded her head in agreement. 'My dad hasn't got a trade an' he's always regretted it.' She went on quickly in defence of her father, 'It wasn't his fault, though, it was the war. He was learning woodwork, but he got called up at eighteen and never finished his apprenticeship. When he came back from the war he was too old to start again, and there were no jobs anyway.'

'I think I'll go in for plumbing. Me mam said there'll always be work for plumbers as long as the water doesn't dry up on us.'

Polly giggled. 'That sounds just like your mam.'

'I know it's a few years off, but when I'm workin' an' I've got a few bob in me pocket, will yer come to the pictures with me, Polly?'

'Of course I will.' She gave him a dig in the ribs. 'What picture shall we go an' see?'

Ada was polishing the dressing table in John Roscoe's bedroom when he came in to stand beside her. 'I've got a very big favour to ask, but knowing how you dislike upsetting Agnes, I'm going to call her up and discuss the matter in front of you both.' He smiled and raised his brows. 'Does that meet with your approval?'

'I only work here, Mr John, you're the boss.' Ada

continued polishing the already gleaming dressing table. 'Whatever you do is all right with me.'

'Good!' John went on to the landing and leaning over the curved bannister rail, called down, 'Agnes, would you come up for a moment, please?'

Ada grinned when she heard Aggie puffing up the stairs, muttering loud enough for anyone to hear: 'What the bleedin' hell does he want now?'

Waiting on the landing, John gave a silent guffaw. As far as he was concerned, Agnes could call him fit to burn and get away with it. She'd been part of his life for so long, he regarded her as family. The only real family he had. He'd offered to set her up in a little house in any area she chose, and pay her a weekly allowance so she would never have to work again. But the old woman, as outspoken as ever, had told him precisely where he could put his money. She'd also told him she was grateful and loved him like a son. But Agnes Theresa Connelly had always worked to keep herself and would do so until the day she died.

Aggie reached the top stair and glared at him. 'If yer must live at the top of the ruddy house, get a bleedin' lift in!'

'Get in, woman, and stop harping.' John waved an arm towards his office. 'In there, if you please.' He turned to Ada who was trying hard to keep a straight face. She couldn't believe the things Aggie got away with. No other boss would put up with it. 'Ada, would you honour us with your presence?'

They entered the office together to find Aggie seated in John's chair behind the desk. 'Sod that for a joke, Mr John! Those bleedin' stairs will be the death of me. Me heart's poundin' like mad an' I can't get me breath proper.'

'Then just sit where you are, I'll stand. Ada, you can perch on the corner of the desk.'

'I'm all right, I'll stand.' Ada winked broadly at the old lady sitting in style behind the desk. 'After all, I haven't just walked up those you-know-what stairs.'

'If you must blame someone for having to walk up those you-know-what stairs, then blame Ada,' John said, rubbing his hands together and smiling. 'Because you are head of the cleaning staff, she insists that no business is conducted without you being present.'

'My God, what an education does for yer,' Aggie huffed. 'Teaches yer a lot of big words that yer feel yer have to use 'cos yer've learned them, and yer'd hate to think yer'd wasted yer time. But yer not half longwinded, Mr John. Get on with it, for God's sake.'

'I belong to a card school in the club I go to. Three friends and myself have been playing at the same table for years. On several occasions I have been invited to the home of my friends for a night of whist, but I have never returned their hospitality. I would like to do so now by inviting them here one night.' He quirked an eyebrow at Agnes. 'Am I being brief enough for you?' When she nodded, he went on, 'I would need to ask for your help in providing some refreshments. Nothing cooked or elaborate, just a selection of sandwiches and what-nots.'

'Huh!' Agnes growled. 'Can yer imagine me waitin' on anyone? They'd think yer were hard-up, Mr John, if they got an eyeful of me.' There was affection in her eyes as she gazed at him. There was pity in her heart, too, but she wasn't going to let that show. 'I'll give Ada a hand to make sandwiches and get things set out, but I'll not wait on.'

'Hey, hang on a minute!' Ada cried. 'I've never waited on in me life. I wouldn't know what to do!'

'There's no "waiting on", as Agnes calls it,' John said. 'Just serve a selection of light refreshments, a cup of coffee, then leave my friends and I to our own devices. We are all capable of pouring a glass of whisky, and that will be our liquid refreshment through to the early hours. You work an extra hour anyway, Ada, and that's all the time I would need you for.'

He shouldn't have to beg it of me, Ada thought, not after

all he's done for me. But she had grave doubts about what he was asking of her. All his friends would be rich, like himself. They'd expect someone more refined than her, and she didn't want to let Mr John down. 'I'd do it for yer, Mr John, willingly, but I'd only let yer down in front of yer friends. Yer need someone who's used to that sort of thing – someone who can talk proper.'

Agnes jumped in here. 'Ay, girl, there's nowt wrong with the way you talk. Don't ever run yerself down 'cos yer as good as the next one.' She tutted loudly. 'If I was a few years younger I'd do the ruddy job meself an' wouldn't give a sod what me laddo's friends thought about me bleedin' language.'

John rocked on his heels with laughter. 'Agnes, my friends would be delighted with your language. They're not snobs, they have a good sense of humour, and I'm sure they'd find your colourful version of the English language far more interesting than a game of whist.'

Ada was only half-listening to what was being said. She'd do it for him, she decided. She'd help him out like he'd helped her out. It wasn't for her to question why his wife wasn't doing the honours – that was his private life, away from Faulkner Square. But she'd do her damnedest not to let him down. All she had to do was smile and keep her mouth shut. And she had a decent dress to wear now, she wouldn't be letting him down in that respect.

'I'll do it for yer, Mr John,' Ada said, 'as long as Aggie helps prepare and set out the food. But,' her eyes twinkled with merriment, 'if I fall flat on me face with a tray of butties in me hand, and shout, "Oh bleedin' hell", don't say yer weren't warned.'

Chapter Twelve

Ada walked to Faulkner Square in her working clothes, carrying a small case she'd borrowed from Dolly. The cheap case had seen better days and had originally come off Les's rag cart, but it had come in useful today because it was carrying Ada's maroon dress, carefully folded and wrapped in a piece of sheeting. She was wearing the only pair of shoes she possessed but they'd been blackened and polished until she could see her face in them.

'I haven't got any tea brewing,' Aggie said when she opened the door. 'I thought we'd best get crackin' and have a drink later if we've got time.'

'My nerves are a wreck,' Ada told her. 'I just hope I don't make a show of meself.'

'You won't, girl! Mr John will see yer all right, so don't worry.' Aggie spoke with confidence. 'Anyway, I came a bit early to make a start an' I've nearly finished down here. It's only had a quick flick of the duster, mind, but we can't be expected to perform bleedin' miracles.'

'I'll go straight up,' Ada said, her hand on the bannister as she mounted the stairs. 'I want the whole top floor shining for Mr John's friends coming. Will you give the second floor a quick goin' over, Aggie?'

'That's all it's goin' to get, girl – a quick goin' over. I'll be that ruddy quick the room won't know it's been done.'

They met up an hour later, both puffing with exhaustion. 'If he makes a habit of this,' Aggie panted, 'he can get someone else in 'cos I've just about had it.'

'Away with yer! Yer think the world of the man, yer'd never let him down.'

'I know that, girl, an' so does he, but it doesn't do to say

161

it out loud. An' I'm so used to moaning, I can't get out of the habit. In fact, if he didn't hear me carryin' on, Mr John would think I was ailing for somethin'. But yer right, I wouldn't let him down as long as I was able to put one foot in front of the other. He's never let *me* down, yer see, girl.'

Aggie moved away from the wall she'd been leaning against. 'One of these days I'll tell yer just how good he's been to me, but tonight we haven't got time. So let's shake a leg an' get those refreshments ready.' As they walked to the back of the house where there was a small staff kitchen, Aggie muttered, 'Bleedin' toffs an' their bleedin' refreshments, they make yer sick. Why can't they just have sarnies like the rest of us?'

Mr John had ordered all the foodstuff from Coopers. Everything was of the best quality. Ground coffee with an aroma that had Ada sniffing up in appreciation, boiled ham that made their mouths water, and smoked salmon that had Aggie pulling a face and saying it was a good job she wasn't rich because she couldn't stand the bleedin' stuff.

The small delicate cakes were an eye-opener to Ada. As she placed them on the glass cake-stand she said, 'I've never seen cakes like this. I wish the kids could see them.'

Aggie chuckled. 'They don't sell them round our way, either. There'd be no call for them 'cos they're too flamin' dear.'

They hadn't heard the front door open and jumped when they heard Mr John say, 'I ordered extra cakes so you could take some home with you.'

Aggie rounded on him. 'Are you tryin' to give me a bleedin' heart attack? If yer want to get rid of me, there's easier ways than frightenin' the ruddy life out of me.'

'I'm glad to see you're in a happy mood, Agnes. Not that I've ever seen you unhappy, but tonight you're like a bright star shining in a dark overcast sky.'

'God strewth! The man's lost his marbles!' But the

affection in Aggie's eyes belied her tongue. 'Have you been hittin' the bottle?'

'Not yet, Agnes, but later on I shall probably have a dram or six.' He winked at Ada. 'And how is Mrs Perkins tonight?'

'Gettin' more worried by the minute,' she admitted. 'We'd better take these upstairs then I can get washed an' changed.'

'There's plenty of time yet, don't get flustered. I'll make a few trips upstairs with these, while you go and do what you have to do.'

Ada didn't need telling twice. She knew that the dress would give her confidence and couldn't wait to put it on. She made a dash for the hall, picked up the case and headed for the staff toilet. If anything went wrong tonight it wouldn't be for want of trying. She didn't have much but she intended making the most of what she did have.

It was fifteen minutes later when Ada put in an appearance. She looked so different from the woman who'd gone through the toilet door, that Aggie and Mr John stared at her in amazement. Her rich dark hair had been piled on top of her head, leaving her face exposed and revealing her striking features: black, perfectly arched eyebrows above her wide deep brown eyes, a slightly turned-up nose and a firm square chin. And for the first time for as long as she could remember, she was wearing lipstick. It was the cheapest they sold in Woolworth's, but it was worth the money because it accentuated her full lips. And the dress which fitted her to perfection completed the picture of a very attractive woman.

She stood uncertain, wondering why neither of them said anything. Perhaps she didn't suit the dress after all, or perhaps her hair looked a mess. Oh dear God, she'd made a laughing stock of herself.

'I don't believe it.' Aggie came towards her, arms outstretched and a tear threatening. 'Yer look bloody lovely!'

Ada closed her eyes as the older woman held her tight. She felt so relieved she had to bite on the inside of her mouth to stop herself from blabbering. How well she'd look if Mr

John's friends arrived and found her in tears.

Aggie let her go and turned around. 'Well, what d'yer think of her?'

Mr John was slowly shaking his head from side to side. 'As you said, Agnes, she looks bloody lovely.'

The old woman put one arm across Ada's shoulders and pointed the other at Mr John. 'Yer'd better stop this swearing lark 'cos it's becomin' a habit with yer. I'm goin' to have to watch meself or yer'll have me at it as well.' She gave Ada a squeeze. 'Anyway, yer shouldn't swear in front of a lady. And by God, this mate of mine looks every inch a lady.'

'She does indeed, Agnes, she does indeed.' John could think of many words to describe how Ada looked – words like beautiful or magnificent, but he knew if he uttered them she'd scuttle away like a frightened rabbit. 'My friends will be very impressed.'

'Just don't let them get their hands on her, that's all,' Aggie warned. 'And no swearwords or dirty jokes in front of 'er, d'yer hear? I've heard plenty of tales about what blokes get up to when they're out on the town without their wives. Yer can't bleedin' trust them.'

'Agnes.' John held out his hands. 'I can assure you my friends are the epitome of respectability and integrity.'

Aggie's jaw dropped. 'The only word I understood in that little lot was me own bleedin' name! Honest to God, Mr John, sometimes yer sound just like a ruddy dictionary on legs.'

The exchange between her boss and her mate had the effect of calming Ada's nerves. How could you be nervous and laughing your head off at the same time? 'If you two intend gettin' the boxing gloves on, would yer leave it until tomorrow, please, when we've got more time? I'll even be referee, if yer like, but right now there's far too much to do.'

'Not for me there isn't!' Agnes took her arm from Ada's shoulder. 'I've done me whack an' I'm goin' home, 'cos that's where I live. Mr John will tell yer what's what, girl, an' yer'll

manage fine. The way you look, the men won't know, or
care, whether they're eatin' brawn or smoked bleedin'
salmon.' She put a finger under Ada's chin and raised her
face so their eyes were on a level. 'You look lovely, girl, just
like a film star. I know Mr John won't let no harm come to
yer, but just in case one of his mates misbehaves, then put
yer coat on an' scarper. Yer don't need to take nothin' from
no one. Okay?'

'I'll be all right, Aggie. I'm quite capable of lookin' after
meself. I'm sure everythin' will run smoothly.'

'Right, I'll be on me way then.' Aggie planted a kiss on
her cheek. 'See yer temorrer, girl.' As she passed Mr John on
her way out, she whispered, 'You take care of her, d'yer
hear?'

'You have my promise, Agnes.' John touched her arm.
'You're fond of her, aren't you?'

'More than fond, Mr John. She's the daughter I never
had.'

Ada felt shy after Aggie had left and she was climbing the
stairs with Mr John. 'If yer'll tell me what to start with, an'
how to fold the serviettes, I'll be grateful. And if you want
me to offer them a whisky when they arrive, yer'll have to
show me how much to pour into the glass. Once yer've
showed me, I'll be fine.'

'I'll get the whisky, it's in the office.'

Ada was rearranging the trays of sandwiches when John
came up behind her and touched her shoulder. She spun
around to find him standing with his head tilted and a half-
smile on his face. 'I just want to thank you once again for
helping me out, I do so much appreciate it. And also to tell
you how very lovely you look.'

Ada closed her eyes. It had been so long since a man had
paid her a compliment or looked at her with admiration in
his eyes, she filled up with emotion. She struggled for
composure, telling herself she was just feeling sorry for
herself. But the tears wouldn't be stopped and they trickled

through closed lids to run down her cheeks.

John looked on in dismay as the tears flowed. He felt so helpless, didn't know what to do or say. In the end he took her by the shoulders and asked, 'Have I said something to upset you?'

'No! It's just me bein' childish.' Ada brushed the tears away. 'This has been buildin' up for a long time. I've had nothin' but heartache and money worries for so long, and when yer down in the gutter yer lose pride in yerself, yer feel worthless. I'd even forgotten what it was like to be a woman. But tonight, in me new second-hand dress which I'm big-headed enough to know looks good on me, and with me hair done decent, I feel like a woman again. I can even remember what it was like to be loved and wanted.' The tears continued to roll and she used the backs of her hands to wipe them away. 'I'm sorry, Mr John, yer must think I'm a very stupid woman.'

'Oh, Ada, my dear.' John pulled her towards him and rocking her like a child, he told her, 'You're far from worthless, or stupid. You're a very attractive and desirable woman.'

Ada's head was resting on his chest and she could smell the scent of expensive soap and the whiff of cigars. She felt so contented and at peace with herself, so safe and secure in a man's arms, it was as though all her troubles had melted away. Then came the intrusion of the front-door bell and she sprang back. 'Oh my God!' Her hand flew to her mouth. 'I'm sorry, Mr John, I don't know what came over me.'

'My fault, Ada, not yours.' John cursed his friends at that moment. 'Now just keep calm and I'll go down and let them in. Take their coats as they arrive and put them on the coat-stand in my office.' He started to walk away, stopped, turned and kissed her cheek, then hurriedly left the room.

John's friends turned out to be so pleasant and friendly that Ada was soon at ease with them. As she was to tell Polly later, they all spoke frightfully far back, but they treated her as an equal. Serving the refreshments was a doddle as each of the four men jumped up to help whenever she approached the table with trays or cups. And the many admiring glances cast her way filled her with a confidence she never thought she'd be capable of. She heard Mr John getting his leg pulled a few times about being a dark horse, and where had he been hiding her all this time. But her boss had a ready answer to them. She was on his staff, and was a respectable married woman with two children.

'It's time you were on your way, Mrs Perkins.' John took his fob-watch out of his waistcoat pocket and frowned. 'It's nearly half-past nine. Your family will be getting worried.'

'Yes, I'll be on my way if yer sure there's nothing else you need.'

'No, we'll be getting down to some serious card-playing now and some heavy drinking.' He rose from his chair. 'I'll see you out.'

'Oh, yer've no need to, Mr John. I can let meself out.'

'Mrs Perkins, you are the most obstinate woman I know. Now get your coat and I'll see you to the front door.'

His three friends left their seats to shake Ada's hand. 'Thank you for looking after us, Mrs Perkins,' said Jack Grimshaw, 'and for adding a touch of glamour. Hopefully we'll see you again.'

'Hear, hear,' chorused one of his colleagues, while the other said, 'It's been a delight to make your acquaintance.'

Ada smiled her thanks and left the room followed by John. They didn't speak as they descended the two flights of stairs but when they reached the front door Ada said, 'There was no need for yer to come down, Mr John. I could have banged the door behind me.'

'I know, Ada, you're a very capable woman. You were excellent tonight, did me proud, and I'm deeply grateful to you.'

When he made no move to open the front door, Ada reached for the handle. But she didn't turn it. Instead she spun around and faced him. If she didn't clear the air now she'd never be able to look him in the eyes again. 'Mr John, about what happened tonight, I don't know what came over me. I don't want yer to think I'm in the habit of crying on the shoulders of strange men, or that I'm a cheap, flighty woman, 'cos I'm not.'

'Ada!' John placed a hand on her arm. 'You did nothing wrong, it was me who should be apologising. But I'm not going to apologise for doing something that I enjoyed and seemed right at the time.'

'It won't happen again, Mr John, I promise yer.'

He took her hand and held it between his. 'If Agnes was here she'd say, "That's not a promise, it's a bleedin' threat!".'

Despite her nerves and shyness, Ada smiled. 'Oh, Mr John, can yer imagine what Agnes would have said if she'd seen us? We'd have both got our backsides slapped.'

'I doubt it.' There was a smile on John's face but his words were deadly serious. 'She'd probably have said there was no harm in two lonely people taking comfort from each other.'

Their eyes locked and what Ada saw in his caused her heart to miss a beat. 'I'd better go, yer friends will wonder what's goin' on.'

'Have you got the cakes for the children?'

Ada nodded. 'Yes, thank you, Mr John, they'll be over the moon with them. Now I'll bid yer good night.'

'Good night, Ada, and take care.' He waited until she was opening the wrought-iron gate before saying, 'Whenever you need a shoulder to cry on, Ada, mine is always here. Remember that.'

Polly's eyes were heavy with sleep when Ada got home, but the sight of her mother, looking as she'd never seen her looking before, soon chased away the yawns. 'Oh Mam, yer don't half look pretty. I bet Mr John got a shock, seein' yer all dolled up.'

'I don't know about him gettin' a shock, but he said I looked nice. An' yer should have heard Aggie, she said I looked bleedin' lovely. How anyone can look lovely an' be bleeding at the same time, only God and Aggie knows.'

'And you do look lovely, Mam!' Polly rested her elbows on the table. 'Tell me all about it. What were Mr John's friends like an' what did they have to eat?'

'Smoked salmon, would yer believe?' And so Ada began her tale, only leaving out the part she was ashamed of. How she was going to face Mr John tomorrow she couldn't imagine. He must have got the impression she was a right trollop. In fact, for all she knew he could be having a damn good laugh with his friends about her right this minute. But even as the thought crossed her mind, Ada knew she was doing the man a grave injustice. He'd only ever shown her respect and kindness, even to taking the blame for that moment of madness.

'And have yer brought some cakes home, Mam?'

Ada's eyes looked blank for a second. Her mind had been split in two, one part telling Polly all about the evening, the other concerned with her indiscretion. 'Er, yes, they're in the case. I put them in one of the boxes they came in, but they've been upside down in the case so they're probably broken up by now.'

But apart from one or two small iced decorations being broken off, the cakes were almost perfect. Polly gazed at them in awe. They were the smallest cakes she'd ever seen – one mouthful and they'd be gone. But they were so dainty, all different shapes and iced in pretty pastel-coloured icing, she thought it would be a shame to eat them. 'There's eight there, Mam. Who are they for?'

'Mr John gave me them for you an' Joey, but I think we should share them between us, don't you?'

'Oh, yeah! You had to work for them, Mam, so yer should have the most.' Polly was eyeing the pale lilac one which had a lump on the top and a small green leaf. But by rights her mam should have first pick. 'You choose what you want.'

'I thought if we had two each, I could give the other two

to Dolly an' Les. They've been very good to me, Polly, an' it would be a small way of showin' my appreciation.'

Polly clamped her lips tight, a thoughtful expression on her face. 'I'll just have one an' give the other to Steve. He always shares with me.'

'We can't leave Clare out, that would look terrible.' Ada began to laugh. 'I suggest you an' me have one now an' put the box away. Joey can have two in the mornin' an' I'll pass the other four over to me mate.'

'Which one d'yer want, Mam? You have first pick.'

Ada saw her daughter's eyes on the lilac cake. 'I'll have the yellow one.'

Polly let her breath out and reached over to the box. She held the small cake in the palm of her hand before taking a bite. Her face assumed a look of pure bliss. 'Oh Mam, there's marzipan on the top, *an'* cream. Mmmm . . .' She stopped chewing so she could savour the taste for as long as possible. 'Mam, what did Aggie say yer looked like?'

'Don't yer ever repeat that, me girl, or I'll box yer ears.'

'I won't, Mam, but what was it?'

'Bleedin' lovely.'

'That's just what this cake tastes like, only better.'

Lost in the luxury of her yellow iced fancy, Ada couldn't disagree. Later, as she lay in bed, the tiredness she'd felt disappeared. She was going over the events that led to her ending up in Mr John's arms. She could remember standing crying like a baby, then the next minute her head was resting on his chest. She hadn't moved towards him, she'd been rooted to the spot. So it was Mr John who had brought about the embrace, not her.

Ada plumped her pillow and turned on her side. She'd be able to look him in the eye tomorrow because she'd done nothing wrong. Then a voice in her head said she could have stopped it, so why hadn't she? *Because it all happened so quickly, I didn't have a chance*, she answered angrily. Then the voice asked what would have happened if the front-door bell hadn't sounded? The answer to this didn't come so quickly. She re-lived the moment of contentment she'd felt wrapped in his arms, the manly smell of him, and his concern and gentleness. All the things that had been missing from her life for so long. And no harm had been done, no one had been hurt. She was still a young, red-blooded woman; was it so wrong to enjoy the company and admiration of a man? She loved Tommy with all her heart, always would. But she couldn't deny her needs.

'In the name of God!' Dolly Mitchell stared down at the cakes in the box. 'One of them would fit in my feller's eye! If that's what the toffs eat then I'm glad I'm as common as muck. Give me a ha'penny cream bun to one of them any day.' But for all her words, Dolly's mouth was watering. 'Still, seein' as yer were good enough to think of us, I'll have one.'

Ada laughed at the expression on her neighbour's face when her teeth sank through the icing into the soft marzipan, then downwards through the cream and soft sponge. Three mouthfuls and the cake had been demolished. Licking her fingers, Dolly said, 'I take me words back about the cream bun, girl. I always thought I was born to better things an' now I'm sure. That cake was bloody lovely. Next time Mr Roscoe's entertainin' toffs, ask him if yer can bring an assistant. Tell him I won't need paying as long as he supplies me with a load of cakes.' She eyed the remaining fancies with a scheming glint in her eye. 'My feller doesn't know about them, so if I eat the one yer brought for him, he won't know the difference. What the eye don't see, the heart don't grieve over.'

'Don't you dare!' Ada cried, closing the lid of the box. 'If I thought yer were mean enough to do that, I'd take them back home with me and bring them in tonight.'

'Huh! Some mate you are, Ada Perkins.' But Dolly cast aside her craving and after giving Ada a pretend look of outrage, picked up the box of tempting pastries and carried it through to the kitchen. 'If yer don't trust me, yer can check with Les when yer see him, just to make sure I haven't diddled him.'

'And I'll check with Steve and Clare, too,' Ada told her. 'I'm not doin' without meself just to feed your face.'

'Da-da-de-da-dah.' Dolly pushed her tongue out as far as it would go. 'Little Goody Two-Shoes, anyone would think yer'd never done nothin' wrong in yer whole life.'

Guilt brought a flush to Ada's face. Her neighbour was only being her usual funny self, and any other day Ada wouldn't have taken it to heart. But today it touched a raw nerve. 'I'm far from bein' an angel, sunshine, an' I'd be the last to say I am. But I've never pinched a cake off me husband, so there!'

'I won't need to pinch it off my Les.' Dolly grinned, pulling a chair out and sitting down. 'I'll do a swap with him.'

'How d'yer mean, yer'll do a swap with him?'

Dolly wagged her head and tutted. 'Surely to God yer know how to get what yer want off yer husband? Just put him on a promise!'

'A promise of what?'

'I don't have to spell it out to yer, do I? Ye gods, yer've been married for fifteen years – if yer don't know what I mean by getting round yer husband, then I'm wasting me bloody breath.'

The penny dropped and Ada rolled her eyes to the ceiling. 'I was slow there, wasn't I?'

'Not slow, girl, dead bloody stopped! I hope yer weren't as slow off the mark last night?'

'I most certainly was not! I did very well, an' it was all down to the dress I got off you an' Les. I felt so good in it I'd have served the Queen an' not turned a hair. But I'd have been well out of me depth in me old workin' clothes, so I'm really grateful to you an' your feller.'

'Only too glad to help, girl. I'll keep me eye out, an' if

anythin' else decent comes along I'll give yer the nod.'

'Yer a smasher, Dolly.'

'Yes, girl, I know.'

Tommy couldn't believe his eyes when Ada walked into the ward on the Sunday. She'd sat up late into the night to get the green coat finished and she was wearing it open over the maroon dress. And she'd gone to pains over her appearance. Her hair was piled up on top of her head and she was wearing lipstick. 'Oh love, yer a sight for sore eyes.'

Ada leaned closer to whisper, 'All off Les Mitchell's second-hand cart. I had to turn the coat inside out 'cos the material was faded, but it's come out fine. The whole lot only came to one and tuppence – and that includes the reel of cotton.'

'If we were out in the garden I wouldn't be able to keep me hands off yer.' Tommy was still very pale and thin, but his breathing seemed easier today. 'I'd be pulling yer into the bushes so I could give yer a big hug.'

'And I'd be letting yer,' Ada said. 'In fact, I'd be the one doin' the pullin' and the huggin'.'

'Yer still love me then, Ada?'

'What sort of question is that! Of course I still love yer, yer daft ha'porth. It's only me clothes that's different, not what's in me heart. There's only ever been you for me, love, an' that'll never change.'

'D'yer know, seein' yer like that takes me back to our courting days. Yer used to wear yer hair up like that then, remember? An' all the fellers used to whistle after yer.'

'It's a long time since a feller whistled after me, Tommy Perkins! If yer saw me in me workin' clothes, yer'd know why. I only got dressed up like this 'cos I've seen some of the young nurses in here an' I thought I'd better pull me socks up.'

Tommy laid his head back. 'I feel a lot better for seein' yer like this. I've been worried in case yer were just putting a brave face on for me, but I'm easier in me mind now, knowing you and the kids are all right.'

'Yer'll see the kids for yerself next Sunday.' Ada was pleased when his face lit up. 'It'll only be through the window, but they're dying to see you even if only to get a wave off yer.'

'You're full of surprises today, love. But they're the sort of surprises I need. Do me more good than all the medicine in the world. In fact, you *are* my world, love – you an' the kids.'

Chapter Thirteen

'Sit down an' take the weight off yer feet for five minutes.'
Aggie waited until Ada was seated on one of the round, black
leather-covered office stools before handing her a cup of tea.
'Yer not gettin' a saucer, saves washing up.' There was
affection in the smile she bestowed on the younger woman.
'I've got somethin' to tell yer that might make yer cry yer
eyes out or jump up an' down for joy. And I want to tell yer
now instead of springin' it on yer, sudden like.' She wiped a
hand across her chin where tea had dribbled down. 'I won't
be comin' back after Christmas, girl, I'm packin' in work.
I've had a bellyful an' it's time to call it a day.'

'Oh Aggie, no!' Ada was horrified. She'd worked with the
old woman for ten months now and she was like family to
her. 'Don't leave, please! If the work is too much for yer, I'll
help yer more.'

'I'm seventy-eight, Ada, and I've done my whack.' Aggie
tried not to let it show but there was a trace of sadness in
her smile. 'I've never told yer about me life before, girl, 'cos
I thought yer had enough misery without me addin' to it.
Mr John knows because I've worked for him, an' his mam
and dad before him, for nigh on forty years. They were good
to me, his mam and dad, the best friends I ever had. They
took me in an' gave me a job when nobody else would touch
me with a barge-pole. But I'm fond of yer, girl, yer've been
like a daughter to me. So I'm goin' to tell yer me tale of woe,
an' yer'll need a hankie at the ready.'

Aggie put her cup down on the desk and fixed her tired
eyes on Ada. 'I've had a bloody hard life, girl, I can tell yer.
Had to leave school at twelve because me mam took to her
bed and there was only me to look after her. I've never

regretted it, mind, 'cos I thought the world of her. But she never got better and died when she was only thirty-two. At fourteen I was left to fend for meself an' I've been doin' it ever since. I had no family, yer see, 'cos me mam was never married. I never knew who me dad was, he dumped me mam when she told him she was expectin'. The bleedin' coward scarpered an' left her to face the music. She never saw hide nor hair of him again. And to this day I'll swear it was the shame that killed her.'

Ada was shaking her head slowly, her heart going out to the older woman. 'I feel ashamed of meself. The times I've moaned to yer, tellin' yer all me troubles, when I've had it cushy compared to you. But don't leave, Aggie, I beg yer. I look forward to comin' here every day but it wouldn't be the same without you. In fact, my life wouldn't be the same without you. Couldn't yer come in every day and just sit with yer feet up? I'll do the work an' you can boss me around.'

'I'm sorry, girl, but me mind's made up. There's no way I'd sit an' watch you do all the work, that's not in me nature. I'm as sad as you are, but me body's tellin' me it's time to pack in. Kneelin' down is gettin' to be a nightmare. Once I'm down it takes me all me time to get up. An' those bleedin' stairs are killin' me.' Aggie took a drink of tea to try and dislodge the lump in her throat. 'It'll break me heart leavin' Mr John, I've known him since he was a baby. Walkin' away from him is goin' to be the hardest thing I've ever had to do.'

'So he doesn't know yet?' Ada was grief-stricken but she kept it hidden. Aggie was upset enough without her making things worse.

'No, not yet. It's two weeks to Christmas. I'll pluck up the courage to tell him before then.'

'I don't know what to say, Aggie, I can't take it in yet. But my feelings are selfish ones 'cos I don't want to lose yer. Yer won't just disappear from me life, will yer? I mean, yer will come and see me?'

'Of course I will, girl – a bad penny always turns up.' Aggie sighed. 'Well, I've got that off me chest an' I feel better for it. Now it's back to the grindstone for thee an' me.'

Ada worked with a heavy heart. There were many reasons for her sadness, one being her own loss. She couldn't imagine coming here every day and Aggie not opening the door to her. But Ada's biggest concern was the old woman herself. Who was going to look after her? With neither kith nor kin, who would be on hand to help her when the day came that she couldn't fend for herself?

Ada was on her knees dusting the high skirting board on the top landing, and as her hand moved the soft duster along the wood, all sorts of questions were running through her mind. If Aggie got sick, who'd be there to hear her cry for help? And who'd do her washing and ironing for her, or her shopping? After such a hard life she deserved better than to be left alone in her old age.

In her mind's eye, Ada pictured Aggie lying in her bed, her life slipping away and not a soul to hold her hand or offer comfort. The picture was so clear, so painful, that Ada sat back on her heels and let the tears flow. And this was how Mr John found her when he stepped from the stairs on to the landing.

'Ada, my dear woman, what is it?' John dropped on his haunches beside her. 'Has something dreadful happened?'

Ada cursed herself for her childishness. A grown woman like herself should be able to control her emotions and not be bawling her eyes out every time she had a setback. 'Nothin', Mr John. Take no notice of me – it doesn't take much to set me off.'

'Look, leave that for now and stand up.' John straightened himself and took her by the arm. 'You've no idea how it distresses me to see you on your hands and knees.'

Sniffing, Ada said, 'It's me job, Mr John, an' there's no shame in it. It's the only sort of work I can do, an' it's either that or me an' the kids starving to death.'

177

'In here.' He steered her through to his office. 'Now what's all this about? And don't say "nothing", because you're not the type of woman to cry for nothing.'

Ever since the night he'd held her in his arms, Ada had made sure she'd never put herself in that position again. She'd helped him out several times now when his card-playing friends came, and had enjoyed the evenings. But whenever they were alone she kept a distance between them. The incident had never been mentioned by Mr John, in word or deed, and he'd never changed in his attitude to her. He was still as friendly and solicitous as he'd always been. It was almost as though the indiscretion had never occurred, and Ada was grateful to him for that.

'Honestly, Mr John, there's nothing wrong!' Ada had no intention of betraying Aggie's secret. It was up to the old woman to tell him when she felt the time and place were right. Their relationship was too precious for an outsider to interfere.

John gripped her arms. 'Ada, when I told you to come to me if you ever needed a shoulder to cry on, I meant it most sincerely. So please tell me what's troubling you. I might be able to help.'

'Well, if yer must know, it's just me bad temper,' Ada lied. It wasn't the best excuse in the world but it was the only one she could think of. 'I was late gettin' home from work this mornin' and the kids wouldn't shift themselves to get to school on time. So what does any woman resort to when things don't go her way? She cries like a baby.'

John held her eyes for a few seconds before releasing her arms. 'Why do I have the feeling you're not telling me the truth? Your words tell me one thing but those eyes of yours tell me another.' He walked to stand behind his desk. 'I wish you felt you could trust me, Ada, because I only have your wellbeing at heart. I thought you'd understand that by now.'

'Oh, I do, Mr John. I'd trust yer with me life, an' that's the God's honest truth!' Ada dropped her head. 'An I *was*

178

lying to yer. I wasn't late gettin' home from work an' me kids are the best-behaved children in the whole world.' She raised her eyes to meet his. 'But I wasn't cryin' for meself, an' that is the truth. I was feelin' sad because of somethin' a good friend of mine told me. And yer know women are never happier than when they've got somethin' to cry about.'

'I've not had much experience with women, Ada, so I really wouldn't know. But from my limited experience, I would say you weren't like other women. You've survived where most others would have fallen by the wayside. With your head held high you've shown spirit and strength of character, and I admire you very much.'

But I'm not half the woman the old lady downstairs is. The one who's going to knock you for six in the next few days, Ada thought. And it was thinking of her mate that gave Ada the idea of how to lighten the situation. 'Thank you, kind sir! But this isn't gettin' me job done, is it? As Aggie would say, "This bleedin' cryin' lark doesn't half interfere with work".'

John smiled. 'There's another woman of spirit who I have much admiration for. She tells you things straight, does Agnes, no messing around. I need to have a word with her now, but if I was to call down and ask her to come up, she'd give me a straight answer . . . "Not bleedin' likely, Mr John. You want me, you come down an' get me. If I'm not worth the journey, then sod yer".'

There was heartache behind Ada's laugh. Aggie was going to leave a void in her life, but more so in Mr John's.

John found Aggie in the office on the first floor. 'Have you got a minute to spare, Agnes?'

'For you, Mr John, I've got *five* minutes.' There was fondness in the smile she gave him. 'What are yer after? If it's to ask me to come an' live tally with yer, the answer's "yes, please".'

'If only you'd been born a few years later,' John laughed, 'you'd have been my ideal woman.'

'I'd have made a better job of it than the one yer married to, that's a dead cert. How yer ever came to lumber yerself with a cold fish like her is beyond me.'

'I made my bed, Agnes, and now I'm having to lie on it.'

'Aye, on yer own! What a right bleedin' performance that is! Oh, I know, I shouldn't talk about her like that, but she gets on my ruddy wick.' Aggie put her face closer to his. 'I know someone you'd like to live tally with, an' I'd rest happy if yer were married to someone like her.'

'I could never hide anything from you, could I, Agnes? But I didn't think it was that obvious.'

'Not to anyone else it isn't. But I've know yer too long, Mr John, not to be able to read yer like a book.'

John sighed. 'Well, it's Ada I want to talk about. When I went upstairs I found her crying. I wondered if you know why . She's very fond of you and I thought she might have confided in you.'

'Why didn't yer ask her yerself? Yer've got a tongue in yer head, an' a ruddy dictionary to go with it.'

'I did ask her, or course I did! First she said she was in a temper with her children, then when I suggested she wasn't telling the truth, she admitted it was a lie. Her second excuse was that she was sad over something a good friend had told her. But I have my doubts and decided to ask you. If she's in trouble I want to know so I can help.'

Aggie stared at him for a while, then said, 'Sit down, Mr John, I've got somethin' to tell yer.'

Ada stepped from the bottom stair and was about to put her cleaning utensils down when she cocked her head. It was very quiet, not a sound anywhere. It wasn't like Aggie to be quiet; if she wasn't banging furniture around she was either whistling in tune, or singing out of tune. And Mr John should be down here somewhere – they couldn't both disappear into the blue. Then Ada smiled. They were probably having a sly cup of tea in the kitchen. She'd sneak up on them and catch them red-handed.

But when Ada reached the kitchen, the sight that met her eyes took the smile from her face and stopped her in her tracks. Aggie and Mr John had their arms around each other and although Aggie's face was pressed against Mr John's chest and couldn't be seen, her muffled weeping could be heard. What to do now, Ada asked herself. Shall I slip away quietly so as not to embarrass them? Or shall I offer to make them a cup of tea? *Slip away*, a voice in her head told her. *Your presence would be an intrusion*. So she started to back out of the room, but the movement must have caught Mr John's eye and he turned his head. 'Come in, Ada.'

She saw tears glistening in his eyes and shook her head. He wouldn't want anyone to see him like that. 'No, I'll leave you two alone. Give me a shout when yer want me to brew up.'

'Ada, my dear, don't be embarrassed by my tears because I'm not. Crying isn't only a woman's prerogative, you know. Men have emotions too.'

Then Aggie surfaced. Her hands wiping furiously at her face, and sniffing up loudly, she said, 'Him an' his bleedin' words no one can understand. What was that word that means men can do it as well as women?'

John took a hankie from his breast pocket and handed it to her. 'Wipe your face and blow your nose. The word was prerogative, and it means I can have a bleedin' good cry as well as you.'

Aggie blew loudly into the pure white linen handkerchief. 'What 'ave I told yer about swearin', Mr John? If Ada wasn't here I'd put yer over me knee an' smack yer backside, like I used to when yer were little.'

'I would rather you didn't discuss my backside with Ada, if you don't mind, Agnes. A man must retain his dignity.'

With the tension lifted, Ada made for the sink. 'I think we

181

could all do with a cup of tea. What say all of you?'

Aggie's blotched face grinned. 'I'll have a drop of Mr John's whisky in mine – for medicinal purposes, yer understand.'

'Tut, tut, tut!' John put a look of severity on his face. 'If there's one thing I can't abide, it's a drunken woman.'

'Mr John, shut up an' get the bleedin' whisky!'

He stood to attention and saluted. 'Aye, aye, sir!'

Ada waited until she heard him climbing the stairs. 'Yer told him, then?'

Aggie studied Ada's face before answering. Then she decided if she told her friend the whole story she wouldn't be doing Mr John any favours. So rather than take a chance on him losing both the women he cared about she gave her own version. 'We were standin' here talking and I thought it best to get it over and done with. I'm glad I did 'cos I'll sleep better tonight.'

'How did he take it?'

'You know me, girl. Hard-hearted Hannah! Well, I wasn't so bleedin' hard-hearted when I looked him in the eye an' told him. I started blubbering like a baby an' that set him off. But yer'll be glad to know he's got everythin' worked out. He's goin' to pick me up in his car an' bring me here to see yer, an' whenever you've got the time to spare he'll run yer to my house.' She chuckled gleefully. 'Ay, girl, I can't wait to see the faces on the women in our street when he comes to my house in his big posh car. By God, their eyes will be poppin' out of their heads like bleedin' organ stoppers.'

Ada put her arms around her and hugged her close. 'Your Mr John thinks of everything, he's a really kind man.'

'He's a better man than anyone knows, Ada, an' he deserves to be treated a damn sight better than he is by someone I can't even bear to say the name of.' Her red-rimmed eyes started to blur and she wiped them with the now-sodden handkerchief. 'Ten years ago he said it was time

I retired 'cos I'd earned it. Offered me a weekly allowance for life, he did, an' promised he'd always be there if I needed him. I could have been sittin' pretty for the rest of me days without ever havin' to worry about money. That's the sort of man he is, girl, one in a million.'

'But yer didn't take it, an' I know why,' Ada said. 'Yer wanted to be near him, preferred his company to his money. Right?'

'Yer've hit the nail right on the head, Ada! Let's say I've been his anchor for the last ten years. Someone he could talk to when the sea got rough. An' that's what's grieving me. I feel as though I'm leavin' him in the lurch. But time marches on an' I'm nearing the end of the road. I can't complain. At seventy-eight I've had a good innings. But I want yer to promise to look after Mr John for me. Be a friend to him, don't let him be lonely.'

'Aggie, I've only known him a short time, and I'm only his cleaner! He's known you all his life – I could never take your place. He'd think I had a ruddy cheek if I started to get too friendly.'

'No, he wouldn't, girl, 'cos he's got a soft spot for yer.' Aggie heard footsteps on the stairs and lowered her voice. 'I'll teach yer all the swearwords before I go, then he won't miss me.'

John came in brandishing a bottle of whisky. 'Do you want a glass, Agnes, or will you drink it from the bottle?'

The old woman felt like running and putting her arms around him, she loved him so much, every bone in his body and every hair on his head. Instead, she growled, 'You took yer bleedin' time!'

Polly wrote the first four letters of the alphabet on a piece of paper and pushed it along to Joey. 'Copy them underneath mine, Joey, then I'll tell yer what they are.'

Joey licked the stub of pencil, and with his tongue hanging out of the side of his mouth with concentration, he laboriously wrote the four letters. Then he studied them with a critical eye. 'I haven't done them as good as you, but I'll soon learn.'

'They're very good! Now, what word begins with an "a"?'

Joey's eyes swivelled sideways, a superior grin on his face. 'I know that one, we learned it at school. "A" is for apple.'

'Yeah, but a lot more words begin with "a", yer know. What about "and" and "are". And our Mam's name, Ada?'

This was getting too much for Joey. It was bad enough having words rammed down him at school without coming home to it. 'Ah, ay, Polly, why can't we just 'ave a game of noughts an' crosses?'

'Oh, all right.' Polly turned the piece of paper over and drew lines across and then down it. 'You be the—' A knock at the door brought a look of surprise to her face. It was a bit early for her mam, and anyway she had her own key. 'I wonder who this is?'

'Go an' see!' Joey was disgusted. Whoever it was could have waited until they'd started the game and then he could have cheated while Polly was opening the door.

'Hello, Steve! This is a surprise.'

There was an air of suppressed excitement about Steve as he shuffled his feet. 'Can I come in, Polly? I've got somethin' to tell yer.'

'Yeah.' Polly stood back to let him pass before closing the door. 'I hope it's somethin' nice.'

Steve rubbed his hands together and smiled at Joey before facing Polly. 'I've got a job.'

'Go 'way!' Her pretty face lit up. 'How, when an' where?'

'I asked for the afternoon off school, 'cos me dad heard this plumbing firm on Derby Road were takin' on apprentices. I didn't think old Grundy would let me go, but he did, and am I glad! If I'd left it until after Christmas all the jobs would have gone.'

'Sit down an' tell us all about it.' Polly was happy for Steve but there was also a tinge of sadness in her heart.

Things would change when he started work. He'd be a working man and working men don't play footie in the street. Nor do they have a schoolgirl for a mate. 'What happened at the interview? Were yer nervous?'

'I'll say! Me legs were shakin' and I couldn't stop them. But the bloke who interviewed me was smashin'. He's probably seen hundreds of lads with knockin' knees.' Steve was so thrilled he couldn't sit still. 'I start the Monday after Christmas. The wages are low – only seven and six a week – but yer get a rise every year. I've got to supply me own overalls an' take carry-out every day 'cos I'll be goin' out to houses to mend burst pipes an' things like that. Not on me own, of course, I'll be with a skilled plumber who'll teach me the tricks of the trade.'

Polly grinned. 'So if we get a leak, all we've got to do is knock on the wall an' we'll have our very own plumber?'

'Ah, ay, Polly, give us a chance! The only way I'd know how to stop a leak would be to keep me finger on it, like that lad in Holland did when the dam burst.'

Joey's head was resting on his hand as he listened. 'What's a dam? I thought it was a swearword.'

'A dam's a . . . oh, I'll explain that to yer some other time.' Steve turned a beaming face on Polly. 'I'm lucky gettin' a job before I even leave school, aren't I?'

'Yer dead lucky! I'm made up for yer, Steve, honest I am, except for one thing. I hope yer don't get too big for yer boots and think yer too grown-up to be me mate.'

'I'll always be yer mate, Polly, nothin' will change that.'

They heard the key turn in the lock and seconds later Ada appeared. 'Hello, Steve.' She pursed her lips at Joey. 'And what are you doin' out of bed at this time of night, me bold laddo?'

'I was just goin' to take him up when Steve came.' Polly couldn't get the words out quick enough. 'Steve's got a job, Mam!'

'Oh son, isn't that marvellous!' Ada threw her coat over

the back of a chair. 'Is it the one yer dad told yer about, down by the docks?'

Steve was so proud of himself he could barely conceal his delight. 'Yeah, that's the one. I start the Monday after Christmas.'

A rap on the window brought a smile to Ada's face. 'It's busy here tonight, isn't it?'

'I'll go, Mam.' Polly opened the door to Steve's mother. 'It's Auntie Dolly, Mam.'

'Tell her to go away,' Ada winked at Steve. 'It's too late this time of night for visitors.'

But Dolly was already in the room before Ada had finished speaking. 'Sod off, girl! I'm not a ruddy visitor, I'm yer mate,' she jerked her head at Steve, 'an' his mother.'

'Ay, it's good news about his job, isn't it? Yer'll be laughin' sacks with his wages comin' in,' Ada said jokingly. 'I'll know where to come for a loan when I'm skint.'

'Huh! It'll cost me money for him to go to work! Buying his overalls, payin' his tram-fare an' givin' him carry-out! It's me what'll be borrowing off you, girl.'

'The wages are not that bad, Mam,' Steve protested. 'Yer won't be makin' much on me, but at least I'll pay me own way.'

'I know yer will, son, I was only kiddin'.' Dolly folded her arms and hitched up her bosom. 'Anyway, I didn't come because of that, Ada. I came to tell yer I had murder with that cow in number four while yer were at work.'

'Oh, don't tell me I missed a good fight! What was it over?'

'Well, I started gettin' meself all worked up this afternoon when I saw the nit nurse come out of their house. I mean, there's no need for it. If she can afford to go to the pub every night with her feller, all done up to the nines, she can afford to buy a block of carbolic soap an' a fine-tooth comb to keep the kids' hair clean. Honest to God, their heads are walkin' alive, poor buggers.' Dolly stopped to take a deep breath before coming to the exciting part. 'Anyway, I didn't have enough tea for in the mornin' an' I was on me way to the corner shop about an hour ago, when she passed me, hangin' on to her husband's arm an' gazing up at him like a lovesick calf. And just behind them, playing in the middle of the street were her two youngest, an' all they had on them were dirty vests. No dresses, no knickers, nothing but these filthy vests which didn't even come down to their waists. Bare backsides and bare everythin' else. An' in this cold weather, too. So I saw red, didn't I?'

All eyes were on Dolly, all ears pricked. 'What did yer do, Dolly?' Ada asked. 'Didn't get yerself into trouble, did yer?'

'I got hold of the queer one's arm and dragged her back up the street, her feller shoutin' at the top of his voice as she pulled him along with her. Yer should have heard his language, girl, the air was blue. If yer think I can swear, then yer should hear him – he'd put me in the shade any day.'

'Dolly, will yer get on with it. Me heart's in me mouth!'

'All right, all right! I stopped them by where the kids were playing an' told them they should be ashamed of themselves. I said if they didn't get back in the house, with the kids, then I was goin' for the police. By this time some of the other neighbours had come out an' they all backed me up. Irish Mary said they weren't fit to have children, and if the police were called she'd tell them the children should be taken from them and put in a Home where they'd be fed and dressed properly. The queer one screamed that she'd pull me hair out if I didn't let go of her arm, an' her brave husband was goin' to do all sorts to me. He called me every name under the sun, insinuating I 'ad no father and was a loose woman.'

Steve leaned forward. 'He didn't touch yer, did he, Mam? 'Cos if he did I'll belt him one.'

Dolly grinned as she shook her head. 'I saved yer the trouble, son. I belted him one meself.'

Ada gasped. 'Yer didn't!'

'I did! I fisted me hand an' let him have it right in the middle of his beer gut. He doubled up, holdin' his tummy and groaning. That's when the queer one tried to grab a handful of me hair, so I belted her one, too!'

Ada narrowed her eyes. 'Dolly Mitchell, if this is one of your jokes, I'll kill yer.'

'So help me, girl, every word of it is gospel. Ask Irish Mary if yer don't believe me. She was blazin' mad at seein' the kids with no clothes on. If I hadn't got me fist in first, she'd have done it for me. An' a few of the other women were so mad they got their hands on the two of them an' pushed them in the house, warnin' them that if they went out an' left the kids in the house on their own, they'd fetch the police.'

'Well, I declare,' Ada said. 'Fancy me missing it all.'

'Does me dad know, Mam?' Steve asked. 'I didn't hear yer tellin' him about all this.'

'Yer didn't hear me 'cos I didn't tell him. He'd lay a duck egg if he knew I'd been fightin' in the street. He'd say only fishwives shout, swear an' use their fists. So don't you breathe a word to him, d'yer hear? If yer do, yer won't be turnin' in for work on yer first day 'cos yer'll be in hospital with both yer legs broken.'

'Dolly, don't say that to the lad,' Ada said. 'He's over the moon about gettin' a job an' you talk about breakin' his legs.'

'He knows I don't mean it, don't yer, son? I wouldn't hurt a hair on his head. An' I know he won't snitch on me.' Dolly's smile covered them all. 'I'll tell yer what, though, I didn't half enjoy meself. For a couple of years I've worried meself sick about those kids bein' out in all weathers with not enough clothes on to keep them warm. The eldest is only about five an' they go out an' leave them on their own. It's just not right. An' only God knows whether they ever get anythin' to eat.'

Hitching her bosom up, she said, 'Beltin' them both did me a power of good. Got me own back on them for all those years they've made me worry. Yer see, it is true what they say about everythin' coming to he who waits. Only in this case, it's a she an' not a he.'

Chapter Fourteen

John was sitting behind his desk on the Saturday afternoon when he saw Ada scurrying past. He called her name and when she looked through the open door, he beckoned. 'Just a word, Ada, I won't keep you long.'

'What is it, Mr John?'

'Just to tell you not to worry about food for Christmas because all the staff get a food hamper.'

'Oh, lovely!' Ada's face lit up, then doubt appeared. 'But I haven't been here as long as the others an' I only work part-time.'

'Ada, are you suggesting I don't know these things, or that I am not the boss?' There was a twinkle in his eye which told her the words were in jest. 'All my staff are treated the same, and you are a very valuable member of staff. The hamper will contain all the food you need and there'll be a turkey to go with it. Now, as you appear to be in a hurry I won't detain you.'

'I've nearly finished up here, but I told Aggie to leave the main hall an' I'd do it for her. Save her gettin' down on her knees and turning the air blue when she tries to get up.' She started to walk away, hesitated, then turned. 'Thanks, Mr John, that's a load off me mind. Our Joey's askin' Father Christmas for a scooter an' Polly wants a new dress. They forget money doesn't grow on trees. But if I don't have to buy any food then with a bit of luck they'll have somethin' decent to come down to on Christmas morning.'

'Is she a big girl, your Polly?'

Ada shrugged. 'Just an average thirteen-year-old. People say she's the image of me, same colouring an' everything.'

'Then she must be a very pretty girl.'

'It sounds like blowin' me own trumpet after saying she looks like me, but yes, I think she's very pretty. Then again, every woman thinks their children are the most beautiful in the world, don't they?' She gave him a smile. 'I'd better get crackin'.'

John watched her walk out of sight, thinking how lucky her children were. He'd give all his wealth away if he had her to come down to on Christmas morning. He sighed and went back to his paperwork.

Ada was on her hands and knees scrubbing the hall tiles. She had her back to the front door and the sound of the scrubbing brush deadened the click of the door opening.

'Out of my way!' a voice barked. 'Remove yourself immediately.'

Ada sat back on her heels and turned her head. She recoiled at the sight of the woman who was glaring at her with such anger and spite, it took her breath away.

'Are you deaf as well as stupid? I said REMOVE YOURSELF!'

Ada looked the woman up and down as her own anger grew. She was well-dressed, but that was the only thing in her favour. Her face was so distorted with temper at not being obeyed immediately, that she was positively ugly.

'Get up, you miserable slut! Don't you know who I am?'

That did it for Ada. She didn't care who the woman was, she wasn't taking insults like that. 'Madam, I neither know nor care who you are. But I will not be spoken to like that.'

'Then get your coat, you miserable wretch, you're sacked!'

Ada's eyes widened. 'Oh, an' are you in a position to sack me?' By this time she had an inkling who this dreadful woman was, but her pride wouldn't allow her to bow down to her, job or no job.

Maureen Roscoe hadn't had a good day. There was a dress she adored in Cripps but John had closed her account there and they wouldn't give her credit. To think she had come so low she couldn't even buy a dress without his consent! She'd felt such an absolute fool in front of the friend she was with.

Now she'd come to tell John she would no longer tolerate the situation and he must open her accounts again. If one had standards then one must live up to them. Her temper hadn't diminished in the walk to Faulkner Square, and the woman scrubbing the floor was an ideal target for her venom.

'Yes, I *am* in a position to sack you, and I am also in a position to do this.' She bent her leg back before kicking out and knocking the bucket of water sideways, so most of the water, as she'd intended, went over Ada.

'How dare you!' Ada's nostrils flared with anger as she felt the water seeping through her clothes. She struggled to her feet and faced the woman. 'Who the hell d'yer think you are?'

'I'm the woman who has just given you the sack. Now get your belongings and leave the premises.'

Ada still had the dripping scrubbing brush in her hand and the temptation was too great to resist. She lifted her hand and before Maureen could see what she had in mind, Ada shook the brush several times in her face. Dirty water ran down from her forehead to add to the grey marks already staining her light beige, pure wool tailored coat.

Aggie had heard the commotion and come out from the kitchen just in time to see the high and mighty Mrs Roscoe get her comeuppance. And the old lady derived a lot of pleasure from the sight. Her only regret was that she hadn't been the one to do it. She would have relished the opportunity of repaying the woman for the years of misery she'd caused Mr John. But oh, what joy it was to behold the stuck-up snob with dirty water running down her face and clothes. That should take her down a peg or two . . .

John too had heard loud voices and came down to investigate. He didn't hear it all, but enough to tell him who was at fault. 'What's the meaning of this?'

'This . . . this *person* had the effrontery to object to being asked to move herself out of my way. And when I dismissed her, this –' She waved a hand over her coat, '– is what she did to me.'

'I'll get my things, Mr John.' Ada looked down at her sodden clothes. 'I won't say I'm sorry 'cos I'm not. No one treats me like a piece of dirt, especially someone who hasn't the manners of an alley cat.'

'Did you hear that?' Maureen spluttered. 'Are you going to stand there and allow me to be insulted by a mere cleaning woman?'

'Agnes,' John looked over Ada's shoulder to where Aggie was standing with her arms folded and a look of sheer pleasure on her face. 'Will you take Ada through to the kitchen and find a way to dry her clothes? And you,' he cupped his wife's elbow and steered her forcefully towards the front office, 'come with me.'

'Come on, girl, let's get yer cleaned up an' dried off.' Aggie, her arm tucked under Ada's, chuckled all the way to the kitchen. 'D'yer know, I feel better than when I've 'ad six bottles of stout. Boy oh boy, did you put her in her place, or did you put her in her place! By, it was funnier than watchin' Laurel and Hardy.'

Ada was shivering with cold and nerves. 'I'm glad someone thought it was funny,' she said, her teeth chattering as she held the sodden skirt away from her legs. 'That little bit of fun, as you call it, only lost me me job. But I'd do the same thing again! I wasn't goin' to let her get away with calling me a slut an' a wretch. Who the hell does she think she is?'

'Miss High and Mighty, that's who she thinks she is.' Aggie opened the oven door of the small stove and struck a match. Turning the knob on to high, she said, 'Take yer skirt off an' we'll hang it over a chair in front of the oven. It'll dry in no time.'

'It's not only me skirt – me underskirt and me knickers are soppin' wet too.' Ada was shaking from the cold and the after-effects. She never thought the day would come when she'd do anything like that. To the wife of her boss, what's more! Then a picture of the contorted face flashed through her mind and she said, 'She asked for it.'

'She's been askin' for it for years,' Aggie said, undoing the ties on her overall. 'Many's the time I've felt like throwin' me bucket of water over her.' She passed the overall to Ada. 'Take all yer things off, girl, and wrap this around yerself before yer catch yer death of cold.'

'I can't do that!' Ada looked horrified. 'What if Mr John comes in?'

'So what! The top of yer is dry, so it's only from the waist down an' this overall will hide yer modesty.' While she watched Ada trying to take her knickers off without revealing anything, Aggie began to chuckle. 'Ay, girl, I'm not half glad yer'd done most of the hall an' the water was dirty. It wouldn't have had the same effect if the water 'ad been clear.'

'The water wasn't clear before I started, Aggie, 'cos I'd put a fair amount of Parr's Aunt Sally in it.'

The old woman rubbed her hands in glee. 'It gets better, girl! She'll stink the place down, an' she'll never get the stains off that expensive coat. Let's all say "aa-ah" for poor Maureen Roscoe.'

'What about poor Ada Perkins? I'm the one who's lost me job.'

'Act yer age, girl, yer won't get the sack.' Aggie nodded knowingly. 'You don't know Mr John like I do. Your job's as safe as houses.'

Standing in the front office, John passed his handkerchief to his wife. 'Wipe your face,' he said curtly. 'It's streaked with dirt.'

With a look of disdain, Maureen took the hankie. 'Where is there a mirror?'

'There isn't one in here. There is a mirror of sorts in the toilet, but you are not going out there because Mrs Perkins is probably using it to try and repair the damage you caused.'

'The damage *I* caused? How dare you suggest it was my fault! And just look what she's done to my coat. She's lucky I don't send for the police and have her arrested.' When there was no response from her husband, Maureen went on: 'Anyway, she's sacked now and she stays sacked. That should teach her to disobey her betters.'

John's face was impassive. 'Maureen, have you any idea how ridiculous you look? Wet the hankie on your tongue and wipe the dirt from your face. I can't hold a serious conversation with you whilst trying to control my laughter.'

As he watched her rubbing her cheeks, he asked himself how he had ever thought he was in love with her. She possessed none of the qualities he'd seen in other wives, like warmth and femininity. But he'd been naive when he'd met her, inexperienced in the ways of women, and he'd been easily fooled by her false show of affection. And for that he'd paid dearly.

When she'd cleaned up her face as best she could without the aid of a mirror, Maureen said, 'I'll take this handkerchief home and have it laundered.'

'Don't bother, I'll put it in my wash.' As John reached over and took the hankie from her hand he noted that while her face was reasonably clear of dirt, the spite and anger were still there. 'Can I ask what you came here for? I presume it wasn't just to cause mayhem?'

'I'd been to Cripps and saw a dress I liked, but they wouldn't give me credit. I was absolutely mortified in front of Jennifer, so I came to ask you to restore my charge account. It really is ludicrous that I have to beg for money.'

John raised his hand and studied his nails. 'Beg, Maureen? On the allowance I give you there should be no need to beg, or feel mortified in front of your friend. You get sufficient to enable you to live in comfort. If you can't save out of that to buy yourself a dress, then you'll have to learn to be a better housekeeper. Many women would give their eye teeth for the income you receive.'

'Are you telling me you won't give me the money to buy the dress I want?'

John nodded. 'There are a few other things I've got to tell you which you won't like. First, I have no intention of dismissing Mrs Perkins. You were extremely rude to her without justification and she had every right to retaliate. In fact, you got off lightly. Secondly, you will never again come to this house. It is my place of work and also my haven of peace and quiet, away from your whining voice, nagging tongue and your greed.'

Maureen gaped, too stunned to speak. In her mind she saw the scrubber woman as the one to blame. If that little incident hadn't happened, John would have been more amenable and she'd have been on her way back to Cripps to pick up the dress she'd asked the assistant to put to one side for her. Oh, the shame of it! She'd never be able to show her face in the shop again. And it was the most exclusive shop in Liverpool, all the best people went there. It was the thought of never being able to rub shoulders with the élite that caused her to climb down. 'John, darling, don't be so difficult. I'm sorry about that little incident in the hall, but after all she is only a scrubber woman.'

John's eyes were as cold as steel. He was livid, not just on Ada's behalf, but for all the years Agnes had been the victim of this woman's evil tongue. And the old woman had taken it, because she loved him and didn't want him upset. 'I won't even bother to answer that, you're beneath contempt. But I will continue from the point I'd reached when you interrupted me. I've been thinking for quite a while how ridiculous it is to keep the house on Queens Drive going just for you. It has five bedrooms, two bathrooms, a lounge, dining room, kitchen, study and large gardens. It costs a small fortune to run, and what on earth do you need all that space for? Since I spend most of my time down here now, I was thinking of looking for a smaller place for you.'

Two bright red spots appeared on Maureen's cheeks. 'It's not my fault you spend all your time down here! That is your decision, so why should I be turfed out of my home? There's nothing to stop you living there too.'

'There's nothing to stop me, but there's nothing to attract me, either. It's a long time since we held any sort of a conversation because we have absolutely nothing to say to each other, nothing in common. Our marriage has been a sham for ten years and I for one am not prepared to carry on pretending. I sleep alone at home, I sleep alone here. The difference is, I feel more at home here.' John looked at his watch. 'I think you should leave now, Maureen. I won't do anything about the house without discussing it with you first, you have my promise on that. But I insist you never come near this place again.'

It was a very subdued wife John escorted down the hall. He watched until she turned out of the gate, then closed the door and hurried to the kitchen.

'Oh, Mr John!' Ada went bright red as she tried to cover her knees. 'Yer can't come in, I'm not decent.'

'A bit late, I'm afraid, Ada, because I'm in. And you look perfectly respectable to me. How are you?'

'She's a bleedin' hero, that's what she is!' Aggie said. 'An' she's sittin' here worried to death in case she's lost her job.'

'Nonsense! It's an apology I'm offering you, not dismissal. I am so very sorry, Ada. I wouldn't have put you in that position for the world.'

Relief flooded through Ada's body. With Christmas so near she desperately needed her wages. 'I'm partly to blame, Mr John, for takin' it to heart. I should have just got out of the way when she told me to. But it was the way she spoke that got me, as though I was a piece of dirt. If she'd asked in a polite way none of it would have happened.'

'Listen, girl,' Aggie said. 'You did what any self-respectin' person would do. I'd have done it meself dozens of times – she certainly gave me reason to – but I didn't because of Mr

John. An' if he wasn't such a bleedin' gentleman he'd have smacked her backside long before now.'

'All right, Agnes, we'll let the matter drop now.' In his heart John knew the old woman was right, but no matter what his feelings were, it wouldn't be right to discuss Maureen behind her back. 'It will never be repeated because my wife will not be visiting the premises again.'

'Before we let the matter drop for good, Mr John, I'd just like yer to know I'm ashamed of my part in it. I've never done nothin' like that in me life before, never lifted me hand to anyone. An' I'd like to thank yer for stickin' up for me an' hope I didn't cause no trouble between you an' yer wife.'

'You can rest assured that you did not cause trouble between me and my wife.' John could say that truthfully. The trouble had been there long before Ada came on the scene.

'I don't know what to buy yer dad for Christmas,' Ada told Polly as she ran the iron over Joey's trousers. 'It's hard because with him bein' in hospital there's not much we can buy him. I mean, if he was home we could get him socks or a tie, but he'd have no call for them where he is.'

'What about some chocolates?' Polly suggested.

'Yer know yer dad was never one for sweet things.' Ada put the trousers over the fireguard to air off ready for her son to wear to school the next day. 'I know of somethin' that would really please him, but I don't think I'll have enough money to buy it.'

'What's that, Mam?'

'A photograph of me, you and Joey. Some of the other men in the ward have photographs of their families on top of their locker, an' I've often wished yer dad had one. He'd be able to look at us all day long an' wouldn't feel so lonely.'

'How much would it cost to 'ave our photo taken?' Polly had a few shillings hidden away upstairs to buy a surprise present for her mam and Joey, but she'd willingly part with it if it went towards making her dad happy. 'Would it be more than two bob?'

'I couldn't tell yer, sunshine. I've never been to a shop to have me photo taken in me life. There's a place in London Road, I think it's called Jerome's, where they do photographs. Perhaps I'll have time to slip down before I go to work tomorrow night and find out how much they charge.' The thought of seeing the look of pleasure on Tommy's face brought a smile to Ada's. 'Oh, wouldn't it be lovely if we could do that! It would make yer dad so happy.'

'I've got two bob yer can have towards it,' Polly told her. 'It means you an' Joey wouldn't get much, but me dad's more important, isn't he? Stuck in hospital over Christmas, he'll be dead sad.'

'I know, love, I've been thinkin' about that. I won't be able to go in an' see him 'cos there's no trams run on Christmas Day.' Ada looked up from the pillowslip she was ironing, 'I've just remembered I won't be able to go to London Road tomorrow, I've been asked to go in to work an hour early. Mr John's got a couple of women comin' to be interviewed for Aggie's job, an' he wants me to see them 'cos I've got to work with them.' She chuckled. 'He said he's not goin' to interview them on his own in case he takes one on that doesn't know one end of a broom from the other.'

'Ah Mam, can't yer get out earlier and go to London Road?' Polly looked disappointed. 'We haven't got much time, yer know, 'cos yer have to wait for photographs, they don't give yer them there an' then. An' I think it's a great idea to give me dad one for Christmas. It would be a lovely present for him – an' it's a personal thing, isn't it? He'd know we were thinkin' of him.'

Ada nodded in agreement. 'If you promise to run all the way home from school so our Joey's not left on his own, I could leave here at three o'clock an' be in plenty of time.'

Polly's face lit up. 'I'll run like the wind an' be home before our Joey. Ooh, I'm that excited. It was a real brain-wave yer had, Mam. It'll be the best present me dad's ever had.'

A chair had been placed next to Mr John's behind the desk. Four women had applied for the job of cleaner and one of the junior clerks in the ground-floor office had been put in charge of bringing them up one at a time.

'Sit down, Ada.' John remained standing until she was seated. 'Now, I think we should have a way of communicating with each other. If you're not impressed scratch the side of your nose and I'll diplomatically tell the unfortunate individual that we'll let them know if they're successful. How does that sound to you?'

'All I'm worried about is that they'll think I'm someone in authority when I'm only a cleaner, just the same as them.'

'You're in authority today, Ada, on my say so. I've never had to interview a cleaner before because Agnes has been here for as long as I can remember, so I need some moral support. Between the two of us we should be able to choose someone suitable.'

The first woman ushered through the door was a Mrs Flanaghan. She was a big woman in every way. When she walked towards the desk her whole body bounced. She had a hard look about her, and when she was answering the questions put to her by John, it was obvious she was, by nature, a hard woman. Ada got the feeling she could be a trouble-maker and she didn't fancy working with her, so she scratched the side of her nose and the woman was sent on her way after being told they'd let her know.

The second applicant was as thin as the first had been fat. But she looked a miserable person, never a flicker of a smile. She had a pale face, hooked nose and teeth that were green through lack of cleaning. Oh dear, Ada thought as she scratched her nose again, let's hope one of the other two are suitable. The third was a wiry little woman who seemed to skip across the floor, a beaming smile on her face. Ada's spirits lifted as the woman answered the questions cheerfully. Her name was Frances Delaney but her friends called her Fanny. Yes, she'd been a cleaner for twenty years and had always satisfied her employers. When asked her age and she said forty-four, John had to bow his head to hide a smile. She'd taken at least ten years off her age, just like Agnes had always done. Then he asked a question he hadn't asked the others and which surprised Ada. 'Mrs Delaney, do you use bad language?'

'Oh no, sir!' Fanny looked suitably shocked. 'I've never used bad language in me life. If I never move from this chair, not one swearword has ever passed me bleedin' lips.'

Ada's tummy started to shake with laughter and she knew they'd found what they were looking for. There'd never be another Aggie, but she had the feeling that this little woman would be a good substitute.

John turned his head, his eyes bright with laughter. 'How is your nose, Mrs Perkins?'

'Fine, Mr John, the itch has gone completely.'

'I thought it might have.' He faced the anxious-looking Fanny. 'Could you start right away, Mrs Delaney? It would give you time to get used to the routine before our other cleaner leaves.'

The little woman looked so excited Ada half-expected her to leap over the desk and plant a kiss on John's face. 'Does that mean I've got the job, sir?'

'Yes. If you turn up tomorrow at half-past five, Mrs Perkins here will give you details of what she wants you to do.'

'Oh, thank you, that's the gear, that is! Just in time for Christmas, too! Yer won't regret it, mister, 'cos I'll work me bleedin'—' Fanny's hand covered her mouth, her eyes wide with fright as she imagined herself losing the job because of one word. 'I'm sorry, sir, but I'm that excited it just slipped out. It won't never happen again, I promise yer.'

'That's all right, Mrs Delaney.' John wasn't going to tell her she'd got the job because she'd used Agnes's favourite swearword, and because she'd knocked ten years off her age. 'Mrs Perkins will take you downstairs and give you details of working hours and wages.' He stood up and held out his hand. 'It was nice meeting you and I'm sure we'll all get on together.'

Fanny's mouth was gaping as she shook his hand. Blimey, he was a right toff, this feller. She couldn't remember anyone offering to shake her hand before. She was going to enjoy working for him 'cos he was a real gentleman.

'Yer late tonight, Mam, I've been on pins.' Polly took her mother's coat and hung it up. 'Did yer manage to get to London Road?'

'Yes, an' I've made an appointment for the three of us to be there tomorrow at half-past four. It'll be a rush, I know, but it's the only time they can fit us in.' It had been a good day all round and Ada was in a very happy frame of mind. 'The photographs will be ready for me to pick up on Monday afternoon, so I'll have them to take in to yer dad before Christmas. And,' she smiled, 'it's only one and ninepence for three photographs.'

'Three? Ooh, can I have one, Mam?'

'Of course yer can, seeing as how you're paying towards them. One for yer dad, one for you and the other I'd like to buy a frame for an' put it on the mantelpiece. I was lookin' at the ones they had on show in the window an' they're a decent size, not like the ones yer get with an ordinary camera.'

'Ooh, I wish it was next Monday. I can't wait to see them.'

'Don't be wishin' yer life away, sunshine, it'll go over quick enough. But I've got to admit I can't wait to see them meself.' Ada glanced towards the kitchen. 'Have yer got the kettle on, Polly?'

'Yeah, it's nearly on the boil.' Polly tilted her head and gazed at her mother. 'Yer look happy tonight, Mam. Have yer had a good day?'

'From five o'clock on it's been nothing but one big laugh. I'll tell yer about it while we're having a cup of tea.'

The tea appeared in no time. 'That was quick! Are yer sure the water was boiled?'

'Yes, *an*' I stirred it with a spoon.' Polly pulled the chair around to face her mother. 'What was the one big laugh?'

Ada pulled a face when describing the interviews with the first two. 'I couldn't have worked with either of them. I'd have been terrified of the first one, she looked as though she could floor yer with one finger. And I'd have been sick every time I looked at the second one – her teeth were as green as grass.'

'Yuk!' Polly shivered at the thought. 'There's no need for that!'

'That's what I thought. If she couldn't afford toothpaste she could do what we sometimes have to do – use salt! Anyway, the third one was just what the doctor ordered.' Ada repeated the interview word for word, and when she came to, 'not one swearword has ever left me bleedin' lips', Polly went into hysterics.

'Oh Mam, that's not half funny. She sounds like Sarah Jane.'

'Yer should have heard her when Aggie arrived an' we were standing in the kitchen. The two of them got on like a house on fire an' they had me in a pleat.' Ada looked smug. 'What with gettin' the photographs sorted out and then finding a cleaner that I know I'm goin' to like, I'd say, all in all, it's been a good day.'

'What's her name, Mam?'

Ada chuckled at the memory. ' "Mrs Frances Delaney, but yer can call me Fanny".'

Chapter Fifteen

'Ay, that's a good photo, girl, if ever I saw one. Good of all three of yer.' Aggie held the sepia-coloured photograph at arm's-length to study it from all angles. 'Your Polly's the spittin' image of you.' She turned her head to where Fanny was standing by the sink waiting for the bucket to fill with water. 'Come an' have a gander at this, Fanny. They look like ruddy film stars.'

Fanny rubbed her hands down the side of her overall as she peered over Aggie's arm. 'Ooh, the state of them an' the price of fish! It looks real good, an' I bet it would look even better if I could see the bleedin' thing! Hold it a bit nearer, Aggie, the people at the Pier Head can see it better than me. Mind you, me eyesight's not as good as it used to be.'

It was a very good photograph and Ada was thrilled with it. She was surprised it had turned out so well because they'd never been in a studio before and had been so apprehensive they'd been terrified to move. Their bodies and faces were so still they must have looked like dummies. But with infinite patience born from experience, the man had got it right in the end. He'd sat Ada between the two children, said something to amuse them, clicked the camera and caught all three with smiles on their faces.

'I can't wait to see Tommy's face when he sets eyes on that. He'll be delighted. I'm goin' to try and get a cheap frame for it so he can stand it on his locker. They were definitely worth the money – one and ninepence for three isn't bad at all. And I've ordered an extra copy for our Polly. She wants to give it to a friend as a Christmas present. The man in the shop promised to have it ready the day after tomorrow.'

'If I'd known that, girl, I'd have asked yer to order one for me,' Aggie said. 'I'd like to put one on me sideboard.'

Ada felt a pang of sadness for the old woman who had no family of her own. 'Oh Aggie, if I'd been thinkin' straight I'd have got one for yer. See if Mr John will ring Jerome's and ask them to make it two copies. There's a number on the back of these so they'd know which ones he meant. If he rings now he might catch them before they close.'

Aggie's face brightened. 'Yeah, I'll do that. Mr John won't mind.'

Fanny was still studying the photograph. 'Is the little feller like his dad? Yer can tell the girl's yours, but he's not a bit like you.'

'Ay, Fanny Delaney, what are yer trying to suggest? That I had a fling with the ruddy milkman?' Ada gave her a playful push. 'He takes after his dad – fair, with blue eyes. He's got his dad's disposition, too – very quiet and easygoing.'

'We'll be easygoin' out of the door if we don't get started on some work,' Aggie said. 'With three of us, Mr John will expect the place to be shining.' She held up the photograph. 'Can I take this to him? I won't let it get dirty.'

'Yer'd better not or I'll flop yer one! And don't bend it, either, or yer'll crack it.' Ada put the bag containing the two photographs in her shopping bag and placed it at the side of the sink. 'I'll get started upstairs.'

John held the photograph between his two hands. 'They're a fine-looking family, aren't they, Agnes?'

'And nice with it, Mr John. From what Ada's told me about her Tommy, he's a good husband and father. If the kids grow up to be like him they won't go far wrong.' Aggie took the photograph from between his hands and turned it over. 'That's the number so they'll know which one yer talkin' about. Just make the order two instead of one.'

'I'll do that, Agnes, and you can tell Ada I'll collect them when they're ready, save her the trouble.' He looked at the woman who'd been part of his life for as long as he could remember. 'Your last week, Agnes.'

'Don't remind me.' The sigh was long and deep. 'I feel sad about goin'. I won't half miss it. But I can't go on for ever, no one can. When yer time's up there's nowt yer can do about it. The only consolation is that it happens to everyone eventually.'

'You've still got a good few years to go, Agnes, so just sit back and enjoy them. I'll visit you often to make sure you've got everything you need and to bring you up-to-date with all the news. In fact, you'll probably get sick of the sight of me.'

'I'd never get sick of the sight of you, Mr John, an' you know it. Yer just like me own flesh an' blood.' A broad grin suddenly appeared on her face and she said, 'Yer'll have fun an' games with that Fanny – she's a caution if ever there was one. Yer should hear some of the tales she comes out with! Half the time I don't know whether to believe her or not. She can have yer splittin' yer sides laughin' one minute, then yer hair standin' on end the next. She loves goin' to the pictures to see horror films an' she gives yer all the gory details. According to her, there's blood and guts everywhere, even in the front stalls! Wouldn't be my idea of a nice night out, but there yer go, it wouldn't do for everyone to be the same. And for all that she's a good soul an' a ruddy good worker. Ada won't have no problems with her.'

'Yes, I think we got lucky with her.' John took the earpiece off the hook at the side of the telephone. 'I'd better ring this shop before it gets too late. It's almost six o'clock now and most shops close at six.'

'Ada said they're mad busy with people wantin' their photo took before Christmas,' Aggie said over her shoulder as she crossed the room. 'So they might be workin' late to get all the orders done in time.'

She was halfway down the hall when she remembered that she wanted him to ask how much her copy would be, so she could pay Ada, and she did an about-turn. Mr John was talking as she neared the door and she heard him saying he wanted to change the order to three copies. Oh lord, she thought as she went to quicken her step, he's got it wrong. Then like a flash of lightning she knew who the extra copy was for. And shaking her head with sadness she turned and walked away.

Ada was happy when she walked into the hospital two days before Christmas and saw the corridors and wards had been decorated with bunting and Christmas greetings. It didn't half make a difference – the place looked more cheerful. And what she had in her bag for Tommy would cheer him up even more. He'd been in hospital nearly a year now and had only seen the children once, and that through the window. But now he'd be able to look at them all day and every day.

Tommy was watching the ward door when Ada walked in and his face lit up. 'Yer a sight for sore eyes, love.'

'And you, sweetheart.' She bent to kiss his forehead. 'I think the nurses have done a good job with the decorations. The place looks a lot brighter.'

'Ay, credit where it's due! Some of the patients helped as well!' Tommy pointed to a paper chain hanging near the window. 'That was made by me own fair hands an' I'm dead proud of it.'

'You look much better today,' Ada said, pulling a chair to the side of his bed. 'Yer've got more colour in yer cheeks.'

'I'm just about the same, love, no better no worse. But I can't complain – at least I'm alive.'

'Don't start gettin' downhearted, Tommy, 'cos yer were told at the beginning it was going to be a long job. Yer've just got to be patient, we all have.' Ada sat down and opened the clip on her bag. 'I've got somethin' that'll cheer yer up.' She brought out a package wrapped in red and white Christmassy paper and handed it to him. 'It's yer present from me an' the children. An' I'm to tell yer it comes with all our love and kisses.'

206

Tommy took the parcel from her and turned it over before running his hand around the edges. 'It feels hard.' He looked puzzled. 'What is it?'

'Now there's not much point in Polly wrappin' it up all nice so yer'll get a surprise when yer open it, if I'm goin' to tell yer what it is. She spent ages on it – with the help of Joey, of course. He wouldn't be left out.'

Tommy's eyes and face became eager. And Ada could see him as the young man she'd fallen head over heels in love with the first time they'd met. 'Can I open it now?' he asked, 'or do I have to wait until Father Christmas comes down the chimney?'

'You're opening it right now, love, 'cos I've been waiting for this moment. And I've got strict instructions from the kids that I've got to remember every word yer say when yer see it. And what yer face looks like.'

Tommy tried to be patient and not tear the wrapping paper, but he was so excited he was all fingers and thumbs. In the end he ripped the paper off in one go and found himself staring down at the faces of the three people he loved more than anything in the world. He didn't move, didn't even blink, as he drank in the sight of the two children he hadn't been able to touch, whose voices he hadn't heard, in almost a year.

Ada waited with her heart in her mouth. She'd imagined what his reaction would be . . . joy, happiness and laughter. But never this long silence. She couldn't bear the suspense any longer. 'Don't yer like the present, Tommy?'

When he turned his head, tears were brimming from his eyes and running down his cheeks. He tried to speak but was too choked with emotion.

'Oh, Tommy, love, don't get upset.' Ada reached for his hand. 'Look, don't cry, love, or yer'll start me off.'

Tommy pulled the end of the sheet up to his face and wiped his eyes. 'I'm sorry, love, but I can't help it. They've grown so much since I've been stuck in here, and it grieves me to know I've missed a year of seeing them grow. A year without their hugs and kisses, givin' young Joey a piggyback or pulling Polly's curls.' He stared down at the photograph. 'By the time I get out of here they'll have forgotten me. I'll be a stranger to them.'

'Of course they won't have forgotten yer, yer daft nit! They talk about yer all the time! Never a day goes by that they don't ask when yer comin' home.' Ada shook her head. 'I shouldn't have brought the photograph, it's only upset yer.'

'Oh no, love! It's the best present yer could have given me. I'm sorry for being so miserable, but seeing their faces after so long . . . well, it really got to me. But don't tell them I cried, will yer? Say I'm over the moon 'cos I can see them every day now. And tell them I'll kiss them good night every single night.'

'Ay, an' what about the one in the middle?' Ada knew she'd break her heart when she got outside, but right now she had to cheer him up. So she told him about the hamper Mr John was giving all the staff. 'Aggie said there's always a bottle of port or sherry in the hampers, so I'll be askin' Dolly an' Les in for a drink. I'll have to invite Steve and Clare, too, 'cos our Polly would have a right cob on if I left Steve out. Even though he's startin' work soon, he's still her best mate.'

This brought a smile to Tommy's face. 'I've always had the feeling that those two would end up gettin' married, yer know. They've been inseparable since they were toddlers.'

'She could do worse than marry Steve, he's a good lad. But she's only thirteen, there's a lot of water to flow under the bridge before she thinks of gettin' wed.' Ada pressed his hand and smiled into his face. 'She's a good girl, that daughter of ours – a real grafter, if ever there was one. Hail rain or snow she's out on a Saturday an' Sunday with the flowers. I used to worry about her bein' out in bad weather but she never comes to no harm, she seems to thrive on it. And she looks so proud when she hands over her few bob every week. Honest to God, Tommy, it brings a lump to me throat.'

'That's why she's doin' it, love, to help yer out. I bet her few bob comes in handy.'

'I'll say it does!' Ada thought before she said any more. She didn't want to set him off worrying. She relied on the three shillings her daughter turned up every week; without it she'd be back getting tick from the corner shop. And once you started that, your money was spoken for before you got it. 'It means I'm not scrimping from day to day. I manage fine on what comes in and I'm glad to say I owe no one a farthing.'

'I think you've done wonders, Ada, an' I'm proud of yer. But I'll be glad when I'm able to work again and you can take life a bit easier.'

Ada was pleased he was taking an interest, and wanting to leave him in a cheerful frame of mind, she went on to tell him about the antics of Aggie and the new cleaner, Fanny. What harm did it do if she did exaggerate? If it made her Tommy happy, Ada would gladly have stood on her head. In no time Tommy's smile turned into a full-blown laugh. And he was still chuckling when it was time for her to leave and they wished each other a Merry Christmas, both saying he'd be at home for the next one.

When Ada looked round before going through the ward door, Tommy was putting the photograph on the locker at the side of his bed. Sympathy welled up inside her as she watched him turn it until he had it at an angle where he could see his family without moving his head.

'Ada, can you spare a moment, please?' John caught her eye as she was passing his office. When she entered the room he motioned for her to sit on the chair he had placed on the opposite side of his desk, then he strode across the floor and closed the office door. 'Don't worry, Ada, there's nothing sinister in my motives.'

'Mr John, I never thought there would be.'

John sank into his chair. 'So you're not afraid of me ravaging you?'

Ada laughed. 'Oh no, Mr John! Anyway, I haven't half got a loud scream – they'd hear me in New Brighton.'

He smiled. 'I told Aggie I'd be asking you in here, so she'll be listening out, no doubt.'

'But why did yer do that?' Ada looked puzzled. 'I won't be more than a few minutes, will I?'

'That's entirely up to you. You can leave any time you wish. But first things first.' His smile was both shy and sad. 'I'm delivering Aggie's hamper to her house tomorrow because it'll be far too heavy for her to carry. While I'm out in the car I'll drop yours off for the same reason.'

'What time will it be? I'll have to make sure someone's in to take it off you.'

'I thought I could leave it at your neighbour's . . . Mrs Mitchell, isn't it?'

Ada didn't like that idea. She knew Dolly was struggling for money and intended giving her some things from the hamper to help her out. But to have it delivered there looked as though she was bragging. 'I wouldn't want yer to do that, Mr John. Yer see, Dolly's . . .' Ada stopped when he held up his hand.

'I know what's in your mind, Ada, and I wouldn't be so insensitive. I have a hamper for Mrs Mitchell as well.'

Ada gasped. 'Oh, Mr John! It's goin' to cost you a fortune buying these hampers for everyone. Fanny said she's gettin' one too.'

John rubbed a finger over an ink-stain on the desk. 'Now we come to the serious part, the reason I asked you in.' When he raised his head his eyes met hers. 'Can I talk to you as a friend, Ada?'

'Of course yer can, Mr John.'

'Before I start, I want you to know I'm not looking for sympathy, but a little understanding. You see, in two days it'll be Christmas, when families get together to celebrate. I don't have a family, Ada, no one to exchange presents with. Since my parents died I've never had a real Christmas, with presents under the tree and everyone excited and happy. You have probably realised by now that my wife and I don't have an ideal marriage. Her idea of Christmas is to invite her own circle of friends around, all of whom are extremely well-off. They exchange expensive presents, each trying to outdo the others. It doesn't, and never has appealed to me, so this year I will not be spending the festive season at home. Nor will I be forking out for expensive gifts for people whose lifestyle I don't particularly like.'

'I hope none of this has got anythin' to do with what happened when yer wife called here, Mr John.' Ada looked horrified. 'I'd go mad if I was the cause of trouble between you and Mrs Roscoe.'

'Rest assured it has nothing to do with you. Let's just say I haven't been lucky in my choice of wife.' John sat back in his chair and lacing his fingers he put his hands behind his head. 'I'm not telling you this to burden you with my problems, Ada, but to ask for your understanding. I have more money than I need and I get a lot of pleasure out of seeing people happy. Especially those who are not so fortunate. So this Christmas, while I may not be celebrating, I will have the pleasure of knowing that I've helped make it a better time for a few people. Is that so wrong?'

Ada's head was spinning. If he wasn't going home for Christmas, would he be spending it here, all alone? Oh, the poor man! Mind you, having had a taste of his wife, she couldn't say she blamed him. Then she realised John was waiting for her answer. 'No, it's not wrong, Mr John.'

'In that case, will you allow a lonely man a little indulgence?'

'What does that mean?'

'I suppose another way of asking would be, will you spoil me by giving me my own way?'

'It all depends,' Ada said, feeling out of her depth but wanting to help a man she was heartily sorry for. 'What is it yer want?'

'I usually give a bonus to the men who have worked for me for many years, just as a show of appreciation. The amount depends on the length of time they've been here. And Agnes, she too will be getting a bonus.' John was nervously fingering his tie. 'But I wondered if, in your case, you would allow me to give you your bonus in a way that would give *me* a great deal of pleasure?'

'I don't want no money off yer, Mr John. Yer giving me enough as it is. And I'm not entitled to a bonus – I haven't been here that long.'

'As well as being a valuable member of staff, Ada, I look on you as a friend. And although I know any extra money you received would be very welcome, I'm going to ask you to let me spend it in a way that would make me feel very happy.'

'Oh, I don't know, Mr John. I really don't feel I can take any more off yer.'

'I wasn't thinking of buying anything for you, Ada, but for your children. Every Christmas the shops are full of toys and I've never had a child to buy for. You mentioned that your son had asked for a scooter, and Polly wanted a new dress. Will they be getting them?'

Ada shook her head. 'I can't afford them. I've explained it all to the kids and they were good about it. I'd give them the world if I could, and they know it. They also know that what I haven't got I can't give.'

'Then let me get the presents for them.'

'I couldn't do that! How would I explain to them that me boss had bought them presents? An' if they told the neighbours, they'd think there was somethin' fishy goin' on.'

'I wouldn't be buying the presents, Ada, it would be your bonus money buying them. All I'm asking is that you let me choose them. Just for once I'd like to join the crowds of happy people who enjoy the excitement of being jostled as they search for a present that will put a smile on the faces of their children when they see what Father Christmas has brought them.' His eyes were pleading. 'Ada, you've no idea what pleasure it would give me.'

Ada was torn. She was thinking of Tommy, lying in hospital. It should be him who had the pleasure and not Mr John. But if what her boss said was true, and she'd be getting a bonus anyway, then in a way it would be her paying for them. And the kids didn't get much out of life, it wouldn't be fair to deprive them. 'Ooh, yer haven't half set me a poser, Mr John, I can't think straight an' that's a fact. One part of me is sayin' I shouldn't be takin' anything off yer, and the other part is tellin' me to pocket me pride an' think of the children. An' then there's you to consider. I don't want to let you down.'

'I'm not going to persuade you, Ada, you must do what you think is best for yourself.' A lock of his dark auburn hair fell on to his forehead and he pushed it back. 'I'll abide by your decision.'

All alone at Christmas, Ada was thinking. That shouldn't happen to anyone, let alone a man as kind and generous as him. It was then she made up her mind. If she had the money she'd buy him a present, but as that was out of the question she couldn't deny him the one thing he'd asked for that wouldn't cost her anything. 'All right, Mr John, an' I thank you from the bottom of my heart.'

A sparkle came into his hazel eyes. 'I'll drop them off at Mrs Mitchell's when I deliver the hampers tomorrow. And so as not to blemish your good name, I'll mention that I'm only the messenger – that you'd ordered them and paid for them yourself. I'll leave you to explain to her about the bonus.'

Ada stood up and pushed the chair back. 'Will you ask her to keep them in her house until the kids have gone to bed? I don't want them to see the things until Christmas morning.' She wrung her hands nervously. 'I don't know what to say. "Thank you" doesn't seem enough for all you've done.'

John put his palms flat on the desk and pushed himself up. 'I have done very little, Ada – nothing that needed exertion or energy. But thanks to you, I'll have reason for going to the shops tomorrow and elbowing my way through the crowds. I'm really looking forward to that!'

Ada returned his smile. 'I'd better get back to work, but I'll see yer later.' She wanted to say more but didn't know how to say it. It was only when she neared the door she took her courage in both hands. 'Mr John,' she didn't know he was close on her heels, his intention being to open the door for her. So when she turned, their bodies collided and she would have lost her balance if he hadn't caught her in his arms. He held her close for several seconds, their eyes locked. Then with the look on his face of a young boy doing something he knew he shouldn't, he brushed his lips across her cheeks before dropping his arms and moving a step back.

Ada was surprised at how calm she felt. 'It was a good job yer were there to catch me.'

With a low sigh of relief, John took his cue from her. 'Ada, if I hadn't been there it wouldn't have happened. I was trying to overtake so I could open the door for you.'

'And I turned around to ask yer something. If I don't, I won't sleep tonight and it'll spoil Christmas for me.'

'What is it, Ada?'

'Yer not stayin' in that big barn of a house on yer own over the holidays, are yer? It'll be as miserable as sin!'

John laughed. 'I'm not that much of a martyr, my dear. No, I'm staying at the Adelphi until the day after Boxing Day. I've invited my wife to have lunch with me on Christmas Day, because even though I will never live with her again, she is still my wife and I felt I had to make the effort. She will not be staying long as she is having her usual party in the evening.' He tilted his head. 'Why, would you be concerned if you thought I was there on my own?'

'Of course I would! We haven't got much, as yer know, but you'd have been welcome to share it with us.'

'And there's nothing I would like better. What you have is a house full of warmth and laughter – it would beat the Adelphi any day. But it wouldn't be wise, my dear. I'm well-known in the area and whilst it wouldn't worry me one iota, we have to think of your reputation.'

Ada put her hands on her hips and stooped slightly to present a pose favoured by Aggie. 'Sod me bleedin' reputation, Mr John!'

This brought a loud guffaw. 'Very good! But you don't really mean it, do you?'

'Well, what you say is probably true, I'd be the talk of the street. But it wouldn't have stopped me asking yer. The only neighbours I care about are the Mitchells and Irish Mary, and I've invited them over for the afternoon so we'd be well chaperoned.'

John looked puzzled. 'Irish Mary? Who's she when she's out?'

'She's one of your tenants, Mr John, Mary Hanrahan.'

'Oh yes, I remember her. Is she a good friend of yours?'

Ada found herself enjoying the exchange. She missed having a man to talk to, and with Mr John it was so easy – he never got on his high horse or spoke down to you. She could still feel the touch of his lips on her cheek but wasn't the least bit embarrassed. He hadn't meant any harm, just a friendly peck. 'Irish Mary's a very good friend of mine.' Then Ada put her hands on her hips again and rounded her shoulders. 'But for Christ's sake, Mr John, don't you go buyin' her no bleedin' hamper!'

'That Mr Roscoe must be made of money!' Dolly Mitchell pointed to the two big boxes on the table. 'It took him all his time to carry them in; there's everythin' in there except bread.' She delved into one of the boxes which had been opened. 'Look, even a box of chocolates! I've never 'ad a box of chocolates bought for me since I was courtin'. Once Les got the ring on me finger all 'is gentlemanly habits disappeared.' She chuckled. 'Like me waistline did three months after the weddin'.'

Ada was peering into the opened box. 'There's things in there I haven't had for years. It'll see us well over Christmas and all the following week. He's saved us a good few pounds, Dolly, hasn't he?'

'You ain't kiddin', girl. There's at least five or six pounds' worth of stuff in there. I felt like gettin' down on me knees and grovelling to him. This will be the best Christmas we've had since Adam was a lad. He's a real swell, is your Mr John.' She gave her cheeky smile. 'D'yer know what he said? He was payin' me back for the use of me china when he was round collectin' the rents. Swore they were the best cups of tea he ever had.'

Ada tutted, 'I'll take that remark with a pinch of salt.' She glanced over to where Clare had her head buried in a comic. 'Did he bring the other things?'

Clare pricked up her ears. She was sulking because her mam wouldn't let her take the items out of the hamper. 'What other things?'

'Ay, buggerlugs, just go about yer business.' Dolly tapped the end of her nose as she glared at her daughter. 'This'll fall off one of these days.'

With a petulant toss of her head, Clare went back to her comic.

In a low voice, Dolly said, 'I'll get Les to carry them in about ten o'clock. Is that all right?'

'I'll make sure Polly's in bed. They don't know they're getting them an' it'll be a real surprise.' Ada felt guilty without quite knowing why. She was only telling the truth. 'I'd have been better off with the money, I suppose, but I wanted to give them something extra special to try an' make up for their dad not being here. It just won't be the same without him.'

'Never mind, girl, he'll be here for next year.' Dolly raised one shoulder and grimaced with pain. 'These ruddy stays are killin' me! Yer know, girl, what we women have to go through to look nice, it should be against the law.'

'I don't know what the hell yer wear them for if they hurt,' Ada said. 'Why don't yer take them off?'

Dolly's tummy began to shake. 'I don't know why I think it's funny 'cos the joke's on me. But when I haven't got me stays on, my feller says I look like a pregnant elephant.'

Ada opened her eyes and her mouth wide. 'D'yer know, I wondered what it was yer reminded me of!'

Dolly clamped her lips together and wagged a finger in Ada's face. 'Any more lip out of you, girl, an' I'll clock yer one.'

Ada backed towards the door. 'I'd better leave while I'm still in one piece. I'll see yer later.'

There were two men on Ada's mind on Christmas morning, filling her with different emotions. Sadness because Tommy wasn't there to see the excitement on the faces of his two children as they came through the door and saw the brightly wrapped presents under the small tree. He would have been as happy and excited as they were. And the other emotion was one of gratitude for Mr John. Without him the children would only have the small presents she'd brought from Woolworths. Joey let out a high-pitched cry when he saw the scooter standing against the table. 'Oh ay, Mam, look what Father Christmas has brought me! Oh, isn't it the gear!' He put a hand on each end of the handlebar and a foot on the footboard. His eyes were as wide as saucers and he was so happy he could hardly contain himself. 'Polly, look what I've got!'

'Aren't yer lucky?' When Joey was happy, Polly was happy. 'Yer'll have all the kids in the street jealous.'

'Mam, can I take it out?' Joey imagined himself speeding down the street on the red and blue scooter while every kid in the neighbourhood stood on the pavements green with envy. 'Go on, Mam?'

'Not until after yer've had yer breakfast and are well wrapped up, 'cos it's bitter cold out. Anyway, you've still got some more presents to open.' Ada looked to where Polly was sitting with a present on her knee. 'Aren't you going to open yours, sunshine?'

Polly could tell by the feel that it was a dress, and she thought her mam had probably bought it from the market. She hoped it was pretty because Steve was coming with his mam and dad later and she wanted to look nice. She pulled at the paper and a piece of it came away in her hand, revealing a small square of blue velvet. With a gasp, she tore the rest of the wrapping off. 'Oh, Mam!' With tears blurring her eyes, she held up the blue velvet dress which was set off by a white lace collar. 'Oh, it's beautiful!' Holding the dress to her, she ran to throw an arm around Ada's shoulders. 'Oh, thank you, Mam, thank you.' She rained kisses on her mother's face. 'You're the best mam in the world and I love yer. I just wish me dad was here to see me new dress.'

'And my scooter,' Joey said, as he turned the handlebars and made noises as though he was driving a motor bike. 'Me dad would let me go out if he was here.'

'Yer dad would be out in the street with yer, sunshine, just like a big soft kid.'

Polly laid the dress down and without a word she left the room. She was back within seconds with a slim, square gift-wrapped parcel. 'This is for you, Mam, from me and Joey.'

Joey propped the scooter by the table and came to stand beside Polly. If he was giving his mam a present he wanted to see what it was.

Ada gazed down at the silver and blue box. 'This is a pretty box. I wonder what's in it?'

'Open it, Mam!' Polly was hopping from one foot to the other. 'I hope yer like it.'

Ada removed the lid and cried with delight as she lifted

the pale blue voile scarf from the tissue paper. 'Oh, sunshine, it's really lovely! I couldn't have chosen better meself.'

'I thought I'd get that colour 'cos it'll go with both yer dresses. We'll be real swanks this afternoon.'

Joey frowned. 'That's not fair! I've got nothin' new to wear.'

Ada grinned. 'Yes, you have. Look at the parcels under the tree. There's a new shirt for you and an underskirt for Polly. And there's a box of games each.'

There were shrieks of delight as the children pushed each other out of the way to be first at the tree. And amid the laughter and joy, Ada's mind went back to the two men she had cause to be grateful to. Tommy, for his love and giving her these two lovely children, and John for being their friend when they needed one.

As John patted his lips with the table napkin, he surveyed his wife's heavily made-up face. Why she had to plaster it on so thick he would never know. It didn't do anything for her, except perhaps make her look slightly ridiculous. He tried to keep Ada out of his thoughts but he couldn't help comparing the two women. Free of powder, rouge, mascara and lipstick, Ada's skin was fine and clear. She was completely natural, in looks and manner. A far cry from the woman facing him now. He'd gone out of his way to be pleasant and courteous, but the meal, for him at least, was a mistake. Maureen would never change, didn't even try. Her only conversation, when she wasn't criticizing the make-up and clothes of the other diners, was fashion, bridge parties and dinner dances.

'I don't know why you'd rather stay here than come home.' Her mouth was petulant. 'I really can't keep making excuses for your absence.'

'Then don't try. Tell your friends the truth – that we have separated. I have no intention of ever coming home, Maureen, as I have told you on numerous occasions. I will continue to support you, but further than that I will not go.

And if we are to be realistic, you don't really want me home, do you? You want the respectability of having a husband, but you don't really want the man. Never have done.'

Maureen's eyes narrowed. 'I think you've got a bit on the side, some cheap slut tucked away somewhere.'

'And who could blame me if I did? Certainly not you! But if that's what you want to tell your friends, by all means do so because I really could not care less. Now, I'll ring for a taxi for you.'

Chapter Sixteen

Charles Denholme was well wrapped up against the bitterly cold wind when he stopped for his Saturday buttonhole. He looked extremely smart in his heavy navy-blue overcoat, navy bowler, thick scarf wound around his neck and fur-lined gloves.

'Hello, Polly,' he said cheerfully. 'How are you on this very cold day? Like a block of ice, I'd say, standing in this open spot.'

'I don't mind, Mr Denholme, yer get used to it.' This wasn't quite true as Polly's feet were freezing, even though she'd lined the soles of her shoes with cardboard. And even with woollen mittens on, her purple fingers were stiff and sore. 'I saved this nice red carnation, in case yer came.'

Charles peeled off one of his gloves. 'Did you have a nice Christmas, Polly?'

'Oh yes, it was really marvellous.' Her face glowed with the memory. 'Yer should see the dress me mam bought for me, it's really beautiful. Blue velvet it is, with a lovely white lace collar. I look proper posh in it. An' our Joey got a scooter. He was that excited he wanted to take it out in the street to have a go on it, an' it was seven o'clock in the morning.' Her face lost some of the glow. 'It would have been the best Christmas I've ever had if me dad had been home.'

Charles, both gloves now secured under his chin, reached into his pocket for the usual threepenny piece he kept specially for Polly. 'Your father wasn't at home, then?'

'No, me dad's been in hospital for a year. I thought I'd told yer about that, Mr Denholme.'

Charles shook his head. 'No, I had no idea.'

'Yeah, he's been really ill.' Polly pushed the carnation into the buttonhole of his coat and gave him a wide smile. 'But he's goin' to get better soon, that's what me mam says.'

'He must have been very sick to have been in hospital so long.'

'He's still very sick, but not as bad as when he went in. I wish he'd hurry up an' get better 'cos I don't half miss him.'

Charles lowered his gaze. 'Does your mother work, Polly?'

The girl nodded. 'Me mam's got two jobs. She had to, yer see, or we'd have had no money to live on. That's why I work on a Saturday and Sunday, to help her out.'

Charles sighed inwardly as he took in the light material of the coat which was no barrier against the biting wind, and the wafer-thin soles of her shoes. He thought of his own two children, Rebecca and Justin. They were roughly the same age as Polly, but there the resemblance ended. They'd be curled up in front of a huge fire right now, with a bowl of fruit and a dish of sweets to hand. They had everything their heart desired and he couldn't imagine any circumstances where they would stand in the freezing cold to earn a few coppers selling flowers. They would consider it beneath their dignity. But perhaps he shouldn't judge them too harshly, they'd been born into wealth and had never known any other life.

'I'll have to go, Mr Denholme, I've got a customer.' Polly grinned. 'I daren't let her go 'cos there's not many of them around today.'

Charles pulled his glove on and turned up the collar of his coat. 'Yes, and I'm due at the Club. My colleagues will think I'm not coming. I'll see you next week, Polly.'

She gave him a wave and moved over to the customer who was trying to decide whether to splash out and have carnations or settle for the more modestly priced marguerites. Polly was delighted when she finally settled on the carnations and rewarded the woman with a bonny smile.

Then she walked behind the buckets to pass the money over to Sarah Jane.

'We're not doin' so bad, girl, considerin' the weather.' Sarah Jane was muffled up to the eyeballs. A thick shawl covered her head and came down to cross over on her chest, another covered her shoulders and a blanket was wrapped over her knees. With her hands tucked inside the blanket, the only part of her body exposed to the elements was her face. 'I was expectin' trade to be lousy.'

'Like me Auntie Mary said, people don't get their wages until Saturday an' they've got to shop no matter what the weather's like. Either that or do without food.' Polly stamped her feet up and down to get the circulation going. Her chilblains were playing her up now, but they'd be a lot worse when she got home and into the warmth. 'You shouldn't be sittin' here all day, Grandma, yer'll catch yer death of cold.'

'I've been doin' it for sixty years, girl, an' as I haven't caught me death yet, I can't see me catchin' it now.' Sarah Jane grinned, showing her toothless gums. 'Me ma used to say I was too slow to catch cold, an' I had to reach this age to prove her right.'

'Surely yer won't be goin' to the pub tonight?' Polly said. 'Yer should stay in an' keep warm.'

'It's warmer in the pub than in me room. An' when I've got a couple of bottles of stout down me, I'll be glowing with warmth.' She gave a hearty chuckle. 'Both inside and out.'

Polly shook her head as she went to serve a customer. She worried about the old woman, but what could you do with someone who was as stubborn as a mule?

While Polly was wrapping a bunch of flowers, Irish Mary came up behind her and nudged her arm. 'Sure, do me eyes deceive me, or is it really the workin' man himself I see walking down the street?'

Polly took the woman's twopence, smiled her thanks, then turned her head to see Steve approaching with a beaming smile on his face. He was wearing a donkey jacket over his

223

overalls and his hands were dug deep in his pockets. 'I didn't expect yer, Steve.'

'I told yer I'd come straight from work an' give yer a hand to clear away.'

Polly was so thrilled to see him, a warm glow spread through her body. 'I thought the weather would put yer off.'

'I promised to come an' I always keep a promise. If I'd been knee-deep in snow, I'd still have come.'

Before Irish Mary moved away, she whispered, 'That's true love for yer, me darlin', so it is.'

Polly blushed to the roots of her hair and hoped Steve hadn't heard. If he had, he didn't seem put out by it. 'Go an' say hello to Sarah Jane, she's been askin' me how yer were getting on at work.'

'Hello, son.' The old woman looked pleased to see him. 'By, yer don't half look grown-up now. A proper handsome man, that's what yer are. If I were fifty years younger I'd be flutterin' me eyelashes at yer.' Her hand appeared from under the blanket to give him a pat on the arm. 'On second thoughts I'd better say sixty-five years younger. That would be nearer the mark.'

At the next stall, Florrie grinned. 'Ay, Sarah Jane, yer can be had up for cradle-snatchin', yer know.'

'Of course I know,' Sarah Jane called back. 'Didn't I visit yer in jail when you were had up for the very same thing?'

Florrie laughed good-naturedly. 'One of these days I'll get the last word in with you, Sarah Jane.'

'Yer'll have to be up early in the mornin' to do that, me girl!'

Steve gazed around, happy to be back with the flower-sellers and listening to their rowdy humour as they tried to entice the passers-by to buy their flowers. As his mam would say, they were the salt of the earth. They appeared as tough as old rope, would argue and fight with anyone. But when you got to know them you found the tough exterior hid a soft centre. He'd seen it many times while he'd been helping them during the school holidays. He remembered the day an old lady passed, weaving from one side of the pavement to the other, a hand pressed to her forehead. He'd thought she was drunk, but Nellie knew otherwise. He'd stood in amazement as Nellie and two of her friends rushed to help the woman. They sat her down on one of the stools and fussed over her until she came round. And when they found her confusion was due to losing her purse, they'd clubbed together and given her sixpence so she could buy a cup of tea in the Kardomah and pay her tram fare home.

'How did work go, Steve?' Polly came to stand next to him but kept her eye open for potential customers. 'Are yer getting on all right with Mr Wilkinson?'

Steve grinned down at her. 'He's not exactly a laugh a minute, but he knows his job well. And he's very patient with me, makes sure I see every move he makes. I suppose that's more important than crackin' jokes all day. An' I did manage to make an impression on him today. It wasn't a definite smile, mind yer, but it shows he must have some humour in him. I was tellin' him somethin' me mam had said, an' his cheeks moved upwards. It was the nearest I've got to gettin' a smile out of him.'

'Take yer mam to work with yer, that should do the trick,' Polly said. 'If she can't make him laugh then no one can.'

'She'd be more likely to get me the sack.' Steve hunched his shoulders and shivered. 'God bless us, Polly, it's freezin' on this corner. Yer get the full blast of the wind.'

She pulled a face. 'I'll not be sorry when the day's over. I've never been as cold as I am today.'

'There's not long to go now, then we'll run all the way home to warm ourselves up.' He made two attempts to speak before the words finally came out. 'D'yer want to come in ours tonight an' we can have a game of cards with me mam an' dad?'

Polly's face brightened. 'Yeah, okay! Me mam doesn't go out tonight so I won't have to mind our Joey. But I won't be able to stay very late 'cos I'm up early to go out with Auntie Mary.' She thought of something that could take the shine off her happiness. 'Yer don't play for money, do yer?'

'I'd have a job, seein' as how I'm skint an' happy. I have to work a week in hand, don't forget.' As Steve looked down into Polly's pretty face he wouldn't have swapped places with anyone. He was never happier than when he was in her company and couldn't wait for the next two years to pass so he could ask her to be his girl. He'd always known she was the one for him, ever since the day her mother had asked him to walk her to school and he'd held her hand all the way. 'We play for matchsticks.'

'Oh, that's all right then,' Polly laughed. 'I can pinch some of those off me mam. I can give her them back out of me winnings.'

'Aggie!' Ada's face was a picture when her old friend opened the door to her. 'What in the name of God are you doin' here?'

'Get in, girl, and let's keep the cold out.' Aggie closed the door and turned to grin into Ada's startled face. 'I got bored, didn't I? Lookin' at four bleedin' walls all day, it's enough to drive yer mad. So when Mr John called to see me, I asked him to run me up so I could have a natter.'

'But yer've only been retired a week!' Ada said as she took her coat off and hung it over her arm. 'I had visions of yer sittin' in yer rocking chair in front of a big fire with a bottle of stout on the table beside yer an' a glass in yer hand.'

'Come through,' Aggie took her elbow. 'Fanny's got the kettle on for a cuppa.'

Fanny turned from the stove when the couple entered the room and there was a huge grin on her face. 'She's checkin' up on us, Ada. Thinks we can't manage without her. Bleedin' cheek!'

'Ay, don't talk about cheeks to me!' Aggie was beginning to feel like her old self after a week of not knowing what to do with herself. 'When yer've sat on yer backside for a week, like I have, yer soon come to realise that the cheeks on yer face are not the only ones yer've got. I mean, yer can't sit on them, can yer? The one question I've been askin' meself all week, is, where would we be without our bleedin' backsides? Go on, answer me that!'

'Ooh, that's too hard for me,' Ada said, trying to keep a straight face. 'I was never very clever at geography at school.'

Fanny was pinching her top lip, her mind ticking over. 'Ay, is there such a word as backsideless?'

The three of them burst out laughing and it was as though the week without Aggie had never been. Fanny poured the tea out and handed the cups over as she eyed Aggie thoughtfully. 'Yer didn't by any chance fall out of that rockin' chair, did yer? 'Cos I heard someone in the pub last night saying, "she's off her rocker". They weren't talkin' about you, were they, Aggie?'

'Ho, ho, very bleedin' funny, Fanny Delaney! Yer'll cut yerself on that tongue of yours one of these days.'

'I did that yesterday, girl. I thought there was a bit more meat on the mutton chop and sank me teeth into it. Trouble was, it was me tongue hangin' out and I nearly bit the bleedin' thing off.'

Once more the three of them doubled up, and that was how Mr John found them. 'Can I join in the fun?'

'What did yer bring her down for, Mr John?' Fanny had soon learned that there was no reason to fear her boss. He wasn't a slave-driver like most men she'd worked for. 'We'll get no work done while she's here.'

John was smiling and Ada thought how young he looked sometimes. 'She pulled rank on me, Fanny – said she was older than me and I should respect and obey my elders.'

'She said all that without swearin'?' Fanny pulled a face. 'No, Mr John, our Aggie doesn't speak that posh.'

Ada made for the broom cupboard where the cleaning utensils were kept. They'd wasted enough time. After all, they were getting paid to work and it wasn't right to impose on Mr John's good nature. 'I'll start upstairs. Is there anythin' particular yer want doin', Mr John?'

'Only a list of what you want from Coopers. You haven't forgotten that tomorrow is my turn to be host to my card-playing friends, have you, Ada?'

'No, Mr John. I might be getting on a bit, but me memory's still in good working order. I'll give your bedroom a good going-over now, then I'll have a bit more time to prepare the food tomorrow night. Don't worry, everything's under control.'

'Ada, I'm not in the least worried. I have every faith in you.'

Aggie dug Fanny in the ribs. 'It's enough to make yer puke, isn't it? Talk about teacher's ruddy pet! He's never told *me* he's got every faith in me!'

'Perhaps there's a reason for that, Aggie.'

'What d'yer mean, Fanny?'

'Well, I mean like, perhaps he hasn't got *no* faith in you!'

Ada grinned at Mr John as she passed him on her way out of the kitchen. They never spoke, but it was silently agreed between them that it was good to have Aggie back, even if it was only on a visit.

Ada was waiting to receive the visitors the following night, and she greeted them with a smile. They treated her with the greatest respect, were always friendly and had insisted she call them by their first names. The first through the door was Simon Ellis, a solicitor. As she took his coat, Jack Grimshaw came bounding up the stairs, his craggy face smiling as always. They exchanged pleasantries, complained about the cold weather and then made a bee-line for the fireplace where a bright fire was roaring up the chimney.

'My wife thinks I'm crazy coming out on a night like this,' Jack said, rubbing his hands together briskly. 'She said it isn't fit for man nor beast. I asked her which category I came under and do you know it took her a while to answer!'

'Wives do have a habit of putting you down,' Simon laughed as he spread his hands out in front of the flames. 'My wife is excellent at cutting me down to size.'

Ada was smiling at them from the doorway when she heard Mr John's voice growing louder as he neared the top of the stairs. Ada was expecting him to be with George Moss, the regular fourth member of their card school, but the man being led towards her was a complete stranger.

'George has gone down with a bad cold, Ada, so Charles kindly offered to take his place for tonight.' John made the introductions. 'Charles Denholme, Mrs Perkins.'

Charles didn't see the hand Ada extended to him, he was too busy inspecting her features. He had to be right. The name was the same, the rich dark curly hair, and those deep brown eyes. He reached for Ada's hand and gripped it tight. 'You're Polly's mother!'

Ada was taken aback. How on earth would this man know Polly? 'You know my daughter?'

'Oh, Polly and I are very good friends.' Charles was delighted. 'I buy my buttonhole from her every Saturday.'

A smile spread across Ada's face. 'You're *that* Mr Denholme – Polly's favourite customer! Wait until she knows I've met you.'

John was telling himself it was ridiculous to be jealous of Charles; after all, he was married and so was Ada. But was it really necessary for him to hold on to her hand for quite so long? 'How did you know Ada was Polly's mother, Charles? You couldn't possible have just made a guess at it.'

'Have you ever seen Polly, John?' Charles asked. 'They are as alike as two peas in a pod.'

John didn't need that piece of information; he was aware of the likeness. His knowledge came from the photograph he had hidden in his desk drawer. But that was his secret and must remain so. 'Then Polly must be a very pretty girl.'

'She's more than that, old man.' Charles released Ada's

hand. 'She's a very special girl and I've grown quite fond of her. If I'd known Mrs Perkins was going to be here tonight, I'd have insisted she bring Polly in the blue velvet dress she got for Christmas.'

Ada was dumbstruck. 'She told you about that?'

Charles laughed. 'And about Joey's scooter. But you mustn't think she goes around repeating everything you say or do, because she doesn't. It was I who asked her what she got for Christmas. And with her in her blue dress, and you in that dress, you must make a very attractive couple.'

Ada could see John was getting fidgety and sought to bring the conversation to an end. 'Oh, Polly's dress is much nicer than this. I got this off the rag and bone man.'

Charles roared with laughter. 'You both have the same sense of humour, too!'

'I'll see to the drinks, Mr John,' Ada said. 'Your friends will think they're being neglected.'

'Quite right, Ada!' Jack called. 'I've usually had at least two whiskies by this time. Why the hell is Charles monopolizing you? We've known you longer than him – tell him to get to the back of the queue.'

Charles took it in good humour. They all belonged to the same Club and had known each other for years. He didn't seek out Ada's attention for the rest of the evening, but his eyes watched while his mind wondered. When it was time for Ada to leave, she bade them all good night and promised Charles she would tell Polly how they'd met. Then, accompanied by John, she made her way downstairs.

'Thank you, Ada, you have my gratitude as usual.' John held the door open for her. 'I don't know what I'd do without you.' He leaned forward and kissed her cheek. 'Good night, my dear.'

'Good night, Mr John.'

John was surprised the next day when one of the office girls came up to say there was a Mr Denholme to see him. What on earth did Charles want? Why wasn't he at his office? 'Show him up, please, Mary.'

He rose from his chair when Charles entered the room, bringing a draught of cold air with him. 'This is a surprise, Charles. Are you so rich you don't have to work like us poor devils?'

Charles laughed as he unwound the scarf from his neck. He was a very successful shipping merchant, and although he did go down to his office most days, it was only to fill in his time. He had very good managers and the business would go on without him. 'Have you any of that excellent whisky left, John? It's jolly cold out there and I could do with something to warm me up.'

'Come through to the lounge, it's more comfortable in there.' John motioned for Charles to precede him. 'And more importantly, the whisky is in there.'

When they were seated in front of the roaring fire, Charles crossed his legs and cupped his hands around the glass. 'I've come to ask about your housekeeper, Ada Perkins. I believe housekeeper is the right word?'

John looked surprised and none too pleased. 'If you are asking if she is my mistress, the answer is no. I'd be a very happy man if she was, I have to admit, but if she were here now she would tell you she is my cleaning lady. And being the person she is, I'm afraid that is all she will ever be. So if your interest lies in that direction, I must warn you that you would be wasting your time.'

Charles's look of shock turned to one of amusement. 'My dear fellow, I am perfectly happy with the wife I have! Victoria and I may have our differences from time to time, but she satisfies my needs, if you follow my meaning. I have no call to look elsewhere.' He swirled the whisky around in his glass as he brought to mind the face and voice of Maureen Roscoe. He'd only seen the woman a few times, that was on the rare occasions their gentlemen-only club was open to lady visitors. A most unpleasant woman, he recalled, both physically and socially. No one would blame John for taking a mistress – in fact, most people probably thought he did have one. 'She's a very attractive woman and I for one wouldn't blame you. Like Polly, she's a bit rough around the edges but a little polishing would have them both shining like diamonds.'

'I wouldn't want to change a thing about Ada,' John said. 'I like her just the way she is – lovely, warm-hearted, funny and down-to-earth. What you see with Ada Perkins is what you get. She doesn't pretend to be anything but a working-class housewife who has been forced to go out to work to keep her family together. No lies, no fancy trappings.' He thought for a while before adding, 'For instance, when she told you she got her dress off the rag and bone man, she wasn't joking as you thought. That is precisely where she did get it, and another one which looks just as attractive on her. And she wouldn't be ashamed to tell you that the rag man lives in the house next door. They are both tenants of mine and that is how I met Ada. Her husband had been taken into hospital and she wasn't able to pay her full rent. She didn't try and hide like other tenants would have done, she faced me and told me she didn't have enough to pay her rent, and asked if I would give her some time. She'd found a cleaning job for a few hours each morning, but the pay was only twelve and six a week. An amount you and I would pay for our cigars. I was impressed by her honesty and offered her a job here. And that is the whole story, except I have to say it was the best thing I ever did in my life.'

Charles looked dazed as he shook his head. 'You and I live in ivory towers, don't we, John? It's a case of – I'm all right, mate, to hell with everyone else.'

'Perhaps I see a little more of life than you, Charles, because I have property in the poorer parts of the city. I do what I can to help, but with the best will in the world you can't help everyone.' John refilled their glasses before settling down again in the comfortable brown leather upholstered armchair. 'So there you have the full story of Ada Perkins. I hope that satisfies your interest?'

'Oh, it's not Ada I'm interested in – it's her daughter, Polly.'

'*What!*' John went to rise from his chair, his face flushed. 'But the child is only thirteen years of age!'

Charles saw by John's face that his words had been misconstrued, and he hastened to put things right. 'I say, steady on, old man! I am not a bounder, I do not abuse young children! I can assure you that my interest in Polly Perkins is one of a desire to help her. She's very intelligent, pretty as a picture, has a good head on her shoulders and has an easy, graceful manner. With a little help she could make her mark in the world, become someone, instead of leaving school and going to work slaving in a factory for a pittance. And what a waste that would be.'

He leaned forward and rested his elbows on his knees, his glass between his hands. 'So now I'll tell you how I think I can help Polly, and see if you agree.'

Chapter Seventeen

Fanny was scurrying along the hall with a full bucket of water when the knocker sounded. 'Sod it! The same thing happens every time the bleedin' bucket's full. They couldn't knock when it was empty – oh no, they 'ave to wait until it's flaming well full.'

Ada tutted when Fanny opened the door. 'Yer slowin' down, Fanny. I've been standin' here all of twelve seconds.'

Tufts of grey hair had freed themselves from the confines of Fanny's mobcap and were sticking out in several places. She tucked them in as she waited for Ada to pass. 'Yer bleedin' lucky I answered the door at all. Why d'yer always turn up when I've got me hands full? D'yer do it accidentally on purpose?'

'Yeah,' Ada laughed. 'I lift the letter box to see what yer doin' and pick the time when it's most inconvenient.'

'Awkward bugger, that's what yer are, Ada Perkins. I've never worked with no one as awkward as you.' Fanny winked as she lifted the handle on the bucket. 'Ay, have yer been misbehavin' yerself? I wouldn't be surprised if yer in for the chop 'cos Mr John's waitin' for yer upstairs. He said as soon as yer put yer foot in the door, I 'ad to tell yer he wanted to see yer.'

'Then why didn't yer?'

'Why didn't I what, girl?'

'Tell me as soon as I put me foot over the door? It's you who'll get the sack, Fanny Delaney, not me! Keeping me here natterin' instead of passing the message on. I'll tell Mr John it was your fault. I'm not takin' the blame.'

'God, but yer can't half talk, girl! If yer not careful, Mr John will think yer late an' dock half an hour off yer wages.'

Fanny eyed the stairs with disgust. She was no more fond of them than Aggie had been, even though she was younger and far more sprightly. 'You go up first, girl, then I can take me time.' When Ada was halfway up, she called, 'Ay, remind me to tell yer about the picture I saw this afternoon. It was called *The Gold Diggers*, with Ruby Keeler and Dick Powell. Dead funny it was, had me laughin' sacks.'

Ada turned around when she reached the landing. 'You won't half miss me if I get the sack. Yer'll have no one to tell about the pictures yer see.'

'Don't worry, girl, Frances Delaney is here, I'll stick up for yer. If Mr John sacks yer, I'll have a word in his ear. He thinks very highly of me, does Mr John, he's always asking me for advice.' She put her foot on the next stair, muttering, 'He doesn't bleedin' take it, like, but I appreciate him askin' for it.'

Ada was smiling when she knocked and entered Mr John's office. 'You wanted to see me?'

John stood up and her happy face brought a smile to his. 'You look full of the joys of spring, Ada.'

'Anyone would be hard put to be miserable when Fanny's around. She's a real case.'

'What's she been saying now?'

'She said if yer sack me then she'll have a word with yer 'cos yer think very highly of her. Always asking her for advice, yer are.' Ada then gave a very good impersonation of Fanny's voice. 'He doesn't bleedin' take it, like, but I appreciate him askin' for it.'

'There are times when I could do with some advice, so I'll keep Fanny in mind.' It's strange, John was thinking, that the only time I can enjoy a good laugh is when I'm in the company of my cleaners. Then he told himself there was nothing strange about it. They were normal, down-to-earth people who had learned to laugh in the face of adversity. You didn't need money to laugh. 'Will you close the door, Ada, I have something to discuss with you.'

'I hope it won't take long, Mr John, 'cos I haven't even started work yet.' Ada closed the door then sat facing him. 'Yer not gettin' yer money's worth out of me.'

John chuckled. 'If you never did a tap, Ada, I'd get my money's worth just from looking at you. I won't embarrass you, suffice to say you are the best thing that's ever happened to me.' He moved a pile of papers to the side of his desk to give him space to rest his elbows. 'Now what I have to say has nothing to do with me, I've merely been asked to be the messenger.'

'A messenger for who, Mr John?'

'Charles Denholme. You remember, you met him last night?'

'Of course I remember! Me an' Polly were talking about him before I left the house. She was dead chuffed when I told her I'd met him.'

'Your daughter seems to have made quite an impression on Charles. He came to see me this morning because he'd like to help her.'

Ada looked puzzled. 'How d'yer mean, he'd like to help her?'

'Well, he reckons Polly's got the brains to get on in life. He said she's bright, pretty, and excellent with people.' John rapped a knuckle on the desk top. 'It's a funny world, isn't it, Ada? He's known your daughter longer than I've known you.'

With a flick of her wrist, Ada brushed this aside. 'Our Polly *is* bright – she always comes first or second in class. But what's that got to do with Mr Denholme?'

John stretched his arm across the desk and held out an open palm. He waited with baited breath until one of Ada's hands was lying in his, then he held it tight, not knowing who needed the comfort more, himself or Ada. 'Remember I play no part in this other than being the messenger. I promised Charles I would put his proposition to you, and there my involvement ends. But I think you should hear the full story before making a hasty decision. What Charles is suggesting is that Polly goes to work in his house as a junior housemaid.'

'What!' Ada didn't wait to hear any more. 'My Polly's only thirteen – she doesn't leave school until next Christmas! An' how does he think being a maid will help her get on in the world? A junior housemaid is only a skivvy!'

'Ada, in fairness to Charles I think you should listen to all he had to say before passing comment. From what I gathered, Polly would not be a skivvy. She would help his housekeeper for part of the day, then she would take lessons with Charles's two children. They are roughly Polly's age and they have a private tutor. Her education would be of the best, that is one thing I'm convinced of.'

'But she'd be out of place with Mr Denholme's children. She doesn't have posh clothes like they'll have, an' my Polly's too proud to be looked down on.' Ada squeezed her eyes tight, trying to take it all in. 'She'd have to make their beds an' wait on them, then sit next to them in her shabby clothes while they're havin' their lessons with this tutor feller! No, I wouldn't put my daughter in that position, Mr John, I love her too much for that.'

'If you'll let me finish telling you what Charles had to say, then you'll have a clearer picture in your mind. She would receive five shillings a week wages, her clothes would be bought for her, and she'd have her own room. Even though she would be expected to do some housework to earn her keep, Charles said she would be treated as well as his own children.' John ran a hand across his brow. 'He seems genuinely fond of Polly, and I formed an opinion that he hopes your daughter's warmth and personality would rub off on his own children. He has no illusions about them; he says they are spoiled rotten and could learn a lot from Polly. Actually, he said she could run circles round them.'

But Ada was shaking her head. 'No, I'm not losing Polly. It's bad enough being without Tommy, I couldn't bear to be without me daughter as well. Tell Mr Denholme I'm thankful to him, but I need me family around me. We might not have any money, but we've got somethin' that money can't buy, somethin' worth more than all the riches in the world. And that's love, Mr John.'

'Ada, I understand how you feel, but I think there is some merit in Charles's offer and I don't think you should dismiss it out of hand. Polly would receive a good education that would enable her to get a decent job, that is something worth thinking about. Also, she'd only be two minutes away from here in Percy Street, and she could see you whenever she wanted. If it turned out she was unhappy there, she could walk out of the door whenever she wished. There is nothing binding to keep her there.'

'I can't win, can I?' Ada looked lost. 'If I say she can't go I'll spend the rest of me life blaming meself for keeping her back. But I can't bear the thought of her not bein' there every day when I get home. She's the only one I can talk to. Our Joey's too young an' I only see Tommy for half an hour once a week. I don't know what to do for the best, Mr John, an' I want to do the best for both me kids.'

'You can always talk to me, Ada, I've told you that. But this is a family matter and I don't want to persuade you one way or the other. All I'll say is, you must do what you want to do.'

'Oh, Mr John, since when have people like me been able to do what we want to do? I'd like to put a joint of meat on me table every Sunday, that's what I want. I'd like to take the children into town and buy them new clothes instead of second-hand ones, that's what I want. I'd like me coal-hole full of coal, me rent up-to-date and money always on hand for the gas meter. Those are all things I want but can't have.' As she spoke, Ada had been looking down at her clasped hands lying in her lap; now she raised her head and looked him in the eyes. 'No, Mr John, there'll always be people like me, millions of them, who'll never be able to do what they want to do. Once yer on the bottom of the scrap heap, that's where yer stay.'

John shot out of his chair and rounding the desk he dropped to his knees beside her chair and put his arms around her. 'My dearest Ada, I could give you all the things you want in life, but I know you wouldn't accept them from me.' Gripping her shoulders he turned her to face him. 'There is one thing you can do for me, and that is to stop calling me Mr John. You've no idea how it grates every time I hear it. If I can call you Ada, why the hell can't you just call me John?'

'Because you're me boss, that's why. It wouldn't be right!'

'To hell with what's right and what's wrong! If it make you feel uncomfortable in front of Fanny, then by all means stick with Mr John. But in the privacy of these rooms, it's to be just plain John from now on. Will you do that to please me?'

Ada nodded. 'Yes, John.'

'Thank you.' He held her close for a brief second and then kissed her cheek before straightening himself up and returning to his chair. 'About this other matter, Ada, why don't you talk it over with your husband and see what his feelings are? If he's dead against it, forget the whole thing. If he's in favour, then the time will come to ask Polly what she would like to do. After all, it's her life we're talking about and the final decision must be hers.'

'Yes. I think that's the best thing. I'll have a good talk with Tommy on Sunday an' we'll take it from there.' Ada sighed as she pushed her chair back. 'I'd better get your rooms done, Mr John, or yer'll be sleeping in an unmade bed tonight.'

'Ada, who is this Mr John?'

That brought a smile to her face. 'I'll have to remember . . . John.'

'I don't know what to say, love, I really don't.' Tommy had listened in silence, weighing up every word. 'I can understand how you feel about her bein' looked down on, but our Polly wouldn't stand for that, she'd soon put them in their place.' His pale face broke into a smile. 'If she's the same girl I remember, if she couldn't put them in their place she wouldn't stay around to be insulted. She'd put her coat on an' walk out with her nose and head in the air.'

'I'm sorry she ever met this Charles Denholme,' Ada said, 'then none of this would have happened. Not that I've anythin' against the man, he's probably very nice and his intentions are genuine. I know our Polly likes him – she calls him her favourite customer. But I'd miss her, Tommy, I don't know what I'd do without her. She's intelligent enough to have a serious conversation with an' we get on so well together.'

'This Mr Denholme must think she's clever or he wouldn't be botherin' about her. I wish I'd had the chance he's offerin' Polly. Then I wouldn't have had to work for peanuts.' Tommy saw the lost look on his wife's face and wished he could take those words back. With him not at home, she needed Polly, and he should have thought of that before opening his mouth. 'Look, love, you're the one who has to make the choice 'cos it's you that it'll affect the most. It's all well and good me lyin' here tellin' yer what I think. I'm not the one goin' to be left with doin' two jobs and havin' our Joey to worry about. It would be too much for yer an' I think yer should forget the whole thing.'

'I've tried doin' that over the last few days, but I can't. I keep thinkin' how our Polly could do so much with her life if she had a decent education. It would open up a whole new world to her, Tommy, an' I'd feel guilty for the rest of me days if I denied her the chance.'

Tommy didn't know what to say. Whichever way it went, one of his family was going to be sorry. 'What does Mr Roscoe think? He knows this Denholme bloke – he should have a better idea than us.'

'Mr John thinks highly of him, but he said he doesn't want to get involved. He advised me to talk it over with you and see what your reaction was before mentioning it to Polly.'

'He's got a point,' Tommy said. 'Seeing as you an' me don't know which way to go, perhaps it would be best if yer sat Polly down and had a heart to heart with her. The girl might not want to go an' we'll have had all this upset for nothing.'

'I'll do that, love.' Ada felt some of the pressure lifting. 'An' I'll write yer a letter an' tell yer what she says, save yer having to wait until next Sunday to find out.' She gave a long sigh. 'Now let's talk about somethin' else, cheer yer up a bit.'

'What's Fanny been up to?' Tommy was smiling as he asked because he knew Ada would have a funny tit-bit for him.

'Yer mean Fanny an' Aggie! Oh yes, me old mate turned up one night – Mr John brought her in the car. She opened the door to me as bold as brass an' within minutes her an' Fanny had me in stitches. It was just like old times.'

'Aggie's missin' yer, is she?'

Ada turned her head to make sure there were no nurses in the vicinity before doing her impersonation. 'It's bleedin' miserable, girl, just sittin' all day lookin' at four bleedin' walls!'

Ada climbed the winding stairs to the top deck of the tram, knowing it would be quieter there. She needed a clear head to think things through properly before she got home. The remark made by Tommy about him not being able to get a decent job because he hadn't been given the chance his daughter was being offered, stuck in her mind. Perhaps she should encourage Polly to take up the offer, try to make something of herself. She deserved it, God knows, because she was such a good kid and it would be nice to see her getting on in the world. But oh, how she'd miss her! Not only because of the help she was around the house, but for her ever-present cheerfulness and ready laughter. And what about Joey? He'd be lost without his beloved sister. But, Ada asked herself, were those things important enough to deny the girl the opportunity of a lifetime?

By the time Ada stepped off the tram she had decided she wouldn't try and sway Polly one way or the other. The girl must decide for herself. But as soon as she stepped into the living room she was given a stark reminder of what she would miss if her daughter wasn't there. The table had been set for tea, with a plate of sandwiches and a Victoria sponge cake, and the kettle standing on the hob was just on the boil.

'Sit down, Mam, an' I'll pour yer a drink out.' Polly turned her ever-ready smile on her mother. 'How was me dad?'

'Just about the same, sunshine, but perhaps a bit more talkative. He sends you an' Joey a big hug an' a kiss.'

'Did he like the flowers?'

'He was delighted,' Ada said. 'Over the moon with them.'

'What about me, Mam?' Joey enquired. 'Did he ask how I was gettin' on in school?'

'He always asks, son, never fails. An' I always tell him you're goin' to be as clever as our Polly, near the top of the class.'

Joey grinned. 'I'm goin' to be cleverer than our Polly 'cos I can beat her at cards, so there!'

Ada glanced from one to the other and asked herself how she could even think of breaking the home up more than it was already. Then her sense of fair play told her to stick to what she'd planned. Let Polly decide for herself.

When tea was over, Ada carried the dishes out. 'I'll wash these few things, Polly, it won't take me a minute.'

'Can me an' Polly have a game of snap before I go to bed?' Joey asked, his face begging her to say yes. 'I promise I'll go to bed when yer tell me to.'

'Yes, okay, son, but seven o'clock sharp yer up those stairs 'cos it's school temorrer.'

Ada rinsed the few dishes and left them on the draining board while she attached the hose pipe to the tap to fill the dolly tub. She'd leave the washing in steep all night and get most of the dirt out. Then when she came in from her morning job she could rinse it out, put the things through the mangle, and providing it wasn't raining, she could have them out on the line before ten o'clock. With decent weather, the washing would be dry before she had to leave for Faulkner Square.

As she waited for the dolly tub to fill, Ada's thoughts went back to Charles Denholme. With a bit of luck Polly might turn his offer down flat. That would save a lot of headaches and heartaches. Then a voice in her head told her that she was being selfish, thinking of herself instead of considering her daughter. And once again Ada determined to let the girl choose for herself without any interference.

'Mam, our Joey's yawning his head off. Shall I take him up?' Polly watched as her mother plunged the dolly peg up and down in the water. 'Yer look tired, Mam. Leave that an' I'll do it when I come down. You sit and put yer feet up while yer've got the chance.'

'No, you take Joey up, an' when yer come down I'll have a fresh pot of tea made an' we can sit an' have a natter.'

There was a grin on Polly's face when she came downstairs. 'He's a holy terror, our Joey. I was halfway through the story when I saw him close his eyes an' drop off. And he let me creep as far as the door before tellin' me he was only pretendin' to be asleep, then he made me go back and finish the story. The little tinker.'

Ada poured out two cups of tea and handed one to her daughter. She sighed with relief when she sat down. 'It's lovely to sit in peace and quiet, rest me weary bones.' She sipped at the tea, gazing at Polly over the rim of the cup. 'Did yer see Mr Denholme yesterday?'

Polly nodded. 'Yeah, I told yer, he came as usual. He doesn't half have a lot of clothes, Mam. I've seen him in about six suits. What it is to be rich, eh?'

'Did he have anythin' to say?'

'I told yer last night he said he'd met you, don't yer remember?'

'Yes, you told me that. But did he have anythin' else to say? Like telling yer he went to see Mr John?'

'No, we didn't have that long to talk because I was busy. Anyway, he wouldn't tell me that, would he? Him and Mr John are friends, so he probably calls to see him quite often.'

Ada's tummy was churning over but she knew if she didn't do it now she never would. 'He had a reason for calling to see him this week, Polly, and his visit concerned *you*.'

Polly's eyes flew open in surprise. 'Me? Why would he go to see Mr John about me? I don't even know your boss, Mam, so what would Mr Denholme want to see him about me for?'

'Well, now he knows I work for Mr John, he probably thought his proposal would stand a better chance if it came through someone who knows the family.'

'Yer've lost me, Mam. I don't know what yer talking about. What d'yer mean by his proposal?'

'He wants to offer you a job in his house, as a junior housemaid.'

Polly laughed. 'He's quick off the mark, isn't he? I've got another eleven months to do at school.'

'He said you'd be taught alongside his two children, who have a private tutor.' Ada had trouble keeping her voice neutral. 'You'd work so many hours a day with the housekeeper, then you'd join his children for lessons. You'd be paid five shillings a week and have yer clothes bought for yer.'

Polly's eyes brightened with excitement. 'A private tutor! That would be marvellous, Mam – just think what I'd learn! I might even be taught how to speak French!'

'So the idea appeals to yer, does it?' Ada's heart plummeted. 'Yer think yer'd like it?'

'Oh, yeah! An' I'd be able to give you the five shillings a week, plus what I get at the weekends. We'd be well-off, Mam!'

'There wouldn't be any weekend job, Polly, 'cos yer'd have to live in. Yer'd probably get a day a week off, but I really wouldn't like yer to take that as gospel. Yer'd have to ask Mr Denholme about yer hours and things, but it is a live-in job.'

'Yer mean I wouldn't live here no more, not with you an' Joey?'

'No, sunshine, yer wouldn't. The job he's offering is what they call going into service, an' that means living in.'

'What about helping Sarah Jane on a Saturday, or Auntie Mary on a Sunday? Couldn't I do that, neither?'

Ada shook her head. 'No, love, yer couldn't.'

Polly dropped her head while she thought it all through. 'How would you manage without me? Who'd look after our Joey for yer an' run all the messages?'

'I'd have to manage, that's all. I know next door would see to Joey for me, so that would be one worry less.'

The mention of Steve's mother had Polly shaking her head vigorously, sending her curls flying in all directions. 'No, I don't want to go. In fact I'm not going! I'd be worried sick leaving you with all the work to do, an' our Joey would miss me somethin' shocking. And I'd be lettin' Sarah Jane and Auntie Mary down. I couldn't do that, Mam, I'd feel terrible. And another thing, I'd never get to see Steve.'

An hour ago, Ada would have been relieved and happy at Polly's words. But after listening to her daughter's reasons for refusing, she could only feel sadness. The girl had been delighted at the prospect at first, Ada could tell by her animated face and the eyes sparkling with excitement. It was only after she'd had time to think about the people who, in her mind, she'd be letting down, that the flame of excitement was dimmed. And while Ada loved her for her thoughtfulness, she didn't think the reasons given were the right ones to be turning down Mr Denholme's offer. Polly was thirteen years of age, far too young to worry about how people would manage without her. She couldn't live her life around other folk, she had to start thinking of herself.

'Polly, if it weren't for worrying about me an' Joey, and Sarah Jane and Mary, would yer consider taking the job?'

'Oh yeah, then it would be different. But I'm not leaving me mam an' me brother, or me friends, in the lurch. That would be selfish, just thinkin' about meself.'

'Most of us have a selfish streak in us, sunshine, it's only natural. Take me, for instance, I don't want yer to go because I'd miss yer so much an' I'd miss the help yer give me. That's being selfish, thinkin' of meself and not takin' into considera- tion that you'd be betterin' yerself if yer took the job. Yer dad wants yer to take it, he was all for the idea. Yer see, he reckons if he'd had a decent education he'd have been able to get a good job and he'd have made a better life for all of us.'

'Me dad did his best, he couldn't have done no more.' Polly was quick to defend her father. 'He's a good dad, the best in the world! And we *did* have a good life – we were happy until he got sick.'

'I'm not running yer dad down, sunshine. Yer know I love the bones of him. But he thinks if yer given a chance to get on in life then yer should grab it with both hands. An' it's not as though yer'd be goin' to the ends of the earth. If yer didn't like it, or were homesick, yer could walk out of the door and be home in ten minutes.' Ada leaned forward and smiled into her daughter's face. 'An' if I missed yer too much I could always march up there an' drag yer home.'

Polly was thoughtful as she ran a finger round the rim of her cup. 'I'd like to know a bit more about it. I like Mr Denholme an' I know I could get on with him. He's a toff, but he's not stuck-up with it. But what about his wife an' children? If they're snobs I wouldn't want to be in the same house as them.'

'Guessing and wondering isn't goin' to get us anywhere, so put it out of yer mind for now. Tomorrow I'll ask Mr John to arrange a meeting with Mr Denholme at Faulkner Square. That's on neutral ground an' yer'll be on equal terms. I'll be with yer 'cos there's questions I want answers to as well. Me an' yer dad love yer, Polly, an' I know he'll be relying on me not to let yer go anywhere unless I'm sure in me own mind that it's the right place for yer to be.'

'Before yer do that, Mam, are yer sure that if I didn't like it I could just walk out of the door? I wouldn't even think of goin' if I was tied down and had to put up with it even if I hated it.'

'You have my promise on that, sunshine. But what I'll do, I'll ask Mr John to sit with us. He's got more on top than us, he'd know what questions to ask. An' he'd make sure you understood everything that was going on.'

Polly suddenly started to giggle. 'I think Mr Denholme might be gettin' more than he bargained for. Instead of a girl going to him to be interviewed for the lowly post of junior housemaid, he's got to come to Faulkner Square to be interviewed by three people to see if he is suitable! I wouldn't be surprised if he told Mr John we could all take a runnin' jump.'

'That's his privilege, love – but after all, he was the one who started the whole thing.' Ada laughed. 'That'll teach him!'

Chapter Eighteen

'Charles, the whole idea is ridiculous!' Victoria Denholme looked at her husband as though he'd gone mad. 'In the first place you have no right to offer a girl a job without my first seeing her! I'm the one who has to deal with the staff. What if I don't think she's suitable?'

Charles tipped the ash off his cigar into an ornate glass ashtray before answering. 'I didn't tell you about her before because I wasn't sure her family would allow her to take the post. I think she's very suitable, Victoria, and I'm sure you'll agree I am entitled to have some say in who we take into our employment? I have never interfered before, because as long as the house was running smoothly I wasn't that interested. However, I *am* interested in helping this young girl and I expect you and the children to welcome and respect her.'

'I really don't know what's come over you, Charles,' Victoria said, a hand to her forehead. She was a very elegant woman, tall and slim, with blonde hair and startling blue eyes. 'You tell me she's the girl you buy your flowers off – in other words, a barrow girl! In the next breath you tell me she's not only coming to live in, but that she's to be taught alongside the children. I must say, I find the whole thing intolerable and ask that you cancel the arrangement immediately.'

'I'm sorry, darling, I don't often refuse you but on this occasion I'm afraid I must.' From the depth of his armchair, Charles spoke quietly. 'Polly is a delightful child and once you meet her I'm sure you'll be enchanted by her.' He looked at the gold watch on his wrist. 'She'll be here, with her mother, in an hour's time and I want you and the children to give them both a warm welcome and treat them with the utmost respect.'

Victoria shook her head. 'No, I can't do it.'

There was an edge now to Charles's voice. 'Can't – or *won't*, Victoria?'

'You're asking too much, Charles. You get this notion into your head that you want to help this . . . this waif, and we are all to suffer for your grand display of benevolence.'

'Did you say, waif, Victoria? Oh dear, you are in for a shock. Polly is from a working-class family, and proud of it, but she has a lot of virtues I find sadly lacking in my own children. And I have to say, darling, that you disappoint me. I thought you would be happy to help someone less fortunate than ourselves. We live a very sheltered life in this house, we have never wanted for anything. We buy the best clothes, the best food, and are waited on hand and foot, our every whim catered for. But we were fortunate, you and I, to be born into wealthy families. We didn't have to toil for our money, it wasn't earned by the sweat of our brow. It was always there and we've taken it for granted. But I believe it's time that we, as a family, stood back and gave a thought to how fortunate we are. I began to step back the day I met Polly Perkins. I began to wonder what would happen if I was suddenly broke, absolutely penniless. Would either of my children do what Polly does, to help me out? Would they be prepared to stand on a street corner selling flowers to earn the princely sum of one shilling per day? I reached the sad conclusion that they would not. So while we think we have everything that we want in life, there are many things we do not have. I hope that when you meet Polly Perkins you will understand what I mean.'

'It would appear to me, Charles, that you care more for this girl than you do your own children.'

'No, Victoria, you are wrong. I am fond of Polly, but I love my children dearly and she could never take their place. But they are ignorant of how people outside our circle live. So while Polly will be gaining an education otherwise not open to her, it is my hope that Justin and Rebecca will learn something from her.' Charles saw the look of bewilderment on his wife's face and said softly, 'I do love you, Victoria, and I hope that you love me enough to trust my judgement and have an open mind when Polly comes. Don't shut your heart to her, my darling, give her a chance for my sake.'

When the bell sounded, Victoria went into the hall to see the maid making her way towards the front door. 'I'll answer it, Lucy. You return to the kitchen to help Mrs Nightingale prepare the dinner.' While waiting for the maid to reach the end of the long, wide hall, she was telling herself that Charles was really going too far with this nonsense. Why, he'd practically ordered the children to like this girl. It was so unlike him she just couldn't comprehend the whole sorry situation.

Victoria opened the door and looked down into two smiling faces, identical except for the age difference. 'Mrs Perkins?'

Ada nodded. 'This is me daughter, Polly.'

'Come in, come in.' Victoria was at a loss. They weren't at all what she had expected and she was unsure whether she should shake hands or not. She decided against. If the girl was coming to work here it wouldn't do to get too familiar. 'Mr Denholme's in the drawing room, please come through.'

'Polly!' Charles's smile was wide as he left his armchair. He took the girl by the shoulders and with a cheeky grin, asked, 'Have you got your blue velvet dress on?'

'Don't be daft, Mr Denholme, course I haven't! I've come straight from school an' I couldn't go to school all dolled up, I'd have got me leg pulled soft.'

'Only because they'd be jealous, Polly.' Charles turned to her mother and extended a hand. 'Ada, it's good to see you. This is Victoria, my wife.'

Stunned by the whole proceedings, Victoria moved forward and held out her hand. 'I'm delighted to meet you,

Mrs Perkins.' She glanced sideways. 'I wasn't aware you and my husband knew each other.'

'I work for Mr Roscoe and met your husband through him.'

'Ada is housekeeper to John,' Charles explained. 'She helps feed his friends when they have a card night and I met her when I made the foursome up one night.'

Polly's brows drew together. Her mam wasn't a housekeeper, she was a cleaner! She helped when Mr John had friends in, but she wasn't his housekeeper! Polly was about to say so when a look from her mother silenced her.

'Victoria, will you ring for tea while I take Polly through to meet the children?' Charles put his hand on the girl's elbow. 'I'm sure Ada would welcome a cup of tea.'

'Charles, the children are in the middle of a lesson!'

'Mr Westly won't object to a five-minute interruption. Come along, Polly.'

'Are yer comin', Mam?'

'No, sunshine, you go with Mr Denholme an' I'll wait here for yer. There's nothing for yer to be frightened of.'

The look of desperation on the girl's face as she was led from the room, and the look of love on her mother's, wasn't lost on Victoria. Charles had been right when he said she was in for a surprise. It had been one surprise after another since she'd opened the front door. The girl she'd referred to as a 'waif' and 'barrow girl', was far from fitting either description. Her clothes were shabby, yes, but with her pretty face and friendly smile you didn't really notice what she was wearing. And although she showed no deference to Charles as her future employer, her easy manner with him had never been over-familiar.

'Sit down, Mrs Perkins, please.' Victoria pushed a button at the side of the elaborate fireplace and when the maid appeared, she said, 'Tea for four, please, Lucy.'

Ada was on pins, thinking of Polly. ' I hope my daughter's

all right. She's not usually nervous but she was shakin' like a leaf coming down the street.'

'Won't you miss your daughter, Mrs Perkins? That is, of course, if she does come to work here.'

'I'll be heartbroken and that's the truth. But I wouldn't tell Polly that for the world, 'cos if I did she definitely wouldn't come. And I don't want to stand in her way. She's a good girl, Mrs Denholme, one of the best.' Ada gave a nervous, tearful smile. 'But bein' a mother yerself, yer know every mother thinks her children are the best.'

'I believe your husband is in hospital?'

Ada sighed. 'Yes, he's been in over a year now, and the doctor reckons it could be another year before he comes home, maybe even two.'

'Oh dear.' Despite herself Victoria was warming to the woman. She sat back and crossed her shapely legs. 'It must be a very trying time for you. I do hope your husband proves the doctor wrong and is quickly back home.'

'This is my son, Justin, my daughter, Rebecca, and their tutor Mr Westly.' Charles could feel Polly shaking and gave her arm a comforting squeeze. 'And this is the young lady I told you about, Miss Polly Perkins.'

Justin dutifully left his chair to shake hands, followed by Mr Westly. But it took a stern look from Charles to bring Rebecca to her feet. Her face was sullen and she barely touched Polly's hand before returning quickly to her desk and bowing her head over a book.

Polly kept the smile on her face even though she was more nervous than she'd ever been. The snub from Rebecca had cut deep but Polly wasn't going to give her the satisfaction of letting it show. She didn't think she'd like being in the same house as a girl who looked down her nose at her, which was a pity really because the boy, Justin, seemed pleasant enough and the tutor's smile had been friendly.

'What subject are you on today, Mr Westly?' Charles

asked. 'Perhaps Polly would be interested.'

'History.' Tom Westly pointed to the open book in front of him. 'We were discussing the Battle of Hastings. Have you heard of that, Polly?'

'Oh yeah, it was in 1066.' A surge of relief flooded Polly's body. She'd have felt such a fool if she hadn't known what he was talking about. 'We did that in school last year.'

Charles and the tutor looked at each other, surprise on their faces. 'Are you good at history then, Polly?' Tom Westly asked. 'Or was it just luck that I asked that particular question?'

'I was top of the class in history in the exams before Christmas.' Polly knew she was bragging and also knew the reason why. It was to get her own back on snobby, smarty-pants Rebecca. 'And I was top in geography and arithmetic.'

'Jolly good!' Charles patted her shoulder. 'Perhaps you could write an essay for Mr Westly, so he can see how good you are at English.' He chuckled. 'Write a story about Sarah Jane, and the other ladies.'

'Yes, I like writing stories.' Polly looked up at him and grinned. 'I'll ask me mam to buy me a notebook.'

The thick Liverpool accent had Rebecca raising her head, a sneer curling her top lip. Slowly, and pronouncing every word carefully, she said, 'I will ask MY MOTHER to buy me a suitable writing book.'

Oh, she's not getting away with that, Polly thought. So with the smile glued firmly on her face, and her accent deliberately thickened, she raised her brows at the girl. 'Ooh, er, is yer writin' a story as well?'

Charles's loud guffaw filled the room, Justin chuckled and Tom Westly, behind the hand that was hiding his smile, was praying fervently that Miss Polly Perkins would become one of his pupils. Because he had a feeling that with her in the class, lessons would never be the same. But she'd made an enemy in Rebecca. And Tom knew to his cost exactly how wicked Mr Charles's daughter could be when things didn't go her way. She would lie her way out of trouble without flickering an eyelid and didn't care who got hurt in the process. Right now she was glaring at Polly, angry that she'd been made a fool of. And if looks were anything to go by, Polly would be in for a rough ride.

Ada linked her arm through her daughter's as they walked down Percy Street. 'Well, that's all signed, sealed and delivered. Mr Denholme seems made up that yer've agreed to go.'

'I did tell him though, Mam, that if I didn't like it after a month, I'd leave. He said he understood but was sure I'd settle down once I got used to the run of the house.' Polly glanced sideways. 'There's only one fly in the ointment and it's that Rebecca. She's not half stuck-up, speaks frightfully far back an' looks down her nose at yer. I can see her givin' me a dog's life . . . that's if I let her get away with it.'

'How old are the children?'

'She's the same age as me, thirteen, an' her brother's fifteen. Posh names they've got, haven't they? Imagine a boy in our street with the name of Justin, he'd be a standin' joke! But then this Justin probably doesn't even know streets like ours exist. Still, he seems all right.'

'I wouldn't worry about the girl, sunshine,' Ada said, trying to sound bright and happy even though she was hurting inside. 'She can't do yer no harm. If she tries anythin', just tell Mr Denholme, or his wife – she seems a genuine person. And the house is beautiful, like a palace.'

'Oh Mam, yer should see the room that's goin' to be me bedroom. It's got a cover on the bed to match the curtains, an' guess what? There's a wash-basin in there so I can wash meself in private.' Polly forgot her misgivings about Rebecca as she went into raptures over all the beautiful things she'd seen. The large gilt-framed paintings and mirrors, ornaments and statues, lovely curtains that came right down to the floor and carpets your feet sank in. 'Ay, Mam, I didn't like those statues of the men and women with no clothes on, I thought they were rude. I wouldn't like them in our house, would you?'

'Our house is a bit small for things like that, sunshine, even if we had the money to buy them.'

'Yeah, it's not half a big house. Our whole place would fit in the kitchen. They've got a cook called Mrs Nightingale, the maid Lucy, an' a woman comes in every morning to do the heavy work, like cleanin' the fireplaces and lighting the fires. It's a dead cushy life they've all got, that's for sure, especially when yer think of how hard you 'ave to work.'

'Don't worry about me, love, I'm quite happy where I am. I just hope you don't get too used to it 'cos I don't want to lose yer.'

'No fear of that, Mam! If yer ever hear me talkin' as though I've got a plum in me mouth, give me a clip around the ear. It's all right for them 'cos they're used to it, but it's not for me.' Polly nudged her mother's arm. 'Rebecca thinks I'm as common as muck but I don't care. I'm not goin' to change to suit her, she can like it or lump it.'

'How did she get on?' Fanny asked before Ada had time to mount the top step. 'Did she get took on?'

Ada nodded. 'She starts next Monday.'

'There's no need to look so down in the dumps, girl,' Fanny said as she closed the door. 'She's not in prison – she can do a runner if she doesn't like it. Anyway, his lordship's waitin' for yer, he said yer've to go up right away.'

'I'm sorry I'm late, Fanny, but I'll work twice as quick to make up for lost time.'

'No need, girl. I got here half an hour early an' got stuck in. You see to the top floor an' leave the rest to me.'

'Thanks, Fanny, yer'll never see what I buy yer for yer birthday.'

'Never mind me bleedin' birthday, I've had enough of them to last me a lifetime! Just remember me in yer will.'

Ada turned on the fourth stair, her hand on the bannister. 'I know, I'll leave yer me grandfather clock. It's a priceless family heirloom, been in the family for generations.'

'Now yer talkin' my kind of language, girl! Somethin' I've always wanted is a grandfather clock, it would look a treat in me kitchen. Mind you, I'd have to throw everythin' else out to get the bleedin' thing in, but if yer want to be posh yer've got to put up with little inconveniences like not bein' able to sit down.'

Ada reached the bottom of the second staircase and stopped for a second to take a deep breath. I'm not going to break down, she vowed. Not until I'm in my own bed where no one can see me. But when she walked through the office door and John came towards her, his hands outstretched, it only took the look of concern on his face to set her off.

'Oh, John.' She screwed up her face in an effort to control her emotions but to no avail. The tears began to flow and she covered her face with her hands, all the while telling herself she was acting like a child instead of a thirty-five-year-old woman.

John closed the door before coming to stand in front of her. When the tears turned to sobs, he took her in his arms. 'Ada, my darling, what nonsense this is. We can't have you upset like this. Let me ring Charles and tell him the whole thing's off.'

'No, I don't want you to do that,' Ada sobbed. 'If Polly ever leaves of her own accord, I'll be very happy. But I'm not goin' to ruin her chance of gettin' a decent education.' Ada's mind was wrestling with an added problem. She had no right to be standing in the arms of a man who wasn't her husband. She should break away now and make sure it didn't happen again. But she didn't break away. She needed the sympathy, the understanding and the comfort of his arms. And there was no harm in being hugged, they weren't hurting anyone. John's life was as loveless as her own. They both needed warmth and affection and all they were doing was answering that need.

John held her until her sobs subsided, making soothing noises and kissing her hair. Then when she had calmed down, he stood back and cupped her red, swollen face. 'Take your coat off, darling, and I'll ask Fanny to make a pot of tea.'

'No, yer mustn't do that. I've given Fanny enough work to do without expecting her to wait on me.'

'Then I shall wait on you.' John leaned towards her and although she could see what his intention was, Ada didn't turn away. His lips, for the first time, covered hers, and the kiss lasted several seconds. Then he moved back and gazed into her eyes. 'Oh, my darling Ada, if only things were different. I could give you so much, take all the cares from your shoulders.'

'I have a husband, John, and I love him very much. Perhaps I'm being selfish taking the comfort you give, the comfort I'm desperate for, when I can give yer nothin' in return.'

'But you do like me, Ada?'

'Oh, I do like you, John. In fact, I'm very fond of you.' Ada gave a weak smile. 'Yer a lovely man, an' it would be hard not to fall for yer.'

'You don't object to my embrace or kisses? They don't repel you?'

'No, John, I don't object. I thought yer knew me well enough to know that if I didn't want yer to kiss me, I wouldn't let yer. I need affection, I've been starved of it for too long. But I don't have to tell you how it feels to be all alone, with no one to hold yer hand and no shoulder to cry on. You've had ten long years of it yourself.'

John pulled her to him. 'I keep telling myself that it is ungallant of me to try and woo a woman whose husband is ill in hospital, but, God forgive me, I can't help myself. I will never do anything to hurt you, all I ask is for your affection.'

'You already have that, John, and my respect. When I met you I was so low I couldn't go any lower. You've made me feel like a woman again, and I'll always love yer for that.'

'Then will you let me make life a little easier for you? I have had this in mind for several months but was afraid I'd frighten you off. I spend all my time here now, and I really need someone to get my shopping in, cook for me, see to the laundry and keep the flat clean.'

'But I do most of that now, John! You don't need to take anyone else on just to do the shoppin' and cooking.'

'I wasn't thinking of taking anyone on for up here; I want nobody but you in my rooms. I will take another cleaner on to help Fanny on the other two floors, and you can give up your morning job and work full-time for me. I worry about you leaving the house these dark mornings at some ungodly hour, then going home from here in the evenings in the dark. It isn't safe, there's some unsavoury characters about.'

'I can't give me mornin' job up, I need the money! An' before yer say anything, John, I'm not takin' charity from you. That would definitely put a different complexion on our relationship.'

'I would have to be very stupid to offer you charity, Ada, my love, knowing how proud you are. What I am offering you is a job that will enable you to work days. Except, of course, on the evenings my friends are coming. I would need you then.' He saw the doubt and questions on her face and went on quickly, 'I am not creating a job just for you, although I have to admit I would enjoy having you around all day. And there would be plenty for you to do. I would even ask you to answer the phone and take messages if I were absent.'

'I wouldn't be able to get here until after nine because I take Joey to school.' Ada was thinking about the money. She couldn't afford to have a drop in her income; it took her all her time to manage as it was. 'I don't know what to say, I can't make up me mind.'

'Then let me make it up for you. From Monday you will become my secretary-cum-housekeeper. Hours to suit yourself, as long as the work is up to standard, of course, and the wage two pound a week.'

Ada gasped. 'It's not worth two pound a week! Yer could get someone for a lot less than that.'

'I'd get my money's worth out of you, Ada. Cleaning, washing, ironing, shopping, cooking and answering the phone . . . I'll have you worn to a shadow in a matter of weeks.'

'It sounds marvellous,' Ada said, 'but there's two little niggles in me mind an' I won't be happy until they're sorted out. First, the job isn't a made-up one, just because yer feel sorry for me, is it?'

'That's one little niggle you can lay to rest . . . I do not feel sorry for you, Ada. I have many feelings for you, but sorrow isn't one of them. Now, out with the second.'

'What will people think? I don't know any of the staff downstairs 'cos I've never seen them, but what about Fanny – and Aggie? I can't see them believin' yer need a house-keeper-cum-secretary. Yer'd have a secretary that had never answered a phone in her life.'

John smiled shyly. 'They both know about it. Agnes has known for weeks, there's not much I keep from her. And she said, and I quote her very words, "It's the best bleedin' idea yer've ever had". And I had a word with Fanny tonight when she came on. She knows someone who is looking for a cleaning job and the woman is coming tomorrow for an interview. You see, my darling Ada, I was determined that you weren't going to carry on with your present workload. And I do need someone here to look after me. I'm sick of eating out.'

Ada smiled. 'I'm a good cook, John, I'll see yer well-fed.'

Relieved, he took her hand. 'Ada, if it was poison you served up, as long as you had cooked it, I'd eat it.'

* * *

Rebecca crossed the landing to her brother's room and walked in without knocking. She closed the door and stood with her back to it. 'You're a coward, Justin. You went back on your promise because you are afraid of displeasing Father.'

'I didn't hear you knock, Rebecca. Isn't it polite to knock before entering someone's bedroom?' Both children had inherited Charles's dark colouring and features, but Justin was already as tall as his father and broader of shoulder. 'What is it you want?'

'We both agreed we didn't want this . . . this common girl in our house and we intended to make it plain to her by our manner. But you reneged on our agreement and were practically fawning over her.'

'Steady on, Rebecca, I think your imagination has taken over. It was you who said we didn't want Polly here. What was it you called her – a guttersnipe? Anyway, I didn't agree to anything, I just let you talk on as you usually do. I find it easier to say nothing when you have a bee in your bonnet.'

Rebecca was livid. 'Oh, it's *Polly* now, is it? A dirty, common flower-seller, and you have no objection to sitting next to her at the table, or in the study? She probably has filthy habits and is entirely lacking in etiquette.'

'Miaow! Your claws are showing, my dear sister, and it does not become you. I for one have no objection to Polly, I thought she was pretty and friendly. I also think she'll be lots of fun.'

Rebecca moved to stand in front of him and drawled, 'Oh yeah, I'll ask me mam.'

Justin laughed. 'I rather think you'll live to regret trying to make a fool of Polly. She does speak with a heavy accent, I agree, but I don't find it in the least unpleasant. And accent aside, I think she's probably a damn sight more clever than you or I will ever be.' He picked up a book from the tallboy and flicked through the pages. 'Close the door on your way out, Rebecca, please.'

Grinding her teeth, Rebecca banged the door. She'd get rid of the girl with or without her brother's help. There were ways of getting rid of staff you didn't like, she'd done it before.

Chapter Nineteen

'Of course I'll mind the little feller for yer,' Dolly said. 'He can 'ave a bite to eat with us, save you worryin'.' She grimaced as she pulled at a bone in her stays which had worked its way through the material and was digging into the flesh beneath her breast. 'I must be barmy wearin' these things when they give me hell. Walkin' round in agony just for the sake of vanity, I want me flamin' bumps feeling.'

'I wouldn't care if yer looked any different with the blinkin' things on, but yer don't!' Ada said. 'Yer look the same, with or without the stays on.'

'Thanks, pal! Yer certainly know how to make a girl feel good. Just like my feller.' Dolly jerked her head in the direction of Les who had his head buried in the *Echo*. 'He's always payin' me compliments, too! It's no wonder I've got a bleedin' inferiority complex.'

Ada laughed. 'You, an inferiority complex? That'll be the day, Dolly Mitchell. I wish I was as sure of meself as you always seem to be. It would be a good one who could get the better of yer.'

Les lifted his head and nodded. 'Yer right there, Ada, I've been trying for seventeen years to get the better of her but I don't stand a snowball's chance in hell. She's got an answer for everything.'

'Oh, I wouldn't say that, light of my life! There's one place in this house where yer always get yer own way.' Dolly's thumb pointed upwards to their bedroom. 'Yer've got no complaints in that department 'cos I'm very co-operative.'

A blush was covering Les's face as he winked at Ada. 'See what I mean about her havin' an answer for everything? My best bet is to just sit tight an' say nowt.'

'Yer have my sympathy, Les. I don't know how yer put up with her.'

'Ay, whose side are you on? I've just offered to do yer a favour, 'cos yer supposed to be me best mate, an' all I get is the height of abuse from yer!' Dolly folded her arms across her tummy and hitched up her bust. As she did so a look of pure bliss crossed her face. 'Oh God, that's lovely! The ruddy bone's not diggin' in now.'

'Dolly, take the flamin' things off! I'm blowed if I'd put up with that just for the sake of lookin' an inch thinner.'

'It's all right for you talkin', Ada Perkins, but yer'd soon change yer tune if yer had my tummy.' Dolly gently rubbed the sore spot. 'I'd better get them off, though, otherwise I'll end up with a ruddy big sore an' have to go to the doctor's.' She began to chuckle. 'Can yer imagine the poor man's face if I 'ad to undress in front of him? He'd think he needed a new pair of glasses.'

'A doctor's used to seein' all sizes and shapes, Dolly, he wouldn't think nothin' of it.'

'Oh, aye – would you like to show him one of yours?'

'I wouldn't have to, sunshine, would I? 'Cos I'm not stupid enough to wear somethin' that was killing me!' Ada began to button her coat. 'I'd better get in before Polly thinks I've got lost.'

'Our Steve's in there. He took a pack of cards with him so they could have a game of rummy.' Dolly tilted her head. 'I don't think he's very happy about Polly leaving, he looked dead miserable when she told him.'

'He'll still see her, she'll be comin' home regularly.' Ada closed her eyes. 'Don't start me off, Dolly. I've shed enough tears today to sink a flamin' ship!'

'Yer'll get used to it, girl, an' it's not as though it's for ever. Time passes quickly an' she'll be home before yer know it. An' you being able to pack up yer morning job should make yer happy. No more gettin' up at half-four – yer won't know yer born.'

'I know, I keep pinchin' meself to make sure I'm not dreaming. Anyway, will yer see me out, Dolly?' Ada looked across to her neighbour's husband. 'Bye for now, Les. An' put yer foot down with this one, d'yer hear?'

'I'll do that, Ada!' he called after her. 'I'll put me foot down with a firm hand.'

Ada stepped into the street and looked up at her friend. 'I didn't want to say anythin' in front of Les, but I'll pay yer five bob a week for minding Joey for me. Is that all right?'

Dolly waved a hand. 'I don't want nothin' off yer, the little feller's no trouble. And what he eats is harmless.'

'I want to pay yer, Dolly, and I can afford it. Mr John is making me other wage up, and I'll be gettin' a few bob off Polly even though I won't have her to keep. So while I won't be on Easy Street, I'll be able to manage fine with just Joey an' me.'

'I won't say the money won't be welcome, girl, 'cos an extra five bob a week would be a godsend. But I couldn't charge yer for mindin' the little feller for a few hours – I'd feel mean. After all, we're friends, an' yer don't charge friends for doin' them a favour.'

'Dolly, count it as doin' a little job. I go to work an' I get paid, so why shouldn't you? If it weren't for you minding Joey, I wouldn't be able to take the job, would I?'

'Are yer sure yer wouldn't be leavin' yerself skint?'

'Quite sure. If the time ever came that I couldn't afford to pay it, yer know I'd tell yer. But Mr John has his friends in once a month now an' I get an extra few bob for that.'

'I'll put Joey to bed when yer have to go out at night, an' I'll sit with him until yer come home. That way I'll make sure I get me fair share of the cakes an' sarnies.' Dolly hugged herself, a beaming smile on her face. 'Five bob a week's not to be sneezed at, girl! I might even buy meself some new stays.'

'You dare, an' I'll clock yer one,' Ada said. 'I'm not givin' yer good money so yer can inflict pain on yerself.' She turned to move away. 'Is that a bargain then, Dolly?'

'It's the bargain of a lifetime, girl, an' I thank yer. In fact, me whole family will thank yer 'cos there'll be extra grub on the table.'

Ada slid her front-door key into the lock. 'I'll see yer tomorrow, Dolly. Good night an' God bless.' She closed the door behind her as Polly opened the living-room door.

'I've been worried about yer, Mam!'

'I slipped next door and stayed longer than I intended.' Ada shrugged off her coat. 'Hello, Steve.'

'Hello, Mrs Perkins. I've been hearing all about Polly's new job.' Steve laid down his hand of cards. 'She's goin' up in the world, isn't she?'

'It depends what you mean by goin' up in the world, sunshine.' Ada could see the hurt and disappointment in his eyes. 'Having plenty of money an' living in a big house doesn't always bring happiness. We may have nowt, but we're better off than some of them.'

'Steve's being daft,' Polly told her. 'He thinks I'll start speakin' posh and go round with me nose in the air. But I won't, will I, Mam?'

'I should hope not, love, because me an' yer dad wouldn't like that. We love yer just the way yer are.'

'An' I love you and me dad, an' nothing will ever change that. Same as Steve is me best mate. He always had been an' always will be.'

'There you are, Steve. She can't say fairer than that, can she?'

But Steve wasn't happy. Why couldn't things have stayed as they were? He'd been waiting for what seemed a lifetime for Polly to reach fourteen so he could take her to the pictures. Then everyone would know she was his girlfriend. But that dream had faded into the distance when she'd told him there was a fifteen-year-old boy in the house and she'd be taking lessons with him and his sister. Justin . . . what a stupid name for a boy, he must be a right cissy. But cissy or not, he lived in a mansion, had plenty of money, and worst of all he'd be living in the same house as Polly and seeing her every day. All this was enough to send Steve into the depths of despair.

When Polly was seeing him to the door, he blurted out, 'Yer'll still come to the pictures with me when yer leave school, won't yer?'

'Of course I will! I said so, didn't I?'

'Things were different then, yer weren't leaving home.'

'I'm not leaving home! At least, I am for a while, but I'll be back. This will always be my home no matter where I am. The only reason I'm goin' is because I want to learn as much as I can.' She would have liked to explain to him how her brain was eager for knowledge, and how much she knew she could learn from Mr Westly that she'd never be taught in a classroom of forty children. But the downcast look on Steve's face stopped her from saying these things. 'Providing me mam will let me, an' if you still want to, I promise I'll come to the pictures with yer on me fourteenth birthday. That can be me birthday present from yer.'

'I'll hold yer to that promise, Polly.' Still Steve lingered. 'Have yer still got the ollie, the bobby dazzler?'

'It's in me drawer upstairs, I wouldn't part with it.'

'An' I've still got the card yer gave me.' He couldn't think of anything else that would keep her, so he stepped into the street. 'I'll see yer temorrer night, eh?'

'Yes, temorrer night. Ta-ra, Steve.'

'Ta-ra, Polly.'

When Ada walked through the ward door her hand was ready to wave to Tommy, who was always watching for her. But he was lying flat in his bed and when she approached his smile was weak. Ada's heart sank. 'What's wrong, love, are yer tired?'

'I feel a bit off today, but it's nothing to worry about.' He struggled to a sitting position, his breathing laboured. 'I got yer letter.'

Ada forced a smile. 'She starts temorrer an' she's had me moth-eaten over what to take an' what not to take. I managed to get her two half-decent dresses from the market yesterday because she said she'd look a nit if she had to wear her gymslip.'

'I'm glad she's goin', love, even though I know it's piling more work on your shoulders. At least she's getting a start in life, which is more than we ever got.'

'I know it's not quite the thing to say when you're lying here in hospital, but we haven't done too badly, Tommy. We've got each other an' two lovely children. What we've lacked in material things we've made up for with love.'

'The day I met you was the luckiest day of my life,' Tommy said, a trace of sadness in his voice. 'You've given me all the love a man could ever ask for, and you've given me two lovely children.'

'Ay, come on, don't be getting maudlin! Yer sound right down in the dumps today.' Ada was shocked by Tommy's appearance but she was determined not to let it show. 'I've got some news that should cheer yer up, seein' as yer worry about me working too hard.' She told him about her new job and how Dolly was going to mind Joey. 'So I can have a lie-in from tomorrow – be a real lady of leisure.'

'I'm glad about that, love, 'cos I have been worried about yer. If I ever get the chance, I'll thank Mr John for bein' so good to yer.'

Ada didn't allow the feeling of guilt to stay. 'What d'yer mean, if yer get the chance? Yer mean *when* yer get the chance. He always sends his regards and says to tell yer he's looking forward to meeting yer.'

Tommy didn't have the strength to stay in the sitting position and he slid down in the bed. 'I'm tired today, love, although God only knows why 'cos I haven't done anythin' to make me tired.'

'Perhaps yer didn't get a good night's sleep? I think it's best if I leave, then you might be able to drop off.'

When Tommy didn't protest, Ada became more worried. He definitely seemed to have deteriorated a lot since last week. She bent to kiss his brow and whispered, 'I'll see you next week.'

'Write to me before then. I enjoyed gettin' yer letter – it made the week seem shorter.'

Ada nodded. 'I'll get Polly to put a note in with it. Joey isn't up to writing yet, but he can sign his name on Polly's, that'll please him no end.'

Tommy reached out to take her hand. 'I love you, Ada, more than yer'll ever know.'

'And I love you so much, sweetheart, if I said it a million times over it wouldn't be enough. And the children idolise yer, so you just hurry up an' get better so we can have yer at home with us.'

Once in the corridor, Ada hastened to the Matron's office. There was no reply to her knock so she paced up and down outside until a passing nurse said she'd try to find Matron for her.

'Yes, Mrs Perkins?' Matron approached, short and stocky with dark hair, her walk brisk and efficient.

Ada cleared her throat. 'It's about me husband, Matron. He doesn't look well today.'

'Come into the office.' When they were both seated, the usually stern face showed signs of sympathy. 'Your husband isn't well, Mrs Perkins. He has deteriorated within the last few days. The doctors are baffled because he was responding to treatment and there seems no reason for the setback. It's not unusual for a patient to have a short relapse, then recover and respond once again to treatment. We are hoping this will happen in your husband's case. So there's no cause for concern at the moment and he certainly isn't in any immediate danger. But if you are worried, and it would put your mind at rest, then I suggest you ring the ward each day and speak to Sister.'

'Yes, I'll do that.' Ada stood up. 'Thank you, Matron.'

'We would certainly notify you of any major change in your husband's condition – that is normal hospital procedure.'

'I understand, thank you.'

Weary in mind and body, Ada walked slowly to the tram stop. She wouldn't say anything to the children; it was no use upsetting them. Better to wait a week and see if Tommy's condition changed. She sighed as she boarded the tram, asking herself what her husband had ever done to deserve this. And on the long journey home she prayed that God would listen to her prayers to make him better.

At half-past eight the next morning, Polly stepped into the street clutching the old battered suitcase of Dolly's. Inside the case were three changes of clothing . . . socks, knickers, vests and dresses. She was wearing the only coat she possessed and the only pair of shoes. Ada had managed to find a small handbag on a second-hand stall at Paddy's market, and inside was a comb, a handkerchief and a shilling piece.

'Well, that's it, Mam.' Polly was smiling but her quivering lips told of her inner fears. 'I'll be home the first chance I get.' She bent to gaze into Joey's face. 'You be a good boy for yer mam, d'yer hear?'

Joey's face crumbled. 'Don't go, our Polly! I don't want yer to go.'

Ada put her hand on his shoulder. 'Come on now, sunshine, big boys don't cry. Give Polly a nice kiss and tell her she's got to come an' see yer soon.'

Polly put the case down and held him in her arms. 'I promise I'll see yer in the next three days.' Thinking of the shilling in the handbag she made another promise. 'An' I'll bring yer some sweets.'

'Come on, Polly, you don't want to be late on yer first morning.' Ada gave her daughter a quick kiss, eager for the girl to be gone before the tears started. 'An' don't forget what I've told yer. No one is any better than you so don't let them treat yer like a skivvy. They may have more money than you an' they may speak posh, but God made us all, we are all equal in His eyes. So while I'd expect yer to be polite and respectful, an' do yer job properly, just remember you're as good as any of them. An' please, if yer get a spare half-hour, let us know how yer gettin' on. I'm working days now, an' it's only a stone's throw to Faulkner Square.'

'I'll try, but I'll have to see what me jobs are first, get used to the routine.' Polly picked up the case and said, 'I love yer, Mam, and you too, our Joey.' With that she walked quickly away, her back straight and her head held high.

Ada watched until Polly turned the corner at the top of the street, then she took Joey's hand and led him indoors. 'Come on, sunshine, it's time for school.'

Polly's heart was pounding as she rang the bell. It took sheer willpower not to turn around and run away. And when the maid, Lucy, opened the door with a surly expression on her face the urge to flee became greater. It was her mother's parting words that forced her feet to take her into the hall and keep the smile on her face. She was as good as anyone and she wasn't going to let them get her down. 'Good morning, Lucy.'

There was no polite greeting in reply. 'You're to go to the kitchen and take your orders from Mrs Nightingale.'

Oh well, Polly thought, shrugging her shoulders, if that's the way she wants it that's the way she can have it. She made her way to the back of the house and when she entered the kitchen and found Mr Denholme there, her spirits lifted. 'Good morning, Mr Denholme.' Polly gave him a beaming smile. 'Good morning, Mrs Nightingale.'

Whether it was the presence of her employer, Polly would never know, but the cook managed a brief smile and an even briefer, 'Morning.'

'Polly, my dear.' Charles's pleasure at seeing her was

genuine. 'Welcome to the Denholme household. Here, give me the case and I'll have Lucy take it up to your room.'

But Polly held on to the battered suitcase. She was supposed to be a junior maid, Lucy wouldn't be very happy at having to wait on her. 'No, I'll take it up, Mr Denholme.'

Mrs Nightingale was bristling. 'Lucy's busy serving breakfast, Mr Denholme. She can't be spared at the moment.'

Polly's eyes and the cook's tone of voice weren't lost on Charles. He warned himself to be careful not to put the girl in a position where she was out of favour with those she had to work with. 'We'll leave the case here, then, Polly, and you can take it up when Cook has told you what your duties are. I have already explained to Mrs Nightingale that today is not a normal day, and that tomorrow you will be at her disposal from seven-thirty until ten o'clock when the children begin their lessons. So now that I have seen you arrive safely, I'll leave you in the capable hands of Mrs Nightingale, who I am sure will advise and help you. I will be going into the office until lunch-time, but if you have any problems, my wife will be here to listen to them.'

'Thank you, Mr Denholme.' Polly watched him leave with dismay. She was aware from Lucy's lack of welcome and Mrs Nightingale's cold response that she wasn't wanted. Why, she didn't know. She'd done nothing to upset them, so why had they taken a dislike to her?

'Come along, Perkins, don't stand there looking gormless.' The cook pointed to the end of the long kitchen table. 'There's yer overall, put it on an' start on those dishes in the sink. Lucy will be bringing more through as the family finish their breakfast.'

Polly put the overall on and rolled up her sleeves. Her mam had told her to be polite, but the cook wasn't polite. She hadn't asked her to do the dishes, she'd ordered her to. And a smile wouldn't go amiss, either!

She was up to her elbows in soapsuds when an arm came around the side of her and dropped a stack of plates into the sink, causing the water to splash all over Polly's clothes. She turned quickly, intending to ask the person responsible why she couldn't have left the plates at the side instead of throwing them in the water, but Lucy's raised eyebrows and look of hostility was daring her to complain. It was almost as though she wanted her to lose her temper. So biting on her bottom lip and rubbing the back of her hand across her chin where the suds had landed, Polly turned her back on the maid, deciding she wouldn't give her the satisfaction. If she walked out now she'd be giving in to them. And she'd have to face the questions that would be asked of her from her family and friends, and the teachers at school. They'd think she was a failure, not up to doing the job. So with tears stinging the back of her eyes, she worked hard to keep up with the mounds of dishes that kept appearing.

It was a quarter to ten when Victoria Denholme walked into the kitchen and took the cook and maid by surprise. The only time their mistress appeared was at about four o'clock each afternoon to discuss the following day's menu. They weren't expecting her now as they sat at the long, scrubbed white table, drinking tea, eating toast and enjoying a light-hearted conversation while Polly stood at the sink finishing off the pans and cutlery. She had her back to the door and didn't realise Mrs Denholme was in the room until she heard her speak.

'Mrs Nightingale, has Polly had a drink and something to eat?' Victoria's face was stern. She could tell at a glance that the girl had not been included in the conversation and in all probability hadn't even been asked if she would like a drink.

'No, Mrs Denholme.' The cook looked shamefaced. 'I was waiting for her to finish the dishes then I was going to make her some fresh toast.'

'Really, Cook, you do surprise me – and I have to say I'm disappointed. You were well aware that Polly's due in the study at ten o'clock. Now please make her something to eat while she goes to her room to freshen up. And from now on it is up to you to see she is never late for the first lesson of the day. Do I make myself clear?'

'Yes, Mrs Denholme.' The cook glanced over to where Polly was watching and listening. 'Go to your room, Perkins, and get washed and comb yer hair.'

Polly smiled at Mrs Denholme on her way out. It was a smile of gratitude. Victoria waited until she was out of earshot before looking first at the cook, then the maid. 'Her name is Polly and that is how I would like you to address her, do you understand?'

When their mistress had left, the cook turned on Lucy. 'If we're not careful we could end up losing our jobs. Mr Charles is taken with the girl, and from the sound of things, so is the mistress. I've no intention of being turfed out on the street, Miss Rebecca or no Miss Rebecca. So in future I'm goin' to treat Polly as I treat you. After all, the girl's done me no harm.'

'But you know what Miss Rebecca said,' Lucy cried. 'And yer know how wicked she can be.'

'Oh, I know how wicked she can be all right! I'll never forget what she did to the maid we had before you. Got poor Rose the sack, that's what the little faggot did.'

'I know,' wailed Lucy, 'an' she told me she'll get *me* the sack if I don't do as she says.'

'You can please yerself,' grunted Mrs Nightingale. 'Me, I'm goin' to do as I'm told by them what pays me wages, not what snooty Miss Rebecca tells me. If you've got any sense yer'll do the same. Get out of that young madam's clutches before it's too late and yer find yerself on the street lookin' for work.'

Justin was already behind his desk and Polly blushed with a mixture of embarrassment and pleasure when he smiled and raised his hand in greeting. 'Good morning, Polly.'

'Good mornin', Master Justin. Good mornin', Mr Westly.'

'And good morning to you, Polly.' The tutor gave her a

warm smile. 'Did you manage to do the essay? It would help me understand what stage your education has reached.'

Polly produced a book from behind her back. 'I've written a story about me friends. I hope it's what you want.'

'I'll check while you're doing the lesson I've set for today, which is a question and answer one on geography. You did say you were quite good at geography, did you not?'

Polly grinned, feeling that in this room she was amongst friends. 'Well, I know New Brighton's over the water, Mr Westly.'

He chuckled. 'That's as good a place to start as any.'

Justin too was amused. 'Jolly good answer, Polly. I must remember to tell Father, he does so enjoy a joke.'

Mr Westly took the cheap penny exercise book and as he placed it in front of him he nodded to the extra desk that had been placed on the left of Justin, which meant he would be sitting between Polly and his sister. 'That's your desk and you'll find everything you need inside. Master Justin will help you.'

Polly's bright smile flashed again. 'I'll just watch what he does an' copy him.'

'Don't copy my answers,' Justin said. 'I'm a real dunce.'

'In that case you'd better copy me.'

Polly's remark had them laughing and it was at that moment Rebecca barged into the room. She was in a filthy temper because her mother had refused to buy her a new party dress, and walking in on the happy scene added fuel to her anger. She gave each of them a withering look before crashing down on the chair behind her desk. 'Close the door, Perkins.'

Mr Westly shook his head in dismay, Justin gasped, and Polly froze. They could sack her on the spot, do anything they liked, but there was no way she was going to be spoken to like that.

'I said, close the door, Perkins.' The words came through teeth clenched with rage. 'Are you deaf?'

'No, I'm not deaf. I heard you all right, but I have no intention of closing the door. You were last through it, you close it.'

'I should jolly well think so!' Justin, for the first time in his life, was ashamed of his sister. He'd put up with her tantrums over the years because it seemed the easiest thing to do. But she really had gone too far this time. 'Good for you, Polly!'

'She's a servant.' Rebecca had quite a pretty face, but right now it was marred by the look of insolence. 'She gets paid to do as she's told.'

'Not while she's in this room, Miss Rebecca.' Tom Westly dared to speak out because he knew Justin would back him if the girl went running to her father with the lies that came so readily to her lips. 'Polly is a pupil, just as you are.'

'How dare you put a common flower-seller on a level with me! Apologise right now or I shall tell Father the minute he comes in.'

'There's no need to wait for Father,' Justin drawled, deciding he'd had enough of his sister's bad temper and equally bad manners. 'I'll go and fetch Mother.'

'Don't bother, Master Justin.' Polly pushed herself up from her chair. 'I'll close the door, but it'll be on me way out. I don't have to put up with the likes of your sister. My mam told me to be well-mannered and polite, but our neighbour's cat's got more manners than Miss Rebecca. And,' she added defiantly, 'it's nicer-looking.'

Tom Westly was enjoying himself more than he ever had in the eight years he'd worked with the Denholmes. What a pity it would be if young Polly walked through the door and never came back. He wasn't in a position to do anything about it, but the young master was. 'Master Justin, I think perhaps you should go for your mother. I believe Miss Rebecca owes Polly an apology.'

Justin was halfway across the room when his sister pushed past him and banged the door shut. She knew she'd gone too far and didn't relish a tongue-lashing from her parents. 'For heaven's sake, all this fuss over closing a stupid door! Now, can we get on with our lessons? This is supposed to be a classroom.'

Knowing this was the nearest to an apology they were likely to get, Justin touched Polly's arm. His eyes were kind, sympathetic and bright with suppressed humour. 'Sit down, Polly, please. I'd say the match was a draw, wouldn't you?'

Polly couldn't help but smile as she mouthed, 'I'll do better next time.'

If Ada had known the problems her daughter was having, it would have been another burden to add to her worry over Tommy. She couldn't get him out of her mind. When it got to one o'clock she could bear it no longer. 'John, can I ask yer a big favour?'

'My dear Ada, of course you can.' He studied her face. 'I have noticed you've been very quiet today, but I put it down to your being upset over Polly. Is something else bothering you?'

'It's Tommy. He wasn't a bit well yesterday and when I asked the Matron she said he'd had a relapse. I was wonderin' if yer'd ring the hospital for me an' see how he is?'

'Shall I get the number and you can speak to them yourself?'

Ada shook her head. 'I'm no good on the telephone, I wouldn't know what to say. And I'm a coward, too, I'd be frightened of gettin' bad news.'

'The news won't be any different if I ring, my love, but you poppy off to the kitchen and I'll get through to them.'

Ada was spooning carrots into a vegetable dish when he came into the kitchen. 'His condition is still the same.'

'Is that all they said?'

'Ada, hospitals are renowned for not giving information over the phone. But had Tommy's condition worsened, they would have said so. If you're concerned I'll ring again later, just before you go home.'

'No, John, that won't be necessary. As you said, if he'd got any worse they would have told yer. But would yer mind ringing again temorrer for me? I am worried about him.'

'I'll ring every hour if it will ease your mind.' John ran a finger down her cheek in a soft caress. 'If I could I would take all your cares and worries away. You know that, don't you, my darling? You know what my feelings are for you, how deep they are.'

Ada took his hand and pressed it to her face. 'What I do know, John, is that I couldn't have managed the last year without your kindness and affection. I would have been the loneliest woman in the world.'

Chapter Twenty

'Yer look worn out, girl! Here, sit yerself down.' Dolly moved a newspaper off the couch and pressed on her neighbour's arm. 'Take the weight off yer feet for a few minutes.'

Ada's sigh told of the weariness she felt. 'I could do with goin' to bed and not gettin' up for a month.'

'I don't know how yer've kept up.' Dolly pulled a chair from the table and turned it to face her friend. 'Yer've certainly had yer bellyful of worry the last six months. It's a wonder yer haven't had a nervous breakdown. Me an' Les were sayin' that only last night.'

'I haven't had time to have a nervous breakdown, Dolly. What with goin' out to work, tryin' to get to the hospital a few times a week, and me housework and shopping on top, it's been a nightmare!'

'But Tommy's on the mend now, isn't he? That should make yer feel a bit easier in yer mind.'

'The doctor said he's slowly beginning to respond, but to me he doesn't look any different. And it's getting on for two years, Dolly – two long years. But if I'm tired and fed up, can yer imagine how Tommy feels? It's enough to drive him mad, lying in that place not knowing how long he's in for, or even if he's ever goin' to get better. He's got to the state where he's lost interest in everything except me and the kids. At one time he used to talk about comin' home and gettin' a job, but he never mentions it now.'

'Wait until he picks up a bit more, then he'll come on in leaps and bounds, you'll see.'

'I could cope better if I wasn't so blinkin' tired all the time.' Ada smothered a yawn. 'I never realised how much I relied on our Polly until she'd gone. They say yer never appreciate what yer've got until yer lose it, and it's true, both in Tommy's case and our Polly's.'

'She's settled in all right, hasn't she? An' I'll tell yer what, they don't half dress her well. That coat she 'ad on the other night when she came to see our Steve must have set them back a pretty penny – real velour it was.'

'Yes, they're good to her, no doubt about that. An' she gets on well with them all, except the daughter – she can't stand her. But I'll say one thing about our Polly, she's got her feet firmly on the ground. She won't let them change her.' Ada's expression was proud. 'She still wears her old coat when she goes down to help Sarah Jane. I thought Mr Denholme would put a stop to that, but no, when she has a few hours off she comes to see me for ten minutes then she's down to Bold Street to give her adopted grandma a helping hand.'

'There's nowt like seeing life from both sides, girl, it'll stand her in good stead when she gets older.' The wooden chair creaked in protest when Dolly leaned her weight back on it. 'I'll 'ave to go down and meet this Sarah Jane one day, see what she's got that I haven't. Our Steve thinks the world of her, goes down on a Saturday straight from work come hail, rain or snow. Yer should see the bleedin' face he pulls if I ask him to do a job, but he'd do anythin' for her.'

'She is a love,' Ada said. 'A real colourful Liverpool character – got an answer and a joke for everything. But I don't think Sarah Jane is the main attraction. Steve knows our Polly will get down there if she possibly can.'

'Aye, they've never wavered in their friendship, those two. She didn't forget his birthday last week, sent him a nice card. An' he's savin' up to take her to the pictures the week after next, on her fourteenth birthday. I told him he's got to ask you first, so when he does, don't let on I've said anything, pretend to be surprised.' Dolly pursed her lips and nodded her head. 'I'm beginning to think there's a good chance of me becomin' Polly's ma-in-law one of these fine days.'

Ada lifted her hands in mock horror. 'Heaven forbid that that should happen to a daughter of mine. A fate worse than death.'

'Don't get bleedin' cocky, Ada Perkins, or I'll biff yer one! Anyway, how come yer home this time of the day?'

'Mr John said I looked terrible and made me leave early, with strict instructions to go to bed the same time as Joey.'

'He's a good boss to have, that feller. Yer certainly landed on yer feet with him.'

'He's the nicest man I've ever met, Dolly, and that's the truth. I'd have been in Queer Street without him.'

Dolly was smiling but her eyes sent out the signal that her question was serious. 'Nicer than Tommy?'

'I wasn't counting Tommy, he's me husband and I love him. But that doesn't mean I can't see Mr John for the kind man he is, does it?'

'No, it doesn't, girl, as long as yer don't forget yer've got a husband.'

'I'll never do that,' Ada said. 'Not in a million years.'

Ada was thinking of her husband as she ran the iron over one of John's shirts. Her worries about him hadn't lessened, because as far as she could see he wasn't improving at all. And after two years, surely to God if he was going to get better there would be signs of it by now, but she couldn't see any light at the end of the tunnel.

She was so deep in thought she didn't hear John come up behind her, and when he touched her cheek she nearly dropped the iron. 'Yer gave me the fright of me life!'

'You were miles away, in a little world of your own.' He cupped her chin and gazed into her eyes. 'If you have any worries, my love, I wish you'd share them with me.'

'I was thinking about Tommy.' Ada turned her head and went back to her ironing. 'I can't understand it. He never talks about coming home now, doesn't seem to have any will to live.'

John caught a movement out of the corner of his eye and turned to see Polly standing inside the door. How long she'd been there he didn't know, but there was a strange look on her face. 'Hello, Polly, come on in, don't stand at the door.'

Ada looked up with a smile. 'Hello, sunshine.' She shook the shirt before folding it neatly and hanging it on the clothes maiden. 'I'm glad to see yer.'

There was no answering smile on Polly's face as she stepped further into the room. 'Isn't me dad goin' to get better?'

'Yes, of course he is!' Ada glanced nervously at John, wondering how much her daughter had heard, but she could read nothing from his face. 'Fancy askin' a question like that.'

'Yer telling me lies, Mam.' Polly was near to tears. 'I've just heard yer telling Mr John he doesn't want to get better.'

'No, love, you misunderstood. I said he's taking a long time to get better, that's all.'

'You didn't, you didn't! I heard what yer said! You've never lied to me before, Mam, but yer lying now.' With that Polly took to her heels and fled, leaving Ada with a look of despair on her face.

'What have I done? She'll never speak to me again.'

'You did nothing wrong, Ada. All you did was try to spare your daughter's feelings – something any mother would do.' He gave her shoulder a squeeze before making for the door. 'I'll give Charles a ring and explain what happened because she's bound to be upset.'

Polly kept on running until she could run no more. Her eyes blurred with tears, her mind screaming, she had no idea where she was until she stopped to catch her breath and found herself at the top of Bold Street. At the bottom she would find Sarah Jane and Auntie Mary, who she knew would welcome her with open arms. The need of comfort from people she loved was overwhelming, and after rubbing her hands across her eyes, she began to walk. But she had only taken a few steps when she asked herself how she could explain her tears without telling them her mam had lied to her. And she couldn't do that, not to her mam.

Pretending to be looking at the display of glass and china in a shop window, Polly tried to sort out all the questions that were going around in her head. Was her dad going to die? Was she never going to see him again? The thought was too horrible to contemplate and she felt like screaming. And why did her mam say she'd misunderstood when she knew what she'd heard? She was old enough to be told the truth; she had more right than Mr John, who didn't even know her dad!

Then Polly allowed another thought to surface. What was Mr John doing in the kitchen while her mam was ironing? Why wasn't he in his office, working? And there was something about the way they were standing, not like worker and boss. They seemed on very friendly terms – in fact, a stranger would be forgiven for thinking they were man and wife.

Polly shook her head, watching her reflection in the shop window. No, she mustn't think things like that, she was just being bad-minded. Her mam loved her dad, she wouldn't do anything to hurt him. And Mr John was a nice man, he was probably just being kind in asking how her dad was getting on. But that didn't alter the fact that she'd heard her mam say he wasn't going to get better and then she'd denied she'd said it. I know what I heard, Polly thought, going over the scene in her mind. I'd just reached the door when I heard me mam's voice saying, 'He doesn't talk about coming home any more. He doesn't seem to have the will to live.'

Polly gasped as the words came over as clearly as if she was hearing them now. Oh, me mam was right, I *did* misunderstand. I called her a liar and it was me that was wrong!

She turned from the shop, and with her head bent she walked slowly in the direction of Percy Street. She'd go to her own room where it was quiet and she could sort out the jumble that was in her head. Tomorrow she'd try and get some time off to go and tell her mam she was sorry. And she was sorry because she loved her mam very much.

Polly went in the back way hoping to escape to her room without being seen. But Mrs Nightingale was hanging a tablecloth on the line and pounced as soon as she saw the girl. 'Mr Charles has been waitin' for yer. He said I was to send yer to the drawing room the minute yer came in.'

'But it's me two hours off! I've still got an hour to go.'

'Polly, do as yer told, there's a good girl.'

Charles and his wife were waiting for her. And it was Victoria who crossed the room to take the hand of the girl she'd grown fond of. 'Polly, my dear, we've been quite concerned about you, haven't we, Charles?'

'We have indeed.' Charles leaned forward and rested his elbows on his knees. 'Mr Roscoe rang to say there had been a misunderstanding and you had fled in a tearful state before anyone could stop you.'

'It was my fault, Mr Charles. I got it all wrong and was horrid to me mam.'

Charles waved her to a chair. 'Sit down, my dear, and tell us exactly what happened.'

With the telling came the tears. 'I never should have said what I did to me mam 'cos she's the best mam in the world and I love her very much. She's had to work very hard to keep me and our Joey since me dad went in hospital.' Polly gave a grateful nod to Victoria as she took the handkerchief held out to her. 'But yer see, Mr Charles, I was all mixed up! Why doesn't me dad ever talk about coming home any more? And why hasn't he got the will to live? That means he wants to die, doesn't it?'

Sobs were shaking her body now and Victoria sat beside her and put a protective arm across her shoulders. 'There now, my dear, don't take on so or you'll make yourself ill.'

'But he musn't love us any more! If he loved us he wouldn't want to die, would he?'

Charles rubbed his forehead and sought the words to take the pain from the young girl. 'Wipe your eyes, Polly my dear, and blow your nose. Then I'll tell you something which will make you feel better.'

Polly was puzzled but did as she was told. 'What is it, Mr Charles?'

'I rang the hospital while we were waiting for you and I managed to get hold of one of the doctors. Your father's condition is stable, my dear, which means he's holding his own. He isn't making the recovery they'd hoped for, but he certainly isn't at death's door, which is what you seem to think. So now you have the truth, right from the doctor.'

'But why didn't me mam say? Why does she keep telling me an' Joey that he'll be home soon when she knows he won't?'

'Because she loves you too much to ask you to share the burden she's been carrying for so long. She's been protecting you, Polly, you and your brother. She didn't want to hurt you.'

Polly rocked back and forth, her cries pitiful. 'And I called her a liar, Mr Charles. She won't love me no more.'

'It would take more than that to destroy the love she has for you. But she is very upset, according to Mr Roscoe – not for herself, but for you.'

Polly sprang up from the chair. 'I want to go to her! She often says you should never go to bed on a quarrel 'cos yer don't know what's going to happen and yer might never get the chance to say yer sorry. So can I go and tell her I'm sorry, please, Mr Charles? I'll run all the way there and back so I'll be here to help Cook with the tea.'

'I'm not the one to ask, Polly, my wife deals with the staff.'

'Oh, please, Mrs Denholme, say I can go.'

'Of course you can. You mustn't let the day go by without

making it up with your mother.' Victoria reached out a hand to smooth the dark curly hair. 'And you must spend some time with her, don't rush back. I am quite capable of pouring tea and passing cakes around.'

In an impulsive gesture, Polly wrapped her arms around Victoria and gave her a big hug. 'Oh thank you! You an' Mr Charles are so good to me . . . like another mam and dad.'

When she'd left, Charles caught his wife wiping a tear from her eye. 'She has that effect on me, too, my darling, but as Polly would say, only cissies cry.'

Now she'd been caught out, Victoria let the tears flow. 'She said we were like another mam and dad, wasn't that sweet? And d'you know something, Charles, I wish she *was* our daughter. I can't remember a time when Justin or Rebecca gave me a hug like Polly just did.'

'Our children are what we made them, Victoria. Because of the difference in lifestyles, we didn't do for our children what the likes of Polly's mother did for her. From the day ours were born, they've had a nanny to do everything for them, change their nappies, take them for walks in the pram, dress and feed them and put them to bed. Those are the things that bind a child to its parents and unfortunately, it's too late for us to change. But we can't blame Justin and Rebecca, we can blame ourselves.' A twinkle came into Charles's eyes. 'I'd prefer to be called Dad instead of Father, which sounds so stiff. But I rather think you'd draw the line at being called Mam.'

'It would certainly startle our friends, but I've thought about it many times since Polly came to us. Mother is just a word to describe the person who gave birth to you, whereas Mam sounds as though you love the person who gave birth to you.'

'There are quite a few people in this house who will be sorry when the time comes for Polly to leave us. Mrs Nightingale actually sings when she's working now, and to my amazement Mr Westly has developed a sense of humour.

Mind you, he probably had it all along but has never had any occasion to show it.'

'Polly's not leaving, is she?' Victoria looked shaken. 'I thought she was staying with us.'

'She'll have to leave one day, darling, she has a family who love and miss her. I must say her mother has been a brick letting her come at a time when she could have done with her help. To put the child's needs before her own is a sign of how much she loves her.'

'I'd miss her if she left,' Victoria said, 'and so would Justin. He gets on famously with her, and she's been so good for him.'

'Yes, but unfortunately the same can't be said of Rebecca. I was hoping they'd become friends, but our daughter hasn't warmed to Polly at all. Still, my darling, there is still time.' Charles held out his hand. 'Come and sit on my knee and give me a kiss. Let's be daring.'

'Don't be childish, Charles.' But even as she was speaking, Victoria was nestling down on his lap. 'What if one of the servants come in?'

Charles chuckled. 'D'you remember me telling you about Agnes – she worked for John and his parents for about forty years? Well, John told us about a favourite saying of hers. It goes something like this: "Sod off! Yer nothin' but a bleedin' nuisance". So that's what I'll say to any person who walks through the door and spoils the kiss you are about to give me.'

'Charles, really! I don't know what's come over you.'

'Freedom, my lovely Victoria. The Pollys and Agneses of this world don't have the wealth we do, but they have a damn sight more fun. Now kiss me, you wanton wench!'

Rebecca stood with her ear pressed against the door, listening to every word. The praise being heaped upon Polly cut her like a knife. Fancy her mother saying she'd like a common flower-seller for a daughter! Well, she had no intention of ever being a sister to Polly Perkins! In fact, she'd have been long gone if the staff had done as they were told. They'd be made to pay for their lack of obedience, but there was time for that. Her first priority was to get rid of Polly. And it had to be done in such a way that the girl left in disgrace . . .

'What are you doing there, Miss Rebecca?' Mrs Nightingale's face was grim. She was beginning to dislike this young madam for all the trouble she caused. She complained about everything under the sun. The toast was too well done, the tea was cold, her bathwater wasn't hot enough. It was a pity she wasn't old enough to get married, they'd be well rid of her. Mind you, heaven help the poor man who got her; she'd have him in an early grave with all her moaning and groaning. 'Eavesdropping, are yer?'

'What business is it of yours, might I ask?' Rebecca's eyes were cold as steel. 'Have you no work to do?'

Mrs Nightingale decided to tell a lie. You could only take so much impudence from a chit of a girl, and she'd taken enough. 'I do have work to do, but I need to discuss it with Mrs Denholme first.'

Rebecca waved a hand as though in dismissal. 'They're busy, you can come back later.'

'No, I can't do my work without your mother's approval so I'll wait here with you.'

Rebecca glared. 'In that case, *I'll* come back later.'

'Shall I tell your mother you wish to see her?' Mrs Nightingale asked, her voice heavy with sarcasm.

'Don't bother, I'll see her later.'

My God, the cook thought, I've never known such wickedness in one so young. I'd be doing myself a favour if I kept out of her way. Now, what was I after before spotting Miss Rebecca up to her tricks? Oh yes, the duster I left on the table earlier.

Polly walked straight into her mother's arms. 'Oh Mam, I'm sorry, I'm sorry, I'm sorry!'

'There now.' Ada held her close. 'It was a storm in a teacup, sunshine, so let's forget it.'

'Mr Charles rang the hospital, Mam, an' the doctor said me dad's stable. That's a good sign, isn't it?'

'Yes, sunshine, that's a good sign.' Over her daughter's shoulder, Ada met John's eyes. She smiled and gave a slight nod. 'One of these days I'll go in the ward an' he'll be sittin' up and smiling. Then we'll know he's on the road to recovery.'

'It's been a long time, Mam, an' I still miss him as much as ever.'

'It's been the longest two years of me life, sunshine, but please God, it will turn out right in the end.'

John coughed. 'Why don't you go in the drawing room?' he suggested. 'It's more comfortable and you and Polly can have a good talk.'

'I think Polly should be at work.' Ada held her at arm's-length. 'Am I right?'

'Mrs Denholme told me not to hurry back, to stay and have a nice long talk with yer. They've been ever so good to me, Mam.'

'All the more reason why you shouldn't stay too long. Never take advantage of a person's kindness, sunshine, just remember that.'

'She can stay long enough for you to tell her what you've planned for next week, on her birthday.' John led the way into the drawing room. 'I'll leave you two together.'

'No, Mr John, you stay,' Ada said. 'After all, it was your idea.'

'Mam, I'm going to the pictures with Steve on me birthday. I promised him ages ago.'

'I know, he came and asked my permission to take you.'

Polly gasped. 'He didn't!'

'He most certainly did, like a proper gentleman.'

Polly giggled. 'I bet he went the colour of beetroot – he doesn't half blush easy. What did you say to him, Mam?'

289

'I asked him to consider takin' me instead, but he wasn't having any. So I had to agree to him taking you. Anyway, that's his birthday present to you. Now what about mine?'

'You don't need to buy me a present, Mam, just give me a card. That's enough, honest it is.'

'I don't think yer'll turn it down when yer know what it is, sunshine. I think yer'll be over the moon.'

Polly's face came alive with excitement. 'Go on, Mam, tell us!'

'Mr John said I can throw a party for yer here on the Sunday. You can invite all yer friends . . . Steve, Sarah Jane, Irish Mary, Auntie Dolly, and of course our Joey. And if yer don't mind, I'd like to invite Aggie and Fanny. You wouldn't mind that, would you, love?'

Polly's mouth gaped. 'Oh, Mam!'

'Yer can thank Mr John for letting us have the use of his flat. It would be no use tryin' to get them all in our house, it's too small.'

When Polly ran to throw her arms around him, John was so filled with emotion, he closed his eyes. 'Oh, thank you, Mr John. That's a lovely birthday present.'

'There's a condition attached.' John's hand hovered over her head. He wanted so much to touch her but was afraid of getting too close. 'You can have the use of my flat if I am invited as a guest.'

'Oh yes, you can be the guest of honour.' Polly was delirious with happiness. 'Can I ask Mr Charles and Mrs Denholme?'

Ada pulled a face. 'Oh, I don't think so, sunshine. I don't think they would appreciate Aggie's and Fanny's interpretation of the English language. Yer know what they're like for swearing, and I wouldn't like to have to put a gag in their mouths.'

'Why don't we let Charles and Victoria decide?' John was now grinning from ear to ear. 'I'll put it to them straight and let them make up their own minds. I've got a feeling they would find it hilarious. I know for certain that Charles would.'

'Yer will tell them about the swearin', won't yer?' Polly was now having misgivings. She loved her friends dearly and would never be ashamed of them, but she had her doubts about Mrs Denholme. 'I mean, yer will tell them out loud what they say?'

'Every bleedin' word,' John said, sending them into gales of laughter.

Chapter Twenty-One

There was a spring in John Roscoe's step as he walked briskly along the hall. It had been a fruitful morning and he was feeling particularly pleased with himself as he bounded up the stairs. He waited until he reached the top landing before allowing the smile of well-being to spread across his face. 'Ada?' He hung his bowler hat on one of the curved branches of the highly polished mahogany hallstand. 'Where are you?'

'In the bedroom!' Ada was changing pillowcases when he entered the room. 'I've nearly finished in here, then I'll see to your lunch.'

John gazed at the woman who had brought him more happiness in the last twelve months than he'd ever known. Her very presence filled his heart with contentment and set his mind at rest. He walked over to the bed and with a smile that was both sad and gentle, picked a feather from her hair. He held it in front of her nose. 'You're sprouting feathers, my darling.'

'As long as it's only feathers I'm sprouting, and not horns, I don't think I need worry.'

'Look, leave things as they are and come in the drawing room. I have something to tell you.'

'Can't it wait? You know I have a routine, John, an' I like to stick to it. If I get here finished, I can serve you yer dinner then spend an hour on the ironing before cleaning the kitchen.'

When Ada went to pick up another pillow to change, John took it out of her hand and threw it on the bed. 'Will the world collapse if you don't do the ironing until tomorrow? And will I die of starvation if I have to wait half an hour for my dinner? No, my love, those things are not important. What I have to tell you is something that I think will please you enormously.'

As Ada allowed herself to be led out of the room by the hand, she still protested. 'You know I won't leave until all me work is done an' I don't want to be late gettin' home on account of Joey.'

'You really are the most stubborn woman, Ada. You know I wouldn't care if the dirt was meeting me at the door.'

'I would, 'cos I get paid to keep it clean. We've been through this a dozen times, John, and yer know how I feel. I will not take your money unless I earn it.'

'All right, my darling, have it your own way.' John sat on the couch and pulled her down beside him, keeping her hand fast in his. 'Now, don't you want to know about my very successful morning?'

There was fondness in Ada's smile. 'You look like a little boy who's been given a present. So out with it before you burst.'

'First things first, eh? Charles and Victoria are delighted with the invitation to Polly's party and accept with pleasure. What is more, Justin insists that as he's a friend of the birthday girl, he too should be invited.'

'Oh dear!' Ada anchored a wayward strand of hair behind her ear. 'I don't think that's a very good idea at all. I'd be worried stiff every time me friends opened their mouths! I know Justin's a bit older than Steve and Polly, but they're used to bad language, and he's not.' A look of defiance crossed her face. 'If he comes he'll just have to put up with it 'cos I'm not ashamed of me friends an' I'm not goin' to spoil the party for them by asking them to mind what they say. If the Denholmes don't like it, I'm afraid it's just too bad.'

'Ada, my love, don't start worrying about something that may never happen. I'm sure the party will be a huge success and everyone will have a whale of a time.'

'I wish I could share your optimism, John, but as I can't I'll just spend the next few days worrying meself sick. You don't know what Dolly Mitchell's like when she's had a few drinks down her. She doesn't care what she says or who she says it in front of. She's me best mate, I'm very fond of her and think she's hilarious. But then I'm used to her an' a bit of bad language doesn't upset me.'

John put an arm around her waist and drew her close. 'Then the Denholmes are in for a lesson on what life is all about, and I'm quite sure it's a lesson they'll have fun learning.'

Ada sighed. 'I just hope yer right. Now, can I get back to me work or is there something else yer have to tell me?'

John nodded. 'Sit back and relax, my love, and enjoy what I have to say. I've been to Coopers and ordered everything for the party. It will be delivered on Saturday afternoon. And I've been to see Agnes to ask if she'll come on Sunday afternoon and give Fanny a hand to set the table.'

Ada gasped. 'Yer had no need to do that! I can see to the table meself, I don't need any help. Oh, fancy you doin' that, John! Agnes and Fanny have been invited as guests – I can't expect them to help with the work.'

'They won't be just helping, my love, they'll be doing it. You see, you won't be here.'

Ada pulled her hand free. 'Why won't I be here? It's me daughter's party so of course I'll be here!'

John took both of her hands and held them tight. 'You won't be here, my lovely Ada, because you'll be giving Polly the best birthday present you could ever give her.' When her deep brown eyes widened as they gazed at him, John couldn't resist the temptation to lean forward and kiss her cheek. 'I got the name of Tommy's doctor off Charles, and I rang and spoke to him. He was very understanding and has agreed that Polly can go in and see her father for a short visit on Sunday.'

'Oh, my God!' Ada's face drained of colour. 'Oh John, are

you sure? They told me they don't allow children in the isolation wards.'

'They don't normally, but this is a special dispensation. Tommy will be moved out of the ward into a side room for the visit. I will drive you both there and wait outside for you.'

Ada closed her eyes as she tried to come to grips with what John had told her. He was right, it was the best present Polly could ever have. She could see her daughter's face now, alive with excitement when she heard the news. After two years she was going to see her father again; she'd be able to talk to him and touch him. It was too much for Ada and with a cry, she turned to John and put her arms around his neck, seeking the comfort only he could give her.

'What can I say to you, John? You've been so good to me since the day we met. In fact, I don't know how I'd have managed without you. But what you've done today is something I'll never forget – and I'll love yer for it for the rest of me life.'

John held her away from him and gazed into her eyes. 'I'll never ask for more than you want to give, my lovely, darling Ada, but would you accept a kiss from a man who deeply cares for you?'

'Oh yes, John!' Ada closed her eyes and when she felt his lips cover hers, she wound her arms around his neck and returned his kiss with feeling. She was confused, not thinking straight. All she knew was that this man could give her the strength and the comfort she needed. And all he asked for in return was a kiss. She could hear his heart beating as he held her close, and when his kiss became hard with passion, she responded with passion. It had been so long – too long – and she could feel her body stirring and responding, to his needs and her own. Then John broke the kiss and moved away from her, his breathing heavy.

'I'm sorry, my darling, I overstepped the mark. Now I should say the gentlemanly thing, that it won't happen again, but that would be a promise I'm not sure I could keep. I love you, my darling Ada, with every part of me.' John didn't face her, but he took one of her hands in his and stroked it gently. 'I would give everything I possess just to spend the rest of my life loving and caring for you. But I know that is not possible; you have a husband and you love him deeply. So you must set the pace for our relationship. I'll take whatever you want to give, and you must see that I don't take more.'

Ada covered the hand that was holding hers. 'John, there are two of us in this relationship and we are both responsible for our actions. If I didn't care for yer, there wouldn't *be* a relationship. We both need what we give each other and so far we have hurt no one. I do love Tommy, and I always will. But over the last year my feelings for yer have gone through different stages. I liked yer from the minute yer came into my little two-up two-down house and made yerself at home. Then over the months when yer showed me such kindness, my feelings turned from liking to fondness. Now that fondness has turned to love. I never thought it possible to love two men, but it has happened. It may not be the same kind of love, but it's love just the same.'

John turned to face her. 'Can I ask you a question, Ada? And I would be grateful for a truthful answer.'

Ada grinned. 'I don't often tell porky pies, John, and when I do it's usually to get someone out of trouble. I will never lie to you, I give you my promise on that.'

'If things were different, if you were single, would you really consider marrying me?'

'Yes, John, I would.'

'Then I'll have to be satisfied with knowing that, and settle for what I've got, won't I?' He cupped her face. 'One little kiss then you can go about your work.'

Ada was halfway to the bedroom when she turned. 'I'll never forget what yer did today, and neither will Polly. You're so kind and caring, and in my book, John Roscoe, you're a man and a half.'

* * *

Polly was relieved of her kitchen duties on Saturday so she could have a lie-in on her birthday. It was nine o'clock when she came down the stairs and she immediately looked on the long hall table to see if there were any cards for her. She pulled a face when she found the table bare, disappointed that there was no card from Steve, or her mam and dad. Then she perked up, thinking any post for her would be in the kitchen.

Mrs Nightingale's face gave nothing away. 'I haven't seen no post. I think Mr Charles picked it up.'

Polly knocked timidly at the door of the drawing room and waited until Mr Charles told her to enter. With a sinking heart she pushed the door open and started with surprise to find Charles, Victoria and Justin waiting for her, their faces beaming as they each held out a brightly wrapped parcel and cried in unison, 'Happy birthday, Polly!'

Feeling shy and embarrassed, Polly remained rooted to the spot. She hadn't expected anything like this. A birthday card, yes, but not the whole family waiting specially to congratulate her. Well, not the whole family, but then she wouldn't expect to see Rebecca; the girl avoided her as though she had the plague.

Victoria was the first to move. She kissed Polly warmly and said, 'Have a lovely day, my dear. I'll put your present on the couch and you can open them all later.'

'Thank you,' Polly croaked. Then her sense of humour came to the rescue. 'Now I know how Cinderella felt, but where's me glass slipper?'

'You're much prettier than Cinderella.' Charles laid his bulky parcel down before giving her a tight hug and kiss. 'I hope you have the bestest birthday ever.'

'Ay, that's bad grammar, that is.' Polly shook a finger in his face and kept her own face straight. 'I'm goin' to tell Mr Westly on you and he'll give you a hundred lines to do.'

Justin came up behind his father, a blush covering his

face. 'Happy birthday, Polly.' He shoved a small square parcel into her hands. 'Here's a small gift for you, I hope you like it.'

'Oh, I know I will, Justin, thank you. And you, Mr Charles and Mrs Denholme, you're all very good to me.' Polly laced her fingers and rested her chin on them as her eyes focused on the presents. 'Shall I open them now?'

'If you wish,' Charles said, 'or would you like your cards first?'

'Ooh, have I got cards?'

'You certainly have – about twenty!'

'Twenty!' The word came out in a shriek. 'I've never had twenty birthday cards in me life! I don't know that many people!'

'You must do, my dear,' Victoria said, 'because all the envelopes have your name on.'

'Ooh, er, what shall I do first?' Polly was torn. 'Shall I open me presents or look at me cards?'

'If I were you, I'd open the presents first,' Charles suggested. 'Then you can take your time opening the cards.'

'Would you like me to take them up to my room and leave you in peace?'

'Most certainly not!' Charles said indignantly. 'I know it's your birthday, but we want to enjoy it as well.'

'I should jolly well think so!' Justin was really enjoying this. He was having more fun than he'd had on his sixteenth birthday two weeks ago. 'How can we see if you like them if you're stuck up in your room?'

Polly smiled at him before sitting on the edge of the couch. 'All right, I'll open yours first.' She pulled at the end of the bow of ribbon and when it came away, she put it beside her. 'I'm not going to throw that away, it's too nice.' She undid the wrapping paper and revealed a small square black velvet box. Overcome with shyness, she lifted the lid to find a string of pearls nestling on ivory satin padding. 'Ooh, er!'

Justin looked anxious. 'Don't you like them?'

'They're beautiful.' Her eyes wide, Polly lifted the necklace out and draped it across her palm. 'I've never had anythin' so beautiful in all me life! But they must have cost yer a lot of money, Justin, and yer shouldn't have spent so much on me.'

'They didn't cost that much.' Justin looked well-pleased with himself. He just hoped his mother wouldn't spoil it by saying it was she who had chosen the necklace and his father who had paid for it. 'As long as you like them, that's all that counts.'

'Oh, I do!' Polly put the pearls carefully back in the box. 'I'll wear them for me party tomorrow.' She then picked up the parcel Victoria had given her. It was soft to the touch and she guessed it would be an item of clothing. But in her wildest dreams she could never have imagined a dress so beautiful it took her breath away. In the softest shade of green, the velvet dress had short puff sleeves, a white collar embroidered in different shades of green and a full flared skirt. In its simplicity lay its beauty.

Polly dragged her eyes from the dress to gaze at Victoria. 'I don't know what to say, it's all too much. Yer shouldn't have spent so much money on me.'

'Polly, we want you to have a nice birthday because we're very fond of you, my dear.' Victoria could see the tears threatening and hastened to kneel at the side of the couch. 'I thought the colour would go well with your hair and eyes. And believe me, I got as much pleasure out of choosing it as you will in wearing it. And now, if you will open my husband's present, it'll leave you free to open your cards and see who these friends are that you don't know exist.'

Polly was wishing she had a handkerchief to blow her nose. She was going to cry, she knew she was, and they'd think she was a big baby. Biting on the inside of her cheek, she reached for the heavy parcel. But the tears came before she could open it.

Charles jumped from his chair and came to stand in front of her. He stroked her hair and said softly, 'Don't cry, Polly, my dear.'

Justin came to stand beside him. 'If you don't stop crying, Polly, I swear I'll take the pearls back.'

Sniffing up, Polly smiled through her tears. 'I know I'm daft, but I'm only cryin' 'cos I'm happy.' She wiped a hand across her eyes. 'Anyway, Justin Denholme, yer can't take a present back when yer've given it, so there!'

Victoria smiled as she undid the wrapping on the parcel. Polly was so good for Justin; she brought him out more than anyone ever had. 'Now do you promise not to cry, Polly, before I take the paper off?'

With a stiffened finger, Polly made a cross over her chest. 'Cross my heart and hope to die.'

But her promise wasn't easy to keep when she saw the camel-hair tailored coat. She wasn't a swank, but by golly it would be very easy to swank in a coat like that. She fingered it lovingly before jumping up and throwing her arms around Charles's waist. 'It's lovely.' She stood on tiptoe to plant a kiss on his cheek. 'Thank you, Mr Charles, for the coat and for being so good to me.' She turned and hugged Victoria before giving her a kiss. 'Thank you for the most beautiful dress I've ever had.'

Justin was feeling emotional as he looked on. They weren't a demonstrative family, and hugs and kisses had always been in short supply. That is, until Polly came. These things were running through his mind when Polly turned and gave him a hug. 'I can't kiss you, Justin, 'cos I know yer'd die of embarrassment. But I do thank you for the pearls, they're a lovely present.' She moved away from him with a mischievous twinkle in her eye. 'Give yer mam a big hug.'

'What!' Justin's brows shot up. 'It's not *my* birthday!'

'I know it's not your birthday, soft lad, 'cos I'm the one who got the pearls. But I'm quite sure you didn't go in the shop and buy them, did you? Come on now, be honest and admit it was yer mam who bought them. Oh, you will have paid for them, I'm not saying yer didn't, but I can't see yer going in a shop and choosing them. So yer mam must have done it for yer, and that deserves a big hug. I know I'd give my mam one if she did a favour for me.'

Justin looked as though he wished the floor would open and swallow him up. But Victoria knew what Polly was trying to do and wondered at one so young being so knowing and sensitive. She held her arms wide and smiled at her son. 'Come on, my dear, give your mother a hug to please the birthday girl.'

Charles had been watching and listening in silence. Polly never ceased to amaze him. She showed her feelings openly, gave her love with warmth and generosity. And she had more nous than the lot of them put together, himself included. 'Justin,' he said, 'if you think you're above giving your mother a hug, shall I do it for you?'

His son glared. 'I'll do it myself, Father.' He intended a quick squeeze, but Victoria wrapped her arms around him and held him tight. He could feel the warmth and smell her perfume. And he found he enjoyed the contact enormously.

'There you are,' Polly said, as mother and son broke apart. 'That wasn't so hard, was it?'

'You are one little minx, Polly Perkins!' No one was more amazed than the lad himself when he grabbed Polly around the waist, picked her up and twirled around with her kicking and screaming with delight.

Charles looked across at his wife and when their eyes met, his were saying that the young girl who had come here to be given an education was instead educating them.

'Put me down, you daft ha'porth.' Polly pummelled Justin's back with her fists. 'I'm gettin' dizzy!'

Justin had never had so much fun in his life. 'I'll put you down if you promise to let me look through your birthday cards with you.'

Polly's hands and feet became still. There might be a card from Steve and she wasn't going to show that to anyone. So in her mind she reached a compromise. 'I'll let yer see them after me.'

'It's a deal.' Justin set her down, his boyish face aglow with an emotion he'd never felt before. But then he'd never been so close to a girl before, certainly not one as pretty as Polly Perkins. 'Can we open them in here, Mother, or would you like us out of the way?'

'Don't you dare leave the room,' Victoria said. 'I am as interested in Polly's cards as you are.'

'Oh dear,' Charles moaned. 'Seeing as I too am interested, it seems you are not to have any privacy, Polly.'

'I don't mind, Mr Charles, 'cos you're three of me best friends. But I'd better take me new clothes upstairs first and hang them up.'

'Are you wearing them tonight to go to the pictures?' Charles asked. 'Steve will be bowled over by you.'

Polly shook her head. 'I'm goin' to give him a hand to clear Sarah Jane's stuff away before we go to the pictures. If I turned up in these clothes I'd stick out like a sore thumb. But I'll be wearin' them tomorrow for me party.' She hadn't been told she was to see her dad the next day because Ada wanted to surprise her, so everyone had been warned by John to keep the secret.

Polly was sitting crosslegged on the floor, a stack of envelopes at the side of her. 'Ah, this one's from Sarah Jane, me adopted grandma. I don't half miss her, I'm glad she's comin' to me party.' As she handed the card to Justin who was sitting beside her on the floor, she said, 'Yer do know she swears, don't yer? And me Auntie Dolly, too. When they get together with Aggie, the air will be blue. And you're not used to that, so yer might be offended.'

'That's all right, Polly,' Charles said as he took the card passed to him by his son. 'Mr Roscoe has warned us. My dear wife has promised not to swoon and Justin is to cover his ears.'

'A fat lot of good that will do him, 'cos none of them give yer any warning.' Polly read Irish Mary's card and smiled before she carried on. 'I don't think they know they're saying it themselves, it just comes out.'

The next two cards were from Aggie and Fanny. Then when Polly opened the next one she blushed. It was from Steve and he'd put *With love* on it and a few kisses. She definitely wasn't showing that to anyone. 'This one's private and confidential.'

Charles chuckled. 'From the boyfriend?'

'From me best mate.' Polly wasn't to be drawn. She slipped the card under her leg and lowered her head as she slit open the next envelope. 'Yippee! It's from me dad! Oh, I've been praying I'd get one from him.' She kissed the card before hugging it to her chest. 'If only he was here it would be the best birthday I've ever had.' Then she re-read what was written on the card in a spidery scrawl. *To my own pretty Polly on her birthday. Have a happy day and remember I love you with all my heart. Your loving Dad.*

With tears not far away, she hugged the card. 'Sometimes I think I'll never see him again.'

'Oh, come now, Polly,' Charles said. 'I never thought you were a defeatist. Of course you'll see him again – and it might be a lot sooner than you think.'

'I pray for him every night, Mr Charles, every night without fail. But it's been so long I'm beginning to think God doesn't hear me prayers.'

'What does your father say on his card, Polly?' Victoria asked. 'Is it too private for us to see?'

'Of course yer can see it! Then I'm going to stand it up in me room, right next to me bed, and I can give it a kiss every night.'

Victoria held the card up. 'Your father hopes you have a happy day, my dear. He wouldn't like to think you were sad.

304

So open the other cards before I ring for tea.'

The next two cards were bigger and more expensive than the others, one from Charles and Victoria, and one from Justin. And Polly blushed with pleasure when she found Mrs Nightingale, Lucy and Mr Westly had sent their congratulations. Amongst the last to be opened were cards from her mother, Mr John, and Auntie Dolly. 'I've never had so many cards in all me life. I'll be able to paper me bedroom with them.'

'Take them upstairs, Polly, and we'll have a cup of tea when you come down. I suppose you'll be going to see your mother before you go off to meet Steve?'

'Yes, and I'll take the card me dad sent to show her.' A frown settled on Polly's forehead. 'Me dad can't be so sick, Mr Charles, can he? I mean if he was really sick he wouldn't have been able to write the card.'

'Polly, keep thinking positive,' Charles said nipping the end off a cigar. 'Your father is going to get better, so keep the flame of hope burning. It's been a long time, I grant you, but it'll come right in the end. Now poppy off upstairs, Justin will help you carry some of the things.'

When they were alone, Victoria asked in a low voice, 'Do you think it wise to keep Polly's hopes up? According to John her father is really very ill.'

'Victoria, my darling, Polly is a fourteen-year-old girl. Far better to let her live in hope for a while than burden her with such distressing news. The time for grieving has not arrived yet, and with God's help it never will. Let's all do as Polly does – say our prayers every night and hope that the good Lord hears one of us.'

Chapter Twenty-Two

'I've brought all me cards, Mam, but I haven't brought me presents 'cos I'm goin' straight down to Bold Street. I promised to give Steve a hand before we go to the pictures.' Her face aglow with pleasure, Polly waved the bundle in front of her mother's face. 'Have yer ever seen so many cards, Mam? I wasn't expectin' anything like this many.'

'Did you get the one off yer dad?' Ada was anxious. She'd helped Tommy write it out last week and had posted it herself, but she didn't want Polly to know that. 'He said he was sendin' yer one.'

'Yeah, that one's me favourite. All the cards are lovely, but me dad's is special. I'll leave them for yer to look through and pick them up tomorrow.'

They were standing in the kitchen talking when John came through with a cup and saucer. 'I thought you were talking to yourself, Ada! Hello, Polly, happy birthday, my dear.'

'Thanks, Mr John, and thanks for me lovely card. It's been so exciting I don't know whether I'm on me head or me heels.' Polly went on to tell them of the presents she'd received from the Denholmes. 'They're really beautiful, Mam, but a bit too posh for me. I don't know when I'll get the chance to wear them.'

'Nonsense!' John said. 'A pretty girl deserves pretty clothes. And you'll have the chance to wear them tomorrow.'

Ada was listening, her smile tinged with sadness because she would never be able to afford to buy her daughter expensive clothes. But Polly was level-headed, she wouldn't miss all the finery when it was time for her to come and live at home again. Especially if Tommy got better and came out of hospital. She knew her daughter well enough to know she'd go barefoot if it meant her beloved dad was home. 'Polly, sunshine, will you come early tomorrow to give me a hand with the table?'

'Of course I will, Mam. But you'll have to find me a pinny to put over me new green velvet dress. I wouldn't like to get a mark on it the first time I wear it.'

'I'll sort something out for you.' Ada was thinking that if her daughter knew she was going to see her dad tomorrow, she wouldn't be worrying about any green velvet dress, no matter how beautiful it was. 'If yer could get here around two o'clock it'll give us plenty of time to get everything looking nice before the guests arrive.'

'I'll be here on the dot.' Polly was eager to be away, knowing Steve would be looking out for her. 'Don't let those cards get dirty, will yer, Mam?'

Ada gazed down at the bundle of cards she was holding. 'Is there one from a certain boy in this lot?'

'Some hope you've got, Mam!' Polly chuckled. 'That one's hidden away in a drawer in me bedroom. And I'm on me way now to thank him for it.' She passed John then wheeled around and came back to stand in front of him. On impulse, she put her arms around his waist and hugged him. 'I'm looking forward to me party, Mr John, and I'm ever so grateful to yer for lettin' me have it here.'

'It's my pleasure, Polly.' John put a finger under her chin and tipped her head back. 'Is it all right if I kiss the birthday girl?'

'Ay, I'm not half gettin' a lot of kisses today, Mam. I should have started chargin' a penny a go, I'd be loaded by now.' She hugged John again as he was kissing her. 'The others all got a kiss and a hug, so I don't see why you shouldn't.'

'Don't tell me you got a kiss and a hug off Justin?' John said. 'Now that really would be a surprise.'

'I didn't, no, but I made him give his mam a big hug. He

didn't half blush, 'cos they're not like us, yer know, they don't cuddle and kiss.'

'How d'yer mean, yer made him give his mam a hug?' Ada asked.

'Ah, can I tell yer tomorrow? I want to get down and see Sarah Jane and all the other women. Steve said we'll have to be away for half-five to get to the pictures in time for the first house, so we'll have to have Sarah Jane all cleared away by then.'

'All right, sunshine, you poppy off and I hope yer enjoy the picture.' Ada went to the window to watch her daughter running down the steps. She felt John's arm come round her waist and leaned against him. 'Her and Joey make up for all the hardship, John, they're really good kids.'

'Polly's like you, my dear Ada, she's very pretty.'

'Oh, come off it, John. She's much prettier than I've ever been.'

'Then you don't see yourself as I see you. Next time you look in the mirror take a good, long look, and you'll see my idea of the perfect woman.'

Steve was bending down refilling one of the buckets with daffodils when he heard Sarah Jane cackle, 'Here she comes, Steve – my granddaughter and the girl of your dreams.'

Polly was greeted with loud cheers and shouts of congratulations from all sides. Her face beaming, she kissed each of the women in turn, watched by bemused customers. But for Sarah Jane there was a special kiss and a loving embrace.

'Hey, what about young Steve here? Doesn't he get a kiss? God knows he's been on pins for the last hour and he must have corns on his ruddy eyes watchin' out for yer.'

Polly wagged a warning finger. 'I'm too young to kiss boys, Sarah Jane. Me mam would have me life.'

'Sod that for a bleedin' lark, girl! And yer mam's not here, so what the eye don't see the heart ain't goin' to grieve over.'

'Leave it off, Sarah Jane,' Steve said, his face the colour of beetroot. 'If I'm goin' to get a kiss I don't want it in front of an audience.'

'Goin' to sit in the back row at the pictures, are yer?' The old lady's wrinkles deepened when she smiled. 'That's the best place to do yer courtin'.'

Irish Mary was standing near listening. 'Every dog knows their own tricks best, Sarah Jane,' she said. 'I bet you were a real fly turn when yer were a young girl.'

'I'm saying nowt.' The old lady wore a haughty expression. 'My lips are sealed.'

'Can we hold yer to that promise, Sarah Jane?' Florrie asked, perched on her upturned orange box. 'For the next hour and a half your gob is goin' to stay closed?'

'After I've told yer this,' said the old lady. 'If I put me hand up, it means I want to go to the lavvy. Okay?'

Polly laughed as she went over to Steve. There were a couple of potential customers inspecting the flowers and he was standing by in readiness. Feeling really at home, Polly went into action. 'Aren't they a lovely colour? A bunch of those in yer room and yer'd have sunshine all day long. Just think, only tuppence for a week's sunshine.' Her words and her bright smile did the trick. Flowers were handed over in exchange for money and she was back in business.

Sarah Jane folded her arms and watched with pleasure and interest. The kid was a natural. With that smile she'd sell anybody anything, even if it was the last thing on earth they wanted. And she did it all without being too pushy, just friendly coaxing.

The next hour passed quickly, and at five o'clock Polly suggested Steve started clearing away while she saw to any last-minute customers. He didn't only tidy up for Sarah Jane, he did it for all the ladies and this made him very popular with them. He was brushing around each stall with the long-handled stiff brush when Sarah Jane said to Polly, 'He'll make someone a good husband, that lad, he's a good worker and kind with it.'

Polly bent down to whisper in her ear, 'That's me yer talking about, Grandma. If Steve doesn't become my husband, I'll want to know why. But that little secret is just between you an' me, so keep it to yerself. Yer see, I haven't told him yet.'

'I think he's one step ahead of yer on that score, girl.' Sarah Jane cackled as she crossed her shawl over her chest and stuck her hands inside for warmth. 'But I'll keep it to meself on one condition. That I'm invited to the weddin' and yer make sure there's six bottles of stout for me.'

'You can be guest of honour, Grandma, and I'll make sure yer get twelve bottles of stout. How about that?'

'Twelve bottles!' The old lady's shoulders did a jig. 'Ooh, I don't know about that, girl, 'cos yer see I do have me limits. I'm unsteady on me feet after six, so if yer insist on me havin' twelve I'll be rollin' all over the bleedin' place. I wouldn't refuse, like, 'cos that wouldn't be polite, but I wouldn't be responsible for me actions.'

'Six it is then,' Polly told her with a smile. 'I don't want to see my grandma rolling all over the place. Wouldn't be dignified.'

Sarah Jane took a hand out of the warmth to pull on Polly's coat. 'Here, bend yer head a minute, I want to ask yer somethin'. Can yer get married at fourteen in this country, or is it against the law? Yer see, I just fancy a jars-out, knees-up do.'

'Yer can have yer jars-out, knees-up do tomorrow.' Then Polly remembered Justin and added, 'As long as yer behave yerself.'

'Behave meself! Yer not supposed to behave yerself at a ruddy party, girl, yer supposed to enjoy yerself! Let yer hair down, kick yer legs in the air, have a sing-song an' tell a few jokes – that sort of thing.'

'Oh dear.' Polly wagged her head from side to side. 'Just promise me yer won't tell any dirty jokes.'

'Listen girl, I can promise yer the earth right now, and

mean it. But after a few bottles of stout I'll have forgotten all about any bleedin' promise I made. If I'm not half-cut after a few drinks, it means I'm havin' a bloody awful time, and yer don't want that, do yer?'

Polly saw Irish Mary talking to Florrie and beckoned her over. 'Auntie Mary, will you keep yer eye on Sarah Jane tomorrow night, make sure she doesn't say anything she shouldn't?'

'Oh, come on, Polly, that's a tall order, that is! It would be easier to stop the wind from blowing, the rain from falling down or the stars from twinkling, than it would be to stop Sarah Jane from misbehavin'. Sure, isn't her motto in life that yer say what yer think and to hell with everyone . . . is it not the truth I'm telling, Sarah Jane?'

The old lady nodded. 'Nail on the head, girl, nail on the head.'

Mary winked at Polly, who was looking decidedly nervous. 'Don't worry yer pretty head about it, me darlin', 'cos when Sarah Jane puts her mind to it she can be the life and soul of the party, so she can. She's only having you on, pulling yer leg, and that's the truth of it.'

Again the old lady nodded. 'Nail on the head again, girl, nail on the head.'

Steve came along then, looking very smart after changing into his best jacket which he'd brought with him for the very special day in his life. 'I've cleared everywhere and there's not many flowers left, so Florrie said she'd sort Sarah Jane out.'

'I'll give a hand, too,' Mary said. 'You two forget about everything but enjoying yerselves.'

Polly could feel the butterflies in her tummy as she bent to kiss Sarah Jane. Her first date, and she wouldn't want it with anyone else but the boy who was standing beside her looking as though he'd lost a tanner and found a pound. They were walking away, their arms stiff at their sides and a yard distance between them, when Polly turned her head.

'Don't forget, six o'clock tomorrow.'

'I'll have me dance shoes under me arm,' Sarah Jane called after them. 'You just make sure the bottles of stout are open, 'cos with havin' no teeth I can't open them meself any more.'

Walking up Ranelagh Street, Steve asked, 'Which picture do yer want to see? Boris Karloff or Jeanette MacDonald and Nelson Eddy?'

'Oh, not Boris Karloff – he frightens the life out of me! I don't want to have nightmares, not on me birthday.'

Steve didn't let his disappointment show. He was all in favour of the Boris Karloff thriller, thinking that when Polly got frightened it would be a good excuse to slip his arm across her shoulders and comfort her. 'Okay, then, we'll go to the Odeon to see Jeanette MacDonald.' As he fingered the half-crown in his pocket he hoped the seats in the city centre cinema cost the same as the local flicks . . . fourpence in the front stalls, sixpence at the back, and ninepence if you wanted to go the whole hog and sit in the circle. Still, even if it did cost more to get in the Odeon, he'd still have enough over to buy Polly a box of chocolates from the kiosk in the foyer. And with a bit of luck it might even run to an ice cream when the lights went up at the interval and the usherettes came around. He'd blow caution to the wind and spend the whole half-crown on giving Polly a night to remember. It would mean he'd have to walk to work every day next week but it would be worth it.

'There's no queue, so we can go straight in.' Polly felt like skipping with excitement. She was fourteen now, she could even go to work if she wanted to. That meant she was nearly a young woman. And going out on a date with a boy – well, that showed she was growing up.

Steve bought two tickets for the back stalls before leading Polly over to the kiosk. 'What would yer like, Polly? One of those boxes of Cadbury's Dairy Milk?'

Polly gasped. 'No! They're sixpence a box!'

'I didn't ask yer how much they were,' Steve growled, 'I asked yer if yer wanted a box.'

'Yer can't afford to spend that much on me.' She gave a determined shake of her head. 'I'll have a tuppenny slab.'

'Yer'll have a box, seein' as it's yer birthday.' Steve handed the small silver coin over. 'I'll take one of those, please.'

'Ah, it's yer birthday, is it, love?' The assistant slipped the purple box into a white paper bag. 'Many happy returns.'

'Thank you.' Polly gave her one of her beaming smiles before Steve cupped her elbow and turned her towards the entrance. 'Yer shouldn't have done that,' she hissed. 'Yer can't afford to spend that much on me.'

'I can and I have.' Steve pulled the door open and when he stepped inside he stood for a while to accustom his eyes to the darkness. 'It's started, but it's only a short Buster Keaton film so we haven't missed much.'

'Tickets, please.' The usherette's torch beamed on the two tickets Steve passed over. She tore them in two, kept one half and returned the other. 'Back stalls, follow me.' Her torch now directed to the floor, she moved ahead of them down the sloping aisle.

'D'yer want to sit at the back or near the front?' Steve's voice was urgent. 'Hurry up before she starts waving that torch around.'

'Anywhere suits me. We'll sit where you want to.'

The usherette was waving her torch on two empty seats further down, but Steve's sharp eyes had spotted two empty ones on the back row and they were just what the doctor ordered. 'Come on.'

The couple sitting on the end two seats weren't even looking at the screen; they were gazing into each other's eyes as they held hands. 'Excuse me, please.' Steve heard their dark mutterings at being disturbed but he didn't care as he squeezed past their legs, pulling Polly after him. He'd paid his money, same as them, they didn't own the place.

'You're not very popular,' Polly said as she pressed the seat down and settled herself. 'Did yer hear what he said about people turnin' up late and spoiling the film for other people?'

'Take no notice, they weren't even looking at the flippin' picture. Just starin' into each other's eyes, all sloppy like, stupid nits.'

'Oh, look at the state of Buster Keaton!' Polly's laugh tinkled as she watched the funny man clinging to the side of a moving tram whilst holding on to his straw hat. His wide, unblinking eyes rolled as he tried to keep up with the tram. 'Ay, he can't half run,' Polly said, marvelling at the speed of the comic's legs. 'Just look at him go!'

Steve chuckled and he felt very grown-up when he explained, 'He's not really running that fast, they've speeded the film up.'

'How can they do that?'

He was still explaining when the comedy came to an end; the next feature was a travelogue. 'I hate these, they're dead boring.'

'Ooh, an' I love them!' Polly had a rapt expression on her face as she gazed at the mountains, streams and waterfalls being shown on the screen. 'The world is a beautiful place, isn't it? If only we were able to travel to see those mountains, wouldn't it be wonderful? But we won't 'cos yer need a lot of money which we'll never have. Still,' she turned to find Steve's eyes on her, 'I've got a good imagination so I can pretend I've really been there, instead of seeing it from the back row of a picture house.'

The darkness gave Steve the courage to say, 'You're prettier than a mountain or waterfall. I'd rather look at you any day, than them.'

'Flatterer.' Polly smiled, embarrassed and thrilled at the same time. In another year or two she'd be old enough for Steve to hold her hand and sneak a kiss. She wouldn't make an exhibition of herself, though, not like the young couple sitting next to him. Their noisy kisses and loud whispers were causing people in the rows in front to turn around, tutting at having their enjoyment spoiled.

The lights went up for the interval and Polly could hold her curiosity no longer. She leaned forward to look past Steve but quickly sat back in her seat when she saw the couple were still in an embrace, even though the lights were up! 'They should be ashamed of themselves, they're old enough to know better.'

'Ugh!' Steve grunted. He'd often wondered what it was like to kiss a girl . . . well, not any girl, just Polly. The other lads in the street stood on street corners and whistled after all the girls that passed, but not him. There was only one for him, and he was dogged in his determination to court and marry her. The bloke he worked with, Jim Wilkinson, had laughed when he'd told him of his ambition, said at fifteen he didn't know his own mind and would have dozens of girls before he found the right one and settled down. Steve knew better but kept his own counsel. He'd win Polly or die in the attempt. 'D'yer want an ice cream?'

'No, but thanks all the same. I've still got some chocolates left.'

'Have an ice an' take the chocolates home with yer.'

'No, I couldn't eat one, Steve, honest.' That wasn't the truth, but as her mam always said, a little white lie never did any harm. Polly knew Steve must be leaving himself skint to spend so much on her, and if he forked out any more it would mean him getting to work on shanks's pony instead of the tram.

The lights dimmed and the audience ceased their chatter as the big picture started. It was a romantic musical comedy and Polly spent the next hour and ten minutes with her eyes glued to the screen. She was totally immersed in the story, laughing at the funny parts, crying over the sad bits, captivated by the music and voices of two of the world's most popular singers. She was so involved with the film she didn't even feel Steve take hold of one of her hands. It was only when the music heralded the end of the film, and she turned to say how much she'd enjoyed it, that Polly realised her hand was being held. 'Wasn't it marvellous?' she asked shyly.

'I dunno, I only saw a bit of it 'cos I was watching you all the time. There was more action on your face than there was on the screen.' Steve reluctantly let go of her hand and stood up, pushing the seat back with his legs. 'Why do girls always cry over soppy things?'

''Cos we're soppy things ourselves, that's why.' Polly gave him a push. 'Let's move before we get caught in the crush.' She nodded at the two empty seats beside him. 'I see the courtin' couple have left.'

Steve put a hand on her arm and pulled her into the aisle. 'God, but they were a menace! Honest, they spent the whole time kissing . . . never even came up for air!'

He was holding on to her elbow as they came out of the cinema and began to walk up London Road. Polly glanced sideways at him. 'Did they make yer mad, that couple?'

Staring straight ahead, Steve growled, 'No! If yer must know, they made me jealous.'

'Jealous! Why would yer be jealous?'

''Cos I've never kissed a girl, that's why.'

Polly's big brown eyes widened. 'Yer only fifteen, Steve!'

'What difference does that make? I'd still like to know what it's like to kiss a girl.'

Now the brown eyes held a glint of mischief. 'Have yer a particular girl in mind, Steve Mitchell?'

'Yes, I have someone special in mind, Polly Perkins, an' yer know who it is. I lie in bed at night wondering when I'm goin' to get me first kiss off her.'

'Ooh, er! If I gave yer a kiss in the middle of London Road, me mam would have me guts for garters.'

Steve put a hand on her arm and pulled her up short. 'Just one little kiss, Polly, please? We can go in that shop doorway and no one will notice us.'

'No, Steve.' But Polly's tone was half-hearted and she was allowing herself to be led as she spoke. It was her birthday and it had been a lovely day, getting all those cards and presents, and being taken out on her first date. What better way to round off the day than being kissed by the boy she intended to marry? After all, it was only a kiss. She wasn't doing anyone any harm.

They emerged from the shop doorway in a daze. Steve put his arm across her shoulders and took a deep breath. Then he gave a throaty chuckle. 'I'll tell yer what, Polly, now I know why that couple spent their time kissing. I enjoyed that one kiss yer just gave me far more than I did watchin' and listenin' to those two warbling in the sloppy picture.'

'Oh, I enjoyed the picture.' Polly let him take her hand and they walked up the road swinging their arms between them – two happy young people walking on clouds. 'But if I had to choose, I'd choose the kiss.'

Steve's chest expanded with pride and he seemed to grow in stature. He'd remember Polly's fourteenth birthday for the rest of his life, as the day he got his first kiss and the day he knew in his bones that she felt the same way about him as he did about her. 'You are my girl, aren't yer, Polly?'

'Yes, Steve, I'm your girl an' you're my boyfriend. But don't tell yer mam 'cos she'll pull me leg soft.'

'Polly, me mam's been pullin' me leg about you since I was about ten years of age! I know she acts daft, but yer can take it from me that she's all there, doesn't miss a trick. But I won't tell her, not until yer've come back home to live and we can see each other every night.' Steve's eyes swivelled sideways. 'When are yer comin' home, Polly?'

'I don't know, I haven't thought about it.'

'But yer fourteen now, yer can get a job!'

'I know that, Steve, but I can't just walk out on the Denholmes after they've been so good to me. I can't just pack me bag and march out of the door without so much as a by-your-leave. It wouldn't be right.'

'But I thought the idea was that as soon as yer were old enough to work, yer'd be coming home. I want yer to come home, Polly, 'cos I hardly see anythin' of yer.' Steve's happiness diminished a little. He thought Polly would be back living next door to him within the next week. 'Yer'd be earning more money if yer got a proper job, and besides, yer mam could do with yer helping in the house.'

'I know all that, Steve – I don't need you to remind me!' Polly could sense a tension in the air and wished she hadn't spoken so abruptly. Steve had helped to make it a perfect day for her; she didn't want it to end in a quarrel. 'I'll tell yer what I could do, I could stay until the Easter holidays, in about four weeks' time, and then leave. There's no lessons for ten days because Mr Westly is going on holiday. That would be the best time to leave, but I'll have to have a word with me mam first, see what she says.'

'You do want to come home, don't yer, Polly?' Steve's voice was gruff. 'I mean, yer haven't got too used to their fancy la-de-dah ways, have yer?'

Polly didn't answer right away; she needed time to think. Avoiding a quarrel was one thing, but speaking ill of people who had shown you nothing but kindness was a different thing entirely. 'Steve, I don't want to fall out with yer and I still want to be yer girlfriend. But I don't like yer talking about the Denholmes like that. Okay, they've got pots of money and they speak posh. But they're good people, Steve, and they've been very kind to me. You'll meet them tomorrow night and I hope, for my sake, that you'll try and see them for what they are, not what you think they are. Please, Steve?'

'Of course I will. I couldn't refuse you anythin', Polly Perkins.' Steve threw caution to the winds and gave her a quick hug. 'And four weeks isn't such a long time to wait. Mind you, I'll be counting every day, every hour, every minute and every second.'

'Go on, yer daft ha'porth!' Polly gave him a playful push

before cupping her chin in her hands. 'Let's see, how many seconds *are* there in an hour?'

Chapter Twenty-Three

Ada could see her hand trembling as she moved the curtain to look down on the Square. 'I'm a nervous wreck, John. The more time I've had to dwell on it, the more I believe that what we're doin' is wrong. I know yer meant well, and I'm grateful to yer, but I think we should call the whole thing off. Polly doesn't know anything about it so there'd be no explaining to do.'

John was beside her in an instant. 'Ada, you can't call it off, it wouldn't be fair on Polly. She has the chance to see her father and you have no right to deny her that chance.'

'I have every right!' Ada said, her anguish coming through in her voice. 'She's my daughter an' I know what's best for her. I don't want her to experience the pain and sorrow I feel every time I see Tommy, she's too young to carry a burden like that. The man lying in the bed in that hospital is only a shell of the dad she knew.'

'Ada, my darling, I don't like to speak sternly to you, but I feel I must. There are several reasons why it is important that the visit goes ahead as planned and I don't think you've given them proper consideration. Firstly, don't you think Tommy should be given the opportunity to see a daughter he hasn't laid eyes on in over two years? Don't you think it might be the incentive that will give him the will to fight and live? And even if it doesn't, he still has the right to see his daughter – just as she has the right to see her father.' He put an arm around Ada's waist and held her tight. 'There are things that must be said, my dear, even if they distress you. How would you feel if Tommy were to die, never having seen his children again? Joey's too young to understand, but Polly is a sensible young lady and deserves to be told the truth.

She'd never forgive you if she found out you'd denied her the chance to see her dad. And frankly, I don't think you would ever forgive yourself. It would weigh heavy on your conscience for the rest of your life.'

'You're right, John, I know you are. But I can't bear the thought of her face when she sees him! She's only a kid, she'll expect to see him as he was before he went into hospital. And if she gets upset, it won't do Tommy any good.'

'Talk to Polly when she comes, prepare her before she sees him.' John saw Polly turn into the Square and let his arm fall. 'Here she is. I'll go down and open the door while you compose yourself. Try to be brave, my love, for Polly's sake.'

'Hello, Mr John!' Polly breezed in, dressed in her new clothes and wearing a beaming smile. She felt on top of the world. 'Miss Polly Perkins reporting for duty.' She bounded up the stairs, shouting, 'I hope yer've got a pinny for me, Mam, 'cos I'm all dolled up.'

As soon as she entered the room and saw her mother's face, Polly knew there was something not quite right. 'What's wrong, Mam?'

'Sit down, sunshine, I've got somethin' to tell yer.'

John poked his head around the door. 'I'll be in the office if you want me.'

'No, don't go away!' There was panic in Ada's voice. 'You're part of this; you can help me explain to her.'

'Explain what, Mam?' Polly looked puzzled. 'Has me party been called off, or something?'

John looked across to see Ada nervously clutching and unclutching her hands. 'Would you like me to tell her, my dear?'

Ada nodded. 'Please.'

Her new clothes and party forgotten, Polly could feel a band of fear grip her heart. 'It's me dad, isn't it? Something's happened to him.'

'No, my dear, nothing has happened to your father.' John

sat beside her and took one of her hands in his. 'I'll start, then perhaps your mother will feel able to carry on.' When he looked into the deep brown eyes that were begging him to tell her that everything was all right, John almost lost courage. But it was something that had to be done and they didn't have much time. 'I was trying to think of a present to give you on your birthday, something special, and I came up with an idea that I thought would please you more than anything else. So I rang the hospital and spoke to one of the doctors who attends to your father. He agreed that you could visit this afternoon as a special treat.'

Polly let out a cry as she pulled her hand free to cover her mouth. She was silent for a while, then in a voice that was merely a whisper, she said, 'Oh, Mr John! You mean I'm going to see me dad?'

'Yes, my dear. But your mother is afraid the visit might be too upsetting for you.'

'Too upsetting for me? Too upsetting to see me own dad! Oh, Mr John, I'd give all me cards and presents back if it meant I could see him, honest.' Polly turned to Ada. 'Why d'yer think that, Mam?'

When Ada didn't reply, but bent her head, John took the fob watch from his waistcoat pocket and gave a sigh. 'We really don't have much time. Perhaps you should get your coat on Ada, while I finish telling Polly.'

Ada rose from the chair, but before she left the room she stood in front of her daughter. 'I'm sorry, sunshine. I know I'm a coward lettin' Mr John do me dirty work, but it's because I love yer so much I can't bear to see yer hurt.'

Mixed emotions filled Polly's head and heart as she watched her mother walk through the door. Why was her mam so sad? Surely, it was a time for gladness, when father and daughter would meet for the first time in two years? It certainly wasn't a time for tears. 'Mr John, I don't understand why me mam's acting so strange. I would have thought she'd be over the moon – I know I am.'

'Like any good mother, she's trying to protect you. You see, Polly, your father has been, and still is, a very sick man. He won't look like the man you remember and that is what your mother is afraid of. But I believe you are a sensible girl, and although you may get a shock when you see him, I believe you are strong enough to cope with that. Just remember that inside, he is still the dad you love and who loves you deeply.' John waited until Polly had had time to absorb his words, then he asked, 'Am I right in thinking you are strong enough, and brave enough, to face whatever shock is in store for you? And don't forget, whatever you feel you must not let it show.'

'Of course I'm strong enough!' Polly was near to tears but was determined not to let them flow. 'No matter what he looks like, he's still my dad and I love him.'

Ada came in the room then, buttoning her coat. 'Coward that I am, I've been standing outside listening. Are you sure, Polly?'

'Mam, how can yer doubt that I'd give everything I've got to see me dad?' Polly jumped up and ran to put her arms around Ada. 'I'll go in there with a smile on me face, and no matter how sad I feel, that smile will stay there until I get outside. I won't upset me dad, I promise.'

Ada looked over her shoulder at John. 'Thank yer for being my crutch again, John, my shoulder to cry on. I don't know what I'd do without yer.'

Polly spun round. 'And I thank yer for the best birthday present anyone could have given me. The best I've ever had in me whole life.'

John inclined his head as he pulled his waistcoat straight. 'We'd better make a move or Agnes will be here to start on the table.'

'Are you comin' with us, Mr John?'

'I'm running you there in the car, but I won't be coming in to see your father. The doctor was only persuaded to let you in because it's a special day. They certainly wouldn't have given permission for me.'

Polly linked his arm as they walked on to the landing. 'You've been good to us, Mr John, and me and me mam won't ever forget it.'

John hesitated before stepping down the first stair. 'Polly, I'll tell you something that might help you keep that smile on your face, shall I? Seeing you again after so long might be just what your dad needs to give him the strength to fight his illness. I know if I was your father I'd fight like hell to get back home to you, Joey and your mother.'

John stood beside the car and smiled at the two nervous faces. 'I'll sit in the car until you get back. I'll be warm and comfortable so don't hurry on my behalf. And give my best wishes to Tommy.'

'I'm frightened, Mr John,' Polly admitted. 'Me tummy's turning over and over.'

'And don't you think your father's tummy will be turning over too? He's about to meet the pretty daughter he hasn't seen for over two years. He'll be more nervous than you are, so don't keep him waiting.'

Polly linked arms with her mother as they neared the hospital doors. 'I am frightened, Mam, I can't help it. I've never been in a hospital before.'

'Yer dad won't be in the big ward. They told Mr John they'd move him to a side ward just for the visit.'

'Will I be able to give him a kiss and a hug?'

'I don't know, sunshine, we'll just have to take things as they come.'

'I told Mr John I'd be brave, but I don't feel very brave right now. And I can't even raise a smile.' Polly's lips were trembling. 'Oh Mam, I'm goin' to let yer down, I know I am. And that means I'll be letting me dad down as well.'

Ada waited until they were in the corridor before pulling Polly to a halt. 'D'yer know what I've just remembered? Mr John's left three crates of stout in the kitchen. If Aggie and

Fanny spot them they'll be rotten drunk by the time we get back and there'll be no table set.'

'They wouldn't do that, Mam!'

'Oh yes, they would! I can see Aggie standin' in the kitchen and shouting to Fanny, "Come an' see what I've found, Fanny! Sod the table for a minute an' let's have a bleedin' drink".'

Polly began to chuckle and so it was that when the nurse took them into a small side ward, Tommy saw a beaming smile on his daughter's face. 'Hello, sweetheart,' he whispered.

Polly ran and put her arms around him. 'Oh Dad, it's lovely to see yer.' She was shocked by his appearance, and all she could feel through the material of his pyjamas was bones. But she gritted her teeth and strengthened her determination not to let him see how upset she was. 'Thank yer for me birthday card, it was the nicest one I got.'

'I'm glad yer liked it, yer mam chose it for me.' Tommy patted the side of the bed. 'Come and sit by me so I can take a good look at yer.'

'Hey, hang about!' Ada said. 'What about me? Isn't yer wife allowed a kiss? If I'm to be left out in the cold I won't be bringing Polly no more.'

'I'm sorry, love, I wouldn't leave you out for the world. It's just seein' me daughter after so long, I can't believe it's happening.'

When Ada leaned over to kiss him she thought he looked brighter. He was certainly glad to see Polly; happiness radiated from him. 'I'll let yer off this time. In fact, I'll sit as quiet as a mouse and let you and yer daughter catch up on the last two years.'

'*Our* daughter, love, our daughter.' Tommy had hold of Polly's hand and his eyes drank in every feature of her pretty face. 'She hasn't half grown, she looks like a young lady now. And she's prettier than ever, just like you were when I first set eyes on yer.'

'She's younger than when we first met,' Ada said, 'but

she's growing up all right. She went out on her first date last night.'

Tommy didn't seem very pleased at that. 'You're a bit young to be goin' out with boys, aren't yer, Polly? I'm surprised at yer mam for letting yer.'

'Dad, I only went to the first house at the pictures with Steve Mitchell from next door.'

Tommy looked relieved. 'Oh well, yer won't come to any harm with Steve, he's a good lad.' Tommy swept his arm down the length of her. 'Yer looking very posh, sweetheart. Who bought yer clothes for yer?'

'I got them off the Denholmes for me birthday.' Polly was still shocked by his appearance but the more she looked at him the more she could see in him the dad she knew and loved. And he was glad to see her, she could tell that. Without stopping for breath, the words pouring from her mouth, she told of all her cards and presents, her visit to the Odeon with Steve and, of course, the box of Cadbury's and the offer of an ice cream. She almost told him about the courting couple, just to give him a laugh, but had second thoughts when she remembered the stolen kiss in the shop doorway. 'And tonight I'm having a party at Mr John's.'

'Yeah, I know about that 'cos yer mam told me last week.' Tommy took a deep breath. He was feeling tired now with all the excitement, and was calling on what little strength he had left to help him through the visit. God knows when he'd see Polly again, if ever, and he wanted to keep her with him as long as possible. 'It's good of Mr John to let yer have a party at his house.'

'Yeah, he's a nice man. Like Mr Denholme, he's nice, too.' Polly wound one of her curls around a finger and tilted her head. 'I wish you were comin' to me party, Dad.'

'I wish I was comin' too, sweetheart. I'd be able to see our Joey, I bet he's grown that big I wouldn't recognise him. And of course, Dolly and Les Mitchell. It would be a treat to see them again.'

'And don't forget their son, Steve.' Polly gave him a cheeky wink. 'I can't let yer forget him when he spent all his hard-earned money on me last night. I bet the poor feller's got to walk to work every day this week.' Another cheeky wink. 'Mind you, I think I'm worth it.'

Tommy gazed at the pretty face and his heart filled with pride. She was a beauty, his daughter, and she had such a nice, sunny disposition. 'I've been in here so long I've lost track of time. I keep forgetting that the young ones are growing up. I remember Steve playin' footie in the street, now he's a working man.'

'Oh, yer wouldn't know him now, love,' Ada told him. 'He's a head taller than his dad, and Dolly said she has to stand on a chair to give him a clip around the ear.'

'Dolly still the same, is she?'

'Yeah, she'll never change, will Dolly. Mind you, I wouldn't want her to, she keeps me going. I'd have been lost without her since Polly left. She looks after Joey and gets me shopping in for me. She's a good pal, is Dolly.'

'Mam, I could come home, yer know.' Polly saw the opening and took it. 'Now I'm fourteen I can get a job, and with me bringin' in a wage yer wouldn't have to work such long hours.'

'No, yer don't need to do that, sunshine. I manage all right. I don't work nearly as hard as I used to.'

'You'd be daft to leave where you are, Polly,' Tommy said. 'Just look at the clothes yer've got on, yer mam couldn't afford to buy that sort of clobber. And anyway, I thought the idea was for you to get a good education so yer'd end up getting a decent job, one with prospects.'

'I've packed a lot into this year, Dad. I'm way ahead of where I'd be if I was still at school. I could work me way up to a decent job, I know I could. And if me mam needs me, that's more important.'

'Leave it for now,' Ada said. 'We'll talk about it some other time.'

'Yeah, okay, Mam.' Polly was glad the subject had come up because now her mother wouldn't be surprised when she mentioned it again. Anyway, it was selfish to be thinking about herself when it was her dad she should be giving all her attention to. 'How long are yer going to be in here, Dad? Me and our Joey don't half miss yer, and me mam misses yer although she tries not to let it show.' She took one of the pale thin hands in hers and brought it up to her lips. 'We never thought yer'd be away all this time.' She met his eyes and smiled. 'You are tryin' yer best to get better, aren't yer? I mean, trying really hard?'

'Yes, of course I am, sweetheart. I'll pick up one of these days and then I'll be on me way home, you'll see.'

'Cross yer heart and make a promise, Dad?'

'I promise, sweetheart.'

Ada heard the tiredness in Tommy's voice and saw the heaviness in his eyes. This visit was taking a lot out of him, draining him of what little strength he had. 'I was warned it had to be a short visit, so we'll have the doctor on our tail if we stay too long.'

'Ah, ay, Mam! We've only been here a few minutes!'

'According to that clock on the wall in the corridor, we've been here half an hour, sunshine, and I think we should go now and let yer dad get some rest. There'll be other times. I'm sure they'll let you come in to see him again soon.'

Polly was reluctant to leave. She looked down on her beloved dad and felt like crying because he looked so pale and thin. But he'd made her a promise he was going to do his best to come home as soon as he could. And her dad never broke a promise. She gave him a hug, careful not to press too tight, and kissed his cheek. 'That's from me.' She repeated the action and whispered, 'And that's from our Joey.'

John stepped out of the car when he saw them approaching.

He scanned their faces anxiously. 'Well, was he glad to see you?'

'Oh, he was, Mr John, he was over the moon! I told him about all the cards I'd got, and me presents, and he thought I looked a real toff in me new clothes.' Nerves were making Polly speak quickly, saying anything that came into her head. 'He knows all about the party and he said he wishes he could be there. And he told me to thank yer for being so good to me and me mam.'

John looked at Ada and raised his brows. 'Ada?'

'As Polly said, he was very happy to see her. You were right, John, it was the best present you could have given, to both of them.'

'And how is Tommy in himself?'

'He seems just the same.' Ada's eyes told him not to question her too much in front of her daughter. 'But with the excitement and all the talking, he was getting tired and I thought it was time to leave.'

'But he's going to get better, Mr John,' Polly said as John held the car door open for her. 'He promised, didn't he, Mam?'

'Yes, he promised, sunshine, and he crossed his heart.'

Polly sat on the back seat of the car and looked up at John. 'And me dad never breaks a promise, Mr John.'

Chapter Twenty-Four

'The car's just pulled up, Aggie.' Fanny was pulling her pinny off as she ran into the kitchen. 'Get rid of yer apron so they can see us in our glad rags.'

'Don't forget what I've told yer, d'yer hear?' Aggie, in her wisdom, had decided not to ask how the hospital visit went. And she had passed strict instructions on to Fanny. 'I'll box yer ears if yer even mention it.'

'Aggie, yer've told me at least a dozen times and I'm not bleedin'-well deaf!'

Aggie put her pinny on the kitchen table and ran a hand down the front of her best dress. It had a navy blue background and was patterned with small white diamond shapes. 'Do I look all right?'

'Yer look the gear, Aggie, the bloody gear! Anyone would think it was *your* party.'

Aggie gave her friend's dark green dress the once-over. 'Yer don't look so bad yerself, Fanny. In fact, if you an' me don't get a click tonight I'll eat me bleedin' hat.'

'Yer haven't got a hat, Aggie.'

'I know that, soft girl! D'yer think I'd have offered to eat it if I'd really had one? I once saw Stan Laurel eat his in a picture, but he gets paid to be daft, I don't.'

'Come on, they're comin' up the stairs.' Fanny pulled her out on to the landing. 'Let's greet them, proper like.'

Polly was the first up the stairs and Aggie threw her hands up in mock surprise. 'Well, I never! Fanny, I didn't know we had a princess comin' to the party.'

Polly raised the first smile since leaving the hospital. How could you keep a straight face with anyone like Aggie? 'Don't be actin' the goat, Aggie, it's only me in me posh new clothes.'

'D'yer know, I didn't recognise yer. Honest, yer could knock me down with a ruddy feather.'

Fanny slapped her on the back and cackled, 'Providing the feather was stuck to a rolling pin, eh, girl?'

'Oh, very funny.' When Ada and John came into view, Aggie jerked her thumb at Fanny. 'Ay, Mr John, because this one here's got her best bib an' tucker on, she thinks she's the bleedin' belle of the ball. She hasn't done a hand's turn since she came in 'cos she's frightened of gettin' her ruddy dress dirty! Left me to do the lot, she did, the lazy cow.'

'Don't yer take no notice of her, Mr John. I've done a damn sight more than me whack.' Fanny feigned indignation. 'Pulled me ruddy guts out, I have, an' that's all the thanks I get for it.'

Ada and John stood at the bottom of the flight of stairs and both of them said a silent prayer of thanks to God for these two women who were beaming down on them. In an instant they had managed to lift the cloud of depression that had been hanging over them on the journey home. Ada had been worried that Polly wouldn't be in the mood for a party, but she could see her daughter laughing at the antics of the two older women and she gave a sigh of relief.

'You two haven't been at the stout, have you?' Ada, her hand on the bannister, made her way up the stairs. 'I told Mr John he should hide it from yer.'

'Yer couldn't hide nothin' from me, girl,' Aggie said. 'I know this place like the back of me hand, every bleedin' inch of it.'

Fanny elbowed her friend in the ribs. 'Yer sly bugger! Yer didn't tell me yer'd seen any bottles of stout.'

'I didn't tell yer for the simple reason I hadn't seen them.' Aggie's tummy was shaking with laughter. 'How could I see them when Mr John had put them in the pantry and covered them with a cloth?'

They were all laughing except for Fanny, who was scratching her head. She just couldn't figure that out. 'If yer hadn't seen them, how d'yer know where they were?'

'Yer as thick as two short planks, Frances Delaney! I've got no time now to spell it out for yer, so get yer feller to explain it to yer in bed tonight.' Aggie grabbed her by the scruff of the neck. 'Let's show them how we've set the table out.'

'Oh, I say, that looks a treat.' John smiled his pleasure as his eyes travelled over the table. 'You've done a splendid job.'

Ada put her arm through Polly's. 'Doesn't it look lovely, sunshine?'

Polly was speechless. She had never seen such a colourful variety of food before. There were dainty sandwiches that you could eat in one bite, iced fancies in every colour and shape imaginable, trifles in posh, stemmed glasses, and there were lots of little pastry things but she didn't know what was in them because she'd never seen anything like them before. But the main attraction, set in the middle of the table, was a huge pink iced birthday cake with her name written across it in blue. And around the cake was a wide, shiny blue ribbon with a big bow in the front.

'Oh Mam, I don't know what to say. I feel like crying.'

'Don't you dare!' Ada said. 'And if yer want to thank anyone, then thank Mr John. It's all his doing.'

Polly slipped her arms around John's waist. 'If I said thank you a million times over, Mr John, it wouldn't be enough.' She reached up to kiss his cheek. 'You're ever so good to me and I am grateful.' Wiping away a stray tear, she added, 'I wish me dad could see it.'

'He will see it.' John fingered one of her curls. 'I've asked Charles to bring his camera to take some photographs. When the film is developed your mother can take one in for your father.'

Aggie could see Polly was getting very emotional and decided it was time to intervene before the tears started. 'Excuse me for interruptin', like, but would yez mind getting yer coats off and doing whatever yer have to do to make yerselves pretty? The guests will be arriving any minute.'

When Aggie and Fanny were alone, Fanny leaned towards her friend. 'Yer know what yer said about gettin' me feller to explain it to me in bed tonight?' She waited for Aggie's nod. 'Well, that won't be no problem because talking is all we do in bed these days. My feller's got no romance in him. The day he was fifty, he said to me, "That's yer lot, girl. I'm too old to be messing about now. I haven't got the will, the energy or the inclination, so yer'll have to make do with yer ruddy memories".'

Aggie chuckled. 'I'd have thought you'd have had better things on yer mind at that age, too!'

'Sod off, will yer, Aggie. I was only forty-six – I had plenty of life left in me.' Fanny glanced around furtively to make sure they couldn't be overheard. 'So I set me hat at the coalman. Great big man he was, flamin' muscles on him like Tarzan.'

'Yer didn't, did yer?' Aggie looked horrified. 'The flamin' coalman! Frances Delaney, I'm ashamed of yer.'

'Oh, nothin' came of it so don't be gettin' yer bleedin' knickers in a twist.'

'I should bloody well hope not! You a married woman an' all.'

'It wasn't bein' a married woman that stopped me, Aggie.' Fanny was laughing inside so much she had to take a deep breath before she could carry on. 'It was worryin' about what excuse I could make to my feller about me havin' black hand-marks all over me body.'

John stood in the doorway watching the women double up with laughter. Aggie he loved dearly, she was part of his life. But Fanny, only the size of sixpennyworth of copper, was fast catching up in his affections.

The Mitchells were the first to arrive and Steve was goggle-eyed when he saw Polly in her green velvet dress, set off by the link of pearls. He thought she looked beautiful, but he couldn't rid himself of a niggling jealousy.

'My God, girl, yer look a proper toff,' Dolly said. 'Turn around an' let's have a good look at yer.'

Her face beaming, Polly did a spin. 'Isn't it lovely, Auntie Dolly?'

'It certainly is. They didn't buy that from Paddy's market!' Dolly glanced at her son. 'Doesn't she look a treat?'

'Yeah, she looks all right.'

Dolly opened her mouth to ask if that was the best he could come up with, but the words never left her lips. Hadn't she been thinking the same thoughts as she guessed were going through her son's mind now? That Polly was going up in the world and it was difficult to imagine her wanting to go back to the life she knew.

Ada looked anxious as she pulled Dolly to one side. 'Was our Joey all right when yer left him with your Clare? I feel dead mean not letting him come to his sister's birthday party, but he goes to bed every night at six o'clock; he wouldn't be able to keep awake until ten, or whatever time the party finishes. And it's school tomorrow, too!'

'He was fine, girl, so don't be worrying. I told him if he went to bed like a good boy for our Clare, you'd bring him loads of stuff home.'

'I will, too. And Polly's going to see him tomorrow, so that'll make him happy. We'll have to have a bit of a do for his birthday so he won't feel left out.' Ada turned to her daughter. 'Polly, will you take the coats into the bedroom, sunshine, while I show Auntie Dolly the table?'

Polly nodded, then handed Mr Mitchell's overcoat to Steve. 'You carry that an' I'll take your mam's.'

As soon as they were in the bedroom, Steve asked, 'Who bought yer the beads?'

'Justin gave them to me.' Polly fingered the link of pearls. 'They're nice, aren't they?'

'What did he give yer them for?' Steve asked, anger and

jealousy fighting for supremacy. 'He hasn't got his eye on yer, has he?'

Polly giggled at the thought. 'No, we're mates, that's all.' Then she saw how flushed his face was, and the hurt look in his eyes didn't escape her notice. If she'd known he would be upset, she wouldn't have worn the blinking necklace. 'It's only a cheap one – he probably bought it at Woolworths.'

'I don't know why he had to buy yer anything! If he starts gettin' fresh with yer, I'll thump him one.'

'Justin wouldn't know how to get fresh with a girl, he's very young for his age. Yer'll see for yerself when he comes tonight, he's just a nice lad.' Polly moved closer and smiled up at him. 'Anyway, aren't yer forgetting something? I've already got a boyfriend and I'll never swap him for anyone else. These,' she lifted the necklace, 'don't mean as much to me as your birthday present did. You gave me a lovely night out, a night I'll remember all me life.' Her brown eyes twinkled. 'And the best part was me first kiss.'

That brought a smile to Steve's face. 'I couldn't get to sleep last night thinkin' about it. Is there any chance of pinching one now, so I'll have something to think about in bed tonight?'

Polly glanced towards the open door. 'It'll have to be short and sweet.'

The kiss was short, but it was sweet enough to satisfy Steve and restore him to good humour. A fact that wasn't lost on his mother. She knew how her son felt about Polly, had always felt, and she didn't want to see him hurt. In fact, even though she loved the girl as if she was her own daughter, Dolly determined that if she ever let their Steve down after leading him on, Polly wouldn't half get a piece of her mind.

Fanny came panting up the stairs. 'There's two women at the door, said their names are Sarah Jane and Irish Mary.'

Polly clapped her hands in delight. 'Why didn't yer bring them up?'

'Because I couldn't get them both on me back! Ooh, yer daft nit!' Fanny jerked her head in disgust. 'That Mary will make it up here, but there's not a snowball's chance in hell of the old lady climbin' all those stairs. She needs a couple of strong men to help her.'

Steve was already on his way down, shouting over his shoulder, 'Come on, Dad, give us a hand.'

'I'll come with you,' John said. He'd heard so much about Sarah Jane, he couldn't wait to meet her. 'We'll get a chair out of the downstairs office for her sit on and we'll carry her up.'

Sarah Jane, wearing her uniform of long black skirt, cream blouse and black woollen shawl, was acting shy. 'Hello, sir, are you the Mr John I've heard so much about? I'm very pleased to make your acquaintance.'

Standing near, Mary closed her eyes. This was a side to the old lady she'd never seen and she wondered how long it would last. She'd give it ten minutes at the most.

John took the old lady's hand and smiled. She was everything Polly had said. A heavily lined face, toothless gums, hair scraped back and held in place with a tortoise-shell comb and spotlessly clean. A typical Liverpool Mary Ellen, and he had an artist friend who would just love to paint her. He'd ask Walter the next time he saw him, John thought, and if the old lady was agreeable, he'd commission the painting for himself.

Steve came out of the office with a chair. 'Here you are, Sarah Jane. Sit yerself down and we'll carry yer up.'

Les Mitchell winked at the old lady as he bent to grip one of the chair legs. 'I've heard of people being carried around, but this takes the cake, this does.'

Sarah Jane caught her breath when her feet left the ground. She grabbed hold of Steve's shoulder for support and shrieked, 'If I fall off here an' break me bleedin' neck, I'll have yer guts for garters. D'yer hear what I said, lad?'

'Sarah Jane, the whole street heard yer!' Steve chuckled.

'If yer fell an' broke yer neck, yer'd have a hard time havin' me guts for garters, wouldn't yer?'

'Don't be givin' me cheek, lad, or I'll clock yer one. And don't be looking up me skirt, either. If yer so interested, I've got me pale blue fleecy-lined bloomers on.'

There's going to be some fun tonight, John thought, bringing up the rear with Mary. Wait till Aggie and Fanny get together with this one! As she walked beside him, Mary was thinking, this poor man doesn't know what he's let himself in for.

And while both their minds were on her, Sarah Jane was secretly enjoying herself. Her eyes were everywhere. It's like a bleedin' palace, she thought, and I'm being carried through it as though I was a queen. Just wait till I get to the pub tomorrow night and tell them. I bet they won't believe me! Still, if they don't they can sod off.

Rebecca Denholme heard the front door slam and ran to the window to make sure her parents and brother were on their way to the stupid party. The fuss that everyone had made over Polly Perkins's birthday, anyone would think she was somebody important, instead of a common flower-seller. But she wouldn't be so highly thought of after tonight, not when they found she was a liar and a thief.

Rebecca moved away from the window and walked to the ornate fireplace, her eyes on the small, fragile, beautifully crafted china figurine on the mantelpiece. It was her mother's favourite – a slim girl with long flowing hair and a pink ballgown swirling around her ankles. When they discovered it was missing in the morning, the whole house would be in an uproar, her mother distraught. But it wouldn't be missing for long because her father would be so angry he'd have the house searched. And they'd find it in Polly's bedroom, in a drawer in the tallboy, hidden under clothes. This time tomorrow the thorn in Rebecca's flesh would be gone, driven out by her father who wouldn't tolerate a thief.

With the figurine held close to her side in case Mrs Nightingale chose this time to come and build up the fire, Rebecca crept up the stairs feeling elated. She'd waited a long time for this but tomorrow her patience would be rewarded. She was so deep in thought she didn't hear the front door opening, and when her name was called she nearly fell backwards off the top stair.

'Steady on, Rebecca, you very nearly toppled over.' Justin walked to the foot of the stairs and smiled at his sister. He'd been annoyed with her earlier when she'd flatly refused to go to the party, but he wasn't one for harbouring ill feelings. 'You haven't been at Father's port, by any chance?'

With her hand behind her back, Rebecca ignored the jest and asked, 'What are you doing back?'

'Father forgot his cigar case, and you know how grumpy he can get if he hasn't a cigar to chew on.'

'I don't know why he bothered to send you back for it, he'll be home very soon. There's no way he and Mother will be able to stand those dreadful people.'

Justin sighed, unwilling to get involved in that argument again. Rebecca could be quite tiring at times. 'Good night, sister dear.' He spun on his heels and went into the drawing room. He found the cigar case on the small side table where his father had said it would be, picked it up and slipped in into his pocket. When he reached the door, he turned to look back in the room, a puzzled expression on his face. Then he shrugged his shoulders and reminded himself that his parents would be waiting for him at the corner of the street.

The atmosphere at the party was very stiff and formal, and Ada groaned with dismay. The three Denholmes were seated on the couch, and facing them were the ones she called her gang. This included the Mitchells, Aggie and Fanny and Sarah Jane and Mary. Conversation between the two groups was so stilted it was agonising. John was doing his best, as was Charles, but they were fighting a losing battle. And so it stayed until Sarah Jane, Mary, and Aggie and Fanny were on their fourth bottle of stout.

'Give us a song, Mr John.' Aggie waved her glass at him. 'Liven the place up.'

'What would you like, Agnes?' John felt like kissing her for starting the ball rolling. 'How about *Come into the Garden, Maud*?'

'Sod off, Mr John! It's supposed to be a party, not a bleedin' wake!'

Charles could feel his tummy shaking with suppressed laughter. He turned his head to see Victoria's mouth gaping and her eyes wide. He gave her a gentle dig and whispered, 'Sit back and enjoy it, my darling. I think the fun is about to begin.'

Hearing a few swearwords, and with four bottles of stout down her, Sarah Jane was now convinced she was amongst friends. 'I'll sing a little ditty for yer.' She cleared her throat. 'Can we have a bit of hush now for the singer.' Again she cleared her throat before starting, 'Oh, Auntie Mary had a canary, up the leg of her drawers . . .'

Her mouth covered by Mary's hand, Sarah Jane rolled her eyes. Her muffled cry of, 'Are yer tryin' to bleedin' suffocate me?' brought forth a burst of laughter which included Victoria's and Justin's. At last the ice had been broken.

Mary took her hand away. 'Will yer be after behavin' yerself, Sarah Jane. Yer not at the pub now.'

'God strewth!' The old lady feigned anger. 'If I'd have had any teeth, they'd have been down me throat by now.' In an instant her mood changed to one of sweetness and light. She smiled across at Victoria and said, 'Excuse me language, madam, I don't often swear but there are times when it just slips out.' After a nod of her head, she turned to Mary. 'If yer won't let me sing, then get up an' give a turn yerself. I bet yer can't sing a ruddy note!'

'Is that right now.' Mary bristled as she got to her feet.

'Wasn't it meself that was in the church choir back home?'

Sarah Jane screwed her face up. 'If yer start singin' a hymn, girl, so help me I'll drown yer out with Auntie Mary an' her ruddy canary!'

Mary waited until the laughter subsided, then feeling too nervous to face her audience, she fixed her gaze on a picture hanging on the wall. In a voice that rang sweet and clear, she silenced and captivated those who were now listening with admiration and wonder.

> *'Oh Mary, this London's a wonderful sight,*
> *With the people here working by day and by night.*
> *They don't sow potatoes nor barley nor wheat,*
> *But there's gangs of them digging for gold in the street.*
> *At least when I asked them, that's what I was told,*
> *So I just took a hand in this digging for gold.*
> *But for all that I found there, I might as well be,*
> *Where the Mountains of Mourne sweep down to the sea.'*

When the song was finished, Mary lowered her head in embarrassment. But the thunderous applause and the shouts of 'Encore!' brought a smile of delight to her handsome face. She had discarded her shawl for the party and was looking a fine figure of a woman in her form-fitting chocolate-coloured dress. 'Sure, that wasn't me singing, it was the four bottles of stout.'

'Then give her another one, Mr John,' Aggie called. 'It was a real treat, that was.'

'As long as he doesn't give her one of mine,' Sarah Jane said, her face creased in a smile. She leaned forward to pat Mary's arm and her voice was sincere when she told her, 'Yer've been blessed with a fine voice, girl, one I could listen to all night. I'd be beholden to yer if yer'd give us another song.'

'Uh, oh!' Mary shook her head. 'Let someone else have a go.'

Heads turned as eyes sought a likely victim. It was Victoria who spoke first. 'How about you, Charles? You haven't got a bad voice.'

Charles roared with laughter. 'Victoria, my darling, if they don't like John's *Come into the Garden, Maud*, what do you think they'd say about my rendition of *We'll Gather Lilacs in the Spring Again?*'

Dolly was hugging the laughter to herself, wondering whether she dared say what she was thinking. But what the hell, it was only a joke. 'We'd tell yer to sod off an' put yer bleedin' lilacs in water before they died off.'

His shoulders shaking, Charles turned to find Victoria's eyes brimming with laughter. 'I did warn you, my darling.'

'Oh, Charles,' she leaned forward and kissed his cheek, 'I haven't laughed so much in my life.'

And neither had Justin. He couldn't take his eyes off Sarah Jane. At first he'd been disappointed. All he saw was an old lady with a lined face, no teeth and who spoke with a thick Liverpool accent. He couldn't understand why Polly loved her so much. But it wasn't long before he was seeing her in a different light. Her lined face was full of character, her eyes, when not twinkling with laughter, were tender and told of the compassionate nature she had. And as for her Liverpool accent, well, that was part of her. Her jokes wouldn't be jokes if they were told in a posh voice. He wished he was as outgoing as Polly, because then he could do what he felt the urge to do, go over and give the old lady a big hug.

'Ay, Ada,' Dolly shouted, 'get my feller on his feet, he can sing.'

'Not on your life!' Les shook his head vigorously. 'I'm not makin' a fool of meself.'

Sarah Jane started clapping her hands, chanting, 'We want Les, we want Les.'

Pretty soon everyone in the room joined in, making a real racket. Dolly gave Ada the eye-eye, and they advanced upon

342

the poor man. He was pulled, protesting loudly, to his feet. 'Now,' said Dolly, in a whisper loud enough for everyone to hear, 'sing, yer bugger, sing.'

'Ah, ray! I only know one song!'

'That's all we want, son.' Sarah Jane winked at him. 'As long as it's clean enough for my delicate ears. Don't forget I was brought up in a strict Catholic household.'

Polly, sitting on the floor next to Steve, felt her cup of happiness was overflowing. This was turning into a party of fun and laughter, with everyone enjoying themselves. Her fears about Mrs Denholme and Justin had proved groundless; they were joining in the fun with gusto.

Les, his face the colour of beetroot, glanced across at his wife and shook his fist at her. 'Just wait till I get you home.'

'Ooh, er!' Dolly feigned coyness. 'Don't embarrass me in front of me friends, sweetheart. Try and control yer passion until we're somewhere more private, but don't squash it altogether, not now yer've made a promise.'

Ada decided it was time to steer the conversation away from the direction Dolly was taking it. 'Les, what about this song?'

'Okay, you asked for it. I've told yer I can't sing, so on your own head be it.' Planting his feet apart and looking up at the ceiling, he began.

> *'Two little girls in blue, lad,*
> *Two little girls in blue.*
> *They were sisters, we were brothers,*
> *And learned to love the two.*
> *Then one little girl in blue, lad,*
> *Won your father's heart,*
> *She became your mother,*
> *I married the other*
> *And now we have drifted apart.'*

Les had a pleasant voice and the song was well received, but he sat down vowing never to go through that again. And if looks could kill, Dolly would have been a dead duck. But his wife wasn't put off by a dirty look. She came over and clasped his head to her ample bosom, saying, 'I'm proud of yer, my little ray of sunshine. Now, if we can get our Steve on his feet, the three of us can give a duet.'

'Some hopes you've got, Mam,' Steve huffed. 'Anyway, a duet's for two people, not three.'

'Go 'way!' Dolly let her eyes sweep across the smiling faces. 'Yer see, the Mitchells are not only good singers, they're clever as well.'

Ada joined in the laughter as she made her way across to where John was standing. 'It's nine o'clock – shall I carry the food in or would it be better if they helped themselves?'

John had deliberately kept his distance all evening, but now he looked at her with longing in his eyes. 'Whatever you like, my . . . er, Ada.'

'I'll make the tea while you lead them to the dining room. The plates and serviettes are all ready, they can just help themselves.'

Polly jumped up and went after her mother to give her a hand, and Justin took her place on the floor next to Steve. 'You're Polly's boyfriend, aren't you?'

Squaring his shoulders, a smile lighting up his handsome face, Steve nodded. 'Yes, she's my girl.'

'She's always talking about you, said you are more handsome than any of the film stars.'

'Take no notice of her, she's only acting daft.' But Steve was secretly pleased. And he found himself warming to the other boy. 'It's her that should be a film star, she's better-lookin' than any of them.'

'Yes, she's very beautiful. And she's so warm and friendly, always cheerful and smiling.' Justin scrambled to his feet to follow his parents. 'You're a very lucky boy, Steve.'

'Yes, I know.' Steve made no attempt to stir as Justin moved away. He was content to sit and go over what the lad had told him. Polly talked about him all the time, he'd said. And she thought he was handsome.

'Ay, Steve,' Dolly called from the doorway. 'Sarah Jane wants yer to carry her plate for her.'

'Okay, Mam, I'm coming.' Steve walked tall. Justin was right – he was indeed lucky to have a girlfriend like Polly.

It was eleven o'clock when the party broke up. They'd insisted on ending a perfect night by forming a circle around Polly and singing *For She's a Jolly Good Fellow*. She was radiant with happiness, a very pretty girl with a smile that touched everyone's heart.

Charles, Victoria and Justin were the first to leave; they were walking the short distance home. But before they left they shook hands with each of the other guests and Charles gave a little speech. 'To John, Ada and Polly, and to the ladies who worked so hard to make this one of the best parties my wife and I have ever been to, I say a very big thank you. It's been a tremendous evening and I propose we do it again in the near future.'

'Hear, hear!' Sarah Jane said. 'Yer a man after me own heart.'

Charles walked towards her and, putting his arms around her, he held her tight. 'I've been wanting to do this all night, Sarah Jane. You're the prettiest woman in the room and you've stolen my heart.'

'And mine!' Justin finally plucked up the courage. If his father could do it, so could he. He hugged the old lady and planted a kiss on the lined face. 'I think you're lovely.'

Sarah Jane wasn't used to compliments and the only way to stop the tears was by joking. 'Right, I'll hold yer to that. We'll be married at Brougham Terrace on the last Saturday in June. Yer won't mind if I don't wear white, will yer? Yer see, with my complexion, I look a bugger in white.'

Polly put a hand on Victoria's arm. 'Are yer sure you don't mind me staying behind to give me mam a hand?'

'Of course I don't mind, my dear. Go home with your mother and have tomorrow morning off. And I thank you for inviting me to your party, I really have had a marvellous time. And Polly, you are very lucky to have all these people as friends.'

'Oh, I know I am, Mrs Denholme, I love them all. And you're my friend, too, and Mr Charles and Justin. In fact, you're me second family.'

Victoria was quite overcome. 'That is very sweet of you, my dear.'

Charles came up and gave Polly a kiss. 'We'll be on our way now, my dear, but we'll have plenty to talk about when we see you tomorrow.'

'Goodnight, Polly, and thanks.' Justin hesitated, then gave her a quick hug. 'It's been brilliant.'

'Thanks, Justin. I'll see yer tomorrow.'

John had ordered two taxis, one for the Mitchells and the other to take Sarah Jane and Mary home. Steve wasn't very pleased at having to leave with his parents, but cheered up when Polly said she'd be down one night soon.

After they'd waved the taxis off, Ada and John climbed back up the stairs. 'I don't know whether I've got feet on me or not,' Ada groaned. 'It's been a long day.'

'But a very satisfying one, don't you agree?'

'Oh yes, it's been great! But I was very worried at first, thought it was going to be a flop. Isn't it amazing what a few bottles of stout will do?'

John put an arm around her waist as they reached the second flight of stairs. 'It's so good to hold you. It's taken all my willpower to keep away from you this evening.'

Ada pulled free. 'Polly's up there!'

'I know, my darling, I know.'

Tired as she was, Ada was reduced to tears of laughter when they entered the dining room. Aggie was standing with her hands on her hips surveying the table which was littered with dirty cups and saucers, half-empty plates, squashed cakes, half-eaten sandwiches, crumpled serviettes and crumbs everywhere.

'Ay, Fanny, come and see the bleedin' mess in here! We'll be at it until next Pancake ruddy Tuesday! Just come and take a gander.'

'Sod off, Aggie,' Fanny's voice came back from the kitchen. 'I've got me own bleedin' mess in here.'

Polly went to stand between her mother and John. Linking arms with them, she said, 'It was worth it, though, wasn't it? I'm a very lucky girl.'

Chapter Twenty-Five

The heavy brocade curtain fell back into place when Mrs Nightingale removed her hand to stifle a yawn. It had been a long day and she was dead beat. Muttering under her breath, she parted the curtain and resumed her watch for the family returning. 'I should have gone to bed like the mistress said, but I never expected them to be this late. With Polly only being fourteen I thought the party would have been over early.' The cook-cum-housekeeper wouldn't admit to herself that it was curiosity that had sustained her until this late hour. Polly had mentioned that her friends the Mary Ellens had been invited, and Mr Roscoe's cleaners, and for the life of her she couldn't see the party being a success. Mixing people from such different backgrounds was a recipe for disaster. Doomed to failure from the very start.

'At last!' She spied them passing under the streetlamp and, hastily straightening her lace-trimmed mobcap and apron, she scurried to open the door.

Victoria looked surprised to see her. 'Mrs Nightingale, you shouldn't have waited up for us.'

'I thought you might want a drink.' She waited until the three were in the wide hall then closed the door. 'I'll make a tray and take it to your room, shall I, Miss Victoria?'

It was Charles who answered. 'Oh no, we're not going to bed yet, Mrs N., we've got too much to talk about. We'll take tea in the drawing room if you'd be so kind, then you must poppy off to bed.'

They're looking very pleased with themselves, the housekeeper noted as she stifled another yawn. The party couldn't have been a complete wash-out. 'Did you have an enjoyable evening, Mr Charles?'

'Splendid, absolutely splendid! A most entertaining and thoroughly enjoyable evening.' Charles's eyes were full of merriment as he smiled at her. 'I couldn't describe what fun it was, what born comedians Polly's friends are. But if there is a repeat, Doris, which is very much on the cards, I'll make sure your name is on the guest list.'

Mrs Nightingale preened at the use of her Christian name. At one time Mr Charles had always called her Doris, until the mistress stepped in and said she should be given her full title out of respect. After all, if the family didn't show respect for her rank as housekeeper, neither would the junior members of staff. 'Oh, thank you, Mr Charles, I'd like that!'

Victoria made for the drawing room. 'Nothing to eat, Mrs N – just a pot of tea. Mr Roscoe laid on a very good table and I rather think I ate too much.'

Justin followed his mother into the room. 'It was fun, wasn't it, Mother? The parties we give are dull in comparison.'

'I have to agree with you.' She began to giggle. 'Can you imagine Mrs Cecilia Compton-Browne holding a conversation with Sarah Jane?'

Charles came into the room, laughing. 'That is something I would like to see, my darling. And I would be willing to bet Sarah Jane would come off best.'

'I wouldn't take your bet, my love,' Victoria walked to the huge mirror over the mantelpiece and, smiling at her reflection, patted a kiss-curl into place. 'Sarah Jane is a remarkable woman, I have to agree, but—' She broke off and spun round, the smile gone from her face. 'Where's my figurine?'

'Where's what, my darling?'

'My figurine.' Victoria pointed to where the ornament usually took pride of place. 'It's missing.'

'Calm down, darling, it can't have disappeared. It was there when we went out, so there's probably a very reasonable explanation. Perhaps it's been taken to the kitchen for cleaning. Mrs Nightingale will be here in a minute and she'll put your mind at rest.'

Justin's heart began to race. Now he knew why he'd turned around at the door when he came back for his father's cigar case. He'd felt there was something different about the room, but everything seemed to be in order and he'd dismissed the idea. So the figurine was there when he'd left the house with his parents . . . but missing five minutes later. And the only person he'd seen was his sister.

Without a word Justin fled from the room and took the stairs two at a time. In his mind he could see what he hadn't registered at the time – the guilt on Rebecca's face and the furtive way she was holding her hand behind her back. But why would she remove the figurine?

Without bothering to knock, Justin burst into his sister's bedroom. Rebecca was sitting up in bed reading. Normally she would be fast asleep at this time, so the mystery deepened. 'Well, what have you done with Mother's ornament?' he challenged.

Rebecca closed her book. 'What are you talking about?'

'I'm talking about the statue – the girl in the ballgown. It's missing from the drawing room and you are the only one who could have taken it.'

'Don't talk rubbish! If there's anything missing, the only person in this house who would steal it is your friend, Polly Perkins. I bet if you search her room you'll find it.'

Justin breathed in sharply through his clenched teeth. 'So that's it. Well, your little plan has backfired, dear sister, because Polly hasn't come home with us, she's spending the night at her mother's.' He shook his head in disbelief. 'You were hoping we'd get in and go straight to bed, weren't you? Then it would look as though Polly had sneaked down during the night and stolen the statue. But you've slipped up on two counts. One, we didn't go straight to our rooms, and two, Polly isn't even here!'

Rebecca lowered her eyes but her voice was still defiant.

'I don't know what you're talking about. Now please leave my room and allow me to go to sleep.'

'That is precisely what I should do – go down and tell our parents that they'll find the figurine in Polly's room, where you put it. But I'm loath to be the one to tell them that their daughter is a liar and a thief. I am ashamed to think my sister would sink so low, but how much more hurt and ashamed will they be?'

Her head bent, Rebecca made no reply.

'I'll never forgive you for what you tried to do to Polly, but to save my parents from heartache, I suggest you run and get the figurine back now. You can tell Mother you'd brought it up to make a sketch of it. Any excuse will do, but you'll have to hurry before Father sends for the police.'

There was fear now in the eyes Rebecca raised to meet his. 'They wouldn't really send for the police, would they?'

'They certainly will, if they haven't done so already. Apart from being a very expensive ornament, it is Mother's favourite and she'll be completely distraught.' There was anger now in Justin's voice. 'But you know that, don't you? That's why you chose that particular item in your devious plot to make Polly out to be a common thief.' He took a deep breath to calm his anger. 'You've got one minute to retrieve the ornament and return it. I will tell them I woke you from a deep sleep to ask if you could throw any light on the mystery, and you'll explain when you bring it down.'

Rebecca pushed the bedclothes back and slid her legs out of the bed. 'Justin, please may I—'

Her brother cut her short. 'I don't want to talk to you now, I am so disappointed in you. I'll come along when everyone is in bed and tell you how you are going to make up to Polly for what you tried to do to her.' With that he left the room and made his way downstairs.

Victoria was in tears, Charles was pacing the floor and Mrs Nightingale was wringing her hands. 'I never touched it, Mr Charles, I swear!'

'I don't for one moment think you did, Doris. I only asked if you could shed any light on its disappearance.'

Justin forced a smile to his face. 'Panic over, everyone, Rebecca has the figurine.'

There was complete silence for several seconds as the news sank in. 'But why has she taken it upstairs?' Victoria asked. 'It's not a toy, not a plaything.'

'Rebecca will tell you when she comes down.' Justin kept his smile fixed and his voice light, but inside he felt like crying. Did his sister hate Polly so much she would ruin her life . . . brand her a thief? Or was Rebecca so naive she didn't realise what the consequences of her action could have been?

Charles was comforting his wife. 'There now, my darling, all is well. It was very stupid of Rebecca to have caused this upset, and I shall not hesitate to tell her so.' He looked over his wife's shoulder. 'I'm truly sorry you've been upset, Doris, and my daughter will be made to apologise to you tomorrow.'

The housekeeper would have liked to have told him what she thought about his daughter, but she merely inclined her head and left the room. Least said, soonest mended. Anyway, Mr Charles had called her by her Christian name again, and that compensated in some measure for all the upset.

Justin waited until the house had been silent for a while before slipping on his dressing-gown and creeping along the landing to his sister's room. He didn't knock for fear of waking his parents, and when he pushed the door open he could hear muffled sobbing. It didn't strike a chord of sympathy, he was still too angry with her for that. And with the anger was a feeling of horror when he thought of what would have happened to Polly if his sister's plot had been successful.

'Rebecca!' Justin shone the torch he'd brought with him at her. 'Sit up and stop making that noise or you'll waken the whole house.'

Rebecca's tear-stained face emerged from under the sheet. 'Don't shout at me, Justin, please.'

'Shout at you? I could willingly wring your neck!' He tore his gaze away before his resolve melted. 'Have you any idea of the seriousness of the crime you were committing? How you could even contemplate doing that to Polly I will never understand or forgive.'

There was a loud gulp before Rebecca answered. 'I wanted to get rid of her. I don't like her living in this house.'

'But why? Why do you hate her so much?'

'Because everybody makes such a fuss of her. Mother and Father treat her more like a daughter than they do me.' Sniffing up, Rebecca went on, 'They never hug me like they do her, and I can never make them laugh like she does.'

Her brother sighed. 'Rebecca, when did you last give Mother a hug, or Father a kiss? When did you last have a smile on your face instead of a scowl? You and I don't show our feelings like Polly does. She has an affectionate disposition and people are drawn to her. If you want people to like you, you have to put yourself out to earn their liking and respect. You and I would have to work on it, but with Polly it comes naturally.'

'We were all right until she came,' Rebecca said. 'We were, weren't we, Justin?'

'No, we were *not* all right! We thought we were, but Polly has shown me a different life.' Justin was weakening. He realised now that his sister had acted out of jealousy, and she had to learn that doing what she did was not the way to banish that jealousy. He didn't want to think she was wicked, he preferred to believe she was immature for her age, didn't understand that some of the things she had done in her life were very wrong. So when he spoke it was with great patience. 'Think back, Rebecca, to before Polly came. We never heard laughter ringing out from the kitchen as we do now. Lessons were dull, whereas now they are fun. We didn't even know Mr Westly had a sense of humour, he always

354

seemed so serious. These days he is much more relaxed because he enjoys working in a happy atmosphere.'

Rebecca was still prepared to argue. 'Mr Westly is supposed to teach us, not make us laugh.'

Justin was sitting on the side of the bed; now he turned and took her hand in his. 'Rebecca, why are you so jealous of Polly? She has so very little, while you have so much.'

'She's prettier than me.' The words came out before she could stop them. 'Everyone is always saying how pretty she is.'

'Polly *is* a very pretty girl – so why shouldn't people remark on it? You would be just as pretty if you didn't have a permanent frown on your face. You are your own worst enemy, Rebecca, if you did but know it.'

Rebecca was listening intently now. 'Am I really pretty, Justin?'

'You have the features to be attractive, but not the disposition. And only you can change that. You could try taking a few tips off Polly, you'll never have a better example.' He rose from the bed and looked down on her. 'What you did tonight was wicked and inexcusable. I find it hard to believe that a sister of mine would do such a thing, and I'm afraid you're going to have to change if you want to win back my love and respect.'

'I do love you, Justin.'

'Words are cheap, I prefer to see action. In future you will treat Polly as she deserves to be treated, with respect. That is your payment for my silence. So the ball is in your court, Rebecca, it's up to you how you play the game. Now I'll say good night.'

Aggie sat on her rocking chair in front of the fire. It was only nine o'clock but all her work was done and the long day stretched ahead of her. 'What a bleedin' life!' she said to the flames roaring up the chimney. 'I put meself out to pasture too soon, I should have stayed on for a while. Mind you, it was those bleedin' stairs what did it; it was murder climbing them a few times a day.'

She set the rocking chair in motion and let her mind go back to last night's party. Pretty soon a smile was lighting up her face. It was some party all right, a real knees-up. She never thought the day would come when she'd see toffs like Mr John and Mr Charles kicking their legs in the air while dancing to *Knees Up Mother Brown*. It did her heart good to see Mr John enjoying himself like that – he'd probably never had so much fun since he was a kid playing footie in the street. And he had the Perkins family to thank for his happiness; he was a different man since they came into his life.

The rocking stopped and Aggie leaned forward to talk once again to the flames. 'Ay, what about that Sarah Jane! God, she was a right caution, she was! There was me, tryin' to be on me best behaviour an' she was swearing her head off like a ruddy trooper! Anyone would have thought she was in the snug at her local pub! She had them all in stitches, even the toffs. Mind you, a "bleedin' " here and there never did no one no harm.'

Aggie turned to look at the Westminster chiming clock standing on a white lace runner on the sideboard. Blimey, it was only half-nine. She couldn't sit talking to herself all day, even though she had to admit to enjoying a good conversation with herself because that way she never lost an argument. She could go and see Ada and Fanny – that would pass a few hours away – but they'd be up to their necks in polishing and scrubbing after last night. They'd washed all the dishes and tidied around before she left, but the floors and carpets were in one hell of a state.

Suddenly Aggie sat bolt upright. 'I'll go and see Sarah Jane! She said she sets up about this time, with the help of Mary, so I can give her a hand.' She was delighted at the prospect of seeing the old lady again. 'We can have a laugh, and that beats stayin' on me lonesome all bleedin' day.'

Five minutes later, Aggie was walking down the street, a smile on her face and joy in her heart. It wasn't far to walk and when she got to Bold Street the going would be easy because it was all downhill.

At the sight of her, Sarah Jane's face creased into a toothless smile. 'Well, girl, I never expected to see you here! I thought yer'd still be in bed sleepin' off yer hangover.'

'I don't get a hangover after six bottles of stout.' Aggie skirted the buckets and stood beside the stool. She saw Irish Mary waving to her and returned the greeting before bending to whisper in the old lady's ear. 'After seven perhaps, but not six.'

'Ay, I've got a customer.' Sarah Jane pointed impatiently. 'Go and sell her a bunch of flowers.'

For a second, Aggie's mouth gaped. Then she realised that the old lady was in earnest. 'What? I can't do that. I've never sold a bleedin' thing in me life!'

'Well, there's a first time for everything, girl, so now's yer chance. Flog her a bunch of flowers an' I'll mug yer to a bottle of stout.'

Filled with apprehension, Aggie approached the woman who was looking at the tulips. 'Nice those, aren't they?' she said, wondering how she'd let herself be talked into this. 'I like the yellow ones meself, they'd brighten yer room up a treat.' She turned to ask, 'How much are the tulips, Sarah Jane?'

'Tuppence a bunch – an' cheap at half the price.'

With the two coins in her hand, a song in her heart and a smile on her face, Aggie swayed back to the old lady. 'Well, then, how about that!'

Mary came up behind Aggie, laughing. 'She's got you at it, has she? Honest, she could charm the birds off a tree, and that's the truth of it. She says she's never been to Ireland, but if she hasn't kissed the blarney stone, sure it's me hat I'll be eating.'

Sarah Jane tugged on Aggie's coat. 'Ay, yer've got a

customer, don't let her get away. She's looking at the daffodils, and if yer can't persuade her that they'll brighten her room up a treat, it's surprised I'll be.'

Shaking her head in disbelief, Aggie approached the potential customer. 'Can't beat daffodils this time of the year, can yer? We haven't got any sunshine, but with them on yer sideboard yer'll think the sun's crackin' the flags outside.'

This time Aggie did a little jig before passing the coins over. 'I never thought I had it in me!'

'Yer a born saleswoman, Aggie,' said crafty Sarah Jane. 'The minute I clapped eyes on yer, I said to meself, "that one would make a marvellous saleswoman".'

'Go on, pull the other one, it's got bells on.' Aggie laughed down into the wrinkled face. 'Which pub do yer drink in, so I'll know where to go to collect the bottle of stout yer owe me?'

'The Crown.'

'Go 'way! I don't live far from there! Will yer be there tonight?'

'Tonight, tomorrow night, and every other night if I can get someone to help me sell me flowers.' A sly look crossed Sarah Jane's face. 'It's me legs yer see, girl, they've given up on me. It takes me five minutes to get off the stool an' by that time the customer's done a disappearing act.'

'Ay, me heart bleeds for yer, yer poor old soul.' Aggie wiped away an imaginary tear. 'Yer can tell me all yer troubles tonight when yer buy me that bottle of stout.'

'Ay, if yer want to work for me, girl, yer'll have to learn to keep yer eye to business.' Sarah Jane managed to keep her face straight but her shoulders were shaking with suppressed laughter. 'There's a woman there waitin' to be served. Buck yer ideas up, girl, or yer'll be turnin' me into a teetotal against me will.'

Aggie moved away, thinking how glad she was she'd thought of coming down here. It beat sitting on her own all day talking to two flaming walls. She called over her shoulder, 'Does eight o'clock tonight suit yer?'

'Down to the ground, girl, down to the ground. Oh, by the way, those pink carnations are threepence a bunch.'

Polly wasn't looking at what she was doing and dipped her pen too far down in the bottle of Quink. She ended up with ink all over her fingers and a look of disgust on her face. Holding her fingers away from her dress, she went to Mr Westly's desk. 'Can I go an' wash me hands, Mr Westly?'

There was a twinkle in the tutor's eyes when he told her, 'You can go, Polly, but you may not.'

Looking puzzled, Polly returned to her desk. What did he mean, 'You can go, but you may not?' Was he telling her she could, or could not go? She'd have to ask again; she couldn't sit with inky fingers all afternoon. From her chair, she asked, 'Mr Westly, did yer say I could go or not?'

Tom Westly grinned, Justin chuckled aloud, and even Rebecca laughed. Polly looked at each of them in turn, and although she laughed with them she didn't know what she was laughing at. 'I'm glad you three find it funny, but I'm sittin' here with ink all over me. I only asked if I could go and wash me hands.'

'Polly, you should know the difference now between can and may. Suppose you asked if you could stand on your head. Now it is possible for you to stand on your head, but I wouldn't allow it.'

Polly was chuckling by now. 'I *can* stand on me head, if yer must know, and I'll stand on me head to wash me hands if that's what yer want.'

Tom dropped his head and took a few seconds to quell his laughter. She really was a treasure, was Polly Perkins. 'I think you would have great difficulty in washing your hands whilst standing on your head. But I only used that as an instance. There are many things we are capable of doing, but we are not always allowed to do them. Now does that make it any clearer?'

'Well, it's clearer than it would be if yer were telling me in French, Mr Westly, but if yer want the God's honest truth, I still don't know whether I can go and wash me hands or not.'

Hooting with laughter, Justin looked across at his sister. She was enjoying the exchange, and he had to admit there was a difference in her attitude to Polly. There had been no snide remarks and no sneers. He just hoped it wasn't a flash in the pan and the improvement would continue.

'Polly, if you ask if you *may* go and wash your hands, the answer will be in the affirmative.'

Dropping her smile, Polly put on a refined accent. 'Mr Westly, *may* I go and wash my hands?'

'You *may*, Miss Perkins.'

'Thank you, Mr Westly.' As she was passing his desk, Polly leaned over and looked in his face. 'I could have been there and back by now, Mr Westly, even if I had washed me hands standing on me head.'

Polly left a room ringing with laughter. And when Justin had controlled his mirth, he leaned sideways to say to his sister, 'Do you now see what I mean, Rebecca? Polly doesn't mind people laughing at her because she laughs at herself. That is her secret, it's what draws people to her. I only hope some of her warmth and humour, and her capacity for giving, rubs off on me.' He winked broadly. 'If I get some, I'll share it with you.'

Chapter Twenty-Six

Fanny had come up for her cup of tea and was perched on one of the stools in the kitchen with her legs dangling a foot off the ground. 'Is that tea nearly ready, missus? I'm parched!'

'Hold yer horses, Fanny, yer've only just come up! I can't make the flamin' water boil any quicker. The trouble with you is everything has to be done on the double.'

Fanny grinned as she pushed her mobcap up out of her eyes. 'Oh, now, girl, I don't like everythin' done on the double, not when I'm enjoying meself. Mind you, it's so long since I was pleasured in that way I've forgotten what it felt like.'

Just then the kettle started to whistle and as Ada picked it up to pour the boiling water into the teapot, she tutted, 'I don't know how yer can say yer've forgotten, when it comes into yer conversation at least once every day.'

'Ah, ray, that's stretching it a bit, isn't it? I don't harp on it, I only mention it in passing. If I didn't I'd forget I ever had it, let alone what it felt like. And yer wouldn't want me to go to me grave not remembering the only act I ever got a thrill out of, would yer? It was the only thing my feller was ever any good at.'

Ada handed her a cup. 'D'yer think yer can stop talking long enough to drink that? Yer were moaning a few minutes ago about being parched but a dry throat doesn't stop yer gabbing, does it?'

'The only chance I get for a natter is when I come up here for me cuppa.' Fanny sipped gingerly on the piping hot tea before holding the cup out to Ada. 'Put a drop more milk in, girl, cool it down a bit.' She eyed her friend thoughtfully.

'You look a bit down in the dumps, girl. Is anythin' the matter?'

'I always feel low after I've been in to see Tommy. I'm really worried about him – there's been no improvement at all. And when I ask the Sister, all I get is "there's no change".'

'Yer'll go in one day and there'll be good news for yer, take my word for it, girl.' Fanny finished her tea, slipped from the stool and went to stand the dirty cup in the sink. 'I'd better get on with me work or I'll never finish in time.'

She had almost reached the door when Mr John came breezing in and her thin face lit up. 'Looking all dandified again, Mr John!'

John fingered the red rose in his buttonhole. 'Put there by Aggie's fair hand. She's in her element down there with Sarah Jane, they get on like a house on fire.'

'Yer know they're boozing buddies, don't yer?' The mobcap was pushed back again. It was far too big for her but she just couldn't be bothered putting a tuck in it. 'In the pub every night they are, drinkin' their bottles of stout and talkin' about old times.'

John nodded and smiled. 'It's given Aggie a new lease of life. In her own words it's better than sitting in her bleeding rocking chair just waiting to die. She said when the good Lord decides to take her, He can get on the twenty-six tram and pick her up from Bold Street.'

'She'll probably insist He takes Sarah Jane with her so she'll have someone to talk to when she gets to heaven,' Ada put in. 'I've always said Aggie would argue with Our Lord.'

'Heaven, did yer say, girl? Bein' a bit optimistic, aren't yer? If you heard how those two carry on at the pub, yer wouldn't give much for their chances. Blimey, the things they come out with would make yer hair curl!' Fanny's high-pitched laugh rang out. 'If she ever does get to heaven, the Angel Gabriel better 'ave a few crates of stout in or there'll be ructions.' Her two palms pressed on her tummy she doubled up with laughter as her imagination ran riot. 'I can just see Aggie sittin' on a stool next to Sarah Jane, both with wings on their backs and playing harps.' She had to take a few deep breaths before she could carry on. 'I can hear Sarah Jane sayin' to Aggie, "Sod this for a lark, girl. Let's give 'em *Down by the Old Bull and Bush*".'

John's laughter was loud, but Ada covered her mouth to keep hers at bay. 'Fanny Delaney, you'll never get to heaven, you won't.'

'I know that, girl, so there's no point in bein' good, is there?' With a wave of her hand Fanny left the room, and they could hear her tittering as she ran down the stairs.

Ada put the plug in the sink and turned the tap on. 'I don't know who's the worst, Fanny, Aggie or Sarah Jane.'

'Much of a muchness, I'd say.' John came to stand beside her and rubbed a finger lightly down her cheek. 'Are you all right, my love?'

'Yes, I'm fine. You go and do what yer have to do and I'll bring yer a drink through when I've washed these few dishes.'

John was standing in the window looking thoughtful when Ada carried his drink in. 'Here, let me take that.' He took the cup and saucer from her and set it on a small side table. 'Don't rush away, Ada, stay for a short while and talk to me.'

'I've got a lot to do, John. I haven't started the ironing yet.'

'To hell with the ironing!' He quickly covered the distance between them and grasped her two hands. 'I didn't mean to eavesdrop, my love, but I couldn't help overhearing you tell Fanny you were worried about your husband.'

She tried to pull her hands free but John held on tight. 'I don't want to talk about it, John, I only get upset.'

'But why didn't you tell me this morning that you were worried? I would never have gone out and left you if I'd known.'

'I can't come moaning to you all the time, it wouldn't be fair.'

'Talking about your sick husband isn't moaning, Ada. And I'm saddened that it was Fanny you confided in, and not me.' He put a finger under her chin and lifted her face. 'You need to talk, my darling; don't keep it bottled up inside of you. Sharing your fears will help ease your mind.'

Ada gave a deep sigh. 'I was hoping that seeing Polly would give Tommy the will to fight what ails him, but it hasn't. In fact, he appeared weaker than ever yesterday, and he showed no interest whatsoever in anything I had to say. He just seems to have given up on life.' She dropped her head. 'I'm sorry, but I'm going to cry, I can't help it.'

'Then cry, my darling.' John pulled her into his arms and stroked the back of her head. 'My shoulder is always here for you to cry on.'

Polly was in a dilemma. She'd promised Steve she'd be living back home by Easter, which was only two weeks away, and she hadn't been able to pluck up the courage to tell the Denholmes she was leaving. I mean, after they'd bought her those lovely clothes for her birthday, how could she turn around and say she was leaving them? She couldn't hurt them like that. They'd been so good to her, treated her more like one of the family than a servant. And she really was very fond of them, they were like a second family to her. Even Rebecca's attitude had changed over the last few weeks, and although they weren't bosom pals at least the other girl was more friendly.

Polly lifted her hands out of the soapy water and reached for the tea towel. It was her night off; Steve was coming to meet her straight from work and they were going for a walk. He was bound to ask if she'd told the Denholmes yet and she was dreading having to say she hadn't. She'd tried over and over again to explain the situation to him, but no matter what she said he couldn't understand why she liked living with posh people who spoke as though they had a plum in their mouths. He said he'd be happy when she was living next door again and they could see each other every night, and if she liked him as much as he liked her, then she wouldn't let anything or anybody stand in her way. He even said her place was at home helping her mother, which made her feel more guilty.

'If you want to get off, Polly,' Mrs Nightingale's voice broke into her thoughts, 'yer can leave those dishes and Lucy will finish them off.'

'No, I'm all right, but thanks all the same.'

'I thought you were seeing yer boyfriend tonight?' The cook pursed her lips. 'You should be looking happy instead of having a face on yer like a wet week.'

'I've got a bit of a headache,' Polly lied. 'It'll go away when I get out in the fresh air.'

'Then put that cloth down and get away early while yer've got the chance. Lucy won't mind finishing them off – yer can do the same for her one night when she's got a date.'

Polly made up her mind quickly. She needed to talk to someone – and who better than the mother who'd always been there when she needed her? Her mam would understand and tell her what she thought was the right thing to do so she wouldn't upset or hurt anyone. 'I think I'll take yer advice, Mrs Nightingale. I'll walk over to see me mam and be back by six o'clock to meet Steve.'

Standing in front of the mirror in her bedroom, Polly ran a comb through her hair as she tried to analyse her feelings. The trouble was, she wanted to please everyone and that wasn't possible. She didn't want to hurt Steve because he was her boyfriend and she knew in her heart of hearts, young as she was, that he was the only boy for her. But she didn't want to hurt anyone else, either, and she just wished Steve could understand that. Polly put the comb on the tallboy and slipped her arms into her coat. She'd wait and see what her mam said, that was the best thing.

Polly's heart felt lighter as she walked the short distance from Percy Street to Faulkner Square. Once she'd got it all off her chest, her mam would advise her and everything would work out fine.

She was surprised to find the front door ajar, then noticed that the front steps had not long been scrubbed, so Fanny was probably in the kitchen. She thought about calling out to announce her arrival, but decided against it. If the little woman saw her she'd keep her talking and Polly didn't want to waste any precious time. So she ran lightly up the stairs and made her way to the drawing room where she could hear voices. There was a greeting on her lips but it was never uttered as she took in the intimacy of the scene before her. Mr John had his arms around her mam and was stroking her hair as he whispered words Polly was too shocked to hear. She felt as though she'd been turned to stone, horrified at what she was seeing. For what seemed like an eternity, but in reality was merely a few seconds, she was rooted to the spot, unable to move or speak. She wanted to run towards the couple who were unaware of her presence, to scream and hit out at them, tell them they were wicked and she hated them for what they were doing when her dad was lying in hospital. But her feet refused to move and her mouth stayed silent. Then her stomach started to churn and she knew she was going to be sick. So she forced herself to quietly walk along the hall, down the stairs and out into the street. Her head was thumping as she hurried to the nearest side entry, and once out of sight, she bent double and retched until her tummy and throat ached. She tried to blot out the picture of her mam in Mr John's arms, but it wouldn't go away, it was imprinted on her mind. She thought of her poor dad in hospital, and at that moment came the hatred for the man and woman she'd seen wrapped in each other's arms. She'd never speak to them again, didn't ever want to set eyes on them. Ten minutes later she emerged from the entry, white-faced and red-eyed, but with her head held high.

'Have yer got a cold?' Steve asked, his face anxious as he

gazed at Polly. 'Yer eyes are all red and puffy.'

'Yeah, they've been running all day, and me nose.' Polly had decided not to tell a soul what she'd seen. She felt so sad, so let-down and lost, but the secret would stay with her. The only emotion she could feel for her mother was one of disgust, but she was still her mother and she wasn't going to discuss her with anyone, not even Steve.

'I don't want to stay out long, Steve, 'cos I don't feel so good. I'll get Mrs Nightingale to make me a hot drink and go to bed early.'

'Have yer told the Denholmes yet that yer leaving?'

Polly knew the question would come and had been dreading it. She didn't want to live at home now, not after what she'd seen tonight. Every time she looked at her mother she'd see her in Mr John's arms and she couldn't live with that. Not without making her feelings of abhorrence known. To pretend everything was all right would be living a lie and Polly knew she could never do that. The only thing that would take her back home now was if her dad came out of hospital.

'No, I haven't said anything yet. In fact, Steve, I think I'll stay on a bit longer. I like it there, they're very good to me, so why leave a place I like to go and work in a factory?'

Steve put a hand on her arm and pulled her to a stop. 'But you promised, Polly! You can't go back on a promise. I've been looking forward to seeing yer every night, counting the flippin' days.' He was so disappointed and hurt he was near to tears. 'Anyway, what's wrong with workin' in a factory? Do yer think yer too good for that now?'

'No, of course not! I'm not a snob, Steve Mitchell!'

'Then why won't yer come home? If you asked me to do something, and I was able to, then I'd do it 'cos of the way I feel about yer. I thought yer felt the same about me.'

'I do, Steve, honest. And I *will* come home – but give me a bit more time, that's all I ask.'

'No, Polly, you made a promise and I want yer to keep it.'

Hurt and jealousy were two of the emotions Steve was feeling. Hurt because she was letting him down, jealousy because he believed the longer she stayed with the Denholmes, the more chance there was of losing her. She'd get so used to living the good life she'd never settle down again in a two-up two-down terrace house. And that is all he'd ever be able to offer her. 'Come home, Polly, please?'

Polly came very near then to telling him the real reason why she didn't want to live at home any more, but something kept her back. 'It cuts both ways, yer know, Steve. You want me to give in to you, but you won't give in to me, will yer? I'm only asking for a bit more time.'

Steve shook his head. 'The longer yer stay there, the less chance there is of yer ever leaving. Yer've changed already, can't yer see that? Now yer think yer too good to work in a factory. Next thing, yer'll be thinkin' yer too good for me.'

Polly closed her eyes. This was the worst day in her life. But she had to hold out, she couldn't bear the thought of having to face her mam every day, knowing what she did. 'I never said I was too good to work in a factory, Steve, and I certainly don't think I'm too good for you. Ever since we were kids I've known there was something special between us and I still feel the same. You are the only boy I've ever wanted, or will want.'

'But yer still won't come home?' Steve's eyes were begging. In his mind's eye he could see Polly on her birthday dressed up in the finery bought by the Denholmes. And he could see Justin in his suit of fine wool, the likes of which Steve would never be able to afford. 'Not for my sake, Polly?'

'I could ask you the same thing, Steve. Give it a bit longer, just for my sake.'

Steve shook his head. He was so hurt he wanted to hit out. 'No, Polly, I won't give it a bit longer. You either keep your promise or that's it, we're through.'

'Oh, you can't say that, Steve!'

'I've said it and I mean it. Are you coming home for Easter, Polly, or not?'

'Can't we talk about it another time, Steve? I don't feel very well right now.'

'No, no more talking. Yer've been fobbing me off for weeks. You and me are finished.' Steve turned on his heels. 'Goodbye, Polly.'

Polly watched him walk away, tears streaming down her face. She wanted to run after him, promise him the earth, but pride and her mother's secret held her back. And because she needed to vent her anger on someone, she placed the blame on her mother's shoulders. The woman she'd always idolised, who she thought could do no wrong.

Ada was on her knees dusting the carved spindles of the staircase when John came on to the landing. 'I'm going out for a few hours, Ada, but I'll be home for dinner.' He usually stopped to chat for a few minutes, tell her where he was going and why, but today he volunteered no information and after a brief wave he was on his way. It crossed Ada's mind that he appeared distant, as though he had something on his mind, but she put it down to him having an important appointment to keep.

John tapped his fingers on the steering wheel as he drive through County Road and Rice Lane towards Fazakerley. Whether he was doing the right thing remained to be seen, but to him there was no alternative. He wouldn't be able to live with himself if he didn't do all in his power to stop the anguish that Ada was suffering and had suffered for so long. He turned into the hospital gates, telling himself he wanted Ada more than he'd ever wanted anything in his life before, but the price was too high. He wasn't so selfish he would wish another man dead so he could have his wife.

The nurse looked surprised to see him. 'I'm sorry, sir, but it's not visiting time.'

'I am aware of that, my dear, but I would like to see Mr Perkins on a very important matter.'

His air of confidence and his impeccable attire swayed the nurse. 'I'll have to ask Matron but I'm sure it'll be all right.'

With a stern look on her face, Matron eyed John up and down. 'You may see Mr Perkins but I must ask that you don't stay too long. He is very weak and tires quickly.'

Tommy was lying flat on his back staring at the ceiling when he heard the nurse talking. He turned his head on the pillow to see her walking down the ward with a man by her side. There was something vaguely familiar about the man's face but Tommy thought he must be imagining things; the well-dressed stranger certainly wouldn't be coming to see him. So he was surprised and curious when the pair stopped at the foot of his bed and the nurse told him, 'You have a visitor, Mr Perkins.'

'You may not remember me, Mr Perkins, it's many years since we met. I'm John Roscoe – does that ring a bell?'

'I thought yer looked familiar but I couldn't place yer. Now I know, yer our landlord and me wife works for yer.'

When Tommy tried to sit up the nurse moved quickly to help. She propped him up on the pillows and gently warned, 'Don't overdo it, Mr Perkins, take it easy.' She smiled at John before hurrying to catch up on her duties.

'Have yer been visitin' someone in here, Mr Roscoe?' Tommy asked, looking puzzled. He couldn't think of any other reason for the man to be here.

John shook his head. 'No, I came to see you. But it's not very comfortable standing, so shall I fetch one of those chairs?'

Tommy waited until John was settled, then asked, 'There's nothing wrong with Ada or the kids, is there, Mr Roscoe?'

'No, they're fine.' John ran a finger around the crown of the bowler hat he was holding between his hands. 'Before I tell you why I'm here, I would be grateful if we could dispense with formalities. I'm John and you're Tommy, is that all right with you?'

'It suits me.' Interest was beginning to stir in Tommy. What the hell had the bloke come for?

'I believe Ada will have told you the circumstances under which she came to work for me so I won't go over those details again. My real reason for coming to see you is to set the records straight. I want you to hear me through without forming any conclusion until I have finished what I came to say. Will you do that, Tommy?'

'Yer've got me fair flummoxed, John, but yes, I'll listen to yer.'

John sighed. 'This isn't easy for me but I'm doing it for Ada's sake, and the children.' He held Tommy's gaze. 'Yesterday, I held your wife in my arms and I kissed her.' He heard the sharp intake of breath and held up his hand. 'Please hear me out. I held her, as I have often done in the past, to comfort her. She was crying, and my shoulder was there for her to cry on. The last two years have been hard for Ada, worrying about you and trying to earn enough money to keep the home together. And I was also looking for comfort as my own marriage was causing me great unhappiness. So we were two people in need of comfort, warmth and companionship. We helped each other. But your wife has never betrayed you, she loves you deeply.'

John ran a hand across his forehead, hoping his words were doing justice to the situation. 'I am not going to lie to you. I will admit that I'm very fond of Ada – she is everything I would want in a woman. It is because I hold her in such high regard that I am here today. Her happiness is more important to me than anything else, and her happiness lies with you.'

Tommy looked at the now bowed head. His emotions were all mixed up together, but through them all came respect for the man who had the guts to come here today and say what he had. 'Have you finished, John?'

'No, I've set the record straight regarding Ada and myself, but I haven't told you why she was crying yesterday, and on many other days during the last two years. She feels that you've lost the will to live, that you don't want to get better. Is that true?'

Tommy's head dropped back on the pillow. 'After two and a half years in this place, anyone would lose the will to live. And what would I have to offer my family if I did get better? I'd never be able to work again. I'll never be fit enough to do labouring, which is all I'm good for. I'd be a burden on Ada, and the children. They'd have to work to keep me, and what would that do to a man's pride?'

John leaned forward. 'If that's the way you're thinking, Tommy, then you'll never get better! You've got a wife in a million and two lovely children – isn't that enough for you? I'd give my right arm to be in your shoes, believe me.'

'It's easy for you to talk, John, if yer don't mind me saying so. You've never seen yer kids running around in second-hand clothes, never seen them shivering because there's no money for coal to light a fire. It pulls a man down when he can't support his family in even the bare necessities, takes his pride away, makes him feel he's a failure. In fact, it makes him feel they'd be better off without him.'

'Now you're going to get some plain talking from me, Tommy! Don't you know that while you're lying here feeling worthless, your wife and kids are saying prayers every night for you to get better? They may as well save their breath because from what I've heard, you've made up your mind you're never going to get well. Doesn't say much for the love you profess to have for them, does it?' John was letting his anger show. 'You said you'll never be able to get a job, but how do you know that? There's plenty of light jobs you could do, if you had the mind.'

'Oh, aye, and who's going to employ someone who's had consumption? They'd send me packing with a flea in me ear.'

'I'll give you a job,' John said. 'A job as a rent-collector that would have you out in the fresh air every day – just what you need.'

'I don't want yer to offer me a job out of pity.'

'For God's sake, man, why are you so stubborn? I wouldn't offer you a job out of pity, but out of friendship. Your wife and children, and your neighbours, the Mitchells, have become like a family to me. If I offered Les Mitchell a job, d'you think he'd turn it down because he thought I was only feeling sorry for him? Not on your life he wouldn't. He'd grab it with both hands and be thankful.'

Tommy was silent as his thin fingers plucked at the cover on the narrow hospital bed. Then, after a thoughtful few minutes, he said, 'Ada's told me how good yer've been to her and the children. And to the Mitchells, Sarah Jane and them all. You're a good man, John, and I'm grateful to yer. But with the best will in the world I can't just wave a magic wand and make meself better.'

'I'm not suggesting you can, Tommy. But if you start thinking positive it would help. Don't be a defeatist, tell yourself that you've got a job to go to when you get home, a loving wife and two beautiful children. Make up your mind you're going to fight this illness. Don't be content to just lie there and die.'

They heard loud brisk footsteps and when they looked up, Matron was marching towards the bed. 'I think Mr Perkins is due for his nap now.'

John stood up. 'I'm coming, Matron, and I thank you for allowing me to see my friend. I just want one more minute and then I'll follow you.'

Feeling like a schoolgirl being dismissed by her teacher, the Matron meekly left them alone.

'Just keep this in your mind, Tommy. Your wife has waited over two years for you. In that time she had never denied or betrayed her love for you. She needs you, so don't let her down.'

'John, did yer mean what yer said about givin' me a job, if I ever get out of here?'

'I don't make idle promises, Tommy. Of course I meant it.'

Tommy stuck his hand out. 'John, ye're a real gent.'

Chapter Twenty-Seven

It was a week to the day that Polly had seen her mother in the arms of Mr John and since Steve had stormed off and left her. She hadn't seen either of them since and it had been the most miserable week of her life. Mr John had rung to say her mother was worried that she hadn't been to see her, but she'd told Mr Charles to tell him she had a tummy upset and would go when she felt better. She couldn't make that an excuse for much longer and she was dreading her mother coming around to see her because Polly knew she'd have to tell her the real reason . . . that she didn't want to see her ever again for two-timing her sick dad.

But although she wouldn't let the thought linger in her mind, Polly missed her mam something terrible. It was like a continual ache in her heart. And she grieved over Steve, too. She'd toyed with the idea of going down to see Sarah Jane on Saturday, knowing he'd be there, but her pride held her back. Besides, nothing had changed; she still had no intention of going back home to live.

The change in Polly was causing concern to everyone in the Denholme residence. Her laughter no longer rang out, and when she forced a smile it didn't reach her eyes. She looked pale and drawn and showed little enthusiasm for her work in the house or in the classroom.

While Polly sat on her bed feeling alone and unloved, Charles and Victoria were discussing her in the drawing room. 'There is definitely something worrying the child, Charles, but what?'

'I don't know, my love, I wish I did. When I ask, she says she's all right. I can hardly force her to tell me anything against her will.'

'I know she hasn't been going out on her nights off, which means she hasn't been seeing her boyfriend.' Victoria fingered the amber necklace she was wearing as she crossed her shapely legs. 'I wonder if they've had a tiff and she's pining?'

'I should think there's more to it than that,' Charles said. 'She hasn't been to see her mother for a week, and that's most unusual. I find the whole situation very odd.'

'Another thought, Charles – perhaps she's worrying about her father. Why don't you ask if she'd like to see him? I'm sure the hospital would allow a short visit.'

'I really don't know whether that would be a good thing or not, my darling. She was distressed last time she saw him, remember?'

'I still think it's worth a try,' Victoria insisted. 'She is such a delightful child I don't like to see her so unhappy.'

'I agree we must do something. We can't let things ride or she will make herself ill.' Charles stubbed his cigar out in the heavy glass ashtray. 'Ring for Lucy and ask her to bring Polly down.'

Polly's face was animated as she walked down the corridor beside Charles. She was so looking forward to seeing her father. He would never, ever let her down. They had reached the ward doors when Charles heard her cry out at the same time as she grabbed his arm and brought him to a halt. He followed her gaze and saw Ada sitting on the side of a bed halfway down the ward. She was holding hands with the man Charles presumed was Polly's father, and the couple were smiling into each other's faces. 'No! How can she! How can she do that to me dad!'

Charles was stunned. 'Polly, what is it?'

'I'm going, I don't want to see her.' Polly turned and fled, leaving Charles no alternative but to follow her. She ran as though she had wings on her heels and was standing beside the car before he caught up with her.

'Polly, my dear, you must tell me what is wrong.' Charles put an arm across her shoulders and could feel her shaking. 'Why didn't you want to see your mother?'

'I can't tell you, Mr Charles,' Polly sobbed. 'But I don't ever want to see her again.'

'I can't believe you mean that, my dear. You love your mother very much and she adores you. What has she done to make you behave this way?'

'I used to love her, but I don't any more.'

'Nonsense! You don't fall out of love with anyone unless they've done something very bad to hurt you, and I'm sure your mother would never do that.'

'She has!' Polly wiped away the tears with the back of her hand. 'But I don't want to talk about it, Mr Charles.'

'You must talk about it or you'll make yourself very ill.' Charles opened the car door. 'I'm going to take you home and I insist you tell my wife and I what is worrying you so much. I'm quite sure that somewhere along the line there has been a misunderstanding, and in your mind it's been blown up out of all proportion. Now hop in the car, my dear. The sooner we get it sorted out, the sooner we'll see a smile back on that pretty face of yours.'

Ada ran a finger over the veins in Tommy's hand as she smiled at him. 'I was out of me mind yesterday when Mr John said he'd been to see yer, in case he'd upset yer.' She remembered her feelings of anger and dismay when John had explained he'd been totally honest with her husband and told him everything. In fact, she'd been so upset John had insisted she came to see Tommy today to put her mind at rest.

'I wasn't upset, love, I admired the bloke for his honesty.' Tommy cocked his head. 'You know he's in love with yer, don't yer?'

'We've been good for each other, Tommy, and I'll not deny it. But there's never been any question about it going any further than that. My heart belongs to you and always will do.' Even as she said it, Ada knew that there would always be a place in her heart for John. He'd been so good, so kind, had always been there for her . . . how could she not love him for those things?

'Aye, he told me that, an' all! He was very straight, said I didn't know how lucky I was to have a wife like you and two lovely children. In fact, he went as far as to say I shouldn't be lying here waiting to die, I should buck me ideas up and get better.'

Ada's jaw dropped. 'He didn't!'

'Perhaps not in those words, but what he said amounted to the same thing. And when he told me about the hard time you'd had, how often yer cried over me – well, I was glad that he'd been there to help yer.' Tommy lowered his eyes. 'If anything does happen to me, like say I didn't make it, then Mr John would be good for you and the kids.'

'Don't you dare say that, Tommy Perkins! Yer can get that idea out of yer head right this minute! Me and the kids want you, nobody else, so make up yer mind yer going to get better.'

'Like I told Mr John, love, I can't just wave a magic wand. It's out of my hands, what happens to me.' He raised his eyes and Ada saw there was a brightness there she hadn't seen for a long time. 'By the way, did he tell you that when, or if, I get out of here, he'll give me a job?'

Ada nodded. 'As a rent-collector. It would be just the job for yer, Tommy, out in the fresh air all day. It would do yer the world of good.'

'I know, I've thought of nothin' else since yesterday. It's just a pity that the opportunity didn't come up a few years ago.'

Ada gently slapped the hand she was holding. 'Stop looking on the black side, Tommy Perkins, and get it into yer head that it's not too late. You've got an aim in life now, so start fighting, sweetheart, for me and Polly and Joey.'

★ ★ ★

Lucy put the tray down and looked towards Victoria. 'Shall I pour the tea, ma'am?'

Victoria dismissed her with a wave of her hand. 'I'll see to it, Lucy. You may go.'

Once the door was closed behind the maid, Charles took a seat on the settee next to Polly. The girl was sitting with her head bent and her hands folded on her lap. 'Now, Polly, won't you tell us what your mother is supposed to have done that is so wrong?'

Polly shook her head, and in a low voice said, 'I can't, Mr Charles.'

'If you don't tell us, my dear, we can't help. And we do so want to help you.'

When Polly shook her head and remained tight-lipped, Charles looked at his wife and shrugged his shoulders. He saw her mouth the words, 'Let me sit next to her,' and he pushed himself from the settee and moved across to his chair.

Victoria offered the china cup and saucer. 'Drink this, Polly, it will make you feel better.'

When Polly lifted her face, tears spilled from her eyes and ran down her cheeks to fall in drops on her dress. 'It won't make me feel better – nothing will!'

Seeing the girl looking so agitated and distraught, Victoria handed the drink to Charles and sat herself next to Polly. 'There now, my dear,' she drew her into her arms, 'you have a good cry and when when you feel able, you must tell my husband and I what is causing such distress.'

Polly laid her head on Victoria's breast, and when she felt the comforting arms enfold her, she gave way to her tears. Her sobs were so heartbreaking, Victoria was herself moved to tears. She could feel them running down her cheeks to add to the damp patch on her light beige shot-silk dress.

Charles watched in silence, wanting to help but not knowing how. He could feel himself becoming emotional too, and sipped on the cup of tea he was holding, hoping to move the hard lump that was forming in his throat. He saw Polly wiping at the tears with her hand and took a handkerchief from his pocket. 'Here you are, my dear, wipe your eyes.'

Polly took the hankie and dabbed at her face. It seemed her whole world had been turned upside down and she had no one to turn to. As her mind tried to sort out the sequence of events that had led to this, her tears ceased to flow and her racking sobs became hiccups. She was still in the comfort of Victoria's arms, where she felt safe and wanted. The Denholmes are so good to me, she thought. They are the only real friends I have now. It was this thought that decided her.

Polly drew back her head and looked into Victoria's eyes. In a low voice she said, 'I saw Mr John with his arms around me mam, and he was kissing her.' Her voice grew stronger when she cried, 'He had no right to do that, and me mam's as much to blame for letting him.'

Victoria gasped in horror, then glanced over to see Charles leaning forward, his elbows on his knees. 'Oh no, my dear, you must have been mistaken!'

Polly's head shook vigorously. 'I saw them! They didn't see me, but I stood and watched them. Then I ran away and was sick in the entry.'

'You should have told us this before, Polly,' Charles said, 'instead of making yourself ill. I'm sure there's a perfectly good explanation for what you think you saw, and if you'd mentioned it right away you would have been spared all this heartache.'

Victoria put a finger under the girl's chin and lifted her face. 'Is this why you haven't seen your boyfriend for over a week?'

'No!' Polly pulled her head free and dropped it to stare at her hands. 'Steve's fallen out with me.' Her voice choked, she told them, 'It was on the same day, too. Everything seemed to happen at once and I couldn't bear it.'

'Why has Steve fallen out with you?' Charles asked. 'Did you have a quarrel?'

'He wants me to go back home to live, and he wouldn't listen when I tried to explain. He thinks if I stay here I'll get too big for me boots, and he won't be good enough for me. I didn't tell him about me mam and Mr John, I wasn't ever going to tell anyone, so I couldn't tell him that I'll never live at home again unless me dad comes out of hospital. I wouldn't be happy living in the same house as me mam, not after what I'd seen.'

Clutching the handkerchief, Polly looked at Charles, and the unhappiness in her eyes touched his heart. 'Steve just said we were finished and he walked off and left me. It was terrible, Mr Charles. I didn't know what to do, who to turn to. Now I've lost everyone . . . I won't even be able to see our Joey again, and I can't go down to see Sarah Jane or Irish Mary in case Steve is there.'

'Do you miss your mother, Polly?' Charles asked, his voice soft. 'And Steve?'

'I miss them terrible.' Her nerves shattered, Polly began to smooth out the handkerchief on her lap. 'But none of it was my fault, Mr Charles, I didn't do anything wrong. In a way I can understand Steve 'cos I'd broken a promise, but he should have been more understanding. He can't have everything his own way, that's being childish. But what me mam and Mr John were doing was bad, and I'll never forgive them.'

'Polly, when you are young a tiny insignificant incident can be magnified a hundred times in your mind, until it becomes a disaster. As you grow older you will learn through experience that the only way to deal with a problem is head-on. Talk to the person, or persons involved, tell them of your fears or suspicions and ask for an explanation. It is only fair to those people that you do that.' Charles took out his fob-watch and feigned surprise at the time. He gave his wife a look which asked that she didn't query what he was about to say. 'Look, I should have met a colleague half an hour ago, so I must leave you for a short while. When I get back we'll talk some more.'

'I'm sorry to be such a nuisance to yer, Mr Charles,' Polly said, looking very young and vulnerable. 'I bet you and Mrs Denholme would be glad to see the back of me.'

'Nonsense!' Victoria took the girl in her arms once more. 'You are like one of our family and we care deeply what happens to you. When you are happy, we are happy; when you are sad, we too are sad.'

She waved her husband off. 'Try not to be too long, darling.'

John was sitting at his desk checking an account book when he cocked his head. Was that someone shouting or was he hearing things? He laid his pencil down and pushed his chair back. Someone was definitely shouting, or talking rather loudly. He walked out to the landing and, peering over the bannister, he was pleasantly surprised to see Agnes struggling up the stairs, muttering darkly with each step.

John quickly ran to the kitchen to alert Ada and Fanny. 'Just come and see who's come to visit us.'

The three were at the top of the staircase when Aggie finally reached it. 'These bleedin' stairs don't get any less, do they? I've slogged me flamin' guts out gettin' up here – and what sort of a welcome do I get? Three silly sods grinnin' like gormless idiots.'

Fanny pushed her mobcap back, a look of sheer pleasure on her thin face. 'If you were standin' here with us, there'd be four silly sods grinnin' like gormless idiots.'

'There wouldn't, yer know,' Aggie huffed, ''cos I haven't got enough energy to grin, so there! Another couple of bleedin' steps an' yer'd have been burying me from here. Bloody murder they are!'

'Wasn't it worth the effort to see three of yer best mates?' Ada asked, with a look of tenderness for the woman she'd grown to love. 'We're all glad to see you, even though you are moaning an' groaning.'

'Perhaps when I get me breath back I'll be glad to see yer, but right now I'm puffed out.'

John took her arm. 'Come and sit on the couch and we'll ask Fanny to make a nice cup of tea.'

Aggie had enough strength to pull her arm free. 'Sod that for a lark, Mr John. I came here for a bit of gossip an' I'll not get any perched on your bleedin' couch, that's a dead cert.'

Fanny cackled. 'Come on, girl, into the kitchen with yer. Yer can sit on the stool while I make yer a drink and tell yer about one of me neighbours who's havin' it off with the milkman.'

'Go 'way!' Aggie winked at John as she followed her friend. 'See what I mean, Mr John? Now you couldn't come up with anythin' to beat that, could yer?'

Ada and John shook their heads as they watched the two women disappear into the kitchen. 'What would you do with them?' John asked.

'I know what I shall do,' Ada grinned. 'I intend to find out what's going on between this neighbour and the milkman.'

'And I refuse to be left out,' John said. 'So lead on, my dear, I'll be right behind you.'

Now that she had an audience, Fanny was in her applecart. Her facial expressions and her gestures spoke volumes as she exaggerated the story out of all proportion. 'Her feller leaves for work at half-past seven, her kids leave for school at half-eight, and at nine o'clock the bold laddo is sneaking in her back door! They don't think anyone knows about it but she's the talk of the street.'

'Perhaps she's asked for an extra pint of milk,' Aggie said, keeping her face straight. 'I mean, it doesn't do to jump to conclusions.'

There was a look of disgust on Fanny's face. 'Oh, she's asked for somethin' extra, all right, but it ain't milk and it don't come in a bottle!' Her thin shoulders began to shake.

'I've heard it called some things, but never a bottle! Anyway, whatever he gives her puts a smile on her face that lasts all day.'

Aggie's face was the picture of innocence as she asked, 'Do you get yer milk off him, Fanny?'

Now the little woman's whole body was shaking with laughter. 'Not at the moment, but there's six of us in the street changin' to him from next Monday.'

'Six of yer!' Aggie cried. 'Yer'll kill the poor feller between the lot of yer!'

'Can yer think of a better way for him to die?'

Gales of laughter greeted Charles Denholme. He'd called out on his way up the stairs but when there was no answer he'd followed the noise. 'Well, this is a happy little scene.'

'Charles, my dear fellow!' John took a hankie from his breast pocket and wiped his streaming eyes. 'Come on in.'

Despite the unpleasant task ahead of him, Charles couldn't help smiling. 'Has Aggie been telling you one of her dirty jokes?'

Fanny gasped. Hands on her narrow hips, she glared. 'Hey, it was me what told the joke. I'm not havin' her steal me bleedin' limelight!'

'I'm so sorry, Fanny, please forgive me.' Charles bowed from his waist. 'Am I allowed to hear this joke?'

Fanny's face brightened. 'Well, it's this neighbour of mine, yer see. She's havin' it off with the ruddy milkman! An' as I was—'

Ada cut in. 'I don't think Mr Denholme would be interested in your milk deliveries, Fanny. Perhaps it would be better if Mr John told him, man to man, like.'

'A good idea,' John said. 'We'll go into the office, shall we, Charles?'

His friend nodded. 'I don't have much time and there's something I want to discuss with you.'

'Shall I bring a drink through?' Ada asked. 'Tea or whisky?'

'Thank you, Ada, but no. I really am tied for time.'

'Then let's not waste any.' John motioned for Charles to follow him, and when they were seated at his desk, he asked, 'What is it, Charles?'

'I find myself in a very embarrassing situation, John. I thought very carefully before coming to see you, but there was really no alternative. I have Polly's welfare at heart and at the moment, although she is not sick physically as you have been led to believe, she is very disturbed mentally.'

Charles sat back in the chair and crossed his legs. 'It's been clear for a week now that she was worried and upset about something, but it wasn't until this morning that we could get her to open up and talk about it. I would be grateful if you would hear me through.'

John remained silent while his friend related everything that Polly had told him, but his expression showed that he was shocked to the core.

Charles finished by saying, 'To end her day, her boyfriend Steve told her they were finished because she wouldn't go back home to live. And the child has been existing for a week with all that on her mind.'

John shook his head sadly. 'If only she'd stayed and confronted us, we'd have been able to explain and put her mind at rest. Yes, I did have my arms around Ada, as I have done on many occasions. She'd been to visit her husband the day before and was in a state of distress. I was comforting her, Charles, as you yourself would have done. Oh, I admit I have loving feelings for Ada, but I can promise you there has never been any impropriety. If you knew Ada, there would be no need for me to tell you that.'

John leaned his elbows on the desk and was thoughtful for a while. Then he said, 'I have told her husband everything. He knows I have held and kissed his wife, and he understands that she needed someone to lean on.'

Charles's jaw dropped. 'You told her husband!'

'I may be many things, Charles, but a complete bounder I am not. I love Ada, but I don't want her at the expense of another man's life. And Tommy is the man whom Ada loves. She was upset that day because she said he didn't seem to want to get better. So I took it upon myself to visit him in hospital and I told him a few home truths. I even offered him a job as a rent-collector when he comes out, hoping that will be an incentive for him to fight for his life.'

'I don't know what to say, John. I'm at a loss for words.' Charles let out a deep sigh. 'In your position, I doubt if I would be as generous. I am full of admiration for you.'

'I have received more than I have given, believe me. When Ada came into my life she brought with her her family and friends. From them I have been shown more warmth and affection than I've known since my parents died. They treat me as one of themselves, as a friend; my money means little to them. I have been given so much, Charles, I can't ask for more.'

'Do you mind if I tell Polly everything you've told me? What I've heard puts a different complexion on things, and I do so want to put her mind at rest. She misses her mother terribly, and Steve.'

'Please do tell her, and quickly. Ada hasn't said much, but I know deep down she is worried. I can't help much over the Steve episode, but if we can get mother and daughter back together again, we can concentrate on sorting that out and getting the childhood sweethearts reunited.'

When Charles opened the door of the sitting room, it was to find Polly still wrapped in Victoria's arms. He ruffled her hair before sitting down. 'I've asked Lucy to bring some tea in.' He took a cigar from the silver box, all the time thinking of how best to approach the matter. He had to get it just right. When the cigar was lit, he screwed his eyes up against the smoke. 'Polly, when you were a little girl, who did you go to when you hurt yourself?'

Polly looked surprised. 'Me mam, of course. Or me dad, if he was in.'

'And what did they do to make you better?'

'Sat me on their knee and gave me a cuddle and a kiss. Why?'

'When you don't feel well or are upset, it helps to have someone there to give you a cuddle, doesn't it?'

Polly nodded, wondering where the questions were leading. 'Me mam was always giving me and our Joey cuddles. Especially if we'd fallen over and cut ourselves – she used to kiss it better.'

Charles ignored Victoria's questioning eyes. 'Like today, it helped to feel my wife's arms around you when you were telling us your troubles, didn't it?'

'Oh, yes!' Polly's curls danced around her face. 'You feel safe when you're in someone's arms.'

'Who gave your mother a hug when she needed to be comforted?'

'Me dad was always giving her a hug.' Polly closed her eyes at the painful memory. 'That's before he went into hospital.'

'And after he went into hospital, who was there to hold and comfort her? She would have needed a lot of hugs because she must have been out of her mind with worry. What with your father being so ill and having no money, she would need someone's shoulder to cry on.'

'There was only me 'cos our Joey is too young. I would have given her a hug if she'd cried, but she never cried.'

'Not in front of you, she didn't,' Charles said softly. 'Because she didn't want to worry you, she cried inside.'

Tears filled Polly's eyes. 'I didn't know, she didn't tell me.'

'No, my dear, you wouldn't know, so don't blame yourself.' Charles put the cigar in the ashtray before leaning forward, his elbows resting on his knees. 'I have been to see Mr John, and the day you saw your mother in his arms, she was using his shoulder to cry on. She was upset because the day before she'd been in to see your father and his state of mind distressed her. She needed someone to comfort her,

Polly, and Mr John was doing just that.'

Charles went on to relate the whole of the conversation, ending with John's visit to the hospital. 'So you see, my dear, if Mr John and your mother were being wicked, as you thought, he would hardly have visited the hospital and offered your father a job, would he?'

Polly dropped her head, shame flooding her body. 'It's me that's wicked, isn't it? I should have known me mam wouldn't do anything to hurt me dad.' She began to rock back and forth. 'I'll never be able to face me mam again. She won't love me now, not after what I said about her.'

'She doesn't know, my dear, I only spoke to Mr John. But you'll have to go and see her tomorrow because she's beginning to worry about you.'

'I couldn't face Mr John, he'll hate me now.'

Victoria now had her emotions in check. 'Nonsense, Polly! Mr John is a thorough gentleman. He wouldn't dream of repeating what Charles had told him in confidence.'

'There was one thing he told me that sent him up in my estimation. He said that when your mother came into his life, she brought her family and all her friends. The Mitchells, Irish Mary and Sarah Jane – he's proud to count them as his friends.'

Polly sniffed up. 'I'll go and see them tomorrow, if Mrs Nightingale will let me off for an hour. I'll tell Mr John I'm sorry I thought bad of him and I'll thank him for looking after me mam.'

Charles smiled at her. 'Now we've only got the little problem of your boyfriend. But I think we've had enough for one day, so shall we leave it until tomorrow when our heads are clearer? He's probably as miserable as you are, so we just need to think of a way to get you together without denting your pride.'

Polly jumped up and crossed the room to throw her arms around him. 'You are both so good to me, I will never forget you until the day I die. Next to me mam and dad, and our

Joey, I love you best in the whole world.'

'Oh – and what about Steve, pray?'

Polly blushed. 'I'll let you know when I've had a good talk to him – but I'm not going to run after him. After all, I've got me pride.'

Chapter Twenty-Eight

Charles rapped on the study door with his knuckles before opening it and popping his head in. 'I'm sorry to disturb you, Mr Westly, but do you think Polly could be excused? I know you're in the middle of a lesson, but it is rather important.'

'Yes, of course, Mr Denholme.' The tutor smiled at Polly. 'Put your books away before you leave.'

But Polly didn't move. Her eyes were wide and frightened. 'What d'yer want me for? There's nothing happened to me dad, has there?'

Justin and Rebecca exchanged glances. They'd been talking about Polly last night in Rebecca's room, wondering what was making her so unhappy. To Justin's surprise, it was his sister who brought the subject up. He was even more surprised, and pleased, when she admitted she'd been wrong about Polly. Her admission had earned her a warm hug before they got their heads together to discuss what they could do to bring a smile back to the pretty face, a twinkle in the deep brown eyes and laughter in her voice. But when bedtime came, and they still hadn't found a solution, Justin promised to have a word with his father to see if he knew what was ailing Polly. Now they both waited with bated breath, hoping he wasn't the bearer of bad news.

Charles smiled. 'No, my dear, nothing has happened to your father.'

'Is that what you've been worried about, Polly?' This was the first time Rebecca had addressed Polly directly, and the fact wasn't lost on her brother or Tom Westly.

'One of the things,' Polly told her. 'I've made a pig's ear of me life and because I've been miserable I've made everyone

391

else miserable.' She smiled briefly. 'But your dad's going to sort me out, aren't you, Mr Charles?'

'I'm going to have a jolly good try.' Charles held the door open for her. 'I'm quite prepared to move heaven and earth to get the old Polly Perkins back.'

'Ay, Mr Charles, not so much of the old, if yer don't mind! Yer make me sound like Granny Grunt, sitting in a rocking chair with a shawl around me shoulders and smoking a clay pipe.' There was a hint of the old mischief in her eyes as she waved goodbye and left the room.

Charles closed the door behind him and gestured to Polly to follow him into the drawing room. Once inside he wasted no time in coming to the point. 'You've got a couple of hours, young lady, in which to clear the most serious of your troubles. Firstly, I'm running you to the hospital to see your father.' He saw the bewildered look on her face. 'Oh, I've rung the hospital and got permission, so don't worry. I thought we would cross that hurdle first, before you go and visit your mother.'

'Will you come with me to see me mam?'

Charles shook his head. 'No, Polly, that is something you must do alone. Now, run up and fetch your coat.'

When the nurse told Tommy his daughter was coming to see him, he insisted on being moved from the bed to a chair. He could feel his tummy churning with excitement, and when she came through the ward doors there was a smile of welcome on his face to greet her. 'Hello, sweetheart.'

'Oh Dad, it's lovely to see yer.' Polly nearly smothered him with hugs and kisses. 'And yer out of bed – that means yer must be getting better.'

'I feel better for seeing you, sweetheart.' Tommy's heart was bursting with pride. 'You've grown prettier than ever.'

She smacked his hand playfully. 'I bet yer say that to all the girls, Mr Perkins.'

'Only the pretty ones.' He leaned forward to pat the side

of the bed. 'Sit down and tell me what yer've been up to.'

'Well, Mr Charles brought me. He wouldn't come in 'cos he said we'd want to be alone.' She glanced towards the ward doors. 'There he is, Dad, wave to him.'

As Tommy waved, he nodded his head in thanks, a sign understood by the well-dressed man standing in the corridor. 'He's good to yer, isn't he, love?'

'Oh Dad, yer've no idea how good the whole family are to me. I'm a very lucky girl.'

'They must be very special people,' Tommy said. 'Tell them I said so.'

'You can tell them yerself when yer come home.' Polly shuffled her bottom on the bed until she was comfortable, then she folded her hands in her lap. 'You tell me your news first, then I'll tell yer mine. Not that I've got much, like, but I can always make some up.'

Charles felt quite emotional as he watched father and daughter smiling into each other's eyes. Then he made a quick decision, turned on his heels and strode towards the Matron's office. Her sharp bark in reply to his knock turned to a smile of welcome when she saw the handsome, fashionably-dressed man standing before her.

'Yes, can I help you?'

'I've brought Mr Perkins's daughter to see him,' Charles said easily, 'and I thought while they were chatting I'd have a word with you about his progress.'

Matron waved to a chair standing on the opposite side of her desk. 'Please be seated, Mr . . . ?'

'Denholme – Charles Denholme.'

'Are you a relative?'

Charles raised his brows, looking very much in command of the situation. 'I suppose you could say that.'

'In that case I presume you will know that Mr Perkins's condition deteriorated several months ago, causing great concern.' Matron tucked in a wisp of hair that had escaped from the confines of her starched white cap. 'Mr Denholme, can I rely on you not to repeat anything that is said in this room, especially to his wife?' She waited for Charles's nod. 'The doctor was discussing Mr Perkins with me this morning and he feels there has been a slight improvement over the last few days, in both his mental and physical condition. He is hopeful the improvement will continue, but as it is too soon to say with any certainty, it would be unfair to build up the hopes of his family.'

'I can assure you, Matron, that I shall be the soul of discretion. And I do appreciate your confidence.' Charles rose and pushed the chair back into the recess of the desk. 'I'll call in again next week to see him, if I may?'

'By all means, Mr Denholme. I'm sure Mr Perkins would appreciate a visit from you.'

Polly couldn't contain her joy as the car travelled along Longmoor Lane. 'Me dad looks heaps better, Mr Charles. I bet he'll be home in no time at all.' Her hands waved about as she shifted on the seat in her excitement. 'He wasn't half glad to see me. Oh, and he said to thank you for looking after me so well.'

Charles smiled but didn't take his eyes off the road. 'No thanks are necessary, Polly. Looking after you is a pleasure. But don't be expecting miracles or you'll be disappointed. Your father has a long way to go yet, so be patient.'

'Oh, I will be, Mr Charles, I'll be ever so patient. As long as I know he will be coming home, that's enough to keep me going.'

Charles braked hard to avoid a child who was crossing the busy road without looking either way. After cursing under his breath at the stupidity of a mother who would let a young child roam free, he changed gear. 'Anyway, Polly, my dear, that's one of your worries laid to rest. Now I'll drop you at Mr John's and you can make friends with your mother again.'

'Mr John won't have told her, will he? I couldn't bear it if he has.' The brightness in Polly's eyes clouded over. 'Me dad told me Mr John had been to see him, and I felt real wicked about the things I'd said about him and me mam.'

'I rang this morning and you can rest assured he hasn't said a word to your mother. You will be welcomed with open arms by both of them.'

Polly glanced at his profile. 'I'll pay yer back one of these days, Mr Charles, honest I will. I don't deserve all the kindness yer've shown to me, but I'll make it up to yer, I promise. I don't know how, but I will.'

Charles pulled into the kerb at the corner of Faulkner Square. He switched the engine off and turned to face her. 'Polly, having you in our house has been payment enough. You have brought more into our lives than we have given you.'

He leaned across her and opened the passenger door. 'Out you get, my dear, and don't look so afraid, they're not going to eat you. Give them a big hug, one of your brightest smiles, and in five minutes you'll be wondering why you were worried.'

Polly waved as the car pulled away. Then she straightened her shoulders, held her head high and rehearsed the smile her mam would be expecting to see.

Ada rushed forward, her arms outstretched. 'Oh, I've been so worried about yer.' She smothered Polly with kisses. 'I was going to call at Percy Street tonight, when I'd finished here.' She held her daughter's face between her hands, thinking how grown-up and pretty she looked. 'What's been wrong with yer, sweetheart?'

'I must have eaten something that didn't agree with me, Mam, and me tummy's been upset.' Polly glanced over her mother's shoulder to see Mr John standing outside his office door. He knows I'm telling lies, she thought, yet he looks really glad to see me. Oh, I've been really stupid and wicked. It would serve me right if he didn't like me any more. 'I'll just say hello to Mr John.' Shyly, she approached him, but when she saw only kindness in his eyes she ran into his arms. Lifting her face for a kiss, she whispered, very softly, 'I'm so sorry, Mr John, so very sorry.'

'We're delighted to see you, Polly. We've missed you so much.' John led her towards the drawing room, saying over his shoulder, 'Come and sit in comfort, Ada, and hold your daughter's hand while she brings us up-to-date with her news.'

Polly couldn't wait to get settled on the couch before blurting out, 'I've just been to the hospital to see me dad . . . Mr Charles took me. And d'yer know what, Mam, he looks great! Much better than he did last time I saw him.'

'I bet he was glad to see yer, wasn't he?' Ada felt as though a ton weight had been lifted off her shoulders. She'd been afraid the tummy ache was just an excuse, and the real reason for Polly's long absence was that she preferred the Denholmes' company to hers. But looking now into her daughter's lit-up face she knew how wrong she'd been. Polly was her own person and would never change, not even for a king's ransom. 'Tell us what he had to say.'

'Well, he told me Mr John had been and he was very pleased about that, I could tell.' Polly repeated everything that had been said during her visit to the hospital, her head turning from her mother to John so that neither of them felt left out. As the tale came to an end, she spread her hands out and smiled. 'And when I left him he looked real happy.'

'I'm glad you went. It would cheer him up, seeing you.' Ada patted her cheek. 'And now what's this about Steve? Aggie said yer didn't go down to see Sarah Jane last Saturday, or the Saturday before, and Steve's like a bear with a sore head. When the women asked him where yer were, he just growled at them, sayin' he didn't know.'

The smile slipped from Polly's face and she lowered her head. 'He's finished with me.'

'But why, sweetheart?'

'Because I said I wasn't going back home to live, not yet anyway. He wouldn't let me explain that I just can't walk out on the Denholmes, not after all they've done for me. He wouldn't listen, he just walked off in a huff.'

'Then you did right in not going down to Bold Street,' Ada told her. 'Steve would think you were running after him, and although I love him like my own son, yer must not be the one to give in.'

'If I am allowed an opinion,' John said, 'I believe Steve is jealous. It's all part of the growing-up process, Polly, my dear. He's afraid of someone coming along and taking you away from him, and he thinks the way to prevent that is to have you living near so he can keep an eye on you. He is very young, you both are, but he must learn to curb his jealousy or you'll both be unhappy.'

'It wasn't all Steve's fault, Mr John, I was to blame as well. Yer see, I'd made him a promise and I broke it.' Polly sighed as she turned to face her mother. 'Remember when he took me to the pictures on me birthday? Well, I promised him then that I'd stay at the Denholmes' another month, then go back home. But I couldn't bring meself to tell Mr Charles I was leaving, not after they'd bought me those lovely clothes.' There was spirit in Polly's voice when she went on, 'Anyway, it's not just because they bought me the clothes, it's everything. They took me in and they treat me like one of the family. I can't just throw their kindness back in their faces and walk away – I'm too fond of them to do that. But I couldn't get Steve to understand how I feel. I'd broken me promise to him and as far as he was concerned, that was that. He just took to his heels and walked away.'

'But you miss him, sweetheart?'

'Yes, I do miss him, Mam. I've only ever wanted Steve for me boyfriend, you know that. But if I start giving in to him now, I'll be giving in to him for the rest of me life. And I'm not having that 'cos I've got a mind of me own and I've got me pride. I'm not turning me back on all me friends, so as

Mr John said, it's up to Steve to stop being jealous. If he really wants me to be his girlfriend, then he's got to take me friends along with me.'

'So you won't be coming back home to live?'

'Of course I'll be coming back – it's my home, isn't it? And I don't half miss you and our Joey. But I won't come back just because Steve wants me to.'

'That's the spirit, Polly,' John said, smiling. 'But don't be too hard on the boy, because if you were my girlfriend I'd be jealous of every young lad that looked sideways at you.'

'I won't be hard on him, Mr John. I just want him to know he can't always have his own way, there are other people to consider.' Polly's familiar bright smile showed. 'Aren't I lucky having three dads? I've got me real dad, who I love to pieces, and I've got Mr Charles and Mr John! Not many girls can boast that, can they?'

Her words brought a lump to Ada's throat and tears to John's eyes. 'You have bestowed a great honour on me, Polly, my dear, by making me an adopted father. May I remain so for ever more.'

'Oh, you will, Mr John! You and the Denholmes will always be part of my life.' She tossed her hair back and chuckled. 'Whether yer like it or not, you're all stuck with me.'

'What are you going to do about Steve, sunshine?' Ada asked. 'You've got to go and see Sarah Jane and Irish Mary. You can't stop seeing them because you and Steve have fallen out, it wouldn't be fair.'

'I'll think of something, Mam, don't worry. Mr Charles said there's always a solution if you look hard enough.' Polly's heart was singing now she was back on good terms with her mother. Never again would she doubt her.

'I'd better get going or Mrs Nightingale will be having me guts for garters.' She kissed her mother and John. 'I'll see yer tomorrow.'

Polly was skipping lightly down the stairs when John

called out: 'When you see your friends, tell them there's a party here the Sunday after next and they are all invited.'

Polly turned, her face aglow. 'Is it someone's birthday?'

'I shouldn't need to tell you, my dear, that it's your mother's birthday next Friday. But with most people working, it would be more appropriate to have the celebration on the Sunday.'

Ada gasped. 'How did you know it was my birthday? I've never mentioned it to you.'

'Ada, you are one of my employees. There is very little I don't know about you.'

'But I don't want a party, John, I'm too old for that sort of thing!'

'Nonsense. It will do you good to have all your friends around for a drink and something to eat. We'll ask Dolly and Les, Sarah Jane and Mary, and of course, Aggie and Fanny. It goes without saying that the Denholmes will also be invited.'

'But I don't —'

Ada's words were cut off as John put a finger to her lips. 'Ada, we are definitely going to celebrate your birthday.'

Polly, her hand on the bannister, tutted, 'Will you two make up yer minds whether we're having a party or not?'

'We most definitely are.' John winked down at her. 'You can do the inviting, my dear, and I leave it to you whether Steve is a guest.'

'Yippee!' Polly clapped her hands in glee. 'I'll invite the Denholmes as soon as I get in . . . I think Rebecca will come this time. And on Saturday I'll go and see me mates in Bold Street. Oh Mam, it'll be a lovely party for yer birthday, the best yer've ever had.'

'It'll be the *only* one I've ever had, sunshine,' Ada said, happy to see her daughter looking so bright and cheerful. 'Give my regards to everyone and tell them I'll look forward to seeing them.'

With a wave of her hand, and humming loudly, Polly ran

lightly down the stairs and disappeared from view.

Ada faced John. 'Haven't you done enough for me without this? I'll be forever in your debt.'

'Poppycock!' John held her two arms and gazed into her melting brown eyes. 'Anyway, as your daughter's adopted father, I'm entitled to be part of family events, don't you think?'

Ada smiled. 'It was nice of Polly to say that. She's a very thoughtful girl and I'm proud of her. And she means what she says; she will never forget you or Mr Charles, you'll always be a part of her life.'

John was smiling but his eyes were serious. 'Will you always be part of my life too, Ada? When Tommy comes home, will there be a place in your life for me?'

'There'll always be a place for you in my life, John, a very special place. You've been there when I needed you and I'll never forget that. You need never be lonely because my family is your family.'

'Thank you, my darling.' John cupped her face. 'You see, without you I'd have no one . . . my life would be empty.'

Ada smiled. 'From now on your life will be full. I'll bring Joey with me on Saturday and you can take him for a walk in the park, get to know him. He misses his dad because there's no one to take him to the swings or play footie in the park with him. I think you and him would get on well together. And when he knows our Polly has adopted yer, well, yer'll find yourself with two adopted children.'

John kissed her gently before releasing her. 'D'you know, I haven't played footie for thirty years?' There was a happy smile on his face. 'I'll go to the shops tomorrow and buy a ball. And I'll buy a boat for him to sail on the lake in the park. Yes, I'll enjoy that.'

Polly's nerves were on edge as she walked down Ranelagh Street. She was remembering everything Mr Charles had told her, but it sounded much easier when you were saying it than it was in practice. She patted her coat pocket to make sure her treasured possession was still there, but even that did nothing to calm her down.

Irish Mary was the first to spot her familiar figure. 'Polly, me darlin', sure is it yerself I see? Haven't we all been worried to death about yer, so we have.'

Polly saw Steve straighten up and look her way, but she quickly turned her head. 'I'm all right, Auntie Mary. I had a cold, that's all.'

'Hello there, Polly,' Florrie called in her loud voice. 'We thought yer'd forgotten us.'

Polly smiled as she passed. 'Now, how could I forget you, Florrie?'

Sarah Jane pulled on Aggie's skirt. 'Here she is. I told yer she'd come today, didn't I? She wouldn't forget her old grandmother.'

Polly made straight for the old lady and threw her arms around her. 'Ooh, I haven't half missed you, Grandma.'

The old flower-seller showed her toothless smile. 'An' I've missed you, girl. What's the good of havin' a bleedin' granddaughter if yer never see her?'

Aggie finished serving a customer and came to hand over the coppers to Sarah Jane. 'About time, Polly Perkins! We'd given you up for dead.'

'Well, I did feel like death warmed up with the rotten cold I had.' Polly could feel Steve's eyes on her. 'But I'm all right now.'

'I've dropped a penny, girl, will yer pick it up for us?' Sarah Jane pointed to the ground. 'I think it rolled under me stool.' Polly bent down, and as she did so, the old lady whispered, 'Have you an' Steve fallen out?'

'Yes.' Polly lifted Sarah Jane's skirts. 'I can't see a penny.'

'Well, yer won't, will yer, 'cos I didn't bleedin' drop one.'

Polly tutted as she stood up. 'You were just being nosy.'

The old lady cackled. 'That's one of the few advantages

of old age, girl. Yer can say anythin' yer like an' get away with it.'

'Don't be makin' yer age an excuse,' Aggie said. 'Yer've always been a nosy old cow.'

'Ay, Clever Drawers, you keep yer eye on the business. Look, there's a likely customer there, an' if yer don't move yer bleedin' lazy bones yer'll lose her an' I'll be tuppence down the drain.'

'Sod off, Sarah Jane! Proper ruddy slave-driver yer are.' Aggie winked at Polly before fixing a smile on her face as she approached the woman inspecting the daffodils. 'It's cold today, isn't it, missus? I expect yer frozen through to the marrow, like I am. Mind you, a bunch of them in yer room would make yer feel warm even if yer had goose-pimples on yer you-know-what.'

Sarah Jane nodded her head in appreciation of Aggie's sales talk. 'She's a good 'un, girl, almost as good as you. She's a good drinking partner, too – she can't half shift the stout. I thought I could drink, but sod it, she can drink me under the ruddy table any day.' Sarah Jane turned her head to where Steve was filling up the buckets. 'Hey, tatty head, aren't yer goin' to say hello to me granddaughter?'

Steve flushed and dropped his eyes for a second. Then he gazed at Polly who was waiting with bated breath. 'Hello, Polly. Have yer been sick?'

Polly nodded, letting her breath out slowly. 'I'm all right now, though.'

Sarah Jane gave her a push. 'Go an' talk to him while I keep me eye on Tilly Mint there. She doesn't know her marguerites from her ruddy aspidistras.'

Polly hesitated. She'd vowed she wouldn't be the first one to make a move, but Steve looked so sad her heart was melting. It was Aggie who solved the problem for her. Mr John's old nanny had been watching out of the corner of her eye while at the same trying to convince the customer that a bunch of daffodils was warmer than a shovelful of coal any day. When she'd finally won the woman round to her way of thinking, she gave Sarah Jane her money, then handed a sixpence to Steve. 'Take her to the Kardomah for a cup of tea. Warm yer both up.'

Walking down Church Street there was a yard separating the young couple. But when they reached the entrance to the Kardomah, Steve put his hand on Polly's arm and pulled her to a halt. 'I'm sorry, Polly, for the things I said. I didn't mean them, but I was hurt and disappointed. I haven't half missed yer. I haven't had a proper night's sleep since that evening.'

'I've missed you, too, Steve.' Polly put her hand in her pocket and brought out the marble . . . the bobby-dazzler. Holding it up to him in her open palm, she said, 'I've slept with this under me pillow every night.'

Steve's handsome face split into a wide grin. He fished in his inside pocket and brought out the crumpled birthday card. 'I carry this everywhere with me.'

Laughing with excitement and happiness, the young sweethearts walked into the warmth of the café. They found a table in a secluded corner and Steve, feeling very manly, ordered a pot of tea for two and two toasted teacakes. 'This will cost yer more than sixpence,' Polly said in a hushed voice, 'and I haven't got any money on me.'

'I've got enough. I haven't been out to spend me pocket money for the last two weeks.' Butter trickled down Steve's chin when he took a bite of the hot teacake. 'Don't ever let's fall out again, Polly. I've been so miserable.'

'I didn't fall out, Steve, it was you.'

'I know it was my fault, and I kicked meself all the way home. And when I told me mam, she got so mad I thought she was goin' to box me ears for me.' He grinned at the memory of his mother standing over him with her hands on her hips. 'She said, "Who the bleedin' hell d'yer think you are, tellin' Polly what to do? Serves yer right if she tells yer to go and take a running jump".'

Polly could see Dolly Mitchell in her mind's eye and she giggled. 'I'm glad your mam's on my side.'

'She was right, though. I won't ask yer again to do anythin' yer don't want to do. If you want to stay with the Denholmes, then you stay – as long as I can see yer on yer nights off, and yer promise to be me girlfriend.'

Polly's lovely brown eyes twinkled. 'Mr Charles told me there's a solution to every problem if yer look for it. Well, I didn't have to look for it, he found one for me.'

Steve gazed at her, thinking she must be the most beautiful girl in Liverpool. 'A solution to what?'

'To keeping us both happy. He doesn't want me to leave them altogether, so he said I could work there during the day and go home every night. That means I'll see me mam and our Joey every day, which is what I want, and I'll still be with the Denholmes. I'm very happy working there, Steve, and I've grown fond of them.' Polly's eyes were questioning. 'Does that arrangement suit you?'

'I'll say it does!' Steve felt lightheaded with happiness. 'As Sarah Jane would say, "Down to the ground, girl, down to the ground".' He stretched across the table and covered one of her hands with his. 'Polly, this is one of the best days of me life.'

'And mine.' Polly's rosy cheeks glowed. 'I've got another bit of good news, too. It's me mam's birthday next week and Mr John is having a party for her. I've got to invite Sarah Jane and Auntie Mary, so we'd better get back so I can tell them.' She pushed a curl out of her eyes. 'Me mam will be asking your mam and dad, but I'm inviting you personally. Will you be my partner for the night?'

'I'm hoping to be your partner for a lifetime, Polly, not just for one night.'

'Oh, come on, yer soppy article! The next thing, yer'll be kissing me in the middle of the Kardomah café.'

'Don't tempt me, or I will!'

Polly's eyes rolled. 'D'yer know, I believe yer would! But

yer'll have to wait for a dark night when we can find a shop doorway.'

'Come for a walk with me on yer first night home and I'll find a shop doorway.' Steve grinned as he stood up. 'In fact, I'll find two shop doorways.'

'Go and pay the bill and let's be going. I can't wait to tell Sarah Jane about the party, she'll be over the moon.'

Sarah Jane saw the young couple coming back and noticed the happiness on their faces and the joined hands swinging between them. Thank God for that, she thought, we might get a smile out of young Steve now. 'You two look as though yer lost a tanner and found half-a-crown! It's many a long year since a man put a smile like that on my face, girl, I can tell yer.'

'I'll give you something to smile about, Grandma.' Polly passed on the invitation and Sarah Jane nearly jumped off her stool with glee. 'Oh, that's the bloody gear! Just what I need, that is, a bleedin' good knees-up.' She turned her head and yelled, 'Ay, Irish Mary, get yer body down here for a minute. And you, Aggie, leave the customer to make up her own mind whether she wants tulips or daffs. Pin yer ears back and listen to this.'

Their arms around each other's waists, Polly and Steve stood listening to Sarah Jane giving forth on the delights to come and announcing that they should all club together to buy Ada a present. 'Anyone would think she'd been invited to Buckingham Palace,' Steve whispered.

'Ay, buggerlugs, I heard that! Me legs might be gone, but me bleedin' hearing hasn't. And if I was to receive two invitations, one to the Palace and one from Mr John, it would the Palace one I turned down, so there! And d'yer want to know why?'

'Yer don't have to tell me why, 'cos I know,' Aggie said, nodding her head. 'They don't have no stout at the Palace.'

'Right in one, girl, right in one,' the old lady said, her

wrinkles deepening when she smiled. 'Yer can go to the top of the class.'

'Excuse me, but is anyone serving here?'

They all spun round, and when they saw their customers, their mouths gaped. Polly was the first to recover. 'Mr John . . . Mr Charles!'

Sarah Jane pushed Aggie out of the way so she could see them properly. 'Well, that's what I call real gentlemanly. Yer've come to deliver the invitations in person.'

'Polly is in charge of the invitations,' John laughed. 'And from what I've heard you have all accepted.'

'Accepted?' Aggie drew herself up to her full height. 'Yer couldn't keep us away.'

Irish Mary, the quietest of the group, said, 'I thank you kindly, Mr John and it's proud I am to accept.'

'I'll come on one condition . . . no, make that two conditions.' Sarah Jane kept her face straight. 'That I get me six bottles of stout and Mr John doesn't sing *Come into the Garden, Maud*.' She tutted in disgust. 'It's a terrible bleedin' song, that is.'

Charles's shoulders were shaking with laughter. 'I would think it's on a par with your Auntie Mary and her canary.'

People passing by were stopping to smile with amusement at the exchange between two toffs and the flower-sellers. It was a rare sight.

Sarah Jane narrowed her eyes. 'Are you insulting me, Mr Charles? What did yer mean, it's *on a par*? I don't want to show me ignorance, but I've never heard nothin' like that in all me flamin' life!'

'I wouldn't dream of insulting you, Sarah Jane. On a par means equal.'

The old lady rubbed the side of her nose. 'Yer mean both the bleedin' songs are as bad as each other.'

It was Steve who answered. 'Nail on the head, Sarah Jane, nail on the head.'

'Oh God, we've got another comedian. He's been as

miserable as sin for the last two weeks, now he's crackin' jokes. At least, they would be jokes if they was funny, which they ain't.'

'Ay, Grandma, you leave my boyfriend alone.' Polly wagged her finger in the old lady's face. 'Or yer'll have me to answer to.'

Mary began to move away. 'I've got a living to make, so I'll be going back to me pitch. Thank you for the invitation; sure I'll be looking forward to it, so I will.'

While both men raised their bowler hats to bid her farewell, Steve was trying to pluck up the courage to speak. He felt gawky in his working clothes, but he wanted to please Polly. 'Thank you for askin' me to the party, Mr John, I'd like to come.'

'We'd love to have you, wouldn't we, Polly?'

'Oh yes, he's on the top of my list.' She gazed first at Charles, then at John. 'Are you two off to the club?'

'No, we came for our buttonholes,' Charles told her. 'And as the adopted fathers of the prettiest flower-seller in Liverpool, we would like to be served by her fair hand.'

'What's he on about?' Sarah Jane asked. 'Who's adopted who?'

Polly's laugh rang out clear as a bell. 'I've adopted them! Now I've got one real father and two adopted ones.'

Looking very puzzled, Sarah Jane scratched her head. 'Well, if they're yer adopted fathers, and I'm yer adopted grandma, what relation does that make them to me?'

'It makes us all one big happy family, Grandma.'

'Well, yer better give them two nice buttonholes or they'll be *un*adoptin' yer.' The old lady growled: 'And they can have them on the house, seein' as they're family.'

Polly chose two deep red carnations. She slipped them through their buttonholes and stood back to admire them. 'You look very handsome and I'm proud of you.' She felt Steve's hand cover hers and turned to smile at him. 'Aren't I lucky, with the best family and friends anyone could have?

And the best, most handsome boyfriend? If only I could have one wish come true, it would be that me real dad was here. My happiness would be complete. I'd ask nothing more from life.'

'I told you to have patience, Polly, didn't I?' Charles had rung the hospital that morning to be told that Tommy's improvement was holding steady. But he didn't want to build Polly's hopes up. 'The day will come, my dear.'

'Charles is right,' John said. 'It may be a while yet, but one day you will have him back with you.'

'And when he is home, will you bring him down here one day?' Polly requested eagerly. 'I'd like to see the three of my dads together 'cos I want you all to be friends. You'll like him, I know yer will, Mr Charles. You couldn't help but like me dad, he's so nice.'

'He must be, to have a daughter like you,' Charles said. 'I'm sure we'll all get on famously.'

Polly smiled up at Steve before folding her arms across her tummy and hugging herself. 'Three handsome men to look after me until me dad comes home. Polly Perkins, you're the luckiest girl under the sun.'

Home Is Where
the Heart Is

Dedicated to my family and friends
for their encouragement.

My gratitude to Mary Johnson,
without whose help and guidance
this trilogy of books would never have been written.

Chapter One

A spark from a hissing coal spurted from the fire and landed on the hearth rug by Eileen's feet. Quick as a flash her foot shot out and extinguished it before it had time to singe the rug. She glanced across at her husband who was sitting at the opposite side of the grate, but Bill was so absorbed in the evening paper he was oblivious to everything else. I dunno, Eileen muttered silently, once he's got his nose stuck in a paper, he wouldn't notice if the house burned down around him. If he had a mind like mine right now, he wouldn't be sitting there so calmly. All the family were in bed and it was quiet in the small living room of the two-up-two-down terrace house, except for Eileen's heart, which was pounding so loudly she wondered that Bill couldn't hear it. Eileen sat back in the chair, her hands clasped tightly together. Go on, tell him, she urged herself. You've got to do it sometime, so the sooner you get it over with the better. But her mouth felt like a piece of emery paper with nerves and she didn't think she could speak even if she plucked up the courage.

Calm down, she told herself, taking a deep breath and exhaling slowly. Her gaze swept around the room, taking in the sideboard with a vase and ornament on top of the lace runner, the couch against the far wall and the dining table with its maroon plush tablecloth and four straight backed chairs standing neatly with their seats hidden beneath the table top. When her heart beat had slowed, Eileen licked her dry lips. It's now or never, so best get it over with.

'Bill, will yer put the paper down a minute. I've got something to tell yer.'

Bill Gillmoss lowered the *Echo* until his deep brown eyes were peering over the top. 'What's that, chick?'

'I'm havin' a baby.' Eileen was sitting on the edge of the couch, her hands clasped between her knees. She pushed a wisp of mousey-coloured hair behind her ear as she waited anxiously for her husband's reaction.

Bill stared hard for a few seconds, then threw back his head and chuckled loudly. 'I nearly fell for that! How you can keep a straight face, I'll never know.'

'I'm not jokin', Bill. I went to see Doctor Greenfield today, and I'm nearly two months.'

The smile left Bill's face. 'You're having me on, aren't you, chick?'

Eileen shook her head. 'I wouldn't joke about a thing like that.'

The paper fell from Bill's hand, and for what seemed like an eternity to Eileen, the only sound in the room was the ticking of the clock on the mantelpiece. Then, in a voice thick with shock, he said, 'That's the last thing in the world I expected.'

'Well, I wasn't exactly plannin' on it meself!' Not for the world would Eileen show how frightened she was. It was

2

twelve years since their Edna was born and that was a long time to go between children. 'It's happened, an' there's nowt we can do about it!'

'But we're too old to go through that again!' When Bill turned his eyes on her, Eileen could see he was bewildered. 'The children are all grown up now . . . Billy's nearly sixteen, Joan's leaving school in a couple of weeks, and Edna's twelve! I thought the days of having babies were well behind us!'

You can say that again! Eileen didn't voice her thoughts. As she'd said, it had happened and there was nothing she could do about it. It wasn't like buying a pair of shoes that you could take back if you found they didn't suit you. 'Bill, I'm forty-two, not a bloody hundred and two! An' if I'm pregnant then I can't be too old, can I? If it hadn't been for the war, an' you bein' away for six years, I'd 'ave probably had a few more children by now.' Eileen was close to tears. She'd been on pins all day, having to keep the news to herself until all the family were in bed and she had Bill on his own. She'd been hoping he'd be pleased, then she'd have felt a bit better. It wasn't that she didn't want a baby, she loved children. But the prospect of giving birth scared her stiff. 'It takes two to make a baby, Bill Gillmoss, so don't be lookin' at me as though I've committed a flippin' crime!'

'I know, chick.' Bill was trying to come to terms with the shock. He could see the disappointment on Eileen's face and tried to raise a smile. 'What did Ma have to say?'

'I 'aven't told me mam. I wanted you to be the first to know, seein' as you 'ad a hand in it.'

'I wonder how she'll take it?' Bill reached for his

cigarettes and matches. 'And the kids? It'll be a big shock to them.'

'Bill, I couldn't give a monkey's uncle about me mam and the kids! It's you who's my main concern, and yer actin' as though it's got nothin' to do with you! We, Bill . . . you an' me . . . are goin' to 'ave a baby whether yer like it or not!'

Out of the side of his eye, Bill gazed at his wife. He took in the droop of her shoulders and the troubled expression on her face. He quickly returned his cigarettes and matches to the mantelpiece and moved to kneel at the side of her chair. 'I'm sorry, chick!' He put an arm across her shoulders and pulled her towards him. 'It's come as a bit of a shock, so I need a little time to get used to the idea.' He kissed her lightly on the lips. 'That's what we get for playing mothers and fathers.' Eileen's arms went around his neck, a constant reminder of his days in the prisoner-of-war camp. She'd been able to fill out his skeletal frame and help him over his nightmares, but nothing could put back the dark brown hair he'd had before he'd joined the army. 'I'm worn out, Bill, an' I've got a splittin' headache. Me mind's been in a hell of a state all day. It's not that I don't want a baby, 'cos yer know I'm a sucker when it comes to babies. But it's been such a long time since I 'ad our Edna, I don't relish the thought of goin' through it all again.' She drew away to look into his eyes. 'But if I thought you were 'appy, Bill, then that would be half the battle.'

'Look, as long as you are all right, that's all I worry about, you know that. If you're happy, then I'll be happy.'

They were quiet for a while, wrapped in each other's

arms. Then Bill asked softly, 'Have you thought about the upheaval this is going to cause? We'll have to move away from here, for a start. The house is too small as it is, we'd never manage with a baby as well.'

Eileen jerked up straight. 'I'm not leavin' this little house! I love it here!'

'Chick, be practical! Where would you put a cot? Your ma sleeps in the girls' room, and they can hardly move, and our Billy's feet are almost sticking out of the window in that little box room.'

'I'm not movin' away from 'ere!' Eileen persisted. 'I'd miss all me neighbours.'

Bill sighed. 'Okay, we've got plenty of time to talk about that. The first thing is to tell Ma and the children.'

'That's the part I'm dreadin'.' Eileen hunched her shoulders as her chubby face creased in a smile. 'I never told me mam when I was expectin' the other three, I just left it till she could see for 'erself.' Eileen started to rock back and forth and Bill could hear the springs in the chair creak in protest at the movement of her eighteen-stone body. 'Can yer believe it, I'm forty-two years old and frightened to tell me mam I'm 'aving a baby!'

'Five minutes is all it'll take to tell Ma, and the girls, and when it's over you'll wonder why you were ever worried,' Bill said confidently. 'You can leave Billy to me . . . I'll tell him.'

'Only five minutes, he says,' Eileen huffed. 'Yer can be hung, drawn and quartered in five minutes, Bill Gillmoss, an' that's what me mam will do to me . . . after she's laid a duck egg!'

* * *

'Is this one of your little jokes?' Maggie stood rubbing her chin, a look of doubt on her face. Her daughter was always pulling her leg, and Maggie never knew when to take her seriously. She was only half the size of Eileen, with a trim figure and an abundance of white hair which was always neatly waved. It was her face, with deep worry lines etched on her forehead and cheeks, that told of the sadness she'd suffered in her sixty-seven years. When her husband had died eighteen years previously, she'd come to live with Eileen and Bill, and never for one moment had she regretted it. They'd taken her into their home and surrounded her with love and laughter. They'd given her a reason for living.

'Mam, I know I clown around a lot, but I'd hardly make a joke about havin' a baby, now would I?' While Eileen's heart was thumping like mad, she told herself it was ridiculous to be so embarrassed. Having babies was natural when you were married. And it wasn't as though her mother had never had children of her own because she'd had her and their Rene. When Maggie didn't answer, Eileen leaned forward, so their faces were nearly touching. 'I know yer gobsmacked, Mam, but for 'eaven's sake say something.'

'That's the understatement of the year!' Maggie's mind was in a turmoil. She could see the pleading in Eileen's eyes, begging her to understand and be happy for her. And all Maggie ever wanted was her daughter's happiness. But while she willed herself to say the words Eileen wanted to hear, Maggie couldn't suppress the fear she felt. She'd always worried that the weight her daughter carried round with her would one day put too big a strain on her

6

heart. How was she going to cope with the extra burden of carrying a child?

'Come on, missus!' Making a fist of her hand, Eileen leaned on the table. 'Cat got yer tongue, 'as it?'

'You certainly know how to surprise people,' Maggie said, smoothing down the front of her floral wrap-around pinny. 'But this is one surprise I never expected!'

'I know what's worryin' yer,' Eileen smiled to ease the tension. 'It's the thought of another Easter egg yer'll 'ave to buy, an' another Christmas pressie.'

'What does Bill say?' Maggie asked. 'Is he pleased?'

'Pleased as punch, he is!' Eileen lied. 'When 'e went out of 'ere this mornin', he walked down the road with 'is shoulders back and his chest stuck out a mile. Real proud of 'imself, he is!'

'And do the children know?'

Eileen screwed up her face. 'Haven't told them yet. I'll tell them when they come in from school, so make yerself scarce, will yer, missus? I 'ad to take me courage in both 'ands to tell you, so God only knows 'ow I'm goin' to break it to them.'

'They'll take it in their stride,' Maggie said. 'As long as their tea's on the table, and they can go out and play with their mates, that's all they worry about.' She opened her arms wide and Eileen, blinking back the tears, walked into them. 'Congratulations, love.'

'Thanks, Mam.' Eileen grabbed her mother round the waist and lifted her off her feet. Swinging her round and round, she gasped, 'I always said yer were the best mam in the whole world.'

* * *

7

'Oh, you, Mam!' Joan's hand went to her mouth, her face the colour of beetroot. She was at the age now when sex was whispered about in the playground, and some of the girls in her class sneaked in copies of *True Confessions* magazine. The thought of her mam and dad doing what couples in the magazine did, horrified her. They were too old for that!

'What d'yer mean, "oh, you, Mam"!' Hundreds of butterflies were flying around inside Eileen's tummy, she was so embarrassed. It's worse than going to the flipping dentist, she told herself. 'I thought yer'd be pleased to 'ave a little brother or sister.'

'Well I'm not, so there!' Joan nodded her head to emphasise her words. 'I don't want it!'

'That's just tough on you, then, my girl, 'cos there's nowt yer can do about it.' Eileen raised her eyes to the ceiling. God give me the strength to keep my hands off her.

Edna had been standing with her mouth open, listening and taking in. Now she flew to put her arms around Eileen's waist. 'Ooh, I'm made up, Mam! I hope it's a little girl, and we can call her Susan . . . after that film star, Susan Hayward.'

Eileen patted her bottom, chuckling, 'An' if it's a boy, I suppose yer want it called Alan, after Alan Ladd?'

Edna's brows came together in concentration. She was two years younger than Joan, but they could pass for twins. Both had their mother's straggly, mousey-coloured hair and hazel eyes. And both were as thin as bean poles, as Eileen had been at their age. After a few seconds' consideration, Edna shook her head. 'No, if it's a boy, can we call it Randolph, after Randolph Scott?'

The rafters rang with Eileen's laughter. 'Some 'ope you've got! Can yez see me at the front door, shoutin', "Randolph, yer tea's ready!" I'd be the laughin' stock of the whole ruddy neighbourhood!'

Joan spun on her heels. She didn't know what there was to laugh about. Fancy someone as old as her mother having a baby! It was a good job she was leaving school in a few weeks and wouldn't have to tell her friends. 'I'm going down to Dorothy's.'

'Don't go far,' Eileen called after her, 'yer tea won't be long.'

'Mam, will yer teach me how to knit?' Edna was moving from one foot to the other. 'Then I can make a matinee coat for the baby.'

'We'll see.' Eileen noticed the jerky movements and gave Edna a push. 'Down the yard to the lavvy, now! Yer always leave it till the last minute!'

Eileen, a smile on her face, watched through the window as Edna flew down the yard. 'At least I've made someone happy,' she said aloud. 'And the others will come round, given time.'

Bill threw the spent match in the fire grate, his eyes screwed up against the smoke drifting upwards from his cigarette. Last night, when Eileen had told him she was pregnant, it had hit him like a body blow, knocking the stuffing out of him. He'd been able to think of nothing else all day in work. But by dinner time, although he wasn't thrilled, he'd got used to the idea. And when he was clocking off, he told himself the eagerness he felt to

9

get home was only because he wanted to make sure Eileen was all right. It was when he was stepping down from the bus, the truth hit him. He wanted this baby!

'Well, that's the last of the washin' in steep.' Eileen came through from the kitchen, rubbing her wet hands on the corner of her pinny. 'They'll be ready to mangle and put out on the line in the mornin'.' She turned one of the dining chairs to sit facing the fire and opened her legs wide to feel the heat from the glowing coals. 'Ooh, that's lovely! It's freezin' out there!'

'D'you feel like a cup of cocoa, to warm you up?' Bill asked. 'I'll make it.'

'Nah! Just give us five minutes to rest me weary bones, then I'll make us a sandwich.' Eileen kicked one of her shoes off and groaned with pleasure. 'That's better. Me feet are killin' me.'

'Will you sit still long enough for us to talk?' Bill asked. 'I've got something to tell you.'

Eileen closed her eyes and put her hand to her mouth, her fingers digging deep into the fleshy cheeks. Her huge tummy started to shake, and her words came out in a splutter. 'Yer not goin' to tell me yer in the family way, are yer, Bill Gillmoss?'

Bill had moved to the edge of his chair, thinking Eileen was upset and crying. Now he fell back, shaking his head. 'Aren't you ever serious?'

'Sometimes I'm dead serious, but nobody takes any notice of me, so why bother?' Eileen wasn't smiling now. 'This is not laughter yer hear, Bill, it's bloody hysterics! It's been quite a day for me, I can tell yer. First I 'ad to pluck up the nerve to tell me mam, then start again with our Joan and Edna. I wouldn't go through that again for a big clock.'

'I'm sorry! I should have been here so we could have told them together.'

Eileen tilted her head, gazing at him questioningly through lowered lids.

'What was it yer wanted to tell me?'

'That I'm ashamed and sorry about last night. I was a right bastard and no mistake.' Bill's eyes followed the path of his two fingers as they ran down the crease of his trousers. 'I was an unthinking, selfish swine, and I want you to know I'm sorry. I also want you to know I'm happy about the baby. It'll be nice to have a little one in the house again.'

Eileen folded her arms and they disappeared from view beneath her enormous bust. With two fingers circling the deep dimples in her elbows, she said softly, 'Hearin' yer say that, Bill, has taken a load off me shoulders. Yer looked far from 'appy last night with a right miserable gob on yer!'

'I'm forgiven, then?' Bill smiled sheepishly.

'I'll forgive yer, but thousands wouldn't! I don't know about me mam an' our Joan, though! Me mam's not too 'appy, but that's understandable 'cos she's worried about me.' Eileen stretched her leg out and kicked Bill on the shin, a wicked glint in her eyes. 'But from the look of disgust on our Joan's face, I'd say she thinks yer just a dirty old man!'

'She's at an awkward age. Probably just learning about the birds and the bees, and she was embarrassed. It's romantic when you're sitting in the picture house and

11

Clark Gable and Myrna Loy get in a clinch, but when it's your own mam and dad . . . well, that's different. But when I told our Billy, he was over the moon!'

'God bless 'im,' Eileen grinned. 'He thinks the world of you, an' anythin' you do is hunky-dory with him.'

'I wonder what Cissie Maddox and the neighbours will think?' Bill mused. 'I bet they'll be surprised.'

'Sod Cissie Maddox and the neighbours! They don't keep us, so why worry what they think?' Eileen's round face beamed. 'Mary and Vera are comin' here tomorrow afternoon, an' I can't wait to see their faces. They'll be flabbergasted!'

'So, it's sod Cissie Maddox and the neighbours, eh?' Bill said. 'Only last night you said you'd never leave here because you'd miss them.'

'Well, so I would! Honest to God, Bill, yer can be as thick as two short planks, sometimes! I can fight like mad with Cissie one day, and be all matey with 'er the next. That's what neighbours are like. It doesn't mean because yer 'ave a difference of opinion with them over something that they're not good neighbours. There's not one in this street that I couldn't go to for help if I needed it, an' that's what bein' a good neighbour is all about. So, put that in yer pipe an' smoke it, Bill Gillmoss!'

Chapter Two

'I really enjoyed that.' Bill dropped his knife and fork on to the empty plate and pushed it away. Leaning back in the chair he undid the top button of his trousers and let out a long sigh. 'I've eaten that much I'm stored.'

'Yer eyes are bigger than yer belly.' Eileen started to gather up the empty plates. 'Sit by the fire, 'ave a ciggie an' relax.'

Bill scraped his chair back. 'Did you have a nice afternoon, chick?'

'Great! Mary and Vera were made up about the baby.'

All eyes turned when Joan stood up so quickly her chair banged into the sideboard and the tablecloth dragged askew. 'I'm going out.'

Eileen watched her daughter disappear down the hall and heard the front door bang behind her. 'Oh, dear, someone's not too 'appy.' She shrugged her shoulders and pulled a face. 'Still, yer can't win 'em all.'

'Here, give me the dishes.' Maggie pushed Eileen aside. 'I'll do the washing up.'

'Ah, yer not a bad old stick, are yer, missus!' Eileen smiled fondly at her mother. 'Will yer cover our Billy's dinner with a plate for us, and put it on a pan of hot water to keep warm? He must be workin' overtime.'

'Shall I help me nan?' A few days ago Edna would have been out of the door like a streak of greased lightning to play with her mates. But not now. She'd made up her mind to help her mother all she could until the new baby arrived. 'Nan can wash and I'll dry.'

Eileen waited until she could hear the clink of dishes, then walked to the couch and flopped down. She was thoughtful for a while as her finger traced the pattern in the uncut moquette. Then she tilted her head sideways to gaze at her husband. 'Yer know what, Bill? I've been that worried over the last few days, first about you, then me mam and the kids, I hadn't given a thought to the baby. It was only when Mary an' Vera were talkin' about it, that it slowly dawned on me.' Eileen ran a hand across her tummy, her happiness and excitement growing with each second that ticked by. 'In 'ere, Bill, is our baby! A tiny human being . . . our own flesh and blood. An' here's us talkin' about whether we want it or not. Of course we want it! An' when it comes, we'll give it all the love we've got to give, eh, Bill?'

Bill could feel the sting of tears behind his eyes and he blinked them away. 'Of course we will, chick! And we'll have more time to devote to it than we did with the other three, because they seemed to come so quickly, one after the other.'

'I'm gettin' real excited.' Eileen's chubby face beamed. 'Mary's gettin' Harry to bring 'er up on Saturday with some knittin' patterns for matinee coats. An' she's goin' to make me some baby blankets and pillow cases an' things.

She was that thrilled, yer'd think it was her 'aving the baby.'

'The dishes are done, Mam!' Edna, her socks hanging round her ankles, sat on the arm of the couch. 'I heard yer tellin' me dad that Auntie Mary was comin' on Saturday. Are yer goin' to teach me to knit, like yer said?'

'Course I will.' Eileen's eyes twinkled. 'Tell yer dad what yer want to call the baby.'

Edna pursed her lips, her thin face serious. 'If it's a girl, I'd like to call it Susan, and Randolph if it's a boy.'

When Bill's jaw dropped in amazement, the room filled with Eileen's laughter.

And Maggie, putting the clean plates away in the kitchen cupboard, smiled. Everything's going to all right, she told herself. Then her eyes looked up, and she whispered, 'Please God.'

'I'll cast on for you, then you can take it from there.' Mary Sedgemoor's fingers moved rapidly, pausing now and then to pull a length of the white wool from the ball. 'It's a dead easy pattern once you get the hang of it.'

Edna sat beside Mary on the couch, her eyes taking in every movement, while Eileen's eyes were on Mary's bowed head. Pretty Mary, with her long, blonde, curly hair, vivid blue eyes, teeth like pearls and a figure as good as any film star. They'd been friends since the day Mary had started work in the munitions factory and Harry Sedgemoor, who was the supervisor in the shell department, had brought her along to work on the same machine as Eileen. She'd been Mary Bradshaw then, now she was Mary Sedgemoor. And she was Eileen's best mate.

'There you are, forty stitches,' Mary said. 'And you'll have to keep counting them in case you drop one.'

Eileen took the knitting needles in her chubby hands and groaned. 'It's years since I did any knittin', I don't know where to start.'

'Give yourself a chance! Look, watch me. In . . . over . . . through . . . off! See how easy it is?'

'Everythin's easy when yer know how, kid!' Eileen's hands were so chubby she couldn't keep the wool over her first finger. 'At this rate, the baby will be ready to start school before I've knitted its first matinee coat.'

'You've dropped a stitch already,' Mary tutted. 'Just take your time, Eileen, and you'll soon get into it.'

Edna's mouth was open, her tongue hanging out as she concentrated on knitting with some old wool Mary had brought. She finished a line and ran across to Mary to show off. 'I've done a row, Auntie Mary, aren't I clever?'

'That's very good.' Mary inspected the stitches. 'Just keep on with plain knitting until you get used to it, then I'll show you how to knit a line, purl a line.'

'Anybody home?'

When Eileen heard her sister's voice, a look of relief crossed her face. 'Come in, our kid!'

Rene walked in to see Eileen's huge body perched on the edge of a dining chair, the turban she had tied round her head slipped over one eye, and the knitting needles she was holding in her chubby hands pointing in every direction but the right one. 'I wish I had a camera with me,' Rene laughed. 'You should see yourself.'

'Go 'ed!' Eileen glared. ''Ave a good laugh! I feel a

16

right bloody fool as it is, without you addin' yer twopenny worth.'

'I was only kidding.' Rene produced a parcel from behind her back. 'A little present for you.'

Eileen happily threw the knitting down, her face creased in a wide grin. 'What is it, kid?'

'Open it and see.'

Eileen tore the paper wrapping off, letting it fall to the floor in her eagerness. 'Oh, our Rene, they're lovely!' She stood up and spread the pram set on the table. There was a matching pair of leggings, a coat, bonnet and a pair of mitts, all in a pale shade of yellow. Eileen could feel her eyes fill with tears, and she brushed them away before facing her sister. 'Thanks, Sis, they're beautiful.'

'Not handknitted, I'm afraid, because I'm hopeless with a pair of knitting needles. But I'm glad you like them.'

'Honest, everyone's been so good I can't believe it.' Eileen sat down and motioned to Rene to pull one of the dining chairs out. 'The baby's goin' to be a proper swank.'

'And so it should be,' Mary said. 'Only the best is good enough for a Gillmoss.'

Rene had been eyeing Eileen, trying hard to keep a smile from her face. In the end she could keep it back no longer. 'Have a look at yourself in the mirror, Eileen. That turban is so cockeyed, it makes you look as though you've been out all night on the tiles.'

Eileen's hands moved to straighten the offending turban. 'D'yez know what? I've been wearin' one of these since the bloody war started an' I still haven't found the knack of tyin' it so it stays put.' She whipped it off in disgust. 'Don't know why I wear the bloody

17

thing anyway.' She suddenly started to shake with laughter. 'Imagine me new baby, openin' its eyes for the first time an' seein' me in this! It would ask the doctor to put it back where it came from!'

Eileen put her backside to the old heavy mangle and pushed it back against the wall. 'Well, that's it for another few days, thank God!' She rubbed her wet hands down her pinny, then lifted the corner of it to wipe the sweat from her forehead. 'Will you see to the fire, Mam, while I go down to the lavvy? Then I'll make us a nice hot drink.'

Maggie knelt in front of the fire, carefully placing pieces of coal on the dying embers with the brass tongs. They'd been so busy with the washing, they'd forgotten the fire and now it was nearly out. She'd have to hold a sheet of newspaper in front and hope the draught would help the new coals catch fire. She heard the kitchen door open and called over her shoulder, 'There's not much heat from this, lass!'

When there was no reply, Maggie turned her head to see Eileen standing in the doorway, tears streaming down her screwed-up face. 'What is it, lass?' Maggie asked anxiously. 'What's happened?'

Eileen's body shook with sobs. 'Mam, I'm bleeding.'

'Oh, my God!' Maggie scrambled to her feet. 'Is it much, or just a few spots?'

'It's a big stain on me knickers,' Eileen gulped. 'I'm not goin' to lose the baby, am I, Mam?'

Maggie's tongue flicked over her lips as she looked into Eileen's distraught face. 'I don't know, lass.' She crossed the room and took hold of her daughter's elbow. 'Come and lay down on the couch.' As she eased the heavy legs sideways, Maggie's brain was racing. If only Bill was in, or even one of the children, they could have run for the doctor while she stayed with Eileen. But they wouldn't be home for hours and they couldn't afford to wait that long.

Eileen was sobbing and Maggie's heart went out to her. 'Does Cissie know about the baby, lass?'

Eileen nodded. 'Yer know what our Edna's like, Mam! The whole of flippin' Liverpool probably knows by now.'

'I'll nip down and see if she's in.' Maggie ran a hand through her hair. 'She can sit with you while I run for Doctor Greenfield.'

Cissie, her face full of concern, followed Maggie down the hall and into the living room. She took Eileen's hand in hers and patted it. 'You'll be all right, girl, don't worry.'

'Oh, Cissie!' Eileen looked into the eyes of the woman she'd had many a set-to with when their children were little. They matched each other in size ounce for ounce, and when there'd been a fight, neither would give way to the other. 'I'm frightened.'

'I've told yer, yer goin' to be all right!' Cissie turned to Maggie who was hovering near the door. 'Get goin', Maggie, I'll see to Eileen.'

Maggie ran as quickly as she could, and when she reached the surgery she was gasping for breath. The housekeeper who opened the door took one look at Maggie's distraught face and shouted for the doctor. Within minutes she was seated next to him in his car and they were on their way to Eileen.

Bill stepped down from the bus and his face showed

surprise when he saw Edna waiting for him. 'This is a nice . . .'

'Me Mam's sick.' The words poured from Edna's mouth. 'The doctor's been and me Mam's in bed.'

Bill could feel the hairs on the back of his neck stand up with fear. 'What's wrong?' He had Edna by the arm now and was almost dragging her along in his haste to get home. 'What happened?'

'I dunno! Me Mam was in bed when I got 'ome from school and Nan just said she was sick. Then she told me to meet yer at the bus stop an' tell yer to hurry.' Edna pulled her arm free. 'Let go, Dad, yer not 'alf hurtin' me!'

'I'll go on ahead, then.' Bill's long legs had never covered the ground so quickly and when he neared their house and saw Maggie at the door, wringing her hands, his blood ran cold. 'What is it, Ma?'

Maggie didn't speak until they were in the living room. She put a finger to her lips and jerked her head towards the ceiling as she closed the door. 'Doctor Greenfield thinks Eileen might be having a miscarriage.'

'Oh, no!' Bill banged his forehead with his open hand. 'No, Ma, not that!'

'It's not certain, son, so don't start getting upset.' Maggie touched his arm. 'And for heaven's sake don't let Eileen see you're worried! If she gets herself all worked up it'll only make things worse. The doctor said she's to stay in bed and not do a thing. He's coming back in the morning, but if we need him before, we've got to ring.' Maggie raised a smile. 'Go and cheer her up while I see to the dinner.'

Pulling on the banister rail, Bill took the stairs two at a

time, his heart thudding. When he threw the bedroom door open, it was to see Joan and Edna sitting on one side of the bed, and Billy on the other. 'Hello, chick, how are you?'

Eileen waved her hand. 'Go downstairs now, kids, and let me an' yer Dad have a talk in private. I'll see yez later.'

Young Billy was reluctant to move. He wanted to know what was wrong with the mother he idolised, but his nan wouldn't tell him anything except she was sick. He wasn't a kid any more, he was sixteen now, and that was old enough to be told what was going on. So he hovered at the side of the bed. 'The doctor must 'ave said something, Mam!'

'He doesn't know 'imself yet, son! Perhaps when 'e comes tomorrer he'll know a bit more.' When Eileen looked at her son, it was like seeing Bill when she'd first met him. Billy had the same dark brown mop of hair and the same deep brown, velvety eyes. Eileen used to call them "come to bed eyes". But young Billy was a few inches taller than his dad had been, and he was still growing.

'Go down and 'elp yer nan, there's a good lad,' Eileen said softly. 'Yer can come up again later.'

Bill took over Billy's seat and reached for Eileen's hand. 'Confined to barracks, eh, love!'

'I'm scared stiff, Bill! I want this baby so much I don't know what I'll do if I lose it.'

Bill bent and gathered her warm, cuddly body close. 'Now come on, chick, who's always telling other people "don't trouble trouble, till trouble troubles you", eh? If you do as Doctor Greenfield tells you and stay in bed, you'll be all right, I know you will.'

'I'll stay in bed for the whole six months if need be.' Eileen's voice was choked. 'I'll do anythin' to keep the baby safe.'

'I'll take the day off tomorrow and I'll make sure you stay in bed. I'll see Billy out to work and the girls off to school, so don't you worry your head about anything.'

'I know I should argue with yer, Bill, but I'm not goin' to. I'd like yer to be here tomorrer when the doctor comes. Me mam's very good, an' yer know I love the bones of her, but it's you I need right now.'

Bill and Maggie sat either side of the fireplace, both deep in thought. The rest of the family were in bed and the house was still except for the occasional hissing from the coals and the ticking of the clock.

'I wonder what brought it on?' Bill wondered aloud. 'Eileen's been looking so well!'

'I know what brought it on,' Maggie said, her voice soft. 'It's that ruddy big mangle! I can't move it, and Eileen shouldn't . . . not in her condition, anyway. I'll bet me bottom dollar that's the cause of it.'

'She shifted that mangle on her own?'

'Well, there's nobody else to do it, Bill, so don't start blaming Eileen for what's happened.' Maggie was quick to defend her daughter. 'The damned thing has to be pulled out to turn the handle, and the kitchen is too small to leave it out all the time. You can't swing a cat round out there, never mind having that ruddy thing stuck in the middle.'

'I'm not blaming Eileen, Ma, I'm blaming meself!' Bill

scratched his head. 'Me own common sense should have asked me how she was coping with the washing.' His fist came down heavily on the arm of his chair. 'I've tried to talk her into moving to a bigger house, but every time I mention it she pooh-poohs the idea. But this has put the top hat on it. If she comes through this all right, I don't care what she says, we're moving to a place where she'll have more room to move around . . . a house like Mary's, where there's a wash-house with a boiler and running water.'

Chapter Three

Dr Greenfield snapped his bag shut. 'You can come in now, Mr Gillmoss.'

He'd barely finished speaking before Bill was in the room. 'What's the news, Doctor?' Bill's eyes flitted anxiously from Eileen to the doctor. 'Is she going to be okay?'

'It's far too early to say. The bleeding has slowed down, but until it's stopped I can't give Eileen an internal.' John Greenfield swung his bag from the tallboy and moved to the side of the bed. 'I can't promise anything, all I can do is advise you to stay in bed, have complete rest. If you do that then there's a chance you may keep the baby. But you must do as you're told, Eileen, do you understand?' He waited for Eileen's nod before continuing. 'You mustn't attempt to go downstairs, and no lifting anything.'

'I'll be as good as gold, Doctor,' Eileen answered tearfully. She had known John Greenfield for years and he didn't seem to have aged at all in those years, even though he'd seen service at the battle front when the war was at its height. He was as slim as ever, still had that boyish, lopsided grin and the fine baby hair that had a

25

mind of its own and kept falling on to his forehead. 'I'll do everythin' yer say, honest.'

'I'll make sure she does,' Bill said, 'otherwise she'll have me to answer to.' He scratched his head. 'What about visitors? We've got a full house downstairs.'

'Uh, uh! Not for a few days.' John squeezed Eileen's hand. 'Best to take no chances because we don't want to lose this baby . . .' he started to chuckle, 'although I'm not sure whether the world is ready for another Eileen Gillmoss.'

'Thanks, Doctor.' Eileen wrapped her fingers around his hand, remembering the times she'd gone to him with her troubles, and everybody else's for that matter. And he'd never let her down. 'I'll do everythin' yer said, scout's honour. Yer know I've got every faith in you, always 'ave.'

'I'll be on my way then.' At the door John turned. 'I'll call in tomorrow and I expect you to have behaved yourself till then, okay?'

'Haven't got much bloody option, 'ave I?' Eileen sounded more like her old self, and the two men smiled at each other. 'Even if Cary Grant walked in that door now, I wouldn't move a muscle.' It was too dark in the room to be sure, but John would swear she had a twinkle in her eye when she added, 'On second thoughts, though, for Cary Grant I might just make the effort.'

'I'll see the doctor out, chick, then explain to our visitors. I'll be back in a couple of minutes.'

Eileen heard Bill running up the stairs and turned her head on the pillow when the door opened. 'D'yer want a little bit of useless information, Bill? Well, there's a hundred and twenty-seven flippin' roses on the paper on that wall.'

Bill grinned. 'Aren't you glad you don't have to water them?'

'Have the visitors all gone?'

Bill sat down gently on the side of the bed. 'Your Rene's gone. She's got to pick Victoria up from school at twelve. But Mary and Vera are still here with the children.' He took Eileen's hand and squeezed it. 'Ma's been busy making cups of tea for the last two hours.'

'I could murder a cuppa, right now. Me mouth's that dry with nerves.' Eileen stroked a finger over Bill's hand. 'What d'yer think, Bill? Did the doctor tell yer anything when yer were seein' him out?'

'Only what he told you. He's not going to commit himself and get the blame if he's wrong.' Bill removed his hand and stroked the hair back from her forehead. 'But I've got a feeling in me bones that everything's going to be all right.'

'I hope so, Bill.' Eileen closed her eyes and prayed. I know I'm no angel, God, and I only come to you when I want something. But I'm in real trouble this time and I really need your help. Please don't let me down, and I promise I'll be good from now on.

'What's wrong with me mam?' Edna was sprawled on the couch, her thin legs stuck out in front of her. 'She doesn't look sick to me.'

Bill's finger made a groove in the plush of the tablecloth as he sought the right words to explain. He could feel Edna's eyes on him as she waited for an answer, and knew that Joan, who was standing by the sideboard with her back to him, was also all ears. 'Your mam's not really sick, as such,' Bill said. 'She hasn't got a cold or pains, or anything like that.' Oh, lord, he thought, how do I get round this? Then he decided it was best to tell the truth. If things didn't go right, they'd have to be told anyway. Best to do it now and get it over with. 'It's the baby, you see. Your mam might lose it.'

Edna shot up straight, her heels banging against the front of the couch. A choking sound left her mouth as her eyes widened with horror. 'Lose the baby?' She ran to stand in front of her father. 'What d'yer mean, Dad? How can me mam lose the baby?'

Joan didn't turn round as she waited for her father to answer. There was no look of horror on her face, just a faint smile. She didn't want anything to happen to her mam because she loved her. But as long as she was all right, then Joan would be quite happy if the baby didn't come along.

'I'm not saying she is going to lose it, pet. The doctor said if she stays in bed then everything might be all right.' Bill ran a hand across his forehead as he sighed. 'So you've both got to help me look after her so she gets better. And when you go to bed tonight I want you to say a few prayers, will you do that?'

Edna nodded, her eyes filled with tears. 'I'll say six Hail Mary's and six Our Father's,' she gulped, as a stray tear trickled down her cheek. 'And I'll pray to Saint Anthony as well.'

Bill turned his head. 'You're very quiet, Joan.'

'I never get a word in edgeways when our Edna's

around,' Joan said, her voice kept deliberately low. 'I'll help, Dad. And I'll say me prayers every night.'

'You're both to muck in with the housework,' Bill told them. 'I can't stay off work and we can't expect your nan to do everything.'

'I'll help with the washin' up,' Edna said. 'An' I'll run all the messages for 'er, Dad, I promise.' She sniffed up and wiped a tear away with the back of her hand, leaving a dirty streak across her thin face. 'Can I go up and see me mam now?'

'Well, Eileen, and how are you today?'

Oh, my God, Eileen muttered under her breath as she struggled to sit up when she heard Father Murphy's lilting Irish brogue. Wouldn't you think someone would have warned her the priest was here. 'I'm feelin' all right, Father.'

'Well now, isn't that good to hear?' Father Murphy drew the small wooden chair nearer the bed, his rosy cheeks beaming. 'I've been having a cup of tea and a little chat with your dear mother. She tells me you're expecting the doctor this morning, is that right now?'

'Yes, Father.' Eileen's eyes darted round the room. Thank goodness her mother had been up earlier and tidied around. 'He should be here soon.'

The priest was carrying a square black box in his hand, and before sitting down he placed it carefully on the floor, followed by his black, round-crowned hat. He rubbed his hands together before leaning forward and resting his elbows on his knees. 'With every hour that passes, Eileen, hope grows a bit stronger. So don't look so down in the mouth, for that's not like you at all.'

'I can't say I feel like me, Father. I'm so frightened, me sense of humour 'as deserted me.'

'Now, now, Eileen! Put your faith and trust in the good Lord. Isn't He up there now, looking down on all His children?'

Eileen looked into the face that shone with goodness and compassion, and nodded. 'I know, father. And although I've been naughty sometimes, I've never done anything really bad in me whole life.'

'D'you think I don't know that, Eileen? For sure, you haven't got a wicked bone in your whole body.' Father Murphy looked at his watch. 'I know you can't come to church, so I'll hear your Confession and give you Holy Communion now.' He pushed his chair back and moved to the window to draw the curtains. 'I'm sure you'll feel better after . . . more at peace with yourself.'

Eileen pulled the sheet up to her neck. 'Thank you, Father. Yer an angel.'

'Not yet, Eileen, but sure now, aren't I living in hopes?'

Eileen had been in bed for two weeks, the longest two weeks of her whole life. Apart from the family, the only visitors she'd been allowed by Bill were their Rene, and Mary and Vera. She was sick of looking at the ceiling and the four walls, but not for all the tea in China would she have ventured out of that bed. Not until the doctor said it was safe for her to get up. He was due this morning and she'd been praying he would tell her the danger had now passed. She'd given herself a good wash down and put on her best nightie, the blue one with lace trimming on the neck and sleeves. Her mam had taken her dinkie curlers out and combed the hair that was lifeless and greasy after not being washed for two weeks.

Eileen looked at the alarm clock on the small wooden-topped table at the side of the bed. 'Come on, Doc,' she said aloud. 'If yer don't come soon I'll be a nervous wreck.' Her eyes swept round the four walls. 'Three hundred and fifty-seven flowers on this paper. I used to like flowers, but now I'm sick of the sight of them. Wouldn't care if I didn't see another one for the rest of me life.' Her eyes travelled to the ceiling. 'See, God, all that and not one swear word. I'm bein' good, like I promised.' The sound of the front door knocker reached her and Eileen's tummy started to turn over. She crossed her fingers on both hands, raised her eyes again and whispered, 'Please, please, please.'

'And how is my favourite patient today?' John Greenfield breezed into the room, a smile lighting up his face. 'Fed up to the teeth being in bed, eh?'

'Can't say I'd fancy much more of it,' Eileen answered truthfully. 'But if it's done the trick, then it's been worth it.'

John placed his bag on the tallboy. 'Your mother is bringing me a bowl of hot water up, then I'll give you a good examination.' He saw Eileen's eyes widen, and grinned. 'No need to be embarrassed, I see women like you every day.'

Maggie pushed the door open with her elbow, a bowl of hot water in her hands, a towel draped over her arm. 'Mind the water's not too hot, Doctor.'

'That's fine, thank you.' John slipped his coat off and

draped it over the back of a chair. 'I'll give you a call when I've finished.'

Eileen stayed flat on her back, her eyes following the doctor as he walked towards the bowl of water. 'Well?'

John dipped his hands in the water, the corners of his mouth curved upwards into a smile. He was always glad when he had good news to give a patient, but this time it was extra special because it was Eileen. He reached for the towel and turned to face the bed. 'Mother and baby fine, I'm glad to say.'

Eileen shot up in bed. She joined her chubby hands together, 'Oh, thank you, God, thank you.'

'Been saying your prayers, have you?' John asked.

'To tell yer the truth, Doctor, I think God is makin' everythin' come right 'cos he's fed up listenin' to me and me mam! She's been goin' to Church every day, an' I've said more prayers in the last two weeks than I've said in me whole life.'

'It seems to have paid off.'

'I've been lucky havin' Him, and you, on my side.' Eileen felt weak with relief and happiness. 'Yez make a good winning team.'

'I'm not in the same league, Eileen, but thank you. Now, you can go downstairs today, but only to lie on the couch. You're to do nothing at all until I call again, understand?'

John had moved to the side of the bed, and before he knew what was happening he was being pulled down and clasped in Eileen's big arms. 'Oh, you lovely man.' Eileen kissed his cheek, squeezing him so tight he had to fight for his breath. 'I'll never forget yer for this, honest I won't.'

Trying to regain his balance, John stammered, 'Eileen, I haven't done anything! Any doctor would have told you to do what I did.'

'Ah, but yer not any old doctor, are yer?' Eileen bent her head and straightened the front of her nightdress. 'Yer've been more like a mate to me, over the years.'

'And can I say I couldn't have a better friend?' John held his hand out, winced at Eileen's tight grip, then said briskly, 'But right now I'm back to being your doctor. For the next few weeks you take it easy. No thinking, well it won't do any harm to wash the dishes or rinse a few things through. If you do anything foolish, Eileen, I won't be responsible for the consequences.'

'I won't take any chances, Doctor, don't worry. I've learned my lesson the hard way.' Eileen flung the bedclothes back. 'I'll go down and give me mam a surprise.'

'Take it slowly,' John warned. 'You'll be weak after being in bed for so long.'

'How about yer givin' me a piggy back?' Eileen asked, her face straight.

John looked at the size of the big woman and burst out laughing.

'Would you come and visit me in hospital?'

'Yeah!' Eileen's tummy started to shake. 'I'll bring the baby in with me.'

Edna was the first in from school, and when she saw Eileen on the couch, a pillow behind her head and the quilt from her bed covering her, the surprise on her face brought a chuckle from Eileen. 'It is me, sunshine, not a flippin' ghost.'

'Mam!' Edna flung herself at her mother. 'Are yer better now?'

'I've got to take it easy for a few weeks, but yeah, I'm better now, thank God.'

'An' yer haven't lost the baby?'

'No, sunshine, I haven't lost the baby.' Eileen turned her head to see Joan standing in the doorway. 'I didn't hear a knock.'

'The front door was open.' Joan had come in just after Edna and had heard the exchange between her sister and mother. She felt so disappointed it took her all her time to hide it. 'You all right now, then?'

Eileen's eyes narrowed. She knew her daughters inside out, and this one didn't look too happy. Still, she thought, like Bill said, she was at an awkward age and was probably embarrassed.

'Give yer nan a hand and set the table, will yez?'

Edna rushed to the sideboard to get the tablecloth as Joan turned towards the door. 'I've got to go down to Dorothy's to get a book off her. I won't be long.'

'Ay, skinnymalinks,' Eileen shouted after her. 'If yer not back in five minutes, I'll flatten yer, d'yer 'ear?'

'She'll be halfway down the street by now.' Maggie came in from the kitchen wiping her hands on a towel. 'Anyway, she's neither use nor ornament when she's here! Me and Edna will manage, won't we, love?'

Eileen leaned back on the pillow, muttering under her breath. 'Kids, who'd 'ave 'em?'

* * *

'I could get used to this, yer know.' Eileen grinned as she steadied the plate on her lap. 'I always said I was born to be a lady and get waited on hand and foot.'

Bill turned his head and grinned back. If only he could tell her how good it was to see her downstairs again. He was so happy he felt like a young boy again. When the rest of the family were in bed, he'd tell her how he felt and how much he loved her.

When Maggie saw the look exchanged between Bill and her daughter, an idea entered her head. She looked from Joan to Edna. 'If you hurry up and eat your dinner, I'll mug you to the pictures.' Maggie didn't really feel like going out, but it would give man and wife the chance to be alone. 'Abbott and Costello are on at the Walton Vale.'

Edna's face lit up and her movements quickened, the fork ramming the food into her mouth. 'I'm nearly finished, Nan.'

'Don't speak with your mouth full,' Bill warned. 'How many times do I have to tell you?'

Joan didn't speak, but she was secretly pleased. None of her friends had seen the Abbott and Costello film so she'd be able to swank about it tomorrow.

'I'm ready, Nan,' Edna said.

'Me too!' Joan reached for her sister's empty plate. 'I'll take these out.'

'Leave the dishes,' Bill told her, 'I'll wash them.'

Bill followed them to the door where he pressed a ten-bob note into Maggie's hand. 'Thanks, Ma! Buy them an ice cream in the interval.'

He walked back into the room and took Eileen's plate from her knee. 'I'll see to the dishes before I sit down.

35

Once I get comfortable I won't feel like budging.'

Eileen listened to the clattering of the pots and pans, thinking it was wrong for Bill to have to do the washing up after working all day. Still, it wouldn't be for long.

Bill stood in the doorway, a look of relief and happiness on his face. 'Chick, you'll never know how good it is to see you sitting on that couch. The last two weeks have seemed an eternity.'

'Yer can say that again, Bill Gillmoss,' Eileen said. 'I thought it was never goin' to end. But right now I feel so happy I could sing me 'ead off.'

Bill swung one of the dining chairs round and set it next to the couch. He took hold of Eileen's hand and kissed it. 'I love you, Eileen Gillmoss.'

Eileen fluttered her eyelashes. 'Ooh, yer sound dead romantic! Tell me more, I'm all ears.'

'Well, I haven't got a voice like Issy Bon, but I'll have a go.' Bill cleared his throat, threw back his head and started singing a very passable rendition of the popular singer's "I Don't Want To Set The World On Fire". When he'd finished he bent forward to kiss Eileen on the cheek. 'How was that?'

'Yer sing better than Issy Bon,' Eileen chuckled, 'and yer better lookin' than 'im too.'

'That shows what good taste you've got.'

It was so unusual for Bill to act the goat, Eileen knew he was feeling as happy and as thankful as she herself was. 'Aren't we lucky, Bill?'

'We can certainly count our blessings,' Bill answered. 'We've got each other, the children, Ma, and now a new baby. There's not many as fortunate as us.' Bill clasped his hands between his knees, his thumbs circling each other. Was it the right time to bring up the subject, he asked himself, or should he leave it until Eileen was on her feet? She might start getting upset and he didn't want that. He'd have to be careful and choose the right words.

Bill cocked his head and looked into Eileen's eyes. 'There's only one blot on the horizon, chick, and I think we should talk about it.'

Eileen's brow furrowed. 'What's that?'

'Now don't start getting all het up,' Bill said. 'I wasn't going to mention it until you were on your feet, but time isn't on our side.'

Eileen knew immediately what he was getting at. 'Yer mean about us movin' to another 'ouse?' When Bill nodded, Eileen groaned, 'Oh, not that again, Bill! Yer know 'ow I feel about this house! We came 'ere the day we got married, remember? We didn't 'ave a honeymoon because we couldn't wait to get in our own little 'ouse.'

'Yes, but there were only the two of us then,' Bill reminded her, his voice soft. 'When the baby comes, there'll be seven. It's only a two-up two-down, Eileen, not meant for so many. We had to divide one of the bedrooms into two when the girls came along, and you can't swing a cat round in them. You certainly couldn't put a baby's cot in either of them.'

'I thought we could 'ave the cot in our room.' When Eileen saw the frown on Bill's face, she went on quickly. 'It wouldn't be for all that long. Our Billy's growin' up an' he'll probably get married in a few years.'

'He's only just turned sixteen.' Bill closed his eyes, his fingers pinching at his bottom lip. After a moment's

37

thought, he asked, 'You do love me, don't you?'

'What a daft question! Yer know I love the bones of yer!'

'That means we both love each other. And what do two people do when they're in love? Have you thought about that, chick? With a growing child in our room, there wouldn't be much loving going on, would there?'

Eileen pursed her lips. She hadn't thought about that.

Bill saw the wavering and took advantage. 'Unless you want me to go out and find myself another woman.'

'Over my dead body, Bill Gillmoss!'

'Then think about it, will you, for my sake? And while you're about it, think of the girls and our Billy, too! When they start courting, where will they go to entertain their friends? They certainly wouldn't have any privacy here.'

Eileen's face was a study. None of these things had entered her mind. And the more she thought of it, the more she saw that Bill was right. But she loved this little house so much, she'd never be happy anywhere else. Bill could see Eileen's brain ticking over. 'We'll have to make up our minds soon, Eileen. It could be months before we find a house we like.'

'Let me sleep on it, will yer, Bill? It's not a thing to decide on in a hurry.'

Bill could see the tiredness on Eileen's face and took her hand in both of his. 'It's time you were going back to bed. You've been up long enough for your first day.' He pulled her gently to her feet. 'I'll come and tuck you in.'

Bill drew the covers up to Eileen's chin. 'I'll be as quiet as I can when I come up, so as not to wake you. So have a good night's sleep. And don't worry about moving, for heaven's sake. If you're dead set on staying here, then here we'll stay. I only want what's best for you.'

'I know you do, love.' Eileen felt drowsy as soon as her head touched the pillow. It had been a long day. She turned on her side and curled up. 'I will think about it, Bill, honest . . .' Her voice trailed off as she drifted into a deep sleep.

Bill stood looking down at her. He loved her very much and couldn't bear the thought of anything happening to her. That's why he had to get her away from here, to make life easier for her when the baby came.

Chapter Four

'Ay, ay, Mam!' Joan's voice was high with indignation as she stood before her mother. 'I can't go for an interview in me school socks! I'd be a laughin' stock and I wouldn't get the job.'

'I'm not made of money,' Eileen answered. 'I've already bought yer a new blouse an' skirt, what more d'yer want?'

'A pair of long stockings.' Joan turned to Maggie, her pale face flushed, her eyes pleading for support. 'Tell her, Nan, please? You must see how stupid I'd look in me short socks.'

Maggie looked up from the pram pillow case she was embroidering. She usually refused to be drawn into any argument between Eileen and the children, but this time she could see Joan's point of view. 'She's right, lass. First impressions are always important.'

Eileen sighed. 'Oh, all right. But yez'll have me in the workhouse one of these days with wantin' this, that an' the other.' She reached down to the side of the couch and took her purse from her bag. 'How much d'yer want?'

'Only a shilling.' Joan looked down at her feet. She and

her friend Dorothy were going for interviews at Vernon's Pools in Aintree on Monday and Dorothy had been swanking about what her mother had bought her to wear for the big day. And Joan wasn't going to be outdone by her friend if she could help it. 'Can I 'ave a suspender belt as well, to keep the stockings up?'

'What's the matter with a pair of garters?' Eileen asked.

'Mam, they're old fashioned! I can't go for an interview with pieces of elastic keepin' me stockings up.'

'An' who the 'ell is goin' to see up yer clothes, might I ask?' Eileen looked up to the pleading in her daughter's eyes and relented. 'Oh, all right, you win. Run down to County Road and see what they've got.'

'Dorothy got hers from T.J. Hughes.' Joan's heart was beginning to feel lighter. 'She said they're cheaper there.'

'I'm not goin' into town with yer, sunshine. It gets too packed, especially on a Saturday.' Eileen was four months pregnant now, and after the scare last month she avoided buses like the plague. 'Besides, yer dad and Billy will be 'ome from work about one o'clock an' they'll expect their dinner on the table.'

'I'll nip into Liverpool with her,' Maggie offered. 'Go and get yourself ready, Joan.'

'Ooh, thanks, Nan!' Joan kissed Maggie's cheek in a rare show of affection before running up the stairs singing a tuneless song at the top of her voice.

'I don't know,' Eileen tutted. 'Fourteen an' wantin' a suspender belt. When I was 'er age it was either garters or a knot in the top of yer stocking.'

'Children seem to be growing up quicker these days,' Maggie said. 'I think the war had a lot to do with it. All the men in the army and most women working, there was no discipline. The old saying, "spare the rod and spoil the child" is true, and we'll find out to our cost. They're like old men and women now before they've left school.'

'I ain't goin' to argue with yer on that, missus! A clip round the ear 'ole is what some of them need.' Eileen rummaged through the silver in her scruffy purse, then stretched her hand out, three half-crowns lying in the palm. 'There should be enough 'ere for 'er stockings and those thingamajigs. It's only a couple of coppers on the bus, so there might be enough to go mad an' mug yerselves to a cup of tea in the cafeteria in T.J.'s.'

Young Billy put a cushion behind Eileen's back, his face creased in a grin. 'You take it easy, Mam, I'll help me dad with the dishes.'

Eileen's eyes were tender as she watched him walk to the kitchen. He was a good lad, was Billy. He was nearly as bad as his dad for fussing over her. When they were home, neither of them would let her lift a finger.

'Put me mam's and our Joan's dinner in the oven with plates over them,' Eileen called. 'They shouldn't be long now.'

A knock on the front door brought Eileen to the edge of the couch. But before she had time to stand up, Bill appeared, a tea towel in his hand. 'Stay where you are, chick, I'll get it.'

Eileen cocked her ear for the sound of voices, and when she heard Mary's laugh, followed by Harry's, her face lit up. 'Hi-ya, kid!'

Eileen's arms went across her tummy as two young

bodies threw themselves at her. 'Hey! Let me breathe, will yez?'

'Come away at once.' Mary had to drag the struggling children from their favourite auntie. 'Behave yourselves or we'll go home.'

'Hello, Auntie Eileen.' The two young voices spoke in unison.

'Are you better now?' asked five-year-old Emma. With her blonde curls and bright blue eyes, she was as pretty as a picture and the spitting image of Mary. 'I missed you.'

Tony, a year younger, pushed his sister aside. He was as dark as she was fair, a miniature version of his handsome father. 'I missed you too, Auntie Eileen. Mummy wouldn't let us come to see you.'

'Well, yer see,' Eileen put an arm round each of them and pulled them towards her, 'I haven't been very well. But I'm all right now.'

Eileen looked up at Mary and noticed her eyes were twinkling with excitement. 'You're lookin' very pleased with yerself. Have yez come up on the pools?' Then a frown creased Eileen's forehead. 'Where's Harry?'

'Talking to Bill in the hall.'

'What the 'ell are they standin' out there for?' Eileen raised her voice. 'Hey, you two, get in 'ere! Don't be whisperin' behind our backs.'

She heard Harry's loud guffaw before he marched into the room, stood to attention in front of her, clicked his heels and saluted. 'Reporting for duty, Sir!'

'I'll just finish the dishes,' Bill said, 'I won't be a tick.'

'Eileen looked from Harry to Mary, her eyes like slits. 'What 'ave you two been up to? Yez look as though yer've

44

lost sixpence and found half-a-crown.'

'All will be revealed in good time.' Harry flopped down next to Eileen on the couch. 'Where is everybody?'

'Billy's in the kitchen, me mam an' Joan 'ave gone to town, and our Edna's out playin' somewhere.' Eileen pulled a face at him. 'What d'yer want to know for?'

'Just idle curiosity.' Harry drew Tony on his knee. 'Shall we go and look for Edna and she can take you for some sweets?'

Tony's deep brown eyes looked from Eileen to his father. He wanted to stay with this big woman he adored because she always made them laugh. But a bag of sweets was very tempting. 'Yes, Daddy.'

'Come on, then.' Harry took the small hand in one of his and held the other out to Emma. 'Let's go and look for Edna.'

There's something going on here, Eileen thought. But they'll tell me in good time. 'Give a knock next door, I think she's playin' in their yard.'

Liverpool were playing at home and Billy had gone off to the match with his mates, his red and white scarf worn with pride. Edna was playing hopscotch in the street with Emma and Tony, and Maggie's and Joan's dinners were still in the oven awaiting their return.

'Well?' Eileen asked. 'Whatever it is that's got you two on edge, spit it out before I die of curiosity.'

Mary looked at Bill. 'Shall I tell her?'

Bill nodded, keeping his fingers crossed. Please God let Eileen be as pleased as I am.

'D'you know Mrs Kenny, who lives next door but one?'

Mary asked. 'You know, the old lady who lives on her own.'

'Of course I know Mrs Kenny!' Eileen was more confused than ever. 'But what's Mrs Kenny got to do with us?'

'I was talking to her the other day,' Mary told her, 'and she said the house was getting too much for her and she was thinking of looking for a smaller place.'

Puzzled, Eileen asked, 'So what?'

Bill couldn't contain himself any longer and he spoke before Mary had time to answer. 'Chick, she might do an exchange with us if the landlords don't object.'

While his wife was digesting his words, Bill carried on. 'Just think, a nice house and right by Mary and Harry.'

'But, but . . . she might not want to come here,' Eileen stuttered. 'She's not goin' to move from a posh neighbourhood to here.'

Harry leaned forward, his elbows resting on his knees. 'It's worth a try, Eileen. If you don't ask, you'll never get.'

'And we'd be able to see each other every day,' Mary said. 'I'd be able to help you when the baby comes.'

'It's the chance of a lifetime, we'll never get another one like it.' Bill ran his fingers through his mop of white hair. He'd been to see several houses but Eileen always found an excuse for not going with him. Either she didn't like the area or it was too far from Edna's school. He knew if it was left to her, they'd never move. 'We'd be fools if we didn't try. I know I'd move heaven and earth to get it if it was left to me.'

Eileen's eyes travelled from Harry to Mary, then on to Bill. They were all waiting anxiously for her answer. It was the pleading in Bill's eyes that finally broke her. 'If that's what yer want, love, then go an' see what yer can do.'

Bill shot up straight in his chair as a sigh of relief left his lips. 'You mean it, chick?'

When Eileen nodded, Mary clapped her hands in glee while Harry dropped back in the chair as the tension left his body. 'Thank God for that!'

Bill stood in front of Eileen, cupped her face in his hands and gave her a noisy kiss. 'That's my girl.' He turned to Harry. 'What do we do now?'

'I think the first thing is to ask Mrs Kenny to come and see this house and ask her to let you look over hers. I don't think there'd be any problem with the two land-lords,' Harry raised his bushy eyebrows, 'as long as you've got a clear rent book.'

'Go way, yer cheeky sod! Of course we've got a clear rent book!' Eileen placed her two hands on her hips. 'For two pennies I'd crack yer one, Harry Sedgemoor.'

'That's more like it,' Harry grinned. 'I was beginning to think you'd lost your spunk.'

'Aye, well, yer know what thought did, don't yer? Followed a muck cart and thought it was a weddin'. And any more cracks like that out of you, Harry Sedgemoor, an' I'll be throwin' you on the back of a muck cart.'

'Oh, aye, you and whose army?'

'I don't need an army,' Eileen fluttered her lashes, 'not when I've got my feller to protect me.'

Bill closed his eyes. It was like music to his ears to hear Eileen back to her old bubbly self. And if the house came off, he wouldn't call the queen his aunt.

When there was a knock on the door, Bill cursed as he walked down the hall. The last thing they wanted now was visitors. 'Hello, Vera! And how's my little girlfriend?' Bill looked down at Carol, Vera Jackson's nine-year-old mongol daughter, who had her arms wrapped around his waist. He stroked the fair hair as the large, round eyes smiled up at him.

'Come on in and see Auntie Eileen.'

'Well, look what the wind's blown in!' Eileen held her arms out to Carol and crushed her in a bear-like grip. 'Who's a little smasher, then, eh?'

'Me, Auntie Eileen.' Carol rained kisses on Eileen's face before making a bee-line for Harry and Mary.

Eileen eyed Vera up and down. 'Yer lookin' very well, Mrs Jackson. Gettin' used to bein' on yer own, now, are yer?'

'Well, it's a damn sight better than when Danny was there. At least I'm not living in fear all the time, worrying about him coming in drunk.' Vera slipped out of her coat and held an arm out. 'Look, Eileen, not a bruise in sight! Makes a change, doesn't it?'

'I wonder if he knocks 'is Dutch lady friend around? I bet she won't put up with 'is shenanigans the way you did.'

Vera shrugged her shoulders. 'I couldn't care less, as long as me, the boys and Carol aren't getting it.'

'Well, park yer carcass.' Eileen motioned for Bill to pull one of the dining chairs out. 'We've got some news for yer . . . at least we might 'ave some news for yer, it's not definite yet.'

Vera listened, wide eyed. She was an attractive woman with a slim figure and lovely, long auburn hair. Her eyes changed colour with the light, from pale brown to green.

'Wouldn't it be lovely if you could get it?' Then a thought struck Vera and she began to chuckle. 'Moving in with the snobs, eh? Remember how you used to pull Mary's leg about being stuck up?'

'Ay, don't be puttin' the mockers on it, Vera, we 'aven't got the flamin' 'ouse yet.'

Harry stood up, and straightening the crease in his trousers, said, 'I think Mary should come because she knows Mrs Kenny better than I do. If you'd keep an eye on the children, the three of us could be there and back in an hour.'

'I'll watch out for the children,' Vera said. 'Wild horses wouldn't move me till I know how you get on.'

Eileen clicked her tongue. 'Some people aren't 'alf nosy, aren't they?' She jerked her head at Bill. 'Go on, love, I know yer on pins. Hurry back and let's know what the score is.'

'The children are having the time of their lives out there. Your Edna is teaching Carol how to skip.' Vera crossed to look in the mirror over the mantelpiece and ran a hand over her long, smooth hair. 'Bill's a long time, isn't he?'

'An hour and a half.' Eileen glanced at the clock for the umpteenth time. 'They should've been well back by now.'

'Give them a chance,' Maggie said. She and Joan had been back an hour, had their dinner and washed up. Now they sat waiting. Joan had come in flushed with excitement over her first pair of long stockings and suspender belt, but when she heard the news her purchases quickly took second place in her train of thought. Just fancy, they might be going to live in a posh house like their Auntie Mary's! Now that would really be something to brag about to her friend Dorothy.

The sound of a car braking outside turned all heads towards the door.

'They're here!' Joan was out of the room like a streak of greased lightning, and they could hear her call, 'Are we goin' to live in Orrell Park, Dad?'

'Oh, my God!' Eileen cringed. 'I'll flatten 'er when I get me hands on 'er. Talk about a mouth like the Mersey tunnel, the whole flamin' street will know by now.'

'Eileen, the neighbours probably knew an hour ago,' Maggie said dryly. 'Joan might have a big mouth, but she's not in the meg specks with your Edna around. I'll bet that little madam's been knocking on doors and stopping people in the street.'

Bill was first through the door, his face aglow with excitement. 'Mrs Kenny is coming in the morning. Harry's bringing her in the car.'

Amid the gasps of pleasure and surprise, and the questions being thrown at Bill from all sides, Eileen sat quietly, her heart pounding. This is it, she thought. All the talking about moving to another house had now become a reality and her feelings were not of pleasure, but sadness. Nobody understood how much she loved this little house, how much it would grieve her to leave. 'You're very quiet, chick.' Bill bent to look in Eileen's face. 'You haven't said a word.'

'With this lot jabberin', I couldn't get a word in edgeways.' Eileen forced a smile to her face. Bill looked so happy she didn't have the heart to spoil things for him.

'Is Mrs Kenny really interested?'

Harry came to stand beside Bill and flung an arm across his shoulder. 'She is very interested. And before you say it,' Harry grinned, 'she knows this area very well. In fact, she was born only a few streets from here.'

Edna appeared in the doorway flanked by Emma and Tony, with Carol bringing up the rear. Never one to mince words, Edna asked, 'Did yer get this 'ouse, Dad?'

Mary, who had taken a seat next to Eileen on the couch, turned to look at the group framed in the doorway. 'Good grief,' she groaned, 'will you look at the state of them! Their clothes are filthy!'

'Holy sufferin' ducks!' Eileen's eyes went to the ceiling. 'Didn't you ever get dirty when you were a kid?'

'We've been playing ollies,' Tony said proudly. 'And I beat Edna, didn't I, Edna?'

Harry's loud chuckle filled the room. 'Good for you, son! I'll have to have a game with you, and see if you can beat me.'

Mary shook her head in despair as she searched in her pocket for some loose change. She couldn't bear to see the children dirty. Oh, she knew she was too fussy and was frightened of the wind blowing on them, but she couldn't help the way she was. 'Here's sixpence. Go to the corner shop with Edna and get yourselves an ice cream while we have a talk with Auntie Eileen.' Edna's mouth opened in protest. 'But I want to know . . .'

'Do as you're told, Edna.' The tone of Bill's voice was enough to silence his daughter, and when she reached for the sixpence, Bill put a finger to his lips and said sternly, 'And keep that mouth of yours closed, d'you hear?' Edna, not looking too pleased, nodded as she steered the children out to the street.

'What's Mrs Kenny's house like?' Eileen asked. 'Is it exactly the same as yours, Mary?'

'The house is the same,' Mary answered, 'but it's not in the same condition as ours was when we got it. Remember, ours was nicely decorated and everything. All we had to do was move in.'

Harry sat on the arm of the couch next to Eileen, and with a finger under her chin, turned her face towards him. 'Mrs Kenny is an old lady and her house hasn't been decorated since the year dot. She hasn't been able to do it herself and couldn't afford to have a man in. But there's nothing that can't be put right with a bit of elbow grease. Me and Bill could have that place like a palace in a few weeks. And I'm sure Arthur Kennedy will be more than happy to give a hand.'

'It sounds lovely, Eileen.' Vera clapped her hands in pleasure. 'You won't know you're born with an inside toilet and a wash-house.'

'Ooh, I hope we get it.' Joan rubbed her tummy. She was dying to go to the lavvy but was frightened of missing something. 'If we do get it, and I get the job in Vernons, I can get the train from Orrell Park station to the Old Roan. It's only two stops.'

'Don't count your chickens before they're hatched,' Maggie warned. 'There's many a slip twixt cup and lip.'

'Well, we haven't got long to find out.' Bill was trying to keep calm but his nerves were as taut as a violin string. 'Harry's picking Mrs Kenny up after church in the morning, so she should be here about eleven.'

'That means all hands on deck 'ere for eight o'clock, and we'll go through this 'ouse like a dose of salts.' Eileen pinched at the fat on her elbows, her forehead creased in concentration. 'We'll take a room each so we don't get under each other's feet.'

'To hear you talk, anyone would think the house never got cleaned!' Maggie's face was red with indignation. 'I gave the three bedrooms a good do on Thursday and they're as clean as a whistle.'

'Okay, Mam, don't get off yer bike!' Eileen smiled and her chubby cheeks moved upwards to cover her eyes. 'I'm always tellin' yer that yer the best maid I ever 'ad.'

'Huh!' Maggie grunted as she smoothed down the front of her pinny. 'Half an hour to tidy up and this place will look like a little palace.'

'Listen, I'm not runnin' round like a blue-arsed fly five minutes before Mrs Kenny's due, so yez are all up by eight o'clock . . . Okay?'

Not a voice was raised in protest and Eileen nodded, her layer of chins rippling with the movement. 'Right, that's that sorted out.'

The cleft in Harry's chin deepened as he threw back his head and roared with laughter. 'I'd give anything to be here in the morning. It'll be like a Laurel and Hardy slapstick comedy.' Tears of laughter were shining in his eyes, and his laughter was so infectious there were smiles on everyone's faces. 'Or better still,' Harry was holding his tummy now as his laugh grew louder, 'one of those Keystone Cop films where everyone runs round in double quick motion.'

Eileen reached behind her for a cushion, screwed up

her eyes till she had the target in sight, then aimed at Harry. It hit him full in the face with such force he had to gasp for breath.

'Bull's-eye!' Eileen chuckled. 'That'll teach yer, clever clogs!'

Chapter Five

'You what?' Eileen's mouth gaped. 'We're movin' house tomorrer an' you want me to do a disappearing act? Have yer lost the run of yer senses, Bill Gillmoss?'

'No, chick, I haven't.' Bill stood in front of her, feet spaced apart. The sleeves of his blue and white striped shirt were rolled up to the elbows, there were streaks of dirt across the front and a ragged tear where a pearl button had been ripped off when he'd tried to lift a bedstead on his own. 'I want you out of the way while everything is moved from here and taken to the new house. I'll have me work cut out without worrying about you.'

'I think yer've flipped yer lid!' Eileen snorted. 'Who d'yer think is goin' to make sure everythin' is put in the right place?'

'Don't argue,' Bill said firmly. 'I know where all the furniture has to go and I'm not having you lugging things around in your condition. I've got our Billy and Arthur to help me, and there'll be two men with the removal van. We'll have everything in place by the time you get back.'

'I've never 'eard anythin' so daft in all me life.' Eileen

lifted her hands in disgust. Her gaze went around the room, resting for a while on the large tea chests containing all the bedding and pans, and the smaller cardboard boxes where crockery and ornaments were packed, each item wrapped in a piece of newspaper to prevent breakages. 'Who's goin' to tell yer where all those things go?'

Bill sighed wearily. He'd been on the go since he'd got in from work and he was dead tired. Not that he'd done it all himself, because Harry, Mary, Arthur and Vera had been there all night and they'd worked alongside him to make sure everything was ready for the van which was coming at nine in the morning.

Bill ran a hand across his forehead. 'Your ma and Mary will be there to unpack all the boxes, and if they don't put them where you want them it's not the end of the world. You'll have plenty of time to sort them out later.' He put a hand under her chin and lifted her face. 'Do this to please me, will you, chick? I'll have enough on me plate without worrying about you.' When Eileen opened her mouth to protest, Bill put a finger across her lips. 'It's no good saying you'll just stand by and watch, because I know you too well. If I took my eyes off you for a second you'd be moving this, that and the other, and I'm not taking any chances.'

Eileen folded her arms and rested them on her swollen tummy. 'I don't know,' she grumbled, 'the day we move house, I go on a ruddy picnic?'

Bill held his hand out. 'Come on, chick, let's hit the hay. I'm so tired I could fall asleep standing up. But this time tomorrow night we'll be all settled in our new home.'

Eileen averted her eyes as Bill pulled her up from the

couch. She didn't want him to know that inside she was crying. This was the last night they'd be sleeping in the house that had been their home since the day they were married. But no one seemed sorry. They were so full of the nice new posh house, it was as if they'd already forgotten this little place with all the memories it held.

'This is the most cockeyed bloody idea I've ever 'eard of,' Eileen gasped as she struggled out of the front passenger seat of Harry's car. 'Half past nine in the mornin', an' we're takin' a ferry trip across the Mersey.' As she lowered her feet to the pavement her dress rumpled up to reveal pieces of knotted elastic keeping her stockings up. 'I must be stark ravin' mad to 'ave let Bill talk me into this.'

'It's for your own good, Eileen, so don't be hard on Bill.' Harry bit hard on the inside of his cheek, but it was no good, he couldn't keep the laughter back. 'I'm sorry, Eileen, but you should see your face.'

'An' I'm sorry, 'cos it's the only bloody face I've got.' Eileen glared at him for a few seconds, then her body started to shake. 'I suppose I might as well see the funny side, seein' as 'ow I can't do nowt about it.' She held her tummy as the laughter erupted. 'I 'aven't been on a ferry for years, an' I 'ave to pick a day when there's a bloody gale force wind blowin'.' She wiped a tear away with the back of her hand. 'On top of that, I haven't a clue what number bus to get back to me new 'ouse!'

Harry bowed, waving his hand towards the car. 'No problem, madam. Your car will be here to pick you up at two o'clock.'

Harry helped Vera and the girls from the back seat and slammed the car doors. 'I'll have to move, I'm blocking the traffic. See you later.'

Eileen stood by the rails as the ferry ploughed its way through the choppy waters of the Mersey. Her head thrown back, she breathed in the sea air. 'Yer know, it wasn't such a bad idea after all. I'm really enjoying this. The wind's blowin' all the cobwebs away.'

'Mam, the water looks all frothy.' Edna was hanging over the rail fascinated by the surf made by the ferry breaking the waves. 'It looks like your dolly tub does when you've put Persil in the water.'

Vera, her hand tightly gripping Carol, was pointing out the flock of seagulls that were following the ferry boat. 'Look, darling, see all the birds?'

Carol's eyes were wide as she watched the seagulls swoop and soar, a sight she'd never seen before. She struggled to free herself from Vera's grip so she could join Edna at the rails, but Vera held on tight. 'Mummy will lift you up, otherwise you might fall in the river.'

Eileen turned her back to the rail to watch the receding waterfront of Liverpool. 'Yer can't beat old Liverpool, can yer?' Her eyes rested briefly on the two Liver birds perched proudly on top of the Liver Building, then she turned to Vera. 'I wonder 'ow they're gettin' on? I should be there, yer know.'

'Eileen, they'll manage much better without you, you'd only be in the way. Now, for heaven's sake stop worrying and enjoy yourself.'

Because it was early on a Saturday morning, there

weren't many people making the crossing, so there was no pushing and shoving when the ferry tied up at the landing stage in Seacombe. Having been warned by Bill not to let Eileen overdo things, Vera kept the pace leisurely as they strolled in the direction of New Brighton. They'd been walking for about twenty minutes when they came to a small cafe. 'How about a cuppa?' Eileen asked. 'With me feet swellin', these shoes are pinchin' and me feet are givin' me gyp.'

The smell of home-made scones pervaded the air and Eileen took a deep breath. 'Smells just like our kitchen when me mam's bakin'.'

They ordered tea and scones for four, and when the homely waitress had set the table, Eileen smiled with satisfaction. With the plate of scones came a dish of butter and a bowl of strawberry jam. 'You can be mother, Vera, and pour the tea.'

Carol's eyes were like saucers. She watched carefully what Edna did, then followed suit. It was the first time she'd ever been in a cafe and the excitement and pleasure was there on her face for all to see. 'She's a little love,' Eileen said.

At that moment Carol misjudged the thickness of the scone and ended up with a blob of jam on her nose. She couldn't understand why everyone started laughing but she joined in and her infectious laugh filled the room. Even the waitress, standing by the counter hoping for more customers, had a wide smile on her face.

When they came out of the cafe the wind had dropped and the sun was making a brave attempt to push its way between the clouds. The foursome continued towards

New Brighton, stopping on the way to watch a Punch and Judy show while licking their way through ice cream cornets. And when Edna saw some children paddling, she was over the railings and running across the sand before Eileen could stop her. 'She'll get 'er death of cold, the silly nit.'

'Look, there's a bench here, you sit down while I take Carol for a paddle. She's never been to the seaside before . . . Danny never took her anywhere, and on the money he gave me, I couldn't afford to.' Vera waited till Eileen was seated. 'She may as well enjoy herself while she can, like all the other kids.'

Eileen watched Vera run across the sand, her long hair bouncing on her shoulders, and heard her laugh ring out when Carol screamed with delight. She's a changed woman, Eileen thought. Pity Danny didn't leave her years ago.

With Vera holding their shoes and socks, and their dresses tucked into their knickers, Edna and Carol ran into the water. 'Ow! It's freezing.' Edna ran back, dragging Carol with her. 'It's like ice.'

'You wouldn't be told,' Vera said. 'I've got a cloth here, come and dry your feet.'

Edna eyed the other children splashing about happily. If they could do it, so could she. 'No, I'll 'ave another go.'

Carol picked up a handful of sand and her eyes filled with wonder as it trickled through her fingers. 'Sand, Mummy. Carol likes sand.'

Eileen waited with growing impatience. 'I wish I 'ad me watch with me,' she said aloud. 'It must be gettin' on now.' Ignoring the curious glances of the people walking by, she kept up her one-sided conversation. 'I bet they're wishin' I was there to tell them where everythin' goes.'

Eileen had slipped her shoes off to relieve the pain, and was completely unaware of the sight she made. An eighteen-stone woman, heavily pregnant and shoeless, was enough to cause people to stare. One couple passed, stopped a short way from Eileen, then turned and came back. 'Are you all right, dear,' a man asked kindly, 'do you need some help?'

Eileen looked at him blankly. 'I don't need any 'elp, thank you.'

The man raised his trilby. 'My wife thought we should ask in case you needed assistance. Happily you do not, so we'll wish you a very good morning.'

Vera came back with the children, their faces glowing, their hair windswept. 'Who was that you were talking to?'

'Some feller tryin' to click,' Eileen said, passing it off. 'Anyway, what time is it, Vera? It must be nearly time to make our way back to Seacombe.'

'Eileen, we've got two hours yet!'

'In that case, I'm goin' for somethin' to eat.' Eileen's face did contortions as she squeezed her feet into the shoes. 'There's a smell of chips comin' from somewhere, so let's follow the smell.'

'Eggs, chips and mushy peas, please.' Eileen smiled at the waitress. 'Two adults' and two children's portions.'

When the order came, Eileen covered her chips with Daddies tomato sauce and tucked in with gusto. The plate of bread and butter disappeared quickly, with Eileen using the last piece to mop up her plate. When she'd finished she patted her tummy. 'I needed that. The sea

61

air's given me an appetite.' She scraped her chair back. 'Now, let's get crackin', or we'll miss the half one ferry.'

Everyone was talking at once as Harry helped them into the car. Edna and Carol were telling him what they'd done and seen, while Eileen was firing questions at him. Did the van turn up on time? Did they manage to get everything away in one go? They hadn't left anything behind, had they? Harry shook his head as he drove up Dale Street and turned into Byrom Street. He took his eyes off the road for a fraction of a second and patted Eileen's hand. 'Everything is under control, so don't worry.'

'It's all right for you,' Eileen muttered darkly. 'You wouldn't worry if yer backside was on fire.'

Harry grinned but was too busy concentrating on the road to answer. It was always busy on a Saturday down Scotland Road and County Road, with women getting their week-end shopping in, and his eyes were wary for the absent-minded pedestrians who stepped off the kerb without looking to see if the road was clear. There were Mary-Ellens on the corner of every side street down County Road, their barrows laden down with potatoes, vegetables, fruit and flowers. They were a familiar sight, with their long black skirts and hand-knitted, fringed black shawls draped around their shoulders. Their sing-song voices could be heard over the roar of the traffic, inviting passers-by to inspect their wares and promising to return their money if they could buy cheaper anywhere in Liverpool.

* * *

Vera tapped Harry on the shoulder. 'You can drop me and Carol off anywhere here. We can cut through the side streets and be home in five minutes.'

'I'll run you there.'

'You've got enough to do.' Vera pulled a hankie from her pocket, licked it with her tongue and rubbed at the remnants of tomato sauce and ice cream which had hardened around Carol's mouth. 'Anyway, I want a couple of things from the shops.'

Eileen twisted in her seat as Harry pulled in to the kerb. 'Thanks, Vera, yer a pal! Bring Carol down on Monday to see me new 'ouse. We should be straight by then, please God.'

Vera was walking away swinging Carol's arm when Harry wound the window down. 'I almost forgot, Vera, Arthur said to tell you if it wasn't too late when we finished today, he'd call in and see you. Otherwise he'd try and make it tomorrow.'

Vera's face flamed as she jerked her head in reply and walked briskly away.

Harry faced Eileen, his eyebrows raised. 'What's going to happen there, d'you think?'

'The Lord knows.' Eileen turned to look out of the window. 'You never saw 'is wife, Harry, so yer don't know the 'alf of it. I couldn't believe me eyes the day I went up there. Right brazen bitch she is, with 'er dyed 'air an' thick make-up. An' the 'ouse was filthy . . . God, I'll never forget the smell of bugs. An' that's what Arthur came 'ome to. Prisoner of war for five years an' he comes 'ome to find 'is wife's turned into a prostitute.'

Harry turned his head both ways before crossing the

busy road over Breeze Hill. 'Apparently she hasn't changed, either.'

'No, she 'asn't changed.' Eileen watched the stream of visitors to Walton Hospital turn into the gates. 'I think that's why Arthur an' Vera are drawn to each other, they're both in the same boat. Married the wrong partners.'

'But Vera could get a divorce from Danny on the grounds of desertion, surely?'

They were crossing the awkward humpback bridge at Orrell Park station and Eileen waited till they were clear before answering. 'She probably will, given time. But what other feller is goin' to take 'er on with Carol?'

'Every man is not like Danny Jackson, Eileen.'

'No, I know. An' Arthur Kennedy's one of them.'

'Don't go matchmaking, Eileen, you'll get your fingers burned.'

'I've already been told not to interfere by Bill,' Eileen told him. 'So I just say me prayers every night for two good friends.'

Edna was out of the car before it stopped and disappeared into the darkness of the hall. But Eileen stood for a while weighing up the house that was to be her new home. She turned her head to look up and down the deserted road. No neighbours standing at doors chatting, no girls playing skipping or hop-scotch, no boys swinging from a lamppost by a piece of rope or kneeling in the gutter playing ollies.

Harry put his hand under Eileen's elbow and urged her forward. 'Welcome to your new home, Mrs Gillmoss.'

'My God, it's like Casey's court!' Eileen tried to

squeeze past a tea chest in the hallway, but gave up after a few attempts. She could hear shouting, banging, and furniture being dragged across floors. 'It reminds me of one of Stan Laurel's "another fine mess".'

'Hang on a minute and I'll get someone to help me move this.' Harry put a hand on top of the chest and vaulted over. 'Won't be a tick.'

'Hi-ya, Mam!' Young Billy came down the stairs carrying a cardboard box. 'This has got stuff in for the kitchen.'

The door of the front parlour was closed and Eileen eyed it for a second. This was to be her mam's bed-sitting room. They didn't have enough furniture to put in it, but next week they were going to Hartley's auction rooms in Moss Street to see what they had. You could get some good bargains at Hartley's if you were lucky.

Eileen was getting impatient waiting for Harry. 'Where the 'ell's he got to?'

In the end she opened the parlour door which was the only one she could reach, and poked her head in.

'Watch it, our kid!'

Eileen held her breath when she saw her sister perched on top of a ladder hanging curtains at the bay window. 'I'll hold the ladder for yer.'

'I'm finished now.' Rene tilted her head to make sure the gathers in the curtains were uniform. 'I'm afraid they're not nearly long enough, but they'll do for now. At least me mam won't have to go to bed with nothing covering the windows.' Rene, half the size of Eileen, stepped gingerly down the ladder. 'That's all the windows done now . . . not bad, eh, kid?'

Maggie's bed had been set against a side wall and was

already made up with her hand-crocheted counterpane covering bedclothes and pillows. The only other thing in the room was a small rug placed in front of the tiled fireplace. 'The room looks bare,' Eileen said, 'but when we get some furniture, me mam should be very comfortable in here.'

'She'll be as snug as a bug in a rug.' Rene gave her sister a quick hug. 'Me and Alan are going to buy her a new sideboard as an early birthday present. And we've got a little table she can have for her bedside, so all she needs is a couple of easy chairs or a settee.'

'Yer mean couch, don't yer?' Eileen stuck her tongue out. 'Settee, indeed! We want none of yer fancy posh Old Roan talk 'ere.'

Eileen felt two arms circle her waist and her eyes slid sideways to meet Bill's. 'Did yer 'ear that, Bill? That thing we've been callin' a couch for years, isn't a couch . . . it's a ruddy settee!'

Rene laughed good-naturedly. 'What would you do with her?'

'Right now I'm going to give her a tour of inspection.' Bill turned Eileen round and reached for her hand. 'Come on, Mrs Woman.'

Eileen's head was reeling when she finally sat down. She couldn't take it all in. Couldn't believe so much had been achieved in such a short time. They didn't have nearly enough furniture for such a big house, but what they did have had been placed just where she would have put it herself. The men had done all the heavy work, while Rene had seen to the curtains and Maggie and Mary had sorted the kitchen out. All pans and crockery had been put away in the kitchen cupboards and drawers lined with bright wallpaper. Pictures and mirrors had been hung, photographs lined the top of the sideboard, and in the middle of the dining table stood a vase filled with carnations and roses.

Eileen rubbed two fingers against her temple to relieve the tension. 'I don't know what to say. For the first time in me life, I'm lost for words.'

In front of her, forming a semicircle, were Bill, young Billy, Harry, Arthur, Rene, Mary and her neighbour, Doris, and Maggie. Her eyes moving from one to the other, Eileen shrugged her shoulders. 'Yez know I'm no good at makin' pretty speeches, so I'll just say yer the best mates anyone could 'ave and I love all of yez.'

'I wouldn't thank us until you get our bill,' Harry said, catching Arthur's eye and winking. 'How much did we say, Arthur? Half-a-crown an hour, was it?'

'Yer can sod off, Harry Sedgemoor,' Eileen huffed. Then she straightened her back, thrusting her enormous bust forward. Half closing her eyes, her nose pointing to the ceiling, she put on her posh accent. 'Hi'll give you sixpence to go to the children's matinee at the Carlton next Saturday, to see Tom Mix. Hand you should have henough hover to buy yourself ha quarter of Basset's liquorice hallsorts.'

'I can't wait.' Harry rubbed his hands together. 'Tom Mix is me favourite cowboy.'

Mary gave him a gentle dig in the ribs. 'Let's make a move and leave them in peace.'

'Yes, I'd better go too,' Doris said, 'If Jim's tea's not on the table at five o'clock, he'll give me my marching orders.'

'Have a cup of tea before you go,' Maggie coaxed. 'God knows, you all deserve one.'

'No thanks, we'll have one when we get home,' Mary laughed. 'It's only two doors away.' She waved her hand over Harry's shoulder. 'See you tomorrow, Eileen.'

'Okay, kid! Ta-ra!'

'I'll see them out,' Bill said, 'I won't be a tick.'

'Mam, can I go and get meself ready now?' Billy asked. 'Me an' Jacko are going to a dance at the Holy Name in Fazakerley.'

'Hopin' for a click, are yer, son? Well, with your good looks, yer should get the pick of the crop.' Eileen gave him a broad wink. 'Go 'ed, son, an' get yerself all dolled up. Oh, an' while yer upstairs, see what our Edna's doin', will yer? She's been up there for hours.'

'She's putting her clothes away in the drawers,' Maggie said dryly. 'She's bagged the top two before Joan gets home.'

Eileen groaned. 'There'll be skin and 'air flyin' up there tonight. Still, me an' our Rene were the same when we were young.'

Arthur pulled a chair from the table and sat down. 'How does your Joan like working at Vernon's?'

'She loves it, but 'ow long the novelty will last I don't know because they 'ave to work till nearly ten on a Saturday night markin' the coupons.' Eileen chuckled. 'Yer should see 'er! Thinks she's the whole cheese now she's workin'. Savin' up to get 'er 'air permed, if yer don't mind.'

'I'll stick the kettle on,' Maggie said. 'Me mouth's that dry it feels like emery paper.'

'I'll give you a hand,' Rene said quickly. 'You've done enough for one day. I think you forget you're not a spring chicken any more.'

Left alone now with Arthur, Eileen asked softly, 'How's things with you, Arthur?'

Arthur rolled his sleeves down and dipped into his trouser pocket for his cuff links before meeting Eileen's eyes. 'I was going to say they were just the same, like I always do. But they're not the same, and I'm not going to lie to you.' He fiddled and cursed under his breath while struggling to get one of the cuff links through the two holes in his cuff. In the end Eileen became exasperated.

'For God's sake come 'ere an' let me do it for yer. Bloody 'elpless men are, just like babies.'

Eileen held on to Arthur's arm when she'd successfully fastened his cuff links. 'What's wrong . . . is it Sylvia?'

'She's ill, Eileen, but won't go to see a doctor. You wouldn't know her if you saw her, she's lost that much weight. She's got a terrible cough and her skin's a yellow colour.'

'Call the doctor in,' Eileen told him. 'She can't do much about it if he walks in on her.'

'I'll have to do something.' Arthur heard Bill close the front door and knew he didn't have much time. 'How was Vera?'

Bill would go mad if he knew she was interfering, but Eileen felt so sorry for Arthur and Vera. They both deserved better out of life. She glanced at the clock. 'If yer left now, yer'd 'ave time to call in an' see her, an' still be 'ome for the boys before it gets too dark.'

Bill came in rubbing his hands and calling through the kitchen, 'How about that cup of tea?'

'I won't stay.' Arthur made up his mind quickly. He hated lying to a friend, and Bill was a true friend. And there shouldn't be any need to lie, because God knows, he and Vera did nothing wrong. But Arthur knew instinctively that Bill didn't approve. 'I'll get home, have a bath and listen to the wireless with the boys.'

'Are you coming up, chick?' Bill asked. 'I'm that dead beat I could sleep on a clothes line.'

Eileen pressed her palms on the table and pushed herself up. 'You go on and I'll follow. I just want to get a drink of water.'

Bill was halfway up the stairs when he stopped, his brow furrowed. There was something not quite right, but he couldn't put his finger on it. Then it struck him . . . in all the years they'd been married, he'd never known Eileen drink water before going to bed.

His hand pressing on the banister rail, Bill took the stairs two at a time. The living room was in darkness, but from the light in the kitchen he could see Eileen bending over the sink, her face in her hands. He rushed to her, thinking she was sick, then he saw her shoulders shaking and knew she was crying.

'Chick,' Bill took her shoulders and turned her around, 'what's wrong?'

'Oh, Bill,' Eileen sobbed. 'I didn't even 'ave time to say goodbye to all me friends and neighbours.'

Bill held her close and stroked her back. 'You can go up

any time and see your friends. It isn't as though we've moved to the other end of the world.'

'But I didn't even have a chance to say goodbye to me little house.'

Eileen swallowed at the lump in her throat. 'And I can't go back there any time, can I?'

Bill wiped her tears away with a finger. He'd expected Eileen to be upset, but he just hoped that when she got used to the new house she'd settle down.

Chapter Six

'Sshush!' Martha Bradshaw put a finger to her lips to quieten the children. 'I think this is Mummy and Daddy.' With her good foot, Martha spun her rocking chair round till it was facing the door. Her neatly combed white hair framed a kind face, with blue eyes that showed her eagerness for news. 'Well,' she asked as Mary came into the room, 'how did it go?'

'Eileen looks as though she doesn't know what day it is.' Mary smiled at her mother as she slipped her arms out of her coat. 'She said for the first time in her life she's lost for words.'

'And that's saying something,' Harry piped in. 'Eileen's not usually short a few hundred words.'

'I've been dying to know how you were all getting on.' Since she'd had a stroke during an air raid in the May blitz, Martha had learned to live within her capabilities. Slowly, and in great pain, she had persevered until she had mastered the crutches given to her by the hospital. Now she could at least get around the downstairs rooms under her own steam. And she never complained because she had so much to be thankful for. A loving daughter, the best son-in-law anyone could ask for, two lovely grand-children and a nice comfortable home. It was only at times like this that she cursed her affliction. It would have meant so much to her to have been able to help Eileen. To repay, in a small way, some of the happiness the big woman had brought into their lives. 'It'll be nice having them for neighbours.'

'Can we go and see Auntie Eileen, Mummy?' Tony pulled on Mary's skirt. 'You promised.'

'I didn't promise you could see her today. Tomorrow, perhaps, if Auntie Eileen isn't too tired. We could take Grandma with us, in the wheelchair.'

Tony, so serious for his age, went to stand in front of Martha. 'You'll like that, won't you, Grandma?'

Emma, not to be outdone, stood next to her brother. 'If Daddy gets the wheelchair down the steps, Grandma, I'll push you.'

Tony swung his hip and pushed his sister. 'I'm stronger than you, 'cos I'm a boy.'

Harry intervened before there was a crying match. 'You can take turns. One push the wheelchair down, and the other push it back. Okay?'

'I'll make us some tea.' Mary looked from Harry to Martha. 'Will beans on toast do? I'm too tired to cook anything.' As she turned, Mary's eye caught sight of a man passing the window. 'Oh, there's Arthur on his way home. Why don't you give him a lift, Harry? He has to get two buses to the Dingle, and he must be worn out.'

Harry's mind ticked over quickly. Unless he was very much mistaken, Arthur would be calling at Vera's before he went home, and he wouldn't welcome being offered a lift to the Dingle, which was the other side of the city. 'I haven't got much petrol left, and I'm right down on coupons.' Harry stared hard at Mary, willing her to understand. 'Don't forget I've done a lot of running around today, and I've barely enough juice to get me to work on Monday.'

Mary was filled with curiosity. What was going on? She knew Harry could have taken Arthur home, he wasn't that short of petrol. And it wouldn't be because he couldn't be bothered because Harry wasn't like that. He, Arthur and Bill were the best of mates. They all worked in the English Electric on the East Lancs Road, and in work and out, they got on like a house on fire.

'I'll get the tea on.' Mary made her way to the kitchen. She'd get it out of Harry when they were alone.

When Vera opened the door and saw Arthur on the step, her face lit up for a second before her eyes started to twitch nervously.

'It's all right, Vera, there's no one around,' Arthur said. 'Not a soul in sight.'

Vera glanced quickly up and down the street before standing aside and inviting Arthur in. 'It's only Elsie Smith I'm worried about,' she told him as she closed the door. 'I've told you about her . . . the neighbourhood scandalmonger. She's got eyes on her like a hawk and she doesn't miss a trick.'

'There's no harm in a friend coming to visit you. Surely she can't make anything out of that.'

'You don't know Elsie Smith! She spends her whole life pulling people to pieces, and what she doesn't know, she

75

makes up. If she's seen you coming in here, it'll be all round the street in the morning. She likes nothing better than a bit of juicy gossip.'

'Are you going to keep me in the hall?' Arthur asked. 'Or shall I knock on the Smiths' and tell her my intentions are strictly honourable?'

'Don't be daft, and come on in.' Vera opened the living room door. 'She wouldn't believe you, anyway.'

'Uncle Arthur!' Carol threw down the coloured bricks she'd been playing with and flew to wrap her arms around his legs. 'I've been on a ship.'

'So I've heard.' Arthur smiled down into the happy face. 'Auntie Eileen told me all about it.' His eyes moved to the small kitchen. 'Are the boys out?'

Vera nodded. 'Peter's gone to the flicks, and Colin's got a date with a girl from his works.' She moved Carol's toys from the couch and motioned to Arthur to sit down. 'She must be someone special because he took an hour to get ready. He pressed his own trousers and you could cut your throat on the crease in them. His hair is thick with brilliantine and the shine on his shoes is nobody's business.'

'Love's young dream, eh?' There was a hint of sadness in Arthur's smile. 'I wish I had my time over again, don't you, Vera?'

Vera averted her eyes as a deep sigh left her lips. 'If I had a pound for every wish I've made over the last few years, Arthur, I'd be a very rich woman.' She shivered and wrapped her arms around her waist. 'Have you time for a cuppa, or are you in a hurry?'

'I haven't got the energy to hurry.' Arthur lifted Carol

on to his knee. 'We've all worked harder today than we do in work. But it was worth it to see Eileen's face.'

'What about the boys?' Vera asked. 'Don't you have to get home to them?'

'I told them I'd be late, and one of their mates is going to stay with them until I get back.'

'Right, I'll put the kettle on and make you a sandwich.'

Vera came down after putting Carol to bed. 'The sea air must have tired her out, she was asleep before her head hit the pillow.'

Arthur watched as Vera sat in a chair on the opposite side of the room. Clasping and unclasping her hands, she was clearly nervous and ill at ease. 'Would you rather I left?' Arthur asked quietly. 'You look worried to death.'

Vera dropped her head to stare at her hands. 'No, I don't want you to leave. It's not very often I get the chance to talk to another adult because I've never really made friends with the neighbours.' She looked at him through lowered lids. 'It's just that I worry about what people think.'

'To hell with what they think!' Arthur sounded angry. 'We're two grown-up people who like each other! If anyone is bad minded enough to read anything into that, then I feel sorry for them. It's you and I who count, and you know I'd never do anything to hurt you, or your reputation, don't you, Vera?'

'I know that,' Vera nodded. 'And it's been marvellous to have you to talk to over the last year, because you understand. Mary and Eileen are the best friends anyone could have, but they've got good husbands and a happy,

77

normal life. They couldn't be expected to know how it feels to be on your own, with no man behind you.'

Arthur leaned forward, his hands clasped between his knees. 'No one to hold you when you're feeling blue, and no one to dry your eyes when the tears come.' A lock of his hair had fallen to cover his eyes and he brushed it away in a gesture of frustration. 'Our lives are a right mess, aren't they? But why us, Vera? What have we ever done to deserve this hell?'

'I stopped asking myself that question years ago.' Vera fixed her gaze on the flickering coals in the large, old-fashioned grate. 'It was when I realised that life without Danny had to be better than the one I had with him.' She tore her eyes away from the fire to gaze around the small room. It was spotlessly clean, but the furniture was shabby, the pattern on the lino had almost disappeared and the curtains were so faded it was impossible to see the flowers that had made them so colourful when they were new. 'I haven't got much to show for nineteen years of married life, not in material things, anyway. And it's a struggle from week to week to make the money spin out. But in spite of that I've got a lot to be thankful for. I've got Carol and the two boys. They're good children and I love them dearly.'

Vera had never spoken at such length before and Arthur sat with his chin cupped in his hands, his eyes noting the changing expressions on her face. He didn't interrupt, afraid that if he did Vera would clam up.

'I don't miss Danny at all.' It was as though Vera were talking to herself, speaking her thoughts aloud. 'It's a much happier house without him and his violent temper.

Me and the kids lived in fear of him, never knowing when he was going to lash out with his fists or his feet. The boys hated him, even though he was never really cruel to them. It was me and Carol he always picked on. Carol because he was ashamed of her, and me because I was the handiest. He used me as a punch bag, did Danny.'

'I know,' Arthur spoke softly. 'Remember, I saw a bit of brave Danny's handiwork.'

Vera's head jerked sideways and she looked at Arthur as though surprised at seeing him there. Flustered, her fingers pecked at her lips. 'I'm sorry, I shouldn't burden you with my troubles when you've got enough of your own.'

'A trouble shared is a trouble halved, Vera. God knows I've been glad of you to talk to, to get things off my chest.'

'How are things at home?'

'Sylvia's not well at all. I've asked her to go to the doctor's but she doesn't take any notice of me.' Arthur shrugged his shoulders. 'In fact, if looks could kill I'd have been dead long ago.'

'What a fool of a woman.' Vera sounded angry. 'Doesn't she know how lucky she is?'

'I've gone past caring, Vera. I've nothing but contempt for her and the life she leads.' Arthur sat back and rested his head on the back of the couch. 'It's the boys I'm sorry for. They're growing up now, and when they see their mother going out every night dressed like a tart, how must they feel? And the kids they play with must say something because you know how cruel children can be.' Arthur made a fist of his hand and banged it on the arm of the couch. 'I can't count the number of times I've told myself I should get the boys out of there. I've gone as far as packing a case, but in the end I've chickened out. Sylvia is their mother, after all, and perhaps a bad mother is better than no mother at all. Who am I to decide?'

Vera's heart was full of sympathy for this fine man who, against her better judgement, she'd grown very fond of. She wished she could help him, but who was she to advise when she'd made such a mess of her own life?

'Arthur, it's nine o'clock. I'm not trying to get rid of you, but it takes you nearly an hour to get home and it's late for the boys to be up.'

Arthur breathed in deeply and stretched his arms over his head. 'I don't feel like moving now. You know I like being here with you, don't you, Vera?'

Vera lowered her head and her voice was a mere whisper, 'And I like you being here.'

Arthur stood up quickly. 'I'd better go before I say too much. But thanks for listening to me, Vera. You've no idea how good it is to have someone to talk to.'

'Of course I do! Haven't I just bared my soul to you?' Vera pushed back a wayward strand of hair. 'I've told you more than I've ever told anyone.'

'Another instalment next week,' Arthur laughed. 'Who needs to go to the pictures?'

Vera opened the living room door and stood aside to let Arthur pass. 'I might see you at Eileen's next weekend?'

'Let's not leave it a week before we see each other. I'll call in on me way home from work one night with some sweets for Carol.' Arthur opened the front door, then whispered, 'Would you like to make sure the coast is clear before I go out? Elsie Smith might be lurking in the shadows.'

Vera didn't often laugh out loud, but when she did it was a joy to the ear. Loud and clear it rang out before caution brought her hand up to smother it. 'Blow Elsie Smith! If she's watching through her curtains, like she usually is, it'll give her something to think about.'

Arthur stepped into the street and looked up at Vera who was standing on the top step, her folded arms hugging her slim waist. 'I'm very fond of you, you know that, don't you, Vera? And there's nothing I'd like better than to give Elsie Smith something to gossip about. But I value your friendship too much to risk losing it. So you need never be afraid of me, love.'

'I would never be afraid of you,' Vera said softly. 'I just wish things were different.'

'Who knows what the future holds?' Arthur leaned forward and pecked her on the cheek. 'Goodnight, Vera.'

Vera waited till he was passing the Smiths' house, then called, 'Goodnight, Arthur.' She closed the door behind her and leaned against it, her hand on the cheek Arthur had kissed. 'Why, God,' she whispered. 'Why do you punish me so?'

Elsie Smith let the curtain fall back into place. 'That man's been at Vera Jackson's again. There's something going on there, I'm telling you.'

Fred Smith sighed wearily. 'Is it any of our business?'

Elsie Smith's thin lips formed a straight line. 'It's not decent having a man in the house when the boys are out. There's something fishy there, mark my words.'

Fred put his *Echo* down and faced his wife. 'Vera Jackson's husband walked out on her, so she's a free agent. If she had ten men in the house, or even a red light put up outside, it's got nothing to do with you, me, or anyone else. She's a good woman and a good mother.'

Elsie folded her thin arms across her flat chest, her nostrils flared and her beady eyes mere slits. 'Well, we'll just wait an' see, shall we? But I bet a pound to a penny there's something going on between Vera and that bloke.'

'Why don't you be honest and say you hope there's something going on?' Fred asked softly. 'Brighten up your life if you had something to gossip about, wouldn't it? With your mind, Elsie Smith, I don't know how you sleep.'

Chapter Seven

'I've never been to an auction before.' Mary gripped Eileen's arm. 'You won't ask me to bid for anything, will you?'

'Oh, don't worry about that, kid!' Eileen said confidently, her wide hips swaying and brushing Mary and Maggie who were walking either side of her. She winked broadly at her mother. 'Me and me mam are old hands at this game, aren't we, Mam?'

'Oh, yes, we're experts.' Maggie smiled at Mary. 'Take no notice of her, lass, we're as green as cabbages.'

'This is it.' They stopped outside Hartley's auction rooms in Moss Street and Eileen grunted when she saw the number of people inside. 'Strewth! We'll be lucky to get in, never mind buy anythin'.' She shook Mary's arm free and straightened her shoulders ready to battle her way through the throng. Her foot was inside the doorway when she turned her head. 'Don't bat an eyelid, kid. If yer blow yer nose or move yer 'ead, yer'll find yer've bought yerself a three piece suite.'

'Ay, Mam, take a gander at those two fireside chairs.' Eileen pointed to two sturdy-looking chairs covered in a beige moquette. 'They'd be just the job for your room.'

'The dealers will probably bid for those,' Maggie said. 'They buy anything saleable.'

'Dealers?' Mary asked. 'What dealers?'

'See that woman in the blue coat, the one who looks as though she 'asn't got two ha'pennies to rub together? Well she's a dealer . . . got a secondhand shop down Smithdown Road.' Eileen lowered her voice. 'Don't look now, but there's a feller standin' right behind us, the scruffy lookin' one in the long overcoat, he's got a shop in County Road.'

Mary stole a quick glance at the thin, seedy-looking man standing directly behind Eileen. 'It doesn't seem fair that dealers can come in here and buy. Doesn't give anyone else a chance.'

Eileen saw the crowd parting to make way for an officious looking man. 'Here's the auctioneer. Now the fun starts.'

In spite of being afraid to move or turn her head, Mary was fascinated as the sale progressed. With the lift of a finger a painting was bought for thirty shillings, a three piece for ten pounds, a piano for a fiver. The auctioneer moved things along so quickly, Mary couldn't keep up with him. Then the two fireside chairs came up . . . lot 24.

'Who'll start the bidding at three pounds for the pair?' The auctioneer scanned the crowd. 'Am I bid three pounds?'

The dealer in the blue coat lifted her hand. 'Three pounds.'

'Three pounds five shillin's,' Eileen shouted, red in the face.

'Three pounds ten.' The scruffy dealer behind entered the fray.

'Three pounds twelve and six.' As Eileen spoke she stepped back a pace, jerked her elbow with a force that winded the dealer when it came into contact with his ribs. 'Oh, I'm so sorry,' Eileen fussed, standing in front of the man and brushing an imaginary speck off his coat as he fought to catch his breath. 'I do hope I didn't hurt you.'

While Eileen was being profuse in her apologies, the chairs were knocked down to her for three pounds twelve and six.

'What happened?' Mary asked.

'I lost me balance for a second.' Eileen bit hard on the inside of her mouth to keep a smile at bay. 'Must be all this standin' that did it.' She opened her purse and took out a five-pound note. 'Do us a favour, kid, and pay for the chairs, will yer? Give it to the man sittin' at the table just outside the door. He'll give yer a receipt.' She grabbed Mary's arm. 'Don't forget me change.'

Eileen felt a tug on her coat and for the first time saw the little woman standing beside her. She was an elderly woman with white hair, a heavily lined face and pale eyes that told of a life of hardship. 'It's about time someone 'ad a go at 'im.' When she smiled, Eileen saw she didn't have a tooth in her head. 'Blinkin' nuisance those dealers, they don't give anyone else a chance.'

'Here every week, is 'e?'

'Him an' the other one.' The woman nodded across to the dealer in the blue coat. 'Got the money, 'aven't they, so they get all the best stuff.'

A bedroom suite came under the hammer then, and this

was what Eileen was waiting for. She held out a hand to silence the woman and joined in the bidding. In less than a minute she was smiling happily, the owner of a wardrobe, dressing table and chest of drawers . . . all for seven pounds fifteen shillings.

Eileen turned her gaze back to the woman. 'What are you after?'

'A bedding bale.' A thin finger pointed to a sideboard with several bundles on top. 'We got bombed out in the war, yer see, and lost everythin' we 'ad. It's taken us years to get a home around us again, but we're short on beddin'.'

Mary came back then and handed Eileen the receipt and change. 'Have you bought anything?'

Eileen pointed to the bedroom suite. 'It's old fashioned, but it's solid mahogany and me mam said it will polish up a treat.'

'Are we going now, then?' Mary's face dropped. 'I'm enjoying meself, I think it's very interesting.'

'Me mam's got 'er eye on that little table over there. It'd look nice in front of the bay window with a plant on. Depends 'ow much it goes for, 'cos by the time I've paid for the furniture, I'll only 'ave a few bob left.'

The table started at five shillings, the scruffy dealer bid an extra half crown, but when Eileen glared at him as she upped it another half crown, he dropped out, thinking she'd probably break his ribs next time. Maggie was delighted. That table wouldn't half set her room off. 'Are we going now?' she asked. 'Me legs are getting tired.'

'Hang on a sec.' Eileen twisted round to face the dealer. His face paled and he stepped back a pace. He didn't trust this big woman one little bit. Eileen put on her best smile. 'I wonder if yer'd do me a favour?'

Suspicion showed in the man's eyes. 'What d'yer want?'

Eileen quickly explained about the old lady being bombed out and what she was after. 'I'm sure you're not interested in beddin', so I wondered if yer'd look after the old lady for me, see she gets what she came for?' Eileen crossed her fingers and asked God to forgive her for telling lies. 'I'll be back soon, I'm only goin' outside for a breath of fresh air, but in case I'm not back in time, can I rely on you to see she gets what she wants?'

The man rubbed the back of his hand across his nose. The woman's barmy, he thought, nutty as a fruit cake. But she was also very big, with muscles on her like Popeye, and he had no intention of crossing her. 'Yeah, OK.'

'Oh, you are kind.' Eileen pulled him towards the woman who was listening with her mouth open in amazement. 'This very nice gentleman is going to help you. He'll make sure yer get what you've come for. And he's goin' to tell his lady friend in the blue coat, aren't you, love?'

The glint in Eileen's eyes warned the man not to argue. 'Yeah, I'll give Hilda the wire.'

'Oh, good!' Eileen beamed. 'We're only goin' outside for a bit, so we'll see yez later.'

'What was all that about?' Mary followed in Eileen's wake as she pushed her way through the crowd. 'I thought we were going home?'

'So we are, kid! I'll explain when we're outside.'

But the smile left Eileen's face when she went to pay for the table and bedroom suite. The man took her money without looking up. 'D'yer want it delivered?'

'Of course I want it delivered! D'yer think I'm goin' to carry the blinkin' things on me back!'

'Ten bob delivery charge.' The man held his hand out. 'We deliver in your area on a Thursday.'

'What! Flippin' daylight robbery!' Eileen could see there was no use arguing, so she turned to Mary. 'Well, money bags, I 'ope yer've got ten bob to lend me.'

'I'll pay for me table when we get home,' Maggie said quietly. 'I've got a few pounds put by.'

'Yer burial money is it, Mam?' Eileen patted Maggie's arm. 'Don't act the goat, missus. Yer know I'm only kiddin'.'

Eileen took one of Maggie's arms, Mary the other, and three happy and well-satisfied women marched out of the shop. And they laughed all the way home on the bus when Eileen told them about the bedding bale. Between guffaws that had all the passengers on the bus looking at them, Eileen said, 'The funniest thing of all is, I told that bloke I was only goin' outside for a breath of fresh air an' I'd be back. He'll probably still be there when the shop closes.'

'It looks a treat, Ma.' Bill's gaze swept Maggie's room. The sideboard, a present from Rene and Alan, had been delivered that day, along with the furniture from Hartley's. 'And when it's decorated, you won't know yourself.'

Young Billy was peering over his dad's shoulder. 'Yeah, it looks great, Nan. Proper posh.'

'When it's all finished, I'll invite you in for tea,' Maggie said with pride. 'In fact, we'll have a party.'

'An' 'ave the neighbours talkin'.' Eileen pushed

between her husband and son, sending them flying. 'There'll be no rowdy parties in this 'ouse, missus. It'll be afternoon tea by invitation only.'

Maggie moved the aspidistra plant an inch, then stood back to admire the new table. 'Sets the room off, doesn't it?'

'Yes,' Bill agreed, 'just the finishing touch it needed. Apart from a few odds and sods, the whole house is furnished now.'

'Except for the decoratin',' Eileen reminded him. 'This wallpaper is so dark it gives me the willies.' She linked her arm through Bill's and fluttered her eyelashes at him. 'When are yer goin' to make a start?'

'We've arranged to start scraping at the week-end. If we get all the dirty work done first, it'll be half the battle.' Bill smacked his forehead with an open hand. 'Oh, I forgot to tell you, Arthur didn't turn in to work today. He rang to say his wife was ill.'

'What's wrong with 'er?'

'I don't know. It was his foreman who told Harry.' The three of them worked on different sections in the English Electric, but they met up at lunch time in the canteen. Harry had a good job as a manager, Bill was a joiner and Arthur an electrician.

'I 'ope it's nothin' serious,' Eileen said. 'Arthur told me on Saturday that she looked ill, but she wouldn't go to the doctor's.'

'He'll probably be back at work tomorrow. If not, he's bound to let us know what's going on.'

Eileen pinched at the fat on her elbows. 'I feel sorry for 'im. He's got no friends up there, so he's no one to mind the boys. If 'e didn't live so far away, I'd call an' see if there was anything I could do. But it's bloody miles away.'

'Don't even think about it, chick!' Bill wagged a finger under Eileen's nose. 'You're in no condition to be helping anybody.'

'Bill, I only meant that if they lived nearer, I could 'elp with the boys. See them off to school, like, and let them come 'ere until Arthur got 'ome from work. It's not as if they're babies and need washing an' dressin', for heaven's sake. David's eleven, and Gordon's nine.'

'Me dad's right, Mam,' Billy said. 'You've got to look after yerself.'

'Oh, don't you start!' Eileen jerked her head in disgust, but secretly she was pleased. He was a good boy, was Billy, very caring for a boy his age. 'Anyway, what are we gettin' so het up about? Sylvia's probably got a cold an' will be up an' about in a day or two.'

'In the meantime, you stay out of it, right?' Bill's face was stern. 'No taking it upon yourself to go up there, jumping on and off buses.' Eileen took one look at Bill's set face and nodded.

'Our Billy's 'ad 'is dinner.' Eileen placed the plate in front of Bill. 'I think 'e must 'ave a date, 'cos he threw 'is dinner down and dashed upstairs to get ready.'

Bill eyed the plate heaped with mashed potatoes, cabbage and bacon ribs. 'That looks good, chick! Now a bit of beetroot, or some pickled cabbage would go down a treat with that lot.'

'Who was yer servant before I came along, Bill Gillmoss? Anyone would think yer were born with a

silver spoon in yer mouth, instead of a flippin' dummy.'
Eileen came back with a glass bowl full of deep red
beetroot. 'As it so 'appens, me mam did this today.' She
watched Bill dip his fork in the bowl, a look of
anticipation on his face. 'D'yer remember when I was
expectin' our Billy, an' I 'ad a cravin' for a coconut?
And with Edna it was crab? Well, this time it's beetroot
an' that's why me mam made that. So don't yer scoff the
lot.'

Bill looked up, a smile on his face. 'What a time I had
getting that crab. I think I tried every fish shop from here
to town before I finally got one.'

Eileen asked the question that had been on her lips
since Bill entered the house. 'Did Arthur turn in?'

Bill shook his head. 'Didn't ring up, either.'

'Oh, dear.' Eileen rested her elbows on the table. 'I
wonder what's up?'

Bill had a piece of bacon rib in his hands and was
chewing on the meat. He didn't answer till the bone was
clean and he placed it at the side of his plate. 'Harry
said if there's no word tomorrow, he'll run me up there
tomorrow night.'

'I've got a feelin' in me bones that there's somethin'
drastically wrong,' Eileen said. 'I don't 'alf feel sorry for
Arthur. He's such a nice feller, he deserves a better life
than he's got. An' the kids, too, poor buggers.'

Bill put his knife and fork down and reached across to
pat her arm. 'We don't know how lucky we are, do we,
chick? Always enough coal on the fire, food in the larder,
good kids and a happy marriage. Who could ask for more
in life?'

Eileen grinned. 'Yeah. We could conquer the world, you an' me, Bill Gillmoss.'

Eileen suddenly sat back in the chair, her two hands covering the lump in her tummy. 'This little feller is certainly lettin' me know he's 'ere. Been at it all day, he 'as.'

'Why do you keep calling it a "he"? There's a fifty-fifty chance on it being a girl.'

'Uh, uh,' Eileen smiled knowingly. 'It's a boy all right. A footballer, too! Been kickin' like mad all day.'

'I'll put his name down to play for Liverpool the day he's born then.' Bill smiled back. 'They could do with a good half-back.'

Maggie was sitting comfortably in her new chair listening to the wireless. She hadn't bothered to close the curtains because the street lamp outside the house gave her all the light she needed in the room. It was from this light she saw Arthur pass the window. 'Arthur's here,' she called, as she made her way down the hall. 'I'll open the door.'

Arthur's face was white and drawn as he stood in the middle of the room, his hands nervously running round the rim of his trilby hat. 'I've come from the hospital, that's why it's a bit late.'

'Is Sylvia in hospital, then?' Eileen took Arthur's hat and put it on the sideboard. 'Take yer coat off and sit down.'

'They took her in the Southern this morning.' Arthur sat down heavily, his breath coming in quick gasps. 'Visiting is half seven to eight, and I got the bus right down here.'

'Who's lookin' after the boys?'

'One of the neighbours.' Arthur saw the look of surprise on Eileen's face and nodded. 'I find it hard to believe meself. For two years all they've ever done is pass the time of day. But when the ambulance arrived this morning, two of them knocked on the door and asked if they could do anything to help. I was glad of it too, I can tell you.'

'And Sylvia,' Bill asked, 'what's wrong with her?'

'They don't know yet.' Arthur said, his gaze resting on Edna who was all ears. He shrugged his shoulders. 'They'll know more in a day or two.'

'Have yer 'ad anythin' to eat?' Eileen asked briskly.

'All I've done all day is drink cups of tea. I don't feel hungry, I've gone past it.'

'Rubbish! Yer've got to eat or yer'll be ill yerself.' Eileen dug her elbow in Bill's ribs. 'Give Edna two bob an' she can go for some fish an' chips.'

'Ah, ray, Mam!' Edna complained, frightened of missing something.

'Now then, young lady, you just do as you're told.' Bill passed the coin over. 'The shop's only at the top of the road.'

Maggie had been standing inside the door, now she bustled towards the kitchen. 'I'll put the kettle on and butter some bread.'

Eileen waited for the slam of the front door, then leaned forward. 'Do they know what's wrong with Sylvia?'

Arthur rubbed a hand across his forehead. 'I asked the Sister tonight but she wouldn't commit herself. Said they'd be keeping an eye on her for a few days before doing any tests. But when the doctor said he was sending her to hospital, I asked him what he thought was wrong with her. He didn't want to say anything at first, but I kept on at him that much he finally said he thought it was TB.'

'Oh, dear God, no!' Eileen's face drained of colour. 'People die of TB, don't they?' Too late Eileen realised what she'd said and clamped a hand over her mouth. 'I'm sorry, Arthur, I shouldn't 'ave said that. I don't know what I'm talkin' about, anyway, so take no notice.'

'You've only said what I'm thinking,' Arthur said. 'And the best of it is, the doctor blamed me.' There was bitterness in his voice. 'Threw the book at me for not making Sylvia get some attention before now.'

'But didn't yer tell 'im?' Eileen asked angrily.

'I did in the end. Told him the lot.' Arthur lifted his hand and snapped his fingers. 'And he changed, just like that. Couldn't have been nicer or more understanding. Said it explained Sylvia's terrible colour. Too much drinking over too long a period had probably damaged her liver.'

'Poor woman,' Bill said softly. 'Poor silly woman.'

'Poor woman?' Arthur's nostrils were white with anger. 'Bill, I could kill her with me bare hands! If she had no thought for herself, at least she should have had some thought for her two sons. They're at home now, Bill, crying their eyes out because their mother's sick. She wasn't a good wife, and certainly not a good mother, but she's the only one they've got! That's the only reason I've stayed with her.'

'Doctors don't know everythin', yer know, Arthur.' Tears were stinging the backs of Eileen's eyes. She didn't like Sylvia, but she certainly wouldn't wish this on her.

'She's in the right place in the hospital, they'll sort 'er out.'

'I think the doctor was right,' Arthur said. 'If you'd seen the change in her over the last six months, you'd know what I'm talking about. She lost so much weight she was only skin and bone. And her cough got so bad over the last few weeks she could hardly breathe.' Arthur was silent for a moment, then said, 'If only she'd done as I asked all those months ago, it mightn't have gone this far. But no, she had to go her own way. Out every night dressed like a floosie, coming home all hours the worse for drink. Bleary-eyed every morning, sending the boys off to school any old way. And never without a cigarette dangling out of the corner of her mouth. But for all that, she's the mother of my two sons and they love her.'

'What will you do now, Arthur?' Bill was so affected he had to struggle to get the words out. 'Will you have to stay off work?'

'Mrs Wright next door has offered to see to the boys for me, at least until we know what's happening. They're old enough to see to their own breakfast and get themselves off to school, so it's only for a few hours at night, until I get home.' There was a trace of sadness in Arthur's voice. 'From what I gathered this morning, listening to Mrs Wright and Mrs Summers, they've felt sorry for me since I came back from the army. Oh, they didn't say it in so many words, but it was Sylvia's way of life they objected to and that's why they kept their distance.'

They probably had plenty of reasons for not liking Sylvia, Eileen thought. She was so hard-faced and brazen, she wouldn't worry what the neighbours thought of her. Knowing Arthur was a prisoner of war, and seeing her out with every Tom, Dick and Harry, it was only natural that decent people would distance themselves from her.

Edna arrived back with the fish and chips and put a stop to any intimate conversation. It was when Arthur was leaving, Eileen asked him to let her know if it would be all right for her and Mary to go in and visit his wife. He threw her a look of gratitude and promised to see Bill in work and let him know how the land lay.

Chapter Eight

'Are you going to the shops?' Mary asked. 'I'll walk up with you if you like, give you a hand.'

'No, I got all me shoppin' in yesterday.' Eileen stood in the middle of Martha's room, dressed in her swagger coat that was fast becoming too small. 'I'm goin' up to Bray Street to see all me friends. I didn't get a chance when we moved and they'll think I'm terrible doin' a flit without saying goodbye after being neighbours for all those years.'

'D'you want me to come with you?' Mary asked. 'You really shouldn't be going that far on your own.'

'Our Edna's comin' with me. She'll be 'ere soon. I sent her upstairs to get a proper wash. She said she'd 'ad one, but it must 'ave been a cat's lick an' a promise 'cos she 'ad a flippin' big tidemark.'

'Sit down while you're waiting,' Martha said, pointing to the couch. 'Take the weight off your feet.'

'Mrs B, if I sat down there, yer'd need a crane to get me up. I'll just park meself on yer bed, if yer don't mind.' Eileen lowered herself slowly. 'It's like a mad house down there, I was glad to get out. Bill's started on the hall with our Billy 'elping 'im, Harry's doin' the livin' room an' our

Rene's in the front parlour. Honest, I'll be glad when it's all finished.'

'It won't take long. I've trimmed half the rolls of paper and I'll do the rest when I've got the dinner prepared.' Mary sat down beside Eileen and put an arm across her shoulder. 'Come on, cheer up! Just think how nice it'll be when it's all finished.'

'It's not only that that's makin' me feel miserable,' Eileen admitted, heaving a huge sigh. 'I can't get Arthur an' Sylvia off me mind.'

'It's not good news, is it, lass?' Martha said. 'It must be serious if they've transferred her to Fazakerley Hospital.'

'I keep thinkin' about the boys, poor beggars. They're too young to know what TB is. They know their mam's sick, but that's about all.'

'Look, Eileen, in your condition you shouldn't be getting yourself all upset.' Mary's pretty face clouded with concern for her friend. 'All the worrying in the world won't change things, so try and put it out of your mind.'

'I can't 'elp it, kid, yer know what I'm like. Arthur's 'ad such a lousy time, an' now this on top of everythin' else.'

There was a tap on the window and Eileen held her hands out to Mary to help her up. 'That'll be our Edna. I'd better go an' see if the tide's gone out.'

As soon as they turned into Bray Street, Edna skipped ahead. 'I'm goin' to see Janet.'

'Hey, buggerlugs,' Eileen shouted after her. 'Don't you go doin' a disappearin' act! I'll meet yer in the corner shop about three.' Eileen walked slowly up the street and with each step her heart became heavier. Further up she could see some of her old neighbours standing at their doors chatting, while the laughter of children at play filled the air. God, what a difference, Eileen thought. We may be living in a posh house in a swanky neighbourhood, but give me this any time.

Edna had spread the news and people appeared as if by magic. In no time Eileen found herself surrounded, everyone smiling and asking how she was and how she liked the new house. Putting a brave face on, Eileen gave a glowing report on her new home, stopping only briefly to cross her fingers and ask God to forgive her once again for telling lies. They're not really lies, she reminded Him. It is a nice house, it's just that I wish it wasn't me living in it.

Cissie Maddox pushed her way through the crowd that had gathered. 'Well, at last yer've remembered yer old friends. We were beginnin' to think we weren't good enough for yer now.'

'As if I could forget you, Cissie Maddox.' Eileen eyed Cissie up and down before casting her eyes down to her own swollen body. 'I'm bigger than yer now, Cissie, so watch yerself.'

Cissie stepped forward and to everyone's amazement gave Eileen a big hug. 'I 'aven't 'alf missed yer, Eileen Gillmoss. It's been like a graveyard without that fog-horn voice of yours bawlin' loud enough to wake the dead.'

'Got no one to fight with, eh, Cissie?' Eileen was overwhelmed by the reception and tears were not far away.

'It has been quiet without you, Eileen,' Ada Wilson said. 'Tommy was only saying that this morning.'

'Come an' 'ave a cuppa.' Cissie linked arms with Eileen. 'You can tell me all yer news.' As they neared her house she glanced sideways. 'Good, but yer not half a size! Yer seem to 'ave sprouted in the last few weeks.' Eileen waved goodbye to the other neighbours, saying she'd see them again soon, then turned to Cissie with a grin on her face. 'Yer not kiddin'! Look at me coat, fits where it touches! When I bought it, it was a loose swagger . . . now it's edge-to-edge.'

Eileen left Cissie's half an hour later feeling more cheerful than she'd done for months. She crossed the road to have a word with Tommy Wilson so she wouldn't have to pass her old house, thinking it was no good upsetting herself. It was over and done with now and she'd just have to make the best of it.

Eileen leaned on the counter of the corner shop and gave Milly Knight a beaming smile. 'Like old times, eh, Milly? Am I still good for a bit of stuff on tick?'

'Oh, it's lovely to see you.' Milly's smile lit up her face. 'D'you know, I haven't had a good laugh since you moved.'

'Well, I 'aven't done much laughin' meself, Milly. Between you and me and the gate post, me new neighbours are a miserable lot. Yer seldom see them, and when yer do they just nod their 'eads. I was beginnin' to think they were all deaf an' dumb until I 'eard them at the shops.' Eileen straightened up. 'D'yer want a little impersonation?'

'Oh, yes, please.' Milly's eyes gleamed in anticipation. 'Make it a good one so I can remember it, 'cos from the looks of you, I won't be seeing you round here until after the happy event.'

you were on your way, she was determined to get the last two strips up, and she moved like those blue flies you're always talking about.'

Eileen was still taking it all in when Bill took her arm. 'Come on, there's more to see.'

When Eileen saw the living room it was too much for her and she pulled out a chair to sit down. They'd chosen a pink paper for this room, patterned in diamonds in a darker shade. 'I never thought yer'd get this far,' she said quietly. 'I expected to come 'ome to a right mess.'

'I'm glad Harry gave me a hand with the ceilings last night,' Bill said. 'Having them done was half the battle.'

'Where is Harry? And our Rene, where's she got to?'

'She went upstairs to give Harry a hand. He's started on our bedroom, but I think I'll call a halt. We've done enough for one day.' Bill cupped Eileen's face in his hands. 'I'd have been lost without Harry and your Rene, they've been great. And our Billy's been a real cracker.'

'Where is Billy?'

Bill grinned. 'Getting ready to go out. If I tell you something, will you promise not to say anything to him?'

'Yeah, go 'ed.'

'I overheard him talking to Harry. He's got a date tonight with Mavis Radford.'

'Mavis Radford from Bray Street?' Eileen didn't know whether to laugh or cry. Her lovely son with a girl . . . she didn't think she liked the idea of another woman in his life.

Bill nodded. 'He met her at the Holy Name dance and made a date to take her to the pictures tonight.' Bill saw the look in Eileen's eyes and wagged a finger under her nose. 'Remember, you promised. He doesn't know I overheard him telling Harry.'

Eileen rested her chin on her hands when Bill ran upstairs to tell the workers to knock off. It had been a long day and the extra weight she was carrying around with her had drained her energy.

When Arthur called with his two sons, Eileen was sitting on a straight chair with her bare feet resting on two cushions. 'Yer'll 'ave to excuse me, Arthur, but I couldn't move if I tried.' She smiled at the two boys. 'Come an' give Auntie Eileen a hug.'

If anybody else had asked for a hug, the two boys would have said they were too old for soppy things like that. But they were drawn to this big, cuddly woman, and they didn't hesitate to fling their arms around her.

'Been to see yer mam, 'ave yez?'

'Er, no.' Arthur's eyes sent a warning. 'They don't allow children in the ward Sylvia's in.'

'Oh, did yez 'ave to wait outside?'

Again Arthur answered for the boys. 'I'd been told they couldn't go in, so I left them with Vera for a few hours.' Looking decidedly uncomfortable, Arthur went on quickly, 'I would have brought them here, but I knew you'd be up to your necks.' He turned to Bill. 'I'm sorry I couldn't give you a hand, like I promised, but under the circumstances I know you'll understand.'

'That's the least of your worries,' Bill said. 'You've more than enough on your plate.'

Arthur gazed around the room. 'This looks very nice.'

'Yer should see me mam's room,' Eileen said. 'She's

sittin' there lookin' like Lady Muck.'

'Come on, I'll show you.' Bill led Arthur and his sons out, saying, 'I can't take any credit for this, Rene did it with the help of our Billy.' While they were out of the room, Eileen tried to pull her dress down to make herself more respectable, but as soon as she let go of the material it wrinkled up again over her knees. 'Blast it,' she muttered, 'I'm like a flippin' elephant!'

A few moments later Arthur returned. 'They must have worked hard to have done all this.' There was a faint smile on his drawn face. 'You're a real slave driver, Eileen Gillmoss.'

'Oh, I've been out,' Eileen tried again to cover her knees but the dress wasn't having any. In the end she gave it up as a bad job. 'I'm not soft, yer know, Arthur, I don't stay around when there's work to be done. I've been visitin' me old neighbours.' Her eyes kept straying towards the door. 'Where's David and Gordon?'

'Maggie's showing them some photographs. She must be a mind reader, your mother, 'cos I wanted a word with you on your own.' Arthur sat down and stared at his clasped hands before meeting Eileen's eyes. 'Sylvia is very sick. The boys don't know and I'm not going to tell them, yet, anyway. I've got to take them to Walton Hospital one day next week, the three of us have to be tested to make sure we haven't contracted the disease.'

Eileen gasped, 'Oh, no!'

'It's all right, Eileen, there's not much chance of any of us having it. The boys didn't see enough of Sylvia, and she wasn't affectionate with them when she did see them. So they should be clear. And as for me,' Arthur said bitterly,

'I haven't slept with her, or had any physical contact with her for two years. Except for two nights, when I first came back from the army, I've slept in the boys' room.'

'Thank God for that!'

'I suppose I should say the same thing, but all I feel is sadness. It could have been so different if only she'd given it a chance. But as it is, it's David and Gordon who'll suffer the most and I can't find it in my heart to forgive her for that.'

Chapter Nine

Joan stood on tip-toe as she leaned towards the mirror over the fireplace. With one hand on top of the tiled grate to steady herself, and her Tangee lipstick in the other, she peered at her reflection. This was the first tube of lipstick she'd ever had in her hand and she didn't know where to start. To make matters worse, her mother and sister were watching. She brought the lipstick towards her mouth and puckered her lips. No, that wasn't how the girls in work did it, they stretched their lips.

Behind her, Edna mimicked every action, winking at her mother as she did so. Although she was two years younger than Joan, there wasn't much difference between them in height. In fact, they could be taken for twins. Through the mirror, Joan caught sight of her sister's antics and spun round, her face red with embarrassment and anger. 'If you don't move, I'll clock yer one.'

Edna stuck her tongue out. 'You an' whose army?'

'Mam, will yer tell this one off?' Joan gave her sister one more dirty look before turning to Eileen who was sitting on one of the dining chairs, her elbows resting on the table, watching the performance. 'She's nothing but a blinking . . .' Joan's words trailed off when she saw the look on her mother's face. 'What's up?'

Eileen's jaw dropped with horror as she gazed at the vivid orange slash that covered her daughter's mouth. 'In the name of God, are yer lips under that lot?'

'I might have known you'd say somethin' like that,' Joan said angrily. 'I never do anythin' right, do I? Not like this one 'ere,' Joan glared at Edna, 'she's mammy's girl, can't do no wrong.'

Edna put her two thumbs to her temples, wiggled her fingers and stuck out her tongue. 'Cry baby, cry baby . . .'

'Hey, knock that off,' Eileen warned. 'Get out of 'ere before I get me hands on yer an' give yer a thick ear.'

When Edna had left, Eileen turned sympathetic eyes on Joan. 'Take a good look in the mirror, sunshine, an' yer'll see what I'm on about. Yer must 'ave half the tube of lipstick on, an' it's all over the place, no shape to yer lips at all. If yer Dad comes down an' sees yer like that there'll be ructions. Tell yer what, why don't yer 'ave a swill, then nip up to Auntie Mary's an' ask 'er to show yer how to make yer face up properly?'

'Where's our Joan off to?' Bill asked. 'She's just flown out of the door as though the devil was on her tail.'

Eileen rolled her eyes. 'I don't think I'm our Joan's favourite person at the moment.' Eileen went on to tell him what had happened.

'She's too young to be wearing lipstick,' Bill said. 'She's only fourteen, for heaven's sake.'

'Yeah, but I remember when I was that age, I kept wishin' I was older so I could do the things the girls in work did. Joan's just the same, wishin' 'er life away.

When she gets older she'll be wishin' she could lose a few years.'

Eileen leaned back, causing the chair to creak in protest. She ran a hand across her forehead before resting it on her swollen tummy. 'I'll be glad when the next month's over.'

'Not long to wait now, chick, only two more weeks.'

'Can't come soon enough for me.' Every part of Eileen's body felt drained and weary. She hadn't had a proper night's sleep for weeks because she couldn't get comfortable in bed. And every night, lying awake listening to Bill's even breathing, seemed like an eternity. 'I'll be glad when it's all over.'

Bill stood behind her, his arms wrapped around her neck. 'Shall I bring some pillows down and you can try and get comfortable on the couch?'

Eileen shook her head. 'No, yer never know who'll come.'

'Eileen, you can't spend all the time sitting on a hard chair. I'll get a couple of pillows, you can sit in my chair and I'll ask Ma if we can borrow one of hers so you can put your feet up.' Bill made for the door. 'And Ma said you haven't had your bottle of Stout today, so I'll get you settled then nip up to the Walnut and get a couple of bottles.'

On his way to the pub, Bill called in to the Sedgemoors'. Eileen was really down in the dumps and needed someone to have a good natter to, someone to cheer her up and get a smile on her face.

When Joan came back, Mary was with her. 'Well, the

state of you and the price of fish!' Mary laughed when she saw Eileen, a pile of pillows at her back, stretched between two chairs with a glass of Stout in her hand. 'There's nothing like comfort.'

'You're tellin' me!' Eileen tried to sit forward but the effort was too much. 'I just wish I 'ad it!'

'Look at me face, Mam.' Joan leaned towards her mother. 'Auntie Mary did it up for me. Cream, powder, rouge, the lot.'

Eileen gazed at the thin face and saw, for the first time, the attractive woman her daughter was going to be. 'Now that's more like it. Yer look a real treat, sunshine.'

'Can I go over to Hanford Avenue to show Marjorie?' Joan was so excited she hopped from one foot to the other. 'I won't stay long, I promise. I'll be back before it gets dark.'

'Who's Marjorie?' Mary asked when Joan had gone.

'Someone she works with. They travel to work together.' Eileen winced when she tried to move to a more comfortable position. 'Yer know, kid, I wouldn't go through this again for a big clock.'

Mary pulled a chair forward and sat near her friend. When she smiled, her set of perfect white teeth gleamed. 'We all say that.'

'Yeah, well I mean it. Bill was right when 'e said we were too old for this lark.'

'When you've got the baby in your arms, you'll forget all about the trouble and discomfort.' Mary tossed her head and her long hair fanned out before resting on her shoulders. 'Me and Harry have been talking about sending Emma to learn how to play the piano. There's a woman in Wembley Gardens who gives lessons.'

'But yer 'aven't got a piano!' A smile seldom seen these days lit up Eileen's face. 'I was goin' to say we 'ad one but the leg fell off, but it's a stale joke, isn't it, kid?'

'Not up to your usual standard, Eileen Gillmoss, but under the circumstances it'll do,' Mary told her. 'Anyway, I told Harry we could get a piano cheap at Hartley's.'

'Aye, it'd be nice for a party. Yer can't beat an old joanna for a proper knees-up. Me mam used to 'ave one, before me Dad died, and we used to 'ave some parties at 'er 'ouse, believe me.'

'Who played the piano, your dad?'

'No, me mam! She never 'ad lessons like, but she only 'ad to hear a tune once and she could belt it out on that old joanna of theirs like no one's business.'

'Well, fancy that! I'd never have thought.'

'Oh, there's lots yer don't know about me mam. She was a nice-lookin' woman, always dressed up to the nines, an' the life an' soul of any party.' Eileen pulled a face. 'Then me dad died, she gave the joanna away when she came to live with us, an' she's never played since.'

Bill came back to see his wife more lively and talkative than she'd been for weeks, and he was glad he'd asked Mary to come and sit with her for a while. It had done her more good than all the Stout in the world.

'Where is your mam?' Mary asked as she set the chair back by the table.

'Need yer ask? Gone to the first 'ouse at the Rio, to see James Cagney an' Pat O'Brien in somethin' or other. When she comes in I'll get the whole story, actions an' everythin'. An' if it's a sad story, we'll both end up cryin' our eyes out.' Eileen handed Bill the empty glass. 'I'd 'ave another one, but it might make me laddo, here,' she patted her tummy, 'drunk.'

'Still kicking like mad, is he?' Mary jerked her head back and tutted. 'Look, she's got me calling it "he", now! We'll all get our eye wiped if it's a girl.'

'Now as yer mention it, I 'aven't felt it for a few hours. Must be feelin' sorry for me, givin' me a rest.'

'He probably got bored stiff listening to you two and he's gone to sleep,' Bill laughed. 'Wait till we get into bed and then he'll start.'

'Mam, I 'aven't felt the baby kickin' for days now, should it be like that?' Eileen was sitting on her usual hard chair peeling potatoes into the colander on her knee. The potato knife clutched in her hand, she looked across the room to where Maggie was on her knees wiping the tiled fireplace with a damp cloth. 'I should feel somethin', shouldn't I?'

Maggie fell back on to her heels and turned her head. 'Can't you feel anything at all?'

'Not a thing. The last time I felt it movin' was the day yer went to the Rio, an' that's four days ago. I 'aven't mentioned it before 'cos I thought it might be on account of me gettin' near me time.'

Maggie put her hands on the raised tiles and pushed herself up. With the corner of her pinny she wiped the sweat from her forehead. 'I'm not very well up on these things, lass, so I can't tell you. Perhaps you'd better go an' see Dr Greenfield.'

'No, I won't bother 'im. I'm due to go to the hospital

clinic tomorrow, so I'll wait till then. It's probably nothin' to worry over, so don't say anythin' to Bill. I don't want 'im fussin' round me.'

But Maggie did worry, and on her way to the shops she called at Mary's and asked if she could have a word with her mother. 'What d'you think, Martha?'

'I don't know any more than you, Maggie, but to be on the safe side I'd advise her to see the doctor.'

Mary was hovering by the door, an anxious look on her face. 'Perhaps Eileen's right, and a baby does stop kicking when it's getting ready to be born.'

Maggie was fidgeting nervously. 'She's told me not to tell Bill, but I'm going to have to whether she likes it or not. As soon as I can get him on me own, I'm telling him.'

'I'll slip up later and tell her I'll go to the clinic with her,' Mary said. 'Doris next door will mind the children for a couple of hours. We'll get a taxi to the hospital.'

Eileen lay on the couch in the clinic, her heart pounding as the doctor moved the stethoscope across her stomach and bent to listen for the sound of the baby's heartbeat. He didn't speak and she could read nothing from his expression. Why didn't he say something?

The doctor straightened up and let the stethoscope fall to hang on his chest. 'Well, Mrs Gillmoss, I think we'd better have you in.'

Eileen tried to turn on her side but found she couldn't move. She'd only been able to get on the couch with the help of two nurses. 'Is there somethin' wrong with the baby, doctor?'

The doctor was middle-aged with dark hair falling on to

his forehead, and the brown eyes that looked down on Eileen were sympathetic. 'I can't say, I'm afraid. I want to do some tests and that's why I want you in immediately.'

Worry made Eileen speak sharply. 'Look, will somebody 'elp me off this ruddy couch? I want to know what's goin' on.'

The nurse who'd been standing near the door came forward and with the help of the doctor raised Eileen's back and swung her body round so her legs were hanging over the side. 'Is that better?'

'Never mind about me, what about me baby?'

'I'll tell you that when you've had a proper examination in the morning. I want you to go home now, pack a few things and come straight back.' The doctor bent to look more closely at Eileen's face. 'Hey, they're not tears, are they? Come, come now, there's no point in crying until you've got something to cry about. Dry your eyes and the nurse will help you on with your clothes.'

Mary was waiting by the front door when Harry came in and she quickly explained. 'Eileen wouldn't go back to the hospital till Bill came in from work. Said she wanted him with her.'

Harry gave her a peck on the cheek before turning on his heels. 'I'll run them down.'

'There's no point in you waiting, Harry,' Bill said as they helped Eileen from the car outside the main doors of the hospital. 'I'll stay with her till she's settled in a ward.'

Harry looked at Eileen's downcast face and wished there was something he could say to cheer her up. But what was there to say?

Harry drove through the hospital gates, saw Eileen's face in his mind's eye and instead of turning left, turned the steering wheel to the right and towards Dr Greenfield's surgery.

Through eyes blurred with tears, Eileen saw John Greenfield walking down the ward towards her, and she held out her hands to him. 'Oh, thank God you've come.'

John held her hands in his, and smiled. 'It's a coincidence, really,' he lied. 'I had to visit a patient on the men's ward, and while I was here I thought I'd call and see a friend who was in the Army Medical Corps with me. He's a doctor on the maternity wards now. I happened to mention you'd be coming in any day now, and told him he'd better look after you. Imagine my surprise when he said you'd come in last night.'

'Did 'e tell yer anythin'?' Eileen squeezed his hands so hard, John winced with pain. 'I mean about the baby?'

'Now, you know what we doctors are like, Eileen. Until we're sure, we never commit ourselves. They'll be giving you a thorough examination later today, and then they'll know more.'

Eileen released his hands to wipe away a tear. 'I'm very stupid about things like this, Doctor. Does 'e think there's somethin' wrong with the baby?'

Oh, Lord, John groaned inwardly. How was he to answer that? He was praying that everything would be all right, but it would be wrong to raise her hopes. He let out a long, deep sigh. 'Eileen, you wouldn't want me to lie to you and I'm not going to. Dr Groves isn't certain of anything, and neither am I. If we were, I'd tell you, honest.' John looked at his watch and grimaced. 'I'll have to be on my way. The surgery will be overflowing with patients.'

'Will yer come in again an' see me?' Eileen sniffed. 'I 'ate hospitals, they're all disinfectant and bed pans.'

John smiled. 'I'll slip in as soon as I get a chance. Keep your chin up and stop crying or you'll make yourself ill.'

Eileen saw a nurse walking towards them and muttered, 'If she's got a bed pan in 'er 'and, hit 'er over the 'ead with it for me, will yer?'

The Matron was waiting for Bill when he came through the doors leading to the corridor outside the wards. 'Mr Gillmoss, Doctor Groves would like a word with you. He's in my office.' Her starched uniform crackled as she led the way. 'In here, please.'

Dr Groves looked up from the notes he was reading and pointed to a chair on the opposite side of the desk. 'Sit down, please, Mr Gillmoss.'

Bill, his face haggard, watched the doctor shuffle the papers into a neat pile and place them in the wire tray on top of the desk.

'I've got some sad news for you, Mr Gillmoss.' Dr Groves removed his glasses and pinched at the bridge of his nose. This was one part of his job that he hated. 'I'm sorry to have to tell you that the baby your wife is carrying will be stillborn.'

Bill slumped in his chair and covered his face with his hands. He couldn't speak for a while, and when he did, it was in a whisper. 'Have you told my wife?'

'Not yet. I thought it best to see you first and ask

whether you would prefer me to tell her, or whether you would rather do it yourself. I am prepared to break it to her, but perhaps she would take it better from you.'

'She's going to take it bad no matter who tells her.' Bill closed his eyes as despair and anger built up within him. 'How can it be? She's been so well for the whole time, did everything she was supposed to do. Drank orange juice, took her Glucodin religiously every day and had a bottle of Stout every night.'

'It's one of those unsolved mysteries, Mr Gillmoss. It happens, and nobody knows why. It certainly hasn't been caused by anything your wife did.'

'Then why?' Bill's clenched fist came down heavily on the desk, causing the wire tray to jump several inches in the air. 'Why did it have to happen to her? She was so looking forward to this baby,' his voice broke, 'she wanted it so much.'

The office door opened and Matron came in with a cup of tea, her eyes showing the sympathy she felt. 'Drink this, Mr Gillmoss, you'll feel much better.'

'I can't face her,' Bill said, his head moving from side to side. 'I know I sound a coward, but I couldn't do it.'

'Then I'll tell her.' The doctor pushed his chair back. 'Wait here till I come back.'

Bill's hand holding the cup and saucer was shaking so badly the tea splashed on to his hands. It was the pain of the hot liquid burning his skin that cleared his head. He put the cup down and stood up. 'No, it's only right I should be the one. I couldn't live with meself if I let her down now.'

'Matron will go with you and draw the screens so you'll

117

have a bit of privacy,' the doctor said. 'If Mrs Gillmoss gets upset or hysterical, ask Matron for something to calm her down.'

'Before I go, will you tell me what's going to happen? My wife is bound to ask, and I want to know meself.'

'We will induce labour either tomorrow or the next day. It depends upon how your wife is. It will be like a normal birth, except, except . . .'

'Except that the baby will be dead,' Bill finished the sentence, his voice bitter.

'There's no easier way of saying it, Mr Gillmoss, I just wish to God that there was. But if it helps, John Greenfield will be here with her.' When he saw the surprise on Bill's face, Dr Groves told how he knew Eileen's doctor and about his visit early that morning. 'He rang to ask about the results of our examination, and said to make sure I told your wife he'd be here with her the whole time.'

Matron walked down the ward ahead of Bill and when Eileen saw her hand reach out to draw the screens, she took one look at Bill's drawn face and burst out crying.

Chapter Ten

'I want to go 'ome, Bill.'

'You can't, chick!' Bill looked shocked. 'It's only been two days and the doctor said you'd be in at least ten days.'

'I don't care what the doctor said, I want to go 'ome.' Eileen was a shadow of her former self. The once rosy cheeks had lost their glow, her eyes were dull and her thin hair was lank and lifeless. 'How d'yer think I feel seein' all the happy mothers with their new babies? Honestly, Bill, if I stay 'ere much longer I'll lose me sanity.'

Bill gazed up and down the ward. He'd been so concerned about Eileen he'd never really looked around before, but now he took in the cots at the end of each bed, some with proud fathers cooing down at their new babies. He leaned forward to take Eileen's hand. 'I know it must be upsetting for you, love, but they won't let you out yet.'

'They wouldn't be able to stop me if you signed me out.'

'I couldn't do that! You know what happens if anyone signs themselves out against their wishes, they wash their hands of you. And what would happen if you got sick? I'd be the one to get the blame.'

'You just said it must be upsettin' for me, but 'ow the

hell do you know what it's like, eh, Bill Gillmoss?' Eileen asked angrily, snatching her hand away. 'I'm not sayin' they're not good to me, 'cos they are, the nurses and the other women in the ward. They're only bein' kind and friendly when they bring their babies to me, but they don't understand 'ow much it hurts.' The fire suddenly went out of Eileen's voice and she whimpered, 'I'm not made of stone, yer know, Bill.'

Bill screwed his eyes up. 'I'm sorry, chick, I had no idea.'

'Sign me out, please?' Eileen implored. 'I promise I'll go straight to bed at 'ome, an' I'll be all right.'

The pleading in Eileen's voice was like a knife turning in Bill's heart. But the responsibility was too much for his shoulders alone. He'd never forgive himself if anything went wrong. 'Look, love, I don't like seeing you so unhappy, and I'd do anything for you, you know that. But for my own peace of mind I'd like to have a word with Dr Greenfield first, see what he says. I'll try and get hold of him tonight and ask Mary if she'll slip in tomorrow and let you know.' He saw the disappointment on Eileen's face and knew he couldn't leave her in this state without a ray of hope. 'Whichever way it goes, chick, I promise you'll be home in a few days, even if I have to carry you out. But let me speak to Dr Greenfield first, eh?' Trying to coax a smile, his hand made a cross over his heart. 'Scout's honour, two days at the most.'

The last patient had left and John Greenfield was clearing his desk before going through to his living quarters for his evening meal. It had been a long, trying day, and he was looking forward to putting his feet up for half an hour before making an evening call on a patient he was concerned about. He heard a knock on the front door and his housekeeper's voice saying that surgery was over and would the caller come back tomorrow.

John sighed, pushing his fine, wayward hair off his forehead. He had to go through the hall to get to the dining room and was just in time to see Bill Gillmoss before the housekeeper shut the front door on him.

'Mr Gillmoss.'

Bill was closing the gate behind him when he heard John's voice. He turned and walked back up the path. 'I'm sorry to bother you, Doctor. I left the hospital ten minutes before the end of visiting time hoping to catch you before surgery closed, but I'll call back tomorrow on me way to the hospital.'

'No, come in now. I can spare five minutes.'

The two men faced each other across the desk as Bill explained why he'd come. 'She's heartbroken, Doctor, honestly. In all our married lives I've never known her so depressed. It's doing her more harm than good being in there.'

'They should have left her in the small room where she was the first day, then she wouldn't have had to see the babies in the ward. But, unfortunately, they needed it for an urgent case.' John tapped the desk with his pen, his face thoughtful. 'Eileen would be better off at home with her family around her. I could get a district nurse to call in every day to keep an eye on her, and I could give her tablets to stop her breasts from filling up.' He threw his pen down. 'No, I can see no reason why she can't be discharged.'

121

'Then she can come home?' Bill's whole body slumped with relief. 'Thank God for that.'

'It's up to the doctor on the maternity ward, and it's too late to ring tonight. I'll give him a call first thing in the morning and have a word with him. You're not on the phone, are you?'

Bill shook his head. 'We're not, but the Sedgemoors are.' He gave the number and stood up. 'Thank you, Dr Greenfield, for everything. It's no wonder Eileen says you're the best doctor in the world. You've certainly taken a load off my shoulders tonight.'

'Well, Mrs Gillmoss, you're leaving us today.' The Matron's stern face relaxed into a smile. 'Now isn't that good news?'

Eileen's face dropped on to her chest as a lone tear trickled down her cheek. She wiped it away and met the Matron's gaze. 'It's not that yez haven't been good to me, 'cos yez 'ave. But I want to be with me family, I miss them so much.'

'I understand. I'll get you a list of do's and don'ts, and you must promise to abide by them. An ambulance will be taking you home, but I can't tell you exactly what time that will be. So while you're waiting, sit on the side of the bed and clear your locker out.' Matron walked away a few steps, then turned. 'You've got a very handsome husband, Mrs Gillmoss. Very distinguished looking.'

'Keep yer eyes off 'im, Matron, he's all mine.' For the first time since she'd come in hospital, Eileen didn't have to force a smile. 'Yer don't think I'm daft enough to marry an ugly beggar, do yer?'

Sitting on the side of the bed, her belongings in a small case by her feet, Eileen talked to the group of women who'd gathered around to say goodbye. But her eyes kept going to the clock on the wall at the end of the ward. Come on, ambulance, her thoughts ran, don't you know I'm dying to see me mam and the kids?

When a nurse finally came with a wheelchair, Eileen couldn't get into it quickly enough. She was afraid the doctor might change his mind and keep her in. With her case on her knees, she said to the nurse, 'Home, James, an' don't spare the 'orses.' She waved to the women as she was wheeled out of the ward. 'Look after yerselves! Ta-ra, now!'

Maggie had been pacing up and down by the window for over an hour, and when she saw the ambulance turn the corner she cried, 'It's here.' She hurried to the door, followed closely by Mary, Vera and Carol. Nervously picking at her pinny, she watched the men open the back doors of the ambulance and climb inside. She gripped Mary's arm when she saw her daughter being carried out on a stretcher and Eileen heard her cry of distress.

'Don't worry, Mam, it's not as bad as it looks.'

Mary dashed upstairs to pull the bedclothes back and was standing by the bed smiling when Eileen was transferred from the stretcher. 'Welcome home, Eileen Gillmoss.'

'Hi-ya, kid.'

Eileen thanked the ambulance men, then let out a sigh when they left the room. 'Thank God for that! I've never been so glad to be 'ome in all me life.'

Maggie came bustling in and bent to kiss her daughter. She was shocked by Eileen's appearance but hid it as she straightened the counterpane. We'll soon have her back to her old self now she's home, she consoled herself.

Carol was hanging on to Vera's coat, a puzzled look on her face. Why was Auntie Eileen in bed in the middle of the day?

There was an awkward silence until Vera walked towards the bed. She struggled to find the right words, but someone had to mention the baby no matter how painful. They couldn't carry on as though nothing had happened. 'I'm so sorry, Eileen.'

Those few words were all that were needed to start the four women crying. Maggie went to Eileen and held her close, rocking her like a baby. 'There, there, lass, you cry as much as you want.'

'Why me, Mam? What did I do wrong?'

'You did nothing wrong, lass.' Maggie's tears ran unchecked on to Eileen's head. 'These things happen and nobody knows why.'

Mary and Vera were crying unashamedly. Both would have given anything to be able to help Eileen, the one person they had both turned to when they were in need of a friend. But there was nothing they could do to take the hurt away, only grieve with her.

'It was a little girl, Mam.'

Carol's lips started to tremble. She didn't understand why everyone was upset, except that it had something to do with Auntie Eileen and a little girl. She squeezed between Eileen and Maggie. 'I'm your little girl, Auntie Eileen.'

Through her tears, Eileen saw Carol's face pushed under her mother's arm and her sobbing eased. She ran a hand across her nose, then sniffing loudly she reached out to stroke the fair hair. 'Of course yer my little girl, sweetheart. An' the best little girl in the whole world.'

Using the corner of her pinny to wipe her face, Maggie stepped back to let Carol near the bed. They say these children bring their own love, she thought, well Carol certainly did. She was a Godsend right now.

When Carol sat on the bed and tried to cuddle Eileen, the big woman quickly put her arms out to protect her breasts. 'Not too close, sunshine. Auntie Eileen's got a pain.'

Eileen pulled a face at Vera. 'Me breasts are full of milk an' they're awful sore.' She turned to Maggie. 'We'll 'ave to find an old sheet to tear into strips, an' yer can bind them up for us.'

'I've got an old sheet,' Mary said. 'And I'll do it for you.'

'Thanks, kid, but we've got plenty of old sheets, 'aven't we, Mam? In fact they're all flippin' old.' Eileen tried to stifle a yawn, but it wasn't lost on Maggie.

'I think it's time for you to have a rest.' Maggie reached across and took one of the pillows from Bill's side of the bed. 'Lift your head and I'll make you comfortable.'

'Come on, Vera, we'll go and let Eileen have a bit of peace and quiet, she looks all in.'

It took some persuading to get Carol off the bed. Only a promise that she could come again tomorrow did the trick.

Mary looked back from the doorway. 'Can Harry come

and see you tonight, or would you rather he left it a few days?'

'Now, kid, 'ave yer ever known me refuse to 'ave a man in me bedroom? Tell 'im I'm lookin' forward to seein' 'im.'

Bill gazed around the table as the children ate the hot-pot Maggie had made for their dinner. Usually meal times were noisy affairs, with jokes, laughter and arguments. But tonight, after seeing their mother looking so pale and tired, they were quiet.

'How long will me mam be in bed, Dad?' Billy asked, putting down his knife and fork. 'She doesn't look very well, does she?'

'No, son, she doesn't.' Bill pushed a potato around his plate. His normal hearty appetite had deserted him and if it wasn't for upsetting Maggie, the whole lot would have gone in the bin. 'You know how much she was looking forward to having this baby, all the plans she'd made. I know we were all looking forward to it, and we all feel sad, but it's much, much worse for your mam.'

There was a lump in Billy's throat which wouldn't go no matter how hard he tried to swallow. Embarrassed, he picked up his plate and made for the privacy of the kitchen. 'I can't eat any more, Nan, I'm sorry.'

'That's all right, son,' Maggie called after him. 'None of us are very hungry tonight.'

Edna pushed her plate away and dropped her head on the table, her thin shoulders shaking with sobs. 'Me mam said I would 'ave had a little baby sister.'

Bill ran a hand over her head, his voice soft. 'I know,

love, but your crying isn't going to help your mam. We've all got to pull together now to help her get better.' He turned to Joan, whose hands were lying in her lap, her eyes fixed on her plate. 'D'you hear me, Joan?'

Joan nodded, not trusting herself to speak. She hadn't wanted a baby in the house, but she would rather have had a hundred babies than see her mam looking so unhappy.

'So we've all got to get stuck in and give Nan a hand with the housework for the next few weeks. This house is far too big for her to keep clean, as well as see to your mam and do the washing and cooking.'

'I can stay off school an' help me nan,' Edna said. 'If yer give me a note for the teacher, I won't get shouted at.'

Bill thought about it, then said, 'I don't like you staying off school, but I don't think it would do any harm just this once. You could help in the house and be company for your mam. That's what she needs, someone to take her mind off things.'

'Can I go up an' tell her?' Edna was off her chair and out of the room before Bill had time to stop her. They could hear her taking the stairs two at a time and Maggie shook her head. 'She's a live wire, that one. Just like her mother was.'

'I'm glad they've all gone.' Eileen lay back on the pillows, her face showing her tiredness. 'I knew Mary an' Harry were comin', but I didn't expect our Rene an' Alan. How did they know I was 'ome?'

'Rene's been ringing Mary every day,' Bill said, sitting down on the side of the bed. He took Eileen's hand in his

127

and rubbed his thumb gently over the skin. 'It's good to have you home, chick. I haven't half missed you.'

Eileen's eyes were fastened on the wall behind the door. 'Where's the cot?'

'Gone. Everything's gone, love.' Since he'd got in from work Bill had been dreading this moment. But what had been done was for the best. 'I asked your Rene to come down and clear everything out.' He saw the pain on Eileen's face and said quickly, 'It had to be done, chick! It would have broken your heart if you'd had to do it.'

'Where've they gone?' Eileen could see in her mind all the small matinee coats, the nightdresses and tiny pillow-cases Maggie had embroidered, and the cot and pram sets. She remembered how she'd folded them all neatly away, ready for when the baby came. Tears smarted her eyes. 'Who did they go to?'

'A young couple in Walton. They'd only just got a house and were struggling to save the money to furnish it when the girl found out she was in the family way. Just the sort of couple you would have given them to yourself.'

'Yer've never said anythin', Bill.' Eileen's voice was low. 'But were yer very disappointed?'

'More than disappointed, love, I was heartbroken. But Dr Greenfield had a good talk to me after the baby was born, and although I didn't appreciate what he said then, I've had time to think it over and he was right.'

'What did he say to yer?'

'Not tonight, Eileen, I'll tell you some other time. You've had enough for one day.'

Eileen struggled to a sitting position. 'Tell me now.'

Bill sighed and ran his fingers through his mop of white

hair. 'I know you'll be upset, but he said we were lucky.' When the bed creaked with Eileen's movement, Bill lifted his hand. 'You wanted to know, so hear me out. There's lots of children dying every day, and as the doctor said, it would have been much worse if we had known the baby and grown to love her.' With a catch in his voice, Bill went on, 'We're luckier than some 'cos we've got three children, and we've got each other.'

Eileen was silent as she watched Bill's face working to keep the tears at bay. And without warning her mind went back in time to when Bill was taken prisoner in the war and she didn't know whether he was alive or dead.

Eileen held out her open arms. 'Hold me, Bill.'

After a week of only being allowed to walk round the bedroom or go to the toilet, the nurse pronounced Eileen well enough to go downstairs on the understanding she didn't overdo things. But there was no need for the nurse's warning because Mary and Vera were there every day to give Maggie a hand, and they wouldn't even let Eileen wash a cup. 'This is the life.' Eileen was sitting on the couch munching a Fry's Chocolate Cream bar, watching Mary doing some ironing. 'Nice work, if yer can get it, eh, kid?'

Mary spat on her finger and tested the iron. 'Ow, that's hot!' She smiled at Eileen. 'Serve me right if I burnt meself. Harry's always telling me off about it.'

'You and Vera 'ave been smashin'. An' our Rene, of course. I don't know 'ow me mam would 'ave managed without yez.' Eileen licked some melted chocolate off her fingers. 'But another week should see me back on me feet.'

'You'll do as you're told and take it easy for at least a month.' Mary folded the sheet she'd finished ironing. 'Me and Vera don't mind, we enjoy having a natter.' She didn't say that there was an understanding between her and Vera, and Rene, that Eileen shouldn't be left on her own too much. She never talked about the baby, but the pain and heartbreak could be seen on her face when she thought no one was looking.

Eileen wiped her sticky fingers on the silver paper before throwing it in the fire. 'I'll make it up to yez, kid. When I'm feelin' better I'll mug yez to a meal in Sampson and Barlows.' She gazed at Mary's bent head for a while, then asked. 'What's wrong with Arthur Kennedy these days? Nobody 'as mentioned 'im, an' he 'asn't been to see me. That's not like Arthur.'

Mary put the iron down while she turned a pillowslip. 'Oh, he hasn't forgotten you, he asks about you all the time. But with you being so low, healthwise, Bill thought it better if he didn't come.'

'That's daft, that is, an' mean,' Eileen said. 'Anybody would think Arthur 'ad the plague.'

'Bill was only being careful, and we all agreed with him, even Arthur.' Mary folded the pillowslip and placed it on top of the pile on the sideboard. 'In your condition it was better to be safe than sorry.'

'How did 'im an' the kids get on when they went for a test?'

'Fine. They got the all clear.' Mary could see the line Eileen's thoughts were taking and said, 'That had nothing to do with Bill asking him not to come. It's just Arthur going to the hospital to see Sylvia, Bill was frightened he might have picked up a germ on his clothes.'

'Load of rubbish,' Eileen said. But she wasn't displeased. How could she be, when Bill only had her interests at heart? 'How is Sylvia?'

'Arthur doesn't go in every night now. He said it was a waste of time because Sylvia wouldn't talk to him. He can sit by the bed for an hour and she won't open her mouth. Arthur said it's as though she's blaming him for everything.'

'Does he still take the boys to Vera's?'

Mary's eyes went to the door of the kitchen where Maggie and Vera were preparing the dinner. Her voice low, Mary said, 'I think so, but Vera doesn't say much.'

'I'll 'ave to get meself better soon, won't I, kid? Get up-to-date with all the news.' Eileen was looking more like her old self. She was eating everything put before her and was feeling stronger every day. But inside, the pain and heartache were as strong as ever. She managed to hide it during the day, and only Bill knew how she was suffering. Because it was in his arms she cried herself to sleep every night.

Mary noticed Eileen shiver, and quickly put the iron down. 'Are you cold, Eileen? Shall I put some more coal on?'

'No, I'm all right, kid. Just someone walkin' over me grave.' It was still an effort to smile, but when Eileen saw the concern on her friend's face she managed to raise one. 'I was just thinkin', yer not very good at repeatin' gossip, are yer, kid? I bet yer don't know 'ow many blankets next door 'ave got on their bed, or who the milkman's 'aving it off with.'

'Oh, go way with you,' Mary laughed. 'You should have Elsie Smith for a neighbour. You'd be in your element then.' Mary cocked an ear. 'There's a knock on the door. I'll go.'

Eileen could hear raised voices but couldn't make out what they were saying. She was watching the door when Mary came back with her arm around Edna's shoulders. Eileen cried out when she saw the bandage wrapped around her daughter's head. 'Oh, my God, what's happened?'

Edna ran to sit next to her mother on the couch while Mary explained. 'One of the teachers brought her home. Apparently she fell in the playground and cut her head open.'

'Is it bad?' Eileen held Edna away from her to look closely at the bandaged head. 'Have yer 'ad it seen to?'

Maggie and Vera came hurrying from the kitchen. 'Oh, lord, what is it now?'

Maggie's hand went to her mouth. 'If it's not one thing, it's another.'

'All right, Mam, don't be gettin' yer knickers in a twist.' Eileen put her fingers under Edna's chin and raised her face. 'Tell us what happened, sunshine.'

Edna, her face ashen, said, 'We were playin' football in the playground an' me an' Marie Ashton ran to kick the ball and we banged into each other. I went flyin' and landed on me head.' Edna was reduced to tears and Eileen couldn't get another coherent word out of her.

'Whoever brought her home said she's been to the hospital and has had four stitches in the wound,' Mary said. 'I think it must have been one of the teachers.'

'It was our headmistress, Miss Bond,' Edna sobbed. 'She took me to the 'ospital in her car. An' she said I was to stay off school till the stitches are out.'

'Is it sore, sunshine?' Eileen put her arm around the thin shoulders and could feel her daughter shaking. 'I think yer'd better take some aspirin and go to bed for a couple of hours. You go on up an' I'll get yer a hot drink an' two tablets. When yer dad comes in, he'll know what to do.'

'You stay where you are, I'll see to her.' Vera took Edna's hand. 'I'll settle her down if you'll make a cup of tea, Mary. Weak with plenty of sugar in.'

Bill took his shoes off and let them fall to the floor. 'There's not much I can do, chick. She says it's sore, but I'm not touching the bandage 'cos I'll never get it back on properly.' He stood up and struggled with the stud at the back of his collar. When it slipped from his fingers and fell to the floor, he cursed, 'The blasted thing's rolled under the tallboy and I'm not moving that tonight.'

Eileen was leaning back against the headboard, a worried look on her face. 'Shall I call the doctor out tomorrow?'

'That won't be necessary, unless she's in a lot of pain.' Bill slipped between the sheets. 'And you know what a good actress our Edna is, so only believe half of what she says. She'll do a Bette Davis on you and have everyone running round after her.' He stretched his arms over his head and yawned. 'Ask Mary if she'll be a pal and ring the school tomorrow to find out when the stitches are due to be taken out. I'll have to take a couple of hours off work to take her to the hospital.'

Eileen watched Bill snuggle down in the bed, the clothes pulled up to his chin. 'I've been lying here thinkin',' she said. 'All the runnin' round, movin' to this 'ouse an' havin' to decorate an' buy new furniture, an' all for nothin'. We could 'ave stayed in our old house.'

Bill pushed himself up and held her close. 'It wasn't for nothing, love. We've got a nice house here. You haven't had time to appreciate it, but when you're feeling better you'll see the difference. Ma's got her own room and we've got a bathroom and wash-house. We couldn't ask for anything more.'

Eileen bit on the inside of her lip. 'Don't start shoutin' at me, Bill, but I feel it in me bones that this isn't goin' to be a lucky 'ouse for us.'

'Ye gods and little fishes!' Bill was exasperated. 'You can't blame the house for what happened to you, or 'cos our Edna fell and cut her head. That's just being superstitious. There's no such thing as an unlucky house and you know it.'

Eileen shrugged off his arm. 'Okay, Bill Gillmoss, 'ave it your own way. But don't say I never warned yer.'

Chapter Eleven

'It was a crackin' game yesterday, wasn't it, Dad?' Billy leaned forward to look past Edna who was sitting next to him at the table. 'That goal of Bob Paisley's was brilliant.'

'Yes, it was a masterpiece,' Bill answered with a smile. 'All the lads played well, Liddell, Stubbins, Balmer, every one of them.'

'Yeah.' Billy munched happily on a roast potato. At twenty, he was a replica of how his Dad had looked at his age. And like his Dad he was a fanatical supporter of Liverpool Football Club. 'We play Arsenal away next week, don't we?'

'In the name of God, can't you two talk about anythin' but football?' Eileen asked, a smile creasing her face. Sunday was the one day of the week she looked forward to, when the extension leaf on the table was pulled out and the family sat down to eat together. Her eyes were bright as they looked around the table. Next to her sat Joan, eighteen now, then her mother, Maggie. Opposite, sat Bill, Edna and young Billy. 'I bet if I put a Liverpool shirt down to yez for yer dinner, yer'd eat the blasted thing!'

'I would if it had salt and pepper on.' Billy grinned cheekily. 'And a drop of the old tomato ketchup.'

'Oh, ha-ha, very funny.' Eileen saw Joan pick up her plate and scrape her chair back. 'You've been quick. What's the hurry?'

'I'm meeting Joyce Harrison, we're going for a walk.'

Joan had grown into a very attractive girl. Her figure was slim and curved in the right places, her long legs shapely in the high-heeled shoes she wore. Her fine, mousy-coloured hair was long and straight, and today it was combed to fall across one side of her face in the style of Veronica Lake, one of her favourite film stars.

'Are yer sure it's Joyce yer meetin', and not some feller?' Eileen asked, jokingly. 'Yer've gone to a lot of trouble with yer appearance just to go out with a girl. There's enough make-up on yer face to sink a flippin' ship.'

'I've told you, I'm going out with Joyce.' There was no answering smile on Joan's pink flushed face. She might have inherited the colour of Eileen's hair and her hazel eyes, but she certainly hadn't inherited her sense of humour. It had rubbed off on Billy and Edna, but somewhere along the line it had passed Joan by. 'Anyway, what difference would it make if I was meeting a boy? I'm eighteen years of age, not a kid.'

Bill could see Eileen's hackles rising and stepped in to prevent a row developing. 'You may be eighteen, young lady, but that doesn't give you the right to be cheeky to your mother. We'll have a little respect, if you don't mind.'

Joan bounced out to the kitchen and they heard her

plate being banged on the draining board in temper. Then she reappeared and marched through the room without a glance at anyone. They heard her footsteps running up the stairs and Eileen clicked her tongue. 'She's a bad-tempered little faggot, that one. And selfish into the bargain. Never thinks about anyone but herself. She won't even wash a cup in case she breaks one of 'er flippin' nails.'

'All right, chick, don't get yourself all het up. I know you were only joking about who she was meeting, but Joan obviously didn't. Just forget it.'

'She wouldn't know a joke if it jumped up an' hit 'er in the face,' Eileen grumbled. 'The only time yer get a smile out of 'er is when she's gettin' her own way.'

'Don't be worryin' about her, Mam,' Billy said. 'She's full of herself now, but she'll grow out of it.'

'Our Billy's right, Mam.' A mischievous grin lit up Edna's face. 'Did yer notice she's Veronica Lake today? I wonder who she'll be tomorrow . . . Joan Crawford or Alice Faye?'

Maggie chortled. 'Your mam will never be dead while you're around, lass.'

Bill was trying hard to keep his face straight. 'You shouldn't be making fun of your sister.'

'Oh, come on, Dad, we're only acting daft,' Billy said. 'Mind you, our Joan is a pain in the neck sometimes.' He started to collect the dirty plates. 'Me and Edna will wash the dishes.' He gave his sister a playful dig. 'Won't we, kiddo?'

'No, I'll do the dishes,' Eileen said. 'You two go about yer business.'

'Are you going up to Bray Street, Billy?' Even as she asked, Edna knew it was a daft question. Billy had been courting Mavis Radford from their old street for three years now, and he spent all his free time up there. Except, of course, for the Saturday afternoons Liverpool were playing at home. 'If you are, I may as well wait an' come with you, 'cos I'm goin' to Janet's.'

Edna went upstairs for her coat and when she came down she pulled a face. 'Our Joan's got a right gob on her. Didn't look at me or say a word.' Edna, at sixteen, was as tall as her sister and very like her in looks. But her body hadn't filled out yet, and every time she had a bath she inspected herself for signs that her bust was growing. The girls she worked with behind the counter of George Henry Lee's told her to be patient, that some girls blossomed later than others, but every time she looked down at her flat chest, she doubted they were right.

'What's she doin' up there?' Eileen asked.

Edna nearly blurted out that her sister was doing what she spent most of her life doing, standing in front of the mirror titivating herself up. But it was no good starting her mam off again. 'She's just pottering around.'

Billy came in then and Eileen eyed him with pride. He looked so handsome in his best suit, his black hair sleeked back with brilliantine. 'Can I bring Mavis back for tea, Mam?'

'Of course yer can. She'll 'ave to take pot luck though 'cos I haven't made a jelly or anythin' fancy.'

'She won't worry about that.' Billy jerked his head at Edna. 'Come on, Sis, shake a leg.'

'I might stay at Janet's for me tea,' Edna said as she

followed her brother. 'But I won't be late. I'll be home before it gets dark.'

'Okay, sunshine. Ta-ra!'

It was half an hour later when Joan came down, her hair and make-up perfect, her perfume pervading the air. 'I'm having my tea at Joyce's, Dad. Can I take a key with me, just in case I'm late getting home?'

'We won't be going to bed till after eleven,' Bill said. 'You should be in by then.'

'Oh, I probably will be! But we sit and listen to records in their parlour and the time flies over.'

Listen to records me eye, Eileen thought. She's tellin' lies, but Bill can't see it. 'What sort of records d'yer listen to?' Eileen spoke to Joan's back.

'Er, em, Frankie Laine and, er, Pat Boone.'

'Oh, I like Frankie Laine.' Eileen's voice warned that while Joan might be able to pull the wool over her father's eyes, she certainly wasn't fooling her. 'I'll 'ave to borrow them sometime.'

Bill, oblivious to the undercurrent, handed Joan a key. 'Don't be too late now, d'you hear?'

'Okay, Dad,' Joan answered meekly. 'I won't be late.' She reached the door, then without looking back, said, 'See you later, Mam.'

Eileen saw Billy grimace and bend down to rub his ankle. She saw him mouth the words, 'That hurt!' and Mavis, bending her head until it was on a level with his, mouthed back, 'Well, tell them, then.'

'Oh, aye!' Eileen grinned. 'Tell us what? Come on, Billy, spit it out.'

139

Flushing a bright red, Billy gave one last rub to the ankle Mavis had kicked under the table, then grinned back at his Mother. 'Me and Mavis are getting engaged at Christmas.'

'Well, 'ow about that!' Eileen pushed her chair back and sprang to her feet. Grabbing Mavis in a bear-like hug, she kissed her cheek. 'I'm over the moon, love. Welcome to the family.'

Bill, pride showing on his face, shook hands with Billy. 'Congratulations, son! I'm very happy for you.'

Maggie pushed Bill aside and threw her arms round her grandson's neck. 'Oh, I am happy, Billy. You couldn't have picked a better lass.'

When the excitement had died down, Bill sank into his favourite chair and lit a cigarette. 'So, you're getting engaged at Christmas, eh? And when d'you think you'll be getting married?'

'Why, Dad?' Billy's face was flushed with happiness as he sat with Mavis's hand gripped tightly in his. 'Are you anxious to get rid of me?'

'Of course he's not!' Eileen answered for Bill. 'He just can't wait to be a father-in-law, can yer, Bill?'

'I dread you leaving home, son, if you must know.' There was a glint in Bill's eyes. 'Just think, I'll be the only man in the house, then! I won't stand a dog's chance if the women all gang up on me.'

'Ah, God 'elp 'im! Eileen dabbed her eyes and pretended to sob. 'Let's all say "aaah" for our Dad. All together now, aaaah!'

Mavis squeezed Billy's hand, her shoulders heaving with a fit of the giggles. She couldn't wait to get married and be one of this family. They were always so happy and Eileen was guaranteed to have you laughing before you had time to sit down. Mavis was an only child and she loved her parents dearly, but it was so quiet in their house compared to the Gillmosses'.

When Edna came in and was told the news, she shrieked with delight. 'I'm goin' to be a bridesmaid, goody goody!'

'Hey, give us a chance, we're not even engaged yet!' Billy looked sideways at Mavis and winked. 'Would you want this ugly duckling to be one of your bridesmaids? She'd probably spoil the weddin' photographs.'

Edna spread her elbows on the table. 'When are yer buying the ring, our Billy?' Then without waiting for a reply, she asked, 'Are you gettin' a solitaire, Mavis? When I get engaged, I'm getting a solitaire.'

'Oh, my God!' Eileen put a hand over her heart in mock horror. 'Don't tell me you've got a secret feller hidden somewhere! I couldn't stand two shocks in one day.'

'Don't be daft, Mam. You're not gettin' rid of me that easy.' Edna patted her mother's arm. 'I know when I'm well off.'

'Well,' Billy smiled at Mavis with that special look in his eyes of someone in love. 'Put our Edna out of her misery. Are you getting a solitaire?'

'I don't mind.' Mavis blushed. 'We'll go together and choose it.'

Billy's chest swelled with pride. He was a man now, with responsibilities. 'We'll have to pull our horns in and start savin' like mad, otherwise it'll be a tanner ring from Woolworths.'

141

Rubbing her hands together gleefully, her face creased in a smile of pure bliss, Eileen warned Bill, 'And you, Bill Gillmoss, 'ad better start workin' all the hours God sends, if yer get the chance, to save up for the weddin'. 'Cos when my only son walks down the aisle, I want to be dolled up to the nines.'

'Mam, me and Mavis wouldn't care if you turned up at the church with curlers in yer hair and an apron on, as long as you turned up.'

'What! An' give these toffee-nosed snobs round 'ere somethin' to talk about?' Eileen shook her head before adopting a haughty pose. 'As Eliza Doolittle would say, my dear son, "not bloody likely"!'

Eileen lay on her back staring up at the ceiling. The illuminated clock told her it was turned twelve and she still hadn't heard Joan come in. All the others were in bed and, like Bill, were probably well away by now. She could hear her husband's rhythmic breathing and wished she'd been able to drop off as quickly as he had, then she wouldn't be lying here on pins wondering where Joan had got to.

Through the silence, Eileen heard the soft click of the key in the lock and she glanced sideways at the fingers on the clock. Twenty past twelve. This was no time for a young girl to be coming home.

Eileen turned on her side and pulled the clothes over her shoulder. Wait till the morning, she'd give the little madam the length of her tongue. Her ear cocked, Eileen listened for the soft pad of footsteps on the stairs, but there was no sound. For ten minutes she waited, her anger rising. 'There'll be no gettin' her up in the morning,' she muttered under her breath.

Slowly, so as not to disturb Bill, Eileen slid out of bed and groped for her dressing gown. She closed the bedroom door quietly behind her and holding on to the banister rail lowered herself gently down each of the stairs. If she woke Bill, he'd come down and there'd be hell to pay. When she reached the bottom stair, a puzzled look crossed her face. There was no sound and no light coming from under the living room door. She leaned back against the wall, telling herself it must have been a noise from outside she'd heard and had mistaken it for a key in the door. She was probably wrong about Joan not being in, too. Here she was calling the poor girl for everything when she was probably tucked up in bed and fast asleep. Eileen was about to pull herself up the first stair when she heard a sound, almost like a whisper. No, she shook her head, it's my imagination playing tricks on me again. If I keep this up they'll be carting me off to the looney bin. Then the sound came again, and this time, Eileen knew it wasn't her imagination.

As she opened the living room door with one hand, Eileen felt for the light switch with the other. And when the room flooded with light, she saw the couple on the couch disentangling themselves from each other's arms, surprise and embarrassment written on their faces.

Eileen took in Joan's ruffled hair, the smudged lipstick and the dress riding high on her hips. She opened her mouth to give vent to her anger, but just in time remembered the sleeping household and closed the door softly. Then she stood with her hands on her wide hips. 'What the hell d'yer think you two are up to?'

'Nothing, Mam! Honest, we . . .'

'You keep quiet, young lady, or I won't be able to keep me hands off yer.' Eileen turned her wrath on the young man who was blinking fifteen to the dozen, his face a bright crimson. 'Who the 'ell are you?'

The youth swallowed hard before stammering, 'Me name's Philip Ryan.'

'Oh, it is, is it? Well, Philip Ryan, what 'ave yer got to say for yerself, eh?' When Philip didn't answer, Eileen asked, 'D'yer make a habit of sneakin' into girls' 'ouses when their parents are in bed?'

'It's all my fault, Mam,' said a tearful Joan. 'I asked Philip in.'

'I'll deal with you in the mornin', my girl,' Eileen warned. 'Right now you can get up those stairs.'

Joan looked from Philip to her mother. 'But, Mam . . .'

'Do as yer told. I'll see yer friend out.'

'No, Mam!' Joan had never felt so humiliated in her life. All the girls were after Philip Ryan but he'd chosen her. Now her mother was making a fool of both of them and he'd never look at her again. 'Please, Mam!'

'If yer've any brains in that thick head of yours, yer'll do as yer told an' get up them stairs. An' if yer wake yer dad, then heaven help yer.' Eileen opened the door just wide enough for Joan to slip through, then closed it again. She looked Philip up and down until he squirmed with embarrassment. 'Well, young feller me lad, what 'ave yer got to say for yerself?'

'Joan invited me in and said you wouldn't mind.' Philip's eyes were on his shoes. 'I'm sorry.'

He's telling the truth, Eileen told herself. The poor bugger's probably terrified. Still, I'm not having those sort of goings on in my house. 'No matter what Joan said, yer own common sense should 'ave told yer it's not proper to go into a girl's house without 'er parents knowin', an' sittin' in the dark snoggin'. Yer not that daft that yer don't know what I'm gettin' at, are yer?'

When Philip shook his head, Eileen asked, 'Where d'yer live?'

Terrified the big woman was asking for his address so she could go and see his parents, Philip croaked, 'Childwall.'

'Then yer'd better be off an' see if yer can get a bus.' With a finger to her mouth for him to be quiet, Eileen opened the door. They made not a sound as they crept down the hall, and as Philip stepped down on to the pathway, he'd never been so glad to be out of a house in his life. But Eileen wasn't finished with him yet and he nearly jumped out of his skin when she grabbed his arm in a vice-like grip.

'Yer know that song about the daring young man on the flying trapeze? The one who floats through the air with the greatest of ease? Well,' Eileen hissed, 'if yer ever again pull a trick like yer pulled tonight, yer won't need to get a bus 'ome, 'cos I'll kick yer backside so hard yer'll be flyin' through the air like that feller on the trapeze. Except it won't be with the greatest of ease.' She gave Philip a push. 'Now, scarper before I test me kickin' power.'

As she watched Philip run down the road as though his feet had taken wings, Eileen didn't know whether to feel sorry for him or angry. It was more Joan's fault than his, but what might they have got up to if she hadn't come down when she did?

As she climbed the stairs, Eileen sighed. Didn't her daughter realise that no bloke would respect her if she played so easy to get? It wouldn't have been so bad if Joan had been going out with Philip and the family knew him, but a complete stranger? She needed a good talking to, that young lady, and she'd get it in the morning.

Bill turned on his side and asked, sleepily, 'What's wrong, chick?'

'I've only been to spend a penny. Go back to sleep.'

It was always a rush in the mornings, getting Bill and Billy out to work, then starting breakfast for the two girls. Edna usually left the house before Joan, and Eileen was biding her time until she was alone with her wayward daughter, who'd avoided her eyes and had barely answered when spoken to. But Joan had other ideas. She had no intention of staying around for the ticking off she knew was coming, so when Edna left for work, Joan followed close on her heels, saying, 'I'll walk up the road with you.'

'The cute little faggot.' Eileen spoke to the empty room as she cleared the breakfast dishes. 'But if she thinks she's gettin' away with it, she's got another think comin'. Just wait till tonight, she'll get a piece of me mind.'

But as the day wore on and Eileen had time to think it all through, she wondered if it wouldn't be wiser to let the whole matter rest. If Bill heard them arguing and found out what it was about, he'd go mad. He'd be angry with Joan, but he'd be upset too, 'cos he thought the world of his children. They could do no wrong in his eyes.

In the end, Eileen couldn't make up her mind what to do and sought her mother's advice. After telling Maggie in detail about the events of the night before, Eileen asked, 'What shall I do, Mam? Have a good talk to 'er, or leave it an' see 'ow she behaves in the future?'

'She deserves a good telling off,' Maggie said. 'Fancy bringing a boy in when we were all in bed! And the lies she told, too, saying she was going to her friend's. I'm surprised at our Joan.'

'I'm not,' Eileen said with a sigh. 'She's different to the other two. They're like an open book, tell me everythin'. But not Joan, she's as deep as the ocean. I've noticed her changin' over the years, an' she's a right little snob now. Seems to look down 'er nose at us, as though we're not good enough for 'er. And haven't yer noticed, Mam, that she never brings any friends 'ome with 'er? Our Edna goes back to Bray Street every week to see her old friends, but Joan's never been back once.' Eileen banged the table with her clenched fist. 'It's this bloody 'ouse that's done it! She thinks we've gone up in the world now an' we're too good for our old neighbours. I feel like knockin' some sense into 'er.'

Maggie was thoughtful for a while, then said, 'I'd leave it be, lass. See how she behaves in future. She probably got the fright of her life last night and it might have taught her a lesson.'

Eileen managed a smile. 'I've got me doubts about our Joan 'aving learned a lesson, but Philip Ryan certainly did. I bet he wouldn't touch 'er with a barge pole now.' The smile turned into a laugh. 'I can see the funny side of it now, Mam. Yer should 'ave seen 'im runnin' down the road as though a ghost was after 'im. I wouldn't be surprised if he 'adn't wet 'is kecks with fright.'

With an imagination as good as her daughter's, Maggie could visualise the scene and she chuckled, 'He'll give Joan a wide berth in future, that's for sure. So let's hope they've both learned a lesson and forget it, eh? No good upsetting Bill and causing a bad atmosphere in the house. You'll just have to keep your eye on her, that's all.'

'I'll be watchin' her like a bloody hawk, don't worry. If she steps out of line again, I'll definitely tell Bill an' he can sort 'er out.'

Chapter Twelve

'I'll never be ready in time.' Eileen plumped up the cushion on Bill's chair and glanced around the room. 'Everything's done, but look at the state of me, I look like the wreck of the bloody Hesperus.'

'Don't panic, chick!' Bill was gazing into the mirror, wrestling with the knot in his tie. 'You've got half an hour before they come.'

It was Boxing Day, and young Billy and Mavis were having a party to celebrate their engagement. Because the Radfords' house was too small for the number of people invited, Eileen had happily volunteered to have it in their house. 'We should 'ave put the Christmas tree in me mam's room,' she fretted. 'We'll need all the space we can get.'

The tie now to his liking, Bill turned to his wife. 'Go upstairs and get yourself ready. I'll carry the tree through.'

'Do as you're told, lass.' Maggie's voice came from the kitchen where she and Mary were arranging sandwiches and sausage rolls on plates. 'You're fussing that much, you've got everyone a bundle of nerves.'

'Well, look who's talkin'!' Eileen waddled to the kitchen door. 'And who is it, pray, that's been rushin' round like a blue-arsed fly all day?'

'Not me.' Maggie gave Mary a sly dig. 'I've been as cool as a cucumber.'

'Eileen, for heaven's sake will you move yourself?' Mary covered a plate of salmon sandwiches with a damp tea towel to stop them from going dry and curling up. 'It's a big occasion for Billy and he'll want his mother looking nice.'

Eileen stood to attention and gave a smart salute. 'Aye, aye, sir.'

When she came down later, she gave a twirl to show off the dress Bill had bought her for Christmas. 'Well, 'ow do I look?'

'You look champion, chick.' Bill squinted through the haze of cigarette smoke. 'It looks a treat on you.'

Mary, her head to one side, nodded in agreement. The dress really suited Eileen. It was a loose-fitting crepe dress, deep blue with three-quarter sleeves and a cowl collar. 'It looks lovely on you, Eileen.'

'Me hair spoils it.' Eileen pulled a face at herself in the mirror. 'Old tatty 'ead.'

'Heat the curling tongs on the gas stove and I'll put a few curls in the front,' Mary said. 'It'll only take a few minutes.'

Mary was just putting the finishing touches to Eileen's hair when Harry's car pulled up outside bringing Billy, Mavis and Mr and Mrs Radford. After that, Eileen was in a whirl as the other guests arrived. 'Blimey,' she whispered to Mary, 'where we goin' to put them all?'

Billy had invited four of his mates from work, and Eileen had asked Milly and Jack Knight, Cissie Maddox and her husband George, and Doris and Jim from next door. With her sister, Rene, and her husband, Alan, Vera, Arthur Kennedy, Mary, Harry, and Harry's parents, Lizzie and George, there were twenty-seven people squashed into the living room and kitchen.

'Spread out, will yez, folks? The eats and drinks are in me mam's room,' Eileen shouted, pushing her way through the mass of bodies, her face glowing with happiness. After all, it wasn't every day your only son got engaged. She felt on top of the world in her new dress, and Mary had done her hair a treat. 'Help yerselves an' get stuck in.'

It was later, when all the food had been eaten, the dishes put away, and everyone had a drink in their hand, that Bill made his planned speech and Billy placed the solitaire engagement ring on Mavis's finger. 'A toast to the happy couple.' Bill raised his glass, his face flushed after a few drinks. 'May they have all the luck in the world.' He saw the tears rolling down Eileen's face and added, 'If they're as happy as Eileen and I have been, they won't go far wrong.'

'Go on, yer soppy beggar,' Eileen gulped before wrapping her arms around her son's neck, her tears falling on his shoulder. 'Yer a good lad an' yer've got yerself a smashin' girl.'

'Let's have some music.' Harry looked through the records and put one of Jim Reeves' on the turntable. 'Take your partners, but you'll have to dance on the spot 'cos there's no room to move.'

Eileen noticed Billy's friends looking ill at ease. 'Why don't you young ones go in me mam's room? You don't want to be with all us oldies.'

Billy, his arm around Mavis, took his friends out, followed by Joan. But Edna hung back. 'I'd rather stay here.'

'Go on,' Eileen urged. 'Yer might get a click.'

'Come on, George.' Cissie Maddox pulled her husband up. 'It's years since we 'ad a dance together.'

'Vera?' Arthur held his hand out. 'Shall we?'

Jack Knight winked at his wife. 'How about it, Milly?'

Soon the room, and the kitchen, were packed with bodies swaying to the strains of a waltz, then a quick step. 'I think we should 'ave booked Buckingham Palace,' Eileen whispered in Bill's ear as he held her close. 'There's no room to breathe.'

'It's a good excuse to hold you tight.' Bill nuzzled her neck. 'I feel all romantic.'

'That's the drink talkin',' Eileen laughed. 'It's amazin' what a few pints will do.'

The drinks flowed freely and the noise grew louder. Harry put on a Mrs Mills record of party songs and Eileen gave Cissie the nod. 'Come on, girl, let's give 'em a treat.'

With their arms across each other's shoulders they stood in the middle of the room and belted out the old tunes for all they were worth. The sight of two eighteen-stone women who were more than a little merry, with their mouths doing contortions as they sang, had everybody in stitches as they clapped and cheered them on. They made so much noise, Billy and his friends came through to see what was going on and it wasn't long before their voices joined in.

Everyone was too occupied to notice the sullen look on Joan's face. Why did her mother have to make a spectacle of herself? It was bad enough her being so big and fat without making a show of herself. It made her feel ashamed of saying she was her mother.

One of Billy's friends, Benny, was standing next to Joan and he turned to her with a huge grin on his face. 'They're dead funny, aren't they?'

'D'you think so?' Joan's lips curled. 'I'm going back in the front room, are you coming?'

Benny hesitated, looking to his friends. 'D'you think we should?'

'Yes, come on.' Joan took his elbow. 'The others will follow.'

From the other side of the room, Edna was watching. She saw the look of bewilderment on Benny's face as her sister pulled at his arm and knew he must be wondering what was going on. This was the first time he'd met the girl and he'd only exchanged half a dozen words with her.

She's a fly one, our Joan, Edna thought. But if she messes around with Benny, Billy will have her guts for garters.

Lizzie Sedgemoor and Milly Knight had joined Eileen and Cissie in the middle of the room to add their voices to 'My Old Man' and 'Maybe It's Because I'm a Londoner'. Then they started on all the old Irish songs, raising the roof with their enthusiasm.

Edna laughed and clapped with the others, but her eyes were on the door all the time. Half an hour later, Joan and

Benny still hadn't put in an appearance and Edna was worried. She'd kill their Joan if she did anything to upset her mother or Billy. Edna knew what her sister was like when there were boys around. She'd gone to one or two dances with Joan but was so disgusted with the way she flirted with every boy she danced with, Edna refused to go out with her again.

Bill was laughing at Eileen's antics as he went round topping up glasses. She was now doing her impersonation of Mae West and the audience were doubled up as she hitched up her enormous bust before standing with one hand on her hip and the other patting her hair. 'It's not the men in my life,' Eileen's hips swayed and her eyes narrowed, 'but the life in my men.'

'Aren't you having a drink, love?' Bill stood in front of Edna with a bottle of sherry in his hand. 'How about a sherry with lemonade in?'

'No, thanks, Dad,' Edna said. 'I'm just going up to the bathroom.' She elbowed her way through the crowd but in the hall she stopped at the bottom of the stairs and made sure no one was looking before stepping back to the half-open door of the front room. Not a sound. Oh, dear, Edna sighed, what do I do now? I can't barge in or our Joan will give me the height of abuse and make a fool of me.

Edna made her way slowly upstairs. She sat on the lavatory seat and told herself she didn't care what their Joan did. If she wanted to flirt with boys, that was her business. But tonight of all nights, and with a friend of Billy's, surely she should have more sense.

Edna made her way downstairs and on the pretence of

looking in the mirror of the hallstand, she cocked her ears. Still no sound. Not even the sound of anyone talking. And if they weren't talking, what were they doing?

'What yer doing out here, Sis?' Billy had been on his way to the bathroom when he spotted Edna. He gave her an affectionate hug. 'Why aren't you in there enjoying yerself?'

Billy had had a lot to drink but something clicked in his fuddled mind when he looked at Edna. He remembered someone asking where Benny had got to and now he put two and two together. His eyes went from Edna to the half-open door and without further ado, he pushed the door fully open. 'What the hell d'yer think you two are doing?'

Edna caught a glimpse of Joan and Benny standing in the middle of the room with their arms around each other and their lips locked. She just heard Benny's gasp of surprise before fleeing back to the party to witness Cissie Maddox doing her impression of Norman Evans' 'Over The Garden Wall' sketch.

'Well, I'll not forget our Billy's engagement in a hurry.' Eileen flopped down after waving goodbye to most of the guests. 'It's been one 'ell of a night, eh? What d'yer say, folks?'

'One of the best parties I've ever been to.' Harry's words were slurred, his smile that of a man who has had more than enough to drink. 'We should do it more often.'

'You, Harry Sedgemoor, are drunk.' Mary tried to look severe but there was laughter in her voice. 'You made a show of yourself doing that tango with Cissie.'

Arthur and Vera had stayed behind, with Mary and Harry, to give Eileen a hand to clear away the mess. But first, Eileen had insisted, a cup of tea and a sit down were called for.

'I don't think I've ever laughed so much in all me life,' Arthur said. 'You and Cissie make a very good double act.'

'Don't put ideas into her head.' Bill handed Arthur a cigarette. 'She's bad enough as it is.'

'Hey! "She" is the cat's mother, Bill Gillmoss! I'll 'ave me full title if yer don't mind.'

'Young Billy enjoyed himself,' Vera said. 'You certainly did him proud, both of you. And he's got a nice girl in Mavis.'

'Yeah, I'm made up for both of them,' Eileen said, kicking off her shoes and sighing with relief. 'Our Billy's a good kid an' he deserves the best.'

Mary took Harry's cup. 'Come on, let's get cracking and clear this lot up. The men move the furniture back and the women will wash up.'

'Bloody slave driver,' Eileen grunted, rubbing her swollen feet. 'Me plates of meat are killin' me.'

'You stay put, and me and Mary will wash up.' Vera rolled her sleeves up. 'Half an hour and we'll have the place back to near normal.'

'Except for me mam's room.' Eileen heaved herself off the chair. 'That looks as though a bomb's hit it. She's gone to bed with glasses and half-eaten sandwiches all over the floor, God love 'er.'

'I didn't see much of our Joan.' Bill's brows drew together. 'In fact I don't remember seeing her at all until she came over to say she was going to bed.' He shook his head. 'I must have had too much to drink because I counted four of our Billy's friends when they came, but I only saw three leaving.'

Eileen laughed. 'There were four, but Benny left early 'cos he had promised to go on to another party. Billy said he didn't say goodbye because there were so many people here he was shy. And as for our Joan, she went to bed early 'cos it's work temorrer.' Eileen bent and grabbed hold of the front of Bill's shirt. 'Now, Bill Gillmoss, if that answers all yer questions, get off yer backside an' get stuck in.'

There were no buses running and very few cars on the road as Arthur and Vera walked along Rice Lane. Now and again a group of revellers would pass, on their way home from parties, but otherwise the streets were deserted. Harry had offered to drive them to Vera's, pick up his two boys and take them to the Dingle, but Arthur said it would be better if they walked. Harry was more than a little drunk and it wasn't worth taking a chance.

It was a clear night but bitterly cold, and they walked briskly to keep warm. 'You can't walk all the way home,' Vera said. 'By the time you got there it would be time to go to work. You'd better stay at ours and get a couple of hours' sleep on the couch. The boys can stay till you pick them up after work.'

'What about Elsie Smith?' Arthur chuckled. 'Aren't you afraid she'll label you a scarlet woman?'

'You're not walking all that way home at this time of

night, Elsie Smith or no Elsie Smith. Let her think what she likes.'

But when they reached Vera's front door, Arthur held her arm as she reached to put the key in the lock. 'I'll leave the boys here because it would be a shame to wake them, but I think it would be better if I didn't stay. I don't want you getting a bad name.'

Vera pulled her arm free and opened the door. 'Arthur Kennedy, you are not walking all the way to the Dingle and that's that!'

The fire had died out and there was a chill in the room. 'I'll put the electric fire on to warm the place up. I don't know about you, but I'm chilled to the marrow.'

Arthur stood just inside the door, making no effort to move. 'Vera, what about the children? My two will still be in bed when I leave for work, but Colin and Peter will be up. Aren't you worried what they think?'

'What is there to think?' Vera asked. 'Colin and Peter know you well enough by now, they're certainly not going to read anything into you sleeping on our couch.' She slipped out of her coat and threw it over a chair. 'I'll make us a hot drink and then I'm off to bed.'

Sitting close to the warmth of the electric fire, her hands around a mug of steaming cocoa, Vera asked, 'Have you been to the hospital since I saw you last?'

Arthur nodded. 'Several times. But Sylvia still refuses to see me. The Sister said Sylvia gets so agitated when they mention my name, it's best if we leave things as they are.' He sipped his cocoa. 'When I went on Christmas Eve with some presents from the boys, I was leaving them in the Matron's office when Sister Duffy came in. She said

Sylvia was in a deep sleep, so if I wanted I could see her without her knowing.'

'And?' Vera coaxed, seeing the distress on Arthur's face. 'You'll feel better if you talk about it.'

'I talk to Sister Duffy when she's on duty, she's very understanding. She told me the doctors don't know how Sylvia has hung on for the last two years.' Arthur met Vera's eyes. 'And I don't know meself, after seeing her. She looked so old, like a wizened old woman, it knocked me for six. I wouldn't have recognised her, would have walked past the bed if Sister hadn't been with me.'

'I'm sorry, Arthur.'

'If God has any mercy, he'll take her.' Arthur's voice cracked. 'I can understand why she refuses to see me. Sylvia was always proud of her looks, she wouldn't want me to see her the way she is now.'

Vera could hear the distress in Arthur's voice and she stood up. Holding out her hand for his mug, she said, 'I'll get a pillow and something to throw over you, and you can put your head down for a few hours.'

When she came downstairs, Arthur was still sitting where she'd left him. 'Come on, take your coat off.' Vera put the pillow and blanket on the couch and turned round to find Arthur standing close behind her. There was a look of such despair in his eyes, she held her arms open and he walked into them. 'What would I have done without you these last three years?' he asked. 'You've been a tower of strength, my anchor.'

Vera stroked his head. 'It cuts both ways, Arthur. You've helped me as much as I've helped you.'

When Arthur put his arms around her waist and held

159

her tight, Vera didn't resist. This was what he needed, physical and moral support. But wasn't it what she needed, too?

'I've stuck to the promise I made all those years ago, that I would never do anything to hurt you,' Arthur whispered into her hair. 'But holding you close like this, it's hard to keep that promise.'

'Arthur, there's been times over the years when I've cursed you for making that promise, and for being the decent, honest man you are. If you had made any advance towards me, I wouldn't have turned you away.'

'Oh, Vera.' Arthur's cry was like that of a hurt animal. 'Don't say that or I'll lose what little self control I've got. I've wanted you so much, for so long, there's times I thought I'd go mad with the need for you.' He held Vera from him. 'I think you should go to bed now, Vera, before I go too far. I'm only human and I can stand only so much.'

'I'm not made of wood myself, Arthur.' Vera gave a nervous laugh. 'But seeing as it's Christmas and friends usually kiss each other at Christmas, there's no harm in a little kiss.'

Arthur looked down at Vera's upturned face and cupped it with his hands. His lips touched hers, like a feather at first, then they came back, hard and demanding. Vera could feel the hunger in Arthur's kiss and her body responded. Somewhere in her mind a warning sounded but it was quickly dispelled. For three years they'd kept each other at arm's length, played everything by the book. Surely now they were entitled to a little happiness? Just one hour, no one could begrudge them that.

Chapter Thirteen

'D'you know what I fancy, Mary?' Harry folded the *Echo* and placed it down the side of his chair. 'A bag of chips, with plenty of salt and vinegar on.'

'What?' Mary's finely arched eyebrows rose in surprise. 'After that big dinner you had? Well, you greedy guts!'

'That was four hours ago, pet.' Harry grinned. 'Anyway, it's not so much that I'm hungry, but it's ages since we had chips from the chippy and ate them out of the paper. And you know they don't taste the same once you put them on a plate.'

Mary lowered her knitting to rest on her knee. She was knitting a pullover for Tony and was in the middle of a row of a complicated pattern. 'It's half past ten.'

'What difference does that make? The children are fast asleep, your mam is sitting up in bed reading, and we'd only be a quarter of an hour.'

Mary gazed into Harry's deep brown eyes and couldn't refuse. 'Just let me finish this row. You go and tell me mam and bring me coat off the hallstand.'

They walked up the road, their joined hands swinging between them. They were passing the entry at the top of the road when Harry happened to glance sideways into the dark passage. The street lamp at the corner cast enough light into the alley for him to make out the figures of a young couple locked together in a passionate embrace. He could only see the back of the boy and the long hair of the girl who was pressed up against the wall.

They were past the entry in a few strides so it was impossible to be sure, but there was something familiar about the girl's hair that reminded Harry of Joan. He didn't say anything to Mary as they turned the corner . . . after all, he could be wrong.

There were only a couple of people in the chip shop and Mary and Harry were quickly served. Outside, they stood while they tore a hole in the newspaper wrapping to get to the bag of chips, giggling like school children given a special treat. 'Mmm, don't they smell delicious?' Harry opened his mouth wide and drew in the night air to cool the red hot chip burning the inside of his mouth. 'Lovely, tell your ma.'

'I feel like a big soft kid.' Mary's laugh tinkled in the quiet road. 'It's years since we did this.'

When they were passing the entry again, Harry slowed his pace to look more closely at the young couple. They were still locked in an embrace, but this time Harry could see the boy's hand inside the girl's coat, moving and exploring. He still couldn't see the girl's face but there was no mistaking that hair style. It was Joan all right.

Harry waited until they were in the house before asking casually, 'Did you notice the courting couple in the entry?'

'No, why?'

'The girl was Joan.'

'Joan! In the entry with a boy! Eileen would kill her!' Mary had slipped her coat off and stood with it over her arm. 'Are you sure it was her?'

'Yes, darling, I am sure it was Joan. And they weren't just kissing, either. The bloke was all over her. If any of the neighbours see her, she'll be getting herself a bad name.'

Mary's face clouded. 'Eileen would go mad if she knew.'

'Don't tell her, for heaven's sake.' Harry leaned forward. 'It's none of our business.'

'I've no intention of telling her. She's upset enough as it is, and I'm sure Joan's got something to do with it.' Mary laid her coat over the arm of the couch and sat down. 'Eileen was telling me the other day that she heard Joan and Billy having a terrible row the day after his engagement party, but when she asked what it was about, neither of them would tell her. But whatever it was, Billy hasn't spoken to Joan since. He won't even look at her, never mind speak to her, and Eileen said the atmosphere in the house is terrible when they're both in.'

'Well, perhaps I'm just being bad minded,' Harry said. 'For all we know, she might be courting the bloke. I'm sure she wouldn't go down a dark entry with any Tom, Dick or Harry.'

'No, I'm sure she's not like that.' Mary picked up her coat. 'Stick the kettle on, love, will you? The chips have given me a thirst.'

Bill gave Eileen a peck on the cheek as he struggled out of his coat. 'The hospital rang the Admin up today, with a message to ask Arthur to go there right away. Sylvia must have taken a turn for the worse.'

'Oh, my God.' Eileen wiped her hands on her pinny. 'Mind you, from what Arthur's told me, it would be a blessing if God took 'er.'

Bill walked to the kitchen to wash his hands. 'Harry's going up to the Dingle after tea and I said I'd go with him. See if Arthur needs any help, like.'

'I'll go with yez. The boys might need a woman to comfort them.' Eileen moved quickly for a woman of her size. She set Bill's dinner on the table, asked Maggie to see to the girls when they came in, and hurried upstairs to get changed.

'Am I all right to go like this?' Bill asked when Eileen came down. 'I don't need to put me suit on, do I?'

Eileen looked him over. Bill was very particular over his appearance. Shaved every morning before he went to work, he always had to wear a clean shirt. 'You look fine, love.' She chucked him under the chin. 'Yer vain enough as it is, but I'll still tell yer, you are the handsomest man in Liverpool.'

'Don't be so mean with your compliments, chick.' Bill grinned. 'You mean I'm the handsomest man in the world.'

Maggie had come in and she stood listening. 'I think you both mean the most handsome man, don't you, not the handsomest? Your grammar is terrible.'

'Oh, 'ere she is,' Eileen groaned. 'The walkin' encyclo-paedia. Don't yer ever wonder, Mam, 'ow anyone as clever as you could 'ave a bird brain like me for a daughter?'

164

'Come on, love,' Bill urged. 'We don't want to keep Harry waiting.'

Eileen picked up her bag and stuck it under her arm. As she followed Bill out, she whispered in Maggie's ear, I've always told yer the 'ospital gave yer the wrong baby. I'd sue them, if I were you.'

Arthur opened the door, his face white and drawn. He seemed to have aged ten years overnight. 'It's nice of you to come,' he said as he closed the door behind them. 'I appreciate it.' He put a finger to his lips and nodded towards the living room. 'The boys are in a terrible state. I've just had to tell them that Sylvia died this afternoon.'

'Oh, my God, the poor things. Shall I go in to them?' Eileen asked, her heart bursting with pity.

Arthur nodded. 'If you would, while I have a word with Harry and Bill. I don't want to say too much in front of the lads because they're upset enough.' He waited till Eileen closed the room door. 'Will you tell them in work, Harry? I'll have to take a week off to see to everything, and I'm keeping the boys off school.' He sighed as he ran a hand through his hair. 'There's such a lot to do, me head's splitting. Tomorrow I've got to go back to the hospital for the death certificate, then to Brougham Terrace. When that's done, I've got to see to the funeral arrangements.'

'Are you all right for money?' Harry asked. 'Because I can always . . .'

Arthur shook his head. 'Thanks, but I'm all right. I knew this was going to happen sooner or later, and I've been putting some money by each week.' He leaned back against the wall, his head lowered. 'It's the boys I'm worried about. When Sylvia went into hospital, I honestly thought she was going to get better and I kept telling them she'd be coming home soon. And it wasn't a lie, because the doctor on her ward told me she had a fifty-fifty chance. But in me own heart I've known for a long time that she wasn't going to get better, and I'm asking meself now if I shouldn't have told them the truth. Prepared them, so it wouldn't have come as such a shock.'

'Don't be blaming yourself,' Bill said. 'You only did what you thought was best for them.'

'You did the right thing, Arthur,' Harry said. 'They're bound to be upset, it's only natural. But they're young and they've got their whole lives ahead of them. It may take a while, but they'll get over it.'

Arthur led the way down the hall. He threw the door open and stopped on the threshold, tears forming in his eyes at the sight that met him.

Eileen was sitting in the middle of the couch with an arm around each of his sons. She was rocking gently, kissing one bowed head, then the other. She looked up at the three men crowded in the doorway. 'Gordon and David are comin' 'ome to our house an' they're goin' to stay for a few days, aren't you, boys?'

Two tear-stained faced looked up into Eileen's face and they nodded.

'We can, can't we, Dad?' There was pleading in David's eyes. He didn't want to move from this big woman who gave out so much love and sympathy. It was what he and his brother needed right now.

'Are you sure, Eileen?' Arthur could feel the relief course through his body.

'I wouldn't ask if I wasn't sure.' Eileen winked over the heads of the boys. 'I've told them you've got a lot of runnin' round to do, so they're goin' to keep me company.'

'Can I go and get me pyjamas, Dad?' Gordon slid to the end of the couch, eager to be away in case his Dad changed his mind.

'I'll pack some things for you.' There was gratitude in the faint smile Arthur gave Eileen before making for the stairs.

'Arthur!' There was surprise written on Vera's face. 'I didn't expect to see you.' She looked at his face more closely. 'What's wrong?'

'Can I come in?'

Vera held the door wide. 'Of course, need you ask?'

'Are you alone?'

'Yes, I've just put Carol to bed and Colin and Peter are out dancing somewhere.'

There was a frown on Vera's face. 'What's all the mystery about?'

Arthur dropped into a chair, his whole body weary. 'Sylvia died this afternoon.'

Vera gripped the edge of the table for support. She closed her eyes. 'What can I say, Arthur? Sorry seems so inadequate.'

'I've been expecting it for years but it's still come as a shock.' He was silent for a while, then said softly, 'I thank God once again for Eileen. I was at me wits' end trying to comfort the boys, and then Eileen turns up and takes charge of them. They're in her house now and she said

167

they can stay there until after the funeral. She's fussing over them, giving them the kisses and hugs that they need . . . something a man isn't as capable of as a woman.'

Arthur looked up at Vera and their eyes locked. This was the first time they'd been alone since the night of Billy's engagement party, and the memory of that night filled Vera with a guilt that lay heavy on her heart.

'Vera.' Arthur knew what she was thinking. It was as though, at that moment, he could read her mind. 'Don't reproach yourself, please. If you want to blame anyone for what happened that night, then blame me.' He stood up and put his hands on her shoulders. 'I'm not sorry it happened and I don't feel any guilt. Sylvia hadn't been a wife to me for over five years . . . ten if we count the war years when I was away. She didn't want me for a husband, didn't want me in her bed. So why should I feel guilty about the one and only night I held a woman in my arms? Especially as I love that woman and I hope she loves me.'

Vera laid her head on Arthur's chest as tears rolled down her cheeks. 'I don't regret what happened that night, Arthur, it's just that I feel it was wrong, when Sylvia was so ill.'

Arthur held her close. 'Don't cry, love, please? We're not bad, you and me. Just two ordinary human beings who needed to be loved.'

Vera sniffed. 'I haven't got a hankie.'

'Here, use mine.' Arthur dropped a light kiss on her forehead. 'I'll have to go now, 'cos I've got a busy day tomorrow.'

'If there's anything I can do, you will let me know,

won't you? If you need someone to help on the day of the funeral, you've only got to say the word.'

As Arthur was walking away, Vera called him back. Her eyes on the pavement, she said softly, 'I'll slip up to church tomorrow and light a candle for Sylvia and you and the boys.'

'All hands are swappin' beds tonight,' Eileen said as she took David's and Gordon's coats. 'Joan and Edna, you're goin' in Billy's bed, and Billy can sleep in your room with the boys.'

'Ah, ray, I don't have to sleep in the same bed as this one, do I?' Edna's smile was wide as she winked at the two boys. She felt so sorry for them, they looked so lost and defenceless. 'She snores something terrible, you know, and talks in her sleep.'

'I'm not moving out of my room,' Joan said, her flared nostrils white with temper. 'Why can't they have Billy's bed and he can sleep on the couch?'

'Because I said so, that's why.' Eileen glared at her daughter. How could she be so unfeeling?

'Well, I refuse to move.' Joan tossed her hair back over her shoulder, a sullen look on her face.

Bill had entered the room in time to catch Joan's statement and his face flooded with colour. 'Did I hear you say you refuse? Well, let me tell you this, young lady, while you're living in this house, you'll do as your mam tells you.'

Joan's chair crashed back and she flounced out of the room. Eileen looked at Bill and shrugged her shoulders, then put her arms around David and Gordon. 'Take no

169

notice of her, she's a bad-tempered little madam. I'll make yez a nice drink and then Edna will take you up and show yez where yer sleepin'. An' she'll find an empty drawer for yez to put yer clothes in.'

'Where's Billy?' Gordon asked shyly. 'Will we see him tonight?'

'He's gone up to see his girlfriend,' Edna told him. 'But he promised to be back early so you can all go to bed together.'

'That Joan's a hard-faced little faggot,' Eileen said when all the family were in bed and she was alone with Bill. 'She thinks of no one but 'erself. Not one word did she speak to those poor boys.'

'She certainly needs taking in hand,' Bill answered. 'She's getting far too big for her boots.'

Eileen was standing in front of the mirror putting a few dinkie curlers in the front of her hair. She lowered the comb, her face thoughtful. 'Bill, I've been thinkin'. Arthur's got no family, and neither had Sylvia, apart from a sister in America that Arthur hasn't heard of for years. There'll be no one to go to the funeral, only us and the Sedgemoors.'

'What have you got in your mind, chick?'

'It's the two boys I'm thinkin' of.' Eileen tapped the comb against her teeth. 'I don't want them to think their mother had no friends, that no one mourned her death.'

'So?'

'Couldn't we make it a good turn out, for the sake of the kids? Ask all the people that know Arthur to rally round? Doris and Jim next door, they like Arthur. And there's

Lizzie and George, Harry's parents, I know they'd come if they were asked.'

'Eileen, the funeral will be in the Dingle. How are they all going to get there? It would mean Arthur ordering enough cars for them all and he might not be able to afford it.'

'I've thought it all out.' Eileen sat down and took Bill's hands in hers. 'That's if you'll go along with it.'

'Do I have any choice?' Bill grinned as he squeezed her hand. 'Go on, spit it out.'

'Harry and Jim 'ave got cars, so they could take us. Arthur would only need to order one funeral car for him and the boys. And they could all come back here for a bite to eat.'

'You have got it all worked out, haven't you, chick?'

'I couldn't bear it if there were only a couple of people at the funeral, the church would be empty. It would be so sad for Arthur and the boys.'

'I agree with you and as far as I'm concerned, you can do what you think best. But you'd better have a word with Arthur first, see what his plans are.'

When Arthur came the following day, he looked completely worn out. He'd never sat down, he told Eileen, but now, thank God, everything had been seen to, all the arrangements made. He'd been to the Co-op undertakers and said they had taken everything in hand. The funeral was in three days' time.

'Have yer thought about who's goin' to the funeral?' Eileen asked.

'Not much to think about is there? There's only me and

the boys.' The sadness and bitterness in Arthur's voice brought a lump to Eileen's throat. She was glad she'd sent David and Gordon on a message to Woolworths in Walton Vale. She wouldn't have wanted them to see their dad so downcast. He was all they had left. 'D'yer mean yer not goin' to ask me an' Bill to come? Or Mary and Harry?'

Arthur lifted his head. 'Will you come? I didn't like to ask but I'd appreciate it if you would.'

'Of course we will.' Eileen tilted her head to one side. 'Shall I tell yer what I'd really like to do, that's if yer've no objections, like?' While Eileen was telling him of her plans, Arthur's eyes lost some of their sadness. While he'd been rushing around all day, dreadful visions had been flashing through his mind. A huge church, the coffin in front of the altar, and all the pews empty except for himself and his two sons. He was worried about the effect it would have on David and Gordon.

'Well,' Eileen asked, 'will that be all right with you?'

Arthur opened his mouth but no words would come. He couldn't express his feelings for this mountain of a woman who had a heart to match her size. Many times over the last five years he'd needed her kindness and her thoughtfulness, and she'd never let him down. But what she was offering now was more than a gesture of kindness, it was a lifeline for him and the sons he adored.

'I don't know what to say.' Arthur coughed to clear his throat. 'I should say "no", it's too much to ask of you. But right now, Eileen, I need help more than I've ever needed it.' Arthur pressed two fingers to his eyelids to relieve the pressure. 'I'd be more than grateful to take you up on your offer, and you have my heartfelt thanks.'

'Oh, it's not only me,' Eileen said, her hand waving away his thanks. 'Yer've got some good friends, yer know, Arthur, and they've all offered to 'elp. After all, what are friends for if they're not there when yer need them?' Eileen put her hands on the chair and pushed herself up. 'I'll put the kettle on for a cuppa. David and Gordon should be back soon and they'll be made up to see you.' She stopped by the kitchen door and turned her head. 'When Bill and Harry get in from work, we'll get our heads together and sort things out.'

Arthur took the cup Eileen held out to him. 'I'll give you the money for the food, but won't it be a lot of work for you to make a spread for so many?'

'Nah! There'll only be a dozen and that'll be child's play.' Eileen took a sip of tea, watching Arthur over the rim of her cup. 'Anyway, I'm not doin' the eats. Me mam and Vera are doin' them.' She saw the change of expression on Arthur's face at the mention of Vera.

'Have you seen Vera, then?'

'Yeah, she called this mornin'. She won't come to the funeral because of Carol, but she'll be 'ere to give me mam a hand.'

They were silent as they drank their tea, each wrapped up in their own thoughts and neither knowing that they were both thinking of the same person. And both with hope in their hearts.

Chapter Fourteen

'Can I take your key, Dad, in case I'm late tonight?' Joan was standing in front of her father, dressed up to the nines, with her hair and make-up perfect. 'I'm going to the Grafton and it means getting two buses.'

Eileen was sitting at the dining table, the *Echo* spread out in front of her. Joan never asked her for a favour. She always went to Bill because she knew he was a soft touch, believed everything she told him. But Eileen was wise to her daughter. She'd found her out in so many lies, she now took everything she told her with a pinch of salt.

'What time's the dance over?' Bill asked.

'It'll be late tonight because Ivy Benson and her band are on. About twelve o'clock, I imagine.' Joan saw the look of doubt cross Bill's face and hurried on to say, 'Oh, but I won't stay till the end. I might even be home before you go to bed.'

'Aye, an' pigs might fly,' Eileen muttered, rustling the paper.

Joan turned around and glared. 'I think you forget I'm turned eighteen now, I'm not a kid.'

'Eighteen or not, I don't like the idea of you walking all

175

that way home if you miss the last bus,' Bill said. 'It's not safe for a girl to be walking the streets that time of night.'

Joan's attitude changed and she said meekly, 'I promise I won't miss the last bus, honest, Dad.'

'Make sure you don't.' Bill slipped the front door key off his keyring and handed it to her. 'You be in here by twelve o'clock at the latest.'

Having got her own way, Joan smiled. 'Thanks, Dad.'

'She's got you for a right sucker,' Eileen said when they heard the front door bang. 'You always give in to her.'

'She's too old now to tell her to be in by ten o'clock. You're too hard on her, chick. I remember going to the Grafton with you when we were her age, and your mother never used to worry about what time we got in.'

'Because me mam knew who I was with, that's why she didn't worry.' Eileen glowered. 'We never know who our Joan's with 'cos she never brings any of her friends home. Don't you think it's funny that the only friend of hers we've seen is the one from Hanford Avenue? And that's only every Preston Guild.'

Edna was sitting quietly in a chair by the window, a romantic novel open on her knee. She'd been reading when Joan came into the room, and kept her finger on the line she was up to as she watched her sister through lowered lids. If me mam and dad knew what our Joan got up to, they'd have a duck egg, she thought. She never brought a girl friend home because she hadn't got one. She was only interested in men, and according to what she told Edna each night, in the privacy of their bedroom, it was a different bloke every night. And they were always handsome, like Clarke Gable or Errol Flynn, had plenty of money and were smashing dancers. But if these blokes were all as good as Joan said, how come they were replaced the following night by another film star look-alike? Edna went back to the heroine in her book. If her sister landed herself in hot water it would be her own stupid fault 'cos she was asking for it.

'Bill, wake up.' Eileen shook Bill's shoulder. 'It's one o'clock and our Joan's not in yet.'

Bill turned on his side, squinting in the glare of the light. 'What's that, chick?' He rubbed the sleep from his eyes. 'Did you say our Joan's not in yet?'

'No, and it's one o'clock.'

Bill shot up. 'Are you sure?'

Eileen clicked her teeth. 'Of course I'm sure! I 'ad a feelin' she knew she was goin' to be late, so I stayed awake, listenin' for 'er. But I expected her before now an' I'm worried.'

Bill slid his legs over the side of the bed and reached for his trousers which were folded over the back of a chair. 'She probably missed the last bus and has had to walk.'

'I wouldn't mind if I knew that's what's 'appened, but I've been lyin' here thinkin' all sorts of things.'

'I'll get dressed and go and look for her.' Bill struggled into the legs of his trousers. 'She'll get a good telling off for this.'

Eileen made a pot of tea when Bill went out and as she sat at the table her inside was churning over. It was dangerous for a young girl to be out at this time, you never knew who was hanging around. And when Bill came in, shaking his head, her nerves were at breaking point.

177

'I walked as far as the station, but there's not a soul to be seen,' Bill said. 'It was no use walking any further because I don't know which direction she'll be coming from.'

'Here, get this hot tea down yer.' When Eileen saw Bill's worried face, her anxiety was mixed with anger. If that little so-and-so was out there gallivanting while they were worried sick, she wouldn't half give her what for. 'You go to bed an' I'll wait up for 'er.'

'I couldn't sleep, not knowing where she is,' Bill said. 'I'll stay up with you.'

'It's daft both of us sittin' 'ere an' you need yer sleep more than I do.' When Bill went to object, Eileen said, 'She's probably strollin' 'ome with some of 'er friends, without a care in the world. She won't know we're sittin' here on pins.'

'Well, give me a call if she's not in soon,' Bill said, shaking his head as he walked through the door thinking of what he'd say to his daughter the next morning.

But when Bill came down at half past six, followed closely by Billy, Eileen shrugged her shoulders. 'She's not come 'ome.'

'And you've been up all night?' Bill pulled his braces over his shoulders and fastened them to the buttons on his trousers. 'Where the hell can she have got to?'

'Don't ask me,' Eileen said, putting their breakfast plates on the table. 'I've been sittin' 'ere worried to death.'

'What's up?' Billy yawned, stretching his arms over his head.

When Eileen explained, Billy raised his eyes to the

ceiling. 'I wouldn't worry about our Joan, she's quite capable of taking care of herself.'

'I keep tellin' meself not to worry, that if there was anythin' wrong we'd 'ave heard by now. They say bad news travels fast.'

'I'll have something to say to her when . . .' Bill broke off when there was a knock on the front door. 'This'll be her now.'

'It won't, yer know,' Eileen said, hurrying along the hall. 'Don't forget, yer gave 'er yer key.'

It was Mary standing in the pathway. 'I've just had a phone call from your Joan. She said she missed the last bus so she stayed at her friend's house.'

'I'll break 'er bloody neck for 'er!' Eileen roared. 'D'yer know, kid, I've been up all night, and Bill was up half the night, worried sick?'

'I told her she was very naughty and that you'd be worried,' Mary said, 'but she said she'd explain tonight, and then put the phone down.'

'I'll phone 'er, when I get me hands on her.' Eileen's face was red with anger. 'The little flamer!'

'I'll see you later,' Mary said, hurrying away. 'I've got me mam's breakfast on.'

When she got home, Mary said, 'Eileen's in a hell of a temper. She's been up all night.'

Harry broke off a piece of toast and popped it in his mouth. 'You can't blame her being in a temper. Can you imagine what we'd be like if Emma was Joan's age and she stayed out all night?' He reached for another slice of toast. 'I know you'll say I'm bad minded, but I'd like to bet it wasn't a girl she spent the night with.'

'Oh, you can't say that, Harry!' Mary said. 'The girl's probably telling the truth.'

'And I'm a monkey's uncle,' was Harry's answer.

Joan was first home from work and Eileen was waiting for her, hands on hips. 'Well, what 'ave yer got to say for yerself?'

Joan raised her brows, a look of disdain on her face. If only her mother could see herself. Big, fat, untidy and loud mouthed. I bet she never had many boys running after her when she was young. 'I told Mary to tell you I missed the bus and slept at my friend's house. There's no law against that, is there?'

'Don't you be so hoity-toity with me, you little madam, or yer'll feel the back of me hand.' Eileen gritted her teeth. 'Now, I want to know where you were all night. What's the name of yer friend an' where does she live?'

'Her name's Doreen and she lives in, er, Everton.'

'Whereabouts in Everton?' Eileen asked, trying hard to keep a rein on her temper. 'What's the name of the road?'

Caught unawares by the question, Joan floundered for a second. Then she brazened it out. 'I didn't take any notice of the name of the road but it's up near Liverpool's football ground.'

'Yer can tell that to the marines,' Eileen growled. 'I don't believe a word yer've said. It's a terrible thing to say about me own daughter but you are a liar, Joan, and yer don't fool me for one minute. But I'm not sayin' any more, I'll let yer dad sort yer out.'

There was an uneasy tension round the table as they ate their meal, and as soon as they were finished, Billy and

Edna made for their bedrooms out of the way. Joan stood up to follow, but Bill motioned for her to stay. He moved from the table to his chair and took out his packet of cigarettes, all the time his eyes on his daughter's face.

He waited till his cigarette was lit, inhaled deeply, then said, 'Well, I think you've got some explaining to do, so let's have it.'

Joan put on her timid, little girl look and said she'd left the Grafton early enough to get the bus but it drove away just as she got to the bus stop. 'I was frightened to walk home on my own, Dad, so Doreen said I could sleep at their house. I couldn't let you know because we're not on the phone and it was too late to ring Auntie Mary's.'

Eileen shook her head slowly in disbelief. What a bloody good actress her daughter was! So different in her attitude now she was talking to her father. Eileen could see by Bill's face that he was being talked around and she pushed her chair back in disgust. He's falling for it again, she thought as she ran the water on the dirty dishes. She can twist him around her little finger and he can't see it. 'He's making a rod for his own back and mine,' Eileen muttered as she banged a plate down on the draining board in temper. 'He'll come to his senses when it's too late.'

'Well, I never expected to see you tonight.' Eileen's face showed her surprise when Bill ushered Vera into the room. 'Where's Carol?'

'Colin's having a night in, so he's minding her.' Vera's eyes were shining. 'I've got some news for you.'

'I 'ope it's good news 'cos I've 'ad me belly full of bad

181

news. I need somethin' to cheer me up.'

'Where is everybody?' Vera asked. 'Are they all out?'

'Billy's gone to see Mavis, an' the two girls are upstairs. Edna's washin' 'er hair, and Joan's got a fit of the sulks because we wouldn't let 'er go out. She's probably sittin' on 'er bed callin' me an' Bill fit to burn.' Eileen clicked her tongue. 'The little faggot stayed out all night and 'ad us worried to death. And for once, Bill put 'is foot down an' made her stay in tonight as a punishment.'

Vera couldn't wait any longer to tell her news. 'I heard today that me divorce is coming through.'

'Oh, smashin'!' A smile lit up Eileen's face. 'So yer'll soon be a free agent, eh?'

'Yes.' Vera rubbed her hands together, 'I didn't expect it so soon, but from what the letter said, because I filed for it on the grounds of desertion, and it's four years since Danny walked out, there's no opposition and it will go through quickly.'

Bill came in from the kitchen with a cup of tea in each hand. 'I'm sorry we've nothing stronger to celebrate with, Vera.' He smiled as he handed her a cup. 'It is good news, isn't it?'

My goodness, Eileen thought, he hasn't half changed. At one time the very thought of anyone getting divorced would have horrified him. You made your vows at the altar to love, honour and obey, and in Bill's eyes those vows were not to be broken. Mind you, he wasn't the only one who had changed since the war. I mean, who'd have ever thought the day would come when women would be seen smoking in the street, or going into a pub without being accompanied by a man?

'D'yer think yer'll ever get married again, Vera?' Eileen's face was a picture of innocence. 'Do yer good to 'ave a man about the 'ouse again.'

Blushing, Vera pushed her hair behind her ears. 'Now who would have me, at my age?'

'Ay, don't be runnin' yerself down.' Eileen leaned forward. 'Yer a nice-lookin' woman an' any man with half a brain would grab yer, aren't I right, Bill?'

Bill knew Eileen was probing and his eyes flashed a warning. 'Vera will sort her own life out, given time.' He smiled at Vera. 'Eileen is right about one thing, though, you are an attractive woman, Vera, and you'd make some man a very good wife.'

'If yer did get married again, it would 'ave to be in a register office,' Eileen said, ignoring the look on Bill's face which was telling her to drop the subject. 'They wouldn't marry you in a church.'

'Eileen, if the time ever came when I did marry again, that would be the least of me worries.' Vera wasn't to be drawn. 'But you know what they say about "chance being a fine thing".'

Upstairs, Edna sat on the side of her bed watching Joan file her long nails before covering them with a bright red nail varnish. 'Where did you get to last night?'

Joan completed the painting of one nail before looking up. 'I told you, I went to the Grafton and missed the last bus home.' Her face was thoughtful as she studied Edna's face. 'If I tell you, will you promise not to tell me Mam?'

'I've never clatted on you before, have I?' Edna stood up and turned the bedclothes back. 'But if yer don't want to tell me, then don't bother.'

But Joan wanted to tell her. She'd had such a marvellous time the night before, she was dying to tell someone. 'If you repeat this to anyone, I'll never speak to you again.' She screwed the top back on the nail varnish bottle and put it on the chest of drawers. The sullen look disappeared from her face as she began to speak. 'I did go to the Grafton, and I met this American. He asked me for a dance, then stayed with me when it was over.' Her eyes were bright with excitement. 'He was lovely, Edna, very good looking and very polite.'

'What was his name?' Edna had climbed into bed and was leaning back against the headboard.

'August, but they call him Augie.'

'August!' Edna tittered. 'What sort of a name is that when it's out?'

'If you're going to make fun, I'm not telling you any more.'

Edna held her hand up. 'Sorry! I promise I won't laugh.'

'Anyway, he was with a friend who's going out with a girl from Woolton, and they joined us. The boys are stationed at Burtonwood, and Valerie, that's Augie's friend's girl, often goes up to the base 'cos they've got a bar there and there's a games room. Anyway, she was going back with them last night, and they asked me to go too.'

Edna's mouth gaped. 'You went to Burtonwood?'

'The boys were in a Jeep, and they said they'd get me back home for twelve o'clock. But I was enjoying meself so much, I didn't realise the time until it was one o'clock. I couldn't come home then because me mam knows there's no buses running that late.'

Edna was all ears. 'Where did you stay, then?'

'At the camp.' Joan heard Edna's sharp intake of breath and hurried on. 'I slept with Valerie, so you can take that look off your face. And Augie ran me to work this morning in the Jeep.'

'You're asking for trouble, our Joan. If me mam and dad knew that, they'd kill you.' Edna wrapped her arms around her drawn-up knees. 'I've heard the women in work talking about the girls who go to Burtonwood and they say they're no good. And they say that most of the Yanks have got wives or girlfriends back in America.'

'Augie's not like that,' Joan protested. 'He hasn't got a girl back home, and he didn't try to get fresh, he only kissed me. I was supposed to meet him tonight, but they wouldn't let me out.'

Edna was sorry now Joan had told her. She didn't want to share that sort of secret, not when she thought their parents had a right to know. 'Don't tell me any more, Joan, 'cos if yer get caught and me mam finds out I knew what you were up to, I'd get into trouble, too.'

Edna's words had no effect on Joan. As usual, the only person she was interested in was herself. 'He probably won't want to see me again after letting him down tonight,' she moaned. 'But I've got the phone number of Burtonwood so I'm going to ring him tomorrow.'

Edna snuggled down between the sheets. 'Bring him home and let me mam and dad meet him. If he's as nice as you say, they won't mind you going out with him and then you wouldn't have to sneak behind their backs.'

'I'm not bringing him here!' Joan flashed. 'If he met me mam, I'd never see him again!'

Edna shot up. 'What's wrong with me mam? She's easy to get on with and everyone likes her.'

'But she's so fat and common! She doesn't . . .'

Edna was out of bed like a flash and she slapped her sister so hard across the face Joan's head snapped back. 'Don't you ever say anything like that about our mam. I've a good mind to go down now and tell her what you've been up to.'

'You promised!' Joan held on to Edna's arm and coaxed, 'Don't tell her, please?'

Edna shrugged her arm away as though she found her sister's touch distasteful. 'From now on keep your lies to yourself. I don't want to know what you do, where you go or who you go with. In fact, you can do me a favour and don't even talk to me. Me mam is the best mother in the world, and let me tell you something else, I'm ashamed to say you're me sister.'

Chapter Fifteen

'Yer know, you an' our Billy are like a couple of daft kids on a Saturday.' Eileen was relaxed on the couch as she smiled up at her husband. She tried in vain to cross her legs but gave up in disgust. She should really try and lose some weight, but it would mean going without chips and roast potatoes, a sacrifice too great for someone who loved their food. 'Yez go out of 'ere with yer red and white scarves on, grinnin' like a pair of Cheshire cats. It's a wonder yer don't buy yerselves one of them big rattle things.'

Bill was combing his hair in front of the mirror over the fireplace and his eyes met Eileen's through the glass. 'You must be a mind reader, chick, I was going to ask you to buy me one for Christmas.' Bill grinned as he plucked the stray hairs from the comb and threw them in the fire. 'I don't know why you don't come to the match with us one Saturday. You wouldn't half enjoy it, the atmosphere is marvellous when the Kop start singing. They make up their own words to the songs and they're dead funny.'

'Oh, aye!' Eileen pinched at the fat on her elbows. 'An' 'ow would I get through the turnstile . . . jump it?'

They heard footsteps running down the stairs and both pairs of eyes turned to the door. 'There's no hurry, son, we've plenty of time.' Bill smiled. 'I was just telling your mam she should come with us one day. She'd enjoy it, wouldn't she?'

'I'll say!' Billy chuckled as a thought struck him. 'She'd probably march down the pitch and thump the referee if she didn't agree with him.'

'I think two fanatics in the family is enough,' Eileen said as she looked from father to son with love shining in her eyes. 'My two handsome men.'

'What are you going to do with yourself, chick?' Bill asked as he slipped his coat on. 'Are you going to the shops with ma?'

'Me mam's gone to Mary's to sit with Mrs B for a few hours. Since they got that television she's never away from there. She can't understand 'ow yer can sit in yer own room and watch pictures comin' out of a little box. Mind you, I can't understand it meself, but I wouldn't tell 'er that.'

'I'll get you a television one of these days,' Bill promised. 'It'll keep you company.'

'I can do without one, thank you. We'll need all the money we can get for when me laddo here gets married.'

'I come out of me time in three months,' Billy said proudly. 'I won't know meself, getting a man's wage.'

'We'd better get a move on,' Bill said. 'We'll see you later, chick.'

Eileen went to the door to see them off and when she came back to the living room a wave of loneliness swept over her. God, but it was miserable when they were all out. She sat down at the table thinking that if she was still in her old house she wouldn't have to wonder what to do with herself. All she'd have to do was open her door and there were bound to be neighbours in the street to talk to. Or she could go up to the corner shop and spend an hour chatting to Milly.

Eileen pushed the chair back and stood up. 'I'm not stayin' here on me tod,' she told the empty room, 'or I'll go crazy. I may as well join me mam in front of Mary's television.'

There was a murder mystery on the television and Eileen wouldn't budge until she knew who the murderer was. She kept looking at the clock, telling herself it was time to get the tea started, but her backside stayed glued to the chair until the play was over. 'I'd 'ave sworn it was the feller with the moustache who did the killin'. Yer could have knocked me over with a feather when it turned out to be the girl that did it.'

'It just goes to show,' Maggie said, 'you can't trust anyone.' She took the television very seriously and sometimes Eileen wondered if her mother really knew it was all make-believe.

'It was a good film, was it?' Bill asked as Eileen bustled round setting the table. 'I bet it wasn't as exciting as the match, though.'

'We won again, Mam.' Billy was so happy you'd have thought he'd scored the winning goal. 'And Everton got beat.'

'I just can't understand men.' Eileen stood with the knives and forks in her hand. 'This city 'as got two football

189

teams and yer'd think yer'd be glad when either of them won. But no, the fans are divided into two camps and they're daggers drawn! Harry came back from watchin' Everton with 'is chin touchin' 'is chest because they got beat, an' when he sees you he's goin' to get 'is leg pulled soft. Next week it'll be the other way round an' he'll 'ave the laugh on you. Honest, I wish yer'd grow up.'

Bill had bought the *Echo* on the way home from the match, and he'd been reading while Eileen was talking. 'Hey, Billy, listen to this. It says here that Liverpool might be getting a new manager.'

'Go way!' Billy sat down near his father, his face agog. 'What does it say?'

'They might be signing Don Welsh from Brighton, to take over from George Kay.'

'In the name of God, can yez think of nothin' else but bloody football?' Eileen banged the cutlery on the table. 'Bill Gillmoss, take that coat of yours off the couch and hang it on the hallstand. If the kids left theirs lyin' around, yer'd soon 'ave somethin' to say.'

'All right, chick, keep your hair on.' Bill winked at his son. 'Make a good referee, wouldn't she?'

'We'll 'ave less of the "she", if yer don't mind.'

'I think I'll go out and come in again.' Bill was still grinning. After such a good match it would take a lot to dampen his spirits. 'See if I can get you in a better mood.'

'Yer know, I am in a bad mood.' Eileen was surprised herself. 'And I don't know why, unless that murder film's given me the willies.'

'I'll take you out for a drink tonight, cheer you up.' Bill dropped his head in his hands for a second, wondering whether he dare say what he was thinking. His shoulders started to shake with laughter that he couldn't hold back. 'We could take Harry for a pint to drown his sorrows after Everton's defeat.'

'Ooh, yer can be a bad bugger sometimes, Bill Gillmoss,' Eileen said. 'Yer sit there gloatin' when Liverpool win, but yer've got a right gob on yer when they lose.'

'It's only in fun, chick.' Bill stretched his legs. 'And Harry can give as good as he gets.'

Eileen and Bill were calling for the Sedgemoors at half seven and they were getting ready to go out when Vera arrived with Arthur. It was so unusual to see them together, Eileen couldn't hide her surprise. 'Gettin' daring, aren't yez, walkin' out together? What's brought this about, 'as Elsie Smith died, or somethin'?'

A deep laugh rumbled in Arthur's throat. 'Vera's decided that seeing as how she is now a single woman, we don't have to worry about Elsie.'

'Has yer divorce been finalised, then?'

Vera nodded, her happiness showing on her face. 'All over and done with.'

'Yez are a lousy pair, deprivin' Elsie of a juicy bit of gossip.' Eileen laughed. 'I wonder who she'll pick on now?'

'I don't care as long as it's not me.' Vera stole a shy glance at Arthur before saying, 'We thought you might like to come out for a drink to celebrate. Harry's mam's minding Carol for us, so we don't have to hurry back.'

'Well, you're just in time,' Bill said. 'We're going out

with Mary and Harry so you can join us and we'll all celebrate.'

They sat in the snug of the local pub and Harry bought the first round. Raising his pint glass, he smiled at Vera. 'All the best, and may you have lots of happiness.'

Eileen lifted her sherry glass and said, ''Ear, 'ear.' She put the small glass down on the table and fixed her eyes on Arthur. 'When are yer goin' to make an honest woman of 'er?'

'Eileen!' Bill was shocked. 'It's none of our business!'

'Oh, God, 'ere he goes.' Eileen was sitting on a round stool which was completely hidden under her huge body, so when she slid round to face her husband she appeared to be moving on air. 'They're two of me best mates, aren't they? And best mates don't 'ave secrets from each other, so there!' She nodded to emphasise her words. 'If yer don't want to listen, Bill Gillmoss, then close yer lug 'oles.'

Bill shook his head. 'I give up. What would you do with her?'

Mary leaned forward, her hair swinging from her shoulders to frame her face. It only needed one glass of sherry for Mary to lose her shyness. 'Do what we all do, Bill, enjoy her.'

Arthur was watching Vera's face as he wondered how to answer Eileen's question. It was six months now since Sylvia died, time enough for him to sort himself out and help the boys come to terms with losing their mother. They were beginning to smile again, mixing in with other boys and starting to enjoy life as young boys should. Arthur felt it was time now to look to his own happiness and he had no doubt that it lay with Vera. He knew their feelings for each other were mutual, but each time he'd talked of marriage, she'd said they should wait until she was a free woman before discussing a future together.

Arthur shook his head to clear his mind when Eileen put a hand on his knee. 'Wakey, wakey, Arthur! We've 'ad two more drinks while yer've been asleep.'

Arthur blushed. 'Sorry about that, I was miles away.'

'Well, the men are goin' to drink in the bar so we girls can 'ave a good natter.' Eileen swivelled again to face Bill. 'I can't enjoy meself with my feller breathin' down me neck.'

Bill picked up his pint to follow Harry and Arthur. 'If she gets too personal, Vera, tell her to mind her own business.' He bent and kissed Eileen on the cheek, much to her embarrassment. 'Behave yourself.'

Eileen watched him walk away. 'He's an old stick in the mud, but I love the bones of him.' She hung on to the table as she lumbered to her feet. 'Shove up an' let me sit next to yer. I can only get one cheek of me backside on this fiddlin' little stool and it's gone all numb.'

'If you're after a confession, then you're out of luck,' Vera said. 'I've nothing to tell you.'

'Stop actin' the goat,' Eileen said, her eyes rolling. 'We all know you an' Arthur 'ave fancied each other for years, an' there's nothin' to stop yez gettin' married now.'

'It's not as easy as that,' Vera said. 'I only wish it was. But I don't know whether Arthur realises what he would be taking on. Carol will be with us for life. She'll never marry and leave home like other girls do, and I want to be sure he understands.'

'Vera!' Mary looked at her friend in disbelief. 'Carol's lovely! Any man would be glad to have her for a daughter.'

'Her own father didn't.' Vera sounded bitter. 'He was ashamed of her.'

'You stupid nellie!' Eileen's voice rose. 'Arthur's not Danny! Has 'e asked yer to marry 'im?'

Vera lowered her eyes. She couldn't count the number of nights she'd lain awake going over all this in her mind. 'He's mentioned it several times, but I keep putting him off. Now the divorce is through, though, I've no excuse for putting it off.'

'I don't believe I'm hearin' this,' Eileen said, her voice angry. 'If you're stupid enough to turn Arthur down, I'll never speak to yer again.' She picked up the three empty glasses and snorted, 'This is more like a ruddy wake than a celebration. I'm goin' for more drinks, and I don't know about you two, but I'm goin' to get blotto.'

Eileen banged the glasses down on the bar counter. 'Get those filled for us, Bill, will yer?' She jerked her head at Arthur. 'Come over 'ere a minute, I want a word with yer.'

They were a noisy, happy group when they left the pub at closing time. The drink had loosened their tongues and filled them with a sense of well-being. The three women walked in front of the men, their arms linked, with Eileen in the middle telling one of her endless supply of funny stories. They were too interested to notice the Jeep parked on the opposite side of the road, or the young girl sitting in the passenger seat.

Joan slid down in the seat and lowered her head to hide her face. 'There's my mum and dad.'

Augie viewed the group with interest. 'Which one's your mom?'

Joan heard Eileen's raucous laugh and groaned. How could she tell him that the loud-mouthed, fat woman was her mother? 'The one on the end with the long auburn hair,' she lied.

'She's a nice-looking woman. Why don't we just go out and say hello?'

'No,' Joan said sharply, 'not tonight.'

'Honey, are you ashamed of me?' Augie drummed his fingers on the steering wheel. 'It sure seems that way.'

'Of course not! It's just that since I stayed out all night that time, me mum and I haven't been on friendly terms. And I didn't tell her the truth,' Joan admitted. 'I told her I'd missed the last bus and stayed with a girl friend.'

'Oh, and you thought I'd let the cat out of the bag? Well, since I know, I wouldn't mention it. So there's no reason why you can't take me to meet your folks, is there, honey? We've been going out together for months now, and I would sure like to meet them.'

'I'll take you home soon, I promise,' Joan said, knowing it would be impossible now after the lie she'd just told.

Vera rubbed the sleep from her eyes and looked at herself in the mirror on the window ledge in the kitchen. There were dark circles under her eyes through lack of sleep, and as she ran the cold water to swill her face she thanked God it was Sunday and the boys and Carol were having a lie in. She'd have time to tidy around and make herself

195

presentable before they came down for breakfast.

By ten o'clock Vera had finished her work. The living room was tidy, the fire had been raked out and reset, and she was washed and dressed. But although she'd kept herself busy, she couldn't keep her thoughts away from Arthur. Last night she'd had a good excuse for saying goodnight to him at the bottom of the street because she had to pick Carol up from the Sedgemoors', and as she'd said, it was late. But he was coming this afternoon at two o'clock and she knew he wouldn't listen to any more excuses. Vera took a deep breath and the pain in her chest was like a knife turning. She didn't want to send Arthur away, didn't want to lose him. She loved him so much she couldn't bear the thought of never seeing him again. But the fear in her heart wouldn't go away.

Vera called Colin and Peter as she climbed the stairs. 'Come on, sleepy heads, time to get up.' She knocked hard on their bedroom door. 'It's nearly dinner time.'

Carol was already out of bed and trying, in her own way, to pull her dress over her head. 'That's a good girl.' Vera pulled the dress down and fastened the three pearl buttons at the back. Carol was twelve now, and although she was a big girl for her age, she had the mentality of a four year old. She was able to do most things for herself but needed watching constantly. Vera never allowed her to play out in case she wandered off and got lost, and she'd never asked the other children in the street to keep an eye on her because she knew from experience that children could be very cruel.

'Come on, down we go.' As Vera walked down the stairs behind her daughter, her thoughts were on Arthur.

He was very kind to Carol and very patient, and Carol thought the world of him. But would it work out?

These were the thoughts running through Vera's mind as she stood in the tiny kitchen frying bacon and eggs for breakfast. And when the children were sitting at the table talking she couldn't concentrate on the conversation.

'You're very quiet, Mum,' Colin said. 'Have you got a hangover?'

'I don't drink enough to get a hangover, you know that.' Vera smiled at her elder son. Colin was twenty and, like Peter, favoured Vera in looks. He was courting and spent much of his time at the home of his girlfriend, Glenda. 'I think I'm in for a cold, 'cos my head's splitting.'

Peter rubbed a piece of bread in the bacon dip and his face took on a look of pure bliss when he took a mouthful. 'You can't beat a Sunday breakfast,' he said, with his mouth half full. 'Did you go out with Arthur?'

Vera nodded. 'And the Gillmosses and the Sedgemoors. We had . . .' A knock on the front door took Vera's eyes to the clock on the mantelpiece. Half eleven, and Arthur wasn't due till two. 'I wonder who that can be?'

'Shall I go?' Colin asked.

'No, I'll go.' Vera stood up. 'It's probably a kid to say his ball's gone over the backyard wall.'

When Vera opened the front door and saw who was standing outside, all her strength drained away and she had to hold on to the door to stop herself from sliding to the floor. She opened her mouth but no sound would come.

'Hello, Vera.' Danny Jackson was wearing a smart suit,

his hair was slicked back, and he looked as sure of himself as he ever had.

Vera was staring at him as though he was a ghost, and when she didn't answer, Danny said, 'Aren't you going to ask me in?'

'Who is it, Mum?' Colin came to look over his mother's shoulder, and his face darkened. 'What do you want?'

Danny stepped back a pace. He'd expected to see a boy, not the man Colin had grown into. 'I came to see how you all are. There's nothing wrong with a man wanting to see his family, is there?'

Colin moved Vera aside. 'You've left it a bit late, haven't you? Anyway, we don't want to see you, so go back to where you've been for the last four years.'

Temper flared in Danny's eyes but it disappeared quickly and a smile crossed his face. 'I don't mean no harm. Surely I can come into me own house?'

Vera pulled on Colin's arm. 'Let him in before he starts yelling and the neighbours hear.'

Peter, a trickle of fat running down his chin, stared open mouthed. And Carol, though not recognising their visitor, ran to put her arm around Vera's waist. 'Mummy.'

'It's all right, darling, go and finish your breakfast.' Vera stood by the table, her gaze on Danny's face. What was he doing here after all this time? What was he after?

'Is there a cup of tea in the pot?' Danny walked over to his old chair and sat down. 'How are you, Peter?'

Peter gulped, not knowing what to do. He could see his mother was upset and Colin's face was red with anger. Why had they let him in? They should have chased him, sent him packing. Anyway, he thought, I'm not having anything to do with him.

Peter picked up his plate and marched silently out to the kitchen. Seconds later he reappeared, passed his father without a glance and made for the stairs. 'I'm getting dressed, then I'm going out.'

Colin rubbed his thumb across the corner of his mouth. He could see his mother was in a state of shock and didn't want to make things worse for her, but somebody had to ask the question. 'What did you come for, Dad?'

'I told you. I just wanted to see me family.' Danny's hands hung loose between his legs. 'I didn't come to cause trouble.'

'I'll make a fresh pot of tea.' Vera escaped to the kitchen. This wasn't the Danny she remembered. He was slimmer, quieter, better dressed and not so quick with his temper. The old Danny would have lashed out at Colin if he'd dared answer him back. Perhaps he's changed, Vera thought as she filled the kettle.

'You know me mum's not married to you now, don't you?' Colin fixed Danny with an icy stare. 'You're divorced now.'

'I know, son.' Danny spread his hands out. 'Honestly, I just wanted to see you all. I've wanted to for a long time.'

'You've left it too late.' Colin towered over his father. 'Four years too late.'

Vera came through carrying the teapot, Carol hanging tightly on to her skirt. She saw the anger on Colin's face and felt the tension in the air. The last thing she wanted to see was father and son fighting. 'Aren't you supposed to be going to Glenda's, Colin?'

199

'There's no hurry.' Colin was remembering the times he'd seen his mother taking a hiding from this man. He'd been too young then to stop him, but things were different now, he was a man. 'I want to know what's brought him here after all this time?'

'I'll deal with this, you go and get ready.' Vera nodded, her eyes sending the message that it would be all right. She wasn't afraid of Danny any more. 'Glenda will be waiting for you.'

Vera sat Carol on the couch with her coloured picture book, then poured Danny a cup of tea. She didn't speak or meet his eyes as she handed him the cup. Then she began clearing the breakfast dishes. Anything to kill time until both boys were out of the house. It was only when she heard the door bang, and the shadows of her sons passed the window, that Vera sat down. 'Well, Danny, what did you come for?'

'Why will nobody believe me? I've been wanting to come for a long time because, to tell yer the truth, I've missed you . . . all of you.'

'What's the matter, Danny, did your Dutch girlfriend throw you out? Is that it?'

Danny's expression gave no hint that Vera had hit the nail on the head. It would spoil his plan if she knew the truth. 'Leaving you was the most stupid thing I've ever done in me life, and that's bein' honest. I didn't know when I was lucky. I'd 'ave come back ages ago, but I was too proud to admit I was wrong.' Danny clasped his hands together and gazed into Vera's eyes. He had to make her believe him because he had nowhere else to go. That bitch had thrown him out, lock, stock and barrel. 'I want to know if you'll 'ave me back, Vera?'

Vera studied Danny's face. He's either a very good liar, or he really has changed, she told herself. But as Colin had said, he'd left it too late. Too late for her, and the children.

There was a rap on the window and Vera jumped. 'I'll see who it is.'

'I know I'm early, but I couldn't wait any longer.' Arthur stepped into the tiny hall and bent to kiss Vera's cheek. 'I had to see you.'

Vera put her hand on Arthur's arm, intending to tell him who was sitting in the living room, but changed her mind. Let whatever was going to happen, happen. No whispering, no secrets, everything above board.

Arthur stared at the man who was sitting at ease in the chair he usually sat in. 'Hello.' He let his hand ruffle Carol's hair as she clung to his coat. 'We haven't met before?'

'Arthur, this is Danny.' Vera's voice was calm. 'Danny, this is a friend of mine, Arthur Kennedy.'

The smile left Arthur's face and he stared with dislike at Danny. 'What are you doing here?'

'What's that got to do with you?' Danny glared back. 'Seein' as this is my house, I should ask you what you're doin' here?'

'No, Danny,' Vera said. 'This is not your house, it's mine. Your name was taken off the rent book when you did a bunk and left your family.'

'Well, I'm here now.' Danny's face was turning purple, his breathing heavy. 'I've come back to you.'

Danny could feel his anger rising and lowered his head

to try and control his emotions. He felt like thumping the bastard, whoever he was, but to show his temper now would only jeopardise his chances with Vera.

When he looked up his face showed no trace of the rage burning within. He ignored Arthur and appealed to Vera, his voice soft. 'Couldn't we have a talk in private, like? I'd like to ask yer some personal questions and I don't need a stranger present.'

'Forget it, mate!' Arthur didn't give Vera a chance to answer. 'I'm not going anywhere.'

Danny jumped up, unable to hold his temper in check any longer. 'Don't you poke yer nose in my affairs or I'll flatten it for yer.' He saw the look Arthur gave Vera and his lips curled. 'Oh, I get it!' He sneered, 'He's yer fancy man, is he?'

Vera stepped between the two men. 'You had me fooled for a while there, Danny. I actually felt sorry for you, believing you really missed your family and cared for them. Not that it would have made any difference because I wouldn't have you back for all the money in the world. But I would have felt some sympathy for you. But it was all an act, you haven't changed, not one little bit.'

Danny pushed Vera aside so forcibly she stumbled into the table. His face ugly with venom, he poked his finger into Arthur's chest, roaring like a bull, 'You sling yer hook and leave me an' me wife to sort this out. You've got no business here.'

Arthur pushed Danny's hand away before grabbing him by the lapels of his jacket. 'I'm warning you, don't you dare lay a finger on me. And for your information I am not Vera's fancy man. Oh, I would have been if she'd let me, but your ex-wife,' he stressed the last two words, 'has too much self respect for that. So watch that mouth of yours, unless you want me to close it for you.'

Carol, frightened by the shouting, pulled at Arthur's coat. 'Uncle Arthur, he's bad man.'

Without releasing his grip on Danny, Arthur looked down into wide eyes filled with fear. 'It's all right, sweetheart, you go to mummy. The man is just leaving.'

'Who the 'ell d'yer think you are?' Danny blustered. He hadn't expected this. It had never entered his head that Vera would have a new man in her life.

'I'll tell you who I think I am.' Arthur let go of Danny's lapels and pushed him away. 'I'm the man who's going to marry Vera.'

'Oh, aye!' Danny turned to Vera and the venom she saw in his eyes took her breath away. The mask had slipped and she saw him for what he'd always been. A violent, bad-tempered, wicked man. 'Yer don't believe he'll marry yer, do yer? D'yer think he's daft enough to take her on?' Danny nodded to where Carol was cowering behind her mother. 'He's havin' yer on so he can get what he wants. He'll fill his boots, then bugger off and leave yer.'

'That does it, I'm not standing here being insulted by a loud-mouthed slob.' Arthur nodded to Vera to open the door, and he moved so quickly Danny was caught off guard. Before he knew what had hit him, he'd been spun round, grabbed by the scruff of the neck and propelled through the door and into the street.

'A word of warning,' Arthur said from the height of the top step, 'which I would advise you to heed. If I hear you've been within a mile of Vera, I'll have the police on to you. That's after I've given you the biggest hiding you've ever had in your life.' With that Arthur slammed the door so hard it could be heard the length of the street.

Danny raised his foot in anger but checked himself before it came into contact with the door. If he made a scene the neighbours would be out and he wasn't going to fill their mouths, or give them the satisfaction of saying Danny Jackson had come crawling back and been thrown out.

Danny straightened his jacket, adopted a jaunty air and strode down the street. He wasn't finished, not by a long chalk. He'd come back when Vera was on her own. If that bloke hadn't turned up, another half an hour and he'd have had her eating out of his hand. Oh, he'd be back all right, and next time he'd be here to stay.

Elsie Smith let the curtain fall back into place. She'd seen Danny pass earlier and was still at the window when Arthur went by. She hadn't even started the dinner because she was too frightened of missing anything to leave her spec by the window. 'There's been some right goings-on at the Jacksons.' She folded her arms across her flat chest, the lines on her forehead deepening. 'Danny didn't stay long when the queer feller arrived. I told you there was something fishy going on with Vera and that bloke but you wouldn't have it. But he must have his feet under the table 'cos he's just thrown Danny out.'

Her husband, Fred, turned a page of the *News Of The World*. For two hours now he'd had a running commentary on the comings and goings at next door but one. He thought his wife was going to have a fit when she saw Danny passing, she was that excited. And when Arthur arrived she was so beside herself with curiosity her head nearly went through the window pane.

Fred laid the paper down. He didn't know why he bothered buying the *News Of The World* when his wife contained more gossip than the paper. 'I'm surprised Danny had the nerve to show his face in the street after all this time. He certainly won't get a welcome off any of the neighbours.'

Elsie's thin lips formed a straight, tight line. 'I'd love to know what's goin' on between Vera and that other feller. He's there nearly every night.'

'You'll find out soon enough.' Fred crossed his legs and picked up the paper. If anyone could find out, it was his wife, and she wouldn't rest until she did.

Elsie glared at her husband's back as she passed on her way to the kitchen. He never got excited about anything. All he lived for were the boys, his work and reading the blasted papers.

Elsie opened the oven door to get the roasting tin out. Her husband forgotten, her thoughts went again to the Jacksons. She'd have given anything to have been a fly on the wall when Danny and Arthur met. I bet there was a right bust up, she thought. Anyway, she'd get talking to Lizzie Sedgemoor tomorrow and just casually mention she'd seen Danny. Lizzie was friendly with Vera, so she was bound to know what was going on. Elsie bent to light the gas in the oven, a half smile on her face. Yes, that's what she'd do.

Chapter Sixteen

It was Wednesday afternoon and Mary was sitting across the table from Eileen telling of Tony's exploits at school while they waited for Vera. It was Eileen's turn for their usual get-together when they exchanged gossip over tea and cakes.

'He fell and scraped his knee,' Mary said. 'It looked really sore but he said it didn't hurt. In fact he looked quite proud of himself.'

'You don't know how lucky yer are with 'im. Remember what our Billy was like? A real tearaway, he was!' Eileen grinned. 'He broke more windows in our street playing footie than all his mates put together. We had many a good laugh over our Billy's antics though, didn't we?'

Mary flicked her head, sending her blonde hair cascading over her shoulders. 'If our Tony grows up to be as nice as him, I'll consider meself lucky.'

'Yeah, he's a cracker.' Eileen's eyes shone with pride. 'Yer don't get many like 'im in a pound.'

When the expected knock came, Mary stood up. 'I'll go.'

'I'm sorry I'm late.' Vera cast a nervous glance at Mary. 'I hope you don't mind, but I met Maggie coming back from the shops and when she said she was calling in to see your mam, I asked her if she'd mind Carol for half-an-hour.'

'Course I don't mind.' Mary closed the front door. 'Me mam's always glad to see Carol.'

'Where've you been?' Eileen asked. 'We'd almost given yer up.'

'I called into Mary's for a few minutes.' Vera slipped her coat off and threw it over the arm of the couch. 'I've got something to tell you and I didn't want Carol to hear, so I've left her with your Mam and Mrs B.'

Eileen leaned her elbows on the table and cupped her face in her hands. 'Is it something excitin'?'

'It depends what you mean by exciting.' Vera pulled a chair out and sat down. 'I got the shock of me life.'

'Well, out with it,' Eileen said, shuffling to the edge of her chair. 'If yer keep me in suspense much longer I'll 'ave to run to the lavvy.'

Taking a deep breath, Vera related the events of Sunday, leaving nothing out. She carried on talking through the gasps of disbelief from her friends, until she reached the part where Arthur had banged the door on Danny.

'Well, I'll be blowed!' Eileen bellowed. 'Yer mean the cheeky sod just knocked on yer door, after all that time, an' expected to be welcomed back with open arms? I'd 'ave broken 'is bloody neck for 'im.'

'That's not all,' Vera told them. 'He came back again on Monday when he knew the boys would be out at work. He probably thought if he got me on me own, he could sweet talk me round.'

Vera gazed from Eileen to Mary, then lowered her head to watch her finger making circles on the table. 'He was as nice as pie at first, you'd have thought butter wouldn't melt in his mouth. But when he realised I meant it when I said I wouldn't have him back, he changed his tune and ranted and raved. He even lifted his hand a few times as though he was going to give me a belt, and I didn't turn a hair. I just stood there, staring him out, letting him see that I'm not the least bit frightened of him any more.'

'Well, I never!' Eileen's layer of chins moved when she shook her head. 'I know Danny's a hard clock, but I didn't think he'd 'ave the gall to show 'is face again.'

'It's a wonder Arthur didn't say anything in work,' Mary said. 'He has his dinner with Harry and Bill every day in the canteen.'

'Don't blame Arthur, I asked him not to tell anyone. And he doesn't know Danny came back on Monday 'cos I didn't tell him or the boys. They were angry and upset enough, it was no good making things worse.'

'And Colin stood up to 'im, did he?' Eileen chuckled. 'He'd get a shock seein' 'ow big his sons 'ave grown.'

'Well, it's all over now,' Vera said. 'We've seen the last of Danny Jackson.'

'I wouldn't bank on that,' Eileen said. 'He's got nerve enough for anythin'.'

'No, he'll not be back.' Vera twisted a lock of hair that had fallen across her face. 'When I think of it I feel real proud of meself the way I stood up to him. As cool as a cucumber, I asked him to leave because the very sight of him made me want to vomit, made my skin crawl.'

'That's tellin' him, kiddo!' Eileen touched her friend's shoulder. 'I'm proud of yer.'

'You've got more guts than me,' Mary said. 'I'd have run a mile from him.'

'It was seeing him and Arthur together that gave me the courage. Arthur would make ten of him, any day.'

'But yer won't marry 'im?' Eileen clicked her tongue. 'Yer want yer bumps feelin', Vera.'

Vera tilted her head to one side and her eyes locked with Eileen's. 'Me and Arthur had a good talk on Sunday, and I got a feeling someone had been telling tales out of school. Am I right, Eileen?'

Eileen had the grace to blush. 'Well, yer both me mates, aren't yer? An' if yer think I'm just goin' to sit back an' let two of me mates ruin their lives, yer've got another think comin'.'

'I'm not angry, Eileen, I'm glad you did. You were right about Arthur, and I was wrong. He's a good man and I'm counting my blessings.'

Eileen leaned forward, her heavy bust resting on the table. 'Yer mean yer goin' to marry 'im?'

'Yes. I've told Colin and Peter and they're over the moon.'

'Yippee! I can buy meself a big 'at now!' Eileen brought her clenched fist down on the table, her eyes lost in the folds of flesh on her chubby, smiling face. 'I'll get a good one so it will do for when our Billy gets married.'

Eileen's excitement was contagious and Vera felt happiness bubbling inside her. 'Hey, slow down, Eileen! We won't be getting married for ages. Don't forget there'll be seven of us with Arthur's two boys, so we'll need a bigger house.' Vera knew she sounded like a young girl instead of a forty-four-year-old woman, but she was so happy she wanted to share it with her friends. 'Anyway, Arthur said he's going to court me properly first.'

'Oh, my God, love's young dream.' Eileen was so excited her backside kept leaving the seat of her chair. 'A real Sir Galahad, is Arthur. All he needs is a white 'orse.' She opened her mouth and let out a roar of laughter. 'I can just imagine Elsie Smith's face if he trotted down the street on a 'orse and tethered it to the lamppost.'

Vera joined in her laughter. 'Arthur said he's going to knock on Elsie's door and introduce himself. He's heard that much about her he can't wait to meet her, I'm sure he thinks I exaggerate when I tell him how nosy she is.'

Mary's eyes were all dreamy. 'We've all hoped this would happen, Vera, and I'm made up for you. Arthur's a lovely, kind man and he'll make you a marvellous husband.'

Vera's face became serious. 'You're both used to being spoilt by your husbands, but I've never known it before. I've never been treated as though I'm someone special. Never been waited on, had doors opened for me or been given presents of flowers and chocolates. But Arthur does all those things and it's boosted my confidence, given me back my pride.'

'Keep that up an' yer'll 'ave me bawlin' me eyes out.' Eileen sniffed up. 'Before I put the kettle on, just answer me one question. Do yer love the man?'

A blush covered Vera's face. 'Yes, I love him.'

* * *

'All the excitement,' Eileen laughed. 'Just like yer see on the films, only better like.'

'You're a sucker for a happy ending, aren't you, chick?' Bill had listened in silence, his face changing from surprise to pleasure as Eileen brought him up-to-date with the news. No one could tell a story as well as his wife, even if she did add little details of her own to make it more dramatic. 'I'm very pleased for both of them. In fact it's good news all round, because Arthur's two boys need a woman to look after them. They need a proper home where there'll be a fire lit when they come in and a meal on the table.'

The door burst open and Edna appeared. 'Mam, our Joan must have me new blouse on, I've looked every-where for it.'

Eileen shook her head, tutting, 'She's a little flamer, that one.'

'It's not fair, Mam!' Edna said indignantly. 'I only bought it on Wednesday an' I haven't even worn it meself yet.'

'I'll 'ave a word with 'er when she comes in.' Eileen could understand Edna's frustration. She didn't earn much as a junior shop assistant and had to count every penny. 'When I've finished with 'er, she won't be borrowin' any more of yer clothes.'

'She had no right to take it without askin'.' Edna's face was flushed with the injustice of it. 'I had to save up for four weeks to buy it.'

'I'll have a word with her, love,' Bill said. 'She won't do it again.'

'I don't want it back, she can keep it.' Edna fled from

the room and tears streamed down her face as she climbed the stairs. She'd had her eye on the pink satin blouse for weeks and was so proud when she'd walked out of Etam's with it. And when she'd tried it on in front of the mirror in the bedroom, she thought it really suited her.

Edna sat on the side of the bed, devastated. She'd meant what she said about not wanting the blouse back. Now Joan had worn it, it wasn't new any more, so her sister could keep it. But she'd make her pay for it, right down to the last penny.

Edna snuggled under the bedclothes in the darkened bedroom waiting for her sister. She was dead tired and only determination kept her from dropping off to sleep. The hands on the illuminated clock told her it was a quarter to twelve so she shouldn't have much longer to wait. Billy had not long come in and she could hear him moving around in the room next door. He was a smasher, their Billy, always happy and good humoured. What a pity their Joan wasn't the same.

Edna heard the key in the lock and raised her head from the pillow to listen for footsteps on the stairs. When the door opened and Joan crossed to switch the bedside lamp on, Edna closed her eyes and pretended to be asleep. Through half-closed lids she watched her sister take her coat off, revealing the dusky pink blouse with the lace collar.

Joan hung her coat in the wardrobe and turned to find Edna sitting on the side of the bed. 'I thought you were asleep.'

'You mean you hoped I was.' Edna's face was blazing.

'You can't keep yer hands off anything, can you? Greedy and selfish, that's what you are.'

Joan pulled the blouse over her head and threw it on Edna's bed, a sneer on her sulky face. 'Here, cry baby, take it.'

'Not on your life, I won't!' Edna was off the bed like a flash and shoved the blouse into Joan's face. 'You needn't think I'm wearing this after you.' Her nose wrinkled. 'It stinks of your scent.' Mindful of the sleeping household, she lowered her voice. 'I want the money for a new one and yer can keep this, seein' as you like it so much.'

'That's a laugh,' Joan spoke scornfully. 'Just try and get the money off me.'

'Oh, I don't have to, me mam will!' Edna watched the change of expression on her sister's face and derived some satisfaction from it. 'Yes, I told me mam and dad.'

Joan's eyes narrowed. 'Running to Mummy to tell tales, eh? Why don't you grow up?'

'I didn't tell Mummy and Daddy,' Edna mimicked her sister's voice, 'I told me mam and dad.'

Joan dropped her head. All this fuss over a stupid blouse. But the last thing she wanted was trouble with her parents. So her face took on a look of penitence. 'I didn't think you'd mine me borrowing it, and I'm sorry. I'll wash and iron it for you.'

'Don't bother, I don't want the blouse, I want the money for it.' Edna turned her back in disgust and climbed into bed. 'And if you don't give it to me, I'll tell me mam.' She turned on her side and pulled the bed-clothes up to her ears. She wouldn't have minded if Joan didn't have many clothes, but she had a wardrobe full of them. Anyway, perhaps this would teach her sister not to take something that didn't belong to her. 'Put the light out and let me get to sleep.'

Billy inserted the key in the lock, then turned his head to look at Mavis. 'I can't wait to see their faces.'

Her eyes shining with happiness, Mavis gave him a gentle push. 'Go on, hurry up.'

Eileen's greeting was one of surprise and pleasure. 'You're back early, aren't yer? Did yer mam throw 'im out, Mavis? I wouldn't blame 'er if she did 'cos she must be fed up lookin' at 'is ugly puss. He spends more time at your 'ouse than he does 'ere.'

Billy sat on the couch and pulled Mavis down beside him. 'Where's me dad?'

'Upstairs gettin' his clothes ready for work tomorrow.' Eileen's eyes narrowed. 'Is there somethin' up?'

'Me and Mavis have got something to tell you.' Billy grinned. 'We'll wait for me dad to come down.'

Eileen's heart missed a beat. Oh, Lord, was Mavis in the family way? Then she saw the twinkling in Mavis's eyes and knew she was wrong. She lumbered to her feet, silently calling herself a bad-minded so-and-so. 'I'll give him a shout.'

'Hey, Bill!' Eileen yelled from the bottom of the stairs. 'Get that bag of bones of yours down 'ere, we've got company.'

'Be right down, chick!'

Edna had been lying on top of her bed reading when she heard her mother call. She put the book down quickly and made a dash for the stairs, jumping them two at a time.

'Oh, it's you two! I thought it was someone important when me mam said we had visitors.'

'Ta very much.' Mavis's laugh was high with nerves. 'I suppose we're just a couple of tramps?'

'I should 'ave known you wouldn't miss anythin'.' Eileen pulled a face at Edna. 'It wouldn't be a show without Punch.' Bill came into the room then and Eileen said, 'Here's the man 'imself.'

'What's all the fuss?' Bill smiled a welcome. 'I thought at least it was the Lord Mayor.'

'Our Billy wants a word with us,' Eileen said. 'So sit down an' let 'im get it off 'is chest before he conks out.'

Bill sat in his chair and lit a cigarette before turning to his son. 'Right, we're all ears.'

Billy's adam's apple moved up and down as he tried to dislodge the lump in his throat. 'Yer remember the Bowers that lived opposite to us in the old 'ouse, don't yer? You know, Jean and Gordon and their children, Jane and David?'

'Billy, I'm not goin' forgetful in me old age, of course I remember Jean and Gordon.' Eileen looked puzzled. 'What about them?'

'They're emigrating to Canada. They've been trying for over a year and they've just heard they've been accepted.'

Eileen's mouth fell open. 'Yer not thinking of goin' to live in Canada, are yez?' She felt weak with fear. 'Oh, my God!'

'No, Mam, of course not.' Billy's face was creased in a huge grin. 'I wouldn't move that far from you an' me dad.'

Eileen looked up to the ceiling and put her hands together as though in prayer. 'Oh, thank you.'

'What's this leading up to, son?' Bill asked. 'Because it is leading to something, isn't it?'

Billy nodded, then prodded by Mavis, asked, 'Would you mind if we got married sooner than we intended? Yer see, we'd like to try and get their house when the Bowers leave. Mrs Radford said she'd have a word with the landlord, an' she thinks we'd be in with a good chance.'

'Yer mean yer'd be goin' back to Bray Street?' Eileen leaned forward so quickly she nearly toppled over. 'Ooh, yer lucky things!'

'It would be a good start to married life for you.' Bill threw his cigarette end into the fire. 'A nice little house, and near Mavis's family and all your friends.'

'We mightn't get it, but I wanted to ask you and me mam first, before I went after it.' Billy hung his head. 'I feel a bit mean about it really because I've never been able to give me mam much money for me keep. And just when I'm going on full wages and could give more, I up and get married.'

'Let that be the least of your worries, son,' Bill said. 'What your mam and I have never had, we'll never miss. All we want is for our children to be happy.'

'Mam, how d'you feel about it? D'you mind?'

Eileen's eyes were misty as she gazed at her son. He was always so thoughtful and considerate, and she loved him dearly. She wouldn't half miss him when he was gone. She straightened up. This was no time for tears. 'I'm over the moon. I'll be able to come to Bray Street for me holidays.'

Billy stood up and walked over to her. He put his arms around her and hugged her tight. 'Mam, I love you so much I could eat you.' He planted a kiss on her cheek.

217

'Thanks for being the best mam in the world.'

Edna hadn't spoken a word, just sat and taken it all in. Now she asked Mavis, 'What colour bridesmaids' dresses are yer havin'?'

Eileen roared with laughter. 'Practical Annie! If they get married too soon, we'll all turn up at the church in our nuddy.'

'We'll manage,' Bill said, moved by Billy's show of emotion. 'I've got enough put by, unless you want a big posh affair.'

'We'll have what we can afford.' Billy sat down again and took hold of Mavis's hand. 'We're not starting married life off in debt. As long as we've got two chairs to sit on, a table and a bed, that'll do until we can afford more.'

'Bring yer mam and dad down one day, Mavis,' Eileen said, 'and we'll put our 'eads together an' see what we come up with.'

'Let's wait and see if we get the house first, Mam. Everything hinges on that.'

After Billy and Mavis had left, Eileen went into the front room to Maggie who was listening to a play on the wireless. 'Yer've missed all the excitement, Mam.'

Maggie turned the volume down. 'Why, what have I missed?'

'Get yer coat on an' come up to Mary's with me. I'm not goin' through the whole story with you an' then again with Mary. So shake a leg, missus, and let's get the show on the road.'

Maggie folded her arms, 'I'm in the middle of listening

to a play and I want to hear how it ends.'

Eileen made for the door. 'Okay, missus, if yer not interested in yer grandson gettin' married, then it's no skin off my nose.'.

Maggie was out of her chair like a shot. 'I'll get me coat.'

Chapter Seventeen

Vera had never been one for having neighbours popping in for a natter, or perhaps to borrow something. Not because she didn't want to be friendly, 'cos heaven knows there were times when she would have welcomed company with open arms. But she was afraid of Danny. She never knew when he was going to be in one of his foul moods, insulting and sarcastic, so she kept herself to herself. And when he'd walked out on her, she'd felt so worthless she became more reclusive. The only real friends she had were the Gillmosses and the Sedgemoors, and the only neighbour who ever called in was Harry's mother, Lizzie Sedgemoor. So when a knock came on the door on the Thursday morning, Vera opened the door with a smile on her face, expecting to find Lizzie standing on the step.

'Hello, Vera.' Danny's spirits lifted, thinking the smile was for him. 'Is there a cup of tea in the pot?'

'What d'you want, Danny?' Vera half closed the door. 'I thought I made it plain the other day that I didn't want to see you again.'

'I've been down to the docks to ask for me old job

back,' Danny said. 'I start on Monday.'

'I'm glad for you, but will you please go away now? I'm just getting Carol ready to go to the shops.'

'Surely ten minutes isn't going to make that much difference.' Danny's voice was sickly sweet. 'I've got so much time on me hands I don't know what to do with meself. Just a cup of tea and I'll be on me way.'

Vera's brain was ticking over like mad. She knew she shouldn't let him in, Arthur and the boys would go mad, but perhaps it would be quicker than standing at the door arguing with him. She pulled the door back. 'Ten minutes, Danny, no longer.'

Carol left her toys when she saw who their visitor was and ran to put her arms around Vera's waist. 'Mummy?'

'It's all right, darling, we're going to the shops soon. Come to the kitchen and help Mummy make a cup of tea.'

Danny looked completely at ease as he sipped his tea, talking about the old mates he'd seen down at the docks. 'I'll be glad to start work and get a few bob in me pocket. You know I've never been work shy, don't yer, Vera?'

Vera nodded. It was true he'd never been out of work and also true he liked a few bob in his pockets. But what Danny seemed to have forgotten was that she saw very little of the money he earned. He kept most of it for himself, to buy booze and cigarettes while she had to eke out the meagre pittance he gave her.

'When I get meself organised I'll be able to slip you a few bob,' Danny said. 'You can buy yerself some clothes, and something for Carol.' He smiled at his daughter, who was half hidden behind Vera. 'You'd like a new dolly, wouldn't you, love?'

'Carol has enough toys, and anyway, you'll need all your money to get yourself fixed up with somewhere to live,' Vera said to remind him he was no longer part of her life.

Danny seemed not to hear. Instead, he stood up and put the now empty cup on the table. He'd thought out his plan of action very carefully, and that was to keep cool, take things slowly and not to put pressure on Vera. 'I'll be off and let you get on with what you 'ave to do.'

Surprised, Vera followed him to the door. He was as meek as a lamb today but she knew better than to trust him. 'Goodbye, Danny.'

'Thanks for the tea.' With a wave of his hand Danny was off down the street, leaving Vera with a puzzled expression on her face. What she didn't see was her ex-husband's smile of satisfaction. Things had gone just as he planned. Another couple of calls like today, keeping his temper and being pleasant, and he'd have his foot in the door.

'Where are you off to tonight?' Vera asked Colin as they sat around the table having their tea. 'Anywhere nice?'

'Glenda wants to go to the Empire to see Donald Peers.' Colin screwed his face up. 'I don't want to go, but Glenda thinks he's the last word.'

'Go on, yer big cissie,' Peter laughed. 'Fancy going to see him!' He started to warble, 'By a babbling brook.'

Colin smiled good naturedly. 'Wait till you've got a girlfriend, clever clogs, and see the things you'll be doing in the name of love.'

Vera gazed from Colin to Peter. They were good boys,

never caused her a moment's heartache. Sighing, she pushed a potato around her plate. She really should tell them about their dad calling. If she didn't, and one of the neighbours did, they'd think she was underhanded. Taking her courage in both hands, she said, 'Your dad called today.'

The boys' mouths stopped chewing, the smiles left their faces. 'Aw, Mam, yer didn't let him in, did you?' When Vera nodded, Colin said, 'You should have chased him!'

'He only called to say he'd got his old job back. He wasn't here more than ten minutes.'

'Mam, he's trying to work his way back in,' Peter said softly. 'Don't you see that?'

'Yes, I do see that. But he is your father and one day you might feel differently about him.'

'No chance!' Colin said. 'I don't ever want to set eyes on him again and neither does Peter.'

'What about Arthur?' Peter asked. 'You're going to marry him soon, and he won't be very happy if me dad keeps popping up.'

'I'm not going to upset Arthur by telling him, and I don't want either of you to mention it. I don't want anything to do with your dad but I want to satisfy meself that you know what you're doing.'

'Mam, this has been a happy house since he went away, it certainly wasn't while he was here,' Colin said. 'Me and Peter haven't forgotten how he left you swinging to bring the three of us up on your own. Never once did he write to ask how you were managing or if we were all right. We could have been dead for all he cared.' Colin pushed his plate away. 'Me and Peter know what we're talking about and we don't want to see him again. We don't even think of him as our father.'

Peter nodded. 'Colin's right, Mam. When you marry Arthur he'll be our dad. He's been more of a father to us than our real one ever was.'

Colin picked up his plate. 'If he calls again, don't let him in. Tell him what we said and send him on his way.' He stopped halfway to the kitchen. 'Promise?'

Vera nodded. 'I promise.'

Elsie Smith was cleaning the inside of her windows with a chammy leather when Danny passed. Never one to hide her curiosity, she rested her clenched fists on the window ledge. She heard him knock at Vera's door and pressed her face against the glass pane waiting to see if he went inside. He was smiling and Elsie saw his mouth moving but couldn't hear what he was saying. Then she saw his expression change to one of anger and heard him shout, 'Let me in!'

There was silence for a few seconds, then Danny's arms started to flay as though he was shadow boxing. 'Fred's right,' Elsie spoke aloud, her teeth gnashing so hard her false dentures were dislodged. 'He's got a flamin' nerve coming round here throwing his weight around.'

Then Elsie saw Vera being pulled into the street and blows being rained on to her body. One arm of Vera's was covering her face while with the other she was trying to push Danny away.

Elsie threw the chammy leather down and ran to the kitchen where she picked up a long-handled sweeping brush. 'He's not gettin' away with that!'

Danny never knew what hit him. The first blow from the brush sent him reeling against the wall, a look of amazement on his face. When he saw Elsie brandishing the brush he roared with anger, 'Get back in yer house before I flatten yer, yer nosy faggot.'

By this time the noise had brought several women to their doors. Had it been necessary every one of them would have gone to Vera's aid. None would have stood by and let a man beat a woman. But one look at Elsie Smith's face told them their help wasn't needed. Only the size of six pennyworth of copper, she stood her ground, her thin lips pursed, her eyes blazing. Pushing the bristles of the brush in Danny's face, she taunted, 'Go on, flatten me, if yer dare.'

Danny made a grab for the brush but Elsie was too quick for him and side stepped. One of the women called out to ask if she should run up to the police station but Elsie shook her head. Although she looked fierce, she was enjoying every minute of it. Wait till she told Fred! This bit of news would get his nose out of the *Echo*. 'Well? Didn't yer say yer were going to flatten me?'

Danny looked at the group of women who had gathered, their arms folded, their faces telling him they meant business. He spread his hands out and spoke quietly, 'I only want to talk to me wife. What's wrong with that?'

Vera was leaning against the wall, her head dropped in shame. She was rubbing her arms where Danny's punches had landed. It had never been known for Elsie Smith to show compassion, but seeing Vera's distressed face filled her with anger. Once more the brush was pushed into Danny's face. 'Speak with yer hands, do yer, eh?' Elsie jabbed the hard bristles into the now frightened man's neck. 'On yer way, Danny Jackson, before I let yer have it over the head.'

Danny made one more effort. He looked at Vera and pleaded, 'Tell them I only want to talk to yer.'

Vera met his eyes. 'You are not my husband and I do not want you in my house.' Her gaze swept from Elsie to the group of neighbours. 'We are divorced.'

A cackle left Elsie's mouth. 'There y'are then.' She lifted the brush as though to bring it down on Danny's head and he took to his heels and fled down the street with Elsie in hot pursuit, the jeers of the women ringing in his ears.

Arthur knocked on the door and smiled when it was opened by Elsie. 'I've come to thank you.' He held out his hand. 'My name's Arthur Kennedy and I'm a friend of Vera's.'

Elsie shook the outstretched hand, her eyes bright with curiosity. Now she'd find out what was going on between this man and Vera. 'Won't you come in?'

Arthur accepted a cup of tea and although he'd been told what had happened that afternoon, he listened attentively to Elsie's version. 'You were very brave and I can't thank you enough,' Arthur said. 'Vera's had enough troubles without Danny making more for her.'

Fred took an instant liking to Arthur and they got on like a house on fire. Over the next half hour Elsie was in her element listening to Arthur talking about his sons, and how he and Vera were getting married when they could find a bigger house.

A smile crossed Elsie's thin face. Fred had praised her no end when she'd told him what happened. Told her he was proud of her, and he'd never said anything like that to her for donkey's years. And the neighbours had made a fuss of her, too. Everyone said how brave she'd been, but Elsie knew it wasn't bravery that had set her on Danny. In fact, if she'd taken time out to think, she'd never have dared stand up to him. It was the anger that had surfaced so quickly that sent her out with the brush. Anger that a man should raise his hand to a woman. Her and Fred might have had their differences, but in all their married life he'd never once raised his hand to her.

'Guess who's comin' to see me tonight?'

'How many guesses do I get, chick?' Bill smiled. 'There's a helluva lot of people in the world.'

'Yer'd never get it in a month of Sundays.' Eileen passed the sheet of notepaper across the table. 'Jean Simpson.'

Bill raised his brows. 'The girl you've been writing to in America?'

Eileen nodded. 'I worked with 'er in the munitions factory. She married a Yank and went to live over there when the war was over. She's home on holiday to see her family.'

'It costs a few bob to come from there.' Bill handed the letter back. 'She must have married into money.'

'He didn't seem to be short when 'e was here, but then none of the Yanks were. Our poor buggers were on about a shilling a week and the Yanks were loaded.' Eileen folded the letter and grinned. 'Our boys used to complain because the Americans got all the girls. They had plenty of money to give them a good time, and they could get stockings and lipsticks and things that yer couldn't buy here for love nor money.'

Bill took a packet of cigarettes from his pocket. 'What time is she coming and do I have to get changed?'

'Seven o'clock and no, yer don't 'ave to change.' Eileen picked up his empty plate. 'I hope Billy and the girls are 'ome handy so I can get their dinners over with. I'd like the place tidy when Jean comes.'

Eileen had just washed the last plate when the knocker sounded. 'I'll go,' she shouted, wiping her hands on the end of the tea towel Maggie was using to dry the dishes.

Eileen stared open-mouthed at the slim, elegant woman smiling up at her. 'My God, yer look like a film star!'

'You haven't changed a bit,' Jean laughed. 'Still the same Eileen.'

'I don't know whether that's a compliment or an insult.' Eileen closed the door. 'Come in an' meet the family.'

Billy was on his way out but stayed long enough to shake hands. 'You might still be here when I get back.'

'He's a nice-looking boy,' Jean said when he'd gone. 'I wonder who he takes after?'

'Ay, none of yer lip, missus, or yer'll be goin' back to America with two broken legs.'

Joan and Edna came downstairs together, both ready to go out. Joan's eyes filled with envy when she took in Jean's clothes, make-up and hair style. Although her parents didn't know about Augie, she was still seeing him and wanted to question Jean about life in America. See if it really was as good as he said it was. Her face was animated as she listened and she would have stayed longer if Eileen hadn't interrupted.

'Ay, aren't you two goin' out? Me mate comes to see me after four years an' I can't get a word in edgeways.'

Reluctantly, Joan stood up. 'Are you coming again before you go back?'

'I sure am.' Jean spoke with a slow American drawl. 'I want to catch up on all your Mom's news.' She looked from one sister to the other. 'You look like twins.'

Edna was delighted because she thought her sister was very pretty, but not for the world would she let her know that. She was big-headed enough as it was. 'If I thought that I'd put me head in a gas oven.'

Joan gave a sneer. 'I'll give you the money for the gas.'

'We'll have less of that,' Eileen said. 'On yer way before there's skin an' hair flyin'.'

Edna smiled at Jean before leaving. 'I'll probably see you later. I'm only goin' to the Palace with Janet to see Larry Parkes in "Jolson Sings Again".'

Bill chatted with Jean for a while, then said he felt like a pint. 'I'll leave you two girls to catch up on the news.'

After Maggie had retired to her room, Eileen made herself comfortable on the couch. 'Well, how's life in America? Is it like yer see on the pictures?'

Jean laughed. 'For some it is. I'm lucky, Ivan's people have money and we want for nothing. But some of the English girls were in for a shock when they got there. There's a lot of slums, and when I say slums, honey, I mean slums. Far worse than anything we've got over here. And some of the girls I travelled over with found themselves living in houses little better than huts. In fact, hundreds of them have come home again.'

While Jean was talking, Eileen weighed her up. Gone was the bleached hair with an inch of dark root showing, and the eyebrows which she'd always shaved off had grown again and were now nicely arched.

'Well, you seem to 'ave done all right for yerself,' Eileen said. 'Yer look proper glamorous in yer nice clothes.' Her body started to shake with laughter. 'Yer look like that ugly ducklin' that turned into a swan.'

Jean joined in the laughter. 'It was Ivan's mother who waved her magic wand. She nearly had a fit when she saw what her beloved son had married. She didn't say it, but I knew she thought he'd lost the run of his senses. The day after I arrived she tactfully said she'd show me around the shops. By the time she'd finished with me, even Ivan didn't recognise me. My hair had been dyed back to its natural colour and she'd bought me a whole new wardrobe. Everything to her taste, of course, I had no say in the choice of clothes she bought. When she finally decided I was fit to be seen, and not before, I was introduced to the rest of the family and their high-falutin friends.'

'Ah, one of those is she?' Eileen nodded knowingly. 'An' what did Ivan 'ave to say?'

'If you knew his mother, you wouldn't have to ask that. When she cracks the whip, everybody jumps.'

'Yer get on all right with Ivan, don't yer?'

'Yes, he's a good husband and we get along fine. But he's under his mother's thumb and what she says goes.'

'Come in the kitchen while I make us a cuppa.' Eileen heaved herself off the couch. 'We can talk out there.'

While they waited for the kettle to boil, Jean talked of

231

the house she shared with Ivan, the swimming pool in the large garden, the cocktail parties and the daily woman she had to do her cleaning.

Eileen poured the boiling water into the brown earthenware teapot. 'Yer've landed on yer feet by the sound of things.'

Jean wrinkled her nose. 'It's all right if you like that sort of thing.' She turned the conversation to Eileen. 'You've got a nice house here.'

It was Eileen's turn to wrinkle her nose. 'Kid, I'd go back to me old house any day. The people were more friendly. It's too quiet round 'ere for my likin'. All yer ever get from the neighbours is "Good morning, Mrs Gillmoss". I've been 'ere four years an' 'ave never 'ad a proper conversation with any of them, except Mary of course, and Doris next door.'

They carried their tea through and began to reminisce about the days they worked together. 'I still miss it, yer know,' Eileen said. 'I often think about Maisie Phillips and Ethel Hignet. And poor Willy Turnbull, the way I used to pull the poor sod's leg. I'd love to see them all again.'

'You're going to.' Jean laughed as Eileen's mouth dropped. 'I've been writing to Maisie Phillips and I've arranged a little get-together for next week. Maisie, Ethel, you and me. And Mary if she'd like to come.'

'Well, I'll be blowed! You live thousands of miles away an' yer know more than I do!' Eileen rubbed her hands together with glee. 'Ooh, I'm made up, honest. It'll be smashin' seein' them again. I wonder if they've changed?'

Jean tapped the side of her nose. 'You'll have to wait and see.'

Edna came home with her eyes and nose red from crying. 'It was a lovely picture, Mam, but awful sad.' Her eyes landed on Jean. 'Does Larry Parkes live anywhere near you?'

Jean laughed. 'Honey, America is a very big country. I'd say Hollywood was about two thousand miles away.'

Edna looked disappointed. 'He's lovely.' She said goodnight and made her way to bed to dream of the handsome man who blacked his face, loved his wife but loved singing more.

Eileen and Bill had just climbed into bed when they heard Billy's voice as his footsteps pounded up the stairs. 'Mam, are yer asleep yet?'

'What a bloody stupid question!' Eileen grinned at Bill as their son burst through the door. 'In the name of God, Billy, is the place on fire?'

'Mam, we've got the house!' Billy was so excited he could hardly get the words out quickly enough. 'Mrs Radford saw the landlord today and he said we could have it when the Bowers leave.'

'Oh, son!' The bed springs creaked in protest as Eileen rocked back and forth. 'That's marvellous news!'

Billy grinned, running his fingers through his hair. 'I haven't seen the Bowers yet, but I'll call tomorrow and find out if they've got a date for sailing.' He sat on the side of the bed, his heart thumping so loud he thought it would burst out of his body. 'I can't believe it, it seems too good to be true.'

'You're very lucky, son,' Bill said. 'There's not many couples have a house ready to move into when they get married.'

'I've told Mavis there's no more nights out for us, we'll have to save every penny. If I walk to work every day, that'll save a few bob a week and it all mounts up.'

'Have you an' Mavis decided where yer gettin' married?' Eileen asked. 'And is it goin' to be a quiet affair?'

'We're gettin' married at the Blessed Sacrament and I'm goin' to see Father Murphy tomorrow night so he can arrange to have the banns read out.' Billy started to blush. 'Mavis wants a white wedding an' I was wondering if Auntie Mary would make her dress?'

'I'm sure she'd be glad to.' The bed shook when Eileen burst out laughing. 'Mary's goin' to 'ave her work cut out over the next few weeks 'cos she's makin' my dress as well, an' with my size it's once round me an' twice round the gas works.'

'What about the bridesmaids, son?' Bill asked. 'Or aren't you going to have any?'

'We've talked about it, but haven't decided yet. We'll have to go careful 'cos we don't have much money.' Billy eased himself off the bed. 'We'll sort it all out when we know for sure when the Bowers are going. Anyway I'm off to bed. Not that I'll be able to sleep 'cos me nerves are as taut as a violin string.'

'You an' me, too, sunshine!' Eileen said. 'I'm wide awake now.'

'Goodnight and God bless, Mam. Goodnight, Dad.'

'Ooh, I won't 'alf miss him.' Eileen picked at the sheet. 'I love every hair on 'is 'ead.'

Bill lay down on his side and pulled the clothes up to his chin. 'Your husband has got to go to work tomorrow and needs his shut-eye. So if you intend staying awake all night, chick, don't hold a conversation with yourself, please?'

'Don't worry.' Eileen patted his shoulder. 'I'll talk in a whisper an' I won't argue with meself. If I get on yer nerves, just clock me one.'

Bill suddenly remembered what Arthur had told him about Danny fighting with Vera. What with Jean staying until it was time for them to go to bed, he hadn't had the chance to talk to Eileen. He half turned, intending to tell her, then changed his mind. She had enough to think about as it was, and if he gave her anything more to worry about she'd never close her eyes. He'd tell her in the morning. 'Goodnight, chick, try and get some sleep.'

Chapter Eighteen

'Mam, I've got a hot-pot cookin' in the oven on a low light, so will yer keep yer eye on it for me? I'll be 'ome before the gang get in from work.' Eileen, standing in front of the mirror on the wall in Maggie's room, gave her hair a pat. 'I've been in bloody agony all night sleepin' in me dinky curlers, and for all the good it's done I needn't 'ave bothered 'cos me hair still looks a mess.' She winked at Maggie through the mirror. 'Still, we can't 'ave brains and beauty, can we?

'Well, I'm off to see me old mates.' Eileen waddled into the hall where Jean Simpson was waiting. 'Ta-ra, Mam!'

Eileen banged the door behind her and fell into step beside Jean. 'Where are we meetin' them?'

'In the St George Hotel on Lime Street.' Jean slipped her arm through Eileen's. 'It's a pity Mary couldn't come.'

'She meets the children comin' out of school so she wouldn't 'ave been back in time.' They reached the corner of the road and Eileen spotted a bus coming. 'Run on, kid, an' ask the conductor to wait for me.'

Eileen took the seat by the window, leaving about six inches for Jean to balance her bottom on. And when the bus lurched to one side as it went round the dangerous bend by Orrell Park Station, Jean had to hang on like grim death to the seat in front.

'The Americans have no idea what we went through during the war.' Jean had forgotten how much damage had been inflicted when the May blitz was at its height, and as the bus made its way into the city she surveyed with sadness the open spaces where houses and shops had once stood. 'I know they lost a lot of men and we probably wouldn't have made it without their help, but they didn't have the bombing to worry about.'

'My Bill says it'll take twenty years to build the city up again,' Eileen said. 'We're givin' money to the countries we were fightin' so they can rebuild their countries when we're skint ourselves.'

'Ah, look at the poor old Rotunda,' Jean said, pointing a finger. 'I can't see them doing much with that.'

The bus drew to a stop in Lime Street where the two friends alighted. They waited for a lull in the traffic before darting across the busiest street in Liverpool city centre. Eileen paused for a second outside the hotel to smooth the lapels of her coat before following Jean through the doors. Her gaze swept over the people sitting at tables, seeking out her old friends.

'They're not 'ere yet.'

'Yes, there they are.' Jean pointed to a table near the back of the room and started to make her way towards it when Eileen's arm stopped her in her tracks.

'It's not them.'

'Yes it is. Look, they're waving.'

Eileen studied the two grey-haired women sitting at the

table and shook her head. 'My God, they 'aven't 'alf changed.'

Jean pulled Eileen forward. 'They're probably thinking the same about us.'

'I wouldn't 'ave known yez!' Eileen dropped into the seat, her eyes on Maisie Phillips. The bleached blonde hair was now a silver grey, and instead of the heavy make-up Eileen used to say she put on with a trowel, Maisie's face was just lightly dusted with powder. And her old trade mark, the bright orange Tangee lipstick, had been replaced with a soft rose pink. No one had ever known Maisie's true age, she'd been thirty-nine all the years Eileen had worked with her. But looking at her now, Eileen guessed she mustn't be far off sixty.

'Oh, it's lovely to see you again.' Ethel Hignet's ill-fitting false teeth left her gums for a second, then clicked back into place. 'You look very well, Jean, proper posh. And Eileen hasn't changed at all.'

'Yer mean I'm just as fat an' untidy as ever?' Eileen grinned. Ethel was still as thin as a beanpole, and her face as pale as ever. The only difference Eileen could see was the hair. It used to be black and frizzy, now it was almost white and dead straight.

'How's life treatin' yer both?' Eileen asked. 'Are yer still women of leisure, like meself?'

'Worse luck,' Maisie said. 'I couldn't wait to get out of that blasted factory when the war was over, but I'd give anything to be back. Not that I wish the war was still on, but I miss the company.'

'Yeah, me too,' Ethel said. 'Me an' Maisie are always talkin' about the old times, aren't we, Maisie?'

Ethel hasn't changed, Eileen thought. She still hangs on to every word Maisie says. Probably still follows her round like a lap dog. 'See each other often do yez?'

'Every day,' Maisie answered with a laugh. 'We live in the same road now. I got a transfer to Huyton not long after the war finished.'

'D'yez ever hear of Willy Turnbull?' Eileen asked. 'I often wonder what became of 'im.'

'He got married, yer know,' Maisie told her. 'Married a woman whose husband was killed in the war.'

'Go way!' Eileen sat back in surprise. 'I never thought that poor bugger would ever get 'imself a wife, although, God knows, he tried hard enough.'

'Got a ready-made family he has,' Ethel said. 'Took on a woman with three kids.'

'Let's go downstairs to the restaurant.' Jean stood up. 'We can talk while we're eating.' She saw the anxious glances exchanged between Maisie and Ethel and quickly added, 'It's my treat.'

When they'd chosen from the menu, Jean called the waiter over and added two bottles of wine to the order. Then she answered the questions that came thick and fast about life in America. She was full of praise for the country and its people, but as Eileen listened she had a gut feeling that everything in Jean's garden wasn't as rosy as she made out. You don't work with a person for four years without getting to know them inside out, she told herself, and unless I'm much mistaken, there's a bit of sadness behind Jean's laughter.

As the wine flowed, so did the conversation and laughter. Memories of the tricks Eileen had played on them all, especially Willy Turnbull, were talked about with hilarity, causing Ethel's clicking teeth to work overtime. 'Yer gave us many a laugh,' she said. 'Yer were as mad as a flippin' hatter.'

'It was her table manners I remember most,' Maisie laughed. 'The dockers' sandwiches she used to make with the chips in the canteen.'

'Eileen lives in a nice house now,' Jean told them. 'She's gone up in the world.'

'Don't kid yerself,' Eileen huffed. 'If goin' up in the world means bein' miserable, then I'd rather be a ruddy tramp.'

Maisie looked surprised. 'Don't yer like yer new house?'

'Oh, the house is all right,' Eileen said. 'It's the miserable flamin' people in the road.' Then she adopted her posh voice and proceeded to imitate some of her neighbours. With her hand in the air, her little finger crooked, she had them off to a T. Her three friends roared with laughter, causing heads to turn in their direction. Those sitting at nearby tables did their best to look as though they weren't listening, but their smiling faces betrayed them. When Eileen was in full flow, on top form, it was impossible not to laugh.

Jean wiped her eyes and took a deep breath. 'Just like old times. I haven't laughed so much since the war finished.'

'It's done me a power of good, too,' Eileen said. 'It's not often I get a chance these days to show off me talents.' She squinted at the watch Bill had bought her the first Christmas he was home after the war. She only wore it on high days and holidays. 'I'd better be makin' tracks or me mam'll 'ave her knickers in a twist thinkin' I'm not goin' to be home in time to put the dinner out.'

'Can we meet again before yer go back, Jean?' Maisie asked. 'I'd be made up if we could.'

'Yeah, sure,' Jean said. 'I'll drop you a line and make a date.'

Eileen was grinning as she stepped from the bus. It had been lovely seeing her old mates again. She'd have to ask for Maisie's address next time they met, then she could invite her and Ethel down one day. The laugh they'd had today had cheered her up no end, it was as good as a tonic. She looked at her watch as she turned the corner of her road and quickened her pace. The family would be in by now and wanting their dinner. Still, it didn't happen often so they couldn't moan. A mischievous smile crossed her face. They could moan all they liked, it wouldn't spoil the pleasure she'd had.

Eileen took the key from the lock and opened the door. 'I'm home!' Her brow furrowed as she walked down the hall. It was as quiet as a graveyard; where was everybody?

Eileen pushed the living room door open and froze. Edna was sitting at the table with her head in her hands, her shoulders shaking as quiet sobs racked her body. Bill, young Billy and Maggie were standing like statues by the fireplace, their faces grim.

'What's up?' Eileen croaked, her heart doing somersaults. Then she noticed Joan was missing. 'Where's our Joan?'

'That's what we're trying to figure out,' Bill said. 'She

242

went into the shop to see Edna this afternoon and said she wasn't coming home. Told her she was going to live with a friend.'

'Oh, she's pullin' her leg.' Eileen let out a sigh of relief. 'She's probably gone to the pictures straight from work.'

Edna lifted her head, her eyes red-rimmed. 'She wasn't pulling me leg, Mam, she meant it. I asked where her friend lived, but she wouldn't tell me.'

'No, I don't believe it,' Eileen said. 'What would she leave 'ome for? All her clothes an' things are 'ere.'

'There's a lot of her things gone, lass,' Maggie said quietly. 'The first thing I did when Edna told us, was to look in her room. There's only some old things left in the wardrobe and drawers, all her good clothes have gone. She must have been taking them out on the quiet over the last few weeks.'

'I can't make head nor tail of it.' Bill looked anxious. 'You haven't had a row with her, have you, chick?'

'Not a wrong word,' Eileen said, 'I just don't understand it.'

'Well, there's not much I can do tonight, but I'll take an hour off tomorrow and go down to Vernons. I'll see the personnel officer and find out what's going on.'

'She doesn't work there any more.' Edna held an already sodden handkerchief to her screwed-up eyes as a fresh burst of sobbing threatened. 'She said she left there weeks ago and has got another job, but wouldn't tell me where.'

Her face drained of colour, Eileen appealed to Bill. 'Why would she do that to us? She's got a good 'ome here.'

Maggie, unable to bear the look of distress on Eileen's face, turned to the kitchen. 'I'll make you a cup of sweet tea.'

'Bill!' Eileen was becoming hysterical. 'We've got to do somethin'! She can't leave 'ome, she's not old enough.'

'There's not much we can do, chick, if that's what she wants.' Bill sat beside Eileen and took her hand. 'She's nearly nineteen now and we can't stop her doing anything she wants. We've no say in the matter.'

Edna's cries grew louder and Billy went to put an arm across her shoulders. 'Don't cry, Sis, it's not your fault.'

'But she's me sister! Why didn't she tell me what she was going to do an' I could have stopped her?'

Eileen closed her eyes and took two deep breaths before asking, 'Tell me exactly what happened, sunshine?'

Edna wiped her nose on the back of her hand. 'She came up to me in the shop an' said she wouldn't be coming home any more 'cos she's gone to live with a girl she works with. I thought she was having me on at first, but when I saw she meant it, I said you'd find out where she'd gone by asking at Vernons. She just laughed at me and said you'd have a job because she'd left there.'

'The hard-faced little madam.' Despite being worried to death, Eileen felt angry that her daughter would cause them such anguish. 'And that's all she said?'

'Told me to tell you not to worry, that she'd be all right. And she said she'd come and see me again in the shop.' Tears ran down Edna's cheeks and her voice was choked with emotion. 'I asked her to come an' see you, Mam, but she said you'd try and stop her and she'd made up her mind.'

'Didn't she give you a reason?' Bill asked.

Edna shook her head. 'Just said she was old enough now to do what she wants.'

'She deserves a damn good hiding.' Young Billy was beside himself with anger. How dare she upset his mam and dad like this! The trouble was, their Joan had never appreciated how lucky she was. 'She'll be back, never fear. When she realises what side her bread's buttered, she'll be home like a shot.'

Bill could feel Eileen's hand shaking and he squeezed it gently. 'Billy's right, chick. If she's sharing a house or a flat, then she'll have to do half the housework and cough up enough money to pay half the rent and all the bills. And knowing our Joan, she won't like that one little bit.'

'I don't want 'er to come back for those reasons, Bill! She's left 'ome because she obviously doesn't like it 'ere, so let her stay away. If she 'asn't got the decency to face her own family, doesn't care about 'ow much she hurts us, then she needn't bother comin' back.' Even as she spoke, Eileen knew she didn't mean a word of it. But she hurt so much inside she needed to relieve the pain, and the only way she knew how was to get angry. 'Next time yer sister comes in the shop, tell 'er what I said.'

Billy watched his mother walk through to the kitchen and her grief-stricken face filled him with sadness. For all her brave words, he knew she was devastated. 'If I had our Joan here, I'd strangle her with me bare hands,' Billy whispered across the room to his father. 'How could she do this to me mam?'

'Sshh!' Bill put a finger to his lips. 'Don't say too much, son, least said, soonest mended.'

245

Bill stopped at the kitchen door and with a heavy heart watched as Eileen sobbed on Maggie's shoulder, 'Why, Mam? Why 'as she done this? I 'aven't been such a bad mother, 'ave I?'

'Of course not!' Maggie motioned with her head for Bill to leave them be. To let her daughter cry away some of the sadness and hurt she felt. Maggie stroked Eileen's hair. 'One of her friends has probably talked her into it and Joan's been easily led. But it won't last long, the novelty will soon wear off, lass, and she'll come running home.'

Joan walked out of George Henry Lees biting on her bottom lip to keep the tears back. It had been much harder than she'd thought it would be. The look of distress on Edna's face had almost made her change her mind. But it wasn't the end of the world, she told herself. She could keep in touch with her sister and in a few weeks she'd go and see her mam and dad.

As Joan made her way towards C and A, where she was meeting Valerie, for once she was truthful with herself. It was her own fault she'd had to leave home. If she hadn't lied to Augie it need never have happened. But she'd never had the courage to tell him she'd lied. And every time he'd asked to meet her family, instead of being honest with him, she'd told him she didn't get on with her parents. It was Augie who'd suggested she went to live with his friend's girlfriend, Valerie, and it had seemed a marvellous idea at the time. She'd be able to see him every night without worrying what time she got home or making excuses about where she was going.

Joan pulled the sheet over her head to muffle the sound of her sobs.

Valerie slept in the next room and if she heard Joan crying she'd be in like a shot, thinking she was the cause of it. But what had happened that day wasn't the reason Joan had allowed her fears and unhappiness to surface. It had been festering since the day she'd walked out on her family. Today's incident had just been the straw that broke the camel's back.

Since she'd moved in, Joan and Valerie had got into a routine of doing household chores on certain days. And Sunday was the day they stripped their beds and vacuumed and dusted the bedrooms. This morning Joan had finished her room, and as she could hear Valerie talking to Richie on the phone in the hall, she decided to help by starting on Valerie's room. She pulled the bedclothes from the bed, threw the sheets and pillowcases to one side for washing, then opened the drawer in the tallboy where she knew Valerie kept her clean bed linen. She pulled two slips out and was about to close the drawer when she saw some photographs of a soldier in uniform. Without thinking, Joan took the photos out and was looking through them when Valerie came into the room.

'Nice-looking man,' Joan said. 'Is he your brother?'

Valerie snatched the photos from Joan's hands, her face blazing. 'What the hell are you doing, snooping through my things? You have no right to be in here.'

'I was only trying to help,' Joan protested, wondering what she'd done wrong.

Valerie noted the bedclothes on the floor and the two clean pillow slips and her temper evaporated. 'Take no notice of me.' She threw the photos in the drawer. 'I must have got out of bed on the wrong side this morning.'

Joan said, 'I'll give you a hand.' While she waited for Valerie to shake out the sheet, she asked, 'Is the man your brother?'

Valerie let the corners of the sheet drop and looked across the bed. For seconds she just stared, then shrugged her shoulders. 'He's not a soldier any more, he works abroad. And he's not my brother, he's my husband.'

'But, then . . .' Joan stuttered.

'Look, let's get one thing straight,' Valerie said. 'What I do is my business and has nothing to do with you. I love my husband, but he works away for six months at a time and I get lonely. Richie knows I'm married and when my husband comes home our affair will be finished. Now you know, but as I said, it's none of your business.'

There'd been a coolness between them for the rest of the day, and Joan was glad when Augie came to take her out. But as he drove the Jeep towards the city centre, Joan found herself looking sideways at him. Did he know what was going on? If he did, and condoned it, he was as bad as Valerie and Richie.

Joan's thoughts ran on. If he saw no wrong in them cheating on Valerie's husband, then he wouldn't be beyond cheating on someone himself, would he? She took a deep breath. 'Augie, are you married? Tell me the truth.'

Augie took his eyes off the road for a second, surprise written on his face at the unexpected question. 'No, honey, of course I'm not!'

He turned his head away quickly, but not quickly

enough for Joan to miss the colour rising from his neck, or the look of guilt in his eyes. She didn't question him any more, she didn't need to.

Now Joan punched the pillow, the blow containing all the emotions she'd kept at bay for so long. What a stupid, naive fool she'd been! Why had she never asked herself how Valerie could keep such a nice house going, and have a wardrobe full of clothes, on the wages she earned?

Then anger took over. I've often told me mam lies, Joan thought, and right now I regret every one of them. But mine have never hurt anyone, not like Valerie, who was not only cheating on her husband, but in not wearing a wedding ring, was living a lie. There was no excuse for her or for Richie. And as for Augie, well she never wanted to set eyes on him again. He was, as her Nan would say, too sweet to be wholesome.

'Oh, Mam,' Joan cried softly, wishing she could feel the big, soft warm body holding her close. 'I want to come home, but would you have me after what I've done? I do love you, Mam, but I don't know if you still love me.'

Chapter Nineteen

'I think that's about right,' Mary said, holding the material against Eileen's leg. Her friend had come for a final fitting of the dress she was making for Billy's wedding, and all that it needed now was the hem turning up. 'It's about four inches below your knees.'

Eileen, trying to see over her mountainous bust, grunted in disgust. 'I can't see a thing, kid! As long as I'm not showin' the leg of me knickers, then it'll do.'

Mary filled her mouth with pins and began the task of getting the hem straight. It wasn't easy with Eileen being so big in the front. 'Keep still, will you? Otherwise it'll be all cockeyed.' She crawled round on her knees, leaning back occasionally to make sure she was keeping the hem even. 'Move nearer the window and turn around slowly so I can see it at a distance.'

'Bloody 'ell, all this just to look glamorous.' Eileen twirled slowly, then did a quick spin. 'Will I outshine the bride?'

Mary struggled to her feet. 'I can't promise that, but it really suits you.' She surveyed the dress with a critical eye. It was a crepe material in sage green, with three-quarter sleeves and a sweetheart neck. 'I'm glad you didn't get a dark colour like you usually do. That green looks great on you, brings out the colour of your eyes.'

'Help me off with it, kid, or I'll be stickin' pins in meself.'

Mary folded the dress and draped it over the back of a chair. 'I'll sit and finish it off tonight.'

'We've kept yer busy the last month, haven't we, kid? Yer've been a real angel doin' all those dresses. Saved our Billy an' Mavis a lot of money. In fact, let's face it, they wouldn't be 'aving any bridesmaids if it wasn't for you.'

'It's been hard going, but I've enjoyed doing them,' Mary said. 'I'm very fond of your Billy and I was glad to help.'

'He's a real cracker, my son, even if I say it as shouldn't. Got a heart of gold. I was made up when 'e asked if Carol would like to be a bridesmaid. There's not many lads his age would 'ave done that, now, is there?'

Mary gazed at her friend with fondness. Behind all the bluff, Mary knew she was heartbroken that Joan wouldn't be here to be a bridesmaid at her brother's wedding. 'No word from Joan?'

Eileen's eyes clouded. 'No. She's been in the shop to see Edna, and she knows the wedding's in two weeks, but we've not 'eard a dickie bird from her. I'll never forgive 'er for lettin' our Billy down.'

Mary sighed as she pressed back the cuticles from her nails. 'She's a very silly girl. One day she'll need her family.'

'In the beginnin' I expected 'er back every day. Never thought she'd stay away a month,' Eileen said. 'If she walked through that door now, I wouldn't know whether to hug 'er or break her flamin' neck. She's been very naughty not gettin' in touch with me an' Bill, but for all that she's me daughter an' I love her.'

'Is everything fixed up for the wedding?' Mary asked, to get Eileen's mind away from her wayward daughter.

'Yeah, we've sorted it all out with the Radfords. We were goin' to pay for everything between us, but young Billy wouldn't hear of it. He said it's the bridegroom's job to pay for certain things, and he wanted to do things properly. So we're all givin' 'im money as a weddin' present and they can buy furniture with it. Me an' Bill are scrimpin' and scratchin' to give as much as we can. I've got a few pound to come in Co-op divvy, so I'm nippin' to Byrom Street temorrer to pick it up. It's not much, but every little helps, as the old woman said when she did a jimmy riddle in the river.' Eileen laughed at the look on Mary's face. 'If all else fails, kid, I'll 'ave to pawn me weddin' ring.'

'Don't you dare!' Mary said. 'I can lend you a few pound . . . it's unlucky to pawn things.'

'Ah, that's an old wives' tale, kid! This ring of mine was in an' out of pawn that often when the kids were little, it's a wonder it isn't worn out. My Bill didn't know, mind yer, or there'd 'ave been blue murder. But when we got married and moved into Bray Street, we didn't 'ave much furniture. We were goin' to save up an' buy when we could afford. But we 'adn't reckoned on 'aving three kids in four years, an' it put a halt to our gallop. It was hard goin', tryin' to make ends meets, I can tell yer. Sometimes it was a case of starvin' or goin' to the pawn shop. Yer know Pobjoys, at Everton Valley? Well, I used to trot along there every Monday mornin' with me weddin' ring an' I'd get enough on it to keep us in food till pay day.'

'But Bill must have noticed you weren't wearing your ring,' Mary said. 'He's not blind.'

'Ah, well, yer see, kid, I was very crafty. I bought meself a tanner ring from Woolies and Bill never knew the difference.'

'You're a case, you are.'

'As the sayin' goes, kid, what Bill never knew never 'urt him.'

'Has young Billy got the key to his house yet?'

'He's hopin' to get it today. If he does, we're goin with 'im tonight to see it.' Eileen laughed, 'Honest, he's so happy he's like a kid with a new toy.'

'He deserves to go through life being happy,' Mary said. 'He's one helluva nice boy. I only hope our Tony grows up to be as nice as him.'

Billy couldn't hide his impatience. 'I'll go on ahead, Mam.'

Eileen, her arm linked through Bill's, nodded. 'Okay, son, but don't go in yer new 'ouse till we get there. I want to see yer face.'

'I don't think I've ever seen anyone so happy,' Bill said, watching Billy racing up the street. 'It does my heart good to see the pleasure on his face.'

'Ay, mister!' Eileen squeezed his arm. 'What about the day we got married? Are yer tryin' to tell me yer weren't as happy then as our Billy is now?'

'Of course I was! But I was more nervous than him. I

was walking round like a headless chicken for weeks before we got wed. Our Billy doesn't seem to have any nerves.'

'It's like history repeatin' itself,' Eileen said. 'The day we got married we moved into our own little 'ouse in the same street.'

Bill glanced sideways. Was Eileen still hankering after the old house after all this time? Mind you, women were more sentimental than men.

Billy was standing with Mavis outside the house the Bowers had moved out of last week. He was hopping from one foot to the other. 'Put a move on, Mam!'

'Hold yer 'orses, son! Give us a chance to get me breath back.'

Billy put the key in the lock, his face glowing with pride. He stepped back to let Eileen go in first, and caught her gazing at their old house opposite with a funny look on her face. 'In you go, Mam. You can be first to set foot in our new house.'

Mavis was giggling with nervous excitement as they toured the small two-up two-down. 'It's not in bad nick, son,' Bill said, looking around. 'The decorating will do you for a while.'

'I won't be doing any papering until we've got some furniture in,' Billy laughed. 'It's no good havin' nice walls when you've no chairs to sit on.'

'Give it time, son.' Bill would have liked to say that with the money they were getting as a wedding present, things would be coming quicker than the young couple thought. But that would spoil the surprise. And anyway, as half the money was coming from Mavis's parents, it wasn't up to him to let the cat out of the bag. 'In no time at all you'll have the house as you want it.'

'Course yer will!' Eileen said. 'In a couple of months yer'll 'ave the place like a little palace an' be as snug as two bugs in a rug.'

'You know, I never knew that palaces had bugs.' Billy fended off a blow from his mother. 'I thought the King and Queen were too posh to have such common things as bugs.'

Eileen pushed him playfully against the wall. 'Watch it, big boy, or yer'll be walking down the aisle on crutches.'

'Help, Mavis, I'm being attacked.'

'You're on your own, Billy Gillmoss.' Mavis winked at Bill. 'I'm keeping on the right side of me mother-in-law.'

'Yer know, I always knew we were goin' to get on well together.' Eileen put her arms around Mavis. 'Welcome to yer new 'ome, sunshine, an' welcome to the family.'

'What time's Harry pickin' yez up?' Eileen was pacing up and down the living room, looking at the clock every few seconds. She had a fixed smile on her face, telling herself to look cheerful even if she didn't feel it. After all, it was Billy's big day and she mustn't spoil it for him. But her heart was heavy. In a few minutes her only son would be walking out of the door and not coming back. What with Joan leaving, and now Billy, the house just wasn't going to be the same. 'I 'ope he won't be late gettin' yez to the church.'

'Mam, will you relax?' Billy showed no sign of nerves as he sat next to his best man, the boy who'd been his friend since schooldays. 'You'd think it was her getting married, wouldn't you, Jacko?'

'Your mam isn't the only nervous one,' Jack replied. 'My tummy is tied up in knots.'

'Yer've got the ring, haven't yer?' Eileen stopped her pacing and stood in front of Jacko. 'I'll kill yer if yer drop it.'

The knocker sounded and Eileen jumped. 'I 'ope this is Harry.'

Harry breezed in, a smile creasing his face. 'I've delivered Edna and Carol to Mavis's, and while I was there Rene turned up with Victoria. So everything is organised at that end. I'll run you and Jacko down now, Billy, then come back for the rest.'

'What about Arthur?' Eileen fussed. 'How's he gettin' to the church with the boys?'

'On the bus.' Harry ran his eyes over Eileen, the cleft in his chin deepening when he grinned. With her green dress she was wearing a wide-brimmed black hat with matching shoes, gloves and handbag. 'You look very fetching, Mrs Gillmoss, if I may say so.'

'Oh, go way with yer.' Eileen blushed. 'Flattery will get yer nowhere.'

'You do look nice, Mam,' Billy said, while his father nodded in agreement.

'Will yer get goin'?' Eileen shooed them out. She was getting more emotional with every passing minute and it didn't help to keep reminding herself that every mother felt the same when one of her children flew the nest. Because deep down in her heart she knew the root of her sadness lay in the fact that Joan wouldn't be there to see

259

her brother married. It just wasn't right, and although no one had said a word, she knew it had marred the happiness of the whole family.

Eileen held on to her hat as she swung her legs round to get out of Harry's car. She heard people clapping and looked with surprise at the people standing inside the gates of the Blessed Sacrament Church. All the old neighbours had turned up from Bray Street and Eileen could feel tears stinging the backs of her eyes. 'All me mates are 'ere.'

Bill gave her a hand and pulled her to her feet. 'Yes, I know, chick.'

'Yer look smashin', Eileen,' Cissie Maddox called.

'Like a mannequin,' Milly Knight said, while her husband winked his agreement.

Ada and Tommy Wilson smiled as she passed. 'I could fancy yer in that outfit,' Tommy said, then feigned a look of pain as Ada dug him sharply in the ribs.

'Behave yerself,' Ada said, a grin on her face. 'A man of your age, yer should be ashamed of yerself.'

'It's lovely to see yez all,' Eileen said, standing on the church step, overcome by the reception. 'I'll see yez later.'

Eileen linked Bill's arm as they walked down the aisle and took their seats in the bench behind Billy and Jacko. She nodded to Mrs Radford, sitting in the pew opposite, before whispering to Jacko, 'Yer've got the ring, 'aven't yer?'

Billy turned around and tutted. 'It's in his top pocket, I've checked half a dozen times.'

Eileen felt like hugging her son, he looked so handsome

in his dark grey suit, white shirt and pale blue tie. And he was so relaxed, completely at ease.

The church was filling up. Maggie arrived with Rene and Alan, all dressed in their best, then Arthur and his two sons. Friends, neighbours and workmates of the bride and groom all slid into the pews on both sides of the aisle. Eileen kept turning her head to wave and smile, while all the time her eyes were peeled for a sign of Joan. Even at this late hour, she hadn't given up hope.

The organ began to play 'Here Comes The Bride', and Eileen forgot everything at the sight of Mavis, her hand on her father's arm, walking down the aisle. Her white satin dress was close fitting to the waist, then billowed out into a full skirt which reached to the floor. It had a square-shaped neck and leg-of-mutton sleeves tapering to fit tightly around her wrists. A long white veil was secured with a spray of orange blossom and her bouquet was a mixture of pink and white carnations.

'Oh, doesn't she look beautiful?' Eileen said, before nudging Bill as the bridesmaids followed Mavis to the altar. Edna led the way followed by Carol and Victoria. Their dresses were in pale blue satin with full skirts, crowns of flowers adorned their heads and their posies were made up of pink and white flowers.

It was all too much for Eileen and the tears rolled down her cheeks. 'Have yer got a hankie, Bill?' She blew her nose and managed to control her emotions until she heard Billy's voice, strong and steady, saying, 'I do.' After that Eileen saw everything through a haze and only regained her composure when they were outside the church once again posing for the photographer.

'Where's me Nan?' Billy left his bride to fetch Maggie who was standing shyly to one side. 'Auntie Rene and Uncle Alan, come on,' he urged, 'we want all the family on this one.'

When the photographer had finished and folded away his tripod, everyone crowded around to congratulate the newly weds and throw confetti. There was so much laughing and so many jokes flying, nobody noticed the lone figure of a slim girl standing looking through the railings at the side of the church. She was wearing a long coat fastened up to her chin and her long hair was hidden under the scarf which was pulled low over her forehead.

Joan feasted her eyes on the happy crowd, lingering for a while on Billy, then finally coming to rest on Eileen. She could feel the rivulet of tears rolling down her cheeks on to her neck but made no effort to wipe them away. Oh, Mam, she cried silently, what have I done? You'll never forgive me now, I know you won't.

Mary and Vera had stayed behind to see to the tables and when they'd finished, they stood back to survey their handiwork. Eileen had borrowed two trestle tables and space had been made for them by moving all the furniture into Maggie's room. They were covered in spotless white sheets, and groaning under the weight of food. Pride of place on one of the tables had been given to the one-tier, square wedding cake, which Maggie had made and Vera had iced. Vera had made a good job of it too, decorating it with little silver shoes, bells and white ribbon. Around it were plates of sandwiches, sausage rolls, meat pies cut in half and two large glass bowls filled with trifle decorated with hundreds and thousands. Lending a splash of colour were four cake stands filled with jelly creams in their stiff, white pleated cases. And where it was possible on the crowded tables, there were small vases filled with purple button daisies.

'We've done a good job, even if I do say so meself,' Mary said. 'Not bad for beginners, eh, Vera?'

'The tables look a treat.' Vera's eyes widened when a knock came on the door. 'We cut that a bit fine, didn't we?'

She hurried along the hall, untying her apron as she went. When she saw Billy sweep Mavis off her feet, she called over her shoulder. 'Quick, Mary, you can't miss this.'

The sheer bliss on Billy's face was a joy to behold. 'Before you say anything, I know it's me own threshold I should be carrying me bride over, and I'll be doing that later, all right and proper. But me mam's house will always be a second home to me, and Mavis feels the same.' With exaggerated groans, Billy staggered along the hall with his blushing bride giggling in his arms. But when he entered the room, he took one look at the tables and lowered Mavis to the floor. He struggled for the right words as he glanced from Mary to Vera. 'I'm speechless.' He gazed at the attractive way the food had been laid out, then gathered them both in his arms and held them close. 'The Adelphi couldn't have done us prouder! What do you say, eh, Mrs Gillmoss, Junior?'

'Oh, lord, aren't we the fine ones?' Mary ran to Mavis and kissed her. 'We were so busy congratulating our-selves, we forgot about congratulating you.'

Vera was pumping Billy's hand when the first of the guests started to arrive and after that the peace of the house was turned into bedlam. Bill was the first to make a short speech and toast the happy couple, then it was Mr Radford followed by a very nervous Jacko. As he told his mates the next day, it was worse being a best man than it was to be a groom. More responsibilities, like, you know.

Then it was Billy's turn. With a glass in one hand and an arm around his bride, he thanked everyone, leaving out not a soul. He looked so tall and handsome, every inch the gentleman, Eileen felt so proud she thought her heart would burst. And when he lifted his glass and asked everyone to drink to his mam and dad, the best parents anyone could ask for, she couldn't hold back the tears, or her feelings.

She rushed to throw her arms round her son's neck, knocking his glass flying and spilling beer on those unlucky enough to be standing near. With her hat pushed precariously to one side of her head, she cried, 'I'm not 'alf goin' to miss yer, son.' She glanced sideways at Mavis. 'Yer will look after 'im won't yer? An' make sure he gets enough to eat?'

With that, everyone burst out laughing and the festivities began.

'Your Carol is so happy she doesn't know what to do with herself.' Arthur was standing next to Vera, a glass in one hand, a plate in the other. 'She looks very grown up today.'

'I'm keeping me eye on her. She's stuffing herself with those jelly creams and she'll be sick if she's not careful.'

'She can be a bridesmaid when we get married,' Arthur said. 'She'll like that.'

Vera lifted her brows. 'In a register office?'

'What's the difference?' Arthur smiled. 'I don't care if we get married in a coal yard as long as you come out wearing my ring.'

Mary pushed her way through the crowds towards them. 'It's like St John's market on Christmas Eve.'

'Or the Grafton on a Saturday night.' Arthur grinned.

'Vera, I've just remembered the parcel that came for Billy,' Mary said. 'Did you give it to him?'

'Oh, lord, I forgot.' Vera put her plate down. 'I'll go and get it.'

She disappeared into the kitchen, returning with a square parcel in her arms. 'Billy, this came for you.'

Billy looked puzzled. 'What is it?'

Talking stopped as everyone's gaze focused on the parcel. 'Where did it come from?' Billy was tearing at the wrapping. 'I thought we'd had all our presents.'

'We don't know who left it,' Vera said. 'Me and Mary were busy in the kitchen when we heard a knock. It only took me a few seconds to dry me hands, but when I opened the door there was no one there, just the parcel on the step. I looked up and down the road but I couldn't see anybody.' Billy threw the wrapping paper to the floor and with everyone gathered round, opened the cardboard box. Inside, packed in straw, was a six-piece tea service. Billy lifted out one of the cups and held it aloft. 'This'll come in handy, save us drinking out of jam jars when we have visitors.'

Eileen peered into the box. 'Isn't there a card with it?'

Billy handed the box to Mavis while he searched inside. After a few seconds he waved a white envelope. 'Mystery solved,' he grinned as he took out the greetings card. But his smile faded when he started to read the message inside. Mavis was looking over his shoulder and her gasp of surprise brought Eileen forward. 'Who's it from?'

Billy handed her the card. 'Our Joan.'

Bill rested his chin on Eileen's shoulder and read the words aloud.

'Dear Billy, Sorry I can't be with you today but I wish you and Mavis all the luck in the world. Joan.'

Without a word Eileen handed the card back to Billy and left the room. Bill saw all eyes in the room follow his wife and he shrugged his shoulders as though apologising. 'She'll be all right, you just carry on enjoying yourselves.'

Bill found Eileen standing by the bedroom window, crying softly. 'Come on, chick.' He held his arms out and Eileen walked into them. 'Don't cry, love,' he whispered. 'You know how it upsets me. And you don't want to spoil things for our Billy on his wedding day. He should be able to look back on today as the happiest of his life.'

'Just give me five minutes to calm meself down, then I'll be all right.' Eileen looked up into his face. 'I'm glad Joan didn't forget Billy's weddin', it'll mean a lot to him. But if she could come to the 'ouse with 'is present, it wouldn't 'ave hurt her to come to the church. What 'ave we done to 'er that she doesn't even want to set eyes on us?'

'I can't even pretend to understand,' Bill sighed. 'But you know how young people do things they're sorry for afterwards but wouldn't for this world admit it. Perhaps that's the way it is with Joan, she doesn't want to eat humble pie.'

Eileen left the shelter of his arms to look at her reflection in the dressing table mirror. 'I'll swill me face and make meself presentable, then I'll go down.'

'Are you all right, Mam?' Billy's head appeared round the door. 'You're not upset over our Joan, are you?'

'Not at all, sunshine,' Eileen lied. 'All mothers are entitled to a little weep when one of their children gets married an' leaves 'ome. No, I'm very glad our Joan didn't forget 'er brother on 'is big day.' She picked up a comb and ran it through the fine, mousy hair. 'You go an' see to yer guests while I titivate meself up. I'll be down in two shakes of a lamb's tail to liven the place up. Give yer a party yer'll remember all yer life.'

Chapter Twenty

'Blimey! I thought you'd be back in America by now.' Eileen stood aside and pulled her tummy in to let Jean pass. Closing the door behind her, she said, 'I've been callin' yer all the names under the sun for not comin' to say ta-ra.'

'As though I'd do that to you!' Jean put her carrier bag on the floor and sat down. 'You know what it's like, going to visit all the relatives and God knows who else. Me mam's had me visiting aunties I've never seen in me life before. Florrie, Maggie, Lizzie, Nellie, Fanny . . . you name them and I've visited them.'

'Terrible name that.' Eileen dropped heavily on to the couch. 'Fancy lumberin' a child with a name like Fanny.'

'She was christened Frances, and that's a lovely name. But her Mum started to call her Fanny when she was a baby, as a pet name, and it stuck.'

'How's life treatin' yer, anyway?' Eileen asked. 'Yer've been 'ome over a month now, aren't yer missin' yer 'usband?'

'I'm missing Ivan, yes.' Jean grimaced. 'But I'm dreading leaving me family again. I wish America wasn't so far away, then I'd be able to see them more often. I never thought I'd miss them, or Liverpool, so much.'

'Well, yer would marry a Yank, kid, so yer stuck with it . . . like Fanny is with 'er name.'

'To tell you the truth, Eileen, I've been seriously thinking of not going back.'

Eileen's eyes opened in astonishment. 'Yer can't do that! Yer can't just walk out on Ivan! That would be a lousy trick, kid, an' I'm surprised at yer for even thinkin' of it. You love 'im don't yer?'

Jean nodded. 'Very much. But sometimes I feel so homesick it makes me ill. I thought I'd get over it, but after five years I still feel the same.'

'He's a good 'usband, isn't he?' Eileen leaned forward, her chubby hands clasped between her knees. 'Looks after yer well?'

'He's a smashing husband. Kind and gentle, and spoils me soft.'

'An' yer thinkin' of walkin' out on 'im? Well, I think yer want yer bumps feelin'. When the novelty of bein' 'ome wears off, yer'll be cryin' yer eyes out for 'im, and it'll be too late.' Eileen clicked her tongue. 'Listen to me, kid. If yer heart's with Ivan, then that's where yer home is. Yer've heard the old sayin', "home is where the heart is", well it's true. So get back to 'im as quick as yer can an' count yer blessings.' She patted Jean's knee. 'Yer know the best thing for curing yer homesickness, kid? Start a family. Then yer'll 'ave no time to sit an' mope.'

Eileen remembered the times during the war when Ivan had helped out their meagre rations with weekly gifts of sugar and meat. 'Tell 'im next time yer come over on holiday, I expect to see 'im with yer. He was a good mate to me, was Ivan, an' I don't forget me mates.'

'You and Ivan think alike,' Jean said. 'He wants to start a family.'

'Then get the next boat 'ome, kid, an' get crackin'.' Eileen grinned into Jean's face. 'You are goin' home, aren't yer?'

Jean nodded. 'If you'll come over and be godmother to our first.'

'Not bloody likely! Bring it over here to be christened.' Eileen wriggled to the edge of the couch. 'I'll put the kettle on.'

Jean bent to take a Sayers cake box from her carrier bag. 'I've brought us some fresh cream cakes to have with a cup of tea.'

'Ooh, no thanks, kid! I ate enough food at our Billy's weddin' on Saturday to sink a ship. I can't walk through the flippin' door now without turnin' sideways.'

Jean lifted the lid of the cake box to reveal four chocolate eclairs oozing with fresh cream. Her face fell and there was disappointment in her voice. 'You mean you won't have one?'

At the sight of cakes Eileen could feel her mouth watering. She snatched the box from Jean's knee. 'To hell with it, yer only live once!' She patted her tummy and grinned. 'What's a pound or two between friends, anyway? Two each, is it, kid?'

Edna raised her brows in surprise when she saw Joan approaching the counter. Her sister had been coming in on a Wednesday to see her, but today was only Monday.

Edna glanced down the long counter to where the senior assistant, Miss Connelly, was serving, and hoped the customer would take her time choosing the coloured braid. 'You'll have to pretend you're buying something.' She slid one of the shallow drawers out of the cabinet behind her and placed it on the counter. 'These are very nice buttons, madam.' She raised her voice for the benefit of Miss Connelly, who was now writing the bill for her customer. 'For heaven's sake, look as though you're interested,' she hissed, 'otherwise you'll get me the sack.'

Joan inspected the variety of buttons, saying, 'I will buy some, they'll come in handy for a dress or jacket.'

Edna's eyes narrowed. Joan looked pale today and her nose was red as though she had a cold. 'It's not like you to come in on a Monday, what's up?'

'Nothing.' Joan put a grey button back and picked up a gilt one to hold against her blue coat. 'I just thought I'd ask how Billy's wedding went off.'

'If you were that interested, it's a pity you couldn't be bothered coming along to see it.' Edna's voice was sharp. 'But then, he's only your brother, nobody important.'

'I did come,' Joan said softly. 'I stood in the side street.'

'You what!' Edna realised she was shouting and her eyes flicked the length of the counter. But, thank goodness, Miss Connelly was busy serving again. 'You mean you went all that way and didn't even have the decency to congratulate our Billy and Mavis? That's lousy, that is.'

'I didn't think I'd be welcome.' Joan handed the gilt button over. 'I'll take four of these, please.' She kept her eyes averted but her tone of voice puzzled Edna. There was definitely something amiss here. Usually her sister looked cocky and full of herself, but today she was very subdued.

'Have you got a cold or something?' Edna asked as she dropped the buttons into a bag. 'You don't look well.'

Joan was about to say something when Miss Connelly appeared at Edna's elbow. 'Everything all right, Miss Gillmoss?'

'Yes, thank you.' Edna stepped aside. 'Would you like to write the receipt out, Miss Connelly?'

There was no excuse for lingering and Joan had to leave the shop without asking the questions she'd been rehearsing all morning, and with four gilt buttons she had no use for.

Eileen laid down the knife and fork and picked up the remains of her lamb chop. She could feel gravy running down her chin as she nibbled at the meat left on the bone, but she wasn't in the mood to care. The silence around the table was getting on her nerves. The only sounds she'd heard in the last ten minutes had been the steady ticking of the clock on the mantelpiece and the occasional splutter from the coal fire. Tea time used to be such a happy occasion, with all the family round the table laughing and joking. Tonight it was like eating in a graveyard.

With a look of disgust on her face, Eileen threw the bone on to the plate and lifted the corner of her pinny to wipe the gravy from her chin. She gazed from Bill to Edna thinking how her family had shrunk in just a few weeks. There were only the three of them now, but surely to God that didn't mean they had to behave like monks who had taken a vow of silence? She was used to Bill being quiet, he'd never been the talkative type. But not so Edna. Usually you couldn't shut her up, yet tonight there was no getting a word out of her. Eileen had tried a few times to get them talking, telling them about Jean's visit, and the cream cakes. Since then, though, there'd been no attempt at conversation.

'What's the matter with you tonight, sunshine? Have yer been gettin' told off in work?'

Edna jerked her head round. She'd been miles away. 'What did you say, Mam?'

'Ye gods, she's goin' deaf as well as dumb!' Eileen pushed her plate away and rested her bust on the table. 'I asked if yer'd been gettin' told off in work? Yer 'aven't opened yer gob in the last half hour, an' that's never been known before.'

A battle had been raging in Edna's head about whether to tell her Mam about their Joan. She'd told her all the other times, but there'd been something different about her sister today and Edna didn't know whether she'd be doing the right thing in mentioning it. Better not, she decided. It was probably only her imagination anyway. She'd wait till Wednesday and see if her sister came in again. She smiled at Eileen. 'I was just thinking.'

'Well, stop thinkin' an' talk to me. Tell me somethin' funny, I could do with cheerin' up.'

Edna put her elbow on the table and cupped her chin in her hand. 'There's not much happened today, it's been very quiet. Except that a woman brought some ribbon back and wanted Miss Connelly to exchange it.' Her face lit up. 'I thought it was hilarious but Miss Connelly didn't see the funny side at all. In fact it put her in a bad temper

274

all day. The ribbon had been used to make a bow, anyone with half an eye could see that 'cos it was all creased, and Miss Connelly said she couldn't exchange it. But the customer brazened it out, saying the ribbon hadn't been used and was Miss Connelly calling her a liar? It ended up with the floor manager coming over to see what the fuss was, and he told Miss Connelly to exchange the ribbon.' Edna picked up her fork and speared a potato. 'So you see, Mam, in George Henry Lees the customer is always right.'

'An' has Miss Connelly been takin' her temper out on you?' Eileen asked, ready to defend her daughter.

'No, but I think she felt like punching the floor manager on the nose for making a show of her in front of the customer.'

'Who was in the right?'

'Miss Connelly was, but you don't argue with the boss. If he says jump, then you jump.' Edna raised her eyes to the ceiling. 'It wouldn't have been so bad if the customer had been nice about it, but she wasn't. She gloated over Miss Connelly's embarrassment and walked out of the shop with a smirk all over her face.'

'Cheeky bitch!' Eileen said.

Bill had been watching and listening with interest. He knew what was wrong with Eileen, she was missing the two chicks who had flown the nest. It was a while since Bill had thought about the baby they'd lost, but he did so now with sadness. If things had turned out differently, Eileen would have had a youngster to lavish her love on and wouldn't be missing the other two so much. 'Is that me nan knocking on the wall?' Edna asked. 'It's either her or next door.'

'It'll be next door, but I'll check to make sure.' Eileen scraped her chair back. 'Be an angel an' clear the table for us.'

Maggie was holding on to the chest of drawers for support, her face grey. 'I don't feel well, lass.'

One look at her mother's face and the blood in Eileen's veins turned to ice. She'd never known her mam to be sick, ever. But she was now, you could see that by just looking at her. Eileen's mind was telling her to move, to do something, but her feet were rooted to the spot with fear.

'I think you'd better call the doctor, lass.' Maggie clutched at her side as a sharp pain cut into her like a knife.

'Oh, my God!' The sight of her beloved mother's face creased in agony galvanised Eileen into action. She stuck her head out of the door and yelled for Bill. He was beside her in seconds, spurred by the urgency in her tone. He took one look at Maggie and rushed to her side. 'What is it, Ma?'

'Terrible pains here, son.' Maggie's hand moved across her tummy. 'I've been having pains for a few days now, but I thought it was constipation. They were nothing like this though, I'm in agony.'

'Who's our doctor?' Bill turned to Eileen. 'I'll ring him from Mary's.'

'We haven't got a doctor.' Eileen was telling herself to be calm, her mam needed her, but it was hard. 'We 'aven't needed a doctor since we moved 'ere.' Her eyes met Bill's. 'D'yer think Dr Greenfield would come?'

'We're not on his panel now. It's too far to ask him to

come. I'll get Mary to ring her doctor.'

Eileen followed him along the hall. 'Ask Mary to tell 'im it's urgent. An' will yer ring our Rene while yer there, I think she should be told.'

Dr Gray came out of Maggie's room and walked to the bottom of the stairs where Eileen and Bill were waiting. 'I think it's appendicitis, Mrs Gillmoss, and I want your mother in hospital right away. Can I use your phone to ring for an ambulance?'

Eileen was biting on her knuckles, fear written all over her face. It was left for Bill to explain they didn't have a phone. 'But I'll take you up to the Sedgemoors', it's only two doors away.'

As the doctor walked down the hall, Bill pressed Eileen's arm. 'Snap out of it, chick, for Ma's sake. Go and sit with her but don't let her see you're worried.'

Eileen couldn't move. If it was anyone else's mother, she'd run to hell and back to help. But this was her mam and her courage had deserted her. Edna was hovering near the living room door, the dirty dishes in the sink forgotten as she studied her mother's face. 'Don't worry, Mam, me nan's going to be all right.'

'Do us a favour, sunshine, an' come in with me to sit with 'er? The state I'm in, I'll only make 'er feel a damn sight worse. I can't 'elp but I'm worried sick. So will yer talk to 'er and try an' cheer her up?'

Edna took Eileen's hand. 'Course I will. Come on, Mam.'

For the umpteenth time, Bill went to the front door to see

if there was any sign of the ambulance. Maggie was writhing in agony and although he tried not to show it, Bill was very concerned. He looked up and down the road and clicked his tongue with impatience. What the hell was keeping them so long? He closed the door and turned to find Eileen beside him. 'You stay in with Ma, I'll keep an eye out for the ambulance.'

'I can't bear to sit and watch 'er in pain when I can't do anythin' about it. I feel so helpless, Bill! I'd take the pain meself if I could, to stop her sufferin'.' Eileen grabbed his arm. 'She's not goin' to die, is she? Tell me she's not goin' to die, Bill, please?'

But Bill couldn't give Eileen the assurance she needed because things didn't look good to him. And the doctor must have thought it was serious to send Maggie to hospital right away. It would be wrong to build up Eileen's hopes. 'I don't know what to think, chick, I really don't.' He brushed a lock of hair from her eyes. 'We'll have to wait and see what the hospital say.'

'It's this bloody 'ouse, that's what it is. It's got a jinx on it. We've 'ad nothin' but bad luck since we moved 'ere.'

'Don't be so childish.' Bill didn't mean to speak sharply but he was too worried to listen to a load of mumbo-jumbo. 'I've no time for silly superstition and I'm surprised at you.'

Eileen's mouth opened, her face angry, but the words died on her lips when they heard the ambulance pull up outside. She shot Bill a withering look, then hurried into Maggie's room. 'They're 'ere, Mam. Once yer in 'ospital, they'll soon have yer sorted out. You mark my words, yer'll be as right as rain in a few days.'

Eileen bit on her lips so hard she could taste blood on her mouth, but she managed to keep the tears back until she saw her mother being lifted on to the stretcher. Then she broke down and it was Maggie who became the comforter. 'Don't cry, lass, there's a good girl.'

Bill was rough as he pulled Eileen out of the way of the ambulance men and bundled her into the back room. 'I'll go in the ambulance with Ma, you stay here.'

'No!' Eileen cried. 'She's me mam an' she needs me.'

'The last thing Ma wants is someone crying over her. And the state you're in, you'd be neither use nor ornament at the hospital. I'll stay as long as they'll let me, to see if I can find out anything tonight. So pull yourself together until your Rene gets here.'

It wasn't often that Bill used that tone of voice to her and it had an immediate effect. 'Yer right,' Eileen sniffed. 'I'm actin' like a baby. You get off in the ambulance and look after me mam.' By this time Bill was running down the hall, Eileen in his wake. 'Tell 'er I love 'er, don't forget now.'

Rene arrived half an hour after the ambulance had left. She'd driven herself up in the secondhand Morris she'd bought six months ago after passing her driving test. She found Eileen sitting on the couch, her body hunched up, her face puffed with crying.

'Bill didn't say much on the phone, so tell me what's going on? What's wrong with me mam?'

Every question brought a fresh outburst of tears from Eileen and in the end it was Edna who had to relate what had happened. 'Me dad said he'd stay at the hospital until the doctor has examined me nan, that's if they'll let him.'

Rene gazed at Eileen. She felt like crying with her sister but knew that would do no one any good. 'You'd better buck yourself up, our Eileen, or you'll end up in hospital as well. It could be something minor, perhaps me mam's eaten something that doesn't agree with her.'

Eileen peered through swollen lids. 'Appendicitis isn't somethin' minor, is it? The doctor's not daft, he wouldn't have sent her away so quick if he hadn't thought it was serious.'

Rene jerked her head at Edna. 'Put the kettle on, love, there's a good girl. I'll stay till your dad gets home, see if he's been able to find out anything.'

Eileen made an effort at normal conversation. 'Did you put Victoria to bed before yer came out?'

'I was getting her ready for bed when Bill rang. Alan said he'd make her a drink, then take her up.'

But when it got to eleven o'clock and there was no sign of Bill, Rene grew uneasy. Alan would be worrying himself sick, as he always did when she was out in the car. If only Eileen had a phone, she could ring him and put his mind at rest.

It was just on twelve o'clock when they heard Bill's key in the lock. All eyes were on the door when he walked in, and from his face they knew he didn't have good news.

'Ma's got a burst appendix.' Bill ran a hand through his mop of white hair. He looked completely worn out and had been dreading having to tell them the news. 'They're operating on her tonight.'

Eileen stretched out on the couch, a cushion under her

head and her old swagger coat covering her knees. Bill had tried to persuade her to go to bed but she wouldn't budge. How could she sleep when she didn't know how her mam was? And there was no point in keeping Bill awake with her tossing and turning, he needed as much sleep as he could get before facing a day's work.

It was getting cold in the room now the fire had gone out, and Eileen tucked the coat around the sides of her legs. 'I should 'ave banked the fire up, it would have kept the chill off the room.' She folded her arms under her bust and sighed. 'Bill was right, I suppose, when he said life must go on. But it's not knowin' 'ow me mam is that's worryin' me.'

Eileen plumped the cushions, then lay staring at the ceiling. 'You know, God, me mam's a good woman. She never misses Mass on a Sunday or Holy Day, never swears or tells lies, and I've never 'eard 'er speak ill of anyone in me whole life. But I don't need to tell You all this 'cos You know everything that goes on.' A lone tear trickled down Eileen's cheek and she could feel the warmth of it on her lips. 'I know I'm always askin' You favours, but this time it's for me mam, and I'm beggin' You, please don't let anythin' bad happen to her. Make 'er better, God, an' send her 'ome to me 'cos I love her so much.'

Chapter Twenty One

'Did you manage to get any sleep?' Bill asked when he walked through the door and saw Eileen sitting at the table, a slice of toast in her hand. 'I was that tired I don't even remember me head touching the pillow.'

'Yeah, I dropped off a few times.' Biting on her toast, Eileen rolled her eyes. Don't count that lie, God, she said silently, 'cos it was only a little white one to stop Bill from worrying.

'I wonder how Ma is?' Bill reached for the marmalade. 'At least no news is good news.'

'That's a daft thing to say! If yer've 'ad no news, 'ow d'yer know whether it's good or bad?'

'Because the police would have been here if there'd been bad news.' Bill spread a thick layer of butter on a fresh piece of toast. 'The hospital always notify the police if they need to contact the family.'

'I'll give Harry time to 'ave 'is breakfast, then slip up an' ask Mary to ring the 'ospital for me. They might let me in to see me mam this afternoon.'

'Go now, chick, before I go to work. Set me mind at rest.'

Eileen had her hand on the knocker when the door was opened by Mary, a dressing gown wrapped around her slim body, her hair all tousled. 'I was just coming down to yours. I rang the hospital because I knew you'd be on pins to know how your mam was.'

'What did they say, kid?'

'You know what hospitals are like, they never tell you anything except the patient is comfortable.'

'Did they say if I can go in an' see 'er this afternoon?'

Mary shook her head. 'I asked that, but the nurse I spoke to said no visitors until the doctor's been on his rounds. She said to ring again at four o'clock.'

'That means sittin' worryin' all day.' Eileen let out a deep sigh. 'I've a good mind to go in this afternoon and pretend I didn't know. Act daft, like.'

'You can ring later if you like. With you being her daughter, they may tell you more.'

'Our Rene will be 'ere about nine, so I'll wait an' see what she thinks.' Eileen backed down the short path. 'I'll have to get back to Bill, but thanks, kid. I'll see yer later . . . ta-ra.'

'I got the same as Mary at first,' Rene said. 'But I wasn't prepared to be fobbed off. I blew my top with the nurse, said it wasn't good enough and I was coming down to see the doctor.'

Eileen looked at her sister with admiration. Rene was so efficient and full of confidence, unlike herself who was as thick as two short planks. How could two sisters be so different in looks and intelligence? 'I bet yer didn't swear once, did yer, our kid?'

'No, but I was damn near it.' Rene huffed. 'I really gave her down the banks. Asked her how she would feel if her seventy-year-old mother had undergone a serious operation and someone tried to fob her off with the usual "the patient is comfortable".'

'What 'appens now?' Eileen asked.

'You're going to get yourself dressed up and we're going to the hospital. We might not be allowed to see me mam because she's bound to be knocked out after the operation, but at least we can see someone in authority who'll tell us how she is.'

'You're on, kid.' Eileen heaved herself up. 'Anything's better than sittin' here worryin' meself sick.'

They knocked at Mary's to let her know where they were going, then called at the florist's in Orrell Lane to buy an armful of colourful flowers. It was a tight squeeze getting Eileen into the small car, but Rene didn't stand on ceremony and pushed her sister none too gently into the confined space.

'Me nerves are shattered,' Eileen said as they walked from the car to the main entrance of Walton Hospital. 'I want to see me mam, but at the same time I'm terrified.'

'Leave all the talking to me,' Rene said, walking briskly down the corridor towards the ward and matron's office. Before knocking on the door, she passed the flowers over to Eileen. 'Here, you hold these.'

'Enter.'

That one word was enough to make Eileen's eyes roll. And when she saw the stern face of the matron she felt her tummy had suddenly been invaded by hundreds of fluttering butterflies.

'I can tell you no more than you were told on the telephone,' the matron said, tapping her desk with the rubber end of her pencil. 'Your mother is as comfortable as can be expected.'

'I think we are entitled to know if the operation was a success.' Rene spoke calmly, even though she was trembling inside. 'I am sure you understand, Matron, we are very concerned.'

Matron gazed from one to the other, her eyes finally resting on Eileen. 'The operation was a success, but I'm afraid your mother's age is against her. If she were a young person I'd have no hesitation in saying she would make a full recovery. But she is over seventy, and a serious operation at her time of life is always dangerous. The doctor was in to see her an hour ago, and he'll be keeping a close check on her progress.'

'When can we see her?' Rene asked.

'I'll have a word with the doctor after he's seen her again, so if you ring about four I'll let you know if he thinks she's well enough to have visitors. She isn't in the big ward yet, we've got her in a side ward where we can keep an eye on her.' The matron stood up to indicate the interview was at an end. 'Give the flowers to one of the nurses and she'll see they are taken to your mother's room.'

Eileen cleared her throat. 'Can we just take a peek at 'er?' She saw the slight hesitation on Matron's face and took advantage. 'Please? It would mean so much to us. We wouldn't let 'er see us.'

'My dear, your mother wouldn't see you even if you went in the room.' The stern face relaxed a little. 'She hasn't come round after the operation yet.'

'Please?' Eileen begged. 'Just a peep.'

Matron led them to a door which was half open. 'Just two minutes.'

Eileen gazed at the still form in the bed, and when she saw all the tubes attached to her mother her legs buckled under her. She fell back against the wall and would have fallen if Rene hadn't caught her in time.

'Come on, Eileen, out!' Rene took a firm grip of her sister's arm and led her to a bench in the corridor. 'Sit there for a minute and calm down.' Rene walked back a few yards. 'Thank you, Matron, I appreciate your kindness.'

'Would your sister like a drink of tea? I can arrange it.'

'No, thank you, she'll be all right. I've got a car outside and I'll have her home in five minutes.'

Mary had been at the window watching for Rene's car and was outside the passenger door in time to help pull Eileen from the restricted space. 'Come on now, all together . . . one . . . two . . . three!'

'Phew! Now I know what a sardine feels like.'

'I expected you home ages ago,' Mary said, taking Eileen's arm. 'I've been worried to death. How is Maggie?'

'We'd have been home long ago,' Rene said, 'but our Eileen was hysterical and we had to sit in the car park until she'd calmed down.'

'Let's get inside.' Eileen pulled her arm free to unlock the door. 'We'll tell yer about it over a cuppa.'

'I tried to tell her that everybody has tubes and things

attached to them after an operation, but there was no getting through to Eileen.' Rene held her cup between her hands and blew on the piping hot tea. 'I was upset meself, because me mam did look terrible, but carrying on the way Tilly Mint here did, doesn't help anyone.'

'Honest to God, kid, I got the fright of me life.' Eileen shuddered at the memory. 'She looked so still, her face as white as a sheet, I thought she was dead.'

Mary could understand how her friend felt. Hadn't she been the same when her mam had the stroke? And if she hadn't had Eileen to help her through that bad patch, Mary would never have coped. With her strength and her humour, Eileen had kept her going. Now her friend was in need of the same support. 'You're expecting too much, Eileen! Just wait a few days and I bet you'll see a difference.'

'Will yer ring up at four o'clock for us, kid? I'm 'opeless on a telephone, the things scare the life out of me.'

'I'll leave Victoria with Irene next door, and me and Alan will go in tonight,' Rene said. 'We'll call in on the way back and let you know how she is.'

'Not on yer life!' Eileen banged her cup down. 'She's my mam, as well.'

'All right, don't bite me head off! We'll pick you up on the way.'

'What! Me get in that contraption again? No, thanks, sis, me an' Bill will get the bus.'

'You'd be better off ringing first,' Mary said. 'You may make that journey down there just to be told you can't see her.'

'I'm still goin', kid.' Eileen sounded determined. 'I'm

288

not sittin' here twiddlin' me thumbs, worryin' meself to death.'

Only Eileen and Rene were allowed in the small side ward, and were told they had ten minutes only. Maggie looked exactly as she had that morning, her face white and drawn, her body perfectly still. Eileen, careful to avoid the tubes and drips, bent to kiss her cheek and whisper in her ear, but there was no response. Maggie didn't even know they were there.

In the meantime, Bill and Alan went in search of the matron to try to get some information. They were not encouraged by what she had to tell them. The doctor had placed Maggie on the critical list. She could have visitors at any time. But only close family, and only two at a time.

'I think we'll keep that under our hat,' Bill said, when the matron had bustled away, her starched uniform making a soft crackling noise. 'I'm going to bend the truth a little.'

When Eileen and Rene appeared, their eyes red with crying, Alan made a motion with his head to tell Bill he agreed. They were upset enough without burdening them with the extra worry.

'We've had a word with the matron,' Bill told them. 'And with Ma being in a side ward, you can come in any time you like. But once she's moved to the big ward you'll have to keep to the regular visiting hours.'

Maggie was taken off the critical list after a week and moved into the big ward. She was still very poorly, but the doctor said he was pleased with her progress so far. It was the longest week of Eileen's life. Each day she sat by her mother's bed talking and trying to be cheerful, while inside she cried. Maggie was a shadow of her former self, her skin didn't fit her face any more, but hung in loose folds, and her eyes were dull and lifeless.

'She's tryin',' Eileen told Bill one night after Maggie had been in the big ward three days. 'Yer can see her makin' an effort to talk and smile, but it's as if she 'asn't got the heart.'

'Honestly, Eileen, I don't know what you expect! Isn't it enough that Ma's getting a bit better every day? Another week will see a big difference, just wait and see.'

'The woman in the next bed is nice, very friendly. She said she'll keep an eye on me mam for us.'

'Can't I go in and see her?' Edna asked. 'I could go tomorrow, it's half day closing. I want to see me nan, and it would give you a break.' Eileen was thoughtful for a while. She could do with an afternoon off, there was all that washing to be done. And the house could do with dusting and tidying, she'd let it go to pot over the last ten days. 'Yeah, okay, sunshine, I could do with getting stuck into some housework. But tell yer nan I'll be in at half seven.'

'I'll get her some nice flowers from one of the stalls by Central Station.' Edna munched on a chip dangling from the prongs of her fork. 'I'm dying to see her, it's been ages.'

'Ah, I was going to ask you to let me come in with you this afternoon.' Mary looked disappointed. 'I've even bought some grapes to take in with me.'

Eileen laid the iron down and folded one of Bill's shirts. 'I was goin' to get stuck into the bedrooms, kid, they look as though a bomb's hit them.' She saw the downcast look on Mary's face, and tutted. 'Okay, we'll go in. But they only allow two visitors at a time, so we'll get there ten minutes late to give our Edna a chance to talk to her nan.'

'I'll go and get me coat.' Mary was already on her way down the hall. 'Be back in two ticks.'

'Remember when we used to come in an' see your mam?' Eileen asked, as they made their way up the long path to the hospital. Half way up, she stopped for breath. 'This ruddy path gets longer every day.'

'I remember very well,' Mary said, linking arms to urge Eileen forward. 'I was as worried as you are, but it turned out all right in the end, just like it will for your mam.'

'This way, kid.' Eileen steered Mary towards the ward door. 'Come in with me an' I'll send our Edna out.'

Maggie was in the fourth bed down, and Eileen's eyes went straight to her. 'Oh, my God!'

Mary followed Eileen's eyes and gasped. Edna was sitting one side of the bed and Joan opposite. She held tight on to her friend's arm. 'Take it easy, Eileen, don't do anything to upset Maggie.'

As they neared the bed, Joan glanced up and the colour drained from her face. She looked around as though seeking a means of escape, then felt Maggie's hand on her coat.

'Sit down, love.' Maggie had seen Eileen and Mary before Joan had, and her initial sense of shock was soon replaced by one of happiness and a strange feeling of calm. 'Everything will be all right, I promise.'

Eileen neared the bed, her mind in a whirl. This was the last thing she expected, but oh, it was lovely to see her daughter. She bent and kissed her mother, then looked across at Joan. 'Hello, sunshine.'

'Oh, Mam.' Tears squeezed between Joan's closed lids. She wiped the back of her hands across her eyes, and her voice choked with emotion, she said, 'I'll wait outside.'

Eileen watched her daughter flee down the ward before turning her gaze to Edna. 'How did this come about?'

'She wanted to come, Mam.' Then Edna blurted out, 'She wants to come home, too, but she's frightened you don't want her.'

'Go out to her, lass,' Maggie said, her voice sounding tired. 'And make your peace with her. Life's too short for arguments and anger. She's a young girl who made a mistake and is sorry, so don't be hard on her.'

'Go on, Eileen, it's what you want,' Mary said. 'I'll just stay a few minutes because Maggie looks tired.'

'I am, lass, very tired,' Maggie admitted. 'All I want to do is sleep.'

'I'll be in tonight, Mam.' When Eileen bent to kiss her cheek she whispered softly, 'I love you, Mam.'

'And I love you, lass.' Maggie smiled. 'Go now and see your daughter before she runs away.'

Eileen sat up in bed, her elbow leaning on the pillow. She watched as Bill undid the knot in his tie and pulled it from his collar. 'Honest, yer could 'ave knocked me over with a feather when I saw our Joan. I didn't know whether to laugh or cry, belt 'er one, or kiss 'er. And to think I wouldn't 'ave seen 'er if Mary hadn't wanted to go to the 'ospital.'

'She's been a very silly girl and I hope it's taught her a lesson.' Bill was standing on one leg, leaning against the wardrobe taking his trousers off. 'That girl had no right to take her in, especially living the life she does.'

'It was the Yank who did it.' Eileen pinched at the fat on her arms leaving hollows that took a second to fill out again. 'He probably thought he was on a good thing with our Joan, but 'e didn't get anywhere with 'er. At least that's what she says, an' I believe 'er.'

'Well she's home now, thank God, so that's one worry off our minds.' Bill tied the cord in his pyjama trousers before throwing the bedclothes back and climbing into bed. 'And Ma looked a lot brighter tonight. I think seeing Joan bucked her up a lot.'

Eileen nestled into his body. 'I asked 'er if she wanted our Billy's room but she said she'd rather share with Edna. And yer should 'ave seen our Edna's face when she said that, she was as pleased as Punch.'

'I was going to mention that to you, chick.' Bill slid his arm under Eileen's shoulder and drew her close. Her body was so warm and comfortable it always relaxed him. Made him feel he was at home and all was right with the world. 'I hope you don't start making a fuss of Joan and leaving Edna out. That wouldn't be fair.'

'As though I'd do that! They're both my daughters and I wouldn't make fish of one and flesh of the other.' Bill felt the bed shake when Eileen began to chuckle. 'Anyway, our Edna wouldn't let me. She can stick up for 'erself, that one, so yer've no need to worry about her.'

Bill took his arm away and pulled the sheet over his shoulder. 'Anyway, you had all your family together tonight when Billy and Mavis turned up, so perhaps we'll see a smile back on your face.'

'Yeah, all back together again, just as it should be,' Eileen said. 'And yer don't 'ave to come to the hossie with me termorrer, 'cos Billy an' Mavis want to come. So yer can put yer feet up an' read the *Echo* to yer heart's content.'

Eileen listened to Bill's gentle breathing, and when she was sure he was fast asleep she turned on her back, her face to the ceiling. In a low voice, she said, 'Thank You, God, You've turned up trumps today. You 'ave given me my daughter back, and me mam's on the mend. You really are me best friend and I'll never forget You. I'm goin' to be so good in future, You won't know I'm the same person.'

Chapter Twenty Two

'Where are you two off to?' Eileen gave a little skip as she followed her daughters down the hall. 'Off flyin' yer kite, are yez?'

Edna opened the door and stepped into the path. 'I'm calling in to our Billy's, then going to Janet's.' A mischievous grin crossed her face as her sister joined her on the path. 'Our Joan's pretending she's going to see our Billy and Mavis, but I don't know who she's trying to kid. She's hoping to see Leslie Maddox, she's got her eye on him.'

'Go way!' Eileen folded her arms and leaned back against the door. 'Well I never . . . Leslie Maddox!'

Joan shot her sister a dirty look. 'Take no notice of her, Mam, she's pulling your leg.'

'Oh, aye? I suppose it's just coincidence that he's standing outside their door every time we go? And if you don't fancy him, why d'you go the colour of beetroot every time he speaks to you?'

'Oh, stop acting daft and let's go.' Joan linked her arm through Edna's and pulled her away. 'We won't be late, Mam, ta-ra.'

Eileen watched as they walked up the road arm in arm.

Since Joan had come back home a month ago they'd become very close, and it did Eileen the world of good to see them so friendly. Now she only needed her mam home to make her happiness complete.

Eileen heard a door bang, then saw Mary coming towards her. 'Hi-ya, kid! Are yer comin' in for a cuppa? Bill's gettin' changed to go to the 'ospital but it'll be another ten minutes before he's ready.' She closed the door after Mary and followed her into the living room. 'Have yer ever noticed, kid, that men are more vain than women? All I've got to do is run a comb through me hair and I'm ready, but Bill takes ages. Mind you, with my tatty 'ead it doesn't look any different after I've combed it.' Eileen gazed at Mary's thick, curly blonde hair and grunted in disgust. 'Every time I look at you I go green with envy.'

Mary pulled one of the dining chairs out and sat down. 'Harry asked if you and Bill would like to come for a run to Southport tomorrow night? We could stop at the Morris Dancers in Scarisbrick for a drink.'

'We don't get back from the 'ospital till half eight, kid, so it'd be too late.'

'One of the others could go in for you, Billy or one of the girls. Come on, Eileen, the weather's lovely and it would do you good. If your mam comes home next week you won't get a chance to go out, not for a while, anyway.'

'It's not certain she will be comin' out, we've got to wait till Monday to see if the doctor gives her the okay.' Eileen straightened the runner on the dining table and gazed at it with a critical eye, making sure the ends that overlapped the table were even. 'I'm keepin' me fingers crossed, kid, and everything else that'll cross. Except me eyes, of course, 'cos I don't want to go around lookin' like Ben Turpin.'

They could hear Bill running down the stairs and Mary decided that she wasn't going to give Eileen time to make excuses. 'I'll tell Harry you'll be ready for seven tomorrow night.'

Harry took the country route to Southport. It was a bit longer than going down the dock road, but the scenery was lovely. Especially when the sun was shining, as it was now.

'It's lovely down these country lanes, isn't it kid?' Eileen gazed out of the window at horses grazing in the field. 'That cottage we passed before 'ad 1819 over the door, and this one,' Eileen pointed as Harry slowed down, 'was built in 1921. Yer'd 'ave a long way to walk to yer neighbours to borrow a cup of sugar, wouldn't yer?'

'An even longer walk to the nearest pub,' Harry laughed. 'We don't know we're born.'

When they neared the Morris Dancers, Harry was about to turn into the car park when Mary tapped him on the shoulder. 'Let's go to Southport first and call here on the way back. There's a smashing pianist plays here on Friday and Saturday nights, but he doesn't start till about nine.'

The fine weather had brought everybody out and Southport was crowded. Lord Street's fine Victorian arcades were bright with flower baskets hanging at intervals the full length of the wide street, and summer dresses, that had been brought out of wardrobes at the sight of the sun, added colour to the scene.

'Yer'd need plenty of money to live 'ere, wouldn't yer, kid?' Eileen paused to look in one of the high-class shop windows. 'Look at the price of that dress . . . nine pounds nineteen and eleven! Blimey, I'd get a full rig-out for that sort of money in T.J.'s, including knickers.'

They strolled up Nevill Street to the promenade and Eileen took a deep breath. She turned to Bill, who was walking behind, deep in conversation with Harry. 'Fill yer lungs with that air, Bill, it'll blow the cobwebs away.' They walked slowly along to the marine lake and Eileen nodded at an empty bench. 'Can we sit down for a while, me feet are killin' me?' She held out one of her legs. 'Just look at me ankles, swollen up like balloons. The warm weather's nice for some, but it sure don't agree with me.'

'You stay here and watch the sailing boats while I go and get the car,' Harry said. 'It'll save you walking all the way back.'

'He's not a bad old stick, your feller,' Eileen said to Mary when Harry had left. 'Nearly as good as my Bill.'

Bill was leaning on the railings around the marina. 'Come and see the swans, there's a whole family of them.'

'Ah, aren't they lovely!' Mary joined him at the rails. 'Come and see, Eileen, the little ones are gorgeous.'

'I'll 'ave to take yer word for it, kid. The spirit is willin' but the flesh is weak. I'm knackered.'

'It's crowded, isn't it?' Bill looked over his shoulder as he pushed his way through the mass of bodies. 'Is it always like this?'

'Every time we've been it's been chock-a-block,' Harry

said. 'When you hear the pianist, you'll know why. He can't half tickle those ivories.' He spotted two empty seats and pointed. 'Grab those seats, quick. The girls can sit, we'll have to stand.'

The pianist was a man in his thirties, very ordinary to look at, but there was nothing ordinary about his playing. He could make the piano talk, and he knew which songs to play to get the crowd singing. After one sherry, Eileen was belting it out with the rest. 'Smoke gets in your eyes', 'Talk of the town', 'Who's sorry now', all her favourites.

'Someone's enjoying themselves,' Harry bent down to whisper in Mary's ear. 'It's a long time since I saw Eileen let herself go like this.'

'She's really enjoying herself.' Mary grinned, watching her friend's mouth doing contortions as she sang with might and main, 'My old man, said follow the van.'

When it was time to leave, Eileen did so reluctantly. 'I was just gettin' into me stride.' And as they made their way to the car she had them in stitches as she swayed from side to side, like a drunk, and slurred the words to 'Show me the way to go 'ome'.

'Woman, you're drunk,' Bill said, trying to keep the smile off his face. 'And there's nothing worse than a drunken woman.'

Eileen threw her arm round his neck. 'Yer've got that wrong, Bill Gillmoss. What yer mean is, there's no one better in bed than a drunken woman.'

Bill spread his hands out. 'What would you do with her?'

Harry scratched his chin. 'Take her home to bed.'

* * *

Maggie came home on the Tuesday. She was as white as a sheet, and so thin her clothes hung loosely, miles too big for her. But she was glad to be home and her relief brought the tears to her eyes.

Eileen was hopping from one foot to the other, her heart bursting with happiness. 'Come on, Mam, don't cry or yer'll 'ave me at it.' She'd missed her mother more than words could describe, but they were both too emotional to tell her now. She would tell her one day, but not until she'd got some flesh back on her bones and some colour in her cheeks. 'You're gettin' in that bed for a few hours' rest before the gang come in. And we'll 'ave a house full tonight, everyone's comin' to see yer.' Eileen slipped her mother's shoes off, then reached under her dress for the top of her stockings.

'I'll do that!' Maggie slapped her daughter's hand away, her face flushed with embarrassment. 'I'm quite capable of seeing to meself.'

'Oh, yer 'ome, are yer?' Eileen grinned. 'Gettin' yer knickers in a twist, as usual. Pity yer didn't leave yer paddy in the 'ossie.'

Maggie smiled. Oh, it was so good to be home with this daughter of hers. 'Just leave me, lass, and I'll get meself into bed. But I would like a cup of tea if you don't mind. The tea in the hospital was terrible.'

'Like maiden's water, was it?' Eileen threw her head back and roared. 'I 'aven't changed while yer've been away, Mam, either.'

Eileen popped her head around the door of Maggie's room to see Joan and Edna sitting on the side of her bed, both talking at the same time. 'Come on, you two, dinner's on the table.' She walked over and put another pillow behind Maggie's head. 'They'd talk the hind leg off a donkey, wouldn't they? I wonder who they take after?'

'Not their dad, that's for sure.' Maggie waved her hand at her granddaughters. 'Go and get your dinner, there's good girls. I'll see you later.'

'I've made some barley broth for you.' Eileen smoothed the counterpane where the girls had been sitting. 'Put a lining on yer tummy and some flesh on yer bones.'

'The girls seem to get on well together,' Maggie said, looking up into Eileen's face. 'Are you happy now you've got all your family together again?'

'They get on like a house on fire. Better than they ever did. And our Joan's not 'alf changed, she even washes dishes and helps with the cleaning.' Eileen put her hands on her hips and smiled down in to her mother's face. 'An' now I've got you 'ome, missus, me family's complete.'

'I'm happy for you, lass.'

'An' I'll be happy if yer eat the broth I'm bringin' in.' Eileen swayed to the door. 'Mary an' Harry will be down later, an' our Billy an' Mavis, so I'd better get me skates on.' She turned and smiled. 'They're all comin' to see you, yer know, missus, not me! What it is to be popular, eh!'

The first visitor that night was Martha Bradshaw, Mary's mother. Harry brought her down in the wheel-chair, pushed her to the side of the bed, then left the two old friends to talk in peace and quiet. They'd missed each other so much and had lots to talk about. 'It's grand to have you back, Maggie,' Martha said. 'The days haven't been the same without you dropping in for a chat.'

301

'I'll soon be up and about, then you'll be fed up with the sight of me,' Maggie answered. 'Give it a week or two, and I'll be trotting up for me afternoon cup of tea.'

'Nan, can we come in?' Edna's head popped round the door. 'Me and Joan are going out, so we want to say ta-ra.'

Martha watched with a smile on her face as the girls kissed and hugged their grandmother, noting how gentle they were, careful not to hold her too tight. And her smile widened when she in turn received a kiss from each of them.

'Ta-ra, Nan!' they chorused. 'Ta-ra, Mrs B.'

'What it is to be young, eh, Martha? Still, we've had our time, haven't we? A lot to look back on.'

Martha looked pensive. 'Good and bad times, Maggie.'

'I'm sorry to break this up.' Eileen bustled in. 'But I've got a room full of people waiting to see her ladyship.'

Maggie raised her brows. 'Who's here?'

'Well, let me see.' Eileen held her hand out and started ticking off on her fingers. 'There's Mary and Harry, Vera and Arthur with Carol, and our Billy and Mavis.'

'It's good of them to come, and I do appreciate it, lass. But you won't let them stay too long, will you? I get tired very quickly.'

'Don't worry, they've been given strict instructions to be in an' out in five minutes. I'm keeping me eye on yer, so 'ave no fear, Eileen's here.'

True to her word, Eileen did keep an eye on her mother. She fussed over her like a mother hen, wouldn't let her lift a cup or make her own bed. Until Maggie put her foot down. 'For heaven's sake, lass, will you let me be? As long as you treat me like an invalid, I'll stay so.'

So Eileen stopped fussing and allowed her mother to move at her own pace. Maggie's progress was slow but sure. After two weeks of good food and plenty of rest, her cheeks and body were filling out. There was still a long way to go, but she was getting there. And when she asked Eileen one afternoon to walk her up to see Martha, Eileen was over the moon. Then a few days later it was a trip to the corner shop. After that they walked a little further afield each day, and both looked better for it. The pallor left Maggie's face and Eileen's chubby cheeks were a rosy red.

The only day they missed their daily walk was when the heavens opened and it poured with rain. 'Never mind, lass,' Maggie said. 'The farmers will be glad of it.'

Eileen set a tray with tea and biscuits, and when they settled she wracked her brains for something to keep her mother amused. 'Did you know our Joan's goin' out with Cissie Maddox's son, Leslie? Seems struck on 'im, too.'

'Doesn't the time fly?' Maggie said, shaking her head. 'It seems like only yesterday that Leslie was in short trousers and his face full of spots.'

'He's as old as our Billy. Done well for 'imself, too. Got a collar and tie job in Liverpool, which suits our Joan 'cos she's always been a bit of a snob.'

'Doesn't take after his dad for the gee-gees, then?' Maggie asked. 'His dad was always fond of a flutter on the horses. Lost more money on them than soft Joe. It's a mug's game, backing horses.'

'I never thought the day would come when me an'

Cissie would be related.' Eileen chuckled. 'Remember the way me an' 'er used to fight? Many's the time we've rolled our sleeves up, stood eyeball to eyeball, threatenin' to knock the livin' daylights out of each other.' Her tummy shaking with laughter, Eileen spluttered, 'I'd 'ave died if she'd laid a finger on me. I couldn't fight me way out of a paper bag.'

'What about Edna?' Maggie asked. 'Hasn't she got a boyfriend yet?'

'She never says anythin', but I've got a feelin' she doesn't go to Janet's so often just to see 'er friend. I think Janet's brother is the attraction there. Edna's been sweet on John since she was a little girl.'

'You still miss the old street, don't you, lass?'

'Yeah, I miss all the old neighbours, like Cissie and Milly Knight. But we can't 'ave everything we want in life, can we? As long as I've got Bill, and you and the kids, I'm 'appy with me lot.' Eileen gave a cheeky grin, 'We did 'ave some good times, though, didn't we, Mam? Never short of a bit of gossip to make life interestin'.'

Maggie huffed. 'You were the one that gossiped, not me!'

'Oh, come off yer high 'orse, Mam, yer couldn't wait for me to tell yer all the news. Yer used to tut-tut, pretendin' yer weren't interested, but yer eyes an' yer lug 'oles were stickin' out a mile.'

The football season had started again, and one Friday night when Billy and Mavis called, Billy asked his dad if he was going to the match the next day. Bill nodded his head vigorously. 'Yeah, wouldn't miss it. It should be a good game.'

'You an' yer ruddy football! Like father, like son.' Eileen turned to wink at Mavis. 'Yer'll be a grass widow every Saturday, like me.'

'I don't mind.' Mavis gazed at the husband she idolised. 'It's his only hobby.'

'I'll meet you outside, Dad,' Billy said. 'Then we can stand together.' His handsome face creased in a smile. 'You wouldn't enjoy the match without me standing beside you singing me heart out.'

When Bill came back from the match he found his wife sitting in Maggie's room with Mary. 'How did Liverpool get on?' Eileen asked. Then she added, 'It doesn't matter, I can see it on yer face. Liverpool won.'

'What about Everton?' Mary asked, rising from her chair. 'I hope they won because Harry always buys me a slab of Cadbury's on the way home. If they lose I only get a commentary on the game. How they could have won if the referee hadn't given a penalty when he shouldn't have done, or a goal had been allowed when anyone with half an eye could see the player had been off-side.'

Bill grinned. 'They were drawing at half-time, but I haven't heard the final result.' He scratched his ear. 'What happens when it's a draw? Do you get a small slab of chocolate?'

'Yes, and all the excuses.' Mary patted Maggie's head before making for the door. 'I'll see you folks, ta-ra.'

'Yer half-an-hour later than usual, Bill Gillmoss, where've yer been?'

Bill opened the *Echo* he'd brought in with him, avoiding

Eileen's eyes. 'I stood talking to Billy for a while. He's having a party for Mavis's birthday next week and wanted to know how to go about getting some beer in.'

Eileen screwed her eyes up. 'Funny he never mentioned it while he was 'ere. And surely he knows 'ow to get a few pints in, the daft article.'

Bill rustled the paper. 'Mavis's birthday is on Thursday, but he thinks they might have the party on Saturday, so everyone can have a lie-in the next day. Anyway, he's calling on Monday night to let us know.'

'I wonder what to buy Mavis? What d'yer think, Mam, somethin' personal or somethin' for the 'ouse?'

'Ask her on Monday. It's better to do that than buy her something she doesn't want.'

Eileen rested her chin on her hands. 'Will yer put the paper down a minute, Bill, an' listen to me? Did yer ask Billy if they wanted to 'ave the party 'ere? We've got a lot more room than them.'

'Eileen, they're married now, with a place of their own. They probably want to show off their house, so let them be, and mind your own business.'

Eileen's chins moved in the opposite direction to the shaking of her head. 'That's telling me, isn't it, Mam? Mind me own business indeed! I've a good mind to clock yer one, Bill Gillmoss.'

'If you do, don't be surprised if you get one back.' Bill let out a hearty chuckle. 'You'll get the one I felt like giving the goalkeeper when he let a goal in that even a child could have saved.'

'My God! No matter what subject we're on about, he always manages to get back to his ruddy football! I give up on you, Bill Gillmoss, yer past the post.' Eileen chuckled. 'Like that ruddy goal yer were on about.'

The following Saturday night Eileen was putting the finishing touches to her hair when Mary and Harry called to take them up to Billy's for the party. Mary looked more beautiful than ever, her long hair bouncing on her shoulders in a page boy bob, her lilac dress fitting her to perfection and her blue eyes shining.

Eileen plucked the loose hairs from the comb and threw them in the grate as she viewed Mary through the mirror. 'Yer lookin' pleased with yerself tonight, kid! Harry come up on the pools, 'as he?'

Mary shook her head, sending her hair swaying across her face. 'No, we're just looking forward to the party.' She held up a small parcel wrapped in coloured paper and tied with silver string. 'We've bought Mavis a link of pearls, I hope she likes them.'

'She'll be made up, kid.' After a last check on her appearance, Eileen spun round. 'What the 'ell's goin' on? You look as pleased as punch, an' Harry's got a grin on 'is mug like a Cheshire cat. Am I missin' somethin'?'

Bill came in then, dressed in his best grey suit, white shirt and dark blue tie. 'Are we all ready? I promised Billy we'd be there for seven.'

'Where's our Billy?'

Mavis took their coats. 'He's just nipped down to the pub for a few more bottles of beer. We were frightened of running short.'

Eileen looked around. 'Are we the first? Our Joan an'

307

Edna should be 'ere, they left the 'ouse ages before us.'

'You're the first.' Mavis patted the coats over her arm.
'I'll take these up and put them on the bed.'

'While we're waiting, chick, would you like to come
over and see Mrs Kenny?' Bill asked. 'When Billy told her
about the party, she said she'd like to see you.'

Bill had a strange look in his eyes that Eileen couldn't
fathom. 'Yer mean Mrs Kenny who lives in our old 'ouse?'
When Bill nodded, Eileen grunted, 'I'm not going in
there! What the 'ell does she want to see me for?'

'Come on, chick, she's an old lady. It won't hurt you to
see her, just for five minutes.'

'Go on,' Mary coaxed. 'She can't eat you.'

Eileen allowed herself to be led along the hall, dreading
the thought of going back into her old house, but afraid to
refuse in case they thought she was being churlish.

Halfway across the road Bill took a key from his pocket.
'She gave Billy the key to save her opening the door.'

Eileen pulled her arm free, a startled look on her face.
'We can't just walk in someone's 'ouse, it wouldn't be
right.'

But Bill ignored her and unlocked the door. There
wasn't a sound as he led her down the familiar hallway.
Eileen stopped at the foot of the stairs and refused to
move as her eyes took in all the things she remembered.
'She's still got the same paper on the walls,' she whispered. 'It looks exactly as we left it.'

'She's an old lady, chick, she couldn't decorate herself
and probably can't afford to pay anyone else to do it.'

Eileen took a deep breath. She shouldn't have let Bill
talk her into coming. Didn't he have any idea what it

would do to her? She made to turn to walk back out, but Bill was expecting it and in one movement opened the living room door and pushed her inside.

Eileen gaped and fell back against the wall. The room was full to overflowing and at first her mind wouldn't take it in. What was Billy doing here when he was supposed to be out buying beer? And surely Mrs Kenny wouldn't have invited Joan and Edna, or Arthur, Vera and Carol? And where was Mrs Kenny?

It was Carol who broke the silence. She freed herself from Vera's grip and rushed to throw her arms around Eileen. 'Hello, Auntie Eileen. We're having a party.'

Eileen absent-mindedly stroked the girl's hair, her mind in a whirl. She cleared her throat. 'Will someone tell me what's goin' on? If this is supposed to be a joke, then I'm not amused.'

Mary and Harry pushed her gently to one side to make room for Maggie. Eileen stared at her mother open mouthed. 'Mam, what are you doin' 'ere? Yer said yer didn't want to come to the party.'

'I don't, lass, but I wasn't going to miss this.'

Eileen gazed at the faces watching her. 'Will someone tell me what's goin' on, please?'

No one spoke as Bill stood in front of her, a key lying in his open hand. 'The key to your new home, Eileen Gillmoss. Or should I say the home your heart has never left?'

Tears sprang to Eileen's eyes. 'Don't do this to me, Bill, please. It's not funny, it's cruel.'

Young Billy couldn't bear to see his mother cry and he rushed forward to put his arms around her. 'Me dad's not pulling your leg, Mam, he wouldn't do that to you.' He looked over her head and saw Mavis standing just outside the door with a glass in her hand. He motioned for her to pass it over. 'Take a drink of this, Mam, then me Dad'll tell you all about it.'

Eileen pulled a face as she swallowed the whisky, bringing a smile to those who were watching in silence. Bill waited till the glass was empty and Eileen calmed down enough to take in what he was telling her.

Mrs Kenny had reached the stage where she could no longer cope with living on her own, and had finally agreed to live with her son and his wife in Wallasey.

'That's what all the secrecy has been about, chick. She told Billy she was leaving, because she wanted him to tell you how much she'd loved living here, and this put Billy in a quandary because, like everyone else, he knew how you felt about this house. So he told me, and we took it from there.'

When it slowly registered in Eileen's mind that what was happening was true, the corners of her mouth curled upwards. She nodded knowingly as her gaze swept the room. 'An' yer were all in on the secret? That's why our Joan an' Edna were gigglin' when they left the 'ouse, an' why Mary an' Harry looked as though they'd won the ruddy pools!'

'Are you happy now you've got what you've always wanted?' Bill asked. 'Don't I even get a kiss?'

'We 'aven't got the 'ouse yet.' Eileen's grin was getting broader by the second. 'We'll 'ave to wait an' see what the landlord 'as to say.' Eileen heard the titters and giggles her remark brought forth, and her eyes narrowed. Pointing a chubby finger, she asked, 'What's so flamin' funny, Arthur Kennedy?'

Arthur put his arm across Vera's shoulder before shaking his head. 'Let Bill tell you.'

'There's no landlord, chick, I've bought the house.'

Eileen looked for somewhere to hang on to, and her son's arm was the nearest thing. 'What yer talkin' about, Bill Gillmoss? Yer couldn't buy the 'ouse. We've got no money.'

Bill took her hand, forced it open and laid the key in the palm. 'I took a couple of hours off work, went down to the building society and put down a deposit. The landlord wasn't going to rent it again, he wanted to sell.'

'Oh, my God, we'll end up in the work-house.'

Bill explained that the mortgage wouldn't be any more than the rent they were paying in Orrell Park. And with the girls' wages coming into the house, they could pay it off quickly. He closed Eileen's hand over the key and smiled into her eyes. 'By the time the two girls get married, we'll own our own house.'

It took a few seconds for Eileen to sort her thoughts out, then she began to chuckle. 'Oh, you lovely man, Bill Gillmoss, I love the bones of yer. I love all of yez.' Her hand moved to include everyone. 'I've got the best family and the best mates in the whole world.'

Then Eileen saw Maggie standing in front of the fireplace. 'Oh, Mam, I'm forgettin' you! Do you want to come back 'ere?'

'I can't wait, lass.'

The advantages started to spring to Eileen's mind. 'I'll be livin' opposite me son, isn't that marvellous? Our

Joan's feller is only two doors away, an' I think our Edna'll be made up livin' near 'er friend. Then there's Milly Knight, I'll be able to get tick when I'm a bit skint . . . ooh,' her hips swayed, 'we'll all be so happy.'

'Except me and Mary.' Harry gave a lopsided grin. 'We're used to having you near us, now we're losing you.'

'Go on, yer daft ha'porth. Yer couldn't lose me even if yer wanted to. Me and me mam will visit yer, won't we, Mam? An' yer've got the car, so yer can come down whenever yer feel like it.'

'We've got some news for you,' Vera said. 'I'll let Arthur tell you.'

With one arm around Vera and the other around Carol, Arthur's face was the picture of happiness. 'Mrs Kenny has done us all a favour. We've been down to see your landlord and he said we can have your house when you move out. So me and Vera have made arrangements to be married three weeks today and we want you to be matron of honour and Bill our best man.'

Eileen's mouth dropped open and her eyes rolled. 'Don't tell me any more, me 'ead won't take it in. What a day this 'as been!'

'Mam, can we go over to our house now?' Billy asked. 'We can talk while we're having something to eat and drink. And at least we'll be able to sit down.'

'Oh, Mavis, I'm sorry!' Eileen hugged her daughter-in-law. 'We've spoiled yer birthday party.'

'Oh, no you haven't,' Mavis said. 'This is the best birthday present I've ever had.'

'You all go across,' Eileen said. 'Me an' Bill won't be long, we just want to 'ave a look around.'

They stood in the kitchen and Bill explained what he had in mind. 'There's a bloke in work who lives in a house like this, and he's had an extension built on the back. You'd have a bigger kitchen, and an inside toilet.'

'Ay, money bags, don't be goin' overboard. I managed before, an' I'll manage again.'

'The building society said they'll lend us a couple of hundred pounds on top of the mortgage to carry out the improvements,' Bill said. 'And before you explode, I've gone into everything with a fine-toothed comb. We can meet the repayments without skinting ourselves. I'm determined you're going to have a decent place to do your washing. And we'll all feel the benefit of an inside lavatory, especially Ma.'

In the bedroom they stood with their arms around each other's waists. 'It looks just the same,' Eileen said, leaning into Bill's shoulder. 'This room 'as seen a lot of lovin', hasn't it, Bill?'

'It has, and it'll see plenty more.' Bill squeezed her before moving away. 'I think we'd better get over the road. Don't forget it's supposed to be Mavis's party.'

When they reached the bottom stair, Eileen caught his arm. 'Bill, are yer sure? Don't do this just for me. I love this 'ouse, an' I'd be made up to come back again, but not if it isn't what you want.'

'As long as I'm with you, chick, I don't care where we live. Be it a hovel or a palace, as long as you're there, that's my home.'

'I love you, Bill Gillmoss.' Eileen gave him a bear hug that threatened to cut off his air supply. 'Now if you'll hang on a tick, I want to go to the lavvy.'

'Can't you wait until we get to Billy's?'

'Uh, uh.' Eileen was halfway across the living room when Bill called after her.

'I've got to give the key back tomorrow, you know, chick. We can't have it until all the papers are signed.'

Eileen was pulling the bolts back on the kitchen door. 'I've waited five years, Bill, another few weeks won't kill me.'

As she went down the yard, Eileen's eyes drank in everything she saw. The broken drainpipe, the black marks on the wall made by Billy's football, and the lavatory door hanging open, its lock skew-whiff like it had always been. Eileen peeped in at the wooden bench-like seat, and her eyes strayed to the nail in the wall they used to hang cut up squares of the *Echo* on when they couldn't afford toilet paper.

The memories came flooding back as Eileen stood in the middle of the yard with her hand on the old clothes line. She raised her eyes and whispered, 'You've been very good to me this year, God, and I want You to know how grateful I am. When I said I had the best mates in the world, well You come top of the list. I know people think I'm daft for wantin' to come back here to live, leaving a nice big 'ouse in Orrell Park. But part of my heart 'as always been in this little 'ouse because it holds so many happy memories for me. All me children were born in that front bedroom.'

Eileen heard Bill calling for her to hurry and she tugged on the line to let him know she'd heard. 'So You see, dear Friend, when we move back in, with all me family around me, this really will be the home where my heart is.'

Now you can buy any of these other bestselling
books by **Joan Jonker** from your bookshop
or *direct from her publisher*.

FREE P&P AND UK DELIVERY
(Overseas and Ireland £3.50 per book)

Three Little Words	£6.99
When Wishes Come True	£6.99
Victims of Violence	£6.99
The Sunshine of Your Smile	£6.99
Strolling With the One I Love	£5.99
Taking a Chance on Love	£5.99
After the Dance is Over	£5.99
Many a Tear Has to Fall	£6.99
Dream a Little Dream	£6.99
Down Our Street	£5.99
Stay as Sweet as You Are	£6.99
Try a Little Tenderness	£6.99
Walking My Baby Back Home	£5.99
Sadie was a Lady	£6.99
Sweet Rosie O'Grady	£6.99

One Rainy Day

TO ORDER SIMPLY CALL THIS NUMBER

I'll Be Your Sweetheart

01235 400 414

The Pride of Polly Perkin

or visit our website: www.madaboutbooks.com

Home Is Where The Heart Is

Prices and availability subject to change without notice.